Sabella is not Italian. He's Sicilian and part of the clan that has settled in Brooklyn.

"Why are you meeting with this guy?" Rosen says.

"Respect," Charlie says. "If I'm going to make moves in his town..."

"Since when is this his town?" Rosen says.

"You gotta show respect," Charlie says. "That's how the Italians handle things. These Sicilians got hair triggers. Joe the Boss is breathing down their neck in Brooklyn. We let him know we ain't interested in taking over his territory. Just play along."

Rosen shakes his head. Meyer lights another cigarette.

"It's America," Meyer says. "There's plenty for everybody. When we were kids, we were all robbing and stealing. It was the Wild West. We've been handed an opportunity on a silver platter. If we play it right, we all get rich."

"Ha!" Rosen says. "And if we don't?"

"You want to open up gambling in Philly?" Meyer says. "You're going to need Sabella's cooperation. Cut him in for a piece. It's cheaper than a war..."

A *Bloody* BUSINESS

THE RISE OF ORGANIZED CRIME IN AMERICA

by Dylan Struzan

A HARD CASE CRIME NOVEL

A HARD CASE CRIME BOOK
(HCC-139)
First Hard Case Crime edition: April 2019

Published by

Titan Books
A division of Titan Publishing Group Ltd
144 Southwark Street
London SE1 0UP

in collaboration with Winterfall LLC

Copyright © 2019 by Dylan Struzan

Cover and interior illustrations
copyright © 2019 by Drew Struzan

This book is a work of fiction. Names, characters, places, and incidents either are the products of the author's imagination or are used fictitiously, and any resemblance to actual events or persons, living or dead, is entirely coincidental.

Print edition ISBN 978-1-78565-770-2
E-book ISBN 978-1-78565-771-9

Design direction by Max Phillips
www.maxphillips.net

Typeset by Swordsmith Productions

The name "Hard Case Crime" and the Hard Case Crime logo are trademarks of Winterfall LLC. Hard Case Crime books are selected and edited by Charles Ardai.

Printed in the United States of America

Visit us on the web at www.HardCaseCrime.com

Foreword
by Tommy Sobeck Jr.

You should know how this book came about and that it isn't purely fiction. I knew both Meyer Lansky and Jimmy Alo personally. These are the guys who lived through all the events in this book and influenced the way things were done. Charlie Luciano was their friend and partner. They shaped the world of crime.

I met Jimmy back in the '70s and Meyer sometime after that.

We used to gather at the house of one of Meyer and Jimmy's associates—Meyer's family, Jimmy, me, a few close friends that differed from time to time. The food was always terrific and plentiful. Wonderful family. Very hospitable. They had a big house, a big Florida room where we would play gin before dinner. The dining room was big, too. They had a big table that was always loaded with food. Very spacious compared to the condo Meyer lived in at the time.

I remember the occasion when *The Gangster Chronicles* came on. We all gathered around the TV week after week to watch the series...all 13 episodes. That was the spring of 1981. I got a lot of insight from Meyer and Jimmy about the way life was for them back in those days.

One evening, Meyer's granddaughter said, "Tommy should do the movie about you guys." At that time, I was a union field rep for the film industry. I got small movie parts for some of the people we knew, but doing a movie about Meyer and Jimmy, well...I knew I would be out of line even thinking about such a thing in those days so I didn't. Meyer told his granddaughter, "He can do whatever he wants after I'm dead."

Meyer was a man of few words. Those were the rules.

At the end of *The Gangster Chronicles*, he said, "That's the way it really was." That's some endorsement for the show. We all enjoyed it.

I was around both men for over a decade before Jimmy told me to meet him for breakfast at the Singapore Hotel in Miami. After that, there were many breakfasts there, lunches at Vincent Capper's Italian Restaurant on Biscayne Boulevard and 80th Street, meals at Wolfie's Deli, Christine Lee's, Thunderbird, the Fontainebleau, as well as other places around Miami.

Jimmy would always introduce me as "this is my friend." In that way, I met many of their associates and friends. I lived with Jimmy for a year and half while my house was being built in Florida while my wife lived with our daughter in Ocala. This is how this book came about.

Jimmy and I would sit on the benches around the bay and chat. I'd go through books from the library and dog-ear the corners of pages that had things on them I wanted to ask Jimmy. Then we would talk. Nobody had talked about these things in my lifetime.

I wanted to ask Jimmy if I could write down what he said but I knew I had to approach that question gingerly. It was hard for me to do because it required a lot of trust on his part. I could be anybody. When it seemed a good time to ask, I did. He must have realized I would never do anything to hurt him so he agreed to my request. I'm no stenographer so that was a disaster. I told Jimmy that I can't write all this down, so "Can you please let me tape this?" I also wanted to authenticate this so people would know it's not BS. I promised no one would ever hear these tapes or read the book until ten or fifteen years after he was gone. Again, he gave me permission. Initially, I had seventeen tapes but we just kept talking and I kept reading new books until, eventually, there were nearly fifty taped conversations that occurred over a period of ten to fifteen years. I lost track.

Jimmy was still alive when I first talked to Dylan. We chatted on the phone and developed a rapport. By then, Jimmy was comfortable with what we were doing and allowed me to give her a few tapes to listen to so she could tackle the story. At first, she was reluctant to write the book but eventually she decided she wanted to take a crack at it. She came to Florida to meet me and Jimmy. This, too, had to be cleared with Jimmy first but I thought Jimmy would trust her once he met her.

After that, she talked often with Jimmy by phone. Like me, she promised not to write the book until he was "gone." She organized the information on the tapes and did her own research. It took a lot of years to complete the study. Tapes had to be verified. Chronology had to be verified. Putting the pieces of the puzzle together was an enormous undertaking but she did it. I knew she had to feel, smell, and hear the time period of the story. She had to be there. I never pushed her. When Jimmy died in 2001, she started writing this story. It's a helluva read and I hope you enjoy it.

—Tommy

Introduction
by Dylan Struzan

When Prohibition became law in 1919 and the following year it became illegal to make, distribute, or sell liquor in America, Meyer Lansky was barely eighteen and Ben Siegel was a kid of fourteen. Guys like them and Charlie Luciano and Joe Adonis were little more than two-bit hoods when the Eighteenth Amendment went into effect. Meyer had given up a hand-to-mouth job in the tool-and-die trade and opened a car and truck rental business in a garage on Cannon Street. The business was handy when it came to moving trucks in and out at odd hours of the night. Stolen suits, shoes, fur coats—small-time stuff, but it offset some of the agony of being poor. That's the way things were and that's the way things would have stayed had it not been for the opportunity the nationwide ban on alcohol created.

The boys on the Lower East Side set off to do what they always did, satisfy people's desires for illegal goods. They embraced the lucrative world of bootlegging and rumrunning with no idea that it would become big business and change the face of crime in America forever.

This story takes place during the thirteen years of Prohibition, 1920 to 1933, during which time Meyer Lansky became the great architect of organized crime, strategically using Prohibition to rise to a position of power. He advised the ruthless and fearless Charlie Luciano when it came to disposing of the old dons who controlled New York's Italian rackets.

I know how it all went down because Jimmy Alo told me. If you don't know who Jimmy Alo is, don't worry, you'll meet him. I met Jimmy in the spring of 1995 when he was a very spry 91 years of age. I knew his reputation: Vincent "Jimmy Blue Eyes" Alo, a man who'd been referred to as "Godfather," described by U.S. District Attorney Robert Morgenthau as "one of the most significant organized crime figures in the United States." Jimmy had come up starting in the 1920s side by side with Lansky and Siegel and Luciano. He was the last survivor of that generation.

I found Jimmy to be at once complex and engaging, a man of immense personal integrity. I asked questions. He answered politely without ever betraying a confidence. We talked often from 1995 until his death in 2001. I gained his trust and then his friendship. I was privileged to see his world from an insider's perspective. I got to know Meyer, Benny, Charlie, Joe Adonis, Eddie McGrath, Johnny Dunne, all the boys, as Jimmy knew them. No one of Jimmy's stature has ever been so forthcoming and candid.

Jimmy understood the historical significance of his life and that of his friends, and he knew about this book. The last time I saw Jimmy, as he was seeing me out his front door, I poked him in the chest playfully and said, "Jimmy Alo, I am going to write your story." He said, "I know, honey, just wait until I'm gone." I kept my promise.

I thank the historians and writers who have documented the lives of these men. And the *New York Times* for generously putting their archives online. That was a life saver. Yes, I did years of research. But it was all in the service of telling Jimmy's story. And I am wholly indebted to Tommy Sobeck, without whom none of this would exist.

Forget what you know. A lot of it is bullshit anyway. That was

Jimmy's response when I told him I'd read a book about the period I thought was good, you know, lots of interesting facts. He said, "Yeah, no doubt. It has a lot of shit in it, too. Who's gonna question them? The only guy can question them is a guy like me. I lived through the whole thing. I knew them all. I don't think there's anybody around that could tell you what I told you."

What I'm about to tell you, I heard mostly from Jimmy Alo. He wasn't a household name, and that was deliberate. He played it so low-key most people never heard of him. He was Meyer Lansky's best friend—not, as the Italians believe, the guy sent to keep an eye on the Jew. This is the story of Meyer Lansky and the beginning of organized crime. I'm telling it to you the way Jimmy told it to me. I'm telling you this up front so you won't be surprised later on. You be the judge of whether or not it's bullshit.

MEYER LANSKY

© COPYRIGHT DREW STRUZAN

Chapter One
"Shhhh! Speak Easy!"

NEW YORK CITY—1920

Meyer Lansky likes to go it alone, especially since he gave up his former trade in favor of robbing and stealing. Trouble is, robbing and stealing is a cooperative effort. You bring your friends into it, and pretty soon it's a small mob, and pulling little jobs here and there isn't enough. You need to feed the fire. Plus, the other guys, the Italians, they've got a mob too, not so small, and no love for a bunch of tough Jews who think they've got as much right to build this sort of business as any man. But Meyer does think that. Now that the Eighteenth Amendment has passed, Meyer's mind spins with thoughts of possibility. The Goyim's Crusade is laughable, a gag, a bad joke certain to meet with non-compliance. Of this, Meyer Lansky is sure. The government presumes to govern the ungovernable. But pursuing all the possibility that Prohibition offers means branching out and becoming big enough to stave off those larger mobs. It means facing his biggest fear, becoming known.

He steps out from his Cannon Street garage and heads to Ratner's deli to meet a friend, Abe Zwillman. Abe got into the lottery rackets early on. He has a head for numbers. Every Friday, he comes to Ratner's deli for lunch not only to get a proper nosh, you won't find a Ratner's or Katz's in Newark, but to touch base with guys like Meyer so he can keep his finger on the pulse of the Jewish rackets.

Meyer looks forward to the discussions. Today is no exception.

He hustles along the sidewalk filled with pushcarts and shop-pers and the traditional bustle of Jews tying up loose ends before sunset. Once the Sabbath commences, there will be no further work until sunset the next day.

A Black Hat steps in front of Meyer blocking the sidewalk.

"You are Meyer Lansky, yes?" the Black Hat says.

Black Hats are a cliquish clan of Hasids who practice a code of ostracism toward anyone who does not practice their form of Judaism. The discrimination includes other Jews, Jews like Meyer, who clearly do not follow the ancient code. Meyer looks at the rebbe and wonders what has driven him to cross the chasm of his social divide to speak to an apikorsim. The fact that this Black Hat, a rebbe of some note, has not only spoken to him but knows Meyer by name is doubly confusing since Meyer blends into his environment with ease. The Lower East Side is full of Russian Jewish immigrant boys who look just like Meyer; wavy dark hair cut short with the slightest lick of pomade, dark eyes, weak chin, and an absence of joy.

Meyer nods.

"Perhaps we can share a cup of tea." The Black Hat gestures to the café behind them.

Meyer follows the rebbe into a Black Hat café where cus-tomers cling to a hundred-year-old dress code of shtreimels and bekishes and gartels, which are oversized round fur hats and long black silk coats and belts made of long, black woven strands that end with fringe and, when wrapped around the waist, create a physical divide between the heart and genitalia while mentioning God's name. The bustling café is stunned to silence as Meyer and the rebbe sit down together.

The rebbe waves for a round of tea.

After a pregnant pause, the rebbe says, "When you were young, you fought with the Italian boys, yes? Yet you never bent a knee to the Christian. You think I don't notice but I see many things. It is not for us to decide our fate." The rebbe points up. "He decides. And charity averts the severe decree. This is what we learn. This is what I believe."

"You didn't bring me here to discuss religion," Meyer says.

The rebbe strokes his beard.

"We have trouble," he says to Meyer. "You understand this kind of trouble."

"Oh...trouble," Meyer says, the purpose of the conversation crystalizing.

The rebbe inches closer.

"I heard about you since before now," the rebbe confides, "but only now do I have to bother you with our problem. I hope you will not take offense. The laws of kashrut stipulate..."

Meyer says, "I know what the laws of kashrut stipulate, a non-Jew cannot open a bottle of kosher wine. You have trouble at the winery?"

"If only they would stick to the Mevushal wine," the rebbe moans.

For a moment, the two men very nearly see eye-to-eye. The waiter brings tea and sweet cakes. The hot tea and heavy cream and the prayer shawl peeking from under the waiter's white shirt and black vest takes Meyer back to his childhood in Poland where heated conversations among adults sorted the threat of the Czar's soldiers, the pogroms, and the reclamation of Israel. He reaches for the pack of cigarettes in his pocket then decides against it. The entire café is eavesdropping on the rebbe's discussion.

"Do you have any idea who is stealing the wine?"

The rebbe says, "Whoever it is, they know that no one stands guard on Shabbat."

"That's not a tough call in these parts. Every goy around

knows about Shabbat. Ever hear of Shabbat goys?" Meyer says,
exercising his disdain.

The slippery slope of Shabbat is bared. There are exceptions.
Jews use non-Jews, or goys, to do work forbidden by Rabbinic
law on the Holy Day. If the non-Jew is paid by the job rather
than by the hour or day, for example, the Jew can hire the goy.
Or if the situation is of great need, great financial loss, illness,
or mitzvah, the Jew can hire the goy to do the work. Of course,
Meyer is no goy, but to a Black Hat, he's not much of a Jew
either. At once, Meyer casts himself as the Shabbat goy to the
rebbe's dilemma.

"I will speak with my friends. If they agree, we will take care
of the trouble…and for ten percent of the Mevushal wine, we'll
make sure they stay gone. Is this agreeable?"

Ten percent echoes the Biblical injunction of tithing. The
rebbe hears the undertone. His frail frame trembles as he gives
Meyer the nod.

It is late Friday afternoon but not so late that even a Black
Hat couldn't enjoy a leisurely stroll and still arrive home with
plenty of daylight to spare before the Sabbath. Meyer heads
back to the garage on Cannon Street and calls in his gang. The
garage, a stone's throw from the East River, is, by day, a car
and truck rental business. By night, something else. The East
River becomes a convenient conduit for moving booze around
the city.

This afternoon, Red Levine is busy fitting trucks with stolen
plates lifted by local kids. At fifteen, Red lied about his age and
joined the Navy but he soon tired of the inevitable fights over
his Jewish heritage, jumped ship, and made his way back to
New York City. The freckle-faced Levine has worked his way
up from hauling heavy chunks of ice from a company truck to a
client's ice box to acting as Meyer's right-hand man.

The gang filters in as the sun creeps toward the horizon.

Meyer says, "I was approached by a rebbe today. Somebody's been knocking over the winery...on Shabbat. What do you think? Yids or goys?"

"Goys," Red says. "What Yid would be stupid enough to steal Mevushal wine? Nobody who has tasted it, anyway. Nobody drinks Mevushal wine on purpose."

He wipes the filth from his hands and settles in with the other members of the gang. The gang is small but effective. They've been together for years.

Mike Wassell says, "Are the Black Hats too holy to protect their own winery, we gotta protect it for them? Apikorsim. That's what they call us, you know. It's a little rich, don't you think, to look down on somebody and then crawl to them for a favor when there's trouble. What! We ain't holy so it's okay for us to get shot?"

Mike is a quiet kid who has never run from a fight. It's the principle of the matter that gets under his skin.

"My first thought was to let the Black Hats fend for themselves," Meyer says. "I almost told him as much but then I got to thinking. If we let goys kick us around here, we'll wind up like in Poland. This is America. You stand up for yourself."

"For yourself, sure," Mike says.

"I say it starts here with us defending our turf, whatever it is, including a kosher winery."

Red brightens. "Next year in Jerusalem. I should live so long."

Meyer says, "Like I said, these guys strike on Shabbat. If you don't want to go, Red."

"Tonight," Red says, "I observe Shabbat my own way."

Meyer says, "You're extinguishing a fire."

"Don't mock God, Meyer," Red warns. "I turn the key that fires a spark. The combustion engine violates the rabbinical prohibition on work. I'm breaking Shabbat and I know it. If I get shot tonight, you'll know why."

Tabbo, who is by birth Irving Sandler, says, "Why don't you want to protect the winery?"

"I never said that," Mike says. "I never said nothing like that. I said it isn't right to spit on somebody and then ask them to do you a favor. That's what I said."

Red says, "Mike doesn't like pacifists."

Tabbo says, "Who's a pacifist?"

Meyer says, "Black Hats."

"Oh." Tabbo catches on. "I thought they just gave the dirty work to guys like us. That's how I see it."

Sammy says, "Maybe their brains get foggy from wearing those black hats in the middle of summer. Maybe that's why they think they're so much better than everyone else."

Sammy is Red's cousin and the newest addition to the gang.

Red says, "Maybe they're right. Maybe we are thugs suited only for rough stuff."

Red still clings to Jewish tradition. Levine, his surname, was once Levin, a name that comes from the Jewish biblical tribe of Levi. The Levites were tasked with the duties of God's temple and with expounding the spiritual meaning of the sacred writings. This fact hangs over Red like a lion over a gazelle. Most days the gazelle escapes but not always.

Mike says, "And maybe they're wrong. A guy who won't defend himself has no right to ask somebody else to do it for him. If their wine's too holy for the rest of us to touch, then they should be the ones standing out there with guns."

Meyer says, "Yeah, picture that! And here we are just the same. For argument's sake, let's say an Italian or Irish mob is knocking over the winery. You let one mob walk in and take what belongs to us and soon there's ten more riding their coat-tails. That's history. Understand? Our history. Jews. Not just Black Hats. Jews. We stick together and protect what's ours. Einstein is running around the world for Jerusalem! You think we can't take care of one block in Brooklyn? Which one of your mothers doesn't keep kosher? Are you going to look her in the eye and tell her there's no more kosher wine because you think the Black Hats are self-righteous and don't deserve protection?"

Mike hangs his head.

Meyer says, "What's it going to be?"

The silence is broken by a young kid named Ben Siegel. He crashes through the back door brandishing a headline:

4 SEIZED IN WALL ST. BOMB INVESTIGATION

The gang looks up wide-eyed.

"What?" Benny says. "You guys look like a bunch of pissed-off Yids. You shouldn't worry. It was a goddamned guinea that blew up Wall Street. Giacomo Caruso! Damn they love to blow things up. Thank God for the anarchists. The cops got their noses so far up the ass of these rich guys, they could give a damn about Jewish bootleggers right about now."

The pockmarks on the façade of 23 Wall Street are the thorn in the flesh of J.P. Morgan's men, a constant reminder of the September bomb that went off in the Financial District when anarchists made good on their threat. Two-million dollars' worth of damage was inflicted with a hundred pounds of TNT carried in the back of a ramshackle horse-drawn wagon. The explosion sent a fireball tearing through the streets. Thirty-seven Wall Street workers died. Another three hundred were wounded. The horse that drew the wagon was found in pieces everywhere, his shoes smoldering on the steps of Trinity Church. Morgan men insist this is most likely an accident.

Mike looks at Benny and then at Meyer.

Meyer thinks it over. Benny has been around long enough to have established himself. He's proven useful on several jobs. He can be trusted. Maneuvering in the moment is Benny's strong suit and who knows what the boys will face at the winery. Meyer looks to Red. Red nods his approval. Then Mike. Then Tabbo. Finally, Sammy.

"What's going on?" Benny says.

Mike says, "We got a winery to defend."

The boys shuttle across the Williamsburg Bridge in two trucks. The winery is housed in a large brick building in the industrial part of town. Meyer, Red, Sammy, and Benny park in an alley a block away from the winery, jump out of the truck, and meld with the hustle of Jews trying to make it home before sundown. Mike and Tabbo slip their truck in with a host of delivery trucks sitting idle for the Sabbath.

Meyer approaches the winery. The rebbe darts out the front door.

"Thank you for coming," he says shaking Meyer's hand vigorously while pressing a key into Meyer's palm. "We put a new padlock on the door. The Talmud says there is no joy without wine. Obviously, the Goyim Crusade knows nothing of the Talmud."

"Or of joy," Meyer says with a brief smile.

Meyer turns the inch-long key in his hand, glances at the small, round padlock that dangles from a metal strap across the door, and tries not to laugh. Only the most casual of opportunists would be dissuaded by such paltry security.

The boys make their way through the winery under the suspicious eyes of the Hasids who work there. Copper lines run in every direction from large copper pots. The place looks like something from a Jules Verne future. Everything about it is spotless: the equipment, the floors, even the ceiling beams. If cleanliness is next to godliness then the winery is suitable for the Holy of Holies.

Bottles of wine stored neatly in wooden crates are stacked no more than head high; the crates held fast to the brick wall by large straps. If the winery was secured as jealously as the wine, the rebbe would have little to worry about. As it is, a good crowbar and thieves have all they can carry.

Sweat breaks across the rebbe's face. No one unclean has ever passed over this threshold. Suddenly the room is filled with hooligans and weapons.

If this wine is ruined, the rebbe explains, his worn, red-rimmed eyes pleading for mercy, there will not be another batch for nine months. Without wine, the Jews cannot keep their commitment to G-d. The empty vats are sealed, waiting for the next season of grapes. Each harvest must be divided into pulp and skin, and then conveyed to fermentation vats. They must remain pure, nothing at all added. Every pump, pipe, press, connection vat, is sterilized by clean hands, meaning 'holy' hands, and overseen by the rebbe himself. Pressing, juice collecting, filtration, cooling, sampling, opening and closing of the vats, bottling, everything is his responsibility. If polluted, a whole nation could sin.

"The Mevushal is there," the rebbe says pointing. "It is your share to take."

Mevushal is Hebrew for cooked. Mevushal wine retains its religious purity no matter who opens or pours it; no matter who drinks it. The rebbe looks at Meyer, drops his head and mutters a quiet blessing for the winery. With a handshake, he takes to the darkening streets along with his devoted followers.

Red remembers with no small amount of remorse his promise to bring kosher wine home for Shabbat. But it is too late. His mother has already struck the match and lit the Shabbat candles and recited the Shabbat blessing—

> *Blessed are You, our God, King of the Universe,*
> *Who has commanded us to kindle the light of Shabbat.*

The boys position themselves around the winery. Hours creep by like so many days. The mercury drops. The boys shiver behind the ceremonially clean vats. A barking dog signals a passing drunk.

Another hour passes.

Outside, Tabbo says, "I hear something."

"Another bum?"

Mike cranes around, searching the street. It is well past midnight. Moonlight falls between the crevices of the buildings, lighting the alley. Inching down the narrow pocket of land, Mike and Tabbo make out the open cabin of a flatbed truck. Three heads bob and weave as the truck crawls along the deeply creviced back alley.

"It's the Irish," Mike says.

Tabbo squints but the moonlight refuses to yield the details.

"Oh, come on!" Tabbo says.

"Shh," Mike says. "Trust me."

The flatbed stops at the winery's loading door. The three toughs jump from the truck's open seat and saunter to the door, as though enjoying a spring day at the beach. Mike lurches toward them but Tabbo pulls him back.

"Wait," he whispers. "Wait for Meyer's signal."

The interlopers rattle the new padlock, then break out laughing. One of them jams a crowbar between the lock and the door and throws his weight against the load. The door easily breaks free. With a kick, the door swings wide.

The winery is dark and silent.

"Stupid hebes," the tall one says.

Benny tenses, steadying his arm atop a stack of boxes. He sights the leader with his Colt .38, the army version 1911A chosen for its dependability in battle.

The tall one reaches for the light switch on the wall. They've been here before. He flips the switch and lights flicker to attention throughout the small room where the large cache of Mevushal wine sits ready to go.

"Jesus Christ, will you look at this," the tall one says. "They musta known we was comin."

"Let's get the stuff and get out," the thug in the plaid cap says. "This place gives me the creeps."

Sammy recognizes the voice. It is the Schmatte that dates his sister, the Irish kid who fancies himself a gentleman, the stone-cold hoodlum who once put a bullet through Sammy's shoulder as Sammy drove a load of Canadian whiskey through the Schmatte's blockade. Sammy squirms. The movement behind the case of wine catches the Schmatte's attention.

"You little Jew bastard," the Schmatte says. "What are you hiding in the dark for? You over there praying for your god to protect your sacred wine? Don't you Jew boys know that when you killed Jesus, you lost all your heavenly privileges?"

Meyer steps from the shadows.

"Who needs prayers when we have .38's?" he says.

Benny stands, the Colt now trained on the Schmatte's head.

The Schmatte reaches for his handgun but fumbles. The Luger, a brilliant piece of Russian technology brought back by a returning WWI soldier, drops to the floor. The Schmatte scrambles for the pistol. The tall Irish flips the light switch and the winery goes black. Benny squeezes off two shots in the Schmatte's direction. The Schmatte, searching the floor wildly, finally seizes the Luger's steel snout. He flips it, fires in Benny's direction.

A bullet hisses past Benny's ear. The Schmatte makes a run for the open door. Benny aims at his silhouette passing in front of the moonlit window. He fires and takes out the window.

The Schmatte squeaks through the crowbarred door. His gang is close behind.

Mike and Tabbo are ready, Mike at the wheel of his parked truck, Tabbo riding shotgun. Mike hits the gas as the Schmatte jumps behind the wheel of the flatbed Chevy. Tabbo fires on the gang but it is Benny, springing through the winery door, who manages to land a bullet in the Schmatte's back.

The Schmatte slumps forward dropping the Luger which sails into the gutter. The tall Irish scoops the Schmatte onto the truck's bed as the third Irish, already at the wheel, tears down the alley. Benny sends a shot through the windshield. The Chevy fishtails, turns at the corner, and disappears.

Mike charges down the alley. Benny jumps on the running board. The jolt of speed very nearly pulls his arm out of its socket as he desperately clings to the door.

"Come on," Benny yells. "I want this little bastard."

Mike bumps the truck around the corner. Benny forms a vise grip with his arm, his head half inside the cab for leverage. The Irish skid through the intersection, drifting badly around the corner. The tall Irish and the Schmatte are thrown from one side of the truck to the other.

As Mike straightens his line, Benny shoots again, this time clipping the driver's arm.

The Chevy hops the sidewalk and grazes the front of Klein's fur storage, then smashes headlong into the façade of an adjoining shop. The driver overcompensates, slamming the gear shift into reverse. The truck springs from the storefront. As the back wheels hit the street, the driver throws the gearshift into first, cranking the steering wheel away from the sidewalk, but, lacking the room for a clean maneuver, wraps the truck around a lamppost. The wheels splay out at opposite angles. Steam pours from the radiator. The driver slumps motionless along the bench seat. The tall Irish, thrown from the truck in the crash, picks himself up and staggers toward the curb, unable to make sense of his surroundings.

Mike slams to a halt. Benny jumps from the running board. Wild and ferocious, he straddles the half-conscious Schmatte laid out in the middle of the road. He grabs the Schmatte's shirt at the neck and lifts him a foot off the ground. The Schmatte's head flops limply backwards.

Benny says, "Listen, you little piece of shit Mick. Next time you think you're gonna take down a Jew, think again. I'll gut you where you stand. If I even hear you talking about Jews, I'll hunt you down and put a bullet between your beady little eyes." Benny snuggles the Colt up to the Irish chin, slides it across the Schmatte's lips and over his nose then stops the barrel cold between the Schmatte's eyes. "That's a promise from me." He goes a little wild-eyed. "They don't call me Bugsy for nothing."

The Schmatte meets this with a blank stare.

Meyer, Red, and Sammy drive up next to Benny. Benny drops the Schmatte. His head bounces off the cobblestone.

Red says, "Benny, come on…the cops."

Benny sniffs the air and says to the Schmatte, "Whadya know, your shit does stink after all!"

The next morning, a hotwire of gossip moves through the backyards of Williamsburg. By afternoon everyone has heard of Meyer's victory. The rebbe itches to see what's left of the wine but the rules of Shabbat must be honored. He decides to take a stroll. If the stroll should happen to take him by the winery just after sundown, so what?

He passes the wrecked Chevy where neighborhood kids scavenge the remains of the demolished truck. A newspaper reporter interviews the crowd. The kids pose for pictures around the car. A block later, the rebbe is joined by two young Black Hats.

They reach the crowbarred door and huddle in sacred conversation until Shabbat has ended. With a deep sigh, the rebbe takes in the very un-kosher mess. The other Black Hats give the rebbe an "I told you so" glower. Everything will have to be sterilized. Everything.

"Don't judge too harshly until you have the facts," the rebbe says.

Meyer waits for the rebbe outside of the Black Hat café. Eventually, the rebbe arrives, Meyer hands him the key to the winery's padlock, the one thing not broken in the raid.

Meyer says, "We didn't need the key after all."

The rebbe says, "You couldn't have stopped them before they jimmied the door?"

Meyer says, "It wouldn't have made any difference. You won't have any more trouble."

The rebbe says, "You didn't take the wine. I put it aside for you. You didn't take it."

Meyer says, "Do me a favor."

The rebbe says, "What kind of favor can I possibly do for you?"

Meyer writes an address on a piece of paper and hands it to the rebbe.

"Make sure this family always has wine for Shabbat."

The rebbe looks at the paper and nods. The address is a small flat in Williamsburg that belongs to Red's family.

❖

A week later, the gang is flexing their collective muscle on a new idea. The government is storing plenty of liquor in warehouses for doctors' prescriptions for medicinal use. Red works feverishly to repair the dead engine of an abandoned truck he picked up alongside a country road. He intends to use it for the night's excursion to the warehouse. Mike Wassell watches Red work.

Mike says, "Yids in Cleveland bring whiskey across the border. I got a cousin in Cleveland. We could set something up."

Red says, "You wanna know somebody in Cleveland, ask me. I was born in Toledo, ya know."

"And you were raised here, just like me," Mike says.

Meyer strolls out from his makeshift office.

"God took less time making the earth than you're taking with this engine," he says to Red.

Red steps back from the truck and slams the hood. He wipes his hands across the thighs of his trousers.

"Forget it," he says with no small measure of disgust.

Sammy wanders over to look at the problem. He raises the hood. He has a way with mechanical beasts.

"Try to start it," Sammy says.

He watches the levers and gears go through their process. He signals to Red to do it again. The engine is simple, by all counts. He fiddles with the parts. Signals again. Red sparks the starter wire. The motor hums alive.

"It needs a new ring gear for the starter," Sammy says. "I'll put a new one in tomorrow. The rear main thrust bearing needs attention, too."

Sammy drops the hood. He and Mike hop in the truck bed and huddle under a canvas tarp. Meyer and Red jump into the cab, Red at the wheel.

"Worth the wait," Red says, shifting into first gear.

The truck rolls out of the garage into a moonless night. Snow blankets the city. The boys are in search of a government warehouse in Brooklyn where a cache of Kentucky whiskey is stored for medicinal purposes only. The anti-salooners believe a government certificate will control the flow of booze to the masses. Meyer and his gang bank on the idea that it will not.

The truck snakes along Delancey to Bowery, sliding through large patches of ice. Red crosses Canal and makes his way down Broadway until he reaches the sixty-story Woolworth Building. He drives respectfully past the looming Cathedral of Commerce, then floors the gas pedal and heads across the Brooklyn Bridge.

Wind gusts lift the truck and shove it from side to side. Three hundred and fifty-four feet below, whitecaps pock the surface of the East River. The bridge spills into Brooklyn's warehouse district as they leave behind the line of docks and factories and water towers that fuel Manhattan's various appetites. Farms dot the passing landscape. The truck skips a beat of pavement. Red guns the engine but a patch of black ice sends the truck into a skid. The back immediately overtakes the front. Red stiffens. He turns into the skid. Nothing happens. He turns away from the skid. The truck spins in two long ellipses before plowing into the fallow field that runs alongside the road. The truck hops twice before the engine dies leaving only headlights that throw a cockeyed beam across the highway.

Red beats the steering wheel. He looks back at Sammy who motions Red to spark the wires again. It works. Red eases out the clutch. The truck lurches and sways and then pulls free of the muddy bog.

"Goddamn farmers," he says. "They flood these fields on purpose, you know, just to trap guys like us so they make a few bucks hauling us out."

It is 2 A.M. The temperature has dipped another five degrees since they left the garage. Mike and Sammy sit numb and chattering. Red rolls up to the guardhouse of a government warehouse. He flashes his headlights three times and then cautiously pulls forward. He slides the walnut handled pistol close to his leg.

"I thought you boys got lost," the guard says, his red cheeks pinching into a forced smile.

"We're here now," Red says with a hard edge.

The guard has a sagging paunch and drooping eyes. He pants when he speaks, the consequence of a bad diet and too much sitting in a poorly heated box.

"There's one guy inside," he mutters. "We got hit last week. The controller called Washington. They put on another guy as a safeguard. He's up in the parapet. Shouldn't be a big deal for guys like you."

"Parapet?" Red says.

"An office, like, that overlooks the warehouse floor. He can see everything. There's a staircase goes up one side. Just look for the light," the guard says drawing a map with his finger on the palm of his hand. "You can't miss it. One more thing. Under the circumstances, I want another two hundred bucks. I'm takin' a big chance with the guy in the parapet."

Red throws out a scowl as he slides his finger around the trigger of his Smith & Wesson. The price of larceny was agreed upon, five hundred dollars. Meyer passes five one-hundred dollar bills to the guard.

"Five hundred," Meyer says. "Take it or leave it."

"What the hell is this?" the guard says. "I can't use hundred dollar bills. I ain't no Rockefeller."

"You're a clever fellow," Meyer says. "You'll think of something."

It's too juicy a payoff to pass up. The guard grabs the cash.

"Make it look legit," he says.

Meyer signals to Mike who jumps from the truck. Mike slides the slapjack from his inner coat pocket, a gift from his grandfather who got it from a prison guard.

"This is how you deal with men who won't cooperate," his grandfather had said pointing to the vulnerable spot just above the knee. "Slap him here. He'll buckle and drop like a fly."

Mike spent the afternoon whacking everything in sight with the rounded leather head attached to the flexible metal stem. "Wind it up and it will slam a guy with enough force to put him in the hospital," his grandfather had said and then patted Mike on the head approvingly.

Red rolls the truck forward and into the loading dock. Mike whips the slapjack hard and lands it just above the guard's knee. The guard buckles in agony. Mike rips the ring of keys from the belt loop on the guard's uniform. A few minutes later, the gang stands silently inside the warehouse. A dimly glowing desk light reveals the location of the new guard on duty. Sammy sneaks through rows of barrels. Mike follows closely behind. Sammy climbs the wooden stairs. They creak under his weight. The guard stirs. Sammy slides a bottle of chloroform from his coat pocket and douses a handkerchief.

"Harry?" the guard calls. "Is that you?"

"It's me," Mike grumbles.

Sammy creeps up the creaking stairs. The guard, weighing in at about two hundred pounds of sheer muscle, comes to the edge of the stairs and peers down into the shadowy background. Sammy is on him like a monkey on a greased pig but he's hit with a left hook. He fumbles the bottle of chloroform and sends it sailing along the floor. Mike double-steps his way to the top of the stairs and whips the slapjack. It hits the guard's arm. The man rounds to face Mike, his whistle at the ready. The whistle screams. Mike swings the slapjack and misses. The man lands another left hook and Mike flies backward. Sammy still clings to the greased pig. Mike jumps to his feet and swings again this time landing his blow. The guard goes down. Sammy gets the chloroform cloth over the guard's nose. It is enough to make the guard woozy. Mike rescues the bottle, dousing the man and the handkerchief. This time it's enough to knock the guard out.

"Jesus," Sammy says.

Mike says, "What the hell was that?"

Sammy stands, grabs the dime novel from the guard's jacket pocket, Zane Grey's *The Man in the Forest*, and shoves it in his back pocket. The boys descend the stairs and snake back through the maze of whiskey barrels and wooden crates. The warehouse stinks of a heady blend of eau de Jack Daniels and eau de Jim Beam.

"Like old times," Mike says while helping Red heft cases of whiskey into the back of the pickup.

Red laughs, "This ain't nothin' like the ice business. A guy can get frostbite if he ain't careful. There ain't no real money in it, either, workin' for somebody, I mean. The guy with the business takes it all. Thinks he's doin' you a favor by letting you do all the fucking work."

With the truck loaded, they squeeze into the cab with Meyer and Red.

"I heard the guys in Cleveland get counterfeit permits and withdraw the booze. It's legit that way plus the warehouse guys do all the lugging. How come we didn't do that?" Mike says.

"What's with you and Cleveland?" Red says.

"I'm just telling you the way it is," Mike says.

"Counterfeit permits don't make it legit," Red says.

"I know," Mike laughs. "But you slip the guards a few bucks to play stupid and they load the booze for you."

Meyer says, "The guys in Cleveland are more sophisticated. They've been dry for a year. You can learn a lot in a year."

Red says, "The Cleveland Jews bring whiskey across the border, from Canada. My cousin is coming down for Goldman's kid's bar mitzvah. You can ask him about it."

Meyer pulls up the collar of his coat and sits back for the cramped ride home.

The day of Hymie Goldman's kid's bar mitzvah arrives. The thirteen-year-old boy becomes a man. The sour smell of over-cooked cabbage no longer hangs like a gas cloud over the neighborhood. Meyer sucks in the morning air with relief. He pours water from the pitcher on the dresser into the large bowl next to it and then stares into the cracked and yellowing mirror that hangs on the wall. The bare light bulb sears his eyes. He lathers the bristle of his beard and then drags the straight razor along his face. He's eighteen now and making enough money to have his own one-room tenement flat. This brings joy to his father. No son who robs and steals for a living should succeed, not in this world or the next, and he certainly shouldn't rise above his father.

Meyer dresses and heads for the temple to make connections.

Young Levi Goldman stumbles through the singsong reading of the Torah. The joy of the Sabbath has given way to a dry throat and a morbid dread of his father's disappointment.

Red Levine takes a seat next to Meyer. The flame-haired shtarker fiddles with the fringe of his prayer shawl. It's no secret that Red dreams of orthodoxy while quietly admiring the boys with unshorn sideburns, long black jackets, and big round hats.

Meyer doesn't hold it against him. Levitical ancestors aside, somewhere between Red's eighth birthday and the moment he jumped ship in the Navy, the streets of the Lower East Side claimed Red's soul and Meyer knows it.

Levi Goldman looks up and announces to the congregation, "Today I am a man."

The Torah now rests squarely on Levi's shoulders. The celebration moves to the Goldman home where kosher wine flows freely.

Hymie pats Arnold Rothstein on the back and says, "No wine for you? One day I enjoy a glass of wine with my wife. The next day I'm a criminal for doing the same thing as I did the day before. What kind of sense is this?"

Rothstein is a gentleman's gentleman who, nevertheless, never drinks alcohol.

Meyer says, "It's illegal to transport, manufacture, and sell alcohol. There's no law against drinking. There's a lot to be made from this new opportunity."

Rothstein says, "Have you got the chutzpah for the game?"

This is a strange question from an uptown guy in his uptown brown tweed suit and shiny new shoes. What can Arnold Rothstein possibly know of the chutzpah it takes to survive on the street? Survival is not a game. A gamble, yes, but not a game.

An old man shimmies a moth-eaten coat over his sloping shoulders.

He says, "You should check out the Curb Exchange."

Arnold says, "Who needs Wall Street?"

The old man says, "What does Wall Street have to do with this? The Curb Exchange, I said. Every morning I hear the Italians under my window. They make such a racket. Kenmare and Mulberry. See for yourself. But go early. By daylight everybody is gone. Or don't and let the Guineas get the jump on you."

Hymie says, "Prohibition is all about Germans. They're the biggest brewers in America. Overnight they're out of business. No more dollars for the Jerrys overseas."

The old man says, "The war's been over for a year. This is special-interest morality. Social Darwinism. Who are they kidding, these meshugenas? A sober worker is a productive worker."

The old man shuffles out of the house.

"Smarter than he looks," Rothstein says, punctuating the point with a raised eyebrow. He turns to Meyer. "You haven't answered my question."

"Wet blankets," Hymie butts in. "It's in the name. Protestants. Protest. They protest what you want to do, and then they turn their protests into laws."

Meyer shrugs, "We've been making laws for centuries. Six hundred and thirteen of them just landed on Levi Goldman's shoulders."

"What the Protestants lack is the ability to enforce the law," Rothstein says.

"Tell that to the Irish cops," Red says.

Rothstein says, "Fact: There aren't enough cops to stop people from doing what comes naturally. There aren't enough courts to settle the suits even if they could arrest them all. You see where I'm going with this? The rich expect this whole thing to blow over in a year. I'm the guy with connections to the distillers. Let's make haste, gentlemen."

Rothstein slips Meyer his card. It simply says, "Arnold Rothstein," below which is penciled a telephone number.

After the bar mitzvah, Meyer calls his gang together.

"Arnold Rothstein has got contacts with European distillers.

They all play poker together. Rothstein is looking for tough guys to move the liquor," he says.

"We've got contacts with Canadian distillers," Mike says.

"I don't know, Meyer," Sammy says.

"It would take us years to get to know these guys," Meyer says. "We don't have years. Rothstein is already their pal."

Red says, "The Irish are bringing in beer. The Italians got wine. These guys got ties to the old country. Wandering Jews. What have we got?"

Meyer says, "One thing, we're going to be the guys providing quality booze, not this bathtub gin or homemade wine. Got that? We get the real thing and sell to people that know the difference. We get our own distributors and make sure they toe the line. Let the little mobs take the small stuff."

Mike looks around, "We're not little?"

Meyer says, "The Italians are still hanging out in the neighborhood. Half of them don't speak English. We've got the edge. We can maneuver uptown. Take the Tenderloin. You can't manufacture, sell, or transport intoxicating liquors. That's our job description. We've got a car and truck rental business. It's a start. If the Jews in Cleveland figured it out, so can we."

The next morning, Meyer rises before the sun, dons a fine wool coat, and makes his way toward the old man's tenement building. Sure enough, voices pierce the darkness as the Italian Curb Exchange bustles. How had Meyer never seen this before? Tommy the Bull is at the center of the action. Tommy is a fireplug of a guy with the musculature of a professional boxer and a blackjack he keeps tucked in his waistband. He answers to Charlie Luciano directly.

Meyer stops in a shop doorway and smokes a cigarette. A man, fresh off the boat by Meyer's estimation of the guy's immigrant wardrobe, waddles past him lugging two five-gallon cans. The guy drops them in front of Tommy the Bull.

"My cousin runs the still," the guy says. "I drink it myself."

"Yeah?" Tommy the Bull says. "I heard it makes good paint stripper, too."

Tommy the Bull laughs. His good nature keeps the peace, most of the time. He counts out the going rate for homemade wine and sends the immigrant packing.

A truck rolls up and unloads three cases of whiskey. The driver talks with Tommy who whistles and motions another truck halfway down the block forward. The drivers make an exchange, the three cases of whiskey for half a dozen kegs of beer and some rum.

Tommy jots a note on a piece of paper that he stores in the brim of his hat.

The guy picking up the whiskey says, "Hey, Tommy, what do I owe you?"

Tommy hesitates, says, "Gimme a quarter and we'll call it even."

And so goes the tangle of cars and trucks swarming the corner of Mulberry and Kenmare in the wee hours before daylight. Just as Tommy is about to get his break and head in to warm his frozen limbs, a dispute erupts on the sidewalk. A right jab leads to a left hook that sends a trader flying backwards into a case of whiskey. Bottles break and booze spews across the sidewalk. Tommy tries to control the outbreak but he is too late.

"You stupid Kraut!" yells the guy on the sidewalk.

He scrambles to his feet and pulls a revolver held under his belt. The gun explodes, sending a furious echo reverberating along the brick buildings. Tommy clubs the shooter with the worn blackjack. The shooter falls to the sidewalk, splayed in unconsciousness.

"Did you see what he just did!" the incredulous Kraut screams.

"Can it!" Tommy says as the flatfoot brigade pours from the precinct a block away.

Meyer snuffs out the butt of his cigarette on the frozen sidewalk and then slips deeper into the hollow of the doorway from which he's been watching the operation.

Tommy reaches for the roll of fifty-dollar bills he keeps in his inside pocket and peels off two, three hundred worth. He props the unconscious shooter against the wall.

"Shush," he says to the Kraut. "Don't say a word until I give you permission to talk."

Four cops form a circle around Tommy, nightsticks in hand.

"We heard a shot," Tommy is informed.

Tommy crosses each of their palms with greenbacks.

"Everything is under control."

The coppers check the damage, one clocked shooter, one silent Kraut, and a case of lost income. Nothing to get in a twist over.

Tommy folds another fifty and stuffs it in a flatfoot's uniform pocket.

"For good measure," he says. "I'll put aside a few bottles of Bushmills for you."

The posse swaggers back to the precinct. Tommy kicks the broken whiskey bottles into the gutter. He knows Charlie might be watching at this very moment from his second-story office window. If he is, from his vantage point, the whole thing will have looked to him like a Keystone Cops skit.

Meyer emerges from the shadows and passes by Tommy.

"Rough morning?" he says.

"Hotheads," Tommy mutters.

Daylight creeps up from the horizon. Pushcart vendors

clamber along the streets to claim their territories. Meyer grabs a bag of hot pretzels from one of them and makes his way through the car rental garage that serves as the backdrop to the Curb Exchange and then up two flights of stairs to Charlie Luciano's office. The door is wide open.

Meyer says, "Is it always this volatile?"

Charlie says, "Tempers get hot. The hotel bars are shut down but that ain't stopping nobody from wantin' a drink. They serve booze in them little teacups now. Have you seen that? People call room service just so they can drink before they go to dinner. The city has gone wild."

Charlie Luciano recently changed his name to Charlie Lucky because, as he explained to Meyer, "It sounds good, like I'm a lucky guy, which I am, and I intend to keep it that way."

Staying lucky requires some care. The blocks known as Little Italy are run by a guy named Joe "the Boss" Masseria. Joe started shooting his way to the top as soon as he stepped off the boat from Sicily in 1903. He hasn't stopped yet. He is a killer and proud of it. He walks the Italian neighborhood as the victor who defeated the Black Hand and took over the Morello family in 1916. He started bringing in new recruits taken from the splintered crime families of the Black Hand war. Discontent always makes for strange bedfellows. Charlie Luciano was brought in for his fiercely loyal and ruthless mob. Other little gangs followed. In that way, Joe gained strength. He stays strong by ruling with impatience and fury. The younger boys don't mind the hothead if they earn.

"You got any whiskey?" Charlie says. "I got a big order for one of them speakeasy joints around Broadway."

"I can get it," Meyer says. "The good stuff."

"I don't care what it is," Charlie says.

Meyer says, "You should. Broadway means it's fat cats."

"Since when do I give a fuck about fat cats?"

"They have political clout. You make one of them sick and we'll all be thrown under the cart."

Meyer tosses the bag of pretzels to Charlie. Charlie is twenty-three, five years Meyer's senior. In this business, five years is a lot. That's why Charlie plays it close to the vest. He refuses to give the thirty-four-year-old Joe the Boss reason to doubt him unless you consider his relationship with a Jew. Joe tolerates the Jew because he makes him money and because Meyer is tough, but he also suspects his every move. Joe is old-school Sicilian, except for adopting the title Boss to sound more American. The truly Old World Sicilians hate him for this.

Meyer says, "When did you start up the Exchange?"

Charlie says, "It's these guys fresh off the boat. They got no way to make a livin' so they make wine or set up stills and come whining to Joe the Boss for help. What else are they gonna do? Joe gave me the word. I got trucks running in and outta here all the time and now all that crap out there on the street. I put Tommy the Bull on the curb to keep things orderly. You know Tommy."

"Sure," Meyer says. "But what's the logic in putting business out on the street? Illegal business."

"The coppers get their cut. What do they care?" Charlie settles back in the chair behind his desk. He pulls a pretzel from the bag. "Who's your connection for whiskey? The Yids in Ohio?"

Meyer says, "Arnold Rothstein."

Charlie says, "That fancy-pants Yid who runs an antique shop uptown? I hear he's paper rich but cash poor 'cause he gambles like a son of a bitch."

"He has his own pot to piss in which is more than I can say

for us. We're barely removed from the outhouse. He must know something about getting ahead. He plays poker with distillers and mingles with the upper class. He could be useful, Charlie."

Meyer lights a cigarette. Below them, the street buzzes with morning traffic. Tommy the Bull heads to the garage and then pounds his way up the stairs. He pokes his head into Charlie's office and waves an envelope.

Charlie says, "Check out that problem in Staten Island we were talking about, eh, Tommy? I'll get with you later."

Tommy nods, drops the envelope on Charlie's desk and then leaves Charlie and Meyer to their business.

Meyer says, "The Yids in Cleveland have been bootlegging for over a year now. That's how long Ohio has been dry. One year and already they're getting rich running the stuff. Liquor is big business. The distillers everywhere will feel the pinch. We get connected, then we call the shots. What we have going now is nothing compared to what we could have going if we organized this like Rothstein did with gambling. We take the Tenderloin lock, stock, and booze barrel. Joe the Boss will be rich. He won't complain."

Charlie smiles. "Big Bill Dwyer, a stevedore over on South Street, has deals back home in Ireland, Irish whiskey."

"We've got connections with Canada," Meyer says. "How long does it take to get from Canada to New York? How long does it take to get whiskey from Ireland to New York? I say we have the better deal. And we have European connections, too. We're gonna need guys we can trust. You get Vito to use a couple of his guys who are around him, who are closed-mouth, and I'll do the same."

Charlie thumbs through the bills Tommy the Bull left behind in the envelope.

He raises an eyebrow, "The Exchange ain't doin' half bad."

"Small potatoes," Meyer says.

Charlie opens the cigar box on his desk and takes out two Romeo y Julieta cigars. He glides the Cuban under his nose and savors the sweet smell.

"They roll these on the hot thighs of Cuban women," he says.

He performs the ritual of circumcising the cigars then passes one to Meyer. Meyer strikes a match and holds the flame under the torpedo-shaped smoke.

"Forget the hot thighs," Meyer says. "Let's grab the whole megillah while we can."

"The whole megillah?" Charlie says.

"Yeah. Importation, sale, and transportation of intoxicating liquors."

Over the aroma of hot, Cuban thighs, they start working out the details.

Meyer says, "Remember why we moved the craps games indoors?"

Charlie gives a chuckle.

"Who needs the publicity?" Meyer says.

Red Levine's cousin in Cleveland, who knows the Yids running bootleg from Canada, has news to share. "Did you read the paper this morning?"

"Why?" Red says. He made the trip to Cleveland by train and will make the trip back again to New York tomorrow. A pain, but for some things you can't use Western Union.

"They raided a garage in Red Hook where they were making wood alcohol. The gang sent it to Connecticut and all those people got poisoned. Half a glass and you can go blind...or die. Everybody is scared. At least up here bootleggers know our liquor is clean. I can hardly keep up with the demand."

"Who is the main guy up here?" Red says.

"Moe Dalitz," his cousin says and scribbles a phone number on the inside of a matchbook.

Dalitz uses the family laundry business to shuttle booze around Cleveland. Nobody questions the laundry as it circulates between hotels and restaurants. Booze flows across the Canadian border like water over Niagara Falls. According to Red's cousin, Dalitz floats his laundry trucks across Lake Erie on barges, loads them with Canadian whiskey, then floats them back. The mob delivers to Cleveland, Detroit, and Ann Arbor.

"But you gotta be careful," Red's cousin says. "If the customs guys get you, they take your booze *and* your truck."

Red sees Dalitz and makes the case. Then it's back to New York and to Meyer, who has just opened a speakeasy on Broome Street. The speak is not the kind of place that Zelda and Scott Fitzgerald would frequent, even if they were slumming. It is a rundown joint in need of a good fumigation. But with a new coat of paint and scavenged tables and chairs from a failed restaurant, it's not half bad.

Harvey, a broad-shouldered man with a thick moustache, tends bar and oversees a stack of sandwiches, making sure the pile never runs low.

Sammy slides in the back door and lifts a corned beef from the large platter on the sideboard.

"There go the profits," Meyer says.

"I'm hungry," Sammy says.

Meyer gives him a look. Then they all hear a knock at the front door. The bouncer steps up to the door and slides open the small window. One glimpse of Charlie's face is all it takes. The bouncer opens the door wide. Charlie and his boys walk in and fan out.

Harvey hauls a tray of teacups and saucers from the back room.

"It looks like snow," Harvey says, setting the teacups around Meyer's table. "I shoulda taken up baseball. The Yankees and the Robins are in Jacksonville, you know. Jacksonville, Florida. The paper says they're worried about the weather. They're worried about the weather! What's the worst can happen? The sun don't shine for thirty minutes?"

Charlie pulls out a chair and brushes the sawdust from the cuffs of his pants.

"Is this really necessary?" he says.

Meyer says, "It's friendly. Makes the common man feel comfortable. Listen, my guy from Cleveland is coming in tonight. I'd like you to meet him. They've got so many boats running back and forth across Lake Erie people are calling it Jew Lake."

"Sure thing," Charlie says.

Red Levine walks in with Moe Dalitz, the Cleveland connection. He points to Meyer and Charlie. Dalitz strides through the room with the confidence of a man who makes money too easily. He ignores the sawdust clinging to his gray slacks, unbuttons his checkered sport jacket and extends his hand to Meyer.

"You got a nice little concern going here," Dalitz says.

Harvey goes into action with teacups and booze. The piano player slips behind the tall upright catawampus along the wall and dives into a tune. His straw boater bobs along the top of the piano like a target in a shooting gallery. His heavy hands don't tickle the ivories as much as pulverize them.

Dalitz groans, "Warn me if he's going to play *Swanee*."

Meyer says, "What have you got against *Swanee*? That's Gershwin."

"Gershowitz, yeah, I know. He sold a million copies of the

sheet music and two million records. I still might kill the guy that wants to play it." Dalitz grins and slaps Meyer on the back. "Next time this year, you'll be as rich as Gershowitz."

Red leans into the conversation, "You're not going to believe this. Moe has bought up a lot of freight cars. Now he's finagling a piece of the Chicago & Rock Island Railroad."

"A little grease at the rail yard and you'll be pulling in more booze than you can shake a stick at," Dalitz says.

"The line ends in Jersey," Meyer says. "We have a warehouse in Jersey at the end of the line."

"Buy another one," Dalitz says. "You guys interested in the cheap stuff? I know a couple of guys that run a string of brothels in Manitoba. They want into the liquor business. With a name like Bronfman, they probably have the yikhes for it, you know what I mean? The trouble is it takes three years to age whiskey so they've been hurrying the process along with formaldehyde. I can get all you want. You could make a bundle."

Meyer stiffens. Bronf is Yiddish for whiskey, not formaldehyde.

He says, "I'm not looking to embalm my customers. We want first-rate whiskey."

"Okay, okay. I been thinking. There's a guy in Jersey named Abe Zwillman. Maybe you heard of him. He can keep an eye on things on that side of the Hudson." He looks at Charlie. "Abe's having a little trouble with an Italian mob in Northern Jersey. Do you have any influence with the Italian mobs in Jersey?"

"I'll see what I can do," Charlie says. "I might know somebody over there. Who's the guy giving him trouble?"

Dalitz snuffs out a cigarette. "I'll let Abe tell you all about it. I'd probably screw up the facts. I don't want to get anybody in trouble. I'm sure it's just a misunderstanding that can be straightened out with a little persuasion. You'll like Abe. He's a smart guy."

"I know Abe," Charlie says.

"Then you know," Dalitz says and takes another look around the speakeasy. "Nice place you got here. Only don't you think you'd be better off up around Broadway?"

CHARLIE "LUCKY" LUCIANO

Arnold Rothstein

Bootleg on scene of
Wall Street explosion

© COPYRIGHT DREW STRUZAN

Chapter Two
Trust Your Mother but Cut the Cards

NOVEMBER 1920

The Little Jewish Navy opens the Canadian whiskey pipeline wide. While Dalitz loads freight cars and sends them on their way to rail yards in New Jersey, Meyer puts feelers on the street to keep track of speakeasies opening in the Tenderloin district of New York but it is an impossible task. Even the government can't keep track, which is a good thing. Among enterprising capitalists eager to serve the rich, the thinking goes like this: the government has no jurisdiction over a private club. We can do what we want. Just keep it under wraps and don't give out the password to every Tom, Dick, and Henrietta. That's why we call these clubs a speakeasy. Speak softly so the flatfoot on the beat isn't tipped off and we got trouble on our hands. Got it?

The Blind Pig is something else altogether. A Blind Pig is purely lower-class. It's a place where any Joe can pay to see an attraction, like a blind pig, and receive complimentary alcohol. Nobody is selling alcohol. Case closed.

New Yorkers prefer the speakeasy. If you want a quick overview of the city in all its glory, you visit the Woolworth Building. 233 Broadway offers a bird's-eye view of the city. Depending on your economic standing, you can see either how much or how little of the Big Apple you own. The plain farmer's boy, as the papers affectionately call him, thrust the steel frame of his limestone building 761 feet into the air a stone's throw from Wall Street. He modeled the top floor after

Napoleon's Palace in Compiègne and then burrowed into his Cathedral. The view from the 57th floor is stunning, breath-taking, and dumbfounding.

It's midday. A heavy, slushy snow hounds the city for the fifth day in a row which leaves the observation floor devoid of visi-tors, save Meyer and Charlie.

"Ain't that somethin'!" Charlie says, taking in the view.

Twenty-two-point-seven square miles sprawl like an anxious lover, shrouded in a cool, gray mist and filled, at last count, with two million souls. Charlie eyes the man-made maze below. Just five miles north sits the Tenderloin.

Meyer says, "There's a lot of escarole out there."

Charlie says, "I saw the labels them Yids in Detroit are putting on their whiskey. Old Grand Dad. Clever bastards. You can't tell their Old Grand Dad from the American Medicinal Spirits' whiskey."

"Where did you see that?"

"When I was in Brooklyn. Frankie Yale peddles the stuff. You know Yale?"

"Never paid too much attention," Meyer says.

"You might wanna," Charlie says. "He ain't gonna bother the Yids, but the Italians, that's a different story."

The round-faced, Brooklyn-based Yale is moving up the food chain. Like the oil cookstove, he's been increasing his presence in Brooklyn since 1901 and is just as likely to explode. He prizes his prowess and cunning. In the recent war between the Sicilian Morello family and the Neapolitans who were trying to scoop up gambling in Manhattan, Yale kept his dis-tance. His Calabrese ancestry provided a convenient cushion in the largely Sicilian/Neapolitan cleansing. When the fireworks settled, the opposing factions had nearly killed each other off. Yale won by default.

Charlie walks around the bank of windows. Below, the East

River snakes under the Williamsburg Bridge and flows out toward Hell's Gate and the Atlantic Ocean.

Charlie says, "You know how the Irish got strong in America?"

"Politics," Meyer laughs.

Charlie says, "They started with the docks. Then they branched out into politics."

Half a dozen visitors drift in from the elevator.

Charlie says, "Whadya say we get somethin' to eat."

The high-speed elevator descends quickly to the lobby. Meyer and Charlie step out into the slush and mud. A kid, no more than ten, darts across Broadway causing the driver of a delivery truck to slam on his brakes. The truck skids through the soft mud barely missing the young runner before plowing headlong into oncoming traffic. Three trucks ram into each other forming a mangle of windshields, headlights, and metal spokes that stymie a backup of horse-drawn wagons.

The kid barely notices. His military cap is tucked hard under his armpit. The cap's broad band holds the paperwork he is ferrying from a Wall Street broker to a client. His hands are numb from the cold, his uniform soaked from the freezing rain. While other kids opt for a glorious ten cents an hour, this kid works by the piece. By the piece, at a full gallop, he can clear eight dollars in a twelve-hour shift. That's the difference between a pound of beans and a lobster dinner. The kid has chutzpah.

At Ludlow, Meyer hangs a quick left and ducks into Pig Market where, in defiance of New York law, pushcart vendors hawk their wares. An old man huddles over a barrel fire. He looks up and sees Meyer heading his way. The old man's ivories, what is left of them, chatter a love song at the sight.

The old man says, "The kippered herring is very fresh today."

Charlie takes one look at the cold fish and says, "You're kidding!"

Charlie hands the old geezer a five-dollar bill and they head off to Mott Street where the air is scented with sautéing garlic, simmering tomato sauce, and baking bread. Charlie stops in front of a meager establishment, the haunt of manual laborers dressed in holey sweaters and worn trousers sporting paperboy hats shoved high on their foreheads, where they sip soup, twirl pasta, and discuss the pros and cons of anarchy.

"Come on," Charlie says, disappearing into the restaurant.

The owner, a tall, thin Italian with a habit of wringing his hands, escorts his new guests to a back room. Bags of flour and cans of tomatoes and artichokes encroach on the small table meant for staff meals. The Italian spreads the table with silverware, a basket of garlic rolls, and a bottle of Chianti.

"The chicken is straight from heaven," Charlie says.

Meyer says, "They hand out cards at those high society joints around Broadway. The coppers can't go into the joints because they're private clubs. They're springing up everywhere. There's a guy named Waxey Gordon that's moving on these joints. You heard of him?"

He flips a card onto the table. It reads:

THE CLUB NEW YORKER
38 EAST 51ST STREET
NEAR PARK AVENUE

A number stamped on the bottom simulates the mark of a private club with limited membership. A name scribbled along the right-hand side is the code the club uses to either allow or deny entrance.

The paesan that owns the café serves them their chicken on oversized plates along with a fresh basket of rolls. Charlie glides on the aroma then digs in, sopping up the sauce with the lightly battered chicken. Meyer follows suit.

"Well," Charlie says.

"Good," Meyer says absently.

"Good?" Charlie heckles. "Holy, Jesus Christ! This is great. White wine and lemon juice. Reason enough to bring wine into America."

Meyer nods, "Yeah, it's good."

Charlie passes the bread basket. Meyer skates the garlic roll around the sauce in the plate and savors the last bite. Charlie pours more Chianti.

"How many trucks have you got in that garage of yours?" Charlie says.

"Why?" Meyer says.

"We're gonna need a helluva lot more. And tell your friends in Detroit that Colosimo's days are numbered. He won't last out the year. Then they'll be dealing with Torrio and Capone and that's gonna be a whole new ballgame."

The challenge is stimulating. Meyer takes Rothstein's card from his pocket and looks at the number written in pencil.

"That's the Plaza," Charlie says. "Your pal is a regular there."

"Let's see if he's a pal," Meyer says.

After lunch, Meyer rings Rothstein's hotel room.

"Yeah?" Rothstein croaks into the receiver.

"This is Meyer Lansky. I'd like to talk to you about a matter of mutual interest."

Mutual interest is smelling salts to Rothstein's brain. He inhales quickly, slides from the edge of the bed, pads to the window, and then throws open the drapes. The sun pierces his pupils and scorches his brainpan.

"Meet me in the lobby in fifteen minutes," Rothstein says, then reconsiders. "Better make that half an hour, in the tea room. You know where that is?"

"I can find it," Meyer says and hangs up the phone.

Rothstein spends fifteen minutes under a hot shower wringing the stiffness from his neck while Meyer takes a cab from the Lower East Side to Central Park South.

The tea room of the Plaza Hotel is a compilation of white marble floors, mirrored walls, bronze candelabras, gilt-edged Corinthian marble columns, and potted palms. The overhead stained-glass laylight is the size of Rhode Island. The soft glow of its light bulbs diffuses seemliness into the room.

Meyer covers his discomfort by ordering coffee while he waits for the Brain to arrive. Coffee is served from a silver teapot poured into gold-rimmed china cups. He spoons sugar into his cup. The luxury does nothing to allay his awkwardness. To the contrary. It doesn't help that, when he comes, Rothstein strides through the room like Goliath on the battlefield. His medium brown suit cut close to the body but with room to move, white silk shirt, light gray sailor-knot tie, straight-hemmed pants and two-toned oxfords say, 'I belong.'

The waiter rushes to take his order.

Rothstein says, "German toast and orange juice, straight up."

The waiter clears his throat. He is gruff by Plaza standards, perturbed by Rothstein's insistence on something other than finger sandwiches.

The waiter says, "You mean French toast."

"Of course," Rothstein says, "Germans be damned. French toast and orange juice."

He dismisses the man with a glare.

"Did you ever notice that whenever America gets into a war, the menus change? French toast. Liberty cabbage. Liberty burgers. Tell the people what to think and they'll follow you wherever you want them to go. Tell me, what's the gamble, how much do you want, and what's my cut?"

"Connections," Meyer says, "to European distillers. You cut your own deal with the distillers. I'll kick back a couple of points to you on this end."

Rothstein takes a moment to romance his coffee while his brain finishes clearing.

He says, "Why should I settle for a couple of points when I can take the whole hog?"

Meyer says, "That deal you have with Waxey Gordon and his buddy Maxey? If I say you're gonna get a couple of points, you'll get them. Waxey and Maxey won't be your shoeshine boys forever. Trust your mother but cut the cards."

"Word spreads quickly," Rothstein says. "My shiksa wife tells me I'll live longer if I get a steady job. What does she know? She's an actress, had a small part in *The Chorus Lady*." He laughs. "My father nearly dropped dead when I married a red-haired, blue-eyed goy."

"My father's a garment presser. He said I'd die from schmatte's plague if I went into tailoring. He never got over me abandoning the tool and die trade. 'Next to knowing when to seize an opportunity, the most important thing in life is to know when to forgo an advantage.'"

"Disraeli," Rothstein says. "You are educated."

"Nah," Meyer says. "I read a lot."

Rothstein says, "Call me in a week."

Rothstein scribbles an address on the back of his business card and shoves it toward Meyer. "Do yourself a favor; see this man about a suit. If you want to move among the rich, you must shop where Carnegie and Rockefeller shop. Face it, they don't put guys like us on the cover of the *Saturday Evening Post*. You want to blend in."

Meyer says, "I'm not ashamed of who I am."

Rothstein says, "What's shame got to do with it?"

Meyer glances out the window at the slush turned to snow. Forecasters predict the worst winter since 1905. In 1905, Meyer was a kid in the Polish Pale. Manhattan is better.

The waiter returns with a silver tray balanced on his shoulder. He flips open a tray stand and goes about serving the Big Brain his French toast with maple syrup. Even the orange juice commands a plate of its own, fine white china rimmed in gold and embossed with the hotel logo. Rothstein shakes out the pink checkerboard napkin and places it on his lap.

"It's the Plaza," Rothstein says. "Don't look so surprised."

Charlie Lucky and Joe the Boss dawdle over cups of espresso in the corner bakery run by Signora Sabatini. A small man in the corner of the bakery reads *Il Progresso*. The newspaper reports that Umberto Valenti is vying for the presidency of the Unione Siciliana. The newspaper lauds the Unione's virtues, a fraternal organization committed to the needs of Sicilian immigrants. The little man has heard the horror stories that surround Lupo the Wolf, the Black Hand extortionist, who led the Unione until his arrest in 1910. The Wolf is back but it is Umberto Valenti who seeks the presidency.

The little man folds his paper and lays it next to his coffee.

The plump signora pulls loaves of bread from the large oven that lines the back wall of her tiny shop.

"Eeeeeeeeee," the small man screams. "Why you wanna ruin my bread!"

She thumps the loaf's hard crust.

"Perfecto! Sally," she says, clinging to the affectionate form of Salvatore, Charlie's given name, "you please to tell my husband I no ruin his bread! He worry too much."

"She no ruin your bread," Charlie says to the little man.

The husband says, "Charlie, you a smart man. What you think

of this Umberto Valenti? He a big man, no? He gonna be the president of the Unione Siciliana or what?"

Charlie winks, "Not if he knows what's good for him."

The little man blinks hard and slides back behind the news.

Joe the Boss looks about anxiously fearing the rumor that he is the target of a hired gun. There's nothing new in this sensation. The iron fist of Joe the Boss demands payment for any Italian racket in his neighborhood. There is one Salvatore Mauro refusing. Mauro also feels the target on his back. The neighborhood always pays the price.

Charlie checks the time. It's nearly 9 A.M. He and Joe the Boss have lingered in the Sabatini bakery for nearly an hour. The shop bell jingles with the arrival of a new customer. The plump signora wraps a loaf of bread and passes it over the counter. The customer drops the bread into a canvas bag and rejoins the crowd on the street, people in a hurry to get to their jobs.

"Unione! Unione! Is full of peacocks, this Unione," the signora clucks.

She grabs a clean cup from the towel-lined bar beside La Pavoni, the copper torpedo-like brewer shined to a brilliant finish. All the way on the crossing from Italy, La Pavoni sat on the signora's lap. Now it sits on the sideboard next to the bakery case to lure passersby desperate for a real cup of Italian coffee. The lifeblood of the bakery is not bread but the hot water forced through darkly roasted and perfectly ground beans.

Joe the Boss takes a deep breath and relaxes.

"You have another sweet?" he asks the signora.

"Just the thing," she says rushing to the back of the shop.

Through the window, they see Salvatore Mauro making his way down Chrystie Street, nervously looking over his shoulder as he goes. He clings to something in his overcoat pocket. Joe the

Boss unleashes the girth of his belly from its proximity to the small table.

Charlie is close behind him as he exits the café. Like wolves stalking prey, they separate for the hunt. Joe weaves in and out of the crowd, dodging Mauro's glances. Mauro quickens his pace. Charlie cuts through an alley to take Mauro from the front but it is Joe the Boss that gets the jump on the target. Joe jams the nose of a .38 Colt into Mauro's back. One shot and Mauro is down. Blood fills the sidewalk. Mauro struggles weakly as Joe rustles through Mauro's pocket. The bulge he has been nervously sheltering is an envelope full of cash.

Joe grabs the cash and swipes the back of his fingers under his chin. Mauro gets the message.

The scuffle induces momentary bravery among a few of the men on the sidewalk who flail at Joe, trying to disarm him. Joe waves the snub-nosed .38 in their direction. They cower and jump back. Joe escapes into the nearest tenement.

Ten minutes later, the police arrive and surround the block but the shooter is gone. The best any of the fifty-five people who witnessed the murder can remember is that a stocky, evidently Italian man pulled the trigger. Although Joe is arrested, no one can say this is Mauro's murderer. Within hours, Joe is back in the Sabatini bakery sipping espresso.

Across town, the Schmatte, who took pride in knocking over the kosher winery, grumbles in a fit of rage.

"I'm not layin' down for no stinkin' hebes. These little Jew bastards are gonna pay for what they done to Patrick. I'll show that little cocksucker that I ain't afraid him."

When the Sabbath arrives, the Irish gang strikes again. As a token of bravado, the Schmatte leaves his plaid cap perched atop a bottle of Mevushal wine. The word on the street spreads quickly to the rebbe's door. The worry of what might have been lost makes the clock on the wall move more slowly. Eventually the sun sets, freeing the rebbe to take stock of the damage. He finds the plaid cap and takes it to Meyer at the Cannon Street garage.

Benny sees the cap and says, "He's a dead man."

Red sits on the tailgate of an old pickup. A shock of hair sags across his forehead. He is as bitter as Benny but for different reasons.

Red says, "Let's see what Meyer thinks."

Sammy says, "I know this Schmatte."

Benny says, "You know him?"

Red says, "Lots of guys wear plaid caps."

Sammy says, "I recognized him at the winery. He comes around to see my sister. One of his died in the car crash...you remember."

"I remember," Benny says. "It's payback."

"Not until we talk to Meyer," Red says. "Round up a couple of cop uniforms."

Benny smiles.

The first thing Red says when Meyer enters the garage is this: "We have a problem."

He hands the plaid cap to Meyer. Behind closed doors, Meyer listens to the story.

"I sent Benny to get us a couple of police uniforms."

"Get Sammy," Meyer says.

Red pokes his head from Meyer's office and whistles.

"I know this guy," Sammy tells Meyer.

"Do you know where he lives?" Meyer says.

"I can find out easy enough," Sammy says.

"Then do it," Meyer says. "Quietly."

Benny returns with a neatly tied bundle. Red pulls out a

pocket knife to slice through the twine holding the package together. Inside are two neatly folded police uniforms.

Benny shrugs. "Even coppers gotta use a dry cleaner."

The stiff blue jacket is oversized for Red's slight frame but not so much that anyone would think it unusual for a New York City beat cop. Benny's pilfered uniform engulfs him.

"You can't make peace unless you sit down with your enemies," Meyer says.

Benny's face goes red hot. Sammy bursts back in the garage sweating and out of breath. He hands Meyer a paper with an address. Red is shocked by the efficiency.

"It's him," Sammy says.

"Are you sure this is the Schmatte?" Meyer says, doubtful such information could be so quickly obtained.

"It's the Schmatte," Sammy says.

"We aren't in the resurrection business," Meyer says.

"It's his address. I know a guy. That's all I'm gonna say. I'll go with Red and Benny just to be sure."

"Sammy can't sit down with these guys," Benny says. "Nobody can sit down with these guys."

"We don't need a war with the Irish," Meyer says. "We have to play this right. The three of you go. Stake out this guy's house. However long it takes, don't grab him until nobody else is around. Let his gang wonder. Red, when you go to the door, you do the talking. Benny, you keep your mouth shut. In fact, you drive the car. That's what you do best and give that uniform to Sammy. Sammy, you go to the door with Red. Cops on the prowl travel in pairs."

"But he knows me," Sammy says.

"It'll be dark when you knock. Stand back from the door. What's this guy's name, Sammy? You can't knock and ask for the Schmatte."

"James," Sammy says. "James Doyle."

"When Doyle comes to the door, he'll know the score," Meyer says. "He won't risk getting his family killed. We don't need him floating around making more trouble. Handle it."

The week passes slowly. Red and Benny stake out the Doyle household. James comes and goes with no regular pattern. Red talks to Meyer about the move. They decide to dispose of Doyle in the ocean. There are plenty of boats on the sea grabbing booze at the three-mile-limit. Meyer gets Mike Wassell to handle the boat. Mike loads up the souped-up cruiser with window sash weights.

The boys make their move before Shabbat. James Doyle is home eating dinner with his family when Red and Sammy knock on the door. Benny has lifted a paddy wagon for the occasion.

Mike brings the boat to the small spit of land at the end of Cannon Street and waits at the helm while the three men make their move. Red steps from the paddy wagon and raps on the Schmatte's front door with the butt-end of his nightstick. He is careful to use polite force.

The Schmatte's mother peeks through the front window.

Red tips his hat, "We're here to speak to James Doyle, ma'am. We know he's inside."

"My son just sat down to dinner," she says through the open window.

Red smiles, "This will only take a minute."

With his napkin still shoved in his shirt collar, the Schmatte steps between his mother and the kosher police. He scowls at Sammy and tells his mother to go back to her dinner. He steps outside and closes the door behind him.

The Schmatte says, "Well, if it ain't the Jew mob, defender of the faith. What's the matter boys, having a little religious difficulty?"

"A gentleman never forgets his cap," Red says extending the cap to the Schmatte.

The Schmatte reaches for the cap. With a move worthy of a Greco-Roman wrestler, Red grabs his arm, twirls him around, and delivers a bum's rush down the front stoop and into the waiting paddy wagon. Benny puts the pedal to the metal and speeds through the neighborhood to where Mike is waiting.

Within moments, the Schmatte is gagged and bound, bouncing off the deck of the runabout as it slams its way out to sea. When Red finally lets off the throttle, land is barely visible.

Benny rips the gag from the Schmatte's mouth. The Schmatte spits in Benny's face.

Benny says, "Whadya say, can we pass the peace pipe and scurry home like good little choirboys?"

"Do what you want," the Schmatte says. "You'll always be a Jew bastard." He looks at Sammy and says, "I was the best thing ever happened to your sister. The bitch really puts out. I'd never've married the whore though. I couldn't bear the idea of a bunch of dirty little kikes running around my house."

Benny says, "You dumb Mick bastard."

He grabs his pocket knife and drags it hard across the tough cartilage of the Schmatte's neck. It slices deep into the windpipe.

Benny says, "That's one way to shut him up."

The Schmatte gurgles a last breath. A dark stream of blood runs from his neck to the boat's deck. Benny kicks the limp body in a fit of rage. A crimson thread runs to the drain and out into the ocean. Sammy hurls over the stern.

"I'm O.K.," Sammy says, bobbing up to wipe his mouth with the corner of his sleeve. "I'm sorry, Red. When he said those things about Hannah, I wanted to kill him, but when it happened, something awful took over inside. I couldn't move."

"Don't worry, Sammy. Not everybody's cut out for this work. There's no shame. You stick with souping up jalopies and boats."

"That's not it," Sammy says. "I didn't think I was like you and Benny. I didn't think I had it in me. But now I know I do and I'll have to live with that. I guess realizing that kinda scared me, that's all."

Benny hefts the dead body onto the bow. The Schmatte's head dangles to one side. Benny sticks the knife deep at the base of the Schmatte's ribs then pulls it down along his gut. Entrails fall from the carcass, slide across the bow, and fall into the sea.

Benny says, "If you don't cut them open, they bloat and then they float. Now tie the weights on. The fish will do the rest."

The body drops into the ocean.

"That's the last we'll see of him," Red says.

Chapter Three
Survival of the Fittest

SUMMER 1921

The world looked rosy in January of 1921. The *Times* was so taken by the balmy weather that it announced New York was "in the throes of a Southern California winter." Temperatures were beyond mild; they were downright merciful and had been ever since November.

But the compassion was a fraud, Mother Nature's dirty little trick to lure the unwary into a false sense of security. With everyone off guard, she let loose the full force of her fury. Cold fronts rolled down from Canada and slammed the city hard, blanketing streets and buildings with a heavy layer of snow and ice. Hell froze over for weeks on end. Moving bootleg through the country became a test of endurance and natural selection took its course.

In this environment, gangs wither and die like mayflies at sunset. Whenever Meyer hears of a gang's collapse, he mocks: "Survival of the fittest."

It is a notion the streets of New York are no stranger to. The streets get harder daily. The fitter gangs mature and take more to themselves.

"Attrition," Red says.

Sammy says, "Charlie's truck inventory is disappearing faster than Arnold Rothstein's bankroll."

"He's not using Harvard graduates," Meyer says.

The jokes ease the pain of reality.

The winter finally ends, and a too-short spring with it. August rolls around. A wave of heat and humidity strong enough to sweat wallpaper from the walls. Life is again unbearable. Arnold Rothstein makes an exodus to Saratoga where all-night poker games become his ritual. When a streak of bad luck drains his pockets one night, he heads to the hotel for a bacon-and-eggs breakfast. After that, he calls Waxey Gordon. Despite Meyer's warning, Rothstein has chosen to go into business with the two shtarkers.

"Has our ship come in?" Rothstein says.

Rothstein has cut out the middleman by chartering a freighter to shuttle hard liquor and wine from Europe to America. Gordon has the job of making sure the shipment, once it gets to St. Pierre, makes its way to the designated drop-off where he'll distribute the contraband to his dealers.

Waxey says, "You some kinda mother hen? It'll get here when it gets here. Your buggin' me ain't gonna make it happen no sooner. I told ya I'd call when I heard from Greenberg that the captain came through with the goods."

Rothstein drums his finger nervously on the small desk in his hotel suite.

"Have me paged if I'm not in my room," Rothstein says.

"Yeah, yeah," Gordon mutters.

The freighter lands in St. Pierre behind schedule. Maxey Greenberg meets the ship with a flotilla of speedboats. With the cargo accounted for, Maxey spreads the goods among the speedboats and the trek to Montauk Point begins. What was supposed to be a daylight crossing turns into a late-night expedition. It is impossible to see where you are, where you've been, or where you are going. Maxey tries to keep the fleet together using only a searchlight but the swell of the ocean bobs the beam in and out of visibility. The boats bunch together, bumping each other. Fights break out among the captains. This is no well-oiled machine.

Waxey waits at Montauk Point to oversee the disposition of liquor from speedboat to truck. The trucks are lined up along a quiet country road. Rothstein has designated Meyer as distributor for Capitol Wines and Spirits. Benny and Sammy wait in line for their share of the goods.

The local sheriff shows up. Waxey passes him an envelope. They chitchat for a good hour and still the speedboats have not arrived. The sheriff decides he's had enough of the mosquito population and moves on. Two hours later, Waxey catches sight of the flotilla. Maxey signals the truck brigade with two flashes of the searchlight followed by one minute of darkness then two more flashes. The signal almost seems ridiculous now. The waves alone could cause anyone to make the 'appropriate signal.'

"Load 'em up, boys," Waxey says.

The trucks file along the shoreline. Benny and Sammy slog to the bow of the boat carrying Capitol wines and spirits and then slog back and hand off the cases to the boys in their truck. It is nearly ten o'clock in the morning before they pull into the Cannon Street garage.

Red is stretched out in front of an oscillating fan that sways back and forth over a bucket of ice. The cool air waggles his hair and dries his sweat-soaked face. The cheap paper from the pulp magazine he is reading sags from the dampness transferred by his fingers. He strips off his shirt and swabs his face with it. Sweat runs down his back and rings the top of his trousers.

Meyer walks from his office and dips a handkerchief into the bucket's ice water. He slaps the handkerchief on the back of his neck. Red pulls bottles of cola from the bucket and chucks two to Benny and Sammy. Red rolls the cool cylinder of his bottle across his scorching face.

"Can you beat that?" Benny says, envious of Red's setup.

"What the hell happened to you guys?" Red says, noting the water-stained clothes and muddy shoes.

"We didn't know we were going deep-sea diving," Benny says.

"The kid's got chutzpah," Red says to Meyer.

"Is that what you call it?" Benny says. "I call it a sore ass and not enough sleep."

Benny and Sammy go to unload the truck.

"Bring him in closer," Meyer says to Red.

"He's still young," Red says to Meyer. "Tough as nails. Thinks he can solve everything with a gun or a knife. I guess I can't blame him for that. But his temper still gets the better of him."

Meyer says, "Test him. See if we can depend on him."

"He's got a sharp mind for business," Red says. "He likes giving things to people. He gets a kick out of making them happy. He gets heated up over ingrates, though. I'll tell you that. He's fierce about loyalty. Fierce. Ask Moe Sedway, the new guy who I put in the front office to run the rentals. He and Benny are close. Friends from the neighborhood."

Meyer lights a cigarette and looks around.

"Test them both," he says.

The whiskey business has squeezed the rental business to half its former size. The grease monkeys who tend to the end-less maintenance of the cars and trucks no longer laugh when the booze arrives. In fact, they got downright rebellious when the crates of liquor inched up the wall and covered the poster of Olive Thomas. Olive is a grease monkey's wet dream. She per-formed in Ziegfeld's *Midnight Frolic*, an extravaganza set in the roof garden at the New Amsterdam Theatre where girls dance through the audience wearing nothing but balloons. Cigar-smoking customers make short work of their costumes.

Alberto Vargas captured Olive in all her frisky delight, the perfect playmate in kissproof lipstick and a black satin negligee falling seductively from lily-white shoulders. Olive grabs her bare breast tenderly, head tipped back and panting for the red flower held above parted lips. The grease monkeys love her, and don't love the crates covering her up.

But there are crates coming in and it's not a democracy.

"Moe," Benny yells, "get over here and help out with this load of booze."

Moe leaves the front office, and he and Sammy finish unloading and stacking. As for Benny, he has a few things to say to Meyer.

"Waxey oversaw the whole goddamn job. We waited for hours for the ships to come in and then we had to wade out to the boats. You ever try to walk through that shit lugging a case of booze? A monkey coulda done as good a job as that. Why the hell didn't he use the docks? He coulda put all the cases on the docks and we coulda done the job in half the time. He already paid off the sheriff up there. What was the big deal?"

Red gives Meyer the "I told you so" look.

Benny says, "He's got a good bullshit line about the Jews sticking together. He rants on and on about how you can't trust the Italians and how he should be the big man to bring us all together."

Red says, "Living in the same hellhole doesn't make us allies. Waxey is no better than the Italian dons. Besides, bootlegging is bigger than the Lower East Side."

A Hassidic kid stops to press his face against the plate glass window that fronts the garage. He wants to get a look at the famous gaunefs that saved the winery.

Meyer says, "You know the expression frontschwein? It's German for frontline pigs. That's what the German soldiers called themselves, frontschwein. Waxey wants to make us all his frontschwein."

"I thought this was Rothstein's operation," Red says.

Meyer says, "Rothstein can't control Waxey Gordon. Waxey Gordon came out of Benny Fein's gang. While Rothstein was sitting around poker tables, Waxey was out labor slugging. Once Waxey gets a whiff of the money he can make from bootleg, you can bet he'll take control. I'm thinking of bringing Charlie Lucky in as a partner. Charlie has a good lineup of guys. By bringing him in as a partner, we gain his strength."

"And Charlie gains ours," Red says. "And we come under Joe the Boss."

"Not so fast," Meyer says. "We have nothing to do with Joe the Boss. Put yourself in Charlie's shoes. Joe the Boss would have killed him by now if he didn't make an alliance. The alliance gives Charlie strength, too. Charlie's had plenty of opportunities to run us out of business over the years and he's never once taken advantage."

Sammy returns with half a dozen fresh cola bottles clenched between the fingers of both hands and a headlock on a brown bag filled with pastrami sandwiches.

"Those bastards kept us waiting out there all night," Sammy moans, dropping the brown bag to the floor and the sodas into the bucket of ice. "The Coast Guard caught up to 'em before they got to the Point. Did you know that, Benny? One of the guys told me. If they'd a had Curtis engines in those boats, that would've never happened."

Meyer says, "The Coast Guard?"

Benny says, "Maxey paid 'em off. They helped some of the other guys unload their liquor. Everybody has their hand out nowadays. Nobody cares."

Sammy says, "Did you hear what I said? Curtis engines. Do you know what those are? They're the engines that powered the war planes. Now that the war's over, the government has fields of planes…and Curtis engines. They're happy to sell them for a song. I read about a guy in Detroit that put one in his racing boat. He hasn't been beat in any race he's entered yet. A Curtis in our boat would put us ahead of the competition *and* the Coast Guard."

Red says, "Detroit?"

Sammy says, "What do you think, Meyer? If you want to check it out next time you're at the library, the guy's name is Gar Wood. He's a big-time racer. I'd sure like to get a look at that boat. You think the Purples know him?"

A million thoughts explode across the landscape of Meyer's mind. First among them is Charlie's warning. Big Jim Colosimo is on his way out. Johnny Torrio and Al Capone are on their way in and Capone wants to own the Detroit River. That won't sit well with the Jewish gang that has been ferrying booze from Canada across that very river.

"I'll see what I can do," Meyer says, turning away from the conversation, but Benny has the last word.

Benny says, "The real game is getting in a position where you control the price of booze, like Wall Street does. That's how those traders all get rich. Supply and demand, only you control the supply and then demand the price you want. What we need for that are exclusive distributorships."

Jake Lansky, Meyer's brother, whistles his way through the garage. Jake, who likes to be called Jack, wants a roadster. He wants to modify the seat into a stowaway compartment where he can hide whiskey. He wants to be like Larry Fay who runs a taxi business that delivers booze to the big hotels. Meyer figures the job is harmless and asks Sammy to help Jack with the modifications. Benny and Red head out; Benny off to get some sleep, Red to find a connection to the Purple gang. It can't be that hard in a population of Yids.

Meyer packs the small duffel that has been gathering dust in his closet. It is just big enough to hold the necessities for a three-day trip but not so big that he can't schlep the contents around Detroit. He stops at the garage to give Red final instructions, just in case. One of Larry Fay's cabbies picks up booze for his afternoon run. Meyer hops the ride back to Penn Station.

Penn's pink granite structure clings to the summer heat and humidity. Travelers scatter in odd bunches under the steel framework fashioned after the baths of Caracalla. The sun saturates the building sending shards of light through the rising steam of the engines. Meyer boards the Limited and socks himself away in the sleeper car. At last, he can grab a little rest.

The train groans out of the station. Interior lights flicker across the black walnut paneling. The city gives way to an endless series of small towns that eventually turn into farmland.

The train clacks rhythmically. Meyer, a Yid from the Lower East Side without an Ivy League to call his own, travels to Detroit to negotiate what might be the biggest corporate deal of his existence.

From Newark to Youngstown, Meyer nods lazily in the bobbing seat. After three sandwiches and too many cups of coffee, the train pulls into Cleveland. Meyer stretches his legs. The train clacks on the remaining 179 miles of track to Detroit.

He is not in search of Gar Wood. He has heard, from Red, that his old nemesis, Charles Auerbach, is the brain behind Detroit's toughest Jewish mob. Auerbach is the festering wound of a bad memory that refuses to be expunged. Auerbach is the reason for an arrest record when Meyer was sixteen. That it ended in nothing but a two-dollar fine doesn't change the fact.

The Professor, as Auerbach is known because of his obsession with rare books, leaves nothing to chance. His gang consists of winners from the life-and-death game of murders, beatings, and the shifting odds of shtarking. Through a few of Red's connections, Meyer finds the Professor running business from the Shady Lane Roadhouse just north of Detroit. It is an old log cabin, well past its prime, but it serves Auerbach's needs. The roof sags. Antlers hang over the door. Meyer braves the makeshift overhang to see what's inside.

In the middle of the smoke-filled room, with a piano going in the corner and figures seated in the shadows here and there, sits a man in a white suit absorbed in a book. He is clinically clean with newly manicured nails. Meyer recognizes him right away. Not much has changed.

Auerbach looks up and stares at the apparition in front of him. He springs to his feet.

"Lansky? Is that you? Are you on the lam?"

A prostitute scurries over, her long hair dyed red. A soft cotton dress falls off her shoulder and plays peek-a-boo with the nipple of her right breast. The Professor waves her away. Somebody moans painfully in an adjoining room. The piano player beats a little harder on the melody of his favorite song.

Auerbach gestures to a seat, but Meyer remains standing.

Auerbach says, "Thank God for the Eighteenth Amendment. Everything freezes around here in winter. People used to go ice skating. Now they drive across the lake to Canada and fill their trunks with whiskey. The trouble is that they aren't very smart. These yahoos don't realize how much weight they're carrying. Do you know that a man can go through the ice around Windsor and by the time they fish him out, he's made it to Amherstburg? Maybe even Lake Erie?"

Meyer says, "Are you the guy selling Old Granddad to Frankie Yale?"

"Same old Lansky. Get right to the point. What is your interest in Old Granddad or Frankie Yale, for that matter?" Auerbach says. "Yale is as cheap as his cigars. He'll cut the stuff two, three times before he sells it. As I recall, you're something of a purist when it comes to crime. You only steal the best."

Meyer says, "Why would Yale come to you?"

Auerbach says, "The history of Brooklyn reads like a regular Roman tragedy. There's no love lost between Yale and Capone. Maybe Yale just wanted to get rid of Capone so he sent him to Torrio. Ever think of that? Capone has his eye on the throne. Yale doesn't need that kind of competition or trouble."

The Professor flips through the pages of the leather-bound book he's been reading. An ornate woodcut of soldiers in battle frames the title: *The Arte of Warre, written in Italian by Nicholas Machiavel, and set forth in English by...*

"Machiavelli had it figured out all the way back in 1523," the Professor says. "The book is invaluable for understanding the Italian mind. You really should locate a copy for yourself if you intend to keep hanging around with that Italian, what's his name? Charlie? Yes, Charlie something."

Raymond Bernstein, a rough-looking character wearing a blood-spattered shirt, yanks a chair from a nearby table. He gives Meyer the once over, then sits down at Auerbach's table. The red-haired prostitute with the peek-a-boo dress brings a fresh bottle of Old Granddad to the table. Bernstein pours a drink and slams it back. He pours another.

Auerbach says, "This is Meyer Lansky, Raymond. He's come all the way from New York. Wants to know why the wops in New York are doing business with us."

A sparkle fills Bernstein's dreary eyes. "Who the hell cares?

Take the money and run. That's what I say. Thirty miles of river, that's what we get in this fekockteh world and somebody's always tryin' to take it away from us."

His eyes are puffy and outlined by dark circles. His thick, dark hair falls loosely around his face, the product of the tussle in the adjoining room.

Auerbach says, "Raymond is the brawn."

Raymond Bernstein scowls and slams another drink.

Meyer looks at Auerbach, "Capone intends to own the River. It's his men you'll be chasing."

"He's nothing," Bernstein says. "I'll stick his head so far down an ice hole he'll be looking at China."

The Professor says, "Raymond knows nothing of Machiavelli or the Romans. Truth is, they never allowed a trouble spot to remain in their realm simply to avoid going to war. They understood that an ignored war doesn't go away. It is merely postponed to someone else's advantage. Guys like Yale and your friend's boss still believe in the glory of Rome. It's in their blood. 'Know your enemy' is just common sense. You can learn from the past."

Meyer ignores the history lesson.

"Why Yale?" he says.

"Why not?" Auerbach says. "What really brings you to Detroit?"

A while back, when Meyer was a young teen, two of Auerbach's whores called the cops to put an end to Meyer's attempts to organize them. Lena Freedman and Sarah Ginsburg were their names. They are indelibly etched in Meyer's memory. Lesson learned.

Meyer says, "Prohibition. What else?"

Auerbach says. "You're not thinking of undermining my business again, are you? I thought we ironed all that out years ago."

"I'm not interested in your business," Meyer says. "I am

interested in cooperation. Who knows how far Prohibition will go. If we cooperate, we can make the most of it. I know a guy who might be able to help if Capone tries to make a move on the Detroit River. Why waste time with a war if you don't have to?"

Auerbach looks at Raymond, "The wheels are always turning in Meyer's mind."

Meyer says, "Are you interested in avoiding war?"

Auerbach says, "I'd be a fool to resist, if it is really avoiding, not merely deferring."

Meyer says, "Then I will get back to you when I put things together." He pauses and then says, "Do you know a guy named Gar Wood?"

Auerbach says, "He filled the newspapers for weeks."

"A friend of mine wants to meet the guy that set the world's record for speed by putting an airplane engine in his boat. He's supposed to be in Detroit."

"That can be arranged," Auerbach says.

Auerbach pulls a folded prescription form from his breast pocket and hands it to Meyer. The workmanship is impressive, like an oversized dollar bill and just as valuable as cash. "Original prescription form for medicinal liquor," it reads. "Issued under authority of the National Prohibition Act." Blanks for "kind of liquor," "quantity," "directions," "name of patient," and other necessary information. The form and the receipt bear a duplicate number stamped in red.

"There's a lot of money in pharmaceuticals," Auerbach says. "If you've got the doctors, I've got the guy with the paper that can move plenty of booze your way."

"I'll get back to you," Meyer says. "I'll have to speak with my associates."

✤

Meyer returns to New York and dumps the contents of his duffel onto his bed. He sorts through the details of the journey and picks up the prescription form. "Ailment for which prescribed."

Benny knocks on the door.

"What are you doing here?" Meyer says.

"You just got back, didn't you? I got something to talk to you about."

Meyer makes coffee. Benny pours out the story of the three-mile-limit. Big Bill Dwyer's latest connection is an Irish ship Captain named McCoy. McCoy runs rum from the Caribbean but you better be sure you get the real McCoy when you go out to get him. McCoy sits just off the shores of Montauk Point in the international waters where no one can touch him or confiscate his shipments.

Benny says, "There's plenty of guys claim to be McCoy but they ain't. They take your money and give ya shite. That's what Big Bill says. They give ya shite. He says make sure ya bring gunny sacks for the booze. I told him we'd line the hull with mink coats. You know what he said?"

Meyer doesn't bite.

"He says 'them bottles are worth more than them varmints.'"

For some reason, this strikes Meyer as amusing.

Benny says, "Let's go. Sammy wants to try out the Curtis engine."

"What Curtis engine?" Meyer says.

"Haven't you been listening? The cruiser will beat any Coast Guard ship on the water if it has a Curtis engine so Sammy bought an engine and put it in a boat. I got a bunch of orders for rum to fill. McCoy has plenty of the stuff. The real thing, from the Caribbean. You want good quality, well, here's our chance to get real rum. Come with us and see how fast this Curtis is."

Meyer shakes his head, "I've had enough travel."

Benny says, "The salt air will do you good."

An hour later, the three men pile into the 45' cruiser. The stripped-down cabin is inhospitable. It echoes and intensifies every gurgle. Sammy fires up the engine. The noise is deafening, even worse in the cabin. Meyer makes his way to the back of the boat and puts a death grip on the stern. Benny slams down the throttle. The cruiser flies wildly along the East River, then out through Hell's Gate. Nautical miles slap by in a dull rhythm of hull to sea until finally the blackness of the Atlantic Ocean appears.

The lights of anchored ships come and go with the roll of the sea. Eyeing what's left of the visible horizon and guessing at the location of Block Island, Benny plots a course to the south, about three miles south, where international waters harbor the rum-laden *Henry L. Marshall*. Just off Montauk Point, two loud cracks sound off the starboard side of the cruiser.

"Thunder," Sammy says.

"That ain't thunder," Benny says. "I know a gunshot when I hear it."

Benny kills the engine and the cruiser's lights. The ocean slaps against the hull, heaving the boat through the black abyss. Sammy listens to the hum of a distant motor.

"They're moving away from us," Sammy whispers.

Benny searches the silence and hears rustling, then hushed voices. Suddenly a light pops on just off the starboard bow. And then another. The outline of a schooner appears in the darkness. Benny gives the ignition a quarter turn to bring up the running lights.

The *Henry L. Marshall* looms in front of them. Four men with rifles line the deck.

"Put your weapons where I can see them," one of them yells.

"Is that Captain McCoy? Bill Dwyer said you were tough," Benny says. "Kinda late for target practice, though, ain't it?"

Sammy throws the bowline to the first mate of the *Marshall*.

Benny says, "We're in the market for about two hundred crates."

"Crates?" McCoy laughs. "We don't use crates. You want crates, you bring your own. Didn't Bill tell ya?" McCoy lets out another boisterous belly laugh. "Let's see the color of your money."

Benny pulls a roll of hundred dollar bills from his pocket and the exchange begins, McCoy's crew forming a brigade of men moving the burlap-wrapped bottles from the hold of the *Marshall* to the three Jews shuffling the same bottles into the stripped-out cabin.

"Stack them wall-to-wall," Sammy says to Meyer.

After the first layer, Meyer's hands are raw and bleeding from the rough burlap. Sammy throws a pair of gloves at Meyer. With the hull full, Benny counts out ten thousand dollars. The *Marshall*'s first mate throws off the bow line. Benny sights the Montauk lighthouse and points the bow toward the light.

Half a mile out, another thunderous crack rips through the night air. This time the hull is breached by a wild spray of bullets. Whiskey spills everywhere. Benny kills the lights and gives Sammy the wheel while he ducks into the cabin to grab an armful of rum bottles.

He pulls the burlap from the bottles and stuffs them in the bottlenecks.

"Meyer," he says, "gimme your matches."

Sammy says, "There's a gas can in the cabin. That's what you really want...and a couple of cans of oil. If you put the oil in the gasoline, you'll really get a kick. Here, I got matches."

Meyer takes over the wheel while Sammy and Benny go to work on the makeshift bombs. Benny tears the sleeve from his shirt, knots the end and stuffs it into the can.

"Head into them, Meyer," Sammy says.

Meyer spins the boat around and opens the throttle. Bullets pummel the hull. Whiskey sloshes across the deck. Benny lights the fuse, then lobs the gas can off the stern. The gasoline explodes, raining down burning oil onto the would-be hijacker's deck. Someone screams. The shooting stops.

Meyer slows the cruiser and turns the boat around. Benny readies for another pass but the blaze aboard the hijackers' boat has already filled the darkness with flames.

Sammy says, "That's why you have a Curtis. Can't beat 'em for speed."

When the boys return to Manhattan, Red is waiting patiently on the stone breakwater at the end of Cannon Street. He jumps to the small spit of land along the stone wall to secure the bow line.

"What the hell happened?" Red says. "You smell like a Caribbean whorehouse."

Meyer says, "Forget about fast engines. Armor plate this thing."

Meyer steps from the boat fueled with a better understanding of what it takes to import and transport booze. They're going to need sailors if they're going to avoid burials at sea, sailors and connections. His first thought is of Charlie Lucky.

He finds Charlie at an opium den on Pell Street where a petite Chinese woman dispenses the "Big Smoke." She wears plain black pants and a frog-button silk jacket. She rolls the opium pill. Her fingernails are long and stained dark from the constant contact with the brown, tarry substance. She primes the pipe then hands it to Charlie. He leans back against a pile of silk-covered pillows.

Meyer sees Charlie drawing deep breaths from the opium pipe. Charlie smiles up at Meyer. He shakes his head, closes his eyes, and dreams of absolutely nothing.

Waxey Gordon

Texas Guinan

Longy Zwillman

Ziegfeld Follies

4

Chapter Four
Don't Get Involved

The Director of the National Republican Club turned Federal Prohibition Director, Ralph Day, threatens to padlock the "all-night restaurants" along New York's boozing forties, the streets from 40th to 49th that surround the Theater District. When guys like Ralph Day make the forties the target of their scorn, the inadvertent side effect is the adrenaline rush from getting through the front door. The experience is downright addictive.

Benny and Sammy make the rounds through the forties, not for the thrill, not even to rub shoulders with New York's most influential, but to introduce themselves as the new distributors.

It is just after midnight. Benny leans against the façade of the Court Theater not far from the Club Moritz, his newest client. The singer at the Moritz swings suspended over the stage. It's the rage.

"You see how that guy rolled over when I made him an offer?" Benny says to Sammy.

"Did you see how he looked at your .38 when your jacket popped open?" Sammy replies.

Theaters dispense a steady stream of business to the clubs that Ralph Day threatens to padlock.

Benny says, "You see these people? They vote. That's what keeps these politicians in line. The Feds will never be able to padlock this town. Three hundred court cases and only one indictment. What does that tell ya?"

Sammy works the brim of his new fedora. He flips it atop his head and tugs it into a slight rake that dips across his right eye.

Sammy says, "Meyer says the Mullan Gage law only succeeded in making a Graft Squad." Meyer is referring to New York's version of the 18th Amendment, 25,000 state and local police officers in charge of enforcing Prohibition.

"Meyer knows what he's talking about," Benny says.

"Those Yids in Brooklyn, Moe and Izzy, bust a hundred joints."

"Pathetic!" Benny says of the fat, cigar-chomping rumhounds of a thousand disguises who make a job of rounding up violators. "Those guys got more costumes than a production house."

A black Cadillac pulls to the curb and stops. The chauffeur scrambles to open the passenger door. Two girls, dressed in matching silk gowns, step from the car's blackness. The breeze plumps the gowns into soft, billowy clouds. Sammy's boasting stammers to a halt as his mind ceases to work so his eyes can gaze desirously at the girls' bare legs.

Then comes the john. There's no mistaking the face or the slumped shoulders that turn a Savile Row suit into a circus-monkey disguise. The brute is none other than Waxey Gordon, who sees Meyer's neophytes taken by his glamorous lifestyle.

"Connections," Gordon says with rasping disdain. "You want 'em; I got 'em. Don't think I don't recognize you, kid. I never forget a face."

Gordon fishes through his inside coat pocket and hands Benny a printed card that reads: Irving Wexler, Real Estate, Knickerbocker Hotel. The girls glom on to Gordon, one on each arm, and the ensemble sways into the Club Moritz.

"Irving Wexler," Benny huffs. "Who does he think he's kidding?"

"If he ain't got the Moritz, he's gonna want the Moritz," Sammy says. "You think he's gonna frequent a place that he don't have some connection to?"

"You worry too much," Benny says. "I got a better idea. Let's check out his operation. He's all but begged us to. Irving Wexler? Knickerbocker Hotel? I gotta see this place."

The boys make short work of the five blocks from the Moritz to the corner of 42nd and Broadway where twelve floors of red brick and terracotta rise to form the Knickerbocker Hotel. Benny is inside before Sammy can object. Orchestral music drifts from the ballroom. A flock of top-hatted and tailed men gather around an oversized fountain where a cherubic, gold cupid plays around a marble bowl. Behind them is a tapestry of Caesar's conquest of Pompeii.

Benny says, "This is where the Pinkertons pinched Monk Eastman. They had a shootout and everything. Right here. Can you beat that? He got ten years at Sing Sing just for robbin' a guy. Ain't that a poke in the eye? What do you think these guys do all day so's they can party like this? Nobody is throwin' them in jail for all the robbin' they do."

Sammy ogles the portable wealth that dangles around the necks of the Astor crowd gathered to celebrate the debut of the daughter of a railroad magnate into New York society. The alleged home of the dry martini is a monument to New York's upper class. Marble pillars and bronze pendant lanterns fill the lobby. A painting of Father Knickerbocker, quaint and out of date in his Dutch costume, reminds hotel guests of the lucrative nature of the hotel turned office building business.

Sammy grabs his fedora and crumples it nervously. He and Benny pass a row of safe deposit boxes, a book stand, a ticket office, and a dining room. Lilies, housed in the flower room, perfume the walkway.

Sammy says, "It was Monk Eastman's partner that gunned him down, in the subway station."

Benny says, "Stop wringing your hat. You look like an immigrant."

Sammy sneaks a peek in the King Cole Bar and blinks hard. The longest "dry" bar in the world is anything but dry. Champagne flows like Niagara Falls, with Rudolph Valentino at the center of the room riding high on his success as *The Sheik*. The women fumble. He spins them around the room, a taxi dancer more intoxicating than the Champagne.

Benny grabs Sammy away. They hop the elevator to the fifth floor where Irving Wexler maintains an office. The floor is quiet. No night guard. Benny works the lock. The door opens easily. The office looks like any other, simple mahogany desk, two-drawer filing cabinet, and a couple of overstuffed chairs.

Benny looks back at Waxey's card.

"This can't be it," Benny says.

He jimmies the inside door that leads to an adjoining room. Jackpot. The stench of Gordon's cheap cigars permeates the room. A gray film covers the windows and clock faces.

There's a noise in the hallway.

"Let's get outta here," Sammy whispers.

But Benny is obsessed with uncovering Waxey's secrets. A quick glance around gives the impression of a bookie room. Benny's gaze stops on the blackboards. They are filled with times and places that fail to jibe with the racing world. A giant nautical map sprawls across a back wall. A wireless consumes half a table. He thumbs through the paraphernalia strewn about the room and makes a mental tab. Code books. Timetables. Tide tables. A list of Coast Guard cutters. Names of ships. Names of captains. Call numbers. Passwords. A map of Long Island with circles around various inlets.

"He's running a goddamn navy here," Benny says.

Benny noses the map. Red-tipped pushpins dot the three-mile limit and circles highlight various docks on the East River and the Hudson. On an adjoining table, Benny finds Waxey's notebooks filled with names of unions and gang bosses and dock workers.

He says, "Little Jewish Navy, my ass. This guy's the real deal."

"Whadya mean?" Sammy says.

"We're freezing our butts off in tin cans picking up crates while he's sittin' at the Ritz calling the shots." Benny runs his finger along Long Island, then through a sea of dots and numbers. "He knows where all the ships are all the time." Benny lifts the headset of the wireless. "He's talking to the ships. No wonder he prances around town acting like he owns the place. He's got one helluva cock to think he can stick it wherever he wants. Fucking Rothstein. This is his doing."

Benny slides the wireless headpiece over his ears and fiddles with the dials.

"Hello…hello?" he says into the transmitter. "Take out those shtarkers in the 45' cruiser."

A voice comes back, "Who is this?"

Benny flips the switch 'off' and flops into the Louis XIV side chair. "You suppose those pirates were Waxey's guys?"

Sammy says, "Maybe. Why would Waxey attack us?"

"Don't be stupid," Benny says. "What a bunch of schmucks we are."

Sammy picks up a code book. The orchestra in the ballroom strikes up again, a waltz to keep the crowd moving through the stifling heat. Someone shoves a key into the front office door. Benny flips off the lights and scrambles for a side door leading to the hallway and finds it secured with a steel bolt.

Someone is in the front office and is working his way toward the inner door.

"Hide," Benny says.

Sammy takes shelter behind the floor-length drapes and chokes back a dusty sneeze. Benny ducks into the bathroom and draws his Colt, pointing it at the door.

The door between the two offices opens. Someone flips on the light. Sammy peeks out from the dusty drapes. It's Arnold Rothstein. Rothstein rustles through batches of papers stuffed in the cubbyholes of the rolltop desk. He thumbs his way through a log book then pulls a pad from his breast pocket and begins to scribble.

A giggle in the front office gives Rothstein a start. It's Waxey and his broads. Waxey barges through the inner door eager to catch the thief rummaging through his operation.

Waxey says, "What the hell are you doing in here?"

Arnold waves his little black book, "Did you think I wouldn't find out?"

Waxey laughs. "You keep your hands clean, don't you? What's your beef?"

A row of pearly white teeth shine in Arnold's stiff grin.

"I make the connections; you make the deliveries. Cutting the booze wasn't part of the deal. We're serving high-class customers."

"Things change," Waxey says. "This way there's plenty to go around."

Arnold shakes his head. "You think like a two-bit operator. The whiskey I ship is top shelf. You don't have to find customers. They find you. The rich know the difference. You cut the quality and you lose the customers who protect us from this wretched law."

Waxey says, "Shemozzle back to your poker game, Arnold. You think your goy wife makes you one of the boys. You're still a dirty little kike as far as they're concerned. Now if you'll excuse me, the broads and me would like to get down to business."

Waxey plays a little grab-ass and somewhere between Angie's silk-covered bottom and the contour of Edie's ample breast, he notices Sammy's shoes poking out from under the curtain. He grabs the closest thing to him sure to cause damage, a heavy glass ashtray with hard corners, and sends it sailing toward the curtain. The ashtray finds its mark with a sickening thud.

Sammy falls to the floor and into the light. He clutches his arm and writhes in pain.

"One of yours?" Waxey says to Arnold.

Benny jumps from the bathroom, his .38 aimed at Waxey's head.

"One of mine," Benny says. "You said come by, so we did. Now what?"

Sammy cradles his arm and struggles to his feet. Gordon reaches for the baseball bat behind the rolltop desk.

Benny says, "I wouldn't."

"You got beytsim, kid," Waxey says. "I'll give you that. You see what kinda business I got. If you got any brains, you'll come in with me. What you're doing with that small-time mob on Cannon Street don't make no sense. I could use a kid like you but don't get the wrong idea. I ain't no wet nurse. Next time you pull a prank like this, you'll be licking the bottom of the East River with a bloated, purple tongue."

Benny maneuvers to Sammy's side then hustles him from the hotel room. Back on the sidewalk, he hails a cab and together they head for Meyer's flat.

"We had a little trouble," Benny says rifling Meyer's refrigerator. "Where's the steak?"

Sammy nurses his arm. Meyer peels Sammy's shirtsleeve back and winces.

"What's wrong with ice?" Meyer says.

Meyer chips away at a large block of ice until the shavings fill a dish cloth. He puts the cold pack on Sammy's arm.

Benny says, "We saw Gordon's setup."

Sammy says, "We broke into his office."

Benny says, "It's a helluva setup at the Knickerbocker."

Sammy says, "It's true."

Benny says, "Rothstein showed up while we were having a look around. He wasn't happy with whatever it was he found in the rolltop. Then Waxey came in with his broads. Rothstein accused him of cutting the booze."

Meyer says, "So what?"

Benny says, "They fought. The Brain is in way over his head. Waxey's got ex-cons to do his dirty work. What's a guy like Rothstein gonna do with that?"

Meyer says, "Gordon's a regular patron saint of ex-cons."

Benny says, "He's on top of the world, Meyer. He struts around Manhattan like some kinda peacock. And he's got cash. He can afford to put streetwise guys to work."

"We've got allies. He can't push us around without a fight."

Sammy tries to flex his swollen arm. It's no use. Purple has spread clear down to his elbow.

"You ain't goin' home," Benny says.

"I have to," Sammy says.

"What the hell do you think you're going to tell your mom? You went a few rounds with Harry Greb?" Benny says. "I never knew a Yid could hold his own in the ring. You can try. They might buy the story."

"I'll just tell 'em that a bunch of canned goods fell on me while I was stocking shelves. It happens all the time."

Meyer says, "Waxey wants to rule over everybody but his mob has no cohesion. He can't fight all of us. That's a fact."

A week passes. The summer heat swelters at 95 degrees.

Fruits and vegetables rot on the pushcarts. Flies swarm the putrid alleys. Sweatshops become death shops.

Reluctantly and with no other discernible option, Arnold Rothstein schleps down to the Lower East Side where rotting garbage and the stench of windowless tenements make his eyes water. He finds Meyer in a stiff-back chair in front of the garage reading. Moe Sedway leans against the brick wall and watches the traffic go by.

"How can you stand it?" Rothstein says.

"What can I do about it?" Meyer says.

Rothstein looks tired, humbled, and tormented.

He says, "Humans are nothing but dubs and dumbbells."

"Is that a personal reflection?" Meyer says. Meyer turns to Moe, "Give us a minute, will ya, Moe?"

"Sure," Sedway says, leaving them to their discussion.

"See the corpses of Jerusalem," Rothstein says, gesturing to the over-crowded ghetto.

Meyer says, "This is the army that lost the war. Now they're stuck doing factory work. The slaves have been chained to the sewing machines."

"My father was a cloth merchant."

"My father is a tailor," Meyer says.

"Discontent," Rothstein says, "the stuff scandals are made of. It was the loophole in major league baseball. They settled out of court, you know. All those ball players got acquitted. The league didn't want anybody looking too closely at where all the money goes."

Meyer says, "You didn't come to talk about baseball."

"What are you reading now?" Rothstein says.

"It's a Roman thing. This guy, Machiavelli, tried to sum up the principles of war."

"Any good?" Rothstein says.

"It's O.K.," Meyer says. "Not sure it's useful for here."

Rothstein says, "I have a proposition. I need you to put a little fear in Waxey Gordon. I'm sure by now Benny told you about the scuffle at the Knickerbocker."

"This business is between you and your gaunef friends. I can't step into the middle of that."

"One hand washes the other," Rothstein says. "I found a guy with certificates of withdrawal. He started in business with a pharmacy. Now he's a lawyer. He's got a setup for medicinal alcohol. This guy reads the Volstead Act for pleasure. You two would get along like gangbusters. You could make a bundle."

"No deal," Meyer says. "On the street, I protect my interests. If you want me to protect yours, you'd have to give me a piece of the business so it becomes my business. That's the way it works. Why would I start a war over something that's none of my business?"

Rothstein looks at his watch, "Can we get out of here? Lunch? Uptown, in a real restaurant?"

Meyer stands and hails a cab.

The "real restaurant" is a private club that occupies a narrow building six stories high. It is one of Rothstein's favorite haunts. They walk up six steps to an arched doorway that gives way to a room lined with quarter-sawn oak panels and fine leather chairs. Heavy beams span the ceiling and rest on ornately carved corbels. Bookcases filled with leatherbound tomes line the walls. The place is full of White Anglo-Saxon Protestant men. Period.

Two Jews entering the establishment for lunch make no sense whatsoever.

"You just have to be on speaking terms with John Knox," Rothstein says, referring to the C-note that gets him into the high-stakes gaming tables behind these closed doors.

They climb a flight of stairs to a dining room. Rothstein settles into a small table. The waiter arrives promptly.

"Brandy for my friend," Rothstein says to the man in the white jacket.

"I prefer whiskey," Meyer says.

"Trust me," Rothstein says.

Meyer looks around. Snifters are the badge of courage, the telltale mark of a successful swindle.

"Whiskey on the rocks," Meyer says. "How about you?"

Rothstein says, "I never touch the stuff. It dulls the senses."

The waiter departs as silently as he arrived.

"Have you ever been to Saratoga in August?" Rothstein says.

"No," Meyer says.

"The sport of kings brings in the real gamblers. Everything is out in the open. It's all chafing dishes and Champagne glasses. I married Carolyn in Saratoga Springs…on a Thursday…1909. Come up. I'll show you the Brook. It is a magnificent gambling house."

"That your joint?" Meyer says.

"The Brook is no joint," Rothstein says. "And, yes, it's mine."

The waiter brings whiskey and runs through the choices of the day.

Rothstein says, "You should try brandy. If I drank, that would be my poison. You can't cut it with more alcohol. What you get is useless. Nobody would buy it. Know your customers, the guys sitting around you. They make the laws…and bend them to protect their interests."

"Brandy?" Meyer says.

"Among other things."

Meyer says, "I can't help you with Gordon unless you bring us in on your end of the business. My associates agree. You bring us in and we will sit down with Gordon and let him know about our association. We'll take care of your customers. Let Waxey and Maxey have the cheap customers. It's not going to hurt your business. Those people will buy from the cheapest distributor anyway."

The man in the white jacket returns. Lunch at the club is the gentlemen's version of a hot dog on Coney Island and a crisp pickle from Gus's. Meyer looks down at the club sandwich of toasted Wonder bread spread with mayonnaise, crisp bacon, chicken, and tomato slices and the side of fruit cocktail. It makes Coney Island look regal.

Rothstein pushes at the meager sandwich removing the bacon, chicken, and tomatoes. He dabbles with the food and finally says, "Deal."

After the dull lunch in WASP heaven, Meyer hops a cab back to Little Italy and calls on Charlie Lucky in the Mulberry Street garage. He breaks down the story of the gentlemen's club. He tells him about the certificates of withdrawal and the pharmaceutical angle. But the real topic of conversation is Waxey and Maxey's operation and Rothstein's discontent.

Charlie has a good laugh.

"You know what Rothstein is good at?" he says. "He knows if you're goin' to Saratoga in August, you should bring a white suit cause white's what you wear after Memorial Day." He laughs again. "And he's good at handling them high-society types which is something you and I ain't no good at. He's got class. So, what? He's a gambler. No shit Waxey and Maxey took advantage."

Charlie shows off a cache of forged whiskey labels and tax-paid stamps. Meyer admires the handiwork.

"A guy from another family came by the Exchange this morning. Not bad, huh?"

"It's good," Meyer says.

"What were you sayin' about Waxey?"

Meyer says, "He's been taking Broadway shows to Sing Sing to create goodwill with the inmates. When the guys get out of the can, they go looking to him for work. He's got a tough mob. It's stiff opposition."

Charlie says, "Yeah? Plenty of guys come outta Palermo, too. They ain't no dandies. They only speak Italian. Where do you think they go for work? Besides, the stiffer the opposition, the better the fight. What's your plan? You gonna pair up with Rothstein?"

Meyer says, "He's got value...connections. I'll meet with him when I'm ready. Rothstein's gotta cough up his certificates of withdrawal and agree to a split on the booze profits."

Charlie shrugs. "I got business to take care of before I can put my gang onto this. Joe the Boss wants a spaghetti dinner. Then we deal with Waxey."

"Who's the target?" Meyer says.

"A guy named Rocco Valenti. Somehow Lupo the Wolf's nephew got shot, now Joe's gotta take revenge."

Meyer says, "I read about that in the papers. They opened fire on city streets. The papers chalked it up to bootleggers but it was Black Handers."

Charlie says, "Yeah. Terranova was gunned down in front of his own house. Joe is his ally. Joe has to take revenge or the Morello family will never line up behind him. That's the way these things work. He ain't got no choice."

"I'm not telling you what to do but if you can, Charlie, try to keep the violence off the streets. We don't need the government handing law enforcement a blank check to clean things up."

"I hear what you're sayin'," Charlie says. "It's a spaghetti dinner. The odds are things will be settled in the restaurant. Who's this guy with the certificates of withdrawal? Can we trust him?"

"The guy's name is George Remus," Meyer says. "I checked him out. He's a lawyer. He scoured the Eighteenth Amendment for loopholes. They weren't tough to find. Lawyers live for this stuff. Seems he's something of a celebrity among the upper class in Cincinnati. He's been around the pharmaceutical business all his life so when the law made prescriptions exempt, he got into the certificate business. I don't know how he and Rothstein connected but you can be sure he's looking for two things: doctors willing to write phony prescriptions and tough guys able to persuade them."

Charlie laughs.

Meyer says, "Remus was in the news a month or so ago. His farmhouse was raided and six of his men were arrested and indicted for violation of the Volstead Act so he must be running booze, too."

"You gonna meet him?"

"Sure, why not?" Meyer says.

After working out the arrangement with Rothstein, Meyer meets Remus at the Red Head, a small speakeasy on the west side of Sixth Avenue where doctors, politicians, bohemians, and entertainers hang out. Rothstein says the lawyer will feel right at home. Jack Kriendler, the proprietor, greets Remus and Meyer at the door. Filled with boozed-up flappers and tipsy college blades, the speak reeks of a fraternity hall atmosphere.

"It's all about the loopholes," Remus says over a teacup of hooch. "I worked in a pharmacy when I was a kid. I owned a pharmacy when I was nineteen. You can get away with a helluva lot."

Remus is gruff. A permanent scowl hangs over squinting eyes. Deep creases run from the edge of his prominent nose to the down-turned corners of his lips. His suit has that slept-in look, pressed-in wrinkles wherever his large frame bends.

"Welcome to the Red Head," Jack says, pouring a second round.

Jack keeps the lights dim. An overhead fan labors to expel the heat. The embossed tin walls are washed in yellow paint. The kitchen, what little there is of it, is in a curtained-off alcove. Jack fills the place with small wooden tables and straight-backed chairs, throws sawdust on the floor and calls it a party. Café society can't get enough of it.

Meyer notices a couple of reporters interviewing Irving Berlin. George Remus notices three women stacked along the wall sipping cocktails and trying to grab Mr. Berlin's attention. They are fashionable by Broadway standards, hair pulled back away from the face, simple black dresses, and long, black gloves.

Remus stares at the cluster of crossed, stockinged legs.

Meyer says, "Let's get down to business."

Remus says, "Business is a simple yes or no."

The proprietor brings a large plate of sliced roast beef, cheese, and onion rolls.

Meyer says, "Business is never that simple, as any good lawyer knows."

Remus says, "Business is Title II, Section 3 of the Volstead Act. The right to withdraw alcohol for medicinal purposes. On my way down here I saw a sign in a pharmacy window, 'Closed for one year due to violation of the Prohibition law.' That's the risk. A year out of your business. You must be sure to dot your i's and cross your t's. If you do, there's a considerable profit to be made. That's where you come in. I sell the certificates to your company, which I will set up legally, a company that allegedly distributes alcohol to pharmacies. As you know, 'Liquor…for non-beverage purposes and wine for sacramental purposes may be manufactured, purchased, sold, bartered, transported, imported, exported, delivered, furnished and possessed.' Be sure you read the law so you know when you're stepping over the line. A bribe never hurts but it doesn't necessarily help, either. What your company does with the certificates is up to you."

Meyer says, "I didn't get off the boat yesterday."

"Listen to what I say," Remus says. "Forty-four hustlers just happened to drop by my house after the raid: politicians, public officials, Prohibition agents, federal marshals. Forty-four! I put out such a shower of green it looked like a St. Patrick's Day parade. A grand each. Take it from me; the government doesn't intend to shut down the sale of alcohol but they do want their end of the business one way or another."

Meyer says, "I have a lawyer who will set up my corporation."

"I don't care as long as you make it worth my while," Remus says, rubbing his thumb and fingers in the ancient gesture.

Remus sends the stockinged ladies cocktails via Jack Kriendler, then tells Meyer, "A word from the wise, keep your name out of the papers. Politicians can read. Once they get your name, they come calling...with their hand out. You can bet on that."

Meyer says, "What happens to our deal if you go to jail? Who has the connection then?"

"Don't worry," Remus says. "If anything happens to me, my wife knows what to do."

"Your wife?" Meyer says.

Remus says, "Never underestimate the ruthlessness of a woman."

Meyer says, "I'll talk with my associates. If we agree to the deal, I deal with you. Not the wife. I will contact you and send a runner with the envelope. You give him the certificates. That's the deal."

Remus laughs, calls for another cocktail. The first three have got him on a roll. He musters the hint of a smile underneath the veneer of cross-examination and then stands and turns to the women.

With the charm of a barracuda he says, "Ladies, would one of you like to dance?"

Meyer disappears into the back alley where he joins Jack Kriendler in a cigarette.

"How's business?" Meyer says.

"It beats cabbage soup."

"You're always here," Meyer says.

"Somebody has to run the show," Jack says. "Meyer, I don't mean to be critical but you don't seem the type to run a joint like this. You have to put somebody out front."

"You need a good bartender?" Meyer says.

"Sure," Jack says. "Send him over."

With that, Meyer closes his speakeasy on Broome Street. His talent is needed elsewhere.

Days go by. The New York Yankees are having a helluva season. Babe Ruth hits one home run after another, thirteen so far. He fills the stadium seats for which he rakes in a cool $52,000. The Yankees meet up with the Cleveland Indians at the Polo Grounds. Meyer takes the day off to watch the showdown.

With the bases loaded, the Babe hits his fourteenth home run. He is six homers shy of Williams and Hornsby. The victory against the Indians puts the Yankees one game behind the Browns, who lead the season. The buzz in the city heats up. The Yankees have a shot at the World Series for the second year in a row.

August rolls around. Temperatures skyrocket. Meyer packs a bag for Saratoga where he explores the 'sport of kings' with

Arnold Rothstein. Charlie stays behind and plans for Rocco Valenti's demise. Before long the news hits the paper, *Thugs Shoot Underworld Leader at "Peace Conference" on Bootleggers' War*. Umberto, aka Rocco, Valenti is dead. According to the *Times*, he is alleged to have arranged for more shootings than any other man in New York.

Meyer reads the story over a mint julep at the racetrack.

Rothstein sips Turkish coffee and says, "Missing the action?"

The question is mildly entertaining. Saratoga nestles into the Adirondacks. Her hills lumber across the landscape in clean, orderly fashion. All activity centers on the racetrack. At the end of the day, the crowds filter out into the local gambling establishments in civilized bliss. It is nothing like the city street where Umberto Valenti jumped onto the running board of a passing cab in an attempt to avoid the bullets filling the air.

The newspaper story rehashes the events of a week earlier, when Joe the Boss escaped a volley of bullets that killed one bystander and wounded five others. This time, an eight-year-old named Agnes Egglineger was wounded in the chest and a street cleaner in the neck. Despite the chaos, Umberto's assassin is cool and collected. He stands still in the middle of the New York traffic and takes careful aim. Even when Umberto jumps on the running board of the cab and the cabbie hits the gas, his shooter remains calm.

One shot later, Umberto hits the street dead.

If it wasn't for the bad publicity and the bullets left in innocent bystanders, Meyer might be impressed with the "conference on a sidewalk." But as it is, the collateral damage is trouble for their burgeoning business. Already, the Italian Squad, organized by Lieutenant Joe Petrosino, is busy gathering information on Joe the Boss and, by extension, Charlie Luciano.

Charlie will have to lay low for a while.

Rothstein finishes his coffee.

"The rich don't jump on running boards in broad daylight," Rothstein says. "They have better ways of taking your money. Gambling. Come on, I'll show you."

The Brook is Rothstein's pride and joy. It lies a mile past the golf course. The Brook was part of the Bonnie Brook Farm until Rothstein bought it. The mansion is surrounded by a working farm and racing stable. The entrance faces west and opens into a large hall furnished with heavy mission furniture. The fireplace, built from rock found on the site, is massive. Heavy beams run across the ceiling.

Rothstein points to the reliable money makers: roulette and chemin de fer. He paints an alluring picture of the elegance and sophistication of a gambling house operator that occupies Meyer's mind for the month he spends with the upper class but always there is something missing in the equation.

When Meyer gets back to the Lower East Side, he sits down with Red and Charlie at the Villa Nova restaurant. Over plates of pasta with marinara sauce, he shares the notion of running a casino in Saratoga. Meyer doesn't stop with August in Saratoga. Gambling joints could be something easily spread all around the country, the perfect complement to the business of bootleg.

"Booze and gambling go hand in hand," he says. "Everybody knows that."

Red says, "I don't know, Meyer. We've just started to get a handle on the booze. Why change horses midstream? Why work for Rothstein?"

Meyer says, "You don't just one day run a joint like that. And I'm not going to work for Rothstein. I'll go up there a couple of times and then we'll open our own joints."

Red says, "I'd like to bump Ben Siegel up a notch. He's been doin' good with everything we give him. We can't take care of all the business, Meyer. We're gonna have to give some of it to other people. One of them should be Benny."

"O.K., Red. Do what you think is best."

"Polly Adler takes her girls to Saratoga," Charlie says. "She makes a lot of dough."

Meyer says, "And puts on quite a show. She parades the girls around the racetrack first thing in the morning while all the men have breakfast at the club. They twirl their parasols and flaunt the goods. She never gets hauled in for soliciting."

"Good madams make good money," Charlie says, "for everybody. The cops are all on the take. Looks like your friend Abe Zwillman is coming up in the world. The guys up there call him Longy."

"That's because his height. He used to protect the pushcart vendors from the micks trying to shake them down," Meyer says.

"He with a guy named Reinfeld," Charlie says. "That's the Italian that was giving him trouble a while back. Willie Moretti is up in Jersey now. He wanted to know if we had anything to do with Zwillman. I told him he's a friend of yours and that he watches over our booze coming in from Canada. That should keep things in line for now. Are you gonna talk to Gordon?"

Meyer says, "That's the general idea. I didn't get into this game to get knocked out by a guy like that."

Summer gives way to fall. The air is crisp. Static electricity snaps Meyer's hands as he slides across the taxi seat on his way to the showdown with Waxey Gordon.

"The Knickerbocker," he says to the cabbie.

Waxey's receptionist is a tall brunette with showgirl sensibility. "Right this way, Mr. Lansky," she says in a Bronxy nasal twang. She ushers Meyer through the reception room and into the heart of Waxey's operation. The blackboards are scrubbed clean; nothing to see except a couple of thugs playing cards and bookkeeper laboring over a set of ledgers.

Bronx throws open another door at the far end of the room. Waxey sits behind a heavy desk and downs Irish whiskey. A cigar burns idly nearby. A couple of girls are perched on the couch. Waxey gestures to a chair in front of the window.

"Take a load off," Waxey says.

Meyer grabs a chair and makes himself comfortable. The girls trade secrets and giggle. The noise annoys Waxey. He gives them a glare and then tells them to beat it. The girls shrug off the insult and leave the suite.

Waxey sizes up the measure of Meyer's success, handmade suit and shoes, Sulka shirt, smart tie, fresh haircut.

"You've come a long way, kid," he says, "but you still got a lot to learn."

Meyer says, "Not too many guys could pull off a thing like this in the middle of Manhattan. You must have a lot of political pull."

"Connections," Waxey huffs. "That's what it takes."

"What does a guy like you need with a guy like Rothstein?" Meyer says. "He's a gambler, a bankroll. He's no street guy."

"That's what I say," Waxey says catching on to the reason for Meyer's visit. "You here to clean up his mess?"

"Rothstein wants out," Meyer says.

"We got a deal," Waxey says. "He musta told you that much. Son of a bitch made me take out an insurance policy with him as the beneficiary in case we got knocked off before we repaid his loan. The guy's got balls in business, just no brains."

Meyer nods, "So cut him loose. You're better off without a guy like that meddling in your business. He's a purist, what does he know about the value of cut whiskey."

Waxey curls his lip in disgust, "You mockin' me?"

Meyer says, "Rothstein is more interested in his image than his purse. He's got to look these guys in the eye every time they play poker. He can't afford to have the reputation of a guy selling cut whiskey."

"I don't give a rat's ass about his reputation. I don't need him meddling in my business."

"I couldn't agree more. Rothstein brought me and my associates in on his end," Meyer says.

Waxey lets out a howl.

"Kid, you're still in the neighborhood. You're still running around with guys you knew when you were sucking your mother's tit. I got guys coming outta the can to do my business. Didn't that upstart tell you what he saw here? You think the guys in Cleveland are wheeler-dealers cause they run Canadian whiskey across the border? I got shiploads of booze coming in from overseas. I got connections to the Caribbean for rum. I got vodka coming from Russia. What the hell do you got? A 45-foot cruiser and a guinea friend."

"You've got it all. What do you need with a stiff-shirt guy like Rothstein?"

"When you put it like that," Waxey says.

Meyer says, "Let's not take this thing to the street. Cut Rothstein loose. There's plenty to go around. They say there are forty thousand speakeasies in this town, maybe more. You go your way and we'll go ours. Me and my associates will take care of Rothstein's little cache of snobs. The rest of New York is up for grabs."

Waxey laughs, "You think you can do better than me with these characters? You think I'm some Daymon Runyon dub? I can't hold my own in the upper classes?" He thumbs the lapel of his suit. "Listen to me, kid. I eat at the finest restaurants, dance at the finest clubs. I got the best lookin' broads in town. I wear suits that cost as much as most guys' annual incomes and there's plenty more where that comes from."

"You work your side of the street and we'll work ours."

"You're smart, kid. You better stay outta my way. I ain't got no qualms about protecting what's mine. I ever find you movin' in on any of my joints, we'll come to blows."

Meyer stands.

"It goes both ways," he says.

Frank Costello

WARNING!
12
MILE LIMIT
14

Joe "the Boss"
Masseria

Chapter Five
Build Capital

AUGUST 1923

The summer of 1923 rolls around. The Big Apple has been through several interesting revolutions. For one, Frank Costello got a judge to throw out the court case against Charlie Lucky's boys who got themselves into some real hot water. Joe the Boss found out about the fix and decided that Costello, an Italian immigrant from Calabria, should demonstrate allegiance to his mob instead of relying on his friends at Tammany Hall.

Moe and Izzy, the fat, cigar-chomping, middle-aged Jewish Prohibition agents, became hometown celebrities almost as popular as Buster Keaton and twice as funny. They dressed as gravediggers, dock workers, stout old ladies, and tuxedoed European royals, then tricked the city's bartenders into violating the Volstead Act. "Yer pinched" is the latest catchphrase among the Broadway set.

Abe "Longy" Zwillman welcomed an alliance with Meyer Lansky and promptly expanded his whiskey running empire. His once senior partner, Joe Reinfeld, found himself in the less enviable position of subordinate but he doesn't mind. He makes enough money to drown his sorrows.

Moe Dalitz immediately saw the advantage of the Zwillman/Lansky alliance. The coup was not so much the alliance but the fact that the rail lines end in Jersey which is Zwillman territory. Dalitz tells his partners in Cleveland that it's time to start thinking beyond boxcars and make the move to owning railroads.

Benny hears about Nucky Johnson, the sheriff in Atlantic

City, who is getting rich allowing rumrunners and booze smugglers access to his shores. The resort town is a stone's throw from Manhattan. That's one advantage. The sheriff is another. But the true advantage lies in the fact that off-season, the whole town is dead. That means no hassles from the cops or any other enforcement agency.

The former journalist turned dictator, Benito Mussolini, marches on Rome sending a wave of Mafioso immigrants to America. These hard-core soldiers provide fresh recruits for the local gangs. Frankie Yale, the local gang leader, uses this infusion of strength to vie for control of the Brooklyn docks.

Charlie Lucky is jerked back into the neighborhood politics that consume the Italian way of life. Joe the Boss calls Charlie and his right-hand man, Vito Genovese, to a meeting in a Brooklyn brownstone. Vito is a throwback to the old country, a native of Naples, while Charlie is the Americanized Young Turk. Although Vito is ten years Charlie's senior, he falls in line under the younger man.

Joe lays out his problem. As he does, he watches for any expressions that might transpire between the two men that would give away their deep-seated nature to exploit the situation. Joe stokes a fire in an apartment he maintains for such conferences. August's temperatures are unseasonably cold, 53 degrees to be exact. The third-story apartment is stark, nothing like his lush Manhattan residence. Should anyone break in, there is not much to discover.

Joe takes a fatherly tone, "Charlie, Charlie. I'm glad you come."

Vito Genovese looks unkempt. His hair sweeps up in an unruly tuft that clings to one side of his head. His deep-set eyes are ringed with dark circles. Joe the Boss needs their strength to succeed in taking over the Italian rackets if he is to become, truly, "the Boss." Joe hovers over a traditional cake, Cassata Siciliana.

"Sit," he says. "I cut you a piece of my wife's cake."

The cake is a Sicilian jewel: sponge cake flavored with liqueur, ricotta cheese, candied peel, and chocolate filling all covered with a marzipan shell topped with candied fruit native to Sicily. Joe opens the small cabinet and removes a gold-rimmed plate. His vest buttons strain under the bulge of his extended gut. He slides the long blade of the knife through the heart of the cake and pulls off a thick slice, then runs his chubby finger along the blade to gather what's left. The lick of icing leaves a greasy shine on his lips.

Charlie says, "You keep eating like that, you're not gonna fit through this door."

Joe says, "What if I get to heaven and I ask St. Peter where to get a good cassata and he say we no got?"

"You worry about what ain't in heaven?" Charlie laughs.

"I worry about lots of things. I worry about Frankie Yale who wants to take over the Unione Siciliana and now he got plenty of soldiers coming in by the boatload from Italy. These guys from the Old Country, they been killing a long time. They handle themselves pretty good. Capisce?"

Charlie says, "He ain't even Sicilian."

"I can taste his treachery. He gets the Unione, he puts his finger in everybody's pie. I worry about Frank Costello. I see how he pays the politicians but he don't pay me. Where is his respect? I worry about your Jew friends. What you think, Charlie, they gonna help you when you need help? We say 'homo homini lupus est.' Vito, you got good Latin. Tell Charlie what this mean."

"Man is a wolf to his fellow man," Vito says.

Charlie says, "You can worry about Yale when he crosses the bridge."

"Yale is a wolf. I have my eye on him, always. Someday I will split his kingdom and he will not be so strong against me."

Charlie nods. "No need to worry about Frank Costello. He is in Harlem with the bucket shops."

"Bucket shop?" Joe says.

Charlie explains the connection to Wall Street and commodities and securities.

"It is a high-class numbers game," Charlie says.

What Joe hears is that Costello is making money, big money, and since Wall Street is part of the Lower East Side, Costello should show his respect.

"Why he change his name to Costello. Is he Irish? He is Frank Castiglia but he hides behind his Irish friends."

Charlie says, "He was raised, so to speak, by a big Irish politician, Tim Sullivan. He was part of Tammany. He's shrewd."

"Never trust a mick."

"I'll talk to Costello."

"Castiglia," Joe says. "Reason with this ingrato. And watch your back with the Jews. You have my blessing to do business with them but don't get too close to the fire. It will burn you."

Since his encounter with Rocco Valenti last summer, with bullets flying on the street and Joe in hot pursuit and Valenti the guy who wound up receiving the death-dealing bullet, Joe has convinced himself he is invincible. It was midday when bullets blazed at the corner of Fifth Street and Second Avenue. Valenti fired wildly, killing one bystander and wounding five others. Joe the Boss ran. His hat filled with bullet holes but not his body, which was something of a miracle considering his size. He bobbed and weaved and escaped with his life. The locals call him "the man who dodges bullets."

Consequently, Joe is convinced that he is destined to become the Boss of Bosses and that Yale is the perfect lever for his ascension. He sends Vito across the street for coffee while he confides in Charlie. He slicks back his hair and smoothes his tie.

Joe says, "You ever smoke a Frankie Yale cigar? What kind of man puts his own face on a cigar box? Who is he kid with this? The Calabrese are proud men, eh, too proud. His nose always point to the sky. But he is a good thief. One time, when he is with Johnny Torrio, he steal very many fur coats. Too bad he get caught. He not so smart as he think. A little bird tells me Frankie Yale wants Big Jim Colosimo dead.

"Everybody think Yale send Torrio to be boss of Chicago. Frankie Yale no want to make nobody strong but himself. I will tell you about Chicago. The young men are restless, no? They smell where the money is but Big Jim has all he wants, enough whiskey to keep his brothels in business. He got his head in the old country and his cock in the girls. The young men gotta get Big Jim out of the way but now Johnny Torrio is there. It is not so easy to kill your boss. Johnny Torrio, he is smart like wolf, too. What's he gonna do? Be careful, Charlie. The Calabrese come from Italy's toe. They like to kick everybody else in the head. Torrio and Yale…" He holds up two fingers tight against each other. "They got a plan for Chicago. You can count on that."

Joe has convinced himself that all roads lead to his front door and that all deals require his network of influence to solidify.

Charlie says, "Capone is Neapolitan."

"That's why he will never control our world. Al, he likes the tarantella, huh? He dance on your chest until he breaks your bones and split open your gut just to be sure you dead. Torrio need a guy like that to be second in command, like you are to me, Charlie. When Lupo the Wolf was in jail, Frankie Yale decide he want the Brooklyn docks. Why? He want to smuggle his paesans from Italy, like Lupo, maybe whiskey and opium, too. He get strong. He make lots of money. We get plenty of trouble."

Vito makes his way up the stairs and through the door of Joe's office. He carries a tray loaded with several cups of Italian coffee, a loaf of bread, and a lump of cheese wrapped in wax paper.

Joe narrows his eyes into tight slits of concentration, "Opium is good business. Arnold Rothstein, he bring opium from Asia hidden in his antiques. I think maybe you smart like fox, too, Charlie. I think maybe you got these Jews lined up for our business. I give you and Vito my blessing to make a deal with this Rothstein for opium. I make you rich men, huh. Then we see who is big in New York, Joe the Boss or Frankie Yale."

Satisfied that Charlie sees the light, Joe sits back in a plump chair and sips coffee.

He says, "I know you like the dream stick, Charlie. Don't forget, I like to chase the dragon once in a while too. Go see this Rothstein and don't forget I like to sample the goods before I buy."

Joe takes the cheese from the wax paper and stands it on a plate. It is a smooth, white provolone in the shape of a pig and neatly tied with brown string.

Vito says, "The Signora sends her gratitude. Provolone from her home town."

Joe pokes a finger into the little white porker.

"Fresh," he says tearing off an ear.

Joe dismisses Vito and Charlie, who shuffle down the stairs and onto the street, where Vito lights a cigarette.

"Let's go home," Charlie says.

Joe watches from the window until they disappear.

Vito and Charlie wind past the rat catcher's shop where a long string of dead rats hangs suspended by their tails. The back wall of the shop is piled high with caged ferrets.

Vito says, "Are you going to make a deal with Rothstein?"

Charlie opens the door to Vito's Packard and says, "I will give it some thought. Right now, take me to Polly Adler's joint."

The Packard's engine hums.

"Why do you think Joe the Boss is so interested in Costello?" Charlie says.

Vito is close to Costello but the chain that links them is weak. Vito clings to Ciro Terranova and Terranova to Costello. It was Vito that connected Charlie to Costello since Costello can fix just about anything.

Vito says, "The Bronx is next door to Harlem. Terranova is strong there. He must be worried about Terranova. If he can get Costello to pay tribute, then Terranova would fall in line."

They pass by Daniel Badger's Architectural Iron Works, a battery of brothels, a deli, the Church of the Divine Unity, Broadway Central Hotel where Rothstein stays on occasion, Union Square, and the temperance fountain built by Adolph Donndorf to keep the good citizens of New York from guzzling alcohol.

Vito says, "Terranova uses Costello because Frank is in bed with all them big Irish politicians. Maybe he just wants to bring the Irish into his orbit so he can use their influence."

A traffic jam slows them through the Tenderloin and stops them in front of Delmonico's. At 40th, passing the Metropolitan Opera House, Vito breaks into his best recollection of "Vesti la Biubba."

"Joe don't trust the Irish," Charlie says.

Vito laughs. "And the Irish sure as hell don't trust him."

At 55th and Madison, Vito parks the car and they hike the half a block to Polly's apartment where the doorman rings them through.

Polly's maid, a small black woman who goes by the name of Lion, opens the door.

"Miss Polly will be here in a minute, Mr. Charlie," she says.

The elegant twelve-room apartment in the middle of what Polly calls "café society country" is sleek and elegantly decorated. Polly, short and Jewish, a madam who got her start on the Lower East Side, likes Charlie not because café society likes to rub shoulders with gangsters but because Polly knows Charlie is a good guy to have in a jam.

Charlie waits in the salon and stares at the twelve-foot Gobelin tapestry that hangs on the wall, a gaudy piece of work in gold and pink and red embellished with floral boughs and blue ribbons and whatnot. Charlie and Vito ignore the whatnot to ogle Venus at the Forge of Vulcan.

A writer of some note saunters through the room. He raises his glass to Charlie, the ice in his glass sloshing scotch onto the floor.

"I assume I have you to thank for this," the writer says.

"Don't blame me, pal," Charlie says. He's still looking at the tapestry. "Polly bought this in Paris. Why anybody would hang a rug on a wall is beyond me."

Polly enters with a tray of cocktails. Her hair is cropped short and styled away from her face. Her eyes sparkle. She wears a red Chinese dress with a gold dragon embroidered across the front. The dragon hugs her short, round body firmly.

Polly says, "Come on, I'll show you the rest of the joint."

"Why'd you move back to Broadway?" Charlie says as they head toward a door at the end of the salon.

Polly says, "You can have the Brooks Brothers crowd. They're a bunch of cheap cake-eaters. My girls work harder for their money than all those men put together. Broadway's got a heart of gold and buckets of Champagne."

The living room walls in Polly's new flat are warm gray, the draperies pale green satin. The furniture is Louis XVI, the lamps jade. A rose quartz elephant sits on the bar behind which Lion mixes a pitcher of Bacardi cocktails. The living room sprawls into the paneled library filled with rare books Polly has collected on her frequent visits to Europe.

The writer, who seems to have followed in their wake, sidles up to the bar and helps himself to more scotch.

He says, "I'm willing to bet it isn't fine businessmen like you that are behind the drive to move the boundary of the international waters from three miles to twelve miles."

"Whadya mean, move the boundary?" Charlie says. "How can you move the boundary?"

"It takes an international agreement. You know how we wound up with a three-mile boundary? The Dutch figured the maximum range of a cannon was roughly three miles. Now that we've forgone cannons, America wants to extend the border to make it harder for the bootleggers to get their goods." The writer hoists his whiskey glass. "Lord help us," he says, and chugs it back.

Charlie shakes his head, "The only guys that'll get hurt with that move are the little guys."

The writer says, "How's that?"

"The little guys don't got the resources for going out twelve miles. It's the boys with the big boats that go that far. You know what they say about a little fish in a big pond. Pretty soon, he's somebody's dinner. Personally, I don't care one way or the other. If I cared, that would mean I got somethin' to lose in keeping it where it is, if you catch my meaning."

The writer tips his glass. "Enough said."

One of Polly's girls comes out for Charlie. Her presence sucks the air right out of the twelve-mile-limit conversation. Vito is at the Victrola picking his way through Polly's record collection. Several hand cranks later, Charlie follows the girl to the peach and apple-green bedroom while Caruso belts out "Vesti la Biubba."

The girl undresses slowly, by Charlie's standards. Caruso manages a complete expression in three minutes twenty-nine seconds when he's in an "O Sole Mio" mood. Three minutes drags out to five. Vito starts another song. Charlie pushes the girl to the bed and takes care of the job of undressing himself in thirty seconds flat. A few minutes later, he's dressed and out the door. He passes Polly fifty bucks which she tucks under the dragon's heart.

"The greatest voice in history," Vito says of Caruso. "Neapolitan. That's my point. It was Naples that put art above family. That's what pisses off the Sicilians but we got the better deal."

Half the day disappears before Charlie comes by the garage driving his latest acquisition, a green Dodge Phaeton with whitewall tires and matching green rims. Charlie flips the top down and waves. Meyer, who has been trying to figure out what's gone wrong with the timing of one of his trucks, drops the job and makes his way to Charlie's car.

Charlie says, "I was at the Cotton Club last night and had a good talk with Madden and Big Frenchy. Big Bill is putting a near-beer brewery in Hell's Kitchen. Did you know you gotta brew the real thing to make near beer? You boil off the alcohol until it's half a percent. You call what's left tonic and sell it legally. Son of a bitch. I had no idea."

"Tonic?" Meyer says with some amusement.

"Does Sammy have time to beef up my engine? I picked this up today. Ciro Terranova, you know him? He just bought a bulletproof car. I figure for him, it's a good idea. Me, I like the wind in my hair so I got this. A little extra speed wouldn't hurt. Let's take a ride. We got stuff to talk about."

Charlie takes the scenic route to nowhere in particular and fills Meyer in on what's going on among the Italian mobs. He passes time with small talk about Joe the Boss' rationale for tribute from guys like Frank Costello and Ciro Terranova and how those boys aren't thrilled with the idea but Joe the Boss is powerful. Once crossed, there is always hell to pay.

Charlie says, "Joe wants into the opium business. He knows that Rothstein is bringin' in good stuff from Asia. He told me to make the connection with Rothstein. See, Frankie Yale, the old greaser in Brooklyn, is workin' an opium racket and getting rich. Yale don't give Joe a piece so he figures our mob should get into the business. If I make a deal with Rothstein, the Italians won't know nothin' about Joe's involvement."

Meyer says, "Sicilians look down on drug dealers. Why would Joe want you to get involved?"

"Joe don't care as long as it lines his pocket. Besides, I'm the guy with the mixed-up mob and connections to Jews. Right there, I lose respect. Joe's the guy at the top. He can pretend ignorance."

Meyer listens. Meyer has bigger plans for their mobs than simple bootlegging. And with Charlie on their side, there were things they could do.

Meyer says, "Drugs are a bad idea. Kids get hooked on the stuff. It runs down society."

"Yeah, and it makes people feel good in this shit life. What's the difference if it's opium or alcohol?" Charlie says.

"Every culture consumes alcohol," Meyer says. "Pretty much. Not many use opium. Not to mention it's a political bandwagon in this country. The Protestants run things. How do you think we got Prohibition? Now they're cracking down on opium."

"And dropping it into our hands, just like alcohol," Charlie says.

"The public isn't for opium," Meyer says. "That's the difference."

"What the public don't know..." Charlie says. "The Chinese don't seem to mind."

"The Chinese had it forced on them and now they're hooked," Meyer says, referring to the British East India Company that forced the Chinese to accept opium as payment for the tea and silk they took from China. The Chinese government quickly regretted their compliance.

"You gotta play it low key," Meyer says.

"If Joe tells me to make a connection, I make the connection, low key or not."

"We can do better with alcohol."

"It don't matter," Charlie says. "You gotta understand these old greasers."

This grates on Meyer. He stares out the passenger window, allowing his thoughts to form. They cross the Williamsburg Bridge and coast through town with barely a notice. The El clangs overhead. Charlie makes a turn toward Prospect Heights. Traffic thins. Wealth kicks in. Neighborhoods go from basic brick to Italianate villa. Charlie's car fades into the true plainness of its stature.

Meyer says, "At least put some distance between you and the business end. Rothstein's got a couple of guys he uses for muscle. You know them. Legs Diamond and his brother."

"Oh, those cuckoos," Charlie says. "I'll see what I can do."

Meyer says, "Something to think about. I'm not telling you what to do but you're moving up the ladder. You gotta think about how others see you. What you do in private is your business but what about when you're smoking? You're vulnerable when you don't have all your senses."

It's true and Charlie knows it. He circles back to the garage.

Benny is hanging around with a couple of Jews Charlie has not seen before, Lepke Buchalter and Gurrah Shapiro. Red is hustling trucks in and out through the alley. Business is brisk.

Lepke's in the middle of saying something: "I didn't know the half of it until I went into the can. I thought I knew it all. I didn't know shit. There's guys in there with experience and nothing but time to talk. It's like Harvard for guys like us."

"Who is this guy?" Charlie says.

"Lepke," Meyer says. "He's O.K. Just got out of the can. The big guy is his muscle. They pulled off a heist last night. They came by to brag."

Charlie is incredulous. "That was these guys?"

A truckload of furs had been diverted by a garbage brigade. White-uniformed street sweepers pushing brooms in the middle of the night had ushered the truck through the blockade. A Model T had followed close behind the truck. The sweepers ran interference, slowing the truck to a crawl while Lepke jumped from the T onto the running board and stuck a .38 in the driver's face. It was then the sweepers pulled rifles from the barrels and took aim at the truck. The driver jumped and ran up a small alley.

Lepke and his mob got away with the furs.

"They were strikebreakers," Meyer says. "Did a lot of union work. Don't get him started on that business. His mother is a union organizer. Lep plans to make a move on management."

Lepke hears the comment and says, "Management is the wolf that runs the pack. Those bastards. Labor is the sheep waitin' to be sheared. Cutters can ruin a whole season just like that. Truckers too. If you don't hit the market at the right time, you're done just like that. Nobody's buyin' mink in the middle of July."

Meyer says, "How about you work your side of the street and

we'll work ours and if we can help each other out, we help each other out?"

Lepke shrugs. "How about we help ourselves to some fried kreplach."

The group schlepps off to Ratner's where lunch is in full swing. High ceilings, arched windows, and utilitarian chandeliers bounce noise everywhere. The room reverberates with complaining and laughter.

Meyer spots Longy Zwillman sitting at a table alone. The Cannon Street gang makes a beeline for the nearly empty real estate. The waiter swings by and drops a handful of menus on the table. Gurrah digs into the pickle plate.

Meyer makes the introductions. Zwillman nods recognition.

Zwillman says, "We got a couple of new Mafiosi fresh off the boat, a guy named Profaci and a guy named Vincent Mangano. You know them, Charlie? We could pick up some business in the Italian market, bring in some wine."

The waiter brings onion rolls and bowls of vegetable soup.

"What makes you the expert?" Lepke says.

Zwillman says, "Newsreels. It's amazing what you can learn at the movies."

Charlie says, "Yeah. It's got Joe the Boss nervous. He knew a lot of them guys in the Old Country."

"Who do we know in Brooklyn?" Meyer says.

"I know a lot of guys in Brownsville," Benny says.

"Italians," Meyer says.

"There's a guy with Frankie Yale named Joe Adonis," Benny says. "You know him, don't you, Charlie? Tough as nails. You want something done, he's the guy to call."

Zwillman butters an onion roll. At the next table, a couple of vaudevillians argue the comparative merits of challah vs. the onion roll, working the argument into a comedy routine.

Zwillman says, "We've got a golden opportunity just like the Russian Jews who revolutionized the rag trade into ready-made. Before that everything was a one-off. They spun gold out of those machines."

"Goldene Medina?" Meyer says.

Zwillman says, "We're a bunch of little mobs all over the place. We can do better. We've got allies from Cleveland to Boston but we haven't leveraged that strength. If we pooled our strength, we could move mountains."

Benny chimes in, "The trouble is that guys on the street are undercutting each other. Some guys are selling the real thing. Other guys are cutting the whiskey two, three times. Fix the price. Make it affordable. Everybody gets rich. That's just good business. Just look at Wall Street or the kosher chicken market."

Charlie says, "Dalitz has the railroads, doesn't he? He ships as much as we can move. We've got the clubs. Bring the little mobs in with us. It's protection for them."

Meyer says, "But protection only goes as far as our combined interest. The more they work with us, the more strength they have."

Charlie hovers over a bowl of borsht and a plate of potato pancakes.

The more the gang talks, the more the business grows. Over soup and blintzes, fried kreplach and onion rolls, reputations merge to take collective aim at amassing enough power to conquer anyone that might rise against them.

Charlie's mind goes to the Italians. The Americanized guys are scattered through a loose association of families led by Sicilians. Many in the Italian mobs don't even speak English. Then there is Chicago where the strongest Italian mob belongs to Big Jim Colosimo who is not the least interested in bootlegging. Diamond Jim, charming whore-master, married a madam and then worked a prostitution ring and gambling houses. When that got old, he divorced the madam and married a singer. He brought in Johnny Torrio and had the bad luck to include Al Capone at Frankie Yale's behest. It's plain the Outfit will dethrone the old-timer blocking the way into bootlegging. Johnny Torrio will be left standing with Al Capone as right-hand man.

The Ratner's crowd dwindles. Meyer pays the tab. Zwillman heads back to Jersey. Lepke and Gurrah bid the gang "Shalom." Meyer and Charlie leave by the back door that leads out to the alley.

Charlie says, "Jews don't think like Italians. Italians are all about family. A guy will appoint his son even if the kid don't know nothing about the street. I've seen it a million times. For you guys, it's all business."

"You don't run it like a business," Meyer says, "before long you'll be out of business."

Charlie says, "Benny is right about Joe Adonis. Here's the thing he don't know, Adonis is close to Capone. They knew each other in the neighborhood when Capone was part of Yale's mob. I just don't trust the guy."

"He could be useful," Meyer says.

Charlie nods, then walks away.

Later that night, Meyer strolls over to Pell Street, a hotbed of opium houses, to make a naysayers investigation. He stands across from the house Charlie frequents and watches. A drizzle of dragon chasers come and go from the den, lost in the sweet haze of forgetfulness. Meyer winds through the addicted and ventures inside.

The place resembles an exotic apothecary. A wooden case with glass doors is mounted on the wall. Inside are stacks of pipes, lamps, curved spoons that look like keys. Copper and bronze boxes. Stacks of silver containers, opium boxes. Around the room smokers and dreamers lounge on the thin mattresses atop wooden bed frames. Some pause to look at the newcomer before returning to their haze. More smokers are stacked in sleepers along a wall divided into compartments resembling a Pullman night train with double-level bunks. The sleepers have already left the station, destination unknown.

The matron, dressed in plain black pants and frog-button silk jacket, gestures to an open bed. Meyer shakes his head.

"I'm looking for someone," he says gesturing to the bodies strewn about the place.

There is nothing fancy about the Pell Street den. The smoking equipment is humble in decoration: a pipe, a lamp, and a needle.

The matron walks toward Meyer, her body parting a sea of smoke. She looks worn. Old. Smoking opium is a messy process. Cooking the chandoo, stuffing it into the bowl of the pipe for the smoker who then puffs the sputtering pellet, leaves sticky bits of the drug scattered everywhere. The eerie underworld of dreamers euphoric with blank stares requires her constant attention.

As for the congregant, a funeral service at Temple Emanu-El has more life than an opium den.

"Nobody here you know. You no smoke?" she says. "You go now."

Meyer has seen all he needs to see. He leaves the matron to her masses.

Chapter Six
Play It Low Key

FEBRUARY 1924

Charlie sinks deeper and deeper into the great oblivion of an opium dream. In this dream, he stands on a small bluff. On one side of the bluff is an open field; on the other, a cliff that plunges to a hellish abyss. A woman calls. Charlie looks around to see a floating figure, a woman dressed in black. Her features are delicate. Her long, black hair blows in the wind, at times framing her face like a hood and then floating free. If it weren't for her delicate nature, she could be the Harbinger of Death. She beckons Charlie to her side. He tries to take a step toward her but can't move. His legs are frozen beneath him.

He is at the pipe again, drawing clouded breaths. The woman on the bluff transforms into a dark angel sitting at the foot of his bed. The angel takes the pipe, tends to the bubbling chandoo, and then extends the mouthpiece to Charlie. She smiles, then shifts, slowly moving away from the dreamer's bed.

She says, "Fire monkey, you rest now. You have good dreams."

Charlie peers out of opium-stained eyes. The angel in black leaves with the smoking bamboo stem. Charlie watches her go. She pauses to look back. Her angelic face dissolves into a grotesque worthy of St. Patrick's Cathedral.

Charlie rides his dream and finds he is floating on a watery surface, maybe the Hudson River, maybe the Atlantic Ocean. He rises above the churning waters. The dread he carries leaves him. The water transforms into the streets of the Lower East Side. A little girl jumps rope next to the dead body of Umberto Valenti sprawled on the sidewalk. A street sweeper works at erasing Valenti's bloody stain to no avail. Valenti looks up from his deathbed and winks. He is free.

Charlie drops his gun, no regrets. He is chasing the dragon in the paradise of opium-eaters and it feels good.

"Charlie," Meyer says to the half-conscious Charlie. "Did you forget? It's Benny's birthday."

Charlie's eyes are glazed, his pupils tight.

Madam Chang says, "You no bother Mr. Charlie. You go now. Nobody want you here."

Meyer ignores the old lady.

"Charlie, you're not going to miss Ben's birthday?"

Charlie smiles and closes his eyes.

A squat, brick-house of a man appears from nowhere. His bare chest is an accumulation of solid muscle sharpened by the discipline of Kung Fu and adorned by a massive dragon tattoo that wraps around his back and creeps down his left arm. Clouds and water compete with the dragon for the canvas of his flesh. His coolie pants billow over muscular legs and massive feet bulge from black satin slippers.

The Chinaman says, "You go...*now.*"

Meyer looks at Charlie. The small brown lump processed from the dried milky juice of unripe seedpods has killed the pain and all conscious thought. By far the worst consequence of Madame Chang's delight is Charlie's eventual return to reality, a return that won't be happening anytime soon.

Meyer steps outside and hails a cab. The first stop is Benny's flat. Benny is sitting on the stoop...waiting. He rushes the cab and piles in.

"Where's Charlie?" Benny says.

"Not in this world," Meyer says.

Benny's disappointment is palpable.

Meyer barks out Polly's coordinates. The cabbie smiles and hustles the boys to the uptown apartment.

Lion answers the door.

"Right this way, Mr. Meyer and you, too, Mr. Benny. My, but them girls do have a surprise for you. We fixed up the bedroom all special like. Miss Polly says all the girls is just for you tonight. All you got to do is relax and let them do all the work."

"Don't spoil the surprise, Lion," Polly says.

The house bursts with a collection of gangsters and society types. Polly sets out a devil's food cake and lights eighteen candles as the crowd breaks into the "Happy Birthday" song. They are quickly interrupted by a Turkish tune on the wind-up Victrola.

A harem worthy of Mata Hari streams from the corridor into the living room. Someone in the crowd weaves the song "Leave Me With a Smile" around the Turkish tune, and the crowd joins in on the refrain. Whiskey sours flow from the kitchen to the guests.

The girls, in pink and peach gauze baggy pants, shimmy and shake their way through the house. Their tops consist of metal medallions strung together with bronze chains that jingle as they walk, fantastic costumes on loan from a theater courtesy of one of Polly's regulars. The crowd breaks out in cat calls and wolf whistles. Polly dons finger cymbals, and summons the house belly-dancer, keeps the rhythm going while the girls surround Benny.

Polly's Mata Hari grabs Benny's hands, places them on her hips, and leads him to the "forbidden quarters," followed by the girls. Heavy purple curtains hang from the ceiling. Satin sheets line the walls. The floor is covered with bolsters and pillows. A bronze dragon atop a short Asian chest belches jasmine smoke while candles light small "alcoves of delight" where the harem retreats to entice Benny to new experiences. The belly dancer shimmies around Benny blocking his view of the other girls. Her belly undulates, a slow series of waves crossing a naughty sea. She rolls her hips in graceful circles while pushing Benny down on the Moroccan wedding blanket cushion. Nervous laughter slips from Benny's lips. He's never had it like this before.

The girls come out from the alcoves and wrap Benny's wrists and ankles with scarves, a mock ritual holding him captive while Mata Hari strips away his clothes and then strips away her costume leaving only the sparkling headpiece, arm brace-lets, necklaces, and two medallions that cover her nipples. Benny is transfixed. Nothing on the Lower East Side ever looked like this.

In the living room, Polly assures Meyer that he is getting his money's worth.

"It's all the rage in Paris," Polly says. "You should try it some-time. It's kinda crazy. The Hindus say it's the anticipation of sex that makes a person go wild. If you wait long enough, your whole body starts quiverin'. Worth waiting for, they say. I don't know. I never tried it myself."

Back in the bedroom, Benny has had enough. The sexual alchemy of Kundalini energy escapes him. This divine sublima-tion is all slow and no go. Mata Hari moves in again but Benny is determined that he has been tantalized for the last time. He jumps up, grabs Mata Hari by the hips, spins her around, and lets loose his frustration.

"Jesus," he says panting from his ejaculation. "What kind of fucking thing was that?"

✿

Charlie rambles through his office spinning regrets over the forgotten birthday.

The phone rings.

"Yeah?"

It is Willie Moretti, a big-mouth Italian from Brooklyn, the guy who tried to muscle in on Abe Zwillman's Jersey operations a few months back. He is the elected mouthpiece of the new greaser in town, dispatched to spread the news that Salvatore Maranzano has arrived in America from Sicily. He says Maranzano wants Charlie to come to Brooklyn for a meeting. He says it is of the utmost importance and that it would be bad judgment on Charlie's part to ignore Don Maranzano's request.

With some disgust, Charlie says, "How can I refuse?"

Willie says, "This invitation is just for you. Maranzano don't want to meet with Joe the Boss. Don't worry, Charlie, I personally guarantee your safety."

"That's reassuring," Charlie says, but he will rely on Vito Genovese for security.

"He's at the restaurant at the foot of the Manhattan Bridge. You know the one I mean? He'll be waiting."

Charlie calls Vito, his underboss, to drive him to Brooklyn.

Vito says, "I don't like it Charlie. You can't trust these Sicilians."

"If I come out feet first," Charlie says, "make sure I get a decent burial."

Vito says, "I'll do better than that."

Vito's Neapolitan pedigree places him outside the Sicilian orbit. He waits outside while Charlie goes in to greet Maranzano. Charlie winds his way through twenty, maybe thirty, guys. Most of them he knows. Some he doesn't. Those he doesn't know have apparently come to town along with Maranzano.

Moretti waves Charlie down. Moretti started as a milkman's

assistant on the streets of Harlem but quickly moved to running gambling games in Italian neighborhoods. That's why Maranzano has given him the job as mouthpiece.

Moretti says, "Don Maranzano is straight outta Castellammare del Golfo. He's got the blessing of Don Vito Cascioferro himself. Imagine that? Don Vito sent him here to take care of things. Maranzano is a 'man of honor.'"

For a time, Vito Cascioferro worked a protection racket in Harlem and Little Italy. He was big in the Morello family until his involvement in the "Barrel Murder" of a Morello gang member sent him scurrying back to Palermo.

Charlie says, "And he's come for his tribute?"

"He's come for more than that, Charlie. He deserves our respect. Hear him out. He makes you think. He's got ideas, big ideas."

Charlie suppresses his dislike of the Sicilian path to honor.

The thirty-eight-year-old Maranzano heads a table filled with his Sicilian cousins. Two pistolas flank either side of him. Neither of them speaks English. Both make a show of their arsenal.

Willie introduces Charlie to the great man from the Old Country.

Maranzano gestures to the chair to his left.

"*Sedersi*," he says. "Salvatore, no?"

"This is America. They call me Charlie."

"They call you what you tell them to call you," Maranzano says.

Charlie's Italian is rusty. He was ten when he emigrated to America and finds little use for the mother tongue except when he is at home, which he tries to avoid as much as possible.

"Sigaro?" Maranzano says pulling a leather cigar case from his breast pocket. "In Spanish, they call it Perfecto."

Charlie takes the cigar.

Maranzano rolls the Perfecto between his thumb and fore-finger, teasing out the rich bouquet. He cuts the tip of the cigar with a gold cutter and then strikes a match which he cradles in front of the cigar. He draws in the heat of the flame and releases a mouthful of smoke into the ceiling above him. Every move is part of a personal ritual to demonstrate his knowledge of all things exquisite.

Charlie strikes a match and sucks his cigar to life with no such ceremony.

Maranzano rests the Perfecto on the fat lip of an ashtray and says in his native tongue, "My father gave me this cigar cutter when I was fifteen years old. He says to me, on my birthday, 'Today you are a man, you should have the tools of a man.' I remember it like it was yesterday. He died in the field not many years later. It was my responsibility to look after my father's house."

Waiters make way for Italian coffees and Zabaione.

Maranzano switches to English, "Let's not mince words. Julius Caesar once said, 'All bad precedents began as justifiable measures.' What we should do and what we can do is not always the same thing. I'll give you an example. Until a few years ago, all cigars were hand-rolled. The American Vice President tells the country it needs a good five-cent cigar. Right away the farmers cultivate cheap tobacco and mix it with filler. Then they make a machine to roll the tobacco. The cigar becomes shorter. Now you got a five-cent cigar but it's no good. You find them everywhere, even in boxes with Frankie Yale's face, eh?"

Charlie waits for the punchline.

Maranzano says, "The man on the street doesn't know the difference between a Perfecto and a Frankie Yale. All he cares about is now he can smoke a cigar when before he couldn't. He spends five cents and smokes it when he reads his newspaper. Men like you and me know the difference between the real thing and a fake, an imposter, a no-good substitute."

Maranzano waits for Charlie to see he is not talking about cigars but about men of honor. Charlie puffs on the fat Perfecto like the common man on a Frankie Yale.

Maranzano says, "In Italy we have fathers. They introduce us to the finer things. America has bosses. They are not the same thing."

"I had a father," Charlie says. "The title is overrated."

The restaurant's owner brings in bottles of cognac. Maranzano raises his snifter in a toast.

"Cento anni di salute e felicita!"

The paesans around his table all raise their glasses.

"Salute!" he says.

The evening drags on with an exorbitant amount of back patting. Maranzano claims he has come to America to save the Sicilian family from certain doom. He inflates the value of the "old ways." He touts the Sicilian spirit that has defeated attempts by foreign nations to take over their island and their culture. He mocks the Neapolitan decision to join forces with their enemies for the good of the country.

Vito Genovese waits outside and empties another pack of Old Gold. The night wears on. He mooches cigarettes from other drivers and shares in idle chat. Finally, Charlie appears with a peace offering, cannoli wrapped in a white napkin.

Vito peels back the napkin. He stuffs his mouth with delight and waits.

Finally, Charlie says, "This guy is so full of hot air he could float back to Italy."

They pop into the sedan and beat a hasty retreat. Vito says

everybody on the street is speculating about the reason for Maranzano's visit and that rumors are running wild.

Charlie says, "Sicilian ambition. Plain and simple."

Vito looks straight ahead and navigates the heavy traffic. They run into a veritable gridlock on the Manhattan Bridge.

Vito says, "Some guy wants to drain the East River and put in a road and a subway and a bunch of garages."

Charlie says, "He should join up with Maranzano."

Charlie stuffs his rage a little deeper into his gut.

He says, "This wannabe Caesar has been here five minutes and already he's got the Sicilians riled up against Joe the Boss. He doesn't like that Joe's mob is not purely Sicilian. You probably already guessed that. The way he talks, we're all a bunch of bastard kids birthed by whores, especially you just because you happen to be Neapolitan."

Vito's lip curls, "Some things never change. This goes all the way back to the Two Sicilies bullshit."

"It goes back to Vito Cascioferro," Charlie says. "He holds a grudge against Joe the Boss since he took over the Morello family."

"What are you going to tell the Boss?"

"I ain't got the answer to that question yet," Charlie says.

Charlie finishes the evening with a phone call to Meyer. The next morning, they meet at a cafe across from McSorley's for breakfast.

Charlie says, "It was a big shindig."

He pokes the yolks of his eggs with the edge of his toast. Last night's meeting still sticks in his craw. He lowers his voice to a near whisper in case of spies.

"This is a guy who has big ideas about taking over the Italian rackets. He's got all the bullshit. He quotes Julius Caesar like he's some kinda saint. He's on a sleigh-ride to become the great

Sicilian Father. He shits in Sicilian. You should have seen them, last night. Everybody was eating out of the palm of his hand. I'm telling you, Meyer, this ain't gonna end well. We can't afford to underestimate these cocksuckers."

His mouth full of egg, Charlie continues, "Last night's show was nothing more than him putting Joe the Boss on notice that he intends to take over the Brooklyn family. He must have Stefano Magaddino's approval. They're cousins. Famiglia, that's what it's all about with these guys."

"Will Joe give up Brooklyn?"

"Are you kidding?" Charlie says. "He's already struggling to keep Frankie Yale as his ally."

"It's gonna be war?" Meyer says.

Charlie says, "Sooner or later. You can count on it. You saw what Joe did to Valenti."

That was two years ago and still the neighborhood buzzes with the story. Valenti had planned to take over. He lost not only the war but his life. Now Vito Cascioferro sends his emissary for the same purpose.

Charlie says, "This guy insulted Joe the Boss in five languages. One thing he don't know is that there's a difference between the Americanized guys and the Italians. We got guys from all over. Vito is Neapolitan. He ain't gonna go for this takeover. And he ain't alone."

"There's more than Neapolitans," Meyer says. "But don't let on."

A heavy dose of laughter comes from a nearby table. Charlie looks up. A group of Irishmen watch a gaggle of women in black dresses and bonnets huddle in front of McSorley's. They look like professional mourners.

The men howl. The women tune their voices to a pitch pipe.

One man says, "It's the old maid brigade. Thank the Lord McSorley's don't let women through the front door."

Meyer and Charlie divvy up the price of breakfast and step outside.

The old maid brigade sings hymns of abstinence a cappella to the passing crowd.

Meyer lights a cigarette.

"Have you talked to Joe Adonis?" Meyer says.

"I'm thinkin' about it," Charlie says.

"We could use a guy on the inside in Brooklyn. That's where Maranzano intends to make his move, isn't it?"

"Yeah. Adonis is with Yale, though," Charlie says. "He ain't part of the Brooklyn Castellammarese. Maranzano won't cozy up to Yale's mob."

"He's still in Brooklyn," Meyer says. "Talk to Adonis."

They walk across town. The conversation drifts to the Hotel Claridge in the heart of Times Square. Prohibition has hit the hotel bar hard, which affects business. Hotels are being forced to find new revenue.

Charlie says, "You can get a room for next to nothing. Five dollars a week. Seven dollars. That's nothing. We could set up offices in the heart of the Tenderloin."

Meyer says, "What's your beef with Adonis?"

Charlie mutters, "His name is Joe Doto."

"So what?" Meyer says.

"He calls himself Adonis. That's gotta tell you something."

Adonis has a reputation with the women. That's a sore point to Charlie, the guy who, as the expression goes, can't get laid in a whorehouse.

Charlie says, "How can you trust a guy like that?"

"Is that it?" Meyer says. "Is that what's bothering you? He gets more tail than you? Look, if Benny thinks he's good on the street, he probably is. Benny says he's friendly with Capone. If this Maranzano thing goes where you think it will go, we could use a tie to Chicago. And who knows, some of his charm might rub off and you could get lucky with the broads in his wake."

"Jesus," Charlie says. "I'll give the guy a call."

By summer, Benny has set up business in the Claridge Hotel. He rents a series of suites that overlook Broadway. The boys come to the hotel to place orders and hang out. They play cards and bring in girls from Polly's house. Benny feeds off the energy.

On a July afternoon, Sammy limps in sporting a black eye and a roughed-up face.

Benny says, "What happened to you?"

Sammy says, "A couple of guys were undercutting us so we gave them an ultimatum."

Benny closes the books and straps on his Colt. He packs off Sammy to the saloon where the dispute went down. The victor, an Italian guy who couldn't be more than a hundred pounds soaking wet, is standing at the bar guzzling beer. The more he drinks, the louder he gets. The alcohol makes him sweat. He takes off his jacket. His shirt is worn and frayed. He slides from the barstool and does a jig.

"And that's how you take care of the Bugs and Meyer mob," he sings.

The bartender sets up another beer.

Benny gives Sammy the look. Sammy nods. It's the guy.

Benny says, "Keep your head. We follow him out the door."

The guy downs another pint and stumbles out the door and down the block. Rounding a corner, he staggers past an alley. Before he can grasp what is happening, Benny is on top of him, pushing him from the street and deep into a passageway that has very little visibility to the outside world.

"You don't want to mess with us," Benny says.

"Who the fuck are you?" the kid says.

"The bill collector."

The kid squints, focusing on Sammy. Benny kicks in the front of the guy's knee. There is a loud pop. The guy's knee buckles and he collapses to the ground. He recognizes Benny and pisses himself.

Benny says, "As of today, you're out of business."

The guy spits at Benny. Benny looks at Sammy, the black eye, the skinned-up face, the limp. He positions himself for a kick to the guy's spine and pauses. The guy on the ground heaves. Puke goes everywhere.

"You know where this guy lives?" Benny asks Sammy.

"Sure," Sammy says.

"You hear that? A word to the wise. We know where you live."

Charlie spends a few days pondering his meeting with the wannabe Caesar before arranging a meeting with Frank Costello. Costello is five years Charlie's senior. In Costello's mind, this is a lifetime. He prides himself on his sophistication. He sees Charlie as little more than a well-dressed guttersnipe who is growing in power, the kind of power that demands respect even from a well-heeled political fixer. Charlie is keenly aware of what Costello thinks. Still, Charlie wants to cover his bases and thus arranges to meet Costello at the Fulton Fish Market early one morning. Vito drives.

"Go around the block," Charlie tells Vito as they approach the market. "And take it slow. Let Frank stew a little. I don't want him to think I'm at his beck and call."

Vito says, "Costello is Calabresi, you know. You can't trust the Calabresi. They got dirt under their fingernails, if you know what I mean. They were always just a bunch of farmers. Lowbrows."

"Yeah well this farmer has got a lot of connections to Tammany Hall."

Vito stews. He slows his trek around the block, idles in a nearby alley, takes a route through the docks, admires the ships in port and tests his knowledge of what is coming in on which ship. It does his heart good to make Costello wait.

Costello peruses the *New York Times*. He checks his watch and hides his resentment. He is a man of punctuality who rises early and takes breakfast amid a string of meetings. He gets a shave and a manicure and has his shoes shined daily promptly at 9 A.M. Then he takes more meetings. The line to see him is long and usually distinguished.

Vito pulls into the fish market and parks. Costello pulls a pair of rubbers from his pocket and stretches them over his newly polished shoes. He hates the smell of fish, fresh or otherwise. He hates the filth. He hates knowing the truth of the miserable journey his dinner has taken from the sea to his plate.

Ciro Terranova runs the market. He is ally to Joe the Boss and friend to both Charlie and Costello. Fulton Market is not only the most important wholesale East Coast market; it is easily one of the largest in the world. Charlie plods through barrels and cartons and endless crates of fish hell with Costello in tow. The guys on the floor shout out "hello" or "good to see you" or "give my regards to Broadway." Already, Terranova has set aside half a dozen bass from the morning's catch for Charlie.

Charlie stops in the tented area where fishmongers bid on the daily catch. The area is empty now, a suitable place for a serious discussion out of earshot of just about anybody.

Charlie turns to Costello and says, "Maybe you heard, there's a new wop in town. His name is Salvatore Maranzano. He's over in Brooklyn. He could smell the money in America all the way across the ocean. I ain't gonna be coy with you, Frank. We ain't got that much in common but what we got, we gotta protect.

Maranzano is looking to situate himself at the top of the food chain. Joe the Boss thinks you oughta join up with us. I ain't lookin' to take nothin' from you, Frank. I make enough money on my own. But I'm askin' you to come in with us as an ally. It's good business. Joe the Boss asked me to speak to you personally. Maranzano is mustering the Sicilians to his side. He's already put the touch on Terranova but don't take my word for it. You can ask him yourself. He'll tell you straight up what's going on. Maranzano ain't got much use for anybody who isn't Sicilian, which is about half the guys in town, including you. Joe the Boss wants to know what side of the fence you're sitting on."

Costello straightens his back; the broadness of his chest fills out. He looks dignified under a full head of trimmed and slicked-back hair.

Costello says, "These old greasers always think they're going to rush in and take over. Half of them don't even speak English. What's this guy gonna do without contacts?"

Charlie says, "He speaks five languages. He'll spill blood if he must. He has his eye on Brooklyn but you can be damned sure that once he gets established there, he'll be looking to spread out. As far as Joe is concerned, you'd come in with me, then you'd have protection. We all know how much we make on bootleg. The way I see it, you got a lot of political connections. We could use a guy like you. We got a lot of muscle. You could use guys like us."

Costello says, "Lots of people have connections. You don't need me."

Charlie says, "I heard you was trained by Big Tim Sullivan personally. Is that so? You got an in with the Irish. We'd like it if you got close to Big Bill Dwyer and Owney Madden. It would be a mutual benefit."

Costello says, "Yeah, when the bullets fly, it's always good to know somebody on the outside who can cover your back."

Charlie says, "I ain't so blind as to think the Irish are gonna jump in the fray to protect a mob of guineas. Not even for a price. What I got in mind ain't that difficult to understand. We're businessmen protecting our interests. If some of us is Irish and some of us is Italian, so what? We got business to think about, not where we come from."

It wasn't that long ago that Costello was selling kewpie dolls to dopes with punch cards. The memory of the bankrupt business still haunts him. He wants to move in bigger circles but to a man like Costello, who did time for a concealed weapons charge, joining up with Joe the Boss doesn't seem to be a logical move. One strike was enough to give him a new motto.

"Violence is ignorance," Costello says.

"Your philosophy ain't no good among these old greasers," Charlie says. "Let's not play games, Frank. Greasers aside, you and I both know there's a lot of money to be made. There's even more when we cooperate."

Costello says, "I'll think it over."

"Take your time," Charlie says. "Call me when you figure it out but keep this in mind, it's better to come in at the beginning of a thing than it is to find yourself capitulating to terms at the end of a .38."

The market winds down from the early morning rush. Ciro Terranova makes his way along the men standing shoulder-to-shoulder cleaning fish. He yells to Charlie and Costello. A guy in galoshes and a long waterproof apron slogs behind Terranova with an ice-laden box of bass. The dead fish are splayed like a geisha's fan in their small wooden coffin. Terranova pushes on the flesh. It bounces back instantly.

"Can't get fresher than that," he says.

Charlie shoves five bucks in the shirt pocket of the galoshes guy and tells him to deliver the fish to the Villa Nuova restaurant. "For my money, they got the best chef in town."

Terranova nods to a delivery truck.

"You make the run," Terranova says. "Come back here when you're done."

Terranova watches the man load the fish and pull away from the market. Terranova knows why Charlie has come. He has not discussed Maranzano with anyone, not even Costello, whom he has worked with in Harlem since Costello's release from prison in 1916. That was in the days of the Morello gang, before Joe the Boss started making his presence known.

Terranova says, "What did you think of the big hoopla in Brooklyn last night?"

Costello balks at Terranova's ease over the greaser incursion. But Terranova is, after all, Sicilian and Sicilians can afford ease.

Charlie says, "He's got some big ideas. Some of the boys are saying he's got the blessing of our old pal Vito Cascioferro. If that's so, we could be in for another war. Maybe you can fill Frank in so he understands what we're up against."

Terranova is an expert on the subject. Even now, he needs the strength of Joe the Boss to survive. With the connection made, Charlie dismisses Costello from the conversation. Costello then winds his way through the fish market and back to the street. He drops the rubbers from his shoes into the trash.

Charlie and Terranova head for a bowl of chowder at the Seafood Bar and Clam House where they shoot the bull, reminisce about old times, and generally reassure each other that come what may, they will watch each other's backs. Then Vito drives Charlie to Brooklyn to collect Joe Adonis. They come back to the Cannon Street garage. Better to discuss business in the heart of the Lower East Side than in Frankie Yale's back-yard. And better to talk in among Jews than Italians. Besides, Charlie, without saying a word, demonstrates to Meyer that Joe Adonis is coming under Charlie's control.

Outside the garage, a bloated dead horse lies, not yet carted away, near a pushcart vendor selling any manner of pots and pans. Blankets hang for sale from an awning frame. A butcher stands in front of his kosher shop fishing for customers.

The stink doesn't stop there. The garage is airing out from Sammy's latest experiment with a smoke machine. He's heard about them from other bootleggers. Attached to the hull of the speedboat, smoldering tins of oil lay down cover for escaping the clutches of the Coast Guard or rival gangs. Charlie waves away the black, billowing smoke and hunts for Meyer.

Sammy says, "It's a takeoff on the smudge pot soldiers used in the war. The Coast Guard might have beefed up their engines but they don't have a defense for smoke."

Charlie says, "You couldn't do this somewhere else?"

Benny saunters in and coughs.

"Jesus, Sammy," he says. "You'll have the whole damned fire brigade here."

Sammy tries to smother the smoke with wet towels.

Benny turns to Adonis, "What the hell are you doing here?"

Adonis says, "Capone is going to be in town next week. He's looking for a night on the town. Take in a fight at the Garden. Pick up some broads. You wanna come?"

"Sure," Benny says. "When the hell are they gonna get that damned horse outta here? The stench is killing me."

"Goldene Medina," Meyer mocks, coming in from a back room.

Benny says, "Did you know the law entitles every Jewish household to ten gallons of wine a year. That's…"

"Twenty-four ounces every Shabbat," Red says.

"That's it?" Benny says. "Twenty-four ounces! And Congress just passed the law…no more medicinal beer."

Charlie says, "Don't get your panties in a twist, Benny. You think the Irish flatfoots are gonna turn in guys makin' beer? Hell would freeze over first."

Benny says, "I wouldn't want to be a druggist right about now. The government sends agents out to check certificates. Longy told me about that. He took an office at the Claridge, you know. Just down the hall from us. We've got a real syndicate taking shape."

Meyer turns to Charlie, "What business does Capone have in town?"

Charlie nods to Adonis to spill the contents of Capone's latest dilemma.

Adonis says, "You heard that Big Jim Colosimo was bumped off. The boys figured they were on easy street without him holdin' them back. All they gotta do is get a handle on the Irish who run the North Side but who are working their way into the Italian neighborhoods. Torrio wants to make nice with the Irish, which ain't makin' Capone the least bit happy. The Irish got the coppers and the politicians. How are ya gonna make nice with guys that have that kind of power? Capone calls in Frankie Yale for support. And Yale tells Capone that the president of the Unione Siciliana is sick and ready to die. You heard of the Unione Siciliana, right? It gives a lot of power to these old greasers. The president has a clear path for putting his fingers into everybody's pockets. Yale wants Capone to put a guy in the Unione but Capone ain't Sicilian and the Unione is strictly run by Sicilians. Capone is backing a guy named Angelo Genna, which has the Sicilians in an uproar. Nobody trusts Capone or Genna."

Charlie says, "Yale's booze funnels through Chicago to Brooklyn. That ain't the end of the story. Joe the Boss sees Yale getting stronger with these ties. Now he wants in on the action. He wants Capone to swear his allegiance to him instead of Yale. He's the Boss. He wants everybody to toe the line under him. That's why Capone is coming to town. There's a lot of turmoil. That's Chicago in a nutshell. Hell, I bet Maranzano was sent over from Italy because of this whole thing. Joe the Boss looks weak in Brooklyn. Why not send in a guy who can take over?"

It's bad news all around as far as Meyer can see. Mining the wealth of Prohibition depends on bootleggers having a good rap. The pieces of the puzzle are, at best, murky and the solution resembles a plan to organize hell. The war will be a boon to the Reformers but for bootleggers, the public outcry will force the government to get involved, which can only be bad news.

Meyer grabs a bottle of Bordeaux from his desk, Chateau Latour, 1899. "Jack and Charlie sent over a bottle of wine from the Red Head in the Village. They bring it in for the high-society types. This stuff is older than we are. Whadya say we see what all the fuss is about?"

Charlie pulls a piece of Victorian hardware from his pocket, a finger-pull corkscrew with a heart shaped center that looks more like stepped-up brass knuckles than a tool for fine wine. Meyer gives him a look. Charlie shrugs. "It comes in handy."

Meyer sends the gimlet screw deep into the cork and pulls. The cork slides out with a pop. He pours the wine into four Mason jars he keeps in his desk drawer. The wine is a light brick color. Even without a chance to breathe, it hits the nose with its sensuous bouquet. Benny doesn't notice. He and Joe Adonis chug the pour and ask for more.

Meyer says, "Beware the Ides of March."

"Whatever that means," Benny says, raising his pinky into the air and chugging another round.

"It means, we got a fifty-fifty chance of not living as long as this wine," Red says.

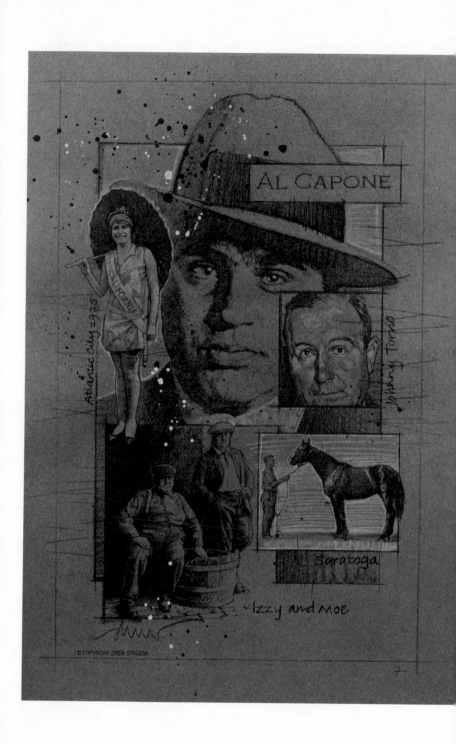

AL CAPONE

Atlantic City 1925

Johnny Torrio

Saratoga

Izzy and Moe

© COPYRIGHT DREW STRUZAN

7

Chapter Seven
Always Touch Base

LATE 1924/1925

Al Capone hops a train and winds his way from Chicago to New York's Penn Station. He's got an appointment in Coney Island, a meeting with his old boss, Frankie Yale. Yale's hangout is the Harvard Inn, a two-story brick building on Seaside Walk. It is the same place where Capone got his face slashed seven years earlier for admiring one of the Harvard Inn patrons who had the misfortune of having what he considered to be a "nice ass."

The "nice ass" blushed. Her brother, having had one drink too many to maintain his hold on reason, chose to take a piece of Capone's face with the edge of his knife. It took an act of god, namely Joe the Boss, to settle the dispute. It was ruled that a guy has a right to defend his sister. End of story.

Capone enters through the grimy front door and looks around. The club hasn't changed at all since the day he fled to Chicago. He makes his way across the dance floor to a back table where Yale holds court. Yale wants to know what's going on in Chicago. He wants to know why Johnny Torrio paid Dean O'Banion $500,000 for O'Banion's share of the once Sieben, now George Frank Brewery, on Pacific Avenue, which resulted in the luxury of the mick's betrayal. He wants to know why he isn't getting more booze. After all, it has been nearly five years since Capone and Torrio set up housekeeping in Chicago at Frankie Yale's behest.

Capone listens to Yale gripe. He still respects his mentor.

Yale smirks that a well-heeled gangster like Johnny Torrio could have stepped into such a wide-open mick trap.

"It was a setup," Capone says.

Five-hundred big ones, Johnny, O'Banion had said, and the joint is all yours.

Torrio laid down the five-hundred in good faith. Chump change. That's how O'Banion had backed out of his partnership with Torrio. About a week later, Elliot Ness and his boys stormed the brewery. The newspapers had a field day. The *Evening Dispatch* ran the story: *Beer Runners Fall Into Police Hands*. Two hundred fifty barrels of beer, ten motor trucks, seven automobiles, and thirty men were captured. Ness hit the front page with a bang.

"Did Torrio think that treacherous old mick was on the level?" Yale shouts.

"O'Banion had a cop on the inside who tipped him off that the brewery was going to get raided but the guy didn't know when. Ness spotted the dirty cop and took him out of the picture. Maybe that's when O'Banion decided to pull out and let Johnny take the hit. It was a good business move on O'Banion's part. I mighta done the same thing myself. Ness busted in, all right, but he got nothin'. The story was all a fabrication for the press. You know the reason for that. If Ness don't get publicity, he don't get no federal money and then what's he gonna do for a livin'?"

Yale yells for ziti and another pitcher of cheap beer. When it arrives, he pours two pints, one for himself and one for Capone. Capone guzzles the beer. His head swims with the dull thud of his days at the club working under Yale. Frustration etches the furrows of his brow. Torrio might have made the blunder of the decade but at least he isn't cheap.

Capone says, "Johnny is too soft on the Chicago micks.

Peace, peace, peace. That's all he thinks about. O'Banion don't give a shit about peace. He's a cocksucking North Sider, for God's sake. Johnnie's got the idea a partner ain't gonna take advantage. This ain't fucking Wall Street. I saw the betrayal in O'Banion's eyes. His head got away from his hat. Them Irish had a good laugh. We grease the cops with a couple hundred bucks; O'Banion comes right behind us with a grand. They run both sides of the law. You know what I mean? Only one way to deal with a cocksucker like that."

Like oil and water, Capone and O'Banion don't mix and now the smooth White Hander has upset the police cart in his own favor. The hell with the Italians.

The Calabrese Yale, with mick problems of his own, nods. "I sent Johnny to Chicago to take care of things…to ensure we would get our fair share of the booze coming across the border. If Johnny can't do the job, you know what to do."

Capone holds his silence in a long stare and then says, "I know you want this double-crossin' mick gone as much as I do."

Yale sloughs off the invitation to do the job.

"O'Banion tried to frame you and Johnny for Duffy's murder," he says. "You gonna own Chicago or fuck around with micks?"

Capone scowls.

Yale says, "Angelo Genna will take control of the Unione as soon as Merlo drops dead. Merlo was never worth spit. He put the kibosh on the O'Banion hit. The Gennas wanted O'Banion taken out way back but Merlo wouldn't have it. Good riddance, I say. When Merlo croaks, you can take care of O'Banion."

The Unione Siciliana was meant to settle problems, just not these problems. Merlo is dying of cancer. His days are numbered. Capone sits back and lights a cigar. He brushes the ash from the sleeve of his brilliant green suit.

"Here." He tosses Yale a Cuban torpedo. "Have some decency. Don't smoke them cheap cigars in my face."

Yale takes the cigar. He lights up and catches a glance at the scar on Capone's face left by Frankie Galluccio's knife. Scarface checks his watch. By all counts, he has been in Yale's club too long.

Capone says, "You oughta come to Chicago and pop O'Banion yourself. Cops can't cross state lines. It's simple. You scratch my back and I'll scratch yours."

"Peg Leg Lonergan," Yale says. "That's my price."

"Done," Capone says.

"What about Johnny?" Yale says.

"Let me worry about Johnny. He will go along with the plan. I'll make sure of it. Now if you don't mind, there's a couple of Jewish guys sluggin' it out at the Garden tonight. This I gotta see. Ain't nothing like a couple of Yids knockin' the shit out of each other."

Capone musters a convincing smile but it is the brutality behind the dark brooding expression that captures Yale's approval. After all, he schooled Capone. He knows what Capone can do.

Capone skirts the dance floor and exits through the front door. Outside is Frank Galluccio, the guy that sliced him all those years ago. Galluccio leans against the wall of the club shooting the bull with Joe Adonis. They amuse themselves by keeping count of the natural blondes, Jezebels, gold diggers, vampers, and teases that walk into the club.

Capone says, "You wrinkle your suit leaning against a wall like that. Makes you look like a bum. Get the car, Frankie. We're done here."

Galluccio runs for the town car.

Capone slides into the back seat. He takes quiet revenge by

making Galluccio his driver. Capone figures that Galluccio is uncomfortable with Capone breathing down his neck. He's right.

"Get in," Capone says to Adonis. "Madison Square, Frankie. And step on it."

"Yes, sir," Galluccio says.

Frankie drops them at a little slop house where Adonis and Capone meet up with Meyer and Charlie. They swarm a small table. A kid no more than fourteen waits the table. The kid collects the orders.

Capone says, "Prohibition is a whore, gentlemen, and she don't care who rides her. All these new guys off the street, they only understand one thing. They wanna earn. The trouble with them old greasers is they don't wanna share, not even when there's plenty to go around."

The cook slaps ladles of chili into scuffed white bowls. The kid lines them up his arm and delivers them to the table. He brings hot coffee, hot dogs, and baked beans. Afterward, apple pie just the way Capone ordered.

Capone drags a napkin across his mouth and says, "Where's the broads?"

Benny says, "Don't worry."

Charlie says, "Polly's broads. They're at the Claridge."

"Then what are we waiting for?" Capone says.

It's a good hike to the hotel, enough to let the chili settle. Capone makes time with the whores. Twice satisfied, he sends them packing.

Charlie says, "Joe A. said you wanted to talk."

Capone says, "I just come from meetin' with Frankie Yale. Now that me and Johnny took care of the obstacle, Yale wants to call the shots. He is hot and bothered over the Unione Siciliana in Chicago. He wants Joe Aiello to succeed Merlo but it's gonna be Angelo Genna. Take my word for it. I got no use for Aiello, that piece of shit. Fuck him. If I'm pullin' strings, then I'm gonna put my own guy up there. What the hell is Yale thinking? Brooklyn ain't big enough no more? He wants Chicago, too? I didn't get rid of Colosimo just to put another greaser in his place."

Meyer says, "What about Johnny? Who does he favor?"

Johnny Torrio fancies himself a diplomat. He, like Meyer, wants to get the violence off the streets.

Capone says, "He's a fool. You see where diplomacy got him, don't you? Making deals with the Irish. I'm married to an Irish girl. There ain't no negotiating. The North Siders ain't interested in a peace deal."

Meyer says, "The last greaser war got us the Italian Squad. Lieutenant Petrosino was put on the street to eliminate the Mafia."

Charlie says, "There's a new guy in Brooklyn. When Mussolini started going through the villages torturing the Sicilians into turning in the Mafioso, he and Joe Profaci fled. They're two big Dons. Maranzano brought his soldiers with him. He sees himself as some kind of general. There will be a war but who needs the heat? We got enough publicity agents."

"Are you with me or not?" Capone says.

"Use discretion, will ya, Al?" Charlie says. "That's all I'm askin'."

"I own the goddamn politicians," Capone says. "I pay 'em enough, don't I?"

"We make enough, too," Charlie says. "We run a very lucrative business."

Madison Square Garden is packed with nearly thirteen thousand frenzied fans. It is the non-Jews who come out in droves to watch Jack Bernstein, the aggressive scrapper from Yonkers.

They want to see him get knocked out. The problem here is that Bernstein doesn't go down easily, not even when he is offered two-and-a-half times the amount he would earn legitimately. Jack refuses to go down without a fight. Tonight, he squares off against the Rockford Sheik. Bernstein sizes up his opponent, the boxer who refused to get wafted into dreamland with a single wallop. Bernstein hopes to succeed where Sidney Terris failed.

The boxers shake hands and return to their corners. The odds favor Bernstein. The bell rings. Immediately the two fighters go in close. The Sheik squeezes the smaller Bernstein making it impossible for Bernstein to get off a good punch.

Capone chomps his cigar in eager anticipation.

Bernstein and the Sheik dance around the canvas. The Sheik is clever. Bernstein has trouble landing his blows. Round after round they clash, bashing each other mercilessly, both too stubborn to go down. It is a match of wits and strength.

In the twelfth round, the Sheik lands a right that leaves Bernstein stunned and wondering what day of the week he's in. The referee sends the Sheik to his corner and declares him the winner by TKO.

Frankie Galluccio chauffeurs Al Capone and Joe Adonis to the Cotton Club. Then he takes them and the two broads they've picked up to the Moroccan. After that, they hit the Plaza and then order room service. A few hours later, Frankie takes Capone to Penn Station.

Capone steps from the car and says, "Give my regards to your sister."

The ailing president of the Unione Siciliana finally succumbs to his death sentence. Frankie Yale heads to Chicago to pay his respects, at least that's the story he tells. He and two others pay a visit to Dean O'Banion's flower shop to order flowers for the Merlo funeral. While they are there, they take the opportunity to shoot and kill Dean O'Banion.

Capone orders $8,000 worth of roses…from Dean O'Banion's flower shop. Torrio drops another $10,000. The Mayor, the State Attorney, the Police Chief, and Cook County board president escort Merlo out of this world as his pallbearers. "Bloody Angelo" Genna sends his condolences to the widow and steps in as the new president.

The Catholic priest recites the Lord's Prayer and three Hail Marys in O'Banion's memory.

A copy of the *Chicago Tribune* is spread across Meyer's desk.

Meyer says, "Dean O'Banion is stretched out in a coffin clutching his favorite rosary…all dressed up with no place to go." He sneers. "The Catholic Church refuses to let him be buried among the faithful."

"They had no problem takin' his money, though, did they!" Charlie says, punctuating the end of O'Banion's influence in Chicago.

When the balmy ocean breezes give way to bitter cold storms in Atlantic City, Meyer sends Nig Rosen over to pay a visit to the local sheriff. The town is dismal. The fat lady languishes in Florida. The diving horse grazes in a Kentucky field. "Little Egypt" is missing. The Harem Revelers no longer dance. The roller carts serve as little more than wicker baskets in which the local snakes lay eggs. The place is a ghost town.

"What do we need with Atlantic City," Nig Rosen had said when Meyer first talked to him about using the city as a port to bring in booze shipments, but the sheriff was making sure everyone knew "The World's Playground" was open for business year-round. It was Moe Dalitz who first heard the call and he passed it on Longy Zwillman who passed it on to Meyer who passed it on to Rosen.

The value of Atlantic City consists of sixty miles of rail running from the Jersey shore to Philadelphia. The Philadelphia and Atlantic City Railway transports tourists. Moe Dalitz thought the sheriff would be interested in more lucrative commodities. Rail service goes both ways—in and out of Atlantic City. Access spreads influence. Meyer asked Nig Rosen to oversee the possibilities.

It turns out that Sheriff Nucky is eager for business. Rosen sets things up and, before you know it, he's walking the boardwalk along the Jersey shore with some of Meyer's guys, waiting for the speedboats coming in from the mothership.

Sammy pays three bucks to see two old mousers with cat-sized boxing gloves taped to their front paws. At the bell, they come out hissing and biting. The bout lasts about a minute, a disappointment greater than Bernstein's knockout by the Sheik.

"Fried clams?" Sammy says to Rosen.

Rosen moans, "I'd rather eat shoe leather."

Heavy gray clouds roll across the pier and head out to sea.

"Come on," Sammy says. "I'm freezin' my balls off out here."

The clam house is a small walk-in joint with scarred wooden floors and fading posters on the walls. A drizzle dampens the boardwalk. The boys take refuge in the restaurant. Rosen orders coffee.

"Tell me somethin'," Sammy says over a bowl of clam chowder. "How come everybody is talkin' about Chicago and the Unione Siciliana? I mean, I know Charlie is Meyer's friend and all, but what's that got to do with us? Why should we care?"

Rosen is stymied.

"Because," he says, stalling for time. "It's these old greasers. It's like...the Jews in Brooklyn were getting hassled by the

Black Hand, who were a bunch of greasers trying to control the chicken market. They wanted the Jews to raise their price but the Jews wouldn't do it because people need the chickens, you know, for religious reasons. The Black Hand was going to blow up their joints until Charlie stepped in."

"We care about Chicago because of Charlie?"

"No," Rosen says. "Not exactly. I mean, I think it has something to do with Charlie but, well, the Unione Siciliana has something to do with all these greasers. Meyer has it all figured out. Maybe you should just ask him."

"Sure," Sammy says.

Hours pass before speedboats roll in. The boys load the booze into the gang's trucks. The rain is falling steadily now. Tabbo pulls up his shirt collar and gives Rosen a look.

"I've got a bad feeling," Tabbo says.

Rosen says, "I told you not to eat the clams."

Twenty miles north of town, the gang encounters agents of the Bureau of Prohibition stopping traffic. Uniformed men wave lanterns at the oncoming traffic. Chase cars flank the stop sign planted in the middle of the street.

Sammy creeps along, suspicious of the barricade and using traffic as his shield.

"Something's fishy," he says.

Rosen shakes his head. He gives the uniformed men the once-over but it is too dark to make out details. The men look legitimate enough. Sammy slows to a crawl. The trucks behind him close ranks.

Sammy says, "Legit or not, I'm bustin' through."

Rosen leans out the window and points a flashlight at Niggy Devine's window. He flashes it three times. Niggy gets the signal but Tabbo, tight on the rear of Niggy's truck, does not.

Sammy slams down the accelerator. He frees the clutch. The

truck squeals into action. The uniformed officers unload rifle fire into the first two trucks as they bulldoze the barricade. Tabbo tries to catch up. He swerves to avoid an agent running for a chase car and loses control. The truck rolls over and slides along the highway in a flurry of sparks.

"Tabbo is down," Rosen yells.

Agents take after Sammy and Niggy. The Ford truck is rattling apart from the speed. Cases of scotch and Cognac clatter and crack in the back of the truck. At $65 a case, it's going to be an expensive night.

Sammy swerves wildly onto a dirt road. The load shifts to one side. Sammy overcompensates, jerking the steering wheel hard right. The load shifts again. More bottles shatter. The countryside reeks of lost revenue.

Running at full speed, the truck sprays rock and debris at the chase cars dogging them from behind. Sammy cranks his neck around. Headlights bounce behind him.

"When I stop, make a run for it," Sammy yells.

"*What?*" Rosen yells back.

"Just do it," Sammy says.

He slams on the brakes. Niggy Devine rams into the back of the halting truck, catching the corner of the rear panel and slinging the truck sideways. The two trucks join together like Siamese twins. Sammy sees the inevitable coming fast. He braces himself. Nig Rosen flies around the cab. The first of the Prohibition cars slams into the back of Niggy Devine's truck, forcing it toward the ditch alongside the dirt road. The truck tumbles over. Niggy rides the rocky road on his shoulder.

The inertia of the crash sends Sammy's truck headlong into a tree. The second of the agents' cars swerves to miss colliding with the booze trucks and plunges into the ditch.

Rosen jumps out the passenger window. Sammy is close

behind. Under a barrage of bullets, they hobble into the darkness. Niggy Devine punches out the front window of his truck with his boots and escapes into the marshland after Sammy and Rosen.

The agents lay down a blanket of fire. The boys huddle close to the ground while their pursuers kick through the debris. Dismayed at what little is left to salvage, they set the shipments ablaze and leave the fractured mob to fend for themselves.

Cognac lights up the night sky.

"I knew it," Sammy says. "Prohibition agents don't walk away from a bust. Let's find Tabbo before the cops do."

Rosen stands and brushes the debris from his clothes and shakes the fog from his head. Who organized the ambush? That's the question of the hour.

The dirt road runs parallel to the main highway. The boys double back for Tabbo and find him hunkered down covered with gashes and bruises. Tabbo shakes himself awake. Nobody, not even Tabbo, knows if he has been beaten or simply injured from the crash.

The local police are slow to show up at the crime scene. They comb the accident for clues and come to the obvious conclusion: rival bootleg gangs. It's just another headline that nobody needs except for the likes of Eliot Ness.

The boys hitch a ride in the back of a farm truck.

Rosen says, "You can drop us at the first food shack that shows up. We can use a good meal."

It is Rosen who drops a nickel in the phone to call Meyer. Tabbo heads for the bathroom to wash the crusted blood from his face. He raises his collar high and pushes back his hair. In the early morning gloom, the ruse almost works. Rosen sends Niggy in for hot coffee and pie.

The waitress studies Niggy's worn leather jacket and raw

skin as she hands him coffee to go. The coffee and pie fill the empty hole of their conversation while they wait for Benny to arrive. Then the four of them slide into Benny's two-tone beige Chrysler and ride silently back to New York.

"They torched the trucks. The Camp Fire Girls on the Jersey shore," Rosen mocks.

"I think it was the Diamond brothers," Sammy says at last.

"How can you be sure?" Benny says.

Sammy laughs. "The hat."

Benny says, "Not again."

Sammy says, "I'm just kiddin' with ya. They had the drop on us from the start. When we ditched the trucks, they couldn't see us but we could see them. It looked like Jack Diamond that was swaggering around lookin' to see what was left. The truck's headlights lit him up pretty good. He started hollerin' about all the broken bottles. He was madder'n hell, and Irish for sure. Eddie, sounded like Eddie, kept tryin' to calm him down. Eddie wanted to salvage what was left. Even with the breakage, they coulda made a good haul but Jack wouldn't have it. He wanted all or nothing so he set fire to what was left."

Tabbo says, "You know what they say. God invented whiskey to keep the Irish from conquering the world."

They roll into the Cannon Street garage. A doctor is on the spot. Everybody is exhausted. Meyer takes stock of the injuries as the doctor peels Niggy's jacket away from the bloody flesh.

"Hold still, son," the doctor says, digging at the embedded debris.

Satisfied that no injuries are life threatening, Meyer and Benny head to the back of the garage and to the quiet of Meyer's office.

"Irish guys," Benny says. "Sammy thinks it was the fucking Diamond gang. Aren't they running dope with Charlie? Ain't they satisfied with dope, they gotta make a move on our business, too? What the hell is wrong with these guys? It ain't like they don't have the cash. Son of a bitch pays more for a suit than he woulda made off our booze."

"I'll talk to Charlie. His business with Legs doesn't involve bootleg. If it is them, they've crossed the line."

Benny, enraged, paces back and forth, ready for action.

"Just be sure you know they did it before you act," Meyer warns. "We can't enforce the law unless we toe the line."

Benny leans close, "I'll be sure. And you can be sure I'll take care of it in a way they won't forget."

The Diamond brothers, Jack and Eddie, frequent a saloon in the Bronx. Jack celebrates his twenty-seventh birthday with a pint and a handful of stories not the least of which is the latest snafu just outside of Atlantic City. Eddie, the younger of the two, keeps his mouth shut while Jack takes credit for their near score on the mob the *Daily News* has dubbed the Bugs and Meyer mob.

"The Jews have this city tied up tighter than a gnat's arse. They want to control Jersey and Philadelphia, too. I guess we showed them a thing or two."

Sammy, Tabbo, and Niggy Devine push into the bar followed by Benny. Jack looks up long enough to smirk at the Jews entering the saloon.

"You Jew boys are a little far from home," he says.

Benny cozies up to the bar.

"Beer," he says.

The bartender draws a pint of near-beer. Benny takes a swig and spits it to the floor.

"Is this what the Irish call beer? No wonder micks rob from Jews."

Jack grins. The joint is quasi-segregated. Irish on one side, guineas on the other. The Jews don't have a side.

Benny says, "You got any sacramental wine back there? In a few hours, it's Shabbat. I'd like to get a jump on Kiddush."

Sammy laughs. It's the most Yiddish he has ever heard Benny utter in a single breath.

Jack glowers. He pulls a revolver and sets it next to him on the table. Red Levine plows through the pub door and gives Benny a nod.

Benny says, "Forget it. It tastes like piss and reminds me of an Irish brothel." He raises a limp finger.

The bartender says, "Take it outside, boys."

Jack tries to stand but he's drunk and unable. One of his boys rushes in from the outside. He is sweating, red-faced. His eyes dart back and forth between Jack and the Jews at the bar. He whispers something in Jack's ear that flushes Jack with adrenaline and sobers him quickly.

The crowd passes around glances. Benny drops a quarter on the bar for the near-beers and then the boys from the Cannon Street garage leave. Outside is an idling car with Nig Rosen at the wheel. The boys pile in. A few seconds later, they pass the assemblage of the Diamond gang hunched over the dead body of their lookout.

Jack and Benny lock eyes as the Bugs and Meyer mob rolls past the scene.

Rosen ditches the sedan. The boys make their way back to the garage independently.

"Looks like the Irish are dropping like flies," Charlie says, entering the garage.

"Better watch out for the Italians," Meyer says. "The police put Frankie Yale at the scene of O'Banion's murder. You should get Joe A. out of Brooklyn for a while. We don't need them making the connection between Yale and Joe A. as murder suspects."

"I got that covered," Charlie says. "Now that Bloody Angelo took over the Unione, he wants to be sure the Irish know that the Italians ain't gonna be pushed around no more like they was with the other guy."

"The Irish aren't intimidated by the Sicilians," Benny says.

Charlie finds newfound respect for Giuseppe Antonio Doto, Americanized as Joe Adonis, and now known as Joe A. They have been spending time together. Joe A.'s ease among the theater crowd pays off in new business for their bootlegging enterprises. Like other Americanized guys, Joe is tired of the old greasers and their tirades over tribute. Yale, grown in the Calabrese criminal world, is 'Ndrangheta to his core: honor, secrecy, violence, solidarity, and mutual assistance. He tolerates this alliance between Joe A. and Charlie Lucky but maintains a disapproving eye. Joe A. borrows a lesson from Yale's playbook, deciding to wait out Yale's conflicts with his rivals to see who winds up on the top. In that way, Joe A. assures himself he will move up the ladder of success bullet-free.

Meyer ticks off the list of greasers like notches on the grip of a .38. They are becoming numerous. Maybe that explains Costello's acceptance of allying himself with Charlie Lucky and Joe the Boss. Between Joe A. and Costello, the ties with Tammany have already proved useful for keeping the heat off the mob.

Nig Rosen says, "The sheriff in Atlantic City is eager to play ball. Why don't we put one of our guys down there where we can make better use of his city? We bring our booze in there, load it into a freight car outside of Philadelphia and ship it all over the Eastern seaboard."

Meyer likes the idea. So does Charlie.

"See what you can do," Meyer says. "Who have we got in Philadelphia?"

❖

Wednesday, September 23, 1925, looks like any other day. Low clouds buffer the bright sun. The temperature is a mild 75 degrees. Emory Buckner, a clean-shaven, Bible-toting, legal eagle, becomes the new United States Attorney for the Southern District of New York. He has been hired to clean up the city. His first job, as he sees it, is to clean up the bureau. Buckner calls it reorganization. The wisecracking rumhounds, Izzy Einstein and Moe Smith, are the first to go. It isn't their record Buckner rejects, 4,932 arrests of which ninety-five percent ended in convictions and five million gallons of confiscated liquor worth an estimated $15 million, but their costumes that gets them early dismissal.

Buckner hires the same sort of man that he sees daily in the mirror, then plants the men as spies everywhere liquor might slide through the cracks. When one of his undercover customs agents gets word about a "rum vessel," Buckner's men are at the ready.

The prime suspect, the *Nantisco*, creeps along the Hudson River heading for the docks controlled by the Irish. Before she can weigh anchor, she is boarded by Buckner's new breed of Prohibition agent. All paperwork onboard is confiscated as ordered by the U.S. Attorney of the Southern District of New York. Buckner intends to establish a paper trail that will allow him to identify all the major bootleggers in New York. The *Nantisco* could be his ticket to ride up the career ladder.

"You'll find what you're looking for in the lumber cargo," the undercover agent had told Buckner.

Unlike Elliot Ness' Chicago brewery bust, the *Nantisco* pays off big-time.

The news of the seizure spreads through New York faster than the influenza of 1918. Buckner collects names of bootleggers, smugglers, and conspirators the way Larry Fay collects a potential client list from the Social Register in the newspaper. This case just might be the career-making investigation of the decade.

"Sir," the voice on the other end of the phone says, "you better come down."

That is how the coroner summons Buckner to view his informant, Edward Starace, the undercover customs guard. Buckner makes his way from his office to the coroner's side where Starace lies in cold storage. The smell of formaldehyde and decomposing flesh swarms over Buckner like the East River over a double-crosser in cement boots.

Buckner's knees wobble.

"This isn't a funeral parlor," the coroner says. "The body isn't, what you might call, viewable."

The skin on Starace's face is black from stagnant blood, the discoloration a result of subdural hematoma.

"Starace was beaten unconscious before he died," the coroner says. "The crosses were carved into his face with a razor blade. Some sort of Irish death ritual."

Buckner steadies himself. He examines every wound and mark. Though the crosses are typical Irish warnings, nothing Buckner uncovers ties Big Bill Dwyer, the biggest Irish bootlegger, to the murder. Buckner is stymied. The investigation comes to a halt. Then one day the phone rings.

"Hello?" a voice says. "I wanna talk to the man in charge. He'll be interested in what I have to say, believe you me. Tell him it's Captain Hans Fuhrmann on the line....You bet I'll hold on."

Hans Fuhrmann tips Buckner to Waxey Gordon's place in the scheme of things. Buckner's zeal for righteousness rises to a boil. He garners a search warrant, collects his men, fortifies them with the local police and heads for the Knickerbocker where Irving Wexler, aka Waxey Gordon, purportedly sells real estate, the same place where Benny and Sammy watched Waxey prove he was Rothstein's superior.

Waxey Gordon kicks back in his Knickerbocker office and leafs through the latest issue of *Time* magazine. He flips back to the cover and stares at the photo of George Gershwin. It is an odd photo for the cover of a magazine. Gershwin's smile curls in disgust. His dark eyes harbor resentment.

Waxey says to his partner, Max Greenberg, "He ain't got a care in the world and still he can't crack a smile. Me, I got plenty of trouble and I'm smilin' all day long."

He throws down the magazine and buzzes his secretary.

"Send him in," he says of the man who has been waiting nearly an hour to see him.

The rather impatient Broadway producer clears his throat and starts to pitch his latest idea for a show. The tall, thin man nervously spins the brim of a straw hat. He spots the cover of the magazine.

He says, "We can get Gershwin to do the music."

Gordon says, "You gonna take his salary out of your pocket?"

The producer offers to cut corners with the costumes and save by keeping the musical numbers to a minimum. He says he knows a set designer that owes him a favor.

Gordon says, "I ain't hiring Gershwin. I don't need no over-paid tin pan piano player on the payroll. Throw a rock and you'll hit ten guys can do the same thing for half the price. The audience won't know the difference."

"They know the difference," he says. "Gershwin is box office."

"You gonna argue with me and then ask for my money? I ain't interested in no Broadway musical. You're taking this show to boys in the can. Got it? Good-looking broads that know how to entertain is all you need. Keep the music loud and it don't matter if the girls can sing or not. Give the boys a good show. You hear what I'm telling ya? Somethin' they can laugh at and drool over. If you ain't got that, get the hell out of my office."

The producer nods and forces a hollow smile.

Gordon says, "Don't look so glum."

"He wrote 'Fascinating Rhythm,' for God's sake," the producer says. "You can't beat that. It's a real toe tapper. It's the best advertising around. His name guarantees…"

Gordon says, "I ain't payin' for Gershwin. You mention him one more time and I'll crack you one right across the face. Get the broads. That's what sells where we're going."

The producer says, "I'll need a choreographer and time to rehearse."

Gordon says, "A bunch of broads kickin' their legs in the air don't need rehearsal."

The producer mops the back of his neck with his handkerchief.

Gordon says, "I'm sure you remember what it's like to shuffle acts around the Catskills. Now get outta here."

The producer cuts a hasty path back to his cluttered office and yells at his secretary, "Goddamn gangsters. Get Polly Adler on the phone."

A minute later, the secretary yells in her best southern drawl, "Miss Polly won't be back until this evening. Y'all will have to call her then."

The producer stares out the window at the Knickerbocker across the street. He can see into Waxey Gordon's outer office. On the street below, a dozen cars swarm the Knickerbocker's entrance, blocking traffic in all directions. New York's finest arrive en masse, escorting Buckner's agents through the hotel lobby.

Buckner, short and squat, is in the lead. Since April, since the *Nantisco*, since his tipster got murdered in retaliation, he has been rabid to nail Waxey Gordon's operation.

The phone rings in the producer's office. The secretary's sister, working the Knickerbocker's switchboard, reports the raid.

"Jesus," the secretary responds. "Jesus H. Christ!"

"What?" the producer says.

"It's a raid on Waxey Gordon," she says.

Buckner's agents swarm into Gordon's outer office then into the main rooms where the heart of the shipping business lives. Nothing is left untouched, not even the toilet paper which is unrolled and searched for hidden messages. The agents confiscate Waxey's maps, codebooks, timetables, ship-to-shore radio, lists of names, even the *Time* magazine with George Gershwin on the cover.

The producer, glued to his panoramic window, grabs binoculars and watches the beehive of activity surrounding the infamous Waxey Gordon.

Benny, having coffee at a café across from the Knickerbocker, watches too.

When the agents finish, Gordon's office is bare.

The man with connections yells at his secretary, "Get the maid up here with some goddamn toilet paper."

Benny ventures into the Knickerbocker lobby. Guests are aflutter. He heads to the King Cole Bar and orders a sandwich. A couple of Wall Street brokers chatter coolly at the end of the bar.

"Did you know that was Waxey Gordon?" one laughs. "Irving Wexler, real estate magnate, my ass. You could tell he was a gangster just by looking at him. Waxey. You gotta love the monikers these guys come up with. Jesus, why not Slippery Jew?"

"Legs Diamond," the other says. "What does a guy called Legs have to do to get that name?"

"He can run," the first one says. "It's a prerequisite to being a gangster."

"Maybe it means he can dance," the other says.

"Nah. You don't have the sense of it. It isn't like Joe College. It's like Scarface, you know. It's a badge of courage for being in the fight."

"They call him Snarky, too, like fancy dresser."

"Yeah, if you think a pea green suit is fancy."

"Rocky."

"Boo Boo Hoff."

"Ice Pick Willie. Now there's a proper name."

They laugh and point to their empty glasses. The bartender pours vodka into a shaker and mixes two martinis.

"Martini di Arma di Taggia created this drink right here," the bartender says, pouring.

"It doesn't matter who the bartender is, it takes a Rockefeller to make it famous," the first one says, then turns to his friend. "I'm walking down Fifth Avenue this morning and I run into one of my clients, nice-looking woman, you know, the kind you could enjoy. She introduces me to her husband. She says, 'Darling, this is Larry.' Larry! When have I ever been Larry? My dick is Larry but only my wife can call it that. Everybody else talks to Lawrence."

The second guy laughs and says, "Larry the Weasel."

"Big Larry," the first guy says. "Hey, do I look like a 'dese and dem' kind of guy?"

"I don't know. What kind of clients do you have?" the other one says.

"I don't care as long as they pay the bill," the first one says.

Benny shoves his sandwich aside and pays the bill. He takes

the Knickerbocker's outlet to the Times Square subway station. The moniker conversation chips away at his sense of accomplishment. The suit, the hat, the tie, the handmade shoes have not erased his Bugsy image.

The subway rattles through the underbelly of the city. Benny is lost in a haze of confusion and bad judgment. He overshoots his exit and is forced to hoof it back to the Cannon Street garage.

Meyer looks up from his newspaper with raised eyebrows.

Benny says, "The Knickerbocker was raided. Buckner had his whole damned mob in there. Tore the place apart...Irving ...the real estate guy...was all that was left of his office. I hung out in the bar for a while. I gotta say, you were right. I was wrong."

Benny hangs his head in derision coupled with rage.

"Waxey isn't worth your regrets," Meyer says.

"Not Waxey," Benny says.

"Irving neither," Meyer says.

"You got it wrong," Benny says. "Two Wall Street assholes were in the bar drinking martinis. These fucking cocksuckers. Fucking arrogant assholes. I'd like to introduce them to Snarky or Ice Pick Willie and see how they'd fare. You know what I'm saying? Cocksucking pigs."

Meyer waits for Benny's rant to get to the point.

"They were laughing their heads off that we're too fucking stupid to use a nickname that don't insinuate us. Bugsy. That's a helluva reputation. You're in this, too! The Guy, the Little Guy. People call you that. Not Meyer. See this is all a game to those lawyers. They take our money and laugh all the way to the bank. They thought Waxey meant Slippery Jew. Fucking cocksuckers!"

"Why do you let people put a label on you?" Meyer says.

"I don't let nobody do nothin'. You know that."

"Then why are you so worked up?" Meyer says.

"They called us slippery Jews," Benny says.

"They called Waxey a slippery Jew. What do they know?"

"Weren't you the guy told me I should forget using Bugsy and use my name?"

"Did I?" Meyer says. "I simply mean that your name is who you are. Nicknames, those are just labels for those that need to know. They call me the Guy when somebody might be listening. It's better than saying Meyer Lansky. Bugsy, that's different. It means something different. You aren't buggy. You have a hot temper but you aren't buggy. At least, you don't want people to think you are."

"Why not?" Benny says. "It scares the shit out of them."

"Those that need to be scared already are, just hearing Benny Siegel. Forget these guys. We've got business to take care of."

Meyer's calm erases Benny's rage as it has so often in the past.

The evening edition of the *New York Times* runs the news that an International Bootleggers' Ring is under investigation. Liquor found among the lumber cargo of the *Nantisco* has led investigators to the Knickerbocker and Longacre Buildings, where thirty agents swarmed the premises.

Buckner begins to link together a conspiracy involving M. Greenberg, I. Wexler, C. Kramer and A. Ross. The agents find a customer list and a key to a code that reveals a business in alcohol: American whiskey, Scotch whiskey, Champagne, and gin. They also find large maps of the Atlantic Ocean that show harbors, shipping lands, and various points that Buckner senses are drop-off spots.

As details are uncovered, the finger of blame turns to Mrs. H. Fuhrmann as the informant. She was angered when the bootleggers refused to turn over her husband's salary for the liquor shipment. The newspaper reported that her husband was with the raiding Prohibition agents when they entered the offices at the Knickerbocker and Longacre Buildings. The Government has put the couple into hiding.

Chapter Eight
Part of Something Is Better Than All of Nothing

WINTER 1925

'Tis the season for dutiful parents to lay their hands on the perfect holiday gift so that their children, lost in comparisons, will be able to hold their heads erect when they return to school. Times Square swarms with resolute shoppers. Arnold Rothstein passes time in front of the Argosy Book Store on 59th Street while his wife braves the crowds. Behind the Argosy's holly-trimmed, oversized plate-glass window, a tiny steam locomotive skirts the display at regular intervals while Saint Nick and his reindeer soar overhead. Christmas and Chanukah square off on competing sides of a cotton mountain. *Dennison's Christmas Book* touts celebration ideas from church decorations to party planning. *The Story of Chanukah* sits beside a Mother Goose offering of *Rhymes For Jewish Children*.

Rothstein snickers. The news is out. Mother Goose has judiciously excluded one of his childhood recitations:

Jack sold his gold egg
To a rogue of a Jew
Who cheated him out of
The half of his due
The Jew got the goose
Which he vowed he would kill
Resolving at once
His pockets to fill

The *Morgan Journal* claims Chanukah is the "true children's holiday." Rothstein watches the pack mules loaded down with bags from Bloomingdale's and Bergdorf Goodman hopping from store to store to fill the empty hands of eight days of tradition and decides the *Journal* might be right.

"Ho, ho, ho," shouts Bloomingdale's Santa.

The corner newsboy, a pugnacious urchin with a red nose, drowns him out.

"Federal agents closing in on Volstead violators, read all about it!" the kid shouts.

Arnold trades the rhyme in his head for the latest headline. He steps to the curb to read the Volstead article. The bankroll in him gloats over Waxey Gordon's bad luck but the Big Brain, as Rothstein is called, worries about collateral damage.

Two of New York's finest dawdle over a can of ash, spreading a thin layer over the ice-covered cobblestones.

"You missed a spot," grumbles the round Irish cop with a heavy brogue as he pushes the trolley holding two cans of ashes. "We wouldn't want Mrs. Vanderbilt to stub her little toes now, would we?"

"Them people have servants that carry them from store to store," the other cop says. The sweat-soaked shirt trapped under his heavy blue wool coat creates an icy chill whenever he pauses, so he presses on. "It ain't human havin' that much money. Look what it does to them."

He works the wooden-handled shovel around the calluses of his hands and digs another scoop from the can.

Rothstein scours the front page for any hint of what Emory Buckner and his men have learned from the Knickerbocker raid and finds nothing. No bond-runner nor fixer nor chiseler, thus far, has been able to break the silence surrounding the case. Buckner has, as the *Times* reports, padlocked the lips of his aides. Only Waxey Gordon knows the details of what Buckner uncovered and he isn't talking.

Rothstein grouses.

"What's wrong?" his wife says, her voice soft and sweet.

"What's right?" Rothstein says.

A year ago, Emory Buckner was as wet as the next guy. Then he accepted the U.S. Attorney position and went dry as a Quaker convert. He refused to employ any man unwilling to embrace the path of teetotaler.

Carolyn, Rothstein's raven-haired shiksa wife, entwines her arm with her husband's. Together they shuffle along the icy sidewalk.

Rothstein says, "I want to buy you something."

Carolyn says, "Christmas or Chanukah?"

"Don't be ridiculous," Rothstein says. "Holidays are for children. What do you say we invest in a piece of real estate for your neck?"

"Liquid assets?" Carolyn smirks. "Why don't we just stop by the pawn shop and buy back what I used to own?"

Rothstein frowns. "You're a cynic, Carolyn," he says, "just like my mother."

They plod across the ashes of Broadway and past the arched entrance of the Lyric Theater where the Marx Brothers appear nightly in *The Cocoanuts*.

Carolyn hums the introduction to Berlin's melody then sings, "'If you told me that I'm the lucky young man…'" She chucks her husband under the chin. "You know what they say, lucky in love, unlucky at cards."

"Don't even joke," Arnold says.

Ratner's deli throbs with a boisterous hubbub of controversies. Nig Rosen, the six-foot-something of a shtarker sitting across from Meyer Lansky, eavesdrops on the morning's kvetch at the next table. Henry Ford's latest anti-Semitic remarks in the

Dearborn Independent, with a readership of over 700,000 people, fuel fears on the state of Jewish workers in America.

A heavyset clothes-cutter, still smarting from the insistence on piece-work, contemplatively scrubs his thick, black beard. The era of the craftsman is dead. In its place rises mighty mass production that threatens to dissolve skilled labor and empower the moneyman.

"Management takes the lion's share," he says. "The rest of us can take what they hand us or starve. Somebody should take Ford to the cleaners just like he's taken his factory workers."

A choir of complaint runs through the restaurant. Tempers soar in defense of the young Jewish lawyer at the center of Ford's accusations and just as quickly, a ray of hope electrifies the room. The young lawyer is Aaron Sapiro. He has clapped Ford with a million-dollar libel suit in reprisal for his insults in the *Dearborn*.

Three tables away the conversation boils into violent debate. "Sapiro has an obligation to all Jews, not just to himself. Let Ford put that flowery signature on a million-dollar check for the evil he's done. What's a million dollars to a goy like Ford?"

The clothes-cutter says, "What? A Jew can't set the standard for a fair price without it being a conspiracy? A Jew doesn't deserve a decent wage for breaking his back in the field? God should see to it that all the factory workers in Detroit find out what a mamzer Ford really is and then they should quit. Let him build his own cars; see how much he's worth without a factory full of slaves. And let me tell you something else. He made it plain knowledge in the book about his life that he never liked the farm. His father wanted him to take over the family farm but he refused. He's too good for this work so he's going to deny the people that do it a decent wage? Ach."

Rosen says, "Ford's factory workers are the best paid of any."

Meyer says, "Of course they are. It's good strategy. It doesn't change the fact that Henry Ford blames the Jews for the war. Or that he claims Jews engage in the 'needle trades' because they have an aversion to manual labor and an abhorrence of agricultural life. Hypocrite. He complains that Jews have a desire to arrange their own affairs and therefore refuse to live outside of cities. What does that mean except that he wants us out on the farms where he can control how much we earn? He bought that newspaper to further his own views. Do you know that he's been dropping anti-Jewish pamphlets from airplanes all over Germany? Who needs a devil when you have Henry Ford?"

The waiter brings menus, an unnecessary inconvenience that dries up the conversation. The menu is freshly minted, a list of daily specials printed in red and stacked neatly into small paragraphs resembling upside down pyramids.

The waiter says, "New paper, same old choices. The salmon is fresh."

Meyer nods.

Rosen orders vegetable soup and plenty of onion rolls.

The waiter scribbles on a white pad, collects the menus, and heads to the kitchen.

Rosen says, "Why is your garage full of Fords?"

"They're basic, black, and everyone has one. Ford wants us all to look the same. Let him pick me out of the crowd."

The Mutt and Jeff Club, as the waiters quietly refer to the late morning conclave of Nig Rosen and Meyer Lansky, has convened because Meyer insists the two sit down every Monday to touch base over a nosh.

Meyer says, "We're ready to make some moves in Philadelphia."

"What are you talking about?" Rosen says, which is what he always says when Meyer proposes an idea that hints of something he doesn't like.

"Opportunity," Meyer says, undeterred.

Meyer passes the pickles.

Rosen shifts uneasily in his seat. He slaps too much butter on his onion roll.

"Have you been following the case Buckner is building against Gordon?" Meyer says.

"Yeah, so?" Rosen says. "What's that got to do with Philly?"

"Gordon is done in New York City. He has business in Philadelphia. He might shift his base of operation."

"He'll never leave New York. It's too profitable," Rosen says.

"We could stand to put a few guys in Philadelphia. Do it while Gordon is busy searching for the ship captain that fingered him."

The waiter brings the salmon and soup.

Rosen says, "I gotta go with Texas Guinan on this one. I'd rather have a square inch of New York than all of Philadelphia."

Texas, the one-time chorus girl turned proprietor, runs the 300 Club on 54th Street where George Gershwin is known to play piano for a lark. The club is the latest hangout for Vanderbilts and Whitneys and Morgans. They just adore the quick-witted Queen of the West.

"That's not the point," Meyer says. "We've come too far to let the likes of Waxey Gordon get the upper hand in a major city. We want to bring you up the ladder. Understand? You're not afraid of the competition, are you?"

"There's a sucker born every minute," Rosen says, stealing another of Guinan's favorite phrases.

"Philadelphia is sixty miles from Atlantic City. The sheriff is on the take. You truck the booze coming in through Atlantic City to Philadelphia and send it by train all over the country."

"We've got that in Jersey," Rosen says.

"Don't put all your eggs in one basket," Meyer says.

"Is this Charlie Lucky's idea? Send a Jew to Philadelphia? Keep the guineas in New York?"

Meyer says, "Charlie and I talked it over. I want you to handle our action. This isn't your personal Diaspora. It's a job."

Rosen cranes forward and scoops spoonfuls of soup.

"We're gonna need that guinea friend of yours," he says at last. "You trust him?"

Meyer says, "You don't have to worry about Charlie. When summer rolls around, take your wife for a nice vacation in Atlantic City. Make your moves from there."

The conversation three tables away boils over again, this time about the Scopes Monkey Trial.

The old man says, "It took that jury only nine minutes to override the Constitution of the United States!"

Meyer says, "Pack a bag and meet me at Penn Station at six."

The taxi deposits Meyer and Charlie at the main carriageway of Penn Station at 5:30. They disappear into the bustle of a thousand passengers making the mad dash through seven acres of travertine-covered steel supports. Steel stairs to the lower platform disperse the crowd among rows of idling trains.

Meyer pays cash for three tickets to Philadelphia then checks his Omega Militar wristwatch. Time is on their side.

"Coffee?" Meyer says.

Charlie looks at the huddled hordes packed tightly among the wooden benches and nods.

Nig Rosen enters the station and weaves his way through the crowd to the arcade where a small cigar shop serves as a meeting place for these expeditions. Sunlight filters through the sloping, glass-paneled roof illuminating the way to the arcade. Meyer and Charlie pick up Rosen from the cigar shop, then fall in line at the café where eager customers eye the crowded counter.

A whistle blows. Steam pours from a departing train. The concourse bustles like a beehive in mid-spring. Two waitresses scurry between the stainless-steel wall of the kitchen and the long, snaking counter that cuts the room into four even sections. The boys shimmy up to an open space. A bleached blonde in a tight black uniform stands on tiptoes to reach across the counter and pour the coffee.

In a twang that speaks of farmland she says, smiling, "What can I get you boys?"

Meyer says, "Just coffee."

Rosen says, "What kind of sandwiches have you got?"

Fifteen minutes later, Rosen wraps half a roast beef sandwich in a triple layer of paper napkins and they're off for their connection.

The *Limited* rattles through a hundred miles of rolling green hills then pulls into the City of Brotherly Love. Despite the late hour, Max "Boo Boo" Hoff is at his desk. Hoff runs his business from the second floor of the Sylvania Hotel. The room is burdened with clutter and smells of pastrami, newsprint, and beer. The walls are filled with a haphazard array of photos and newspaper clippings, a plethora of shots of Max and his corral of fighters.

Max wears a freshly pressed houndstooth suit, the kind made from cashmere, with a three-button jacket in place of the traditional two. The wiry boxing promoter paces a well-worn semicircle defined by the black tether of the heavy telephone held fast in his right hand. Max's ear is pressed hard to the phone's receiver. He grunts inauspiciously into the phone then spots Rosen coming through the door, two other men behind him. Max drops the receiver from his ear making an easy catch with his left hand and gives the giant of a shtarker the once over. Max knows the value of a good pair of fists.

Max says, "You ever think of getting in the ring?"

His bowtie bobs up and down along his Adam's apple as he speaks.

Rosen furrows an insulted brow not because he resents the

question but because he disdains the Marquess of Queensberry rules. Fair play is strictly for suckers.

Max lifts the receiver to his ear and waves the boys toward a worn-out couch slammed against the back wall. Rosen swats a stack of newspapers from the couch. A mudslide of newsprint fills the floor.

Max says, "Jack, I gotta go." He punches the phone's switch hook and bawls, "I had those papers in order."

Rosen says, "Now they're outta order."

Max stiffens and musters an insincere smile. He and Rosen go way back to the old neighborhood. Max knows better than to cross the giant Jew.

Meyer says, "We didn't come all the way from New York to stir up trouble."

The hand-tailored suit, freshly polished oxfords, Sulka shirt, and satin-banded fedora begs to differ.

"Then what did you come for?" Max says.

"I'm Meyer Lansky and this is my business associate, Charlie Luciano."

Max raises an eyebrow unsure what to make of the Jewish/Italian alliance. He listens.

"Yeah? What brings you to the cradle of liberty?"

"Respect," Meyer says without a moment's hesitation.

Max steps back. His gaze moves from Meyer to Rosen to Charlie and back again. His chest expands like an outraged puffer fish.

Max says, "I knew a rabbi once who used to say, 'Beware of those who come bearing respect.' Should I be worried?"

"Let's cut the bull," Rosen says. "You know who these guys are."

Every Jewish bootlegger along the Eastern seaboard knows of Meyer Lansky. As Charlie likes to say, 'those that need to know, know.' It is a small world.

"We're making a few connections in Philadelphia," Meyer says. "We want you to know that Nig Rosen represents our interests. We know you're connected to Waxey Gordon and we want you to know we respect that alliance. We're not here to step on anybody's toes. If you have a problem, we want you to talk to Nig about it. He'll work things out."

That's how the conversation begins, with Max doing most of the listening and Meyer doing most of the talking. Eventually, the Italian in the room becomes clearer. It comes as no surprise to Max that Italians are moving quickly and heavily into boot-legging. Given half a chance, the Italians will squeeze the Jews from the field.

Meyer says, "What do you want from this business?"

Max says, "The same thing you want. Money. You think I'm in this for my health?"

That's when the discussion turns to Waxey Gordon's troubles with the law.

Max says, "I don't care what happens to Waxey Gordon as long as it doesn't happen to me."

"Rejoice not at thine enemy's fall," Meyer says, "but don't rush to pick him up, either. The game is getting rougher, Max. It's not just getting out to the twelve-mile limit that's changed things. It's the guys involved. I'm sure your fighters are good for collections at the local bars but what are you going to do when some of these guys want to put you out of business?"

Max chuckles. It's finally plain what this business is all about and he'd be a fool not to take advantage of an obvious protec-tion racket.

"Well, maybe that's right." He shrugs. "Hey, you hear Tunney and Dempsey are going head to head right here in Philadelphia? That's right. His agent got the booking. Most people like the sluggers like Dempsey because they don't understand thinking fighters like Tunney. Don't get me wrong. Tunney's got as solid a left jab as Dempsey ever had but Tunney doesn't waste his blows on the air. He lays out his fight like a chess game. Every swing he takes tells him where his opponent is strong and where he isn't. He dissects the guy bit by bit. When he's sure he's figured out the weakness, boom, he lands the punch that ends the fight. I'm putting my money on Tunney. How about you?"

"A C-note on Dempsey," Rosen says slapping a hundred-dollar bill on Max's desk.

Max digs through the cash in his pocket and calls the bet. The money goes in an envelope that Max labels and shoves into his desk. The hour is late. Meyer and Charlie make a move for the door.

Max says, "You hear about George Remus?"

Who hasn't? The tale resounds nightly around every Jewish mother's dinner table. The famous Cincinnati lawyer turned bootlegger took up with a golden-haired shiksa named Imogene. And now that he's in jail, she's in charge of all his money and money-making opportunities. Meyer's relationship with Remus goes way back to the beginning when Remus got those first "certificates of withdrawal." Meyer thanks his good sense for keeping Rothstein as the go-between standing between him and Remus.

Charlie laughs out loud. He has long held that a gangster should avoid marriage at all costs. He likes to say, "Why pay for a house in Yonkers when you can rent a room at the Plaza?"

"Remus was indicted for a thousand violations of the Volstead Act," Max says. "I didn't know there were a thousand violations. Hey…" He hesitates. "I heard…I heard you have the connection…for the certificates."

"You interested?" Rosen says.

"I could be," Max says.

"Doctors don't prescribe much beer," Meyer says.

"Maybe I'm branching out," Max says.

"I'll see what I can do," Meyer says. "We'll be in touch."

"Two years in Atlanta," Max says. "Ain't so bad for the haul Remus made. He'll get back on his feet again."

"Sure," Rosen says. "He can salvage what's left of his business once Imogene and the federal agent she's in bed with finish selling off everything."

The boys bid Max goodbye and stroll along the streets of Philadelphia in search of a good diner.

"You think he's on the phone to Waxey?" Rosen says.

Meyer says, "Waxey is a beer peddler just like Max. If I were in his shoes, I'd be thinking about padding my own account and not Waxey Gordon's."

After lunch, they check into a couple of suites on the top floor of the Sylvania Hotel. Everybody winds up in Charlie's room for a strategy session based on tomorrow's agenda with the leading Italian in town, Salvatore Sabella. He's another guy from Castellammare del Golfo, Sicily. Charlie is hoping the thirty-four-year-old Sabella will see the value in an alliance with him and Meyer. It is a stretch.

"What about this Sicilian...what's his name?" Rosen says.

"Sabella," Charlie says. "He was sent to Philly by one of the Brooklyn families to get a foothold in the Italian rackets here. He's plenty strong, this Sicilian. Has a soft-drink café. Brings in olive oil and cheese. Tough son of a bitch, too. When he was fourteen he killed the butcher he worked for cause the guy would beat him for not working hard enough."

Rosen takes note. Sabella is not Italian. He's Sicilian and part of the clan that has settled in Brooklyn. Charlie's prickly situation comes clear. The wannabe Caesar, Maranzano, is turning the tide against Joe the Boss by asserting his dominance over the Sicilians' clan. Charlie is Joe the Boss' emissary. He needs to tread persuasively but lightly with Sabella.

"Why are you meeting with this guy?" Rosen says.

"Respect," Charlie says. "If I'm going to make moves in his town…"

"Since when is this his town?" Rosen says.

"You gotta show respect," Charlie says. "That's how the Italians handle things. These Sicilians got hair triggers. Joe the Boss is breathing down their neck in Brooklyn. We let him know we ain't interested in taking over his territory. Just play along."

Rosen shakes his head. Meyer lights another cigarette.

"It's America," Meyer says. "There's plenty for everybody. When we were kids, we were all robbing and stealing. It was the Wild West. We've been handed an opportunity on a silver platter. If we play it right, we all get rich."

"Ha!" Rosen says. "And if we don't?"

He has a point. Violence is the backbone of ghetto life and criminal occupation.

"You want to open up gambling in Philly?" Meyer says. "You're going to need Sabella's cooperation. Cut him in for a piece. It's cheaper than a war and who needs the publicity?"

Outside, a patchwork of office lights shine on vacant desks. Streetlights burn brightly over near empty streets. It is 3 A.M. and Philadelphia has closed its eyes for the night.

Charlie pours whiskey and drops ice cubes into the glasses.

Meyer says, "Nig, there's a few things you gotta understand about this move. It isn't the same as when we were kids. I didn't bring you along to muscle these guys…unless that's needed, later. This is a business first and we're gonna conduct it like a business. It's better to get cooperation."

Rosen says, "You think you're going to get cooperation from Sicilians?"

Meyer says, "We've got connections all over the country because of Charlie. We watch out for the guys we're connected with and they watch out for us. You'll be meeting guys like

Sabella now. Philadelphia might be your oyster. We're bringing in Jews and Italians. Listen close. If Charlie says this guy is a friend of ours, it means he is a close associate, an ally. If he says this guy is a friend of mine, it means he's with Charlie one-hundred percent. You introduce people, then you bring them along the same way. Everybody who needs to know will understand what that means."

"When you want to make a deal with an Italian, come to me. The deals you make with the Jews are between you and Meyer," Charlie says. "Everybody is trying to make a buck. You wanna make a deal, you ask the guy if he wants in on it. He says 'yes' or 'no' and that's it. Everybody puts their cards on the table. That way, there ain't no misunderstandings later."

Meyer says, "Protection only goes as far as that deal. Whatever else the guy has going on is up to him. It doesn't have anything to do with our business."

"Ain't our problem," Rosen says. "I get it."

Meyer says, "You've got the idea but not the whole picture. When I say something has to be done a certain way, it has to be done just that way. You don't have to understand. We're working things out, me and Charlie. Sometimes you won't understand until later. That's the way it has to be for now."

Rosen nods. He swigs back a glass of whiskey and lights a cigarette. No territory. Connections. It's an outright criminal democracy. In this business, you can rise. In a hierarchy, a rising star is sure to get knocked back in place.

"Tomorrow, Charlie handles Sabella," Meyer says.

"O.K.," Rosen says. "And later?"

"Come to me first if you have a problem," Charlie says.

"I got the protocol," Rosen says. "Is that it?"

"That's it," Meyer says.

Rosen crushes the butt of his cigarette and yawns.

He says, "What about spreading payola around the casinos? We still doing that? Paying off the neighborhood for good measure?"

"Yeah," Meyer says. "Twenty-five, thirty bucks goes a long way for the common man. Nobody is gonna beef if you're running a respectable establishment."

"Business as usual," Rosen says. "I don't know about you gents but I gotta get some beauty sleep. Don't get up. I'll show myself out."

"We'll meet downstairs at eleven," Meyer says.

The next morning Nig Rosen is waiting in the lobby when Charlie and Meyer step out of the elevator. He stands, tosses his newspaper on the chair where he was reading, and the three of them make their way outside to grab a cab to see Sabella.

The Castellammarese clan is tight. Salvatore Sabella, fleeing a murder charge in Italy, made his way to the U.S. in 1911. Stefano Magaddino, the big cheese in Buffalo, is his father-in-law. Magaddino used to run the Brooklyn family that the wannabe Caesar is now wooing. Magaddino lives in Buffalo for the same reason Sabella lives in Philadelphia rather than Italy. Famiglia. Joe the Boss flexes his strength in Brooklyn but Joe is not famiglia.

Joe Adonis, as part of Frankie Yale's mob, is keeping an eye on the escalating tension in Brooklyn. Yale has nothing to do with the Castellammarese but plenty to do with Brooklyn. Nobody knows just how much power the wannabe Caesar intends to grab from Magaddino but their mutual hatred for Joe the Boss is indisputable. It is the force that binds them. Charlie Lucky, who wants to stay that way, holds out an olive branch to Sabella in the hopes that the Sicilians will see him as an ally rather than an enemy.

"Let him earn," Charlie says.

"And what's our connection?" Rosen says.

Meyer says, "Charlie and I are partners. In Sabella's world, that makes us 'friends of ours.' "

A cab pulls up in front of the hotel. The gang jumps in. Charlie gives the address of Sabella's soft drink café. The cabby shivers. He knows the café is nothing more than a thinly disguised speakeasy where the city's gangsters do business from booths inside. It is a short ride from the hotel to the café.

Meyer and Nig Rosen wait outside while Charlie meets with Sabella.

Charlie tells Sabella about the Jews, points out the cab through the window, and says, "I vouch for them myself."

Sabella rankles.

"I heard you were in bed with the Jews," Sabella says, "but I wouldn't believe it."

"Believe it," Charlie says. "You're hearing it straight from the horse's mouth. I got business with them. These guys are friends of ours."

"That remains to be seen. What do Jews know about olive oil and cheese?"

Charlie says, "They know a helluva lot about whiskey. Me and Meyer are putting Nig Rosen in Philadelphia. He will be moving booze around the city. I figure you gotta be interested in that."

Sabella stares out the window at the Jews.

He says, "I got wine coming in from Italy, what do I need with whiskey? You can't trust a Jew. They'll rob you blind. What kind of shit are you trying to get me involved with? Joe the Boss put you up to this? Another trick to get the Sicilians under his thumb?"

Charlie breaks a smile. "You afraid of the Jews?"

"Whatever gave you that idea," Sabella squawks.

"They're sharp businessmen. I personally vouch for Meyer. He's my partner in the bootleg business. If he says he'll do somethin', he'll do it. You have a problem with Nig Rosen, you call me and Meyer will take care of it."

Sabella looks out at the Jews again.

"They look shifty," he says.

"Bullshit," Charlie says. "They ain't no more shifty than the motley throng coming through unguarded gates. You got that little piece of historical reference?"

"Your Jewish friends teach you that?"

"What if they did?" Charlie says. "The point is that none of us are really welcomed here. We can get our asses kicked back to Italy anytime they want. Why not make the most of it while we're here? Whatever we got going, we got more when we got it together. You wanna come along for the ride? No pressure. You do what you want to do but ignoring bootleg is, in my opinion, a mistake. You can do your business for the Italians but you'll make a helluva lot of money in bootleg."

"What's your proposition," Sabella says.

"Let Meyer and Niggy come in and we'll talk business."

Sabella nods and the negotiations begin.

The day before Christmas, Al Capone's seven-year-old son is stricken with a severe mastoid infection that leaves him irritable and lethargic. His ear bulges and droops. Gooey pus dribbles out. The doctor covers the boy's ear with gauze.

"He needs surgery right away," the doctor says.

Capone calls a New York surgeon and then checks the schedule for the *Limited*. The boy whines and screams from Chicago to New York City. They race to the hospital where Capone's surgeon is standing by. Dutifully, Capone and his wife wait as the boy goes under the knife. When Sonny is safely nestled in his mother's arms, Capone heads to the Adonis Social Club for a pre-Christmas break from domesticity and an opportunity to take care of a little business.

On Christmas Day, the *Times* informs the people of New York that the leader of the White Hand Gang, Peg Leg Lonergan, is dead, killed at a ramshackle Brooklyn cabaret on Twentieth Street. In other words, the Adonis Social Club. The newspaper warns of the probability of a serious gang war between the Irish and the Italians now that the White Handers have suffered the loss of their leader and two of his "aides" who were also killed by the rival gang.

Capone reads the morning paper and smiles, pleased with the night's work. Meyer reads the news and sighs. The violence is too close to home. He folds the paper and wanders to the window of his flat. Snow gently falls on the streets below and, along with it, a hush. The Chanukah spirit evades him. Christmas, too, for that matter. His mind prefers to busy itself with the chance that Frankie Yale has cashed in on his deal made with Capone, Dean O'Banion's murder in exchange for Peg Leg Lonergan.

Meyer heads to the Claridge where Benny punches numbers into an adding machine and Adonis stands by the desk.

"What went on last night?" Meyer says.

"I was there," Adonis says. "That loudmouth Lonergan came in shooting off his trap. Too bad for him Al Capone dropped by. A couple of broads came in, Irish girls. They were with Italian guys. You know Lonergan. He can't hold his liquor or his tongue. He yells at the girls like they're a couple of sailors: 'Fer chrissake!' He tells them to get out and come back with white men. His boys fall out laughing. These guys come to the club to give the Italians a hard time. It's a sport. What the hell? The Irish love a good fight. He should just slap Yale and get it over with but the goddamn mick's gotta get stinking drunk before he walks into the club and roughs up the clientele."

Meyer listens calmly with no hint of his inner concerns.

"He sees Capone and shouts," Adonis continues, "'I can lick

the whole bunch a ya single-handed.' Capone doused the lights. Bullets flew. People dove under tables."

Meyer says, "Was this Capone swapping with Yale for the murder of Dean O'Banion?"

"Nah," Adonis says. "It just happened."

"That's a lot of heat to bring down on the neighborhood," Meyer says.

"The Astors don't hang out in Brooklyn. Nobody gives a damn what happens there."

Meyer says, "The common man cares. Don't kid yourself. He's got sons and daughters on those streets. If you're connected to the trouble, we all fall under scrutiny. You should think of that. Buckner is happy to add us to his little black book. We won't be able to walk down the street without a tail. Who needs it? If you're smart, you'll play it low-key."

The hard-nosed Adonis finds the revelation hard to swallow. Meyer's words are not so much wisdom as they are a mother hen trying to corral her chicks.

Adonis says, "The Irish problem has been neutralized. Ain't that good enough?"

Meyer says, "Where's Capone?"

"He's gone back to Chicago. He's got his alibi. He was at the hospital with his kid, for Christ's sake."

December bleeds into January. Rosen gets busy making connections in Philadelphia. He shuttles back and forth to Manhattan. Meyer keeps up appearances at the Cannon Street garage. He pulls on a heavy wool sweater and lights another cigarette. He has an hour to peruse the newspaper before the Mutt and Jeff Club meet at Ratner's but the newsboy is running late. Meyer will have to wing it without the knowledge of today's news if the boy dallies much longer.

"Dry law conspirators heading to court!" the kid yells, jumping indoors from the winter storm.

He gives his head a toss, shaking wet snow from his brown cap and then folds a paper and sends it sailing through the air toward Meyer's desk. It smashes into a cup of coffee. Meyer looks up from the mess. The kid is gone.

The brown stain highlights the news: *W. V. Dwyer, J. J. McCambridge and 59 others indicted for conspiracy to break dry law, some also indicted for sending men to sea in unseaworthy vessel and for bribery of Coast Guard. E. Caperton accused of using airplane to direct rum ships...*

It is the biggest Prohibition bust ever and still there is no word on the street regarding Hans Fuhrmann, the ship captain who is slated to testify against Waxey Gordon.

Meyer reaches for a cigarette. The pack is empty. He throws on an overcoat and slogs to the corner market.

"Can you believe it?" says the brassy brunette behind the cash register.

Her hair falls gently to her shoulders. Her eyes pierce the icy gloom of the January storm that spreads a shiver through the shop.

"As mild as May," she says, a Marlboro dangling from between her fingers.

She adjusts the shawl collar of a white lace blouse and tugs at the ends of the sleeves. Her name is Anne Citron and her father owns the store. Meyer knows of her but has never been ballsy enough to speak with her.

"Who needs an icebox when you've got January?" Anne prods. "I see they got the gunsel twins, Waxey and Maxey. I'm sure you know that by now." She picks at a piece of tobacco on her tongue. "Doesn't it strike you as odd that the government only rounds up criminals of 'exotic origin'?"

"What?" Meyer says.

She winks. Picks up a small brown bag and rattles it toward the bootlegger.

"I could offer you an almond. My father gets them from a cousin in Israel but you don't look like the kind of guy that celebrates Tu B'Shvat. My cousin worries that those of us born in America are losing our identity. Eretz Yisrael and all that." She raises her eyebrows, gives Meyer the once over. "Almond?"

Anne shoves her pack of Marlboros across the counter to Meyer.

Meyer laughs. "The British gave Yisrael to the Arabs."

He takes a cigarette and lights up.

"Arabs, shmarabs," Anne says. "Look."

She peels back the heavy curtain that separates the market from the back room. The yeasty beer smell that permeates the shop finally makes sense. Anne rips a blanket from atop a sea of gallon jugs.

She says, "What will we eat in the seventh year? Grain, what else? Bran hops, molasses, yeast and water. Eleven percent beer!"

Meyer stares at the jugs in wonder. This is a woman after his own heart.

"The perks of being a grocer's daughter," she says. "George Washington's recipe was in the paper. I thought, what the hell? A lotta people come in here looking for booze."

"Not Jews," Meyer says. "Jews are looking for whiskey. And nobody wants to get poisoned."

"Are you calling me a lousy cook?"

"You want into the bootleg business?"

"You have to know somebody who knows somebody. Do you know somebody?"

Meyer says, "What time do you close this joint? The Marx Brothers are playing at the Lyric."

"What time?"

"Seven-thirty?"

"I'll think about it," she says.

Nig Rosen is deep into a plate of blintzes when Meyer steps into the deli. He doesn't even bother eavesdropping on the morning kvetch.

"We've got a problem with Sabella," Rosen says. "His guys hijacked a couple of our shipments."

"What does he say?"

"Not guilty," Rosen says.

"How do you know he did it?"

"It was our guys on the trucks," Rosen says.

"I'll talk to Charlie. What else? How's Hoff?"

"I wouldn't worry about Hoff. He's a smart fella. Part of something is better than all of nothing. I heard Waxey Gordon made a deal with a Jersey mayor."

"Hague," Meyer says. "A thin-lipped teetotaler. What's he doing making a deal with a bootlegger?"

"The straitlaced types are always trouble. He squeezes the balls of his employees until they cough up a nice little kickback. Gordon is right up his alley."

Gordon has located his new business headquarters a stone's throw from Jersey City and right next door to the end of the rail lines.

Meyer says, "That's not good news. Dalitz brings his freight cars through that yard by Elizabeth. It wouldn't be hard for Gordon to make trouble for us. Be sure you contact Dalitz with the news."

"Done," Rosen says.

They spend the afternoon cruising Jersey City and the surrounding towns. Meyer makes a mental note of each town's relationship to the rail yard. By the time they finish, it is nearly 7:30. Meyer has barely enough time to make it back to the grocer's shop to pick up Anne.

The Lyric Theater is standing-room only but somehow, Anne surmises the how, Meyer has procured front-row seats. A bell rings from behind the stage curtain.

The crowd settles and the curtain slides open. On stage is the Hotel De Cocoanut.

"We want to see you, Mr. Schlemmer!" a bellboy calls.

The audience howls. Schlemmer is the Broadway equivalent of schlammer which is Yiddish slang for a person who beats people up. Groucho, the unscrupulous Florida land promoter known as Henry W. Schlemmer, takes center stage. The bellboy approaches him. He wants to get paid. A volley of jokes ensues.

With that, vaudeville officially invades Broadway.

The sixty men indicted for conspiracy to break the dry law come to trial. Dwyer and 23 others plead not guilty to the charge of sending out a boat that is not seaworthy. Hans Fuhrmann, the elusive sea captain, is shot to death in a New York hotel while waiting to testify against Waxey Gordon. Suicide, the medical examiner calls it. Murder, his widow says, but no one is listening.

Charlie kicks back in his Mulberry Street office and reads the latest news on the case. The phone rings. Joe the Boss is demanding Charlie's presence. Charlie hoofs the ten minutes to Joe's Lower East Side office. The Boss waves Charlie to the hardback chair against the wall. Joe stares out the window and puffs the last of his Cuban torpedo. The smoke fogs the window and adds to the yellow haze on the walls.

Charlie scans the room and stops on the picture of the young bride that hangs behind Joe's desk. She wears a soft, white dress and long white gloves that cover her elbows, white stockings and white shoes. Her veil sits atop a head of thick black hair and cascades down her back to the floor. A bloom of fresh flowers adorns her left arm. Her face is the picture of innocence.

An uncontrollable chuckle escapes Charlie's being.

Joe the Boss turns to confront the source of Charlie's amusement.

Charlie quickly points to the photogravure of the Isola Bella that hangs beside the bride. "Manhattan ain't nothin' like Sicily, eh?" he says.

Joe contemplates the Dragon tree that rises from the dry, rocky hillside above the island's small bay. Then he looks at the bride.

He says, "That is my Mama. We spring from the rocks, huh? We have to be tough to survive. Sally." The Boss uses Charlie's Sicilian name whenever there are Italian troubles to be dealt with. "You see what we have in Brooklyn? I want you to take care of this problem. Cola Schiro is supposed to be the father to this Castellammarese clan but he is a weak man. This we know. Salvatore Maranzano knows it, too. I know this Maranzano from Sicily. He was with Don Vito Cascioferro. You remember him, Charlie? Cascioferro? The devil has his soul. Ferro and Maranzano are up to no good in Brooklyn. Go to Brooklyn and sit down with Schiro. See what's in his eyes but watch out for that due-facce Maranzano. He gonna have the same smooth words as Cascioferro, who used to say, 'You have to skim the cream off the milk without breaking the bottle.' Then he pretends he is interested in protecting the business of his victims. I know his business, this Maranzano. He will put on a good face for his victims. Let us remove his mask before he gets too strong."

Charlie arranges to meet with Cola Schiro at a Brooklyn restaurant but when Charlie arrives, he finds Salvatore Maranzano has taken Schiro's place.

Charlie says, "Where's Schiro?"

"The weather," Maranzano says. "Schiro is not well. You will excuse him for his absence."

Charlie summons Vito Genovese with the wave of his hand.

"Go get Schiro," he says to Vito and Vito is gone.

Charlie orders espresso, stirs in two spoons of sugar.

Maranzano says, "Perhaps the worry has made Schiro ill."

Charlie says, "What does Schiro have to worry about?"

Maranzano says, "Joe the Boss is putting pressure on him. He expects tribute. You must know this for yourself."

Charlie says, "How has this become your business?"

Vito escorts a worn-down Schiro into Charlie's presence.

Charlie says, "When I call you, you come."

Schiro nods. Maranzano watches the compliant family head with disgust.

Maranzano says, "We are men of honor. The Castellammarese stand as one. Who is Joe the Boss to insist that we come at his beck and call?"

Schiro musters strength and says, "We have heard disturbing news from our friend in Philadelphia."

Charlie looks at Schiro then at Maranzano and back to Schiro again.

Schiro stutters, "S-S-Sally Sabella..."

"Do you have business with Sabella?" Charlie says.

Schiro says, "There are certain Jews in Philadelphia telling him how to handle his business. Sabella says these Jews are with you."

Maranzano pushes Schiro's trembling hands aside and sets his glare on Charlie.

Maranzano says, "These Jews claim to have your blessing. Salvatore Sabella is a man of honor. We are bound by our honor to each other. You can see why this would be troublesome news. We want to know if this is true."

Charlie continues to look at Schiro.

"Does Salvatore Maranzano speak for you now?" Charlie says.

The little man trembles. His eyes drop in defeat.

Maranzano says, "Out of respect, I speak for the family. I have more experience in these matters. It is none of my business how Don Masseria runs his family. It becomes my business when he involves the men of our tradition."

Three years of smuggling soldiers from Italy into America has emboldened Maranzano, who relies on the old ways to empower him. He spreads hatred of American ways, calling Joe the Boss a traitor to their tradition. Joe has a mob of disparate backgrounds where Maranzano has a family of pure Sicilians.

Charlie says, "What is your business with Salvatore Sabella?"

Maranzano leans forward and cups his hands over Charlie's. Charlie pulls away. Maranzano musters a fatherly voice.

"I am suggesting Don Masseria not make the same mistake that Mussolini has made. Mussolini thinks he will break the Sicilians by subjecting them to his will but he is wrong. Torture makes the heart resolute. Fear must come only by respect. Without respect, a man is nothing more than a butcher. Mussolini sends out Cesare Mori to instill fear and enforce his will. Mori butchers men who do not stand together. We stand together. You must know the things of which I speak."

He sits back confident he has made his point using Mussolini's henchman as his example. Mori has made his way through Sicily with nothing more than two boxes the length of a man's legs, a leather belt, and a gas mask. With this device, he struck fear in the hearts of the opposition.

Mori's torture device has a simple technique. Bind the arms behind the back. Stretch the man over the boxes stacked one atop the other, strap the thighs tight with the leather belt and secure the chest with a rope run under the armpits. Ankles are secured by two iron rings attached to the boxes. Place the gas mask on the man's face and fill it with salt water. Even the most stoic of Sicilians tends to confess to any sin at this point. If not, a quick tug on the rope, smashing the head on the ground, does the trick. Whipping and burning the feet, twisting the testicles, pulling out fingernails, or applying a vice to nearly any body part leaves Mori with a perfect record of confessions.

Maranzano says, "A father must think about the needs of the family. A father must maintain order. It is difficult to lead. Not everyone is suited to the job. Julius Caesar said, 'War gives the conquerors the right to impose any condition they please upon the vanquished.' We have not been vanquished. If Joe the Boss wishes to be a father over the Castellammarese, let him prove his worthiness not by demanding tribute but by becoming a man of honor."

Charlie says, "You walk the neighborhood and come to places like this for the same food your mother cooked. You hear news of the old country. It is all very clannish but don't let this illusion of Italian camaraderie fool you. Outside is America."

Joe the Boss listens to Charlie's report with the disdain of a rebuffed lover. Joe uses Mussolini's estimation of the Sicilian mindset, " 'Sicilianism is a mental illness.' " And then, resolute, he adds, "We prepare for war."

Rothstein

Buckner

Garment strike   1926

Chapter Nine
We Stick Together, No Matter What

APRIL 1926

"Hello, Sucker. Come right in and leave your wallet on the bar," says Texas Guinan. Patrons at the El Fey buy "Champagne" made from cider and alcohol for $25 a bottle. Watered-down whiskey is a buck a shot. That doesn't stop everyone who is anyone from coming to the El Fey to listen to the quick-witted Guinan, or Larry Fay from laughing all the way to the bank.

Fay made his way to the top using his fleet of taxis to run beer and whiskey to the major hotels and hidden speakeasies of Manhattan. When Owney Madden came out of the can in 1923, Larry Fay joined up with him and Big Bill Dwyer. The El Fey, on 45th Street, is Fay's latest endeavor, for which he lured the wisecracking Guinan away from the Knickerbocker's King Cole Bar. Business has never been better.

Still he sweats the news that Big Bill has been caught up in Emory Buckner's net. It eats away at Fay's confidence even though his Texan star is the darling of café society. The white-hot spotlight that the Knickerbocker bust has cast on his closest associate leaves him sleepless and irritable. With a fair degree of sarcasm, he assesses the celebrity count in his club. Rudolph Valentino. Fanny Brice. Eddie Cantor. Sophie Tucker. And then, for good measure, he stashes his booze in the house next door to the club, where Prohibition agents won't find it.

"Bunch of immigrants," Fay mutters, and then counts out the politicians and judges. "Bunch of hypocrites."

Meyer Lansky walks Anne Citron along the awning-covered entrance of the El Fey. Benny Siegel, with his date, Esther Krakower, are close behind. The girls check their furs and then take stock of the club's clientele.

"You can't fight City Hall," Fay says showing the party to a front-row table. "All you can do is entertain them and hope they remember the favor when you land in front of the judge. So far, it's working."

"Too bad about Big Bill," Benny says.

"Class warfare," Fay says. "Protestants against Catholics. Wait and see. They'll be clapping a padlock on the El Fey soon enough. It's all a show for headlines. I'll shut down here and open someplace else. Word gets around. These same guys will be in the new joint boozing and bragging before anyone else. Nothing ever changes."

Anne says, "We're good enough to work in the factories but clean the dirt out from under your nails and see how far you get. You want something, you gotta take it when it comes your way."

She glances at Meyer with a furtive look and strokes Meyer's manicured nails.

The tuxedoed maître d' pours Dom Perignon, the real stuff, not the cider mix parading as Champagne.

Larry Fay says, "Amen, sister," and whispers to the maître d' that this tab is on the house.

Not more than a dozen blocks away, Emory Buckner, holed up in his Manhattan office, opens an envelope that was discreetly passed to him earlier in the day. The Sergeant at Arms of the United States Senate requests the presence of Mr. Emory Buckner. He is to come to Washington D.C. to testify before a senate hearing on crime.

"The Sergeant at Arms requests!" he says. "And what would

he do if I declined? Arrest me? Can't anybody just pick up a telephone and call?"

"What?" his secretary says.

"I have to go to Washington. Find out when the next train leaves."

"This late?" she says.

"As soon as possible," he says. "If that's now, then now. It's a train. It runs in the dark!"

Buckner packs his briefcase. He throws in a freshly laundered shirt and clean underwear just in case his appearance should drag on.

"You've got twenty minutes," the secretary says.

Buckner races down the hall and runs down two flights of stairs. Outside, he hails a cab. The temperature has dipped to barely forty-six degrees. He kicks himself for leaving his topcoat on the hook behind the door.

"Grand Central. And step on it," he tells the cabbie.

"Just once I'd like a guy who ain't in a hurry," the cabbie says.

Buckner barely makes the train bound for the nation's capital. He falls into a commuter seat. A copy of the *New York Times* occupies the seat next to him. He picks up the paper and thumbs through the pages. He stops short to read about the latest debacle shaming the federal war against bootlegging.

To control the easy money made from bathtub gin, government chemists routinely add poison to all industrial-destined denatured alcohol. The latest chemical concoction used for this purpose has bootleggers stymied in their search for a removal process that frees the alcohol from the poison. Consequently, the death toll mounts and the government, not the bootleggers, is taking the heat for poisoning its citizens.

Buckner snaps the paper closed and grumbles under his breath. It isn't the government's fault. It is the brazen rebellion of the country's citizens—that's what is wrong with this country.

The person sitting across from Buckner looks up from his timetable and notices the *Times* article.

"Shameful," he says out loud and goes back to his schedule.

Buckner's lip curls. He is of the belief that people get what they deserve when they step outside the law, and that includes the poisonings. But his logic doesn't fly with liberals and he knows it. Furthermore, expressing such a thought could weaken his case, so he stuffs his opinion down deep and focuses on the job at hand: cleaning up New York. Which means he needs more federal money.

He pulls a manila folder from his briefcase and reviews his notes. The president is soft on enforcing the unpopular law. Another thorn in Buckner's side.

The train pulls into D.C. Buckner hustles for a cab that takes him to the Capitol Building. He tips his hat to the young ladies sitting on the stone wall leading to the famous steps and ultimately the great white building where justice is served. The girls giggle and go on with their white-bread sandwiches and lightweight conversation. Birds rustle through the trees and swoop down to catch the crumbs thrown by the girls.

The investigating subcommittee convenes in the holy of holies. Sixteen senators set apart from Buckner by tightly spaced desks that face rows of small mahogany tables arranged in neat semi-circles. Buckner settles his briefcase and takes a seat. He removes a stack of folders from the case, and then faces the senators.

His first official act is to state his name. The senators shuffle papers and speak among themselves. Buckner waits patiently for them to get to the point.

Mr. Codman asks if Buckner enforces the Prohibition law. After that he asks if Buckner is having any success. Buckner asks the senator to define success. He explains that enforcing Prohibition in a district like New York is nearly impossible. For two hours, a back-and-forth debate rages.

Then Senator Means asks about the "foreign element" and wonders if they are responsible for the criminal violations. Without mentioning specifics, Means hints at prevailing attitudes: a report by Ellis Island doctors that the Italian face lacks intelligence; an article in the *North American Review* quoting Police Commissioner Bingham as declaring that half the criminal population in New York is Hebrew and another twenty percent are Italian; Henry Ford's declaration that Jews are in crime because they are unfit for hard labor and that Italians are in crime because they are a "riffraff of desperate scoundrels, ex-convicts and jailbirds."

But that's not the whole story, of course, and Buckner gropes for clarity. How does one explain the burden of poverty to a Senator earning $7,500 a year?

On the Lower East Side, four square blocks of Rivington Street and Clinton Street in his Southern District contain 5,800 people, most of them Hebrew. The average garment worker's day wage is $1.68, or 14 cents an hour per twelve-hour shift. Put another way, it takes three hours of work to buy a dozen eggs.

Means presses for specifics of Prohibition violators with regard to trafficking.

Buckner turns to his calculations. Sixty million gallons of illegal alcohol runs through industrial pipelines. Buckner figures a plant at full capacity can produce four thousand gallons a day. That amounts to $75,000,000 a year. He calculates the profits drugstores can garner from their dealings in the trade.

The numbers, the numbers, all the talk is about numbers. Gallons, percentages. But the thing eating away at Buckner's cause, like a moth going at a perfectly good wool suit, is the simple fact that morale is low among his inspectors. They don't care like they once did. The demon spirit has turned out, in most people's eyes, to be benign. Corruption has spread through the ranks.

Which means he needs new soldiers in the ranks. But today, the senators are not inclined to release the federal dollars Buckner needs for the fight. Buckner repacks his briefcase and returns on the next train to New York.

Back on home turf, he hails a cab. The driver takes him past the El Fey, where Texas Guinan stands on the sidewalk securing the club's mascot, a tiger named Mecca, while federal officers close the club. The officers shout and the tiger returns a growl. The spectacle has captured a large audience of onlookers.

Texas turns to Larry Fay and says, "They shoulda padlocked this joint sooner. You can't buy this kinda publicity."

Meyer relaxes in his Claridge Hotel office and scans the paper. Brigadier General Lincoln C. Andres, head of Federal Prohibition enforcement, has informed the House Appropriations Committee that the cost of enforcing Prohibition during the next fiscal year will be $29,120,122.

"He thinks that's high," Meyer says to Benny. "He should be working this side of the street."

"Everybody has a hand out," Benny says. "What does the general think *we* pay for enforcement?"

"It's the cost of doing business," Meyer says and moves to the next story.

"The Irish got cops and politicians. What do the Jews get?" Benny says.

"Lawyers," Meyer says. "You can do a helluva lot more with a good lawyer than you can with a cop or politician."

"Tell that to George Remus," Benny says.

For Remus, who was on trial for a thousand Volstead Act violations, the jury took just under two hours to convict him and send him packing to the Atlanta Federal Penitentiary.

Charles Solomon sticks his head in the suite's door. Charles "King" Solomon is the latest bootlegger to secure a series of suites in the Claridge, the gathering place for Jews unlikely to join the needle trades.

"Is this the place?" he says.

"The king has arrived," Benny says. "Too cold in Boston? You gotta run down here to warm up?"

"*Stock* up," Solomon says. "I hear you are making moves in Philadelphia. I came to make sure you aren't thinking of branching out to Boston."

"We'd let you know," Benny says without a smile.

"Yeah, yeah," Solomon says with a nod. "You know Samuel Bronfman up in Montreal?"

"What about him?" Meyer says.

Solomon lights a cigar and assesses the mood of the room. Meyer folds his newspaper and lays it on the table. In fair imitation of the Lincoln Memorial, he sits back, settles his arms on the chair's armrest, and studies the King.

"I have a connection with him. I can get all the whiskey you need," Solomon says.

"We'll keep it in mind," Meyer says.

It isn't so much Solomon's cheap whiskey that Meyer objects to as the narcotics that are his stock in trade. Solomon rarely deals in opium, the stuff of Chinese dens. He prefers heroin and commercially manufactured morphine for the simple reason that it guarantees return customers.

"What brings you here?" Meyer says.

"That's it," Solomon says. "Checking in to see how things are going."

Meyer nods. It is dangerous to get too close to a drug dealer but foolish to avoid all cooperation.

Solomon offers, "There are no unwilling victims, eh? We give the public what they want. In that way, we stay in business. That's the bottom line, isn't it? Business?"

Meyer says, "Why rock the boat with a crime that's publically despised when you can make as much from one that people love?"

"Don't put all your eggs in one basket," Solomon says.

"What's that, advice from the Easter Bunny?" Benny says.

Solomon says, "I'm on the fifth floor in case you want to find me," withdrawing his head from the office.

A long series of grunts and groans that would sound more at home in Polly Adler's place than bootleg central emanate from a back room. A shaft of light pierces through the room. Meyer rises and closes the shade.

Benny says, "What are we, mushrooms? We have to live in the dark?"

"Whorehouses should be dark," Meyer says, referring to the business in the back room. He fires up a cigarette and tries to ignore the pleasure circus in the back, a couple of Charlie's guys going at it with a couple of Polly's girls.

Meyer says, "Don't get too close to Solomon. We don't need that kind of trouble. Who was it that Buckner busted in Jersey last week? Anybody we know?"

"Nah," Benny says. "Strictly a one-man operation with permits for the denatured stuff. Buckner hired some General to sniff out the guy on account of the government poisoning."

"General Andrews? He has no jurisdiction in Jersey."

Benny says, "They nabbed ten carloads full of this guy's alcohol. The guy's got the permits, all right. The undercover guys couldn't make a move at the yard so they followed the shipment to a plant in Jersey. That's where the guy turns it into bootleg. Buckner calls it an overt act. I had Dalitz send our stuff to a different yard until all this blows over."

Polly's girls wander through Benny's office.

"We're leavin' now. Need anything?"

"A little peace and quiet," Meyer says.

Red Levine wanders out from the back.

"Were you part of that?" Benny says.

"What? The girls? Jews don't make noise when they're having sex," he says.

As the girls exit, before the door even has a chance to swing shut, Charlie Lucky saunters in.

Benny says, "Charlie, what's with your guys jazzing it up with Polly's girls all day and night? All that heavy breathing is steaming up the windows."

Charlie says to Meyer, "You know the Italian in Philadelphia, Sabella?"

"What about him?" Meyer says.

"He's spreading the word among the Mustache Petes that there is money to be made in bootleg. Lots of money. These cocksuckers in Philadelphia are knocking over shipments left and right."

Red leans against the wall and cleans his fingernails with the tip of a switchblade.

Benny says, "What's it got to do with us?"

Charlie says, "A couple of friends of mine were in a restaurant and they heard the guys at the next table, friends of Sabella, planning to jump our next shipment. Apparently, they ain't got no respect for Jews. They're tellin' the old greasers that the Jews are pushing their weight around in Philly."

Benny snarls, "Is that right? These fucking cocksuckers. I can clean up this mess."

With Charlie's blessing, Benny, Red, Meyer, and Nig Rosen board a train to Philadelphia. They settle into a private compartment. The semaphore goes green and the train lurches forward.

Meyer says, "These old greasers are nothing but trouble. One day we'll be forced to take them out of the picture. Maybe not today but soon. If we make Charlie the man, he can clean things up."

Red says, "Why make anybody the man?"

"It's their culture. 'Father' this and 'man of honor' that. They need someone at the top. But it's got to be someone they respect. The Americanized guys don't put a lot of truck in the greasers—they just want to earn, but the greasers have their hands so deep into everybody's pocket that the guys on the street don't make much money, yet they're the ones out there risking their lives. That pushes these guys to do stupid things. That's in our favor. Remember Rothstein and the Black Sox Scandal? Play on the discontent. Same idea. Charlie is fair and square with the guys. He lets them earn, so they don't have to take what belongs to somebody else."

The discussion volleys back and forth between the inadvisability of getting involved and the undeniable fact that they already are involved. The break from the greaser debate comes when Benny hands off a stack of taxpaid stamps to Rosen, who examines the small green strips of etched genius. The fine print reading TAXPAID blossoms in the middle of a four-leaf clover. The banner on one end of the strip reads "80 Proof." The banner on the other end reads "One Quart." Across the top of the strip are the words "Bottled in Bond Under the Supervision of the United States Government in Distillery Bonded Warehouse." La pièce de résistance, as far as Meyer is concerned, is the undulating red type of the distillery name: Old Shylock Distributors.

The booze comes in through Atlantic City just after midnight. The contents are loaded into three unmarked trucks and taken to a warehouse not far from the docks. The counterfeit taxpaids are affixed to the bottleneck, over the cap and down both sides, guaranteeing the contents are pure and legit. The bottles are returned to their original crates. The crates are loaded into the trucks and the trucks are sent on their way.

Benny is behind the wheel of the lead truck. Red rides shotgun. Just outside of Philadelphia, Salvatore Sabella's boys take the bait, hijacking the trucks and leaving the drivers on the side of the road. Nig Rosen comes up from behind and retrieves the drivers. They follow the trucks to Sabella's drop. In a flurry of bullets that takes the lives of two of Sabella's men, they take back what is theirs.

Sabella is left with a nagging suspicion that Charlie Lucky is behind the rout. The accusation is a slippery slope. Accuse Charlie and you accuse Joe the Boss. Neither Sabella nor his boss have the strength to take on Joe the Boss' mob.

Sabella attends two funerals and fumes. He heads to New York where he meets Charlie at the Mulberry Street garage in a rage about the men who were killed in the raid.

Charlie says, "I'll check around, see what I can find out."

Sabella has no choice but to agree. Days pass before Charlie bothers to give Sabella a call.

"The way I hear it," Charlie says as though the information is fresh off the street, "the Jews and the Irish took revenge. Didn't you check the taxpaids? The Jews marked that shipment so they could find the guys that have been knocking them over. You aren't trying to tell me that a mob can't protect what is theirs, are you? Listen, Sally, it ain't worth hijacking the Jew mobs when I can hook you up with the guys bringing in the booze. You hook up with them and they will handle the trouble."

Sabella says, "I ain't interested in doin' business with no kikes."

Charlie says, "Jews aren't interested in your neighborhood stuff; they got neighborhoods of their own."

There's silence on the line.

"The Jews are here to stay. And they know how to make money," Charlie says.

"I'll let you know," Sabella says.

The garment strike that started last December continues to rage. The goal is a forty-hour work week. In a meeting held at the new Madison Square Garden last May, fur strikers gave a ten-minute demonstration of cheering, stamping, hat-waving, hat-throwing, shouting, and whistling and held out for their cause.

The International Ladies' Garment Workers' Union meets. Workers push for a guarantee of thirty-six weeks of labor throughout the year. The manufacturers push back. The ILGWU goes on strike July 1, 1926.

Spurred on by the worker's discontent, the Communist faction tries to seize control of the unions. The Socialist faction fights back. Manufacturers hire schlammers to beat sense into workers who refuse to work. Governor Al Smith creates a Mediation Commission but the ILGWU cannot agree on the commission's suggestions.

The strike enters week 24, becoming the longest strike on record. Cloak makers insist it is impossible to live twelve months on six months' worth of work. Unions hire their own gangsters. Little Augie Orgen and three members of his gang are arrested for shooting one Samuel Lendman, a strike picket. After four more striking garment workers are shot, District Attorney Banton warns garment manufacturers and union heads that he will stop the violence if they don't.

From 34th to 42nd Street, factories groan from inactivity as violence escalates.

"It is bad enough to have a strike," Governor Smith says, "but violence in an industrial controversy is absolutely inexcusable and merits the most severe condemnation."

There it is, out in the open. While the business world keeps tabs on how many bathing suits are sold and worries over the "raw silk situation" in Japan, the violence takes center stage in the news. Nineteen cloak designers are assaulted, intimidated and kidnapped by union officials.

Cloak and suit manufacturers quibble over the selling season's lack of distinctiveness in fabrics. Underwear prices drop. Button manufacturers are encouraged by a new style trend that puts buttons in vogue.

The strike enters its twenty-eighth week. President Coolidge confers with labor chiefs. Governor Smith urges arbitration and calls in Abe "the Just" Rothstein, respected member of the needle trades. Arnold Rothstein contemplates the news. In a moment of clarity, he realizes his father will have no more success than the governor at settling the strike. Negotiators have come upon two immovable and uncontrollable forces, the unions and the manufacturers. Both continue to hemorrhage money that fills gangsters' pockets.

For six months, two mobs have cracked skulls, thrown acid, exploded bombs, and broken bones. Strikers have been jailed for disorderly conduct. The unions reel. Bankruptcy looms.

"Stop futzing around with these guys. Call the other Rothstein," a garment lawyer says.

Arnold Rothstein agrees to the meeting. He leaves the Plaza and hails a cab.

"Lower East Side," he says. "Cannon Street."

It is late on a Friday afternoon. Sabbath is approaching. The cabby swerves through a maze of pushcart vendors rushing to get home. Meyer Lansky looks up from a book about Julius Caesar as Rothstein's cab comes to a halt.

Rothstein takes a seat in Meyer's front office.

"Neither the communists nor the socialists are willing to budge. Management is losing ground. The unions can't get the head-crackers out. My father…" He laughs. "I'm not the neighborhood goyishe kop," Rothstein says which literally means non-Jewish head but which actually means someone who fails to use his head. "I've got a meeting with the union heads and the manufacturers tomorrow. When I walk in, I want to know that Little Augie and Jack Diamond are going to play ball. In exchange, they get a piece of the pie."

"The pie being?" Meyer says.

"Unions," Rothstein says. "What else?"

Jack Diamond is tightly associated with Rothstein. Little Augie is the fly in the ointment. Augie is a hard-headed Hasid in gangster clothing. He has no desire to settle the strike. Only one guy can influence Augie and that's Lepke Buchalter. Only one guy can influence Lepke Buchalter and that's Meyer Lansky. By now, Benny is running around with Lepke Buchalter and Gurrah Shapiro. The fast friends have become the triple threat of the Jewish mobs.

"I'll take care of Jack," Rothstein says. "I've got plenty of what he wants. He's obsessed with getting his mother out of a rundown tenement. If her sisters are in a sweatshop grinding out $1.68 a day, she won't leave. He buys her rugs and settees to spiff up the place but it's like putting a gold ring in a swine's snout. She won't give up the iron bed that flakes paint everywhere…or the chamber pot." Rothstein cops a brogue. "'Can't ya at least put that thing outside when you got compnee?' He'll see the value of settling with the manufacturers if he thinks it will get his mother out of the ghetto. Can you…will you talk to Lepke?"

Meyer says, "Why not you? He can be reasoned with."

"We both know he wants into the unions," Rothstein says.

"Lep's mother was part of the fainting brigade."

Rothstein says, "A fainting woman can bring a union meeting to a standstill."

Jewish mothers are the cornerstone of the fight against deplorable working conditions. The Triangle Shirtwaist factory fire in 1911 brought the battle to a head. One-hundred-forty-six workers died, mostly young girls, trapped behind locked doors that were management's tactic for limiting cigarette breaks. The eighth floor of the Asch Building went up in smoke. Girls jumped out windows to escape the flames only to fall a hundred feet to their deaths. The catastrophe was over in half an hour but for a solid week afterward, the police held lanterns over numbered, rough-wood coffins while relatives searched for loved ones. Seven bodies were so severely burned they were unidentifiable.

"You should go to Augie first," Meyer says.

Rothstein says, "Lepke knows what we want. He's a smart guy. He'll figure out the rest. But I don't think he will listen to me."

Meyer nods. He meets Lepke at Prospect Park in Brooklyn. Meyer lays out Rothstein's plan to settle the strike.

"Augie won't go with it," Lepke says.

They wind their way up Lookout Hill and check the view from Far Rockaway to Sandy Hook. In the opposite direction, the view spreads from the Bay and the Hudson to Jersey Heights and New York City.

Lepke says, "Augie's got one thing on his mind and one thing only, sluggin'. Can Rothstein really make a deal?"

Meyer says, "He's going to try. If I was part of the unions or the manufacturers, I'd settle. If they don't settle soon, the government steps in. Then what do they have? A whole lot of nothing."

It doesn't take a genius to realize what's at stake. Meyer doesn't even have to ask. Lepke calls Little Augie who, in turn, calls in his gang. They meet at Augie's dilapidated office. Lepke lays out the plan. Rothstein will offer to settle the strike in exchange for a piece of the unions.

Augie says, "Unions. Fainting and spitting...what kind of bullshit is that? You have to crack heads if you want change. They'd be stupid to settle for that. I ain't stupid. I ain't about to settle for no piece of the unions."

Gurrah jabs Lepke in the ribs.

Lepke says, "Can't you see the logic in taking a piece of the action?"

"Since when did I die and put you in charge?" Augie says.

Augie picks at the stuffing that leaks through the rips in his armchair.

Lepke says, "This is our chance. You don't have the good sense God gave you."

The hair on Augie's neck prickles to attention.

Augie says, "If God had any sense, we wouldn't be here. Workers will always strike. Manufacturers will never give them an even break. You gonna run to Arnold Rothstein every time there's a strike? You trust this two-bit hustler? The unions are bust. What are we gonna get from them?"

"Management is ready to make a deal," Lepke says. "Unions will be flush again."

"What makes you think so?"

Gurrah Shapiro says, "Part of something is better than all of nothing."

"Shut your mouth, Gurrah. Nobody asked you to think,"

Augie says. "You got my answer. Let Rothstein fall flat on his face just like his father. This strike ain't gonna be settled."

Augie pounds the table with his fist. He is sticking with the obstinacy he learned from his father. The rituals of Judaism were meant to be enforced without compromise or reason.

That evening, Meyer meets Arnold Rothstein at Owney Madden's place in Harlem where the orchestra plays hot jazz and a chorus line of black girls in loose-fitting silk tops and short-shorts wiggle and jiggle their way to center stage. The dancers' hands fly back and forth in a mock Charleston. Long, muscular legs glisten under the hot stage lights.

Arnold Rothstein calls for Champagne. He raises his glass to the ILGWU labor leaders who, despite Augie's position, pronounced the strike settled. Gossip circles rave about Abe the Just and whisper about Arnold Rothstein. For the first time in as long as he can remember, Arnold Rothstein feels good about himself. People who run in certain circles, many of whom frequent the bohemian nightclubs, recognize his accomplishment.

Madden scoots closer to Texas Guinan and raises his glass to Rothstein.

"To the man of the hour. May all our fathers' failures wind up our successes," he says and downs the Champagne.

Rothstein tips the etched amber glass to Madden and sets it down without drinking a drop.

"He never drinks," Madden explains to Texas.

"Never?" she drawls. "What a shame." She raises her glass. "To my father's failure," she says, and drains it.

"Texas, here, has a new club all her own," Madden says, "the 300 over on 54th Street."

"If it's good enough for Gershwin, it's good enough for the likes of you lot," she says. "I got the best broads, the best band,

and the best suckers in town. You gentlemen should come down sometime."

"But don't lay a hand on her broads," Madden says. "She's got a lot of micks on her side who are happy to enforce her rules, make sure nothing happens to them broads. Am I right, Tex?"

"Right as rain," she says.

Rothstein says, "That's highly unusual for this town."

Anne Citron, Meyer's date for the night, scowls.

"Good for you," she says to Texas. "Good for you."

"Did you hear," Madden says. "One of Emory Buckner's agents is calling it quits. He claims sixty-five percent of New Yorkers are violators and therefore the law cannot be enforced."

"The law makes criminals of us all," Meyer says.

The singer, a high-yellow with sleek pinned-back hair and smooth confidence, takes the stage and eases into "Poor Little Rich Girl."

Mae West, draped in silk and surrounded by a group of vaudevillians, makes her way through the club. Madden rises instantly upon catching sight of her.

"Sit down, honey," she says, "you're blocking the view. Can't you see these boys are in love?"

She nods to the singer and then pulls up a chair, shooing the vaudevillians to another table. The singer wraps up her song and takes a bow. The orchestra strikes up a dance number.

Madden says, "You ever hear of the Washingtonians?"

"Those boys in their ivory towers in D.C.?" West says.

"Nah," Madden says. "The bandleader is a guy called Duke Ellington. He's got six guys backing him up. They're playing in a joint over on 49th and Broadway called the Kentucky Club. You know the place?"

"I can't say that I do," she says.

"I talked to the bandleader. He's smart, this guy, I don't mean nigger smart but real smart. He says that white kids anxious to free themselves from the Puritan stranglehold come into the club to listen to something more upbeat."

"White kids need freedom about as much as Henry Ford needs another factory to pump up his bankroll," Rothstein says.

"You're cynical," Madden says.

West fluffs her hair and says, "Don't take it personal but that boy's got it right. It's hard to have fun when you have to be clean all the time. Why do you think people keep drinkin' when it's against the law? It's the only way they can forget their chains."

Madden thinks maybe she's got something there, and maybe Duke Ellington has, too.

Chapter Ten
Never Let Your Guard Down

NEW YEAR'S EVE 1926

"Beau" James Walker performs his first official act as New York's mayor by fanning the party atmosphere of the New Year's Eve celebration in Times Square. The one-time songwriter and son of an Irish-born assemblyman steps up to the microphone and warbles one of his own tunes: "Will you love me in December as you do in May...?" The loudspeakers crackle in the cold.

Benny Siegel leans out the window of his fifth-story suite and shouts, "You'll be lucky if they still love you in the morning!"

"Nobody can hear you," the redhead says.

She sprawls, bare, between perfectly white silk sheets that hug the curves of her body.

"Do I give a shit?" Benny says, slamming the window on the near-zero chill outside. He stokes the hot embers of a flagging fire and throws on another log.

The inebriates below harmonize over the top of the Mayor's song: *Should auld acquaintance be forgot...*

The redhead says, "You remember what happened last time you stood that close to the flame?"

If he could, Benny would blush, but he can't, so he sneers.

The redhead gathers up the silk sheet and twists it around her body. Long, slender legs play peekaboo as she strolls from the bed to the fireplace. By the time she reaches Benny, the silk has dropped down to around her waist using the same

move that got Mademoiselle Fifi busted in the Minsky's Bur-
lesque raid. Benny drops the fire poker and tackles her mid-
stride. She falls onto a mink coat cast thoughtlessly on the long
couch. The fur bristles against her back. Benny grabs her muscular legs and presses them open. He mounts her and thrusts
himself, impatiently, between her chorus girl thighs.

She giggles.

Benny grunts. In a blaze of ecstasy, he falls across her, panting
and spent.

"Goddamn," he says as if Santa got it wrong and misplaced
his lump of coal. "Goddamn," he repeats.

Outside, Jimmy Walker finishes his ballad. The crowd's roar
rattles the windows of the suite. The redhead sits up and gathers
her unruly locks into a short ponytail at the base of her neck.
Benny pours another round of Champagne.

"To Old King Cole," the redhead says, her green eyes flashing
with disgust. "May the old buzzard never rest in peace."

Benny nurses the Champagne bottle.

"Who the fuck is Old King Cole?" he says.

"Haven't you ever looked at the mural over the bar at the
Knickerbocker? Old King Cole, the guy in the mural, that's John
Astor," she says. "The Fourth. The guy that built the Knicker-
bocker. I bet you don't even know where he got his millions."

"Off the backs of factory workers," Benny hazards.

"Wrong!" she says. "His grandfather, John Jacob Astor, was
America's first multi-millionaire." She stares at the blazing fire
and snugs the mink around her shoulders. "The old man made
millions in fur. And then did it all over again in real estate." She
stops with a pregnant pause. "And opium." The word swirls from
her lips like smoke from a pipe. "The grandson, that's the guy
in the mural, inherited a shitload of money, built the Knickerbocker, and then went down with the *Titanic*."

"Jesus," Benny says.

"You only live once," she says, copping a Mae West drawl, "but if you do it right, once is enough."

The roar of the crowd outside dies off. Benny beats a path to the window, the redhead close behind him. Mayor Beau James strokes the countdown to midnight with the beat of his black walking stick.

"Ten, nine, eight…" The crowd counts down in unison.

The iron and wood ball that hangs above Times Square waiting to usher in 1927 glows with 2,500 watts.

"Four, three, two…"

Christmas lights bob in the rustling trees that line the streets. Gentleman Jimmy tips his hat.

"One!"

The ball drops. A cacophony of whistles and cowbells, horns and cheers, deafen the merrymakers in the Square.

Benny turns to the redhead ready to go again.

"Happy New Year!" he says.

Buried in the Times Square crowd of revelers are Mr. and Mrs. Harry Stromberg, as Nig Rosen and his wife are known in polite circles. Already, they've had too much Champagne. They carry their buzz to the Cotton Club where the party is just getting started. By dawn, they drag themselves home for some scrambled eggs and a little hair of the dog. A few hours later, Rosen catches a cab and meets up with the gang at Katz's Deli.

"Is Tunney gonna give Dempsey a shot at getting the title back?" Benny says over a salami sandwich.

It is a simple question with an equally simple answer.

"Wouldn't you?" Nig Rosen says. "A fight like that would pull in a lotta dough."

He scoops another round of sauerkraut and shouts for a bowl of matzoh ball soup to shake the chill. Winter has hammered the Lower East Side with all the fervor of the Manassa Mauler pounding the comers in his infamous saloon fights.

"In a minute," the waiter shouts back.

"Who you gonna bet on?" Benny says.

Rosen clings to his love affair with Dempsey's style. He looks at Meyer.

"Maybe he should stay in Hollywood," Meyer says of the once-tough Dempsey who has undergone plastic surgery at the behest of his shiksa wife.

Rosen says, "He kicked out his manager over something the guy said about his wife. The broad got him in pictures out there. He carries her around on his shoulders. She thinks she can reform him. What a show. After the surgery, he won't get in the ring. Save the face. Dempsey is going soft out there with all those actors." Rosen grabs a pickle from the bowl, a full sour, and bites it in half. "My wife ain't a Jew but she ain't no shiksa either. She'd never try to reform me. She likes mink too much."

Meyer says, "What's going on in Philadelphia?"

Rosen says, "Sabella is as predictable as my wife. Dangle a few greenbacks in his direction and he'll follow you anywhere."

The hijacking of the booze with the "Old Shylock Distributors" stamps and counter revenge attack has done the trick. Still...

"Watch your back," Meyer says.

Joe the Boss Masseria strolls past the neatly stacked and packed streets of Little Italy along with his rising lieutenant, Charlie Lucky. The 5'2", brutish Masseria marvels at America's genius for consolidation. Sicily, with all its sprawling beauty, never offered such compact control. Joe paints a picture postcard image of the business opportunities that surround them. He dreams of grandeur and schemes for conquest and justifies the whole package with indignation.

Joe is on a tear.

"We have a responsibility to our people," he says. "Look at them. Peasants. They shuffle wherever they go, always the head hung down. You should always stand tall and take what you want. If you don't, you are trampled underfoot. Do you know, Sally, there are more Italians in New York than in Sicily. That's a lotta escarole for us!"

Charlie covers his disdain with a smile. The papers have made a fortune wrangling the city's census statistics into "startling facts" that scare sensible citizens. "More Italians than in Naples," the paper said with no word of Sicily. "More Germans than in Berlin. More Irish than in Dublin. More Jews than in Warsaw."

Joe the Boss and Charlie duck into a small café on Elizabeth Street where, over a large plate of pasta and a bottle of fine Chianti, Joe twists a few facts of his own.

"Famiglia," he tells Charlie. "This is our credo. Every family needs a strong leader. Stefano Magaddino was strong in Brooklyn. Now he is strong in Buffalo. He can do them no good in Buffalo. Cola Schiro is weak. A little bird tells me that Salvatore Maranzano is turning heads in Brooklyn. Soon he will head the Sicilians. He will challenge our famiglia. We are not strangers to this way of life."

Joe the Boss hunts for signs of betrayal in Charlie but finds only an impassive stare. Charlie runs through a short list of little birds and comes up with Alfred Mineo as the most likely ally whispering in the old man's ear. Mineo chafes under the reins of his boss, who favors Maranzano's bid for ascendency in the Castellammarese clan. Mineo courts Joe's favor by betraying his boss' trust.

Charlie says, "There's a guy in Yale's mob I've been bringing along. His name is Joe Doto. He calls himself Joe Adonis. He's Napoli. A guy like Maranzano is too busy spreading his bullshit among men of honor to notice a Neapolitan. Doto keeps us informed about what's going on in the Sicilian orbit in Brooklyn."

Joe the Boss rolls the Chianti in his glass.

"And what does this Doto have to say?"

"Maranzano is trouble," Charlie says.

For one thing, the self-important Maranzano flaunts his contempt for Joe the Boss, and he does it in five languages. He quotes Julius Caesar and uses the skills he learned while studying for the priesthood to gather a following. Maranzano eloquently insists the "man who dodges bullets" has abandoned Sicilian tradition by taking the crass American title of "Boss." He insists loudly that Joe the Boss, a gluttonous man, will use his impure mob, spotted with non-Italians, to devour the Castellammarese.

The Neapolitan in Brooklyn makes for a good spy.

Masseria snarls and stuffs more pasta into his gaping mouth.

Joe says, "This is Don Ferro's doing. He wants to come back to America."

Cascioferro fled to Italy to avoid a murder charge. Joe Petrosino, the New York cop heading up the Italian Squad, naively followed him to Palermo where Cascioferro had Petrosino executed in the Piazza Marina.

"Is that possible?" Charlie says.

Joe the Boss says, "Bring the Napoli by my office. I take a look at him."

An old woman slips through the front door of the restaurant.

"White-washed graves," she screams, pointing a bony finger toward the street. "Are we such little dogs that we should be kicked around by ruffians such as these?"

The restaurant's patrons turn as one and watch five hundred hooded men, beating drums and waving American flags, parade past them. The six-million strong Ku Klux Klan is on a mission to inform New Yorkers and New Jerseyans that Al Smith, the Catholic Church, and Demon Rum are the tools of the Devil. As the Devil's tools, they are tearing Americans from their moral roots. The parades target neighborhoods of immigrants to demonstrate the power of white supremacists. Their stake in America flows from the pioneers who built the country and bequeathed to their own children a priority right to control the country. "America for Americans," they tout.

Joe the Boss turns back to Charlie and finishes his wine.

"You talk to Yale," he says. "I want to know what he thinks of this blowhard in Brooklyn."

Charlie calls the doorman of his uptown apartment to have his car brought around. He checks his look in the hall mirror, making sure everything is in place. It is. The elevator takes him to the lobby. The lunch crowd fills the street outside.

The whine of the six-cylinder, high-compression engine of the Chrysler Maxwell is unmistakable. Charlie gives the driver a five-dollar handshake and climbs behind the wheel. He swings the car out into traffic and heads toward the Brooklyn Bridge, which spans the great divide between Castellammarese ambition and Joe the Boss' hold on Manhattan's Italian rackets.

Charlie's mind turns to Coney Island, where he will meet with Yale and try to squeeze blood from the tight-lipped turnip. Yale, one of Brooklyn's most ruthless killers, prefers to keep his opinions to himself. Yale has taken up residence in the Citadel Coffee Shop since his old club burned to the ground. His stiff, round collar and heavy brown wool suit mark him as chronically Italian. He looks up as Charlie comes through the door and rakes the thick shock of hair that falls across his forehead to the side with a sweep of his hand.

Yale says, "To what do I owe the honor of this visit?"

Charlie says, "Joe the Boss is interested in what you know about Salvatore Maranzano. He figures we might be able to help each other."

"He's a real saint, that guy," Yale says. "What should I know?"

Yale looks around his cafe. The locals have come and gone. The place is dead.

Charlie eyes the Young Turk sitting next to Yale, the eager Napoli of whom he speaks. Adonis sports a black suit, white Sulka shirt, and Deco tie. His hair is slicked back, his face clean-shaven. He grabs the arm of the girl serving the table and whispers in her ear. She smiles. He winks.

Charlie rankles at the smooth ease with which Adonis sways the woman.

"Let's not play games," Charlie says. "You know Brooklyn like you know your wife's face. Salvatore Maranzano ain't makin' no bones about how much he hates Joe the Boss. He's trouble. We both know it."

"Lovett was trouble," Yale says of the Irish white-hander bent on controlling Brooklyn's docks. "Willie 'Two-Knife' Altierri buried a meat cleaver in his skull. After that, Lovett's brother-in-law was trouble. Capone put an end to that. There's always trouble."

Yale's pinky ring clinks on the handle of the coffee cup he raises to toast his insight but it doesn't erase the fact that, a few weeks after the white-handers were killed, the Harvard Inn went up in smoke. The predominantly Irish fire brigade was unwilling to save Yale's rundown, two-story dancehall on Seaside Walk.

Yale says to Adonis, "Wait outside."

Adonis leaves the table.

Yale says, "Joe the Boss must be shaking in his boots for him to send you over here to talk to me about the Sicilians. You wanna know about Sicilians? Check out the docks. Maranzano is smuggling soldiers from Palermo. He's a smart fella. You figure a guy like that is gonna be content taking orders from a coward like Cola Schiro? That little wimp pisses his pants at a loud fart."

Yale lights one of his cheap cigars, filling the coffee shop with its stench.

Yale continues, "I got no truck for a guy like Maranzano. I worked too hard for what I got to hand it over to somebody else. If Joe the Boss has any sense at all," he rolls his eyes in disbelief, "he'll make his move while he has the chance. This guy ain't gonna roll over and play dead."

Charlie stands and thanks Yale for his time.

In the crisp winter afternoon, Joe Adonis leans against the building's cool brick front careful not to wrinkle his suit. He smokes and, as the skirts walk by, flirts.

"The real scoop is Maranzano's connections to Cascioferro," Adonis says to Charlie, flashing an easy smile.

Charlie says, "Don't tell me anything out here in the open. You don't know who might be listening. Meet me on the boardwalk at two in the morning. And don't be late. I ain't in the mood for freezin' my balls off cause you're in the sack with some broad."

By midnight, a drizzle has slicked up the streets, but by 1 A.M. it has ended. Adonis leaves the cafe at 1:50 and makes his way to the boardwalk. The Maxwell idles under a street light. Windshield wipers swipe at the rain. Adonis hikes up the collar of his overcoat and walks up to Charlie's car. He taps on the driver's window.

"Get in," Charlie says through the crack.

Adonis slides into the passenger seat bringing with him the smell of Yale's cigars.

Charlie says, "Jesus. It ain't bad enough I gotta smell them cheap cigars around Yale, you gotta stink up my car, too? Open the window."

Charlie releases the handbrake and lets out the clutch. The Maxwell's engine beats smoothly as he drives away. The amusement park fades from view. Darkness surrounds the car.

Adonis rubs his hands in front of the heater vents trying to take the chill off.

Charlie says, "Here's a piece of advice; never let nobody know what you're thinking. You might find yourself takin' the rap for something you didn't do."

Adonis coughs up an excuse. He waxes lyrical about the politicians in Yale's pocket then he attempts a joke about a politician and prostitute.

Adonis says, "The prostitute gives you something for your money."

"Polly Adler tells the same joke," Charlie says.

"Polly's joke is about wives and prostitutes," Adonis says.

"You got it all figured out, don't you, Joe? Listen to me and listen good. Whatever you got to say to me, you say to me alone, not out on the street corner where everybody can hear our business. Got that? Think before you say something you're gonna regret. The action you got in Brooklyn is small potatoes."

Adonis says, "Yale is just as strong as Joe the Boss."

Charlie says, "Don't make me laugh. This ain't about Yale, anyway. Me and Meyer Lansky wanna bring you along in our business. Understand? I took care of my business with Yale. Now I'm taking care of business with you. You wanna stay in that rundown flea-bitten joint of Yale's or you wanna come uptown with us? Make up your mind. But you come with us, you follow our rules. We don't stand for no shit. You do things the way I tell you to do them. No questions asked. Got that?"

Adonis shifts in his seat. He doesn't really get Charlie, who is sitting almost on top of the world yet everything about Charlie is low key: his car, his clothes, the way he handles himself. In a room full of guys, nobody would even notice one of them is Charlie Lucky, the trusted right arm of Joe the Boss.

Charlie says, "Joe the Boss wants to see you. He's gonna bring you in under his wing but you're going to be with me. You're my doing. I'm taking the responsibility."

Another uncomfortable silence.

Adonis says, "If you really wanna know what's going on with the Castellammarese, call Willie Moretti. He's a loudmouth anyway. A guy like you calls him, he'll be all over himself to spill what he knows so he can look good."

"You trust what he knows?" Charlie says.

"With a grain of salt," Adonis says.

"Are you as good a fixer as they say?" Charlie says.

"That ain't hard," Adonis says. "Why do you think I'm always after the broads? These guys, give 'em a few bucks and night on the town and they'll give you what you want."

Charlie gives him a hard look.

"How's your relationship with Capone?" Charlie says.

"Friendly. Why?"

"If I bring you up to him, I don't wanna get no backlash," Charlie says. "You wanna hit Lindy's? I'm starving."

"The Jew joint?" Adonis says.

"I'm hooked on the G-Man Special," Charlie says.

Charlie parks a block away. Lindy's is jammed with the Broadway crowd.

From nowhere, Ben Siegel appears. "What the hell are you doing here?" Benny says.

"Slummin'," Charlie says.

Benny looks at Adonis. "I'd expect you to be at the Lenox

Club. They got broads that…well, what the hell am I telling you that you don't already know?"

Adonis winks. Benny is aroused by the notion of picking up broads at the Lenox.

"You guys go on," Charlie says. "I don't need Joe anymore."

By 6 A.M., Charlie is at the Claridge Hotel talking shop with Meyer Lansky over coffee and doughnuts.

"You were right," Charlie says confessing the value of Joe Adonis. "He goes all the way back to the early days when Capone was part of Yale's mob. By then, I was already hooked up with Joe the Boss. Joe A. and Al are still tight."

Meyer says, "Are the rumors true? Has Capone been knocking over Yale's shipments?"

"That I don't know," Charlie says.

Meyer says, "An alliance with Chicago would be useful."

Charlie says, "Only the feds can cross state lines and only for a federal offense. The feds are busy chasing outlaws, not bootleggers."

Meyer says. "Something isn't right. I can't put my finger on it yet."

On March 29, President Coolidge appoints a new U.S. Attorney for the Southern District of New York. Buckner couldn't compete with the millions of dollars spent on bribery, perjury, and oath violations, and so he resigned. Thus, the padlocking business shifts from Emory Buckner to Charles H. Tuttle, who vows to pursue bootleggers as relentlessly as dope peddlers.

Salvatore Maranzano busies himself with building an army of illegal immigrants while Arthur Flegenheimer, who calls himself Dutch Schultz, and his partner, Joey Noe, make their presence known in the Bronx. Flegenheimer runs his business from a musty saloon. The joint stinks of stale beer and spent cigarettes and urine courtesy of too many drunks who couldn't hit the toilet bowl.

Meyer hails a cab. He and Benny are bound for Harlem and the Dutchman's little nest. An assortment of Italian and Irish immigrants fills the bar. Meyer takes in the collection of thugs the Dutchman has in his mob. They sit around a table shooting the bull. Benny recognizes Eddie McGrath from the docks, an Irish guy with sway among his countrymen. The Dutchman counts on McGrath's influence to smooth the way for his moves on the Bronx docks.

A slender Jew with a calm face leaves the card game to greet Meyer and Benny.

"Bo Weinberg," he says extending a hand to Meyer.

Weinberg breaks into a full smile. The Dutchman emerges from the back room. He rambles toward Meyer with the slow shuffle of a caged gorilla. An over-stretched gray jersey shirt bulges uncomfortably under the cheapest of Sears' suits.

The Dutchman says to one of the boys at the table, "Go get me some cigarettes." The Dutchman turns to Benny. "What are you lookin' at?"

The Dutchman's eyes shift nervously between Benny and Meyer and then between Meyer and Weinberg. The smile drops from Weinberg's face.

Weinberg says, "This is Benny Siegel and Meyer Lansky. You know, the Bugs and Meyer mob."

The Dutchman's face flushes bright red. "You come in here to fix beer prices, too?"

Benny says, "This is a friendly visit, Arthur."

"Arthur?" the Dutchman says. "Nobody calls me Arthur."

The Dutchman leads Benny and Meyer to the back room. The room is littered with bookie notes wrapped in adding machine tape held together by rubber bands. Newspapers, racing forms, wildly scribbled notes on horses and numbers gleaned from the wire broadcasts cover the rest of the mess-filled table. A metal lockbox sits next to the ledgers.

The Dutchman says, "You didn't come for no tea party."

Weinberg stands at the doorway and clears his throat.

"You got my cigarettes?" the Dutchman grunts.

Weinberg lays the carton of cigarettes on the big table in front of his boss. The Dutchman rips open the box and tears into a pack. He lights up and leans back in his chair. He sucks his cigarette dry.

Meyer says, "The word on the street is that you are moving on the docks in the Bronx."

"When I do, I'll alert the press."

Meyer says, "We're interested in making a deal with you."

"What kinda deal?"

"We've got shipments coming in from Europe," Meyer says.

"And?"

Meyer says, "You've got the numbers racket up here?"

"I'm strictly in the beer business," the Dutchman says.

Benny says, "Ain't that Irish typically? The beer business?"

"You worried about the Irish all of a sudden?" the Dutchman says. "They got plenty of power…gumshoes everywhere and Tammany politicians. But I got my connections."

"Can you handle our shipments or not?" Benny says.

The Dutchman sizes up the interest and decides it's a good move to work a deal with the Bugs and Meyer mob.

"I'm in business, ain't I?" the Dutchman says.

The Dutchman shoves another cigarette in his mouth and lights up. His two-bit shirt and four-dollar suit covered with ash rubs Benny the wrong way.

Meyer says, "What's your take?"

"Five percent," the Dutchman says.

Benny gives Meyer a glance.

"We'll be in touch," Meyer says.

The Dutchman goes back to his scratch pad and figures.

Meyer stands and nods to Benny.

"What a schlub," Benny says, stepping outside. "Who does he think he's kidding about the numbers racket? You see that saloon?"

"He's a schlub with Irish connections," Meyer says. "Weinberg knows the score. Get to know him. He's a guy that can be reasoned with."

"What gave you that idea?"

"The way he shook my hand," Meyer says.

September 22 rolls around. Dempsey gets his rematch with Tunney at Soldier Field in Chicago. Al Capone puts fifty grand on Dempsey to win. For six rounds, Tunney holds the lead in points. Then Dempsey pins Tunney against the ropes. Two rights and then two lefts to Tunney's chin and Dempsey has the champ staggering. He throws four more punches. For the first time in his career, Tunney finds himself dazed and on the canvas.

Tunney grabs the rope but doesn't get up. The referee orders Dempsey to a neutral corner but Dempsey hovers over Tunney. A good offense is a good offense.

Five seconds pass, maybe more, before Dempsey moves off and the referee begins the count. By the time the referee reaches "nine," Tunney is on his feet.

In the eighth round, Tunney puts Dempsey on the canvas and the cycle begins in reverse. Even though Tunney doesn't immediately take a neutral corner, the referee begins the count on Dempsey. The fight ends with Tunney holding on to his title as Heavyweight Champion of the World but the controversy over the count has just begun.

Capone shrugs off his losses and gathers his entourage. He has a standing reservation at the Bella Napoli Café. On his way out of the stadium, he runs into the president of the Unione Siciliana in Chicago. He invites the president to join him at the Napoli. The president gladly accepts.

Capone drops into his Cadillac and insists Joe Adonis ride with him.

"Dempsey was robbed," Capone says. "It is a cryin' shame."

"The referee was paid off," Adonis says. "No doubt about it."

Capone growls.

"I heard Charlie was bringing you into the fold," Capone says. "You like the idea?"

Adonis gives a nod.

The Cadillac rolls up to the Napoli. The local riffraff is confronted with two choices: leave or get locked in while Capone enjoys his meal. Joe Esposito, the Napoli's chef and owner, doesn't mind. It's all part of the show and Capone more than compensates for the imposition. Most of the clientele stay and collect stories to tell their grandchildren.

Esposito busies himself in the kitchen. He romances the flavors of food like most men romance women. He brings out the antipasto, the primi, the secondi, and the contorni. Capone and his cohorts eat and drink and eat some more. When it is time for the dolci, Esposito brings out Ossa del Morti, or Bones of the Dead, even though All Soul's Day is weeks away. He places the sweet bread shaped like a skull and tibia and frosted in white in front of Capone.

Capone roars, "My mother used to make this for me when I was a kid."

Capone takes a detour into the kitchen to talk to the chef, then returns to the table and stuffs himself into hog heaven.

Adonis brings the story of his evening with Capone to his new partners: Charlie, Meyer, and Benny.

"It's another goddamned Sicilian nightmare," Adonis says. "There's a fight for the presidency of that damned Unione. A guy named Joe Aiello is making his moves. This Aiello guy is close to the wannabe Caesar in Brooklyn. He wants the Unione to remain strictly Sicilian. Capone wants to bring all the Italians together and call it the Italo–American National Union. Turns out the cocksucker Aiello approached the chef at Capone's regular restaurant and offered him thirty-five grand to poison Capone."

The details read like a Greek tragedy. Aiello brought five of his best men to the Napoli. Over bowls of lentil and escarole soup, they vented their frustrations about the Unione and Capone's meddling. When Esposito served a main course of capon the criticism of Capone grew hotter and bloated, insulting Capone's manhood and power, calling him a castrated chicken. After the meal, Aiello went into the kitchen, as he often did and always with the same purpose, to praise an outstanding meal. And then he did the unthinkable. He told Esposito to make a special treat for Capone and lace it with prussic acid. For taking care of business, Esposito would earn a cool $35,000.

"Don't worry, my friend," Aiello had said. "It will all be over in a matter of minutes. We will all be better off without this gorilla, eh?"

Adonis says, "Esposito thought, 'I should live so long.' He trembled at the thought of Capone coming in for dinner knowing about the bribe. You can imagine. And then he came up with the idea of how to tell Capone of Aiello's treachery. He made Bones of the Dead for dessert, showed Capone the vial of prussic acid Aiello had left behind, and whimpered 'I'm a cook; not an assassin.'"

"Poor bastard," Charlie says.

"Capone went into a fit of rage. When he finally settled down, he told Esposito to leave town until the matter was settled. When Aiello found out that Esposito skipped town, he upped the contract to fifty grand."

Charlie says, "Aiello is a dead man."

"And then what?" Meyer says. "Another Sicilian war?"

"At least in Chicago," Benny says.

The first to try to collect Aiello's bounty is Tony Torchio. Jack McGurn cuts him down before he can even get close to Capone.

Four guys follow Torchio.

Capone's bone pile grows.

Joe Aiello turns to the Irish mob run by Bugs Moran. The peace treaty between Capone and Moran is instantly shattered.

The news floats around Manhattan like the mist on a fall evening, reaching everywhere.

Samuel Bronfman flies into town to wine and dine the powerful Jewish bootleggers. Meyer Lansky escorts Anne Citron to Lindy's where they meet Longy Zwillman from New Jersey, all 6'2" of him, and his blonde date. For all his wealth, Zwillman maintains a modest veneer. For the life of him, Samuel Bronfman cannot understand why but it doesn't really matter. Bronfman has Canadian whiskey and Lansky and Zwillman have the market.

Bronfman pours a round of Champagne and launches into a rant on the Dempsey–Tunney bout.

"Dempsey was robbed," he says.

Meyer says, "Dempsey should have taken a neutral corner."

"Hogwash," Zwillman says. "The ref was paid off. The ref started counting Dempsey out before Tunney went to a neutral corner."

Meyer says, "Tunney wasn't standing over Dempsey when he went down."

Bronfman says, "Who's the better fighter? That's what everybody wants to know. That fight didn't prove anything."

Meyer says, "Tunney took a break. His point: 'Why would anyone want to get up early in the same ring with Jack Dempsey?'"

Zwillman says, "It's a goddamn fact that Tunney got to sit on his backside an extra ten seconds. To a boxer, that's an eternity."

Bronfman spends half his time in Canada and half of his time in Manhattan. The law requires it. He's a citizen of Canada. Now that he's in Manhattan having dinner with his distributors, he goes back to the consequences of Buckner's Knickerbocker raid.

Bronfman says, "Madden must have inherited all of Dwyer's beer business. He's gotta be the top Irish dog."

"He does all right," Meyer says.

Bronfman says, "Frank Costello got off easy. My father never got any respect. Distillers passed out money to anyone who would open a bar in the hotel. We thought that was grand."

Zwillman laughs at the whitewashing Bronfman gives the family brothel.

Bronfman says, "The distillers were the smart ones. They wound up with all the money. Distilling is a science but blending is an art."

"Aging is the science," Meyer teases, remembering the early days of Bronfman's business when he used formaldehyde to age his whiskey.

Bronfman says, "I'm buying Seagram's. I'm going to make it the most popular brand in America. Let the Europeans wallow in their history."

Zwillman says, "You're buying a reputation."

Anne puts down her cigarette and says, "Sam's buying yikhes."

Bronfman says, "Prohibition won't last forever. It didn't last in Canada. It won't last in America. It's worth too much in tax money. You should be thinking about life after Prohibition."

Meyer says, "Puritans still run this country."

Bronfman shakes his head, "Finances run everything."

Zwillman says, "We're bringing in twenty-two thousand cases a month through St. Pierre. Sam wants to put the squeeze on the supply so that once the deal goes through with Seagram's, he'll put his whiskey away to age."

"What do you mean squeeze the supply?" Meyer says.

"Rotgut will disappear when Prohibition ends," Bronfman says. "You see that, don't you? Yikhes or not, with Seagram's we'll have warehouses full of top-shelf whiskey. If you're smart, you won't distribute all you've got. Hold back some cases. When the supply dwindles and the demand rises, you will make a fortune."

"We've got customers…orders," Meyer says.

"So what?" Zwillman says.

The proposition leaves a bad taste in Meyer's mouth. He's built his reputation on supplying only the best. Nobody knows when Prohibition will end or even if it will end. The reformers could keep this going for years. Store more than you need and thieves break in and steal.

Bronfman says, "I've made a deal with a guy. He grew up in the Scotch business. He's got the nose, Meyer." Bronfman taps away at his own. "I'm bringing him in to create a new blend. We're going to change the world of whiskey."

"Ha!" Anne says. "Even in Canada they won't take in a Jew with a nose."

"Who won't?" Bronfman twists his face in confusion.

Anne says, "Do you really think you can buy your way into polite society?" She gives Bronfman a cockeyed grin. "Say it ain't so."

Bronfman says, "Money talks."

Meyer says, "Never loud enough."

Chapter Eleven
The House Always Wins

AUGUST 1927

Like a bear emerging from hibernation, the Dutchman rattles and bumps his way to a Bronx beer drop in a beat-up, aging jalopy. He is obsessed with his 1923 Model T Runabout. He believes the Lizzy, this Lizzy, with the modified cylinder head, oversized carburetor, upgraded manifold and fuel pressure system that transformed the 20-horsepower L-head engine into a fuel-burning, ass-hauling demon, will deliver him from all evil.

Although Henry Ford promises a sleeker, more powerful Model A that will be priced at a "reasonable" $385, the Dutchman curses Ford and the last of the Model T's scheduled to come off the assembly line in June. The Dutchman gruffly resents change.

"If it ain't broke, don't replace it!" he growls at Weinberg, his right hand and strong-arm, who drools over the new top-of-the-line Town Car with a water-cooled, 4-cylinder engine.

Weinberg says, "The pleasure of a nice vehicle offsets the pain. What's fourteen hundred bucks to guys like you and me?"

With a cold stare the Dutchman says, "What kinda sucker you take me for?"

The Dutchman doesn't have anything against Weinberg, or Henry Ford, for that matter. He just likes things to stay put.

He pauses along his journey where the Hutch dumps into the East River and sniffs at the air. He knits his brow into a fierce tapestry of concentration and confusion. A garbage barge lumbers dutifully on its way out to sea. The dock commissioner wasn't thinking of Dutch Schultz when he had the Hutch dredged to a depth of twenty feet to open the five-mile stretch of river to business, manufacturing, shipping and rail service.

The Dutchman's partner in the Hub Social Club, a fast-talking, deal-making dynamo named Joey Noe, wants to expand. The adding machine in the Dutchman's head tallies the cost. If he controls the shipping and rail along the small towns that dot the river from Scarsdale to Eastchester Bay and makes a connection with Meyer Lansky, his profit could double, maybe triple. The mere thought of all that cash makes his fingers break out in a sweat.

He punches the gas and beats a path to the docks where Eddie McGrath waits, impatiently, for the arrival of a whiskey shipment coming in from Ireland. Eddie's connection to the homeland runs through Owney Madden, who took over Big Bill Dwyer's action when Dwyer retired after the bootleg trial.

Eddie scans the horizon but finds only the sun inching its way into view. The Dutchman pulls his jalopy into the empty field across from the docks. The field is littered with old newspapers and an assortment of idle men keeping warm over oilcan fires.

A flock of black birds scatter as the Dutchman trudges across the field. He snorts at the line of longshoremen waiting for breakfast at the small café kitty-corner to the docks.

Eddie flicks a cigarette butt to the ground. He stares at his watch and then looks back at the horizon. The Dutchman walks up behind him.

"Where's the booze?" the Dutchman says, his haircut flopping in the breeze.

"Who the hell knows?" Eddie shakes his head calmly. "Ship captains aren't bankers, ya know."

The Dutchman paws at his stinging eyes.

"Chili peppers," Eddie says. "They're unloading them on the next dock. Those guys get the worst of it. Saw a guy once with a face looked like a baboon's butt. His wife hadda come walk him home on accounta his eyes were swollen shut. Makes you wonder what he did to piss off the dock boss that much."

"I'm goin' for coffee," the Dutchman says without a trace of emotion. "Come get me when the ship comes in."

The sign above the café door reads "Breakfast All Day." The Dutchman elbows his way to a place at the counter. The server swabs up crumbs and coffee rings.

"Tough luck about them anarchists," the server says referring to last night's electrocution.

Nicola Sacco and Bartolomeo Vanzetti, accused and convicted of the anarchist plot that blew up Wall Street, are dead. The papers say so.

The Dutchman says, "Coffee and a roll."

The server throws an extra day old roll on the Dutchman's plate.

He says, "You think they blew up Wall Street? Everybody says they were innocent. Helluva thing, that explosion. They still got pock marks on the buildings."

The Dutchman dips the stale roll into milky coffee and fills his mouth. The chummy server scowls and moves on.

A barrel-chested Irishman barges through the labor pool and taps the Dutchman on the shoulder. The Dutchman spins around grabbing the cold steel of the handgun in his pocket.

The Irishman holds up empty palms. He is the dock boss with whom the Dutchman has an agreement for favored treatment of the load coming in from Ireland.

The Irishman says, "You got my money?"

The Dutchman says, "You got my shipment?"

The Irishman flashes an easy smile and says, "It's only a matter of time so why don't ya be a good sport and pay up."

A bushy shock of gray hair on either side frames the Irishman's tanned face. A steely, shifty look fills his eyes.

The Dutchman drops a nickel on the counter.

"Outside," he says.

They step out into the humid August morning. The dispatcher, perched high on a warehouse roof, hikes a pair of binoculars to his eyes. He searches the river then looks down at Eddie. Nothing.

An idling tug churns the briny waters, unleashing a stench of seaweed and decomposing garbage. Eddie sheds his suit jacket and loosens his tie. He checks his watch. Even a captain avoiding the Coast Guard should have had enough time to make it to the docks by now.

The Dutchman turns to the barrel-chested Irishman and says, "Eddie will take care of your end once he gets the goods. That's our arrangement. That's the way it will stay."

A cocky Italian passes by them heading for McGrath. His suit jacket is basic black, his trousers gray, his shirt white and freshly laundered. He wears it unbuttoned at the neck and with no tie.

Eddie dwarfs the Italian by a good six inches.

"How did you know where to find me?" Eddie says to the Italian, who didn't rat out his accomplices in a jewel heist four years earlier.

The Italian, a guy named Jimmy Alo, is an asset. Since his release from prison, he's been on more than a few payroll heists with Eddie and the boys.

The dispatcher yells through a megaphone, "Here she comes. Here she comes."

Eddie tosses the morning paper aside. It lands with the above-the-fold story showing: *Sacco and Vanzetti put to death early this morning; Governor Fuller rejects last-minute pleas for delay after a day of legal moves and demonstrations.*

Jimmy reads the headline and snorts. The anarchists never stood a chance. Somebody had to be punished for the Wall Street debacle. Jimmy watches as the idling tug throws off its bowline and noses toward the incoming freighter.

Eddie says to Jimmy, "I might have something for you if you play your cards right. You see the guy coming our way, the slobby looking guy? That's the Dutchman. When he gets here, keep your mouth shut. I'll do the talking."

Jimmy nods.

The Dutchman makes quick work of the distance between him and Eddie. He gives the Italian the once over.

"Who's this?" he says.

"He's O.K.," Eddie says.

"How long before the shipment is unloaded?"

"An hour or so," Eddie says. "I'll take care of everything."

"See that you do," the Dutchman says. "When you're done, I got business for you in Jersey." Again, he gives Jimmy an up-and-down look, nods in his direction. "Can he handle himself?"

"Sure," Eddie says.

"Come by the saloon and bring your friend."

The Dutchman passes the dock boss' payoff to Eddie and then he's gone. Moments later, the Dutchman's Lizzy tears across the field and out onto open highway.

The freighter nuzzles up to the dock.

Eddie says, "You mess up…the Dutchman will kill us both. This ain't like the joint. There ain't no bulls to stop a fight. No solitary confinement to cool things off."

"The bulls never stopped nothin'," Jimmy says.

The longshoremen swarm the freighter's cargo hold like ants on a picnic pie. Eddie's booze is the first to come off the ship. The barrel-chested dock boss plants his beefy hands on the back of Eddie's neck and gives him a friendly shake. Eddie passes him the envelope. The older man flips through the stack of bills, satisfied.

Within the hour, Eddie has a fleet of trucks packing off to a variety of the Dutchman's drops around town. The last load he keeps for himself. With an address scribbled on a scrap of paper, he gives Jimmy the task of making sure the booze gets to a Hell's Kitchen warehouse.

"My brother-in-law, Johnny Dunn, is waiting. I'll get with the Dutchman and see what he wants. Stay with Johnny until you hear from me."

Jimmy climbs into the driver's seat of the old beater of a truck cloaked in a bakery disguise. "Quality First" reads the back panel. Trays of bread line the back window. Jimmy grabs a loaf and wags it out the window at Eddie.

"Can you eat this stuff?" he yells.

Eddie laughs, waves him on, and then heads for his tan Chrysler Series 80 cabriolet.

"You lucky bastard," he mumbles to himself turning over the engine.

He hunkers down behind the wheel and makes it to the Dutchman's saloon in record time. His step is quick. He passes the boys at the table, gives a quick knock on the Dutchman's doorframe, and then pokes his head into the back room where the Dutchman and his second in command sit shooting the bull.

"What took ya so long?" the Dutchman says. "And where's the guy I told you to bring along?"

Eddie says, "I sent him to get his piece."

Eddie figures even a guy like the Dutchman respects the

Sullivan Act, which penalizes anyone caught carrying a gun without a permit with a year in prison.

"When I tell ya to bring somebody, you bring him," the Dutchman says. He scribbles a note on a scrap of paper and hands it to Eddie. "There's a guy muscling in on our joint. You know the place?"

Eddie nods. "In Jersey."

"Take care of this bastard and don't come back until you do. I don't care how long it takes."

Eddie holds in a sigh. This better be worth the time it takes to get to Jersey, knock some sense into the guy, and get back. It's Eddie's anniversary and the wife is going to be plenty sore when she finds out that he won't be around to celebrate.

Bo Weinberg says, "Before you do too much damage to this piece of shit, make sure he's not with Zwillman's mob. If he is, we talk to the Little Guy to straighten it out."

"And if he's with Gordon?" Eddie says.

"He don't walk home," the Dutchman says.

The Little Guy is Meyer Lansky. That's what he's being called these days, the Little Guy or just the Guy. That's how powerful he has gotten. This is the first time Eddie has heard the Dutchman defer to anybody. The thought puts zip in Eddie's step.

Eddie climbs into the Chrysler and revs the engine. Just an hour ago he was feeling lucky. Now it's back to normal. If only this was November. The Holland Tube is scheduled to open in November. This is August. The tube would let Eddie zip over to Jersey and back quickly. He might even make his anniversary celebration. But as it is, Eddie will have to take the ferry or bum a ride across the Hudson from a friendly rumrunner. The delay will cost him dearly. He assesses the roll of bills in his pocket. Not quite Tiffany's but probably a pretty good gold necklace with a charm.

He makes a beeline across town for Johnny Dunn's operation in Hell's Kitchen. Johnny and Jimmy are kicking back enjoying a beer when he arrives. The floor is littered with empty bottles.

"Jesus!" he says at the sight. "What kind of help are you gonna be if you're pissed?"

"Ah, relax," Johnny says. "Those are from the boys. Jimmy barely touched the stuff."

Eddie makes a phone call then looks at Jimmy and says, "We got work to do. You got a rod on you?"

"No," Jimmy says.

"Well, we ain't got time to change that. Come on, let's go."

The seatback is Eddie's private vault. Tucked in the springs and horsehair is a metal box just big enough to hold a Colt .45 and two clips of ammunition. Eddie slides the semi-automatic pistol to Jimmy who takes note of the details: 1911, U.S. Army. The wooden grips are barely worn. The action tight. Jimmy loads a clip and cocks the gun for action. He slides the extra clip into his coat pocket.

Eddie says, "We're going to Jersey. There's a guy puttin' the bull on one of our joints. It's my business to take care of him. If you ain't up for it, let me know now."

Jimmy smiles. "I ain't got nothin' to do."

They stop at Moore's for cabbage and corned beef and arrive at the dock just in time to catch the ferry across the Hudson with the rest of humanity. On the Hudson side, a pack of kids, stripped down to their underwear, escape the heat by jumping from the landing.

Eddie flags the guy he called from Johnny's office for the ride to Max's bar, the Paradise. Max is preparing for the Friday night crowd. He sees Eddie and breathes a sigh of relief.

"Paradise ain't what it used to be," Max says in confidential tones.

He yanks the cuff of his shirt over his hand and rubs out a water mark on the glistening mahogany bar. The locals gather around the sizeable slab to be entertained by Max who prides himself on his ability to predict a customer's preferred drink by their occupation. Longshoremen drink beer. Single-minded accountants drink single-malt whiskey, but not the pricy stuff. Accountants, Max contends, want something sensible like Glenlivet.

"For you, Eddie, a Scofflaw," Max says with a grin.

The drink is a combination of rye, dry vermouth, lemon juice, and pomegranate grenadine so-called because of a contest run by Delcevare King, Harvard man, who paid $200 in gold to the person who coined a word for the "lawless drinker of illegally made or illegally obtained liquor."

"Just some cold water," Eddie says. "We'll drink when the job is done. What can you tell me about this guy that's botherin' ya?"

"Skittish guy," Max says as he sets up the water. "Very shifty, if you know what I mean. Normally I wouldn't bother you with somethin' like this. I can take care of myself, you know. I won plenty of rounds in the ring. But I got customers to think about and, well, I just don't need this kinda trouble, Eddie. I figure that's what I pay you for."

Eddie downs the water then gestures for the pitcher.

"You did the right thing," Eddie says. "When is he comin' back?"

"He didn't say...specifically," Max says. "But I don't think he's the dallying type. From the way he looted the till, I'd say he's a desperate character. Maybe a hoppy."

That's another blow to Eddie's evening. What are the chances a hop-headed druggie will strike the same place twice? Eddie looks around the bar. Two old drunks exchange sloppy smiles over beer and cigarettes.

Eddie says, "O.K., Max. If this guy shows up, he won't be around until you got enough to steal so me and my friend are gonna take a seat in the back and wait. Give us a pitcher of beer and a couple of dirty glasses. You go about your business like we wasn't even here. Let's not tip our mitt to this guy."

Max nods.

Eddie and Jimmy take a table deep in the shadows. Eddie pulls out a cigarette. Through force of habit, he hides the flare of the match's igniting phosphorus behind cupped hands. He takes a long draw from the cigarette, leans back in his chair, and fiddles with the matchbox. On the cover it reads, "The Aristocrat of Harlem." A dancing silhouette of a long, lean, and ample-breasted woman, arms waving high above her head, holds his attention.

Eddie says, "If you had to choose, which would you go without, booze or women?"

"I been without both," Jimmy says referring to his stint at Dannemora.

"But if you could choose," Eddie pushes.

"I'd take the broads. You can have the booze."

Eddie says, "There's the difference between the Irish and the Italians."

Jimmy says, "Maybe if the Irish got laid more often they wouldn't fight so much."

"You're one to talk," Eddie says.

Jimmy Blue Eyes is Jimmy's nickname acquired for the shiners he sports from the brawls he engages in around town.

"Should be Jimmy Black-and-Blue Eyes," Eddie mocks. "How come you aren't running beer? There's a lot of wide-open territory around Westchester and White Plains. I can get all the beer you can peddle."

"Payrolls are good business," Jimmy says. "Nobody wants to

take a bullet for somebody else's cash. Besides, they're insured. How the hell did you wind up in with a German Jew? I woulda thought you'd be in with Madden."

Eddie nods, "The Jews control the whiskey business. The Irish bring it in but the Jews got us when it comes to distribution. While you been in the can, they've been busy organizing things. You ever try to organize the Irish? Besides, Madden's more interested in nightclubs."

"You mean chorus girls," Jimmy says.

Eddie laughs as he dances the matchbox across the table.

He says, "Listen, when this guy comes in, we get the jump on him before he knows what's going on. You go to the left and I'll go to the right."

Eddie lights another cigarette and checks the time. The door of the Paradise swings open. A blade of light slices through the room. Jimmy snaps to attention. Three and a half years in Dannemora has left him edgy. The Paradise's door closes behind a shapely blonde with bobbed hair. She coasts over to the bar.

"A sidecar," Max says.

She nods.

"Relax," Eddie says. "This guy would be an idiot to show up before the cash register is full."

Max brings a clean ashtray and a pitcher of water to Eddie's table. Regulars come and go. The place hops with noisy drunks. Max pours and polishes and entertains with jokes picked up from the burleycues on Forty-Sixth Street.

By 4 A.M., a handful of soused souls with legs too rubbery to walk home are all that's left of the crowd. No sign of Max's hoppy. Just as Eddie begins to wonder if Max's story has been concocted to cover a little skimming, the skittish, shifty extortionist finally shows up. He is tall and nervous and alone.

Although it is August and the Paradise is as hot as a Caribbean island, this scarecrow is dressed in a heavy wool suit. The knees bag, the sleeves are too short. The only item remotely suited to the man's frame is the plaid "gentleman's" cap.

He steps up to Max and says, "Where's my dough?"

Max lifts a stack of bills from the register then flashes a look in Eddie's direction. He swallows hard at the realization that Eddie and Jimmy are gone.

"A little light," the bastard says.

And then Eddie and Jimmy are on him. The cold metal of the Army-issue weapon digs hard into his ribs. Eddie grabs the cash and rocks the interloper backwards with the twist of an arm.

The guy screams, "Do you know who I am?"

Eddie says, "The guy who's just made the biggest mistake of a very short life. This joint belongs to the Dutchman and I'm closing your account."

The scarecrow trembles; his knees buckle. Eddie keeps him from tumbling to the ground by hustling him through the back door and into the darkness of the back alley.

Eddie says, "Now listen and listen good. If I ever see you around here again, I'll take your legs right out from under you. You'll be rollin' around on one of them wheelie carts like the soldiers out there who got their legs blown off in the war. You got that?"

There is nothing but wide-eyed terror on the scarecrow's face.

Eddie throws the guy hard against the brick wall of the club, torquing his arm behind his back until the tension of the joints is stretched to near breaking.

Eddie says, "Who are you with?"

"Nobody," the guy says. "It's just me."

Eddie pauses, wondering if the guy is lying or telling the

truth. A lone figure of a man appears from the shadows of the alley.

"He's alone," the man says.

"Dennis?" Eddie says.

"He won't bother you anymore," Dennis says. "I'll see to that."

With a kick and a shove, Eddie sends the scarecrow flying.

Dennis steps into the light. He is a world away from New York but the Irish in him sparks quickly with Eddie.

He grins and says, "The guy is a real cake-eater. He wouldn't touch a hot stove. What brings you to the Jersey shore?"

"He was putting the bull on one of our establishments."

"You want me to take care of him?" Dennis pulls a bottle from his inner coat pocket and waves it at Eddie. "This stuff's shite anyway, real rotgut. But it's great for lightin' up a place like a Roman candle. I know where he lives."

Dennis has the gift of lobbing a petrol bomb with the accuracy of a Babe Ruth home run.

Eddie says, "Last time you nearly blew yerself up."

Dennis rubs his scarred right hand.

"I was a bit pissed," he says.

Eddie says, "I don't need none of your shenanigans coming back to haunt me."

Dennis says, "Have it your way. Did ya see the headlines today? Sacco and Vanzetti…"

Dennis does a mock electrocution, arms and legs shaking and tongue hanging out.

"Say, whadya think, were they really the guys that bombed Wall Street or just a couple of suckers takin' a fall for the real guys? I know a guy says Vanzetti hated his father. Hated the Church, too. Couldn't take all the restrictions so he joined up with the anarchists and boom! There goes Wall Street. Go figure.

Hey, you wanna go for a proper drink? There's a great little joint down the street."

"I'm already in the dog house," Eddie says. "The Missus."

"You're wound too tight. You've always been wound too tight. A little anarchy is good for the soul," Dennis says.

"You're one to talk," Eddie says. "Come on, the Paradise owes us. Let's see what the bartender would serve an anarchist. The ferry don't run until the sun comes up, anyway."

The National Prohibition Law hearings before the Subcommittee of the Committee on the Judiciary United States Senate, sixty-ninth Congress, in April of 1926 resulted in no noticeable change to the landscape of New York's bootleggers.

Representative Mead has done the math. It will take seventy-five million dollars to enforce the law in New York alone. That's over five hundred million dollars for the entire country.

Rather than throw good federal money after bad, the senators choose to amend the amendment in such a way that the burden of enforcement is shifted to the states:

> Sec. 2. Any person who transports or causes to be transported into any State any beverage prohibited by such State as being an 'intoxicating liquor' shall be punished by the United States by imprisonment for not more than ten years or by a fine of not less than $10,000 nor more than $100,000, or by both such fine and imprisonment.

The Advocate runs a contest of its own: twenty-six dollars to the person who can come up with a clever phrase for an "unalterable, die-hard dry." Miss Katherine Greene Welling of New York City comes up with the winning contribution, "Spigot–Bigot."

Jimmy Alo pokes around the small towns just outside of the

Bronx and finds a sheriff willing to take a bribe. Within days he is running Madden's No. 1 brew to the local saloons. The business makes enough for him to buy a brand new 22' Chris-Craft runabout. He and Johnny Dunn strip away the green leather passenger seats to make room for whatever they happen to be running.

They take the Chris-Craft out to the twelve-mile limit where bootleggers swarm the motherships in a feeding frenzy. Over twenty ships are anchored and open for business. They fill the Chris-Craft with rum and gin coming up from the Bahamas and cruise in and out of the inlets along Long Island Sound. The high-gloss varnished mahogany bow reflects a bouncing moon. The 150-mile trip back takes them to the Bronx docks under Irish control.

Some of the Irish longshoremen take offense at the cocky Italian's presence.

"What are you bringing this guy around here for?" one of them says to Eddie. "Guineas multiply like rabbits. You let one of them on the dock and pretty soon you get an invitation to get lost."

"He's with me," Eddie says, trying to ease the tension.

Jimmy ties off the runabout and hefts a case of rum onto the dock.

"Everything O.K.?" Jimmy asks Eddie.

"Everything is fine," Eddie says.

"Everything ain't fine," the biggest dockhand says. "We had enough of you ginzos around here."

Without thinking, Jimmy rushes in and plants his fist hard into the Irishman's gut. The Irishman folds forward and wheezes. Jimmy repositions himself, a ramrod ready for action. The wheezer swings and lands a meat-tenderizing blow to Jimmy's jaw.

Jimmy spits blood. He throws a left uppercut that flies wild. The brawl is on. Sweat, spit, and blood spatter on a growing circle of men not the least of which is Owney Madden and his partner, Big Frenchy DeMange.

Eddie steps back from the circle to save his suit.

"What's this?" Madden says.

"A guy just outta the can," Eddie says.

Madden puts twenty bucks on the guinea just as Jimmy takes a devastating punch to the face. Jimmy sways and falls to the ground. He takes a deep breath and staggers to his feet.

"Put your fists down, man," the Irishman says. "If Eddie says you're O.K., that's good enough for me."

Benny Siegel joins the crowd as the action ends.

"What's this?" Benny says.

"Some guinea just out of jail," Madden says.

"Jimmy Blue Eyes," Eddie McGrath says. "He's all right."

Benny says, "I heard he's a tough little bastard."

Eddie laughs. "Yeah, you could say that."

Madden says, "Siegel, what the hell kinda dance was that you were doin' at the club last night? You had the ladies all fired up."

Benny says, "The Harlem Strut? Ain't you ever heard of it? I got another one for you." He dangles two fingers on either side of his face mocking the unshorn locks of the Black Hats, then shuffles, Groucho Marx style, along the dock. "The Hasidic Shuffle. Drives 'em wild on the Lower East Side!"

"Stick to what you do best," Madden says. "And when you find the time, send over some more of that Canadian whiskey. We're running dry."

Benny says, "You're just jealous."

The various shipments that find their way from the twelve-mile limit to the Bronx docks are divvied-up among the bootleggers.

Jimmy Alo walks away with the growing respect of the Irish. Eddie McGrath connects with a jewel thief and buys his wife the gold necklace of her dreams.

Eighteen people are taken away in the latest raid on the El Fey Club. Across town, Duke Ellington opens at the Cotton Club. It is December and the weather is promising a white Christmas. Owney Madden sits back and takes in the show. Fake banana trees fill the stage, posing as palm trees. No one in New York seems to know the difference.

Plumed hoochie-coochie girls tap and sway and shimmy in a surplus of feathers. They look more like Zulu warriors than a chorus line. The Duke and his boys roll through a dozen numbers. The Duke calls his new musical style "the jungle beat" for the sake of the bohemians trying to escape the moralists' restraints.

Feathers fly.

"Ziegfeld never thought of this," Abe Zwillman says to the table of powerful Jews enjoying Duke Ellington's opening night.

Samuel Bronfman is on one of his goodwill tours. He uses as much as his six-month visa will allow taking in what New York offers while surrounding himself with the Czars of Bootleg, not so much for the business value but for the prestige of their company.

Mae West floods into the club with an entourage. Last year, only fans of the Shubert revues knew who she was, but after writing and starring in her own Broadway show, *Sex*, and spending ten days in the workhouse on the charge of presenting an indecent public performance, she has become a public hero.

She saunters through the Cotton Club in a black satin dress and white mink, takes a seat at Madden's table.

Abe Zwillman turns to Bronfman. He hints at Annenberg's recent acquisition, a controlling interest in Mont Tennes General News Bureau. The racing wire, as the "news bureau" is called, gives the public an opportunity to bet on any race anywhere they choose. The law prohibits gambling outside the racetrack but Annenberg insists that people who can't take time off from their jobs shouldn't be deprived of a strand of hope.

Zwillman says, "New York is cracking down on gambling to keep Tammany happy. It's something to think about."

Walter Winchell buzzes his way into the club. Madden waves him over to rub shoulders with Mae West.

Bronfman says, "Did you hear that George Remus shot and killed his wife? He's calling it justifiable homicide."

Remus seems to be fighting a long run of bad luck. While in jail, he was won over by an undercover Prohibition agent posing as an inmate. Remus let it slip that his wife had control of his millions. The agent quit his job in favor of wining and dining Mrs. Remus. The couple liquidated all that George had acquired. Then Imogene Remus filed for divorce.

Meyer Lansky says, "She gave him a hundred bucks. Remus, worth millions, and she gave him a hundred bucks."

"Every Jewish mother's nightmare," Zwillman says.

"Justifiable homicide," Bronfman says.

Two tables away, Eddie McGrath slides an egg-blue box tied with a white ribbon toward his wife. She tugs at the ribbon then opens the box. Inside the box is a pearl, diamond, and emerald lavaliere necklace.

She takes the necklace from the box. All anger drains from her countenance.

Henry Ford's Christmas present to the Jews is an apology for a recent slew of articles printed in the *Dearborn Independent* asserting that Aaron Sapiro was the principal in a Jewish plot to control agriculture. Aaron Sapiro organizes cooperatives of farmers and fruit growers in California and no accusations to the contrary can change that fact. The defamatory articles bore Henry Ford's name though he denies having penned them. Sapiro filed suit for a million dollars for the libelous allegations.

The trial had occupied the press for months but before Ford could take the stand, he was injured in an auto accident. The trial ended with an out-of-court settlement.

Meyer Lansky picks up the phone and calls Sapiro.

"Congratulations," Meyer says. "I didn't know you could get an apology from an anti-Semite."

Sapiro says, "What's a million dollars to a guy like that? He is the richest man in America. The apology is a small price to pay for the damage he's done by the things that he wrote. That said…"

"Yes?" Meyer says.

"Only in America can we sue…and win."

Meyer says, "You specialize in corporate law? I would like to meet with you and discuss the formation of a corporation that handles grain. Can you come to New York?"

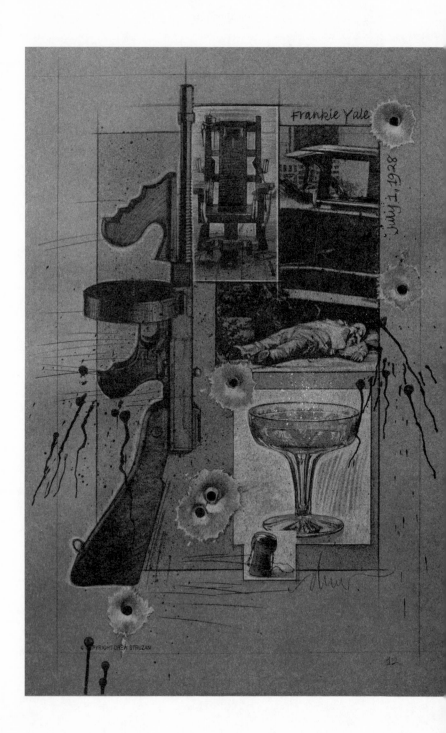

Frankie Yale

July 1, 1928

12

Chapter Twelve
It's All How You Spin the Story

1928

The plaintiff, John Barrett, still in a heated rage over being shot, is in the hospital recovering. Two detectives flank his bed coaxing him to give up the perpetrators. Barrett measures out his accusations carefully. The detectives push harder. Barrett hesitates and then shakes his head.

"No," he says. "You don't know these guys. They'll go after my family."

"Let us worry about that," the first detective says.

"They tried to kill you," the other detective says. "What good are you to your family if you're dead?"

Barrett looks at them with a steely eye, still refusing to talk.

"Either you get them or they get you. That's the jungle we live in. You tell us who to take care of and we will," the first detective says.

"And what good is a family to me if they're dead? I can't live with the guilt."

"It's a little late to think about guilt, isn't it?" the first detective says. "You're already in the mess. Let us help you get out."

Barrett swallows hard. It is Benny Siegel's fault he is in this mess. Benny flew off the handle. He slammed his car to a halt in front of an open field. Red opened the back-passenger door and kicked Barrett into the field. Barrett stood next to the car shouting wild accusations. Benny fumed. The more Barrett shot off his mouth, the less inclined Benny was to listen. Benny pulled out his Colt 1911A and took aim. Barrett began a dash for his life, running zigzag through the open field.

Benny opened fire. Bullets flew wildly through the air, zipping past Barrett. Then two hit their mark, nothing serious, just enough to remind Barrett that crossing Benny Siegel's mob was a dangerous thing to do.

That's what really happened but there is no way in hell that he is going to tell that story to a couple of gumshoes. But sitting comfortably in his hospital bed after surgery while listening to the guys that might be able to do something to Benny has sparked Barrett's desire for retaliation.

"Joe Benzole," Barrett sputters. "And Red Levine. They were in the car."

"An Italian and a Jew?" the other detective says. "What were you doing with them?"

Ah, there it is, the question Barrett was dreading, the one that if answered truthfully will implicate him in a crime.

"Driving around," Barrett says.

"Driving around?" the first detective says, incredulous. "Just driving around? And these guys opened fire on you?"

"Yeah," Barrett insists, confident that neither Benzole nor Levine are the kind of guys to spill the beans about the fur heist that raised Benny's ire in the first place. "Just driving around."

"How did you wind up in the field? Was that before or after they shot you?"

"Before," Barrett says without thinking. "They kicked me out of the car and started shooting. What was I, a rabbit?"

The detective narrows his eyes and bobs his head.

"That's how these things get started," he says. "Anyone else in the car?"

Barrett sits mum.

"Who else was in the car?" the other detective pushes. "Another Italian? Another Jew?"

Barrett curls his lip in disgust, "A Jew named Meyer Lansky."

"That's it?" the first detective says. "Just the four of you?"
Barrett blinks hard.

"Just the four of us. I stand by that."

"Do you have addresses?"

"Yeah," Barrett says. "I know where they live."

The detectives jot down the addresses of the three men
Barrett has fingered, stake out their homes, and haul them in for
questioning. They deny the charges. Admit to knowing Barrett.
Can't imagine why he would make up a story to frame them.

Barrett's accusations still stick and Meyer Lansky, Joe Benzole
and Red Levine, accused of attempted murder, find themselves
sitting in jail waiting to see the judge.

Benny hears of the arrests and grabs Moe Sedway.

"Come on," Benny says. "We got work to do."

The two of them drive to the factory where Barrett's brother
sweats as a cutter of men's suits. The factory toils on. Waiting
for the end of the shift, Benny and Moe occupy themselves
with stories of scores gone wrong: the time Sammy took a
bullet because he fell for a fake Prohibition road stop, the time
Sammy got caught in Waxey Gordon's hotel room spying on
Arnold Rothstein and Waxey beaned him with an ashtray, the
time the Irish kid was knocking over the kosher winery, the
time Charlie went to a spaghetti dinner and lived to tell the
tale, and the time John Barrett got away after stealing a load of
furs and lying about it.

"We ain't the Musketeers," Moe says. "It ain't one for all and
all for one."

"That ain't what pisses me off with the cocksucker," Benny
says. "I would have let him off the hook but he lied. It ain't the
first time. Fucking ingrate. And then he blabs to the cops and
fingers Meyer. He fingers Meyer, for Christ's sake! What else
will he tell the cops? We gotta shut this cocksucker up before
he puts us all behind bars."

The factory bell rings, marking the close of the workday. Benny darts from the car and into the crowd pouring out onto the street. He spies Barrett's brother, collar raised and head lowered. Benny is on him like a cat on a rat.

"Relax," Benny says cutting him from the crowd.

Barrett's brother gives a jerk and tries to run but Benny has his arm and shoves the Colt into his ribs.

"I wouldn't," Benny says. "You can die right here or you can come with me and take your chances."

Fear courses through Barrett's bones. He is the hard-working Barrett, the one who loves his mother. His heart pounds like a dove caught in a snare. He begins to sweat. Benny hustles him into the back of the roadster and tells Moe to hit it.

"It's easier if you cooperate," Moe says over his shoulder.

"I got nothing to do with my brother's business," Barrett says. "What he does, he does. I got no interest in anything. I don't know anything."

Benny says, "You're family, ain't ya?"

Barrett freezes, eyes forward and mouth shut, on the long haul to nowhere. Moe drives beyond the city limits through the small towns on Long Island. Finally, he stops at a phone booth set out beside the road.

Benny ties Barrett's hands behind his back with an eight-foot rope then drags him to the booth like a dog on a leash. He shoves Barrett into the phone booth and chucks a handful of change onto the small shelf beneath the phone.

"I ain't got a lot of patience," Benny says. "You better make it convincing."

The blood has drained from Barrett's body. His skin is pasty and clammy.

"What?" he shivers. "Make what convincing?"

"You standin' here between the devil and the deep blue sea," Benny says.

Benny lifts the receiver, drops in a few coins and dials the operator. He asks for the hospital where John Barrett is recuperating and then shoves the receiver to the brother's ear. The good son speaks.

"J-J-John Barrett," he says to the girl on the hospital switchboard.

She rings the call through to the phone at the end of the ward where Barrett sits recuperating and where detectives stand at the ready waiting to catch more of the mob. The duty nurse answers the phone and then pads down the hall to Barrett's room.

"Your brother is on the phone. Do you want to speak to him?"

Barrett swings his feet to the floor and slides them into a pair of well-worn leather slippers. It takes all his might to hobble down the hall. The detectives shadow him.

"Hello?" Barrett says cautiously.

The detectives step in close.

Barrett turns his back and hunkers down for privacy. His brother is persuasive. Barrett's eyes go wide. He cups his hand around the receiver and whispers a single sentence.

"Don't worry, Abe."

Quivering, John Barrett returns the handset to the cradle and gives the detective a numb stare. He shuffles back to his ward where he sits on the edge of his bed, silent and sullen.

The detective says, "Talk to me, John. Are you going to let these gangsters get away with this? They shot you for God's sake. Stand up to them and put them where they can't hurt anyone else."

Barrett is silent.

"John," the detective says. "Don't you understand what I'm saying?"

Barrett says, "Don't you?"

They stare at each other in silence. An eternity passes. Still, John remains resolute. The detective folds his notepad and tucks it into his coat pocket.

"It's a mistake, John," the detective says. "You'll regret this."

"I regret a lotta things," John Barrett says. "This ain't one of them."

The nurse says, "He needs to rest, detectives. He shouldn't be under this much strain."

Meanwhile, the police precinct in Long Island City clamors through the daily barrage of complaints. The judge shuffles through the list of arrests. One name bleeds into another: a case for attempted robbery, another for felonious assault. It is all a day's work. He calls Joe Benzole, Red Levine and Meyer Lansky to the bench to assess the evidence in the case against them.

The judge looks over the top of his reading glasses at the three accused men. Joe Benzole, looking more like an immigrant than a citizen, is unrefined. Red Levine is rough-hewn. His steely eyes and arrest record convey a violent response to the ghetto's hard knocks. Meyer Lansky, on the other hand, is well-dressed and respectable, with only one prior arrest that resulted in a paid fine. Meyer appears to be, as they say, the brain behind the brawn.

"I see the plaintiff is still in the hospital," the judge says.

"Yes, your Honor," the prosecuting attorney says.

"It says here he was shot while running through a field?" the judge says.

"Yes, your Honor," the prosecuting attorney says.

The judge turns to the defense.

"And these are the accused. Are there any others?"

"No, your Honor," the defense attorney says.

"How do you plead?" the judge says.

"Not guilty, your Honor."

"I don't see mention of a weapon or any witnesses?"

"No, your Honor."

The defense attorney steps forward and points out the obvious. Barrett admits he had business dealings with these men on numerous occasions. If it can be proved these dealings are illicit in nature, New York law does not allow the testimony of a co-conspirator in a crime.

"Can you prove the plaintiff knows the defendants?"

"Yes, sir, we can," the defense attorney says. "Mr. Barrett's character will be called into question. For all we know, he may have shot himself as some sort of reprisal. His wounds were not life threatening."

The judge looks over the defendants and then flips through the papers in the case folder. The court clerk steps up to the bench and passes a neatly folded paper to the judge. The judge reads the contents and sighs.

He looks up from the paper and takes aim at Meyer.

"Don't fool yourself into thinking that I mistake a lack of evidence as a sign of innocence," he says. "Gentlemen, the plaintiff has recanted his accusations. Case dismissed."

The court assistant gathers the case folder for processing and calls the next case. Meyer turns to his attorney and thanks him for his time.

Joe Benzole makes a beeline for the door. Outside, his brother waits beside an idling taxi. Meyer and Red hit the sidewalk without sharing a word between them, hands in pockets, and eyes to the ground. In the distance, the 59th Street Bridge beckons to them, offering relative anonymity.

Meyer boils at his mistake. Persuasion is better served away from the prying eyes of a neighborhood.

A Model A roadster pulls up and honks. Benny is at the wheel, come to rescue the recalcitrants.

"Get in," Benny says. "You look like a couple of lost cocker spaniels."

Meyer shakes off the indignation and climbs into the back seat. Red follows.

Benny says, "That bastard sure could run."

This gets the boys smiling.

"He told the cops that Charlie sent him spiked chicken," Benny says. "Said that's the way with Italians."

"Why would Charlie send a spiked chicken to the hospital?" Meyer says. "What's Charlie got to do with it? It's a made-up story."

"Ingrate," Benny says. "Why didn't he turn me into the cops? I was the shooter. Fucking coward, that's why."

He powers the roadster over the bridge and through town and then back to the Lower East Side, pulling quickly into the Cannon Street garage. Meyer sits silently in the back seat, his mind racing over thoughts of what he should have done. Where did he go wrong with Barrett? And then he has it. He felt pity for the underdog and very nearly went to jail for his miscalculation of Barrett's loyalties. Meyer quietly acknowledges the flaw in his character. Taking a chance on someone is always a risk. Sometimes you lose.

Weeks pass and then a month. Meyer stands in line at the change booth of the Horn & Hardart. He steps up and drops two dollar bills on the counter. The redheaded nickel-thrower behind the cage pulls nickels from the tray without so much as a twist of the head to double-check what her fingers have done. Meyer removes his hat and scoops the nickels into the crown.

He peruses the bank of little windows showcasing high-quality food for a fistful of nickels, then drops enough change to fill his tray with baked beans, Salisbury steak, creamed spinach, a bowl of rice pudding, and a cup of coffee.

Charlie Luciano and Al Capone are huddled in conversation

at a table in the middle of the massive dining room, continuing an ongoing conversation about Frankie Yale and the hijackings he is supposed to be behind that robbed Capone of certain booze shipments coming in through Atlantic City. Long ago, Capone accepted that Charlie and Meyer were far more than partners. Meyer is obviously what the Italians would call Charlie's consigliere. When push comes to shove, the partners inevitably come to similar conclusions on how to deal with a problem, Meyer coming up with strategy and Charlie with logistics.

Meyer navigates the room, defending the cup of hot coffee with his elbow. He takes a seat at the table with Charlie and Capone.

Charlie says, "What do you want me to say, Al? The Prince of Pals ain't so princely? That ain't news. We know why he gave people cash and it wasn't from the generosity of his heart. It was hush money that made Yale a pal to the neighborhood. Is it worth the trouble? That's the question we gotta consider. We got access to all the booze you want."

Capone snarls and gnaws on a cigar. "That ain't the point," he says at last. "It's the principle of the thing."

"Sometimes the principle is gonna foul up somethin' important," Charlie says.

Capone says, "You gotta put your foot down with these guys."

The Broadway crowd coming out of the theaters is lured by the thirty-foot wide stained glass window of fruit and flowers that glows brighter than a genie's lamp. The automat fills with chorus girls, musicians, and press agents happy to dine where ten cents buys a slice of huckleberry pie and a nickel gets a cup of piping hot coffee.

Meyer stirs three spoonfuls of sugar into his coffee.

Charlie says to Meyer, "Al thinks we're too soft."

Meyer says, "Compared to Chicago, I guess we are."

Capone says, "You and me go way back, Charlie. Let's not pretend we don't know how these things work out. The Prince of Pals has gone too far."

Capone unconsciously strokes his scar. The implication is not lost on Charlie.

"He's jealous," Meyer says.

"Who?" Capone says.

Meyer says, "These old Mustache Petes have one thing on their mind. They want to be on top. You're the biggest thing to hit Chicago. You're sitting on top of the world while the prince is sitting on the beach worrying about how he's going to skim more money from the neighborhood. What do you think goes through his mind now that you have more than he does? You owe him for everything you have. He sent you to Chicago. Right? He wants a piece of all you've done. If you don't give it to him, he's going to take it himself."

Charlie nods. "Meyer's catching on to these greasers."

Capone turns to his cherry pie and gashes it with his fork, drawing off an extra-large bite.

Jimmy Walker tramps through the front door surrounded by an entourage of entertainers and Tammany politicians. His mob works the dolphin spouts for the French-drip coffee that Frank Hardart personally roasts and grinds daily. Walker catches sight of Charlie Luciano and Al Capone and steers his group in the opposite direction. He doesn't need that kind of publicity.

Capone looks up and grunts.

Meyer makes short work of the baked beans and Salisbury steak.

Charlie says, "It's the Calabrese in him. When I was a kid, my Ma always warned me about the Calabrese. She'd tell me how they steal the figs off the trees of their enemies. 'That's how farmers get revenge,' she would say. 'They steal the crop and bust up the trees.' He can't take you down no more, Al, so he strikes where he can. He's crazed. He wants revenge for all the pie he didn't get in life."

Capone says, "That's plain stupid."

Meyer nods to Walker. "It's getting a little crowded, don't you think?"

Charlie wolfs down what's left of his huckleberry pie, then the boys rise quietly and slip away.

In the quiet of the Claridge, over brandy and Cuban cigars, they get down to business.

Capone says, "I put a guy in place to keep an eye on Yale, see if it was him jacking my booze. Yale made the guy. I give my buddy the green light to do what hadda be done. He missed. Next thing I know, my guy's dead and Yale's struttin' around like the cock-of-the-walk. I got a little revenge of my own to serve up so don't be surprised when you find Yale in the obituaries. If we put Joe Adonis in Yale's place, we all benefit."

Charlie says, "Joe the Boss will never go for it. 'Keep 'em down and you keep 'em working for you.' That's his motto. He'll split the mob up to dilute the power. Besides, we gotta play it low key. Puttin' Joe A. in Yale's place ain't to our advantage at this juncture. The death of a guy like Yale is big news. You let Joe A. move up the ladder, the papers will have a field day speculating. Once a guy winds up in the headlines and public opinion turns against him, he don't ever get free. I ain't tellin' you nothin' you don't already know."

"I been in the headlines," Capone says. "Didn't hurt me none." He puffs on his cigar for a long minute. "This cocksucker is stealin' my dough and I don't let nobody get away with that. I'll make sure Joe A. ain't nowhere near this when we make our move."

"Your thoughts, Meyer?" Charlie says.

Meyer agrees it's good for Capone to deal with Yale. Local police cannot cross state lines.

Meyer asks, "If Joe the Boss splits up Yale's mob, who will he favor?" Charlie throws out a couple of names, more greasers.

Charlie says, "It doesn't matter who Joe the Boss puts in place. We'll deal with it when the time is right."

Capone follows the twists and turns of their conversation as Charlie ties a formidable noose around the neck of Joe the Boss. Whatever the two partners are planning, it spells the end for Joe the Boss.

"Anthony Carfano is the guy I want to see come up the ladder," Capone says at last. "You don't gotta worry about him."

The conversation stalls.

Then Charlie says, "Jesus Christ, no kidding? Carfano? He's been hustling booze since the early days."

"How do you think Yale knew where my booze was coming from?" Capone says.

Capone is restless. He looks at his watch.

Capone says, "Where the hell is Joe A.? We was hittin' the town, tonight…I'll give you the heads-up. You make sure Joe A. and Carfano got a good alibi, huh? I got an itch needs scratchin'. If Joe A. ever shows up…"

Just then Joe Adonis walks into the suite.

"Where the hell have you been?" Capone says. "I thought we were going clubbing. Whadya waitin' for, sunrise?"

"I was lining up a few things," Adonis says. "Sometimes it takes a little finesse. Come on, the broads are in the car."

Capone turns to Charlie with a smile.

"It's our turn," he says. "Do what you gotta do. I'm with you."

Capone hustles Adonis out the door.

Charlie turns to Meyer.

"Well how do you like that?" he says.

Meyer says, "Make sure Joe A. is close to Carfano when this thing goes down. Another thing, Albert Anastasia is over in the

Brooklyn docks. He and the Dutchman have bumped heads a few times. Maybe we can smooth things out. Make sure they respect each other's territory. I'm sure Joe the Boss doesn't want to open a can of worms on the docks."

Charlie says, "Anastasia is with a guy named Mangano. Don't worry about it. I'll whisper in Joe's ear. He's a smart guy when it comes to doling out territory."

Spring turns into summer. A sweltering heat wave sweeps through the city. Joe Adonis pulls up in front of Carfano's house in his Willys and honks. Carfano looks out the window of his middle-class Brooklyn house and waves. Carfano, the dawdler, takes his time coming out.

Adonis drums the steering wheel and swelters in the summer heat. His eyes wander around the Willys. Not his style. The Willys is a fine car...for a doctor or a lawyer with upscale aspirations and no glamor. Excellent for a professional showing success without the nerve to flaunt it before others. A Stutz Bearcat, now that's a car and the broads love it but Charlie has insisted on everyone playing it low key and so Joe Adonis contents himself with the Willys.

He honks again.

Carfano finally exits the front door and stops on the stoop to adjust his tie. He looks over the neighborhood before deciding to strut down the steps. He pauses in front of the Willys, unbuttons his jacket, and tugs at the brim of his fedora the same way Edward G. Robinson does it in *The Racket*, the latest hot ticket on Broadway.

Adonis grinds his teeth.

"What took ya?" he snarls as Carfano slides into the passenger seat. "I'm gettin' heatstroke out here, for God's sake."

Adonis hits the gas and sails off to Harlem. The beat of Duke Ellington's band fills the street with energy. Inside, the jungle beat sways the audience. A shapely black woman, Adelaide Hall, wearing a flowing white silk dress, makes her way out onto the horseshoe-shaped stage. The audience quiets as she belts out her latest song. Joe Adonis, playing it low key, refuses the seat at the front of the stage in favor of a less conspicuous spot.

Jimmy Durante concedes to a guest appearance. For forty seconds, the orchestra pounds out a vaudevillian tune while Durante rants.

Bubby Miley comes forward as Durante exits the stage and the orchestra dives into "Creole Love Call." Bubby wails his trumpet in a long series of wah-wahs while Adelaide Hall's haunting voice echoes the trumpet's call. The dance floor fills.

Adonis pops the cork on a Champagne bottle and sends the contents to two women at a neighboring table. Before the bottle is empty, he and Carfano have joined them. The foursome dance and drink and dance some more.

It's four in the morning. The Cotton Club gives way to a Plaza suite. After room service, a hot shower, and another bout in the sack, Adonis gives the girls cab fare and sends them on their way.

Charlie meets Adonis and Carfano at Lindy's for a very long lunch. This is a different show, the one that keeps Carfano occupied and publicly visible for the afternoon. Shortly before 4 P.M., the Brooklyn police receive a phone call about the black sedan with four men who have chased and overtaken Frankie Yale, "the Beau Brummell of the Brooklyn underworld," and shot him dead.

Inspector Sullivan and Captain Ryan part the crowd gathered around the crime scene in front of a Brooklyn home. The car carrying Frankie Yale has jumped the curb and smashed headlong into the sidewall of the steps in front of the house. Rubble, bricks, a hedge, several small trees, and a displaced planter are strewn across the yard.

The crash is barely thirty minutes old. It shook the family

inside as they celebrated a bar mitzvah. The police were called. Inspector Sullivan heard the news and raced to the scene himself. Frankie Yale is slumped over the steering wheel. The stench of fresh blood fills the car. Sullivan reaches in and pushes Yale toward the seatback. Yale's head flops to the side. It is the first time the inspector gets a good look at Yale's reputed penchant for fine clothes and diamond jewelry.

"Jesus," the Inspector says. "And I can't even afford a decent steak."

"We're on the wrong side of the law," the coroner says. "Unless you're corrupt and then it ain't half bad."

The Captain takes a break from interviewing witnesses to ogle the diamonds.

"Five'll get you ten it was Capone's American boys done the job," the Captain says.

"What makes you think so?" the Inspector says. "My money's on Joe the Boss."

"Too slick for Joe the Boss," the Captain says.

"You call this slick?" the Inspector says.

The Captain says, "Most of these witnesses put Illinois or Indiana plates on the shooters' car. Revenge killing? All those rumors about Yale hijacking Capone's liquor might be true especially since there was a Thompson submachine gun involved."

"How do you know?" the Inspector says.

"Some of the witnesses heard a rattle, like a Chicago typewriter, they said."

"Keep that under your hat. I'll give Capone a call," the Inspector says, rubbing the back of his neck. "I'm sure he'll be happy to stop by for tea and tell us why he wasn't involved."

The Captain says, "I'll work on Joe the Boss. If Joe don't cooperate then maybe the bullets will tell us something. And yeah, haul in Capone, too. Let him know we made the connection to Chicago."

"You'll need to contact Miami to subpoena him," the Inspector says. "He wasn't anywhere near New York today or any other day for quite a while."

The Captain frowns, "Technicalities are killing us all."

Yale's body is unceremoniously pulled from the car and laid on a blanket at the bottom of the stoop. The coroner signals for a gurney. He pulls the jewels from Yale's body.

"Who's gonna sign for this stuff?" the coroner says, pointing to the jewels that once decorated the corpse.

The sparkle of seventy-five brilliant diamonds on Yale's belt buckle would give even Tiffany pause. Then there are the two diamond rings and the diamond stickpin.

"Jesus," the Inspector says again.

The coroner says, "You shoulda called for an armored car. I'm not risking my neck over this. Give it to somebody with a gun."

"You know what gets me?" the Inspector says. "This guy walks around the neighborhood droppin' cash like penny candy. He gets the nickname Prince of Pals. How do you like that? What do you think they call us?"

The Captain says, "Look where it got him. Our job is to find the killers."

"In your dreams," the Inspector says. "In your dreams but don't let that stop you."

A copper, hands on hips, poses among the debris with the crashed Lincoln and the dead Yale. Cameras pop. Yale is loaded onto the gurney and slipped into the coroner's wagon.

The thirty-five-year-old gangster, the Beau Brummel of Brooklyn, won't be doing any further business in this world. His soul, wherever it is going, will have to go it alone. His bullet-riddled remains, with half an ear blown off, missed out on the sacred Eucharist. The priest is useless now. No lighted candles, no holy water; no clean napkin; no key of the tabernacle;

no final anointing; no dominus vobiscum; in short, no last rites for the man credited by the police as one of three assassins "who invaded the flower shop of Dean O'Banion and killed that outstanding figure of the underworld."

It turns out that Yale was taking care of business at the Sunrise Club, his speakeasy, when a call came in. Yale told his buddy that something was wrong with his wife and he was leaving to take care of her. He jumped into his brand new, coffee-colored Lincoln coupe. Shots crashed through the rear window of Yale's sedan not long after he left the club. He swerved onto 44th Street in a defensive maneuver but failed to evade the assassins.

The four men in the black sedan who showered the Brooklyn streets with bullets didn't stick around to scrutinize their handiwork. They sped off, leaving Yale's Lincoln to ride out its momentum at the hands of a corpse. The car jumped the curb and then plowed into the front steps of Solomon and Bertha Kaufman's home, sending pedestrians scurrying for their lives.

An abandoned Buick matching the description of the car loaded with shooters is found a few blocks away. Inside are the assault weapons: a .38 caliber revolver, a .45 automatic, and a sawed-off pump shotgun. The police give the rundown to reporters.

In Miami, Capone is served with a subpoena. A world of theories floats around town. The consensus seems to be that Yale's gang was hired by Capone to guard Capone's alcohol shipments coming through Brooklyn and Long Island City. The shipments had been regularly hijacked so Capone asked Yale to provide protection. That's the story, anyway.

Brooklyn mourns. The underworld parades its sorrow with streets lined with mourners. Joe the Boss calls his advisors. Charlie Lucky is among the elite that hear the news firsthand. Joe complains about the police suspicions that caused him to be hauled in for questioning then pontificates on what he calls 'the situation.' He praises Al Capone for getting rid of the back-stabber. With Yale out of the picture, Joe the Boss can bring Brooklyn under tighter control just in time to nip Salvatore Maranzano's ambition in the bud.

The police turn the weapons over to a ballistics expert and track the paper trail of the abandoned car. The vehicle that pursued Yale is traced to Knoxville, Tennessee. Through wires to the local police, they discover that the car had been written off as stolen.

News articles wallow in the grisly details. They point to the present murder 'wave' and use it as evidence that the good effect of the Baumes law, which dictates an automatic life sentence to any criminal convicted of more than three separate felonies, has lost its luster. Homicide is on the rise. Even Frankie Yale, who managed to wiggle free from most of his arrests, save the charge for carrying a revolver, isn't immune. The gangster is buried like a big shot which is exactly what he wanted. The two women claiming to be his wife didn't change a thing.

Three days after Yale's demise, the Commissioner and Inspector reveal the role of a Thompson .45 machinegun in the murder. That's when they begin to speculate that gangsters driven out of Chicago are bringing their brand of brutality to New York. The revelation is devastating to everyone involved.

"The news sells papers," Meyer says to Charlie.

Within days, Police Commissioner Whalen announces that he knows the name of the man responsible for Frankie Yale's death. He accuses the "leader of a powerful group of Italians" but withholds the name saying only that the man knows Johnny Wilson and "Little Augie" Pisano and is responsible for a man named Marlow being expelled from a secret order in Brooklyn.

Joe the Boss hears the news and laughs. Two weeks later, the

Boss is picked up for questioning. A week after that, Yale's wife, one of them, accompanied by her lawyer, turns up to claim Yale's personal effects. The newspaper lists the widow's assets as a belt buckle, a diamond ring, and $2,000 in cash and checks.

A ripple of rumors circulates among the boys on the streets. Graft has just gotten more expensive.

A new play by Sophie Treadwell, *Machinal*, debuts at the Plymouth Theater in September. It uses the sensationalized homicide case that made Ruth Snyder, a housewife from Queens, the first woman since 1899 to ride Sing Sing's Old Sparky.

Esther Krakower, Benny's girlfriend, talks Anne into pressuring the boys to see the play. What could a woman have done to deserve the electric chair?

Benny says, "Why the hell do I want to listen to some sad sap tale with some broad moaning about how tough her life is because she hadda make dinner? This is New York, for Christ's sake. All you gotta do is make reservations."

But Esther doesn't back down.

Esther says, "I want to see it. If you don't want to come, don't."

Benny moans, "What's it gonna cost me?"

"Five tickets and then we'll do whatever you like," she says.

"Anne and Meyer?" Benny says. "That's four."

Esther smiles, "And the lawyer."

"What lawyer?" Benny says.

"The one Meyer brought in. The one that got a million bucks outta Henry Ford. This guy I gotta see."

"Can we skip the play and just go to dinner?" Benny says.

Anne glares. Society types love this kind of thing and Esther is looking to fit in. She hopes Aaron Sapiro, the lawyer who won Henry Ford's apology, will add a glint of sophistication to their group. Benny relents. The fivesome head out for a night on the town.

"This guy didn't come all the way to New York to see a play about the Dumbbell murder trial," Benny nearly apologizes.

Esther clamps Benny's arm, "He's a lawyer."

"It's a play, not a murder trial," Benny says. "Besides, Aaron works for corporations, not murderers. Ain't that right, Aaron?"

Aaron ducks the question. Esther hustles Benny through the open doors of the theater. The play is noisy, an exposé of the irritation and frustration centered on Treadwell's view of the deplorable state of female oppression. Adding machines clack and filing cabinets clang until the girl marries her boss whom she cannot stand. Eventually she takes to slumming through New York's speakeasies and succumbs to the advances of a stranger who agrees to help her kill her husband.

"I killed him to be free," she declares.

Like Ruth Snyder, the protagonist is executed in the end. Unlike Ruth Snyder, no reporter observing the electrocution smuggles in a camera under his pant leg to snap a photo for the *Daily News*. The photo, which displays Ruth Snyder's sagging body still strapped to Old Sparky, filled the front page the next day. The paper had to go into a second run to fill the demand. New York hasn't stopped talking about the case since.

Benny cannot get out of the theater quickly enough.

"Come on," he says, grabbing Esther's hand. "We have a table at the Grotto."

The Puncheon Grotto is a dozen blocks from the Plymouth, an easy stroll through the mild September evening. The Grotto, an epicurean haven, is Jack Kriendler and Charlie Berns' second club since the days of the Red Head on East 4th.

The Grotto's success is, in part, the result of the closure of New York's great dining halls which, devoid of their wine and alcohol-based sauces, couldn't manage to stay in business. The Grotto's chefs are free to practice their trade on consenting adults. Everything is open to interpretation from fresh crab, brook trout, and spaghetti with tomato-and-black-truffle sauce, to patisserie with Viennese coffee and thick whipped cream. Tonight, the crab sports a delicate Champagne sauce and the whipped cream is doused with Brandy.

Esther passes her mink stole to the hatcheck girl who runs her fingers through the deep fur.

Benny slips the maître d' a sawbuck. The party is escorted to the best table in the house, not because of the ten dollars but because Jack Kriendler relies on Meyer and Benny to help stock his illustrious cellar with the finest European wines.

The waiter brings a bottle from Charlie Berns' private stock. Berns uncorks the bottle personally.

Aaron Sapiro raises his glass. "Next year in Jerusalem," he says. "L'chaim."

The table resounds: "L'chaim."

Charlie Berns says, "May we never be stuck with nothing but Mevushal wine!"

Anne leans forward and settles her elbow on the table. Her cigarette hangs limply between two fingers. She catches Aaron Sapiro with her deep, dark eyes.

She says, "I just wanna know one thing. Why does Ruth Snyder fry while a guy like George Remus goes free? It's nuts. You know? He killed his wife. Snyder killed her husband. What kinda double standard runs our justice system?"

"What kinda double standard lets a wife throw her husband's business away?" Benny says. "Remus was dead in the water the minute he emerged from prison. His business was long gone."

He casts a knowing smile in Meyer's direction. The business had moved on from George Remus. Pharmaceutical certificates don't wait for those serving time. Connections change. Business goes on, as usual.

"Justice? What's that got to do with justice?" Sapiro says. "The emollient that allowed Remus to wriggle free from his conviction was not justice or even acquittal on the grounds of insanity. The jury was all male. They could relate to George. A good trial lawyer knows it's all in how you spin the story. Think about it. George Remus is sent to the pen for crimes against the Volstead Act. He does his time. Two years, right? His wife takes up with another man and not just any man but a Prohibition agent. That's adultery. Tsk, tsk right there. The wife and the lover sell George's businesses, spend the millions, and leave Georgie a hundred bucks for his trouble. One of the jurors said if they could have acquitted him clean, they would have. 'We decided that the man had been persecuted long enough.' Ruth Snyder is a different story. In her trial, she was the trollop and her husband the victim. The play seeks to tell a different story, a more compassionate tale of the Ruth Snyders in this world. Maybe one day women will become jurors and have a say about what justice might look like to them."

"Ha," Anne says. "We just got the vote eight years ago!"

Sapiro says, "It wasn't the why but the how that convicted Snyder. She tried to kill her husband seven different times and failed. The lovers garroted the husband, stuffed his nose full of chloroform-soaked rags, and tried to make it look like a burglary. He was executed, too, the lover. Henry Judd Gray, I think was his name. George Remus on the other hand, in a fit of rage, got out of his car, walked over, and shot his wife. People understand that action. Planning and deception are different."

Esther says, "She was desperate. She wanted the insurance money."

Anne says, "Snyder made the cover of the *Daily News*. The paper sold half a million copies but her kid didn't get one penny of that money. His mother was a spectacle for all of New York see but he's still left an orphan."

Sapiro shrugs. Tell that to the judge.

❖

Summer fades and with it the memory of Frankie Yale and the press' insistence on the new danger to New York's streets. Brooklyn settles into a new rhythm with Anthony Carfano managing Yale's gambling and bootleg businesses while Albert Anastasia, another Calabrese and leader of the International Longshoremen's Association, becomes ever more aggressive at taking control of Brooklyn's docks, and why not, now that Frankie Yale is out of the way.

Perched on the shore on the Brooklyn side of the Williamsburg Bridge, is a luxurious Italian restaurant that stretches lazily along the East River taking full advantage of a million-dollar view. The brilliance of Manhattan's shoreline outshines the stars in the sky.

Maranzano looks out at Manhattan and raises a glass of Chianti to his Old World friend, Joe Profaci.

"Salute!" he says. "Frankie Yale is no longer a thorn in our side."

"Salute!" Profaci agrees. "Let's hope we've seen the end of his five-cent cigars."

Yale is Maranzano's latest example of everything that is wrong with men who lack honor. Snapshots of Yale's life fill the conversation.

The $50,000 funeral.

The fifteen thousand mourners.

The overcrowded Church of St. Rosalie.

The 250 automobiles, 38 covered with floral tributes.

The hearse.

The hundred policemen lining the five-mile route from church to grave.

St. John's cemetery.

The photograph in the *Daily News* that shows a flood of mourners and Yale's flower bedecked coffin.

The $7,962 that was left behind.

The feuding wives; Yale having neglected to inform the first Mrs. Yale of their divorce.

The diamond-studded belt buckle that the first Mrs. Yale sold for $500 to bring her take to $8,462.

It was a crying shame and a disgrace to men of real honor.

Maranzano says, "Fifty thousand dollars for a funeral. These thugs have no foresight. It would have been better to spend that money on soldiers. And this war between Yale and Capone, what were they fighting over? The Unione Siciliana?"

Profaci says, "What business does a Calabrese and a Neapolitan have fighting over the Unione Siciliana?"

Maranzano says, "They are jealous of Our Tradition. It drives them to destroy us. They will destroy the Unione so they can control all the Italians as one. Capone wants his puppet to control the Unione in Chicago. The old Calabrese didn't like his underling's choice. My fear, old friend, is that men such as these have corrupted the minds of our young. So many have lost sight of what it means to have honor. We must purify Our Tradition."

Profaci takes a fatherly tone, "It is the nature of young men. Respect has to be taught."

Maranzano says, "Joe Masseria is to blame. He has become the Boss, and not the Father the men need. What do you expect from a man with the table manners of a Hun? He is incomplete inside. He is greedy for what does not concern him. The glutton in him cannot be satisfied."

Profaci nods. "Keep clear of him."

Maranzano says, "He will devour us all. Stefano thinks so, too, and Giuseppe Aiello. Capone's threats have sent Giuseppe into hiding. Joe the Boss encourages this foreigner to cut off our existence. We must come together as one if we are going to survive these wild dogs."

The men dip crusty bread in olive oil and speak of Sicily and the good times they enjoyed before Benito Mussolini took control. They gnaw on olives, roasted garlic, artichoke hearts, mozzarella, prosciutto, mushrooms, and marinated artichokes.

Maranzano says, "The artichokes are fresh and plump, no?"

Profaci says, "Business is good. We can still import what we need to eat well."

Profaci spends another half an hour talking about his estate turned hunting lodge in rural New Jersey. Maranzano's longings stir. His Brooklyn house is modest by such standards. His paesan immigrated to America in 1922. Maranzano calculates how long it will take him to catch up with a mansion of his own.

Profaci suggests that Maranzano take a break from the strain of the city by joining him for a leisurely week in the country where they can relax away from prying ears and discuss the current state of affairs.

Maranzano eagerly agrees. His ambition to use Sicilian possibility to thwart the whirlwind known as Joe the Boss is palpable. A cool assessment of Italian rackets could be just the thing he needs to congeal the soldiers into a fighting force capable of defeating the Hun.

The two men finish their meal and agree to meet the next morning for a week-long retreat.

Maranzano slides into his armor-plated Cadillac and tells his driver, a young man he calls Pepito, to show him the town.

"I want to see where the people live," he says.

Pepito takes him through the local neighborhoods before crossing the Williamsburg Bridge and winding through the Lower East Side and through the heart of Manhattan ending in Harlem, blocks from the Cotton Club.

"In America, everybody is a King," Maranzano says.

"Pardone?" Pepito says.

"The Olive Oil King. The Artichoke King. This is how we make our success, by giving people what they need," Maranzano says. "Is everything set?"

"Everything is set," Pepito says.

"Then take me home, Pepito. I am tired now and need to rest."

After dropping him off, Pepito heads for a back alley and a rendezvous with a neighborhood kid. At fifty cents a head, Pepito purchases half a dozen rats. Night falls. Under the cover of darkness, he and his accomplices cross the Brooklyn Bridge and then zip through the maze of warehouses known as the garment district until they come upon the building of a manufacturer that Maranzano has been muscling with little success.

Pepito and the boys pile out of the car and slip into the building. Racks of silk, satin, and lace hang like ghosts animated by a soft evening breeze. Pepito dons heavy leather gloves and, one by one, wrangles the rats from their cage. The boys tie alcohol-soaked rags to the rat's tails and then ignite them. The rats run helter-skelter through the warehouse spreading flames through the clothes. Spring colors burn red hot then turn to ash. Black smoke billows into the night sky. By morning, an entire season is lost.

Maranzano packs his suitcase. He kisses his wife. Pepito takes him to Joe Profaci's Brooklyn home. The two men then head to New Jersey to sort out the details of a Sicilian summit.

The garment manufacturer is still mourning his losses when the cutters and sewers show up for work. Lepke Buchalter, who has had his eye on the unions long before the strikes made such a grab possible, looks on from afar. He smokes a cigarette and assesses the damage. To the union coughing up his fee, this assault strikes quite a blow.

Lepke finishes his cigarette and hails a cab.

"Delancey and Essex," he says.

Over a bowl of kreplach, he makes his complaints known to Meyer.

Lepke says, "I don't scare easily. I'll get to the bottom of this."

Meyer says, "I had a situation just the other day. This guy had a connection but he didn't have the money so he comes to me and Benny. We think it over. It looks like a good investment so we give him the cash. The guy goes out and buys himself a new Chrysler. Payday comes around and he cries 'broke.' I tell him, 'You'll make payments to me weekly.' He misses three payments. We send a couple of cops over to pay him a visit. The guy hightails it into the Claridge and starts crying on Benny's shoulder about how tough his life is and how the deal didn't work out and how his wife is gonna kill him if he gets rid of the car."

Lepke says, "And then Benny told him how he was gonna kill him if he didn't?"

"That's about the size of it." Meyer laughs.

Lepke says, "Did you ever get paid?"

Meyer shakes his head.

"I'll see if Charlie has heard anything," Meyer says. "If it is Maranzano, see me before you do anything, will ya, Lep? The Frankie Yale affair has put us all under the magnifying glass for a while. There's going to be changes made. You'll get your revenge but for now, keep it under your hat."

"O.K., Meyer," Lepke says, a tinge of frustration evident in his promise.

"These things can't be rushed," Meyer says.

"Yeah, I get it," Lepke says. "I don't want to lose what we already got. We just got Little Augie outta our hair."

Meyer stops in to see Charlie. Charlie listens to the story of the garment district fire. He tells Meyer about the Sicilian summit as it was told to him.

"The Sicilians are plotting something. That can't be good."

✻

By early fall, tensions are running high on the streets as a wave of new soldiers fresh off the boat from Italy makes a bid for various Italian rackets. An Italian, known most often as Al Mineo, strolls along Mulberry Street cursing his new shoes and the blister forming on his heel. He stops in front of a bicycle shop to loosen his laces. A row of bicycles glistens in the morning sun. The smell of Dunlop's pneumatic tires fills the air.

Mulberry Street is unusually quiet for a Saturday afternoon. Mineo looks at the miniature "Spirit of St. Louis" mounted on the front fender of the Lindy bicycle. He flips the propeller, amused at the commercialism. It is just the sort of thing the kids love.

Joe the Boss strolls around the corner and catches sight of Mineo eyeing the little wonder.

Joe says, "This is some bicycle, eh?"

Mineo clears his throat and replies in kind, "I am thinking for my son. All the boys want one."

Joe says, "Walk with me."

The bloated blister on Mineo's heel pops. The pain is terrible as his heel continues to rub against the stiff leather. For the sake of his self-esteem, he tries to ignore the pain.

Joe the Boss prods his paesan for news of the Brooklyn Italians.

"Please, may we sit while we talk?" Mineo gestures to his foot. "New shoes."

Joe says, "Never wear new shoes. I have a man who breaks them in for me. I will give you his name."

They stop at the Sabatini bakery. Signora Sabatini hustles a plate of sweet rolls to the table. Joe the Boss eases his large body onto the round seat of the bentwood chair. He makes sure that he maintains a proper view of the street outside. Mineo is left with his back to any trouble that might arise. Instantly, he is nervous. His boss, should he see them together, would certainly see the meeting as treachery.

Mineo's boss openly opposes Joe the Boss. He has sided with

Castellammarese in rebuffing the moves Joe is making to take control of the Brooklyn rackets one mob at a time. The wake of opportunity that followed Frankie Yale's murder has left everyone ambitious and more than a little paranoid.

Joe the Boss says, "Signora, you have any more of those little cheese pigs you get from your hometown? You must try these, Alfredo. They are delicious. Now, what is it that brings you to Mulberry Street?"

"Can I be frank with you?" Mineo spits out carefully.

Signora Sabatini brings a pair of the cheese pigs. Joe grabs a little porker, pinching it hard between his stubby fingers and bites off the little head.

"Try one," he insists.

Mineo manages to nip off the snout before spilling his guts. He does not agree with his boss. The Brooklyn Sicilians are making a mistake pledging loyalty to Salvatore Maranzano. Maranzano is too ambitious, too eager to take control.

The words tickle the ears of Joe the Boss. He latches onto Mineo's private question.

He says, "I understand your concern but you are not alone. Now that Frankie Yale is gone and Anthony Carfano is in place, Brooklyn will remain ours."

"Do I have your blessing to do what must be done, Don Masseria?" Mineo says.

Joe the Boss examines Mineo's sincerity, detects no deception.

"I give you my blessing," Joe says at last, "but let me give you a word of advice, my good friend."

Mineo glances out at the street to make sure he is in the clear before he leans closer to hear the words Joe the Boss is about to utter.

"The Lindy bicycle is too expensive," Joe says. "Do not spoil your son. I have a friend. He will get you a nice bicycle for much less."

Mineo stands and thanks the fat man for his good sense. He puts enough change on the table to cover the expense of eating at the bakery and bids Joe the Boss good day.

On October 10, just as the lamps are being lit and the neighborhood begins to take up residence on the stoops for a bit of cool air, Alfred Mineo makes his move. He stations himself along with two accomplices near the corner of Avenue A and Thirteenth Street.

The fifty-year-old boss that rules over Mineo drives up with his family. He and his wife are being treated for heart disease by the local doctor. This has been their routine for weeks now. Mineo's boss steps from the car. Before he can open the car door for his wife, Mineo draws him into a quarrel.

They squabble. Mineo's cohorts rush in and open fire.

Three bullets lodge in the boss's back, one in his left eye, one in his chest, one in his abdomen, one in his groin, one in his right shoulder and one in his leg. Nine bullets in all. He drops to the ground and bleeds to death. His wife sits frozen in fear, unable to move or open the car door. The sight of her dying husband is too much for her to endure. The four children crouch on the back-seat floor screaming, their older sister draped over the younger ones protectively.

A crowd forms but no one can identify the killers.

The police arrive and take note of the murder and then they dig into the gangster's life. They wonder what a cheese importer with a record of two arrests is doing with three cars and a fine home in the Bronx. Further digging reveals that the family lived in the Bath Beach section of Brooklyn. This neatly ties the cheese importer to Frankie Yale's murder and the murder of Yale's lieutenant, who was buried only yesterday.

Mineo reads the newspaper satisfied that the spotlight has not landed on him. He plots moves on the waterfront. Joe the

Boss celebrates his good luck. One less Sicilian mucking up his dynasty.

"I'm getting old," he says. "I deserve respect."

The Irish, who have long dominated the docks, sense the Italians breathing down their necks. A man named Umberto Anastasia, also known as the "Mad Hatter," heads up the International Longshoremen's Association, but his ambition reaches beyond the maritime union. His resume includes an eighteen-month stint at Sing Sing for brutal attacks on his fellow workers.

Salvatore Maranzano seizes on current events to fan opposition to Joe the Boss.

"Nobody is safe until we deal with this monster," he says.

The ears of the Brooklyn Castellammarese perk up.

Rothstein's Funeral

WHY WE SHOULD VOTE FOR HERBERT HOOVER
TOLD IN TALKING MOTION

Legs Diamond

Jimmy Walker

Chapter Thirteen
If At First You Don't Succeed,
There's Always Gehinnam

NOVEMBER 1928/1929

Arnold Rothstein's mind is having trouble connecting the sound of the gun blast with the pain in his abdomen. He looks down at his bloodstained shirt then up at the smoldering .38 Detective Special and wonders if his father had it right. All his stern, forbidding words. Was this the recompense for ignoring the old man's advice?

Blood soaks the front of his trousers. He tries to sit down but his legs don't seem to bend. His ears ring. He can't understand the words coming from the mouth of George McManus, the guy who has, for the last fifteen minutes, insisted Arnold pay his gambling debt.

George stands in the middle of Room 349 of the Park Central Hotel, frozen with fear. Sweat rolls down his round face. He swipes at it with the cuff of his shirt and wonders what went wrong. Not thirty minutes earlier Rothstein had agreed to meet him here to work out the details of the past-due debt incurred in a poker game.

"You stupid mick," Rothstein says, insisting that forty-six is too young to die. He presses his hand hard on the hole in his abdomen and says again, barely audible, "You stupid mick. What the hell are you doing with a gun?"

George's brother Tom, a retired Detective Sergeant, looks on in disbelief. George wipes the sweat blurring his eyes.

"I'm sorry, Arnold. It just went off," George says.

The smell of burning flesh hovers in the room. Tom grabs the towel hanging from the rail above the washbasin and scrubs the .38 of any evidence that might implicate his brother.

"Don't just stand there," Tom says. "Go on before the paddy wagon comes. You get as far away from here as you can. You got that? Hide, George, and don't tell nobody where you are."

"You dubs," Rothstein sputters as his eyelids flutter.

Tom pitches the .38 through the rotting, soot-ridden screen, a pitch worthy of Lefty Grove himself.

Rothstein's heart pounds. His head aches. Like a cheap truck with a worn-out gasket, he continues to leak. He grabs the back of the desk chair for support. It tumbles sideways under the pressure. Hotel stationery spills onto the floor, blotting the deep red goo that once kept Rothstein running.

"You shouldn't a made me do this," George hisses. "You shoulda paid up!"

"The game was rigged and you know it," Rothstein says.

Tom grabs George's arm. "It's spilt milk," Tom tells Rothstein. "If you'd a given him what you owe him, none of this would have happened."

The brothers dart from the hotel room. Rothstein stands alone sucking in short, painful breaths. His body begins to convulse. He staggers into the hallway and then struggles down three flights of stairs. Blood trails him. He finds himself in the hotel's service corridor. It is nearly 11 P.M. The elevator operator, on his way to work, takes him for drunk until he recognizes this is Arnold Rothstein. Everyone at the Park Central knows that the Big Brain doesn't drink, not even socially.

"Are you sick?" the operator says, only then noticing the crimson track on the floor.

"Get me a taxi," Rothstein says. "Get me to Polyclinic Hospital."

Rothstein leans against the wall and then sinks, slowly, to the floor. His voice is barely a whisper. He rewinds September's poker game in search of the moment when things went wrong: the $322,000 he owed Nate Raymond, the gambler's agreement, the revelation that Nate owed Titanic Thompson. That's it, he thinks. Thompson owed everybody. Then tonight, the McManus clan all present and accounted for in room 349. George McManus had lied about being alone when he phoned Lindy's and interrupted late supper with Inez. The phone call, yes, the goddamned phone call from the dub who took a rigged poker game seriously.

"Mr. Rothstein?"

"Hello?" Rothstein says.

"Mr. Rothstein, are you O.K.?"

Rothstein looks toward the voice. Patrolman Davis has joined the party.

"I want to go home," Rothstein says.

Davis says, "Mr. Rothstein, you've been shot. Who shot you?"

"Get me a cab," Rothstein says. "I live at 912 Fifth Avenue. Get me a cab."

"An ambulance is on the way, Mr. Rothstein," Davis says. "Try to relax."

Rothstein explores his gut.

The hotel manager rushes in with a stack of towels. The patrolman wads them around Rothstein's middle.

"Take me to Polyclinic Hospital," Rothstein says. "Call my doctor. Understand. I want *my* doctor."

"Yes, Mr. Rothstein," Davis says.

Three dozen employees crowd around the famous, limp body to get a glimpse of Mr. Big's demise.

"Is he dying?" somebody asks.

"Well he ain't dancing a jig," somebody else says.

"Who shot you?" Davis repeats.

Rothstein's eyes are glassy; his thoughts fade into incoherence.

Two medics push their way through the crowd dragging a gurney behind them. They gather up Arnold Rothstein and take his vital signs. Rothstein stares blankly at the sky as he is rolled from the hotel to the waiting ambulance.

Several blocks away, at the corner of 57th and Eighth Avenue, George McManus steps into a pharmacy phone booth to make a call. He is on his own. The boys split up as they left the hotel, each hustling away in a different direction. McManus picks up the receiver and drops a nickel in the box and calls the one guy he trusts to get him out of this jam, Tammany's chieftain, Jimmy Hines.

"Hello, Jimmy?" he says. "There's been a little trouble. Arnold Rothstein was shot."

"Don't say another word," Hines says. "Where are you?"

"Fifty-seventh and Eighth Avenue," McManus says.

"Stay put," Hines says. "Understand? Stay put."

"I'm in trouble," McManus says.

"Georgie," Hines says, "we'll have somebody to ya in a flash. Don't move. We'll get through this."

Hines hangs up the phone and calls Frank Costello. Ten minutes later, Bo Weinberg, the Dutchman's right-hand man, flies around the corner and slams to a halt in front of George McManus, who waits hunched at the curb with his hands stuffed into his pants pockets. McManus dives into Weinberg's Buick sedan. The sedan speeds away.

McManus takes a handkerchief from his pocket and swabs the sweat on his face and neck.

"What the hell?" Weinberg says. "Somebody shot Arnold Rothstein?"

Like a boy getting a scolding, McManus drops his head in shame.

"Jesus Christ! You're kidding me, right?" Weinberg says, "*You* knocked off the Great A. R.?"

"Goddamn hebe," McManus says—and then chokes out, "No offence, Bo, but I got payoffs, ya know. These guys lookin' for their money are lookin' at me. Goddamn Rothstein. It's been three months! Three fucking months since the game! He's tellin' everybody the game was fixed. Horseshit. It wasn't fixed. He lost fair and square. He owes me. Three hundred fifty grand. Fair and square."

Weinberg says, "Everybody knows Arnold is paper rich and cash poor. He's a gambler, for Christ's sake."

"He wanted me to wait for the election. Said he's got a winning ticket."

Weinberg laughs. "Yeah? Well, you're gonna have a helluva time collecting if he drops dead. Where did you hit him?"

McManus says, "I wanted to scare him. That's all. The gun just went off."

"Rule of thumb, George, never give a loaded gun to a guy who don't know how to handle himself. In your case, never take a loaded gun when you are hot under the collar. It always winds up bein' somebody's funeral. Who the hell thought it was a good idea to go packing, anyway?"

"My brother," George says.

"The social worker?"

"Tom," McManus says.

"Leave it to a copper," Weinberg says. "That's all they know. There ain't no silver bullets, Georgie. Can't wait to see how Hines pulls this one off. You better hope Rothstein don't die. Now I want you to listen and I want you to listen good. You're gonna lay low for a while. You think you can handle that?"

McManus fumbles with a cigarette. His hands tremble. The wind blows out three matches before he manages to light it. The big Irishman sucks in a lungful of smoke and lets it out slowly.

He says, "Me and this broad got a room at the Park Central."

Weinberg says, "Your blonde alibi."

McManus laughs. "Yeah. How'd you know she was blonde?"

"Look around, George. They're all blonde. Can she handle the heat?"

McManus says, "She handles me, don't she?"

Weinberg motors across the Brooklyn Bridge and winds his way to the Bronx. As the distance from the Park Central Hotel grows, McManus breathes easier. Weinberg stops the car in front of a small apartment.

"This is it," Weinberg says. "Home, sweet home."

He takes McManus inside and makes coffee for them both. McManus paces. He sits. He rubs his hands together as if trying to wash them clean.

"Relax," Weinberg says. "And for god's sake, stay put! There's an old woman who's gonna make sure you got food. I told her you were a sick friend of mine. Cough a lot. She won't get too close. Whatever you do, don't leave the apartment. Don't leave the apartment! And don't call your goddamn cop brother. Let Jimmy do the work."

McManus nods.

Weinberg says, "I'll be back later with some clothes. What size do you wear?"

"Forty-two," McManus says.

"Stay calm, Georgie," Weinberg says. "Everything's gonna be all right."

Rothstein is admitted to Polyclinic Hospital. Detectives swarm the Park Central. A cabbie stumbles on the discarded

Detective Special that got pitched through the window. He stops a patrolman to hand over the gun.

"I picked this outta the gutter," the cabbie says, waving the pistol. "Maybe you're lookin' for it?"

The patrolman grabs the gun. The gutta-percha stock of the .38 special is cracked, the hammer jammed. One cartridge remains in the chamber.

"Where'd you get it?" the patrolman says.

The cabbie points toward the trolley tracks.

"Show me," the patrolman says.

They wade through traffic. The Detective Special had bumped across Seventh Avenue's trolley tracks and found a home against the far curb somehow. The cabbie points to the spot. The patrolman shines his flashlight along the curb. Five unexploded shells litter the ground. The patrolman scoops up the bullets and dutifully stuffs them into his pocket, the wool uniform wiping away any fingerprints that might have been left behind.

At Polyclinic Hospital, nurses and doctors labor over Rothstein's body. The loss of blood has left Rothstein weak and unresponsive. The sun rises. Abe the Just, Arnold's father, sits next to the hospital bed and watches as his son slips away. Abe bows his head and says a prayer for the deceased. It's his duty, like the obligation, according to Jewish tradition, to have his son in the ground within twenty-four hours. The lifeless body of Arnold Rothstein is ushered to Riverside Memorial Chapel.

Charlie Lucky has a cup of coffee and heads to the Claridge Hotel.

"Did you hear about Rothstein?" Charlie says.

Meyer says, "I heard McManus called Jimmy Hines, and that Bo Weinberg drove McManus to a safe house. Hines musta called Frank Costello, who called the Dutchman."

"Yeah," Charlie says. "Tammany owes him. If it wasn't for Costello, Jimmy Walker wouldn't've been mayor. But where does the Dutchman come in?"

"I don't know," Meyer says. "Rumor already has it that this is a hit by the Dutchman. But McManus is a gambler, not a hit man. What the hell was he doing with a gun?"

Charlie says, "Me and George Uffner cleaned out Rothstein's office last night. This morning detectives are crawling all over the place. They won't find nothin'. We can follow the trail to his rackets. Costello shouldn't have no trouble picking up the political connections. The rest we'll sort out with the boys."

Rothstein's body is dressed in a white shirt, a simple dark suit, a purple-striped prayer shawl, dark shoes and socks, and a white skullcap. The body is placed in a mahogany casket with a glass lid. That way, should God look down from heaven, Abraham Rothstein is assured He will see a devout man and a good son lying in repose.

Rothstein is put on display in the chapel. The patriarch reads Psalms over the body of his wayward son. Rabbi Jung rips the shirts of Rothstein's mother and father, his brothers, and his sister. Cantor Jassinowski extols God in song. If he has any aspirations for Broadway, he isn't making them known this day.

"Y'hei shlamah rabbah meen sh'mahyah, v'chahyeem aleynu v'al kohl yisrael, v'eemru: Amein," he sings. May there be abundant peace from heaven and life upon us and upon all Israel.

"Amein," the congregation responds.

"Amein."

Rothstein's casket is taken to Union Field Cemetery in Queens and nestled next to his brother, Harry. His marriage to the

Catholic Carolyn is forgotten and forgiven now that they are forever separated in death.

Amein.

Abraham Rothstein, the man who could not settle the strike in the garment district, makes peace with his God. His son is no doubt in Gehinnam, the place of spiritual purification. Abraham lingers at the gravesite hoping that his son will do the right thing, pay his dues over the course of the year ahead of him. If the price paid is enough, Arnold Rothstein's soul will be free to ascend to Olam Ha-Ba, the world to come.

Amein.

Arnold Rothstein fades from front page news as the presidential election, a race between a Catholic and a Quaker, heats up. The moment Herbert Hoover dubbed the Holland Tunnel the Pope's conduit to the White House, Rothstein had placed his wager on Herbert Hoover to win. He had no illusions a Catholic could ever beat the odds. He stood to make a cool half a million dollars, $570,000 to be exact, when the Catholic Al Smith was defeated.

In death, Rothstein's ship comes in. Herbert Hoover wins by a landslide, 444 electoral votes to Al Smith's 87. Only one problem, nobody knows where Rothstein's winning ticket has gone.

Carolyn, Rothstein's shiksa wife, wails.

Legs Diamond, Rothstein's bodyguard turned drug-dealing partner, wanders through his midtown apartment and laughs out loud. He laughs that McManus can't lay his hands on the $570,000. He laughs that the police think McManus might be innocent. He laughs that two million dollars in narcotics that was part of his deal with Rothstein was seized in a raid on an "alleged Rothstein ring." He laughs that Arnold is gone and along with him the biggest deal of Legs' miserable life.

Legs says, "What a dub."

The waiters at Ratner's Deli dish up the daily news like knish at a Bar Mitzvah.

"They said the Black Sox Scandal would kill baseball. It's the Babe's first season with the Yankees and already he's hit 54 home runs and three more in the World Series. Baseball's dead! Without Arnold Rothstein, rest his soul, the game would be dead. He should have lived one hundred twenty years," one waiter laments.

"People are gullible," another complains.

"Methodists want a dry country," the first says. "It's wet and dry, not Catholic and Protestant."

"It is always about religion," a customer chimes in. "You, being a Jew, should know this."

Meyer ignores the chatter. There are bigger fish to fry. Moses Annenberg is taking the *Racing Wire* nationwide. There are intricacies to this dance that need to be worked out between him and Charlie. Meyer makes plans to spread their network from New York to California.

"It's worth millions," Meyer says to the small table of Jews and one Gentile.

The waiter brings fresh coffee, takes everybody's order. Doesn't bother to hide his disdain when Charlie says, "Bring me ham and eggs."

A look passes among the Jews: Meyer, Benny, Lepke Buchalter, Gurrah Shapiro, Abe Zwillman.

"No ham," the waiter says to Charlie.

"Bacon then," Charlie says.

"No bacon, either," the waiter says.

"Then bring me whatever it is you got," Charlie says.

The gauntlet has been thrown down. The waiter hustles off to the kitchen. Fifteen minutes later, the waiter returns loaded down with plates of blintzes and bagels and potato pancakes with applesauce. The waiter slides a plate of eggs to Charlie and then a plate of Gefilte fish.

Charlie pokes at the white fish patties.

"What's this?" Charlie says.

Everybody laughs, even Charlie.

"Gefilte fish," the waiter says and turns on his heel.

"*Fish?*" Charlie says.

"This is a kosher deli," Lepke says.

"Whadya gotta do to get bacon?" Charlie says.

"You don't get bacon," Lepke says. "Jews don't eat bacon."

Charlie says, "You're kiddin' me, right? You guys eat bacon all the time. I seen ya. You got Pig Market right down the street."

"It's called that because there's everything *but* pigs in the market," Benny says. "Pigs aren't legal."

"Pigs ain't legal? Now I know you're pulling my leg," Charlie says waving down the waiter.

The waiter ignores him.

Benny waves his hand over the Gefilte fish. "Take this away," he says. "Bring him something he'll enjoy while he's still smiling. Trust me, you don't want him rummaging through the kitchen looking for something he likes."

The waiter skulks back to the kitchen. Benny turns to Meyer.

"What's this with the wire?"

"We are going to spread the joy of gambling across the country," Charlie says.

Benny squints, "What the…what are you saying?"

"Annenberg," Charlie says. "He tussles with the politicians over the right of the little guy to bet away from the track. He says the people livin' in poverty got a right to take a chance on getting free from their humdrum lives. Says it isn't right to deprive the little people of a chance to be lucky, on or off the track. He's got a helluva line of bullshit."

Meyer says, "Reformers will never let it happen. They've got a line of bullshit, too. They say they want to protect the guys that go broke gambling. The only guys getting rich are those who control the betting. I've called Costello so we can all sit down with Erickson and work this thing out. Charlie is sending Jimmy Alo to check on the gambling joints out west. I've asked Nig Rosen to go with him."

The waiter returns with roast beef that has been thinly sliced and cooked to a crisp finish. He slides the plate next to Charlie while keeping an eye on Benny's reaction. Benny takes one look at the dish and busts out laughing and slaps Charlie on the back. The stiff-necked waiter sighs relief.

"Never disrespect one of my friends again," Benny says to the waiter.

December kicks in, and with a little help from Bergdorf Good-man and the housekeeper, Charlie Luciano's apartment begins to exude the Christmas spirit. An eight-foot tall Christmas tree adorned in gold and silver dominates the living room. A trailing green vine tied lovingly with a giant red bow hangs on the mirror above the fireplace. Red and gold ribbons twine through a pine garland that stretches from one end of the mantle to the other. Four red candles set in silver candlesticks dot the table where two golden reindeer sit peacefully next to a silver coffee setting. And for good measure, scattered around the couches and chairs are special Christmas pillows with laughing Santas and holly and reindeer.

Charlie shuffles from the bedroom to the living room still in his silk pajama bottoms, silk robe, and fleece-lined slippers. He barely notices the infusion of joy. The morning paper sits folded next to the silver coffee pot. Charlie pours a cup of coffee and settles into an overstuffed chair. He cracks the paper open.

The housekeeper rustles through the refrigerator whistling her version of Mamie Smith's "Crazy Blues."

She yells from the kitchen, "You want blueberry pancakes this mornin', Mr. Ross? I done froze them berries you liked so much this summer."

Charlie Lucky, aka Charles Ross for purposes of his rental agreement, yells back, "Yeah, Bessie, and make extra. We got company today."

"Yes, suh," she says, and then under her breath. "Don't I know it?"

The news of George McManus' indictment for the murder of Arnold Rothstein fills several columns. The article ends with McManus' plea: Not Guilty.

Charlie grins. Tammany is pulling hard on the strings of the judicial system. The beefy Irish gambler will do no serious time if he does any time at all.

Pots and pans clang in the kitchen.

In the bedroom, Polly Adler's whore stretches between the silk sheets of the oversized bed. A fifty-dollar bill waits on the nightstand. The boys mock Charlie saying he makes fifty-dollar whores out of two-dollar whores. The whore smiles and then stuffs the bill into a small silver mesh bag.

She pads to the bathroom and fills the tub with bath salts and hot water. The aroma of sizzling bacon tangles with the smell of perfumed bubbles.

The phone rings. Charlie puts down the paper and takes the call. Willie Moretti, big-mouthed guy who is avoided but tolerated, is on the line with news. Willie is Frank Costello's cousin and that alone affords him some clout.

"Frank told me to call you personally," Moretti sings into the receiver.

Charlie listens.

"You seen the *Plain Dealer*?" Moretti says.

"When would I see the *Plain Dealer*?" Charlie says.

Moretti explains. The *Cleveland Plain Dealer* has rolled out the story of a police bust on an alleged Mafia meeting that was taking place at the Hotel Statler. Twenty-seven men of Italian descent were in attendance. Several were taken into police custody. Moretti, busting with facts, gives Charlie an earful.

"Profaci is up in Cleveland now, bailing out the guys that got pinched. They're calling it a Unione meeting to cover things up."

"A Unione meetin'?" Charlie says.

"It ain't a total lie," Moretti says. "What else are a bunch of wops holed up in a Cleveland hotel gonna call it? They come up with the story that they're all members of the Unione Siciliana, businessmen getting together to help each other out."

Moretti laughs uneasily. The power of the new Sicilian hierarchy forming in Brooklyn has him nervous. Unofficially, Moretti is considered the strength behind his cousin, Costello, but truth be told, Moretti relies on the more powerful Charlie Lucky to back him up should he ever be faced with a situation. After all, Frank Costello has enjoyed a long alliance with Joe the Boss and Charlie Luciano. Why shouldn't he?

Charlie says, "Who called this meeting?"

"I think it was Joe Porrello. I heard he needs the old Mustache Petes if he's gonna survive in Cleveland. The Porrellos got plenty of enemies. The meetin' never got off the ground, though. Some gumshoe spotted the wops right away. Porrello hadda pull thirty families together to put up their houses for collateral just to get everybody out of jail. I wonder what he's thinking now. Good idea or bad idea?"

"How many did you say?" Charlie says.

"Twenty-seven," Moretti says.

"Cleveland," Charlie says. "At the Statler. What the hell."

Moretti says, "Only thing I know is that Joe Porrello is kissing everybody's…well, I ain't gonna say it on the phone. He's got the corn sugar market up there. He wants to keep it. Maybe he figures all that booze coming across Jew Lake is putting a dent in his profits. I don't know."

The sparks that fly through Moretti's brain don't always connect in a useful way. Charlie accepts the comment at face value. The bootleggers that buy Porrello's corn sugar for their stills aren't in the same market as those running Canadian whiskey across the border.

Charlie says, "I'm sayin' why meet at a place like the Statler? That's high society."

"You got me there, Charlie," Moretti says. "It would take a blind man not to spot that many wops in one place."

"Thanks," Charlie says and hangs up the phone.

Charlie puts George McManus on the back burner and ponders the implications of a Mafia meeting in Cleveland. Then he calls Meyer.

Charlie says, "The usual place? About an hour?"

"Sure," Meyer says.

Polly's girl walks from the bathroom snugged in a towel. Charlie looks up with a smile. She straddles his lap, knees sinking into the soft sides of the chair's cushion. With furtive fingers, she tugs at the belt on Charlie's robe. The robe falls open easily. She runs her hands down Charlie's chest, unfastens his pajama bottoms, and begins a slow gyration of her hips.

Charlie says, "I ain't got that kinda time, Doll."

She throws out a pout. He yanks off the towel and stands up. His pajamas fall to the floor. He bends the whore over the chair. Five minutes later, he's in the shower and the whore is on her way home. He skips the blueberry pancakes and leaves the joy of Christmas to the housekeeper. He meets Meyer at a small market in the Village.

Bread and rolls are piled high on the shelf behind the counter. Shanks of ham and tubes of salami dangle from the ceiling. The cool case exhales great meaty breaths each time the sliding door slams shut. Ham, tongue, roast beef, corned beef, and bologna sandwiches roll out with the precision of a Ford factory assembly line.

Charlie ponies up the cash for two pastrami sandwiches.

The guy behind the counter says, "You think George McManus is gonna get the chair for killing the Jew?"

Charlie shrugs, "I guess they gotta prove he did it first."

Outside, Meyer smokes and waits. Charlie pops out of the market and snaps the paper-wrapped sandwich to Meyer. They stroll along First Avenue discussing the news.

"I got a call," Charlie says in between bites. "There was some kinda wop meeting at the Hotel Statler in Cleveland."

"What kind of wop meeting?"

Charlie drops the news of the Sicilian meeting in small doses as he and Meyer press on through Midtown and the Theater District and finally Hell's Kitchen. Kids rummage through garbage and kick tin cans and snarl at the strangers.

"Maybe thirty guys were there," Charlie says. "Supposedly a guy named Porrello wants the Sicilian fathers' nod to take over the city. That ain't far-fetched. These guys like everybody kissing their ring and all that shit."

Meyer doesn't like the sound of it. It doesn't take an Einstein to theorize that the Sicilians are organizing on a national scale. With Joe Profaci and Vincent Mangano, two big New York fathers, making a show at the meeting, this is something Meyer needs to understand.

Meyer says, "Does this have anything to do with Yale?"

"They don't give a damn about no Calabrese. Good riddance, you know what I mean? But don't think their world wasn't shaken by the hit. If Capone can take out a guy like Frankie Yale then everybody's fair game. They'll stick out their chests but you can be sure they're gonna beef up the soldiers around them."

Meyer says, "There's sure to be a backlash against Capone's guy as president of the Unione."

"You can bet that grain o' sand ain't makin' no pearl. Where there's power, there's scheming and killin'. Let's see, Anthony D'Andrea was the guy at the top in the teens. He got bumped off and Mike Merlo took over. Him and Torrio worked together for the betterment of Chicago, so to speak. That's how Torrio and Capone got their foot in the door with all them politicians. Then Merlo died a' cancer. That was '24, I think. One of the Gennas stepped in and proclaimed himself president of the Unione. A year later he was dead. Natural causes," Charlie smiles, "a bullet from the Irish. Then Amatuna declared himself president which Big Al objected to. Amatuna dropped dead in a barber chair from too close a shave, plus two bullets in the chest. That's when Al backed Lombardo as president. Moretti says that Lombardo was at the Statler with the rest of them Sicilians which just goes to show you how they like to keep their cover. The president of the Unione would have to be there, wouldn't he? Profaci was there. You remember me talking about Profaci. The guy's got a chapel in his house with a hand-carved replica of the altar in St. Peter's Basilica so's he can atone for his sins. It's a wonder he ever gets outside. He's among the guys that got pinched in Cleveland. Now he's helping arrange bail for everybody. I can tell ya that he ain't interested in no trouble. He's got a good business bringin' in olive oil and tomato paste for the Italians. He's glad to be away from Mussolini. He ain't like Joe Aiello who has his eye on Chicago. I'd make an even bet that Aiello was at the party, too. When that many Sicilians get together, you can be sure they're scheming to take over the world."

Meyer follows Charlie's story. The greasers brought the Black Hand business to America and subjugated the Italian neighborhoods. Once they got their hands in everybody's pocket, they never let go.

Meyer says, "What does Joe the Boss make of all this?"

"He wasn't invited. That's the first thing. The Sicilians don't like that his mob is mixed up with non-Sicilians. By now, I figure Joe's meeting with Al Mineo to see what he knows," Charlie says. "It could be that the Sicilians are plotting to overthrow Joe the Boss."

Meyer crushes his spent butt on the sidewalk then kicks it into the street.

"What kind of move will Joe make?" Meyer says.

Charlie says, "No doubt he will tighten the reins on the Brooklyn clan. Demand tribute. That's how these old greasers think. Money makes them feel like they're getting the honor they deserve. Brooklyn has to decide if they'll fall in line. When Cola Schiro was in charge, they did as they were told. Maranzano is a different animal. Greaser feuds go way back to the old country. A grudge is for life. Who knows what these guys have against each other, if anything at all. Maranzano fancies himself another Caesar. He's smart, Meyer. And he's got the Sicilians on his side."

It's not something Meyer wants to hear but there it is anyway.

This pushing and shoving between the greasers could turn New York into another Chicago. As the death toll grows, the cry of the public will reach the ears of those in power to do something about it.

They stop at the piers to watch the luxury liners dock. Tugs dance along the Hudson vying for position to take on the next great ship. It is a first-come, first-served business the Irish have dominated ever since the Fighting McAllisters made their stand. Without the small tugs, the big ships cannot maneuver in or out of berths. In this case, it pays to be small.

Meyer is quick to appreciate the irony. His mob is small in comparison to those of the lumbering Italian families. He has allies rather than relatives, agreements rather than obligations. His mob is quick, limber. He and Charlie have been trading favors with Chicago for years. If the Sicilians organize, they will do the same. The inevitable headlines could easily make business too hot to handle.

Charlie says, "Remember the guy that was gunned down in front of the doctor's office? Al Mineo organized that hit. Mineo wanted to move up the ladder. He bided his time while Joe the Boss made his moves and got stronger. Mineo's boss refused to submit to Joe the Boss' demands. Mineo made a quick alliance with Joe. In turn, Joe gave him the nod to take out his boss, which he did. The guy's wife and kids watched from the car as the whole thing went down.

"Suddenly, Mineo becomes Joe's constant companion, advising him about the Castellammarese in Brooklyn. And—" Charlie pounds a fist into the palm of the other hand. "Jesus, I didn't realize it until just now but that move Mineo made on my cousin, Mike…I bet he *knew* Mike was my cousin. He wanted to get something over on me. Like a dog marking his territory. Son of a bitch!"

Charlie turns sullen and stares out at the river, allowing the revelation to sink in.

"Oh, Jesus," he says looking at his watch. "I asked Jimmy to stop by the garage. I want you to meet him. He's the guy I was tellin' you about that came to me about Mike. He's a stand-up guy. Did three-and-a-half out of a five-year stretch in Dannemora for a jewel heist. Never said a word to nobody. Remember when we wanted to stir up a little trouble on the docks for Frankie Yale? He's the guy I sent to take care of business because of his ties with the Irish. He knows how to move among them, Meyer. I told him to come by the garage 'cause he'll be getting his whiskey from Red. Mostly, he's in the beer business. I want your guys to get to know him."

Meyer looks up and down the street.

"We'll never get a cab in this neighborhood," he says.

They hustle north along the river. Cabs line the streets next to the ocean liners' berths. They hand the taxi hailer a dollar and make it to the Cannon Street garage with time to spare.

Moe Sedway is busy with the car and truck rentals in the front office. Moe is eight years Meyer's senior, small and understated except for his heft which makes him self-conscious around the younger, fitter boys. He is relaxed under the heat of business which makes him a valuable player.

Meyer says, "Keep your eye out for an Italian guy. His name is Jimmy Alo. Show him to my office when he gets here. After that, let Red know I'd like to see him."

"Sure, Meyer," Moe says.

Meyer and Charlie disappear into the small office with the potbellied stove. Meyer throws a log into the stove. He and Charlie hover over the flame and try to divine the meaning of the Cleveland meeting as the winter freeze loses its grip on their extremities.

Charlie says, "There's more to the greaser story. A few weeks ago, Aiello came to see Joe the Boss demanding Al back off. Aiello said he offered Al the East side of Chicago. He seemed surprised that Al told him to take a hike. Aiello is demanding Joe the Boss put a collar on Al like it's some kinda test of Joe's leadership. Joe is smart enough not to take the bait, naturally, so Aiello hightails it back to Chicago and sends word back that it ain't safe for Joe the Boss to come to Chicago no more. Aiello was at the Cleveland meeting. Porrello wants to head up Cleveland. What does that tell you?"

Meyer says, "You said Joe the Boss is using Mineo as his consigliere to keep tabs on the Sicilians?"

"I guess I ain't on his dance card anymore," Charlie says.

The news is disappointing. Charlie has been the voice of reason, mitigating Joe's otherwise volatile nature, but even more than that, his position as confidante has provided him and Meyer with vital information for making their own moves. Joe the Boss benefited from this, too. His take of Charlie's business increased. However, Mineo's position has weakened Charlie's strategic influence.

Meyer says, "If Mineo counsels war…the Sicilians can't blame you if Joe the Boss listens to Mineo, nor can they blame you for following the orders of your boss. Should the wannabe Caesar get the upper hand, he will be forced to take that into consideration."

There's a knock. Moe brings Jimmy Alo to the door. Charlie motions him inside.

Charlie says, "Jimmy, you know who this is?"

Jimmy is no fool. Everybody knows Meyer Lansky. He speaks for and to the Jews. He is razor-sharp with ideas and connections around town and across the Eastern seaboard.

Alo nods.

Charlie says, "Tell Meyer how you wound up with the Irish, Jimmy."

Alo shrugs. "Things just worked out. I done a few things with some of the guys, we made a few bucks, I never tried to cheat nobody. I guess they trust me."

Meyer says, "What happened with the guys that were bulling Mike?"

"I told 'em Mike's with me. What are they gonna say? They seen me around. I told 'em a move against Mike is a move against me. I gave 'em my name and suggested they check around before they make a move that ain't in their favor. I guess they did 'cause they didn't bother Mike after that."

Charlie says, "Jimmy, some of the guys are getting together later tonight at the Cotton Club. After that, we'll go to Polly Adler's joint for breakfast. You wanna come along?"

"Sure," Alo says and then Red Levine pokes his head in the door.

"Show Jimmy around," Meyer says. "He's gonna be coming around now for whiskey."

Red nods, catching the drift. He leads Alo out.

"How'd you find this guy?" Meyer says.

"He found me," Charlie says. "He knew Mike was my cousin. He saw what was going on with the greasers. So he asked one of my guys to talk to me. He wanted to come around and tell me about Mike. Mike ain't no gang guy. Those bastards woulda killed him to get his business. I give Jimmy the O.K. to do what he had to do. Jimmy ain't the kind of guy to back down when he's got a .38 in somebody's ribs. The greasers didn't want to mess with Jimmy, so they left Mike alone. There's easier game around every corner. Later, I find out Jimmy's with the Irish, Johnny Dunn and Eddie McGrath, them guys. Tough sons of bitches, the Irish."

Meyer opens the front of the potbellied stove and throws on another log. Embers fly. He attributes the latest surge of greaser interference to the moves of Maranzano. Add to that Mussolini's purge of the Italian Mafia which amounts to little more than exporting Italy's violence to other countries, and there's trouble on the streets of New York, as if there wasn't enough trouble already. The problem for a guy like Meyer is that he sees the greater value in being invisible where these guys imagine being seen is the same as being powerful.

Meyer says, "I don't get guys like Yale. Street violence is bad for business."

Charlie says, "You're preaching to the choir."

Meyer says, "How do we put an end to it?"

"It's gotta be a purge of the old greaser thinking. Sooner or later Joe the Boss and Salvatore Maranzano will square off. They don't back down. They win or die tryin'."

"Then that's the move we wait for," Meyer says, and then responding to Charlie's look, "It's a chess game."

Charlie laughs. He's Italian, not Jewish. He plays cards. Scopa, most of the time, as a kid, around the kitchen table with his siblings when he wasn't occupied with something more important like robbing or stealing. As the name suggests, the object of the game is to "sweep" all the cards from the table. Skill and chance are the defining elements.

Chess, Meyer never tires of explaining to him, is a game of strategy.

Meyer says, "In chess, you want to control the center of the board. The Tenderloin is the center of our board. Our guys earn. Other guys see that. They want a piece of the pie but they gotta come through us to get that piece. We know that the guys who earn have an interest in protecting their territory. It's the Americanized Italians that see the lay of the land. The greasers' biggest mistake is thinking they're the only game in town. They're still playing Scopa. They forget about the Jews and the Irish. That's to our advantage. They call it chess blindness when a player misses a good move or fails to see an obvious danger. Look at the board, Charlie. Then we'll decide how to make the best move possible. I say we should let this conflict come to a head between the greasers. When they declare war, they will disrupt the boys who are earning. The Americanized guys will want the war settled."

"You think so?" Charlie says.

Meyer says, "We have the connections to make a stand against the violence. Costello brought the Irish around with his Tammany connections. Jimmy is connected to the street Irish, the guys on the docks. We must make sure we make our move before the government shuts us all down but not before the boys see what these greasers are really doing. Otherwise, the reformers will come out and bootleggers won't be able to walk down the street."

"Don't forget we got an ally in Capone," Charlie says.

"Let's talk," Meyer says.

Arranging a face-to-face with Capone proves fortuitous. Capone has fled the mind-numbing cold of Chicago to winter in Miami, Florida, where he has purchased a Spanish Mediterranean home built in 1922 by Clarence Busch, the beer baron. It seems only natural that the current beer baron of Chicago fork over the forty grand for the purchase. He puts the house in his wife's name, just in case. His tropical bliss, in the form of seven bedrooms, seven baths, and 30,000 square feet of waterfront property, sits on its own little spit of land.

Capone surveys the landscape and concludes that 93 Palm Avenue is the only place to be when the midwest gets hammered with cold. His Floridian bliss convinces him that he is now the generous benefactor of paradise. Capone thumps his chest with his thumb. Ash from his stogie falls on his shirt. He sweeps off the ash and then gestures toward the blue-green water of Biscayne Bay. He looks Jack McGurn in the eye.

"I want the New York boys to know they have my personal invitation to come down anytime. Anytime. I could use a little company."

McGurn nods. The boss is uneasy. A visit from Charlie would be a welcome relief. He calls in Tony Accardo, his latest recruit, to travel to New York and extend Capone's invitation to Charlie Lucky and his top aides. Accardo packs an overnight bag and heads north.

McGurn, born Vincenzo Antonio Gibaldi in Licata, Sicily, came to America in 1906. When Prohibition rolled around, he set up a speakeasy, the Green Mill, in the middle of Bugs Moran's territory and used his boxing skills to acquire entertainment. Last November, Jack persuaded Joe E. Lewis not to move his act to another speakeasy by slitting his throat and leaving him for dead. His ruthless nature makes him a valued player in the Chicago outfit. Currently, both Capone and McGurn are seething to take the North Side from the Irish. They sit around the pool and toss ideas back and forth. So far, a doable plan has not been forthcoming.

Tony Accardo reaches New York City and heads straight to Charlie Luciano's apartment. He waves two rail tickets and tells Charlie the boss extends his deepest wishes that he will come down to Florida and enjoy a break from the cold.

"It's Miami Beach, for god's sake," Accardo says. "You can walk around in a bathing suit. Bring whoever you want. If you ain't got nobody, there's plenty of broads down there."

For appearances, Charlie doesn't want to jump at the invitation.

Accardo says, "Look outside. Miami is seventy-six degrees and balmy."

He places the rail tickets on the table next to the golden reindeer.

"In case you're in the mood," Accardo says. "The boss calls it 'the Sunny Italy of the New World.'"

Charlie sits down in the overstuffed chair and smokes a cigarette. He and Accardo shoot the bull.

"I been to Florida," Charlie says. "It ain't Italy."

Accardo says, "Then you know about the goddamn Palmetto bugs."

He means the cockroach with black spots for eyes that look more like sunglasses. A grown man will pull a weapon in self-defense. It happens all the time.

Charlie picks up the rail tickets and reads the fine print, passage from New York to Miami, first class.

"I might just go for this," he says.

Accardo is relieved. He moans about Chicago and the Canadian winds that whip across Lake Michigan and freeze to the bone. He says Miami ain't really that bad when you consider a Chicago winter.

When Accardo leaves, Charlie calls Meyer.

By evening they're settled in a Pullman car on the Florida East Coast Railway heading for Miami. Meyer and Charlie kick back and kill time. They take meals in the dining car, after which they play cards in the recreation car where fake palms stand guard over small card tables. When boredom sets in, they return to the private car to talk shop. The twenty-eight-hour journey transforms the landscape from sheet white to impenetrable green.

When Meyer steps from the train, hit with humidity and temperatures in the 80s, he says, "I over-packed."

Capone has drinks and food set out around the pool. He is particularly fond of a new concoction picked up from Havana, a Cuba Libre.

"If you want, I'll take ya down to Cuba. It's the rage for hot shots." Capone runs a Cuban cigar under his nose. "I got just the boat to take us there."

He nods to a 36-foot V-bottom Robinson Seagull dubbed the *Flying Cloud*.

Meyer eyes the chop on the ocean with suspicion. "We just got off the train."

"This baby don't pound over the waves," Capone says. "It's a real smooth ride."

Capone takes a long series of contemplative puffs on his cigar.

"Americans are crazy over the place," he says. "Gambling is legal. Hell, everything's legal. You should see some of the side shows they got in different clubs."

Mae, Capone's wife, makes her way from the house to the pool sporting a mock-sailor top and white linen pants. Her blonde hair, combed to one side, falls to her shoulders. The glow of a budding suntan makes it obvious that she has taken to the Floridian lifestyle with ease.

"Why don't you take your guests out on the boat, dear?" she says. "I'm sure they would enjoy a little fresh air after being confined on a train for that long."

Al smiles. He pulls out a roll of cash from his pocket and puts it in Mae's hand.

"Buy the boy some toys," he says. "And a new outfit for yourself."

Mae looks at Jack McGurn and says, "See that he gets some exercise, will you, Jack?"

"Yes, Mae," Jack says with a convincing smile.

When Mae is well out of earshot, Charlie says, "You heard about the Sicilian meeting up in Cleveland?"

Capone nods, "Just another headache. Lolordo was there. He's headin' up the Unione now."

"I heard," Charlie says.

"I told him he should go. Be my eyes and ears. He said it was some big hoopla on the part of Porrello who wants the backing of the Sicilian fathers. Porrello wanted to impress these yahoos so he booked the conference at a fancy hotel. If there was more to it than that, they never got around to discussin' it before they all got pinched. Apparently, they don't like the Unione being called Italo-American, like Lolordo made it, at my suggestion. These guys don't get it. They want to keep it an exclusive club. They ain't got no vision, these Sicilians."

Capone draws on his cigar and watches his reflection ripple across the surface of the water in the pool.

"Goddamn Sicilians, eh Charlie? Goddamn schemin' Sicilians. You better have both your pockets sewed shut when you meet with those bastards. Come on, I got something to show ya."

They board the *Flying Cloud* and settle into the seats at the stern. Capone fires up the engine. Jack McGurn throws off the bowline. Capone noses the boat northward. McGurn releases the stern line and jumps aboard. Capone motors away from the shore then opens the engine wide. The hull slaps the water hard before the nose rises, allowing the V-hull to break the waves and smooth out the ride.

"Where the hell was this boat when we were running out to the mothership?" Meyer shouts over the roar of the engine.

Capone yells back, "I'm gonna show you my little secret. I'm puttin' in a gambling joint up the Intercoastal, a town called Deerfield."

"What's in Deerfield?" Charlie asks.

"My own peninsula," Capone yells.

It takes nearly forty minutes for them to cover the distance from paradise to Al's gambling dream. He shows off a 53-acre, triangular-shaped tract of land. He plans to build a $250,000 nightclub/casino. Capone slowly navigates the waterways on either side of the land: the Spanish River on the east and the Hillsboro River on the southwest. Red and white mangroves filled with egrets pack the site. Turtles slog through the wetlands. A long, black snake zips through the undergrowth and around the trees to the water's edge and then it is gone.

Capone kills the engine.

He says, "I'm gonna put a joint here just like the one I put in Lake Arrowhead. You know the place? A hundred miles east of Los Angeles and straight up the mountain. The Hollywood set vacations up there. You ever see the movie *Mantrap* with Clara Bow? The whole thing was filmed up there. All them New York Jew directors moved to California for the weather. They film all year round. Smart sons-a-bitches. They're making a bundle off all that sunshine. George Raft thinks he's gonna be the next Casanova. There's lots of broads and they're all hopping from bed to bed. Joe and Benny would be in hog heaven. We put in a tunnel that runs between the brothel and the casino up there so guys can slip from one place to the other for a little action without disturbing the wife, if you know what I mean. It's a helluva place. Show 'em the brochure, Jack."

McGurn pulls a folded pamphlet from his pocket. Club Arrowhead of the Pines, with its Olympic-sized swimming pool and private casino, outshines Saratoga's glory, not quite as lavish, but easily as romantic.

"This will be even better. This is my own private island. All we gotta do is dredge out some of this land. These resort towns are real money-makers. Easier than runnin' bootleg, eh? It's the future for guys like you and me. But, if you want my real opinion," Capone says, "the big money is in the Hollywood unions. You should be thinkin' about gettin' into that business."

Charlie hands the pamphlet back to McGurn.

"Keep it," Capone says. "There's plenty more where that came from."

They float around the island before motoring gently down the Intercoastal waterway. When Capone tires of navigating the boat, he turns the wheel over to McGurn and sits down with the boys. Like a rat going at an ocean liner's mooring rope, Capone chews voraciously on his cigar. His Floridian getaway is no secret. While he claims he is taking a break from business, the truth is the tension between him and the Bugs Moran gang grows daily. Al's rage overflows. There was an attempt on Johnny Torrio's life and he can't let that go. The rot in Big Al's paradise turns out to be his need for revenge on the Irish North Siders.

Capone says, "I want those Irish fuckers dead. They're pushing me hard. They stepped over the line when they damn near killed Johnny and they almost got Jack, too. Fucking cocksuckers. Ain't they ever heard of capitalism? What do they think, we're gonna lay down and wind up selling newspapers barefoot on the streets of Brooklyn? This is America, for Christ's sake."

On the train back to New York, Meyer says, "Al was a little strange, don't you think?"

"A little?" Charlie says. "A guy like Al believes his own bullshit. He's got no common sense. You seen how him and Joe A.

handled the Irish in Brooklyn. Big fucking showdown in a club. What is this, the Wild West?"

"We should consider gambling in Florida, though," Meyer says.

"Who goes to Florida?"

"Rich Jews," Meyer says. "We can expand to Cuba. It could be a good move."

The problem with this idea is Al Capone's presence. The local politicians in Florida want Capone gone but Capone is standing firm.

On February 14 all hell breaks loose in Chicago. A police squad car, gong clanging, pulls up to a beer-drop for Bugs Moran's mob located at 2122 Clark Street, in the Lincoln Park neighborhood of Chicago's North Side. Two cops and two men in plain clothes jump from the vehicle and take the garage by storm.

"Up against the wall," one of them shouts to the seven men in the garage. "Spread 'em."

The men scramble. Frank Gusenberg, one of the guys against the wall, senses something is wrong. He turns to look at the policemen. The cops have Tommy guns.

A German Shepherd named Highball, leashed to a truck's bumper, barks.

"Shut up, ya lousy mutt," one of the cops says.

Just as things begin to click in Gusenberg's mind, the guns go off. The men lined against the wall tumble to the floor like discarded flour sacks, cut down one by one. Highball howls from the blast of the guns.

Frank Gusenberg looks over at his brother Pete but it is too late for Pete. The strike has been fatal. Frank closes his eyes. The would-be cops march out from the garage and load into the idling squad car. The driver clangs the gong and speeds away through traffic.

Highball howls and barks and howls until a woman from the boarding house across the street sends a young girl over to find out why. The young woman nearly faints at the sight of the carnage.

Again, a police gong clangs, this time legitimately. Scores of detectives turn the Clark Street garage into a hotbed of police investigation. Highball is removed from the scene. Frank Gusenberg, still alive, moans. He is rushed to the hospital and stabilized then prodded for information. Despite the fourteen bullet holes that riddle his flesh, he refuses to talk. Three hours later, he is no longer of value to the police, his corpse shuffled off to the coroner and subjected to forensic analysis.

The examination of the bodies is routine. The police have little to go on but their suspicions. Their suspicions light immediately on Al Capone. Detectives interrogate witnesses. Six of the men are tied to the Bugs Moran mob. Police conclude the raid was a beer-distributors' rendezvous. The seven were mowed down in a frenzy of Tommy-gun rage. If the killers meant to murder Bugs Moran, they missed. Moran was on his way to the rendezvous but was running late. When he noticed the police car just outside the garage, he disappeared into a café.

Chicago makes the front page of the *New York Times*. Jack McGurn reads the list of dead men and fumes.

"Shit!" he rails to Capone. "I told the fucking Purples not to give the signal until they saw Moran walk in! He was on his fucking way! Goddamn hebes. Can't tell one gentile from another."

The Chicago Police Commissioner assesses the evidence and declares "a war to the finish." Gangland has yet to believe the Commissioner will do much in the way of cleaning up the streets.

Major papers pick up the story and run with it. The St. Valentine's Day Massacre is big news. Meyer follows the investigation in the *New York Times* and the *Daily News* while relying on a bottle of milk of magnesia to appease the gnawing in his stomach. Unlike Capone, Meyer sees the impact of outrageous violence on their business…and more clearly the more he reads. This event isn't going away any time soon. As days pass, the story gains momentum. Chicago police make use of the latest forensic techniques. Detectives are hoping for a break using the burgeoning science of ballistics. The story rises from the status of a war between rival gangs to that of public menace. Police everywhere are called on to enforce Prohibition with increased muscle.

Five days after the event, Chicago's Police Commissioner orders a strict ban on liquor.

"The lid is on," Commissioner Russell says, "and it is going to stay on."

The police car used in the massacre is discovered on February 22, when an accomplice to the crime tries to destroy the vehicle using acetylene. In the process of lighting the car on fire, he manages to badly burn himself and another man.

Jack McGurn is named as the leader of the execution squad despite his blonde alibi, which leads the police to the Congress Hotel. They can trace a call from the hotel made half an hour after the murder to Al Capone in Miami. Jack Guzik, Capone's fixer and trusted member of the "Outfit," as the Chicago mob is known, is identified as the caller.

February 27, Jack McGurn is arrested in Chicago. A sixteen-year-old kid is the witness against him. Newspapers relive the event with spectacular flourish with an aim to changing public opinion. Gangsters will no longer be shown journalistic mercy. They are proven to be stone-cold killers. They got what they deserved.

Meyer and Charlie meet on the shores of Coney Island.

Charlie says, "What are they killing, cockaroaches?"

Meyer smokes and stares at the surf. Wind whips his hair. His pant legs wag like flags. He ponders the massacre and its consequences. His rage is deep. It isn't the revenge but the way it was executed. The echo of Meyer's warning rings in Charlie's ears. No one will be able to walk the streets if the violence isn't dealt with soon.

Charlie says, "Al ain't just another guy on the street."

"This is bigger than Al," Meyer says.

Bootlegging is big business, run by men with little more than eighth-grade educations who are known mostly for their street smarts and who lack any desire or need to cooperate with others. Capone's blatant disregard for public decency casts a dark shadow across the entire nation. The guys that pulled off the massacre are known as "the American boys." Capone has culled them from different cities, none of which is Chicago. Anonymity is a gangster's lifeblood but this card has been played too often to remain a reliable disguise. Capone has put himself at the center of the government's investigation on crime. Even Buckner's man with a calculator couldn't have seen this coming.

Meyer lights another cigarette as his countenance drops and his mind wrestles with the question, "What now?"

"Al is nuts," Charlie says. "He's always been off. When I heard Yale sent him to Chicago, I just shook my head. Yale didn't stick around long enough to see the monster he created."

"He has to get out of the public eye," Meyer says. "Politicians sweep corruption under the rug. Capone needs a P.R. agent."

"It ain't so easy to clean up the reputation of a guy like Al," Charlie says.

"He has to look like he's reformed," Meyer says. "The coroner in Chicago is putting together a commission with Calvin Goddard. He's a ballistics guy that tied the bullet in a dead man's body to the gun in Nicola Sacco's possession. He's smart. This new science…they can connect a bullet to a gun."

"Jesus Christ," Charlie says. "Fingerprints for a gun. The boys need to make damn sure they deep-six anything used for work."

Meyer nods. The wheels are turning. The big picture expands and shrinks in fits of possibility. Their network is large, built on nine years of struggle and negotiation. Meyer hits the history books. He brushes up on Woodrow Wilson's Fourteen Points for settling World War I and then tackles the Treaty of Versailles. The Capone situation is tricky.

The wave of publicity surrounding the St. Valentine's Day Massacre grows. Capone bristles under the pressure and grouses over the lack of loyalty among those for whom he has done many favors. Charlie and Meyer make a trip to Capone's Palm Island home. Al takes them to his favorite haunt, Joe's Restaurant.

"They've got the best pompano," Al says.

They eat. They talk, nothing heavy at first. The weather. Fishing. Johnny Torrio's return to America.

"That old Fox," Capone mutters. "He took the easy way out, running off to Italy. I shoulda gone with him but I ain't that kinda guy. Johnny left me to take care of business and that's what I done."

They finish lunch and board the *Flying Cloud*. Offshore, they bob aimlessly on crystal-clear water. The soft chop that slaps the side of the boat, the balmy Atlantic breeze, and the memory of perfectly cooked fish calms Capone. Charlie opens the can of worms.

"This thing just ain't goin' away," Charlie says of the slaying. "We're all in this, Al."

"It's Loesch," Capone says of the president of the Chicago Crime Commission. "He's a reformer. Hoover put the pressure on him. He sent word. I gotta clean up my image or else."

Frank Loesch is an ardent crusader against, his words, the alliance between crime and politics. That puts him in league with President Hoover's command to quell Capone's influence and put an end to the kind of violence Prohibition has brought to American cities.

"You have to get the heat off," Meyer says. "Let the publicity die down."

Capone lets out a belly laugh.

"The public is fickle," he says. "They forget all the things I do for them."

Meyer says, "We're businessmen. What we do now will determine whether we stay in business."

"We?" Capone says, standing at the stern of the *Flying Cloud* and staring down at the seaweed threatening to tangle the propeller.

The massacre has changed Capone but not in good ways. He has nightmares. Something in his mind has snapped and that has him worried even more than the latest headlines that tell of police investigations tying the Yale and Marlow murders with shooters from Chicago.

Charlie says, "The best thing you can do is lay low, Al. Let things cool off."

Capone turns on his heel, takes the cigar between his chubby fingers, and points to Meyer.

"You've always been the brains," he says. "What do you have to say?"

Meyer says, "I have an idea but you might not like it."

"Spit it out," Capone says.

"Wall Street robs the people blind and nobody takes note. Brokers blend in to hide their crimes."

Capone bellows, "They got the lawmakers in their pockets! I got lawmakers, too."

Charlie says, "When the public starts squawkin', the government's got no choice but to step in."

"Tell me somethin' I don't know," Capone says, once again putting Meyer under his gaze.

"They're looking for a weapon," Meyer says. "Let them find one. Yours. A clean one, of course. We've got a judge in our pocket."

"Are you willing to do a year in the can?" Charlie says. "It would be easy time."

"Sounds like a lotta hogwash to me. The defense attorney called all that ballistic evidence tommyrot."

Meyer says, "They can match the weapon to the bullet they pull out of a body."

Capone says, "We need a crematorium."

Charlie says, "Who has time to load up seven bodies after they shoot them?"

Meyer says, "We have powerful mobs. We set the example, act like gentlemen in public. Our guys toe the line. Let the other mobs run amuck. Let them take the limelight."

Capone's mind sharpens to the task.

Charlie says, "All those greasers that got pinched in Cleveland laid low. They didn't make it into the papers after that."

Meyer says, "Loesch said you need to clean up your image, right?"

"That's right," Capone says.

"If you decide to take a year in the can, it looks like Loesch has cleaned up the city. Hoover can relax. Take the heat off."

"There's more," Charlie says, and turns to Meyer with a nod.

Meyer says, "You control the press. People believe what you tell them to believe. You tell them that you've reformed, they'll believe it. The common man just wants his booze. He doesn't want to know how it gets to him."

Capone gives Meyer the eye. He rubs his chin. The can. What if someone hears his screams in the middle of the night?

Charlie says, "We ain't tellin' ya what to do, Al. Just throwing around ideas. You spread goodwill around and in a year Valentine's Day will be all hearts and roses again."

"Easy for you to say, Luciano." Capone is tired of the discussion. "This ain't like the time Frankie sliced my face and Joe the Boss told me to take it like a man."

Charlie says, "This ain't nothin' like that. This is a lot worse."

They motor back to the estate and sit beside the pool. Palms sway overhead.

By morning, Meyer and Charlie are on their way back to New York.

Charlie says, "What was with that 'we set the example'?"

Meyer says, "Al's troubles are the tip of the iceberg. If the greasers in New York go at it, we're gonna have our own trouble. The whole country's been whipped up over the massacre. We're criminals. This is not a holy war we're fighting. When we have differences with other mobs, we need to sit down and settle them like businessmen. Why should we let this all go to hell? We've got booze. We've got gambling. We've got the wire. A year in the joint is nothing compared to losing what we've got."

"Easy for the guy to say who ain't goin' into the can."

"It's not personal. It's business. If we get Capone off the street, the public will rest easier," Meyer says. "We'll all rest easier."

Charlie gives him a look.

Meyer says, "Owney Madden's got connections with journalists. Al goes in. He gives a couple of interviews. Journalists will jump at the chance to make their career. All Al has to do is stick to the script. Then we bring everyone together. We can meet in Atlantic City. The place is empty in May. You can throw a rock and never hit anybody.

"We solidify our alliances and show our strength. Capone will think these guys are behind him, too. We make a peace treaty. Capone likes that shit. Present it like a bootleg conference. Don't tip our mitt. Bring in the top guys in the country. They can pat each other on the back. Then we'll know who is with us and who isn't."

"I gotcha," Charlie says. "These are the guys who will back us up when we wanna put the dons six feet under."

Meyer culls the fourteen points of Wilson's speech to Congress following World War I to fashion a gangster's treaty.

An end to all economic barriers between countries becomes the basis for maintaining open cities. With open cities, no mob becomes so strong that it can cut out all other mobs.

A readjustment of the frontiers of Italy should be effected along clearly recognizable lines of nationality translates into, let the Sicilians remain a closed mob. Likewise, all mobs retain the freedom to organize themselves as they see fit without interference from any other mobs or families.

In cities where territories are already defined, any mob that wants in must sit down with the controlling family and make their deal.

When a dispute erupts, "Don't walk out until you work it out." Those involved will sit down and hammer things out peacefully. And though wanton violence will no longer be tolerated, criminal justice will remain. Appropriate measures for infraction of the agreed-upon rules will be determined by consultation among mob bosses.

Articles of agreement begin to take form. Meyer and Charlie hammer out the details. Meyer travels to various cities asking each mob boss what he would need in an agreement if he were to sign. Mobs begin to line up. At the top of the food chain are Chicago and New York. Chicago becomes responsible for everything west of the Mississippi and New York everything to the east.

Meyer and Charlie begin to strategize the demise of the dons. They agree that a purge is necessary to clean out the defectors, but not a massacre. Each mob has the right to clear out the dead weight in true Machiavellian terms: only this once and then the purging is done. The signal will be the death of both dons.

"This is one hell of an undertaking," Charlie says. "Can't wait for it to be done."

"What makes you think we'll live through it," Meyer says.

Meyer calls Anne.

"Have you seen *Animal Crackers*?" he says.

"I've been busy," she says.

"It's at the 44th Street Theatre," he says.

"I know where it is," she says.

"Do you want to go?" he says.

After a moment, she says, "Why not?"

"I'll pick you up at seven," he says. "We can have dinner afterward."

Despite the Marx Brothers' antics on stage, Anne broods, mumbles under her breath. She does this more than once, which puzzles Meyer. Anne's usual playful wit has gone silent and Meyer cannot crack the code. They step outside into the cold night air.

"Where do you want to go?" he says.

"Somewhere with a good, stiff drink," she says.

The Grotto, where Jimmy Walker is already entertaining half of New York society, is a short walk from the theater. They settle in. Anne orders a Manhattan.

She tells the waiter, "Don't be stingy on the refills, either."

Anne downs one round. The waiter brings more. She toasts to Jimmy Walker. She toasts to Prohibition.

"Let's stick with toasting Israel," Meyer says.

Anne gives a soft snort. She rolls her eyes then stares at her empty glass. Minutes pass before she looks up and directly into Meyer's eyes.

"Shit, Meyer. I'm pregnant," she says.

Meyer's stomach turns. His mind goes numb.

The reception hall on the Lower East Side is nothing short of spectacular. The walls have been given a fresh coat of paint. The floors shined to a brilliant gloss. Tables, covered in white linen, fill the room. Long tables spread with a buffet of everything kosher edge the room.

Benny stops in front of a wall mirror to check his tie. Both he and Meyer have forgone the traditional kittle, a white robe worn over the suit as a symbol of purity.

"Why are we doing this again?" Benny says looking around the hall. "Oh, yeah, cause you knocked Anne up. Now we're both diving into the semblance of respectable men."

"There are no unwilling victims here," Meyer says.

Benny readjusts his tie again.

"There's cautious and then there's you," Benny says. "You're in a league of your own. You think Anne knows what she's marrying into?"

"You think Esther does?"

"She had me pegged from the beginning," Benny says. "Esther knows which way the wind blows. You can count on that."

The first of the guests arrive. The men greet Meyer and Benny with handshakes and slaps on the back. Women giggle slyly. The hall fills with noisy anticipation.

Anne and Esther enter the hall from a back room. Anne appears angelic in a white dress adorned with three rows of lace ruffles that fall from the waist. Lace covers her arms and a band of lace skirts her neck. She wears white stockings and white shoes. Her head is covered with white lace, cloche-style, tied at the ear and allowed to fall to the shoulder and back. It is simple by Fifth Avenue standards but brighter than most Lower East Siders can afford.

Esther wears her mother's wedding dress, something borrowed, a throwback to days in Eastern Europe, but not so much as to be unfashionable. The something blue is the garter around her stockings. Around her neck is something new, a simple pearl necklace Benny purchased from Tiffany's.

The girls cut through the crowd and cling to their soon-to-be husbands. The entire assembly migrates to the outdoor patio where the chuppah, a small canopy supported by four poles, has been erected. Meyer and Benny take their place under the chuppah.

The rabbi nods to the mothers of the brides and grooms. It is their job to come forward and break a plate reminding everyone assembled that, as Humpty Dumpty already knows, all the king's horses and all the king's men cannot put a broken plate back together again, nor a broken marriage, nor a scandalized reputation, nor anything else that gets shattered along the way.

The brides are escorted to the chuppah by friends and family amidst song and lighted candles. They circle the grooms three times. The rabbi offers a blessing that is sealed with the first cup of wine shared by the bride and groom.

This elicits a smile from the otherwise somber Red Levine. His mind wanders back to the first time the boys protected mevushal wine. Red never expected any of them would live this long but here they are anyway.

The rabbi offers a sanctification prayer.

Ring in hand and visible to the chosen witnesses, first Meyer and then Benny recites, "Behold, you are betrothed unto me with this ring, according to the Law of Moses and Israel."

They place the rings on the forefingers of their wives' right hands.

Anne feels a tickle in the pit of her stomach as the rabbi reads from the ketubah, the ancient marriage contract. The rabbi holds up the ornately hand-decorated documents for all to see. The ketubah assures the bride that her husband will fulfill his duties: procreative, protective, financial.

Seven blessings are required over the second cup of wine. The brides and grooms drink again and then a glass is placed on the floor and crushed ceremoniously underfoot by the grooms.

The crowd yells, "Mazel tov!"

The celebration kicks into high gear and runs late into the night, long after the newlyweds leave for their honeymoons. About midnight, Meyer and Anne step from their car into the cool sea breeze of Atlantic City. A white-gloved doorman at the Ritz–Carlton Hotel yanks the suitcases from the car while Anne takes in the ocean view.

"Welcome, Mr. and Mrs. Lansky," the manager says, stepping from the hotel. "We have prepared the Presidential Suite for you. If there is anything you need, anything at all, please don't hesitate to call."

Anne wanders through the suite. She flops on the bed. Opens the closets. Picks up the exotic triple-milled French soaps of lavender, chamomile, and honey. Runs hot water in the giant claw-footed tub then throws handfuls of pink sea salts on top of it. She drops her travel clothes in a pile and slips into the bath.

Meyer pokes around the suite. A mink coat is draped over a bedroom chair courtesy of Nucky Johnson, who makes his home in an eight-room suite in this very hotel. Nucky runs the city out of this hotel.

"Something for you," Meyer says bringing the coat into the bathroom.

"Where did that come from?" Anne says, sponging hot water across her shoulders.

"Never look a gift horse in the mouth."

He hangs the coat on the hook on the bathroom door and walks out to the balcony overlooking the ocean. Waves sway back and forth along the shore.

"I'm going to take a walk," Meyer yells to Anne.

He strolls along the empty boardwalk. A blend of carnival music and a barker's ballyhoo streams from the direction of Steeplechase Pier. A couple of hawkers in clown suits shoot the breeze in front of the two-story clown face with the cavernous mouth that forms the entrance.

Lucy the Elephant is on display next door, all six stories of her. During the season, dances inside run from 9 P.M. to 1 A.M. In May, the dancehall is still closed. Long lines of roller chairs wait for the season to begin. A photo postcard in a store window touts the pier's diving horse act.

Advertisements fill the sky. Lipschutz sells cigars. SHAVE YOURSELF, exhorts a message from Gillette Safety Razors. EGYPTIENNE STRAIGHTS CIGARETTES. ELGIN WATCHES.

Meyer heads back.

The next morning, the newlyweds rise early and head downstairs after breakfast in their room. The sun burns through the clouds. Meyer sees a familiar face among the few passing along the boardwalk, that of Owney Madden. Neither acknowledges the other.

Later in the day, Meyer and Madden huddle near a pile of abandoned fish nets and speculate what sort of reactions they will get from the guys coming to the meeting.

"Have you seen anybody else?" Meyer says.

"Yeah, a few of the guys are around," Madden says. "This place gives me the creeps, though. It's too quiet for my taste. A good jungle show would do this town some good."

Capone is the next to show up, along with his financial advisor, Jake Guzik.

"I heard we got company," Capone says. "G-men are sniffing around. Who tipped them off?"

"They won't find anything," Meyer says.

At the chowder house, Meyer asks Nucky Johnson, "Have we got G-men around town?"

Nucky assures him that Harry Houdini himself couldn't have broken through the town's security.

Anne is out for a walk, too. She stops to introduce herself to Nucky.

"Mrs. Lansky," she says, brushing her ring hand along the lapel of the mink.

Nucky says, "I'm very pleased to meet you."

"Kinda stinky around here, isn't it?" she says.

Meyer says, "The fishing nets are just below us."

Anne leans against the rail of the boardwalk.

"Wasn't that Al Capone I saw walking along the boardwalk? The entire hotel is gossiping about him," she says.

"Probably the whole town," Nucky says.

She says, "What do you think of our new president?"

"Hoover?" Nucky says. "Any guy that thinks he can rid the country of poverty is ambitious. I wish him the best of luck."

"You know what made Hoover so popular among the Jews?" she says.

"I have no idea," Nucky says.

"He promised them a chicken in every pot."

A hundred and fifty miles away, in a small restaurant in Little Italy, Al Mineo dines with Joe the Boss. The conversation is heated but respectful.

"You let Charlie go to Atlantic City with all those Jews?" Mineo says.

"What business is it of yours?" Joe says.

"How can anything good come from business with Jews?" Mineo says.

Joe puts down his fork and wipes his chin.

Mineo says, "Who am I to tell you what to do with your own men? I am nobody. You are Joe the Boss. You have made New York your oyster. It is no secret that Salvatore Maranzano would like the pearl inside that oyster. He calls to the Sicilians. If Charlie is steadfast, like you say, then he will not mind taking a loyalty oath. It is the way of men of honor with their underlings. Let the men show they can be trusted. The boys watch to see what kind of man you are. You deserve the respect of your men. This is what Salvatore Maranzano understands. All his men take loyalty oaths."

Joe says nothing. He finishes his veal and then orders dessert.

Meyer and Anne Lansky 1929

Chapter Fourteen
We All Sign on the Dotted Line

MAY 1929

The sun beats on the thick gray clouds that hang over Atlantic City. The clouds refuse to budge. They remain impenetrable, unyielding. The sixty-six thousand residents sigh. Business will not pick up until the sun fills the sky.

Anne dons her new mink coat. She and Meyer take to the near-empty boardwalk. Anne breathes in the magic of open spaces, and yet it's not without some unease. Manhattan, a city of seven million, offers anonymity. Here, walking this way out in the open with nothing to shelter her prompts the anxiety of exposure. Meyer seems unfettered by this discomfort. They have the perfect cover story, just another honeymoon couple out strolling the boardwalk.

Meyer holds his head erect as though he is on top of the world and runs through the moves that have gotten him to this moment. Charlie calls it the Atlantic City Conference, a gangster gathering of sorts that will, hopefully, tame the beast of street violence that plagues their business. Meyer has asked the right questions of the attendees. His propensity for understanding how far the criminal mind is willing to go in a compromise has served him well. "What do you want from our cooperation?" "What will it take for you to make a deal?" "What will break the deal?" "What do you expect in return?" The odds for dissatisfaction are greatly diminished when the endgame is clearly understood.

"A successful partnership is predicted by a good contract,"

Aaron Sapiro had said. "A good contract manages expectations well."

Meyer spent time visiting allies and associates in Chicago, Cleveland, Detroit, St. Louis, and Boston. Whenever Italians were involved, Charlie came along. The *Racing Wire* breathed new life into old negotiations. The massacre undermined deeply rooted beliefs on the subject of street violence. Meyer was quick to propose cooperation. His reasons run deeper than anyone imagines. He is not only interested in spreading a web of gambling connections across the U.S.; he has plans to make Charlie the man in New York. This is the beginning of Meyer's moves, a considerable undertaking, and he can't wait to get started.

The dominoes of a major conflict between Joe the Boss and Salvatore Maranzano have already begun to tumble. Old ways will give way to the new. The Atlantic City Conference is the melting pot that has the potential to solidify a sizeable amount of manpower. Success here means violence can be contained and the government can return to looking the other way.

Al Capone believes he is a major part of the new face of crime, organized crime, a business not dissimilar to Wall Street and the rest of American capitalism. He arrives with his boys from Chicago, which emphasizes the ongoing teamwork between Chicago and New York. The future depends on what happens here in Atlantic City.

Anne snuggles into Meyer's arm as they walk. The Loop-the-Loop clacks under the strain of a single car bobbing along the wooden track. At Abe Klein's delicatessen, Meyer sees Charlie and Vito Genovese talking shop over the remains of a couple of pastrami sandwiches. Meyer suggests a deli is as good a place as any for lunch.

A kid, maybe ten years old, slops a mop head around the gritty restaurant floor and then stops for a long, curious look.

"Keep your eyes on your work," Abe shouts.

While Meyer orders tongue sandwiches and near beers for him and his bride, Charlie and Vito head out to the boardwalk. A dozen girls play at the ocean's edge. Their jersey tank suits, stretched to the limit, catch the attention of the men on the boardwalk. Fortunately for all parties concerned, the beach censors are nowhere to be found.

Vito heads back to the hotel and Charlie settles into one of the many benches along the boardwalk. He spots Capone, registered here as Al Brown, in a pea-green suit and white fedora walking toward him, Jake Guzik by his side. Guzik keeps track of Capone's cash flow and has come to be known as Greasy Thumb Guzik for the way he greases politicians.

"I told ya he'd be here," Capone says, slapping Guzik on the back. Capone gulps in the ocean air like a fighter on the ropes. He tells Charlie, "I seen ya watchin' the broads. It ain't Palm Island but it ain't Lake Michigan either. Jesus, that water's gotta be cold. I hope they don't freeze nothin' of importance out there. My guys are lookin' to enjoy a little entertainment later."

He drops on the bench alongside Charlie. The bathers run from the shore and huddle in a small circle high up on the beach. They smoke and giggle and talk shop.

The youngest of the girls says, "One of the guys wanted me to put it in my mouth."

Her giggles are a transparent attempt to hide her inexperience. Capone edges closer to the boardwalk railing trying to hear what it is the girls are giggling about. Already he has his eye on one of them.

The redhead says, "That ain't the half of it, Sister. Some of these guys got requests you could never imagine. You'll get used to it."

Another of the girls says, "I heard about a dame that beat a murder rap cause her husband was insisting on a little cock-sucking action."

She is no more than eighteen and sports an infectious smile. Her hair color comes from a bottle of Nestle Colorinse left on too long.

The first girl laughs, "Who kills a guy over sex?"

"Swear to God," the eighteen-year-old says.

The redhead readjusts the contents of her swimsuit and then catches sight of Capone, who offers an approving nod.

Capone turns back to Charlie. "I ain't seen the Bernsteins. Are they coming?"

"They'll be here," Charlie says. "Meyer talked to all them Jews around the lakes."

Guzik, a Jew himself, nods.

Capone finds himself relaxing in the sea breeze. The peace jars him. He is still not sleeping well at night. The photo of the seven men lined up against the brick wall and machine gunned to death that graced the front page of the *Herald Examiner* haunts him. Headlines rage about a city out of control. In the early morning hours of May 8, three bodies were found on a lonely road near Hammond, Indiana. They were badly beaten and shot to death. The coroner had never seen such disfigured corpses. At first, the incident was pinned on the North Side gang as retaliation for the massacre, but a few days later, blame shifted to Capone. Word is that Tony Accardo, dubbed "Joe Batters" by Scarface himself, settled Capone's displeasure with three traitors. The weapon used? A baseball bat.

Meyer joins the group.

"The girls have gone shopping," he says.

"We was wonderin' about the Bernsteins," Charlie says.

"Haven't seen them," Meyer says.

Capone says, "If you will excuse me, gentlemen, I have some business to attend to."

He leans over the railing and shouts.

"You girls better get outta them wet clothes before you catch cold. I got a room full of towels and a pack of boys would love to dry you off."

"Showtime," the redhead says and the girls rise as one.

Capone heads for the President Hotel: six-hundred-fifty luxury rooms, indoor and outdoor pools, private terraces, Turkish baths, and service with a smile. There's no smile on his face, though.

"What's with the big guy?" Charlie says, not bothering to hide his concern. "He don't seem on top of his form."

Guzik hesitates. It's just the three of them and though he would like to dodge the question, everybody's future could be jeopardized by Capone's condition.

"The big guy is hearing voices," he nearly whispers. "Not just any voices. It's Bugs Moran's brother-in-law calling out from the other side. Maybe it's just a phase. But better you hear it from me than someone else."

Charlie exchanges a glance with Meyer. If Capone goes down, Paul "the Waiter" Ricca is the guy most likely to inherit the top position among Capone's mob, him or one of the Fischettis by dint of being both tough and Capone's cousins. Ricca will see to it that any deal formed under Capone will continue in existence as long as he has a say. The Fischettis, it's harder to be sure.

The Atlantic City Conference runs along informal lines. Negotiations occur as a matter of course in walks along the boardwalk, over hot dogs and beer, at champagne celebrations in hotel hot spots, while discussing the value of one whore over another, wherever the men mingle. Conversations boil over and cool down.

Roller chairs rattle across the planks of the Steel Pier. Theaters buzz with the promise of comedy and jazz.

Frank Costello makes sure Frank Erickson makes the rounds talking about the bigger possibilities with gambling. The big Swede wines and dines the idea of the countrywide wire service. He sees the plan the way most guys see the sunrise, a force of nature that shines on all men. He presents his ideas complete with risk, premium, and payoff, beginning with the twenty-nine racetracks scattered around the country.

"It's like this," he says. "Annenberg provides the racing news: charts, tips, workout reports, handicappers' selections, odds, past records, track conditions, weights, rider information. Whatever a bettor or bookie needs to know, the *Racing Wire* puts it in print. When a race is running on the East coast, everybody on the West coast can listen as the race progresses. It's great for our business. Win or lose, everybody pays the bank."

That's one news item. The other, the more important as far as Meyer is concerned, is the discussion about settling matters in ways that avoid violence. Charlie has brought his most powerful guys with him, as has Meyer. As agreed, their mobs set the example. They act like gentlemen. It seems to be contagious.

Capone asserts that he's cleaned up the botched massacre by executing the men responsible, Albert Anselmi and John Scalice. Apparently, Joseph Guinta was thrown in for good measure. The story goes that the three men were shifting their allegiance to Joe Aiello, that cocksucker. The brags John Scalice threw around Chicago before his demise made the story easy to swallow.

In a grand gesture, Capone agreed to allow Joe Aiello to ascend to the presidency of the Unione Siciliana. The illusion

Capone projects is that gangsters in Chicago now answer to a higher, saner power.

Privately, Capone tells Charlie and Meyer, "I took your advice, Charlie. I'm goin' away for a year. I got it all worked out. I gotta let the public see that I'm willing to let bygones be bygones."

The deals continue. Meyer brings Jimmy Alo to Nig Rosen in a more formal arrangement. At Meyer's suggestion, they set their sights on open cities, especially those on the West Coast: San Francisco, Los Angeles, and Reno.

At the end of the conference, Capone slaps Meyer on the back and says, "Son of a bitch, you put one helluva show together. I got a little show of my own coming up. Keep your eyes peeled."

Anne and Meyer enjoy dinner at the Breakers. The waiter brings a bowl of hot rolls.

Meyer eyes the menu. Anne orders soup with kneidlach, roast chicken, knishes, and candied sweet potatoes.

Meyer nods, "Make that two."

It's a postcard honeymoon if Anne can forget the image of Meyer standing next to Al Capone. But she can't. Tomorrow is life as newlyweds in New York City.

Capone climbs into the back of his touring car, Frankie Rio at the wheel, and leaves Atlantic City. Fifteen miles south of Camden, New Jersey, they pull off the highway and stop at a roadside diner. Something is wrong with the car or, rather, something is going to be wrong with the car.

Rio kills the engine and turns to Capone.

"Are you sure about this, Boss?" he says.

"I'm sure, Frankie," Capone says. "Now call Jack before I change my mind."

Rio hikes the collar of his coat and leaves Capone in the car with two bodyguards. He glides into the diner like any other Joe.

"You got a phone?" he says. "We got car trouble."

The waitress nods to the side door.

"Out back," she says.

He grabs a toothpick from the dispenser at the cash register and leaves through the side door. He calls Jack McGurn.

"We're dropping off the car now," he says. "You know where."

Rio reenters the diner.

"You got a commuter to Philly?"

"A couple of blocks north," she says. "You can't miss it."

Rio tips his hat and leaves.

"O.K., Boss," he says to Capone. "It's all set."

The boys head for the station. They take the commuter to Philadelphia. Once in town, Capone buys rail tickets to Chicago. The lag time between their arrival and departure affords a good excuse to scuttle over to the Stanley Theater to catch a movie. Capone pats his coat pocket making sure the snub nose .38 is in place. They walk to Nineteenth Street and Market.

The Stanley's overly exuberant marquee that covers much of the Market Street facade announces *Voice of the City* starring Robert Ames, who plays an escaped convict, and Willard Mack, the detective tasked with hunting him down. It is a story of betrayal and unlikely partnership. Capone laughs out loud. How much better can it get?

Rio buys two tickets for the movie. Capone looks out over Fourteenth Street and tells the other two boys to get lost. It doesn't take the two detectives long to show up at the theater. They flash their badges.

One of the detectives approaches Capone. There is no trouble. Capone knows what to do. He and Rio hand over their weapons. They are cuffed and driven away. Within sixteen hours of their arrest, they are sentenced to terms of one year each.

And then the show begins.

A four-page article in *The Literary Digest* quotes Capone as saying he had visited Atlantic City to sign a peace pact between him and the Bugs Moran gang. The article runs a fourteen-point peace pact on which Capone and Bugs Moran have supposedly agreed.

"Everybody signs on the dotted line," Meyer had told Al. "The fourteen points are bullshit, of course. You're not going to do any of those things. But certain things will need to be done to give the public peace of mind."

"What things?" Capone said.

Johnny Torrio had suggested giving Joe Aiello the Unione. The fight for power over the Unione was an insignificant war anyway.

"The violence on the streets is what's got everybody upset," Charlie had said. "Tame it down. Bugs Moran ain't got the stomach for war like he had before. Taking out his brother-in-law changed him. You can see it in his eyes. I ain't tellin' ya what to do but we got a situation that ain't goin' away anytime soon. It's this or the war goes on and the government steps in. G-men are already sniffing around. If we all agree to sign on the dotted line, then we all toe the same line. That's just good business. We agree to let bygones be bygones. No more revenge. We settle differences professionally. Get rid of the machine guns. We gotta look like businessmen. Your boys know how to conduct themselves. That's the important part."

"You have a wife and a son to think about," Meyer said. "A good boy, from what I hear."

"I idolize that kid," Capone said.

Charlie said, "Give him the life none of us got."

News of Capone's arrest spreads across the country. Charlie takes a copy of the *New York Times* to Joe the Boss. Joe sits behind his oversized mahogany desk considering the details of his rackets in New York. In his estimation, he has come a long way. With some bitterness, he knows his success is due, in no small part, to Charlie Luciano's bootlegging and drug running and he fears Charlie is growing too powerful.

Charlie sits in the high-back chair that faces Joe's desk. He passes Joe the newspaper. The headline reads: *Capone Enters Jail to Serve One Year*. The article reports the obvious. Capone was picked up for carrying a concealed weapon outside of a theater in Philadelphia. Capone has whined to the press that he has not "had peace of mind in years." Still, the paper reports, "The whole affair went off so smoothly and quickly that it left astonishment in its wake."

"Walsh was the judge," Charlie says. "They call him a hanging judge."

Capone gives a press interview touting a truce with the Irish mob. He says a peace compact was signed in Atlantic City. He connects the dots between himself and Bugs Moran. Chicago's liquor business will no longer be fought on the streets of the city.

Joe the Boss furrows his brow.

"What am I supposed to make of this," he says.

Charlie says, "Chicago isn't going to stand for no more gunmen. Al don't have no choice but to lay low for a while."

Joe says, "Capone is crazy. You can't fight no battles when you can't look your enemy in the eye. How is he going to help me from jail?"

"There's more than one guy in Chicago that we can count on," Charlie says.

Joe says, "It's all this Atlantic City business. What are you doing with the Jews, Charlie? Don't be quick to make bed-fellows with those not your own kind."

Charlie says, "The Jews are the best bootleggers. That's why we do business. I ain't never told you otherwise."

Joe looks at Charlie and worries. Maybe he yearns for the throne. Maybe Salvatore Maranzano has a point: the Jews have corrupted his Sicilian loyalties.

"I got a job for you. Bring Frank Costello and Joe Adonis back here," Joe says. "We got something to discuss."

Charlie nods. The cozy relationship he once enjoyed with Joe has gone sour. Charlie hikes downstairs to the alley where Vito waits in a parked car. The clouds overhead let off a drizzle that soaks the cobblestones and turns the dust on the car to mud.

Vito says, "Everything O.K., Charlie?"

Charlie says, "You know how these greasers are…suspicious of everything. We gotta find Costello and bring him back here."

By the time Charlie and Vito collect Frank Costello and Joe Adonis and make their way back to Brooklyn, Al Mineo has joined the party.

"I'm gonna make this simple," Joe says. "I'm giving you my blessing for this new setup with the Jews on one condition. You swear a loyalty oath to me."

Al Mineo lays a gun and a knife on Joe's desk and then stands off to the side like some altar boy assisting the officiating priest. Charlie does his best not to look surprised. Joe asks Charlie if he vouches for Joe Adonis and Frank Costello. Charlie nods.

"Do you vow loyalty to our family?" Joe says to Charlie

Charlie rubs his hand across his scar.

"I ain't one to criticize," Charlie says. "I always tell you straight. I'm tellin' you straight now. I ain't never done nothin' to compromise this family. No kinda ritual will change that. No kissin' the ring or cuttin' the finger or recitin' no words is gonna make me keep my word any more than I already keep it. And I don't trust nobody that says any different." He casts a glare at Mineo. "Either you trust me or you don't. I vouch for these guys that they'll be loyal. If they cross the line, I will deal with them personally even if it means takin' them out of this world. They're my responsibility."

Joe ponders Charlie's stance. He looks at Mineo, the rejected puppy.

"It's like a baptism," Mineo says.

"I ain't religious," Charlie says. "An oath don't change nothin' that doesn't already exist."

"I'm satisfied," Joe announces. "You know the penalty if you stray."

"I got it all straight in my head," Charlie says. "And you boys?" he turns to Vito, Joe A. and Frank Costello. "You boys understand the stakes here? You know if you ain't gonna be loyal it means somebody will be hunting you with a pistol and that somebody's likely to be me."

The boys nod in unison. Joe dismisses them all and settles back into his daily routine. He never cared much for rituals anyway.

Days later, when Charlie tells Meyer about the ritual, he repeats what he said, "An oath don't change nothin'."

Meyer says, "If it puts his mind at ease and takes the onus off you, what the hell do you care? Let him have his rituals. We've got business to do."

Jack Diamond flounders after the death of Arnold Rothstein. Rothstein elevated the schlammer, and deprived of the Big Brain, Jack is forced to fall back to his own uninspired level in life. He finds himself little more than a tough guy in a very nice suit. Losing the drug deal set him back plenty. His mob takes to hijacking booze to fill the needs of his club, the Hotsy Totsy, the sole remnant of his life with Rothstein. When that isn't enough, Jack moves the mob to Green County where they easily run over the local bootleggers like squirrels on a highway.

The Dutchman suffers a series of hijackings at his beer drops and blames Jack for the inconvenience. Jack ambles around Green County in a snit. He's restless. The Hudson Valley lacks the sophistication to which he has grown accustomed. He misses the nightclub and the action of the big city. He reads the bullshit story about Al Capone and the Irish truce and spits.

"No self-respectin' Irishman, let alone Bugs Moran, would ever agree to no peace pact with Al Capone, not after the massacre," he tells his boy. "All Capone has to do is turn his back and he'd find a knife in it."

He paces and plots. Miles and miles of the Catskills' rolling green hills stretch all around him, an island of green that holds him hostage. He feels marginalized. The insult to Bugs Moran becomes his cause. Jack wants, needs, to show the Jews and Italians that they were wrong for leaving him out of the negotiations in Atlantic City. He wants to punish them for their ignorance. Jack collects the newspapers describing the massacre and relives the carnage as though he was there. His laments fall on Moran's brother-in-law, James Clark, who was among the dead.

"What the hell? James didn't have a gang," Jack says. "Capone wants peace…What a load of shite. Come on, boys, we're going home."

He heads for New York.

On July 13, Jack swaggers into the Hotsy Totsy Club in a red-hot rage.

"Goddamn Rothstein," Jack says to his buddy, Charles Entratta.

"I shoulda been the one to put the bullet in him. Not McManus. Coppers. The whole family. I wonder how they're feeling now with their shiny badges all tarnished from this scandal."

Jack orders another round of whiskey, Bushmills, the only whiskey that comes to America on its own steamship. It's a proper whiskey for a proper toast.

He raises his glass and says, "This one's for you, Eddie." He gulps the shot down. "They just couldn't let you die in peace, could they! Goddamn bastards."

Eddie was Jack's brother. Eddie had tuberculosis. He was a lunger with a bad prognosis. The doctor prescribed Colorado, which proved to be nearly as bad for his health as New York. Driving through the country, Eddie's car was filled with over a hundred bullets. It was a miracle the bullets and the ensuing crash didn't kill him. He came back to New York to recover. In the end, it was the weather that finished him off.

A loud bang yanks Jack from his memories. William "Red" Cassidy is at it again. Adrenaline kicks in. Jack is on his feet. He won't tolerate the disrespect while honoring the memory of his brother.

"They'll let anybody in this joint," Cassidy says, his gaze boring a hole through Jack's mourning mood.

Jack, not the kind of guy to allow reason to get in the way, seizes the moment. He pulls his revolver and shoots. Cassidy stumbles and grabs for his own revolver. Cassidy's bar pal jumps from behind the stumbling Cassidy and fires at Jack. A volley of shots sends patrons scurrying for cover. Jack's partner, leveling several shots at Cassidy, pulls at Jack's arm.

Cassidy and his pal lie dying on the floor.

"Let's go! They're done for," he shouts.

Fifty people witness the event. When the police come around, nobody can remember much. Jack is indicted on a charge of first-degree murder in the deaths of Cassidy and Walker. Within six weeks, the club's manager and three waiters turn up in various parts of the city dead, riddled with bullets. By October, the authorities are still cracking down on everyone in the bootleg business. Jack remains in custody serving his time in the Tombs.

The phone rings in Meyer's apartment. It is early morning and Meyer is still in bed with Anne by his side. Meyer dons his slippers and pads to the living room.

"Hello?"

"You better come now," a raspy voice says. Vito Genovese. "I'll pick you up in five minutes."

Meyer hangs up, rustles through his closet, and throws on a clean shirt and tie and a lightweight suit.

"What is it?" Anne says.

"Go back to sleep," Meyer says.

"Another one of your gangster friends?" Anne says.

"Go back to sleep," Meyer says.

"When are you coming home?" Anne says, sitting bolt upright as she gathers the silk sheets and comforter around her legs.

There is panic in her voice. No one would guess she is six months pregnant. She lives on saltines and black coffee.

"Call your mother," Meyer says slipping on his shoes.

Anne is still screaming as the door closes.

"I don't want to call my mother!"

Vito Genovese is waiting at the curb. Meyer jumps into the idling car.

Vito says, "Charlie's had the shit beat out of him. It's bad, Meyer. Cops picked him off the beach, took him to Richmond Memorial. I got a guy up there now checking things out. Charlie wants to see you. He damn near had his head cut off."

Vito's guy, a bruiser named Harry wearing an orderly's outfit, waits near Charlie's room as the doctors tend to Charlie's wounds. Vito flags Harry down and the threesome huddle in the stairwell at the end of the ward.

Harry says, "The doc's still stitching up his neck. The cops are talking about taking him in on a grand larceny charge. They know who he is and they're hoping he'll spill his guts while he's still loopy. They're taking him to a precinct in Manhattan, a lineup. They want him to identify his assailant. And then they're gonna try for a larceny charge."

Meyer hands Harry a roll of bills.

"Don't worry about that," he says. "You get a place where he can lay low for a while. Don't let him go back to his apartment until we know who's behind this. Get something nice, a place where he can sit in the sun and look out the window. Get a doctor. Make sure he brings morphine. I want the doctor there waiting for Charlie, not Charlie waiting for him."

Vito says, "I know a broad, just the right type. Polly's broad. She's a nurse. She can pick Charlie up from the precinct."

Charlie is shuffled around from hospital to precinct to lineup. The police try but can't get the grand larceny charge to stick, as Meyer knew would be the case. They have no choice but to let him go.

Polly's girl takes Charlie by the arm and maneuvers him into a waiting car. Harry is at the wheel. He drives Charlie to a two-bedroom with a balcony and a view of Central Park. Vito and Harry carry Charlie to the bedroom where Polly's girl gets him out of his clothes and into pajamas and then into bed. The doctor checks Charlie's vital signs. Charlie is stable. The doctor hits him with a syringe full of morphine. Charlie goes out like a light.

Meyer looks at the angry slash on his neck and the gash on his face, both stitched neatly closed. He looks at the doctor.

"How long does it take to die from a cut throat?"

The doctor says, "Minutes. He's fine. Somebody didn't know

what they were doing, or Charlie was able to fight them off, but I'd guess the former. If they'd cut the carotid artery he'd be dead. Charlie would have been unconscious in about three minutes and dead a couple of minutes later. His cut is superficial. They missed the trachea, too. That's a good thing."

"Don't look superficial," Vito says as he tosses a newspaper to Meyer. "Page twenty-three."

Meyer reads the news and shakes his head. Charlie's beating lands on page 23 of the *Times*. That's not so bad. What rankles Meyer is the fact that Charlie is officially identified as part of the criminal underworld. It is an unfortunate turn of events for Charlie's anonymity, something Meyer was counting on as they make their moves with regard to the old Dons.

Harry brings coffee, and while they're gulping it, Willie Moretti stops by. He tells Meyer about Maranzano's new armor-plated Cadillac complete with a machine gun mount in the back seat. Frank Costello stops by. He tells Meyer that the reform vote is dividing between two candidates and that the split is weakening LaGuardia's chances for a win.

"Gentleman Jimmy will owe me," Costello says.

Polly Adler phones to see if Charlie would like another girl. Joe Adonis brings a brochure from the White Star Line just in case Charlie needs a nice, long sea voyage. Vito puts in a call to Lindy's for dinner.

"Steak and lobster," Vito says, "and whatever else you got. You know what Charlie likes better than I do. I'll be down to pick it up."

Charlie sleeps straight through dinner and into the next morning. Meyer sleeps on the couch. The doctor takes the second bedroom and sets up his supplies. By morning, Vito is back resurrecting his role as head cook. Harry makes the coffee.

"You look like shit," Charlie says, groaning his way through the living room.

"You're no Valentino," Meyer says. "Who did it?"

Charlie says, "A couple of mick cops. They gave me a helluva time, I'll tell you that." He looks at the nurse. "Honey, can you cook? Can you whip up some scrambled eggs? Maybe a little toast?"

"Sure, Charlie," the girl says and heads into the kitchen where Vito is already fixing breakfast.

Charlie says, "What did I miss?"

"Willie Moretti," Meyer says.

"What did he want?"

Vito pops two slices of bread into the chrome toaster on the counter and musters a plate of bacon and eggs. The smell of breakfast wafts through the apartment.

"The papers said you tried to bribe a cop with fifty bucks in exchange for a taxi," Vito says, handing Charlie an oversized plate.

Charlie tries to smile but the gash on his face won't let him. "I guess I did."

"They said you were picked up on Fiftieth Street and Sixth Avenue by three guys with guns who threw you in the back of a limousine," Vito says.

"They say a lot of shit," Charlie says.

Meyer says, "From the looks of it, they intended to kill you."

Charlie says, "They said they were looking for Jack Diamond. He's on the lam. Everybody knows that. They accused me of being in a big drug deal with him. Trumped-up bullshit. Jack Diamond is a convenient excuse."

Meyer runs a few theories through his mind. Diamond's shootout at the Hotsy Totsy Club caused a ripple to run through the police department. You can't involve fifty innocent people and expect the law to twiddle their thumbs in public. But that had nothing to do with Charlie.

"The cops were Irish?"

"Yeah, so?" Charlie says.

"Isn't it kind of strange that Jack Diamond is Irish and the cops were Irish? They know where Diamond is," Meyer says.

"Like I said, bullshit," Charlie says.

"You're lucky as hell," Meyer says.

"Is that what you call it?" Charlie says.

"These guys missed everything vital."

"I guess they ain't been to medical school," Charlie says.

Vito says, "Guys that been in the war know how to do it. I spent some time with a guy who was on the battlefield in Europe. You gotta pull the head back and cut deep below the Adam's apple, but you gotta be sure you run your knife clear from one side of the neck to the other. That's the way it's done. Lucky you were tackled by rookies."

"Thanks," Charlie says. "That's encouraging."

"Ain't nothing," Vito says. "The guy told me that cutting a guy's throat ain't the greatest way to kill somebody anyway. I know a guy, a cabbie, had his throat cut. He's fine."

Charlie says, "If they'd a wanted me dead, they'd a shot me. There was nobody around. These guys beat me hard. I don't remember much after that except wandering around and holding my neck to stop the bleeding."

Vito says, "How far was it spurtin'?"

Charlie wrinkles his forehead in disbelief.

"How the hell do I know?" he says.

Meyer says, "Can you identify the guys, Charlie? Could you pick them out in a lineup?"

"I don't know," Charlie says. "They jumped me from behind and beat me up pretty good."

Meyer says, "The Irish like to drink. Sooner or later, something will slip out. Alert our Irish friends and see what turns up."

"McManus has a brother in the P.D.," Charlie says. "They owe Jimmy Hines. Put Costello on it."

Harry says, "There's one lucky son of a bitch, George McManus. The only thing the cops can prove so far is that Rothstein's overcoat was in George's room at the Park Central on the night Rothstein was murdered."

"You know who was in the room with McManus the night Rothstein was killed, don't ya?" Charlie says. "McManus' bagman was there and two of George's brothers, Frank and Tom."

Frank works in the Children's Court system. Tom is a retired Detective Sergeant. If that wasn't enough clout, George's father was a highly respected Inspector. Retired detectives don't need anyone poking into the particulars of the night Rothstein was shot. Neither do the men in blue. Maybe that explains the lack of evidence.

Meyer says, "Jimmy Alo is tight with the Irish."

"That's right," Charlie says. "See what he can find out. If you don't mind, I think I'll get a little fresh air."

Charlie steps out onto the balcony. Birds hustle winter provisions. Pigeons wander the trails like panhandlers. A cool breeze sweeps through the apartment. The doctor emerges from his room. Vito nods toward the terrace.

"Mr. Luciano," the doctor says. "You have a mild concussion. You should take it easy and let your brain settle back to normal. Not to be a killjoy but you might refrain from too much activity during sex."

Charlie looks back at Polly's so-called nurse and says, "Thanks, Doc, but I don't think you gotta worry about that right now. All I want is a good night's sleep."

The doctor leaves a bottle of sedatives on Charlie's nightstand before heading back to the hospital. Meyer steps out onto the balcony.

Meyer says, "It could be that somebody wants to get you off the street."

"What for?" Charlie says.

"I'm working on that. Joe the Boss is making moves in Brooklyn. It's possible that some politician wants to neutralize him and tried to do that by taking you out of the picture."

"I don't know," Charlie says, barely more than a whisper.

Meyer says, "Things will fall into place as we go. Get some rest."

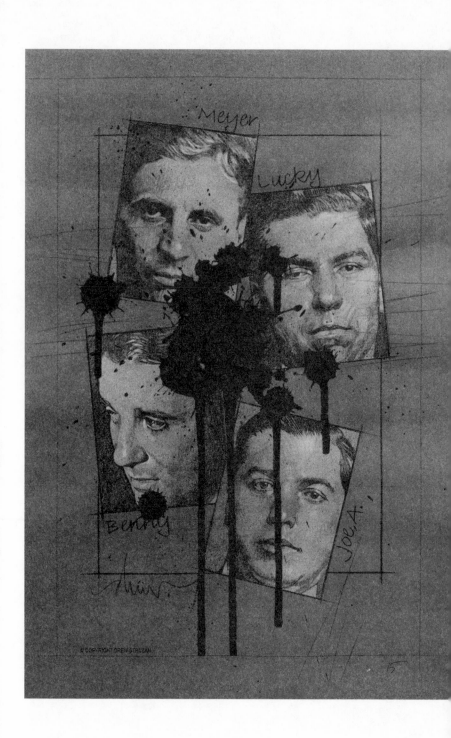

Chapter Fifteen
Let Slip the Dogs of War

OCTOBER 24, 1929

The alarm on the brass and Bakelite clock that sits on the nightstand next to Charlie Luciano's ear buzzes loudly. Charlie rolls over and silences the clock. The buzzing has stopped but his ears still ring. He rolls his aching body to the edge of the bed and lets his feet drop to the floor. He sits slumped over, head in hands, struggling to get his thoughts into today's game. The face of the clock shows it's two minutes past six. Charlie stiffens and rises.

An early-morning chill fills the room. Charlie pads across the red Chinese rug and closes the window, gently. Already Fifth and Madison Avenues swarm with clean-shaven, starched, determined businessmen. In the distance, Broadway's neon signs loom like hanging gray ghosts, reminding anyone who cares to look up that Manhattan is a city of the night. Nobody looks up. The Madison Avenue types focus instead on the gaping hole at Fifth and 34th where the Waldorf-Astoria once stood. The old Victorian has been flattened and hauled away amidst promises of steel girders and limestone walls destined to rise 1250 feet straight up to the clouds. The proposed Empire State Building will out-reach the Woolworth Building by almost 500 feet. Al Smith and the construction committee fiddle with the harebrained idea of putting a dirigible port on the top of the building.

Charlie draws the curtains to muffle the noise below and

block the intrusion of the rising sun. His head still pounds from the paddywaxing he took two weeks ago. His face remains tender. In exactly one month he will be thirty-two years old, middle-aged, running out of time to make his mark. He strolls across the room to turn on the radio, then sees that the clock shows 6:15. Charlie heads for a shower.

The image in the mirror is still something to lament. Black and blue bruises have given way to a sickish green, a color not dissimilar to the minty green of the sink. Charlie turns the hot-water faucet and lathers his face for a close shave. Until the stitches heal, shaving is strictly a personal profession.

He runs the hot water in the shower, grateful for the steam that fogs the mirror. He steps in and lets the hot water beat against the tense muscles of his neck. For a moment, he forgets about Frank Costello and their proposed meeting at this ungodly hour.

The clock shows 6:35. Meaning Frank Costello is at the front desk waiting for the doorman to ring him through. Maybe he already rang once, while Charlie was showering. He towels dry. Costello will just have to wait.

"Green," Charlie says to the face behind the fog. "I look like some kinda goddamn leprechaun."

He pushes the flesh around his limp eye. The knife that cut him went deep, cut something of consequence. Fifty-five stitches will never change that fact. He lets go of the swollen flesh. The droop returns. He slips into a pair of navy slacks and a starched white shirt.

The doorman rings the apartment.

"Send him up," Charlie says and sits in the chrome-plated metal-and-leather lounge chair.

The Murray Hill apartment is everything the ad promised and yet not so much that a man like Joe the Boss would feel threatened by his underling's success. Simple Art Deco design. He'd told the decorator to keep it simple. The bookcase at the end of the room holds exactly two books, one of them the copy of *The Prince* that Meyer gave him, and which Charlie hasn't touched since peeling off the brown paper wrapping.

Costello knocks at the door. He removes his fedora in a gesture of respect. Costello is a man of routine, pressed and buttoned down for the day's work, never late for an appointment. He steps into Charlie's apartment.

The cook hits the living room bearing a silver tray just as Frank Costello sits down. She pours two cups of coffee and leaves the men to their conversation.

"What did you find out?" Charlie says, handing a cup to Costello.

"You won't like it," Costello says. "Everybody's stickin' to the story pretty much the way you heard it. I talked to a lot of guys and they all have the same thing to say."

Costello has risen through Tammany's ranks, trained personally by the great Tim Sullivan, so he seemed the logical choice to find out about the cops that beat Charlie. The paddywaxing, which is another word for an Irish beating, went too far. There must be something more than graft or information on drug trafficking or even the search for a guy like Jack Diamond.

Charlie listens, emotionless, as Costello tells him everything Detective Sergeant McManus was willing to share, everything the Irish cops had let slip in locker rooms and over pints of Guinness.

"The cops see you moving up the ladder," Costello says. "There's somethin' in the air. The cops are being pushed to crack down on drug dealers. You got power in the city and that makes everybody nervous. That's why they grabbed you after Rothstein was knocked off. They got their eye on you."

Days after Rothstein's death, Charlie and a couple of his guys were picked up for questioning. That was before Charlie's paddywaxing. It was before Jimmy Hines arranged George McManus' fix, before McManus was arrested for Rothstein's murder and sent to the tombs to await his trial, before the pistol that flew out of the Park Central window was traced to St. Louis, before any real evidence had been neatly eradicated, before Arnold's wife and mistress began fighting over the disposition of his estate, and before Frank Costello came up with the campaign strategy that paved the way for Gentleman Jimmy Walker to keep his seat as Mayor of New York City, a valuable position that allowed Tammany to continue running its political organization the way it had always run things, by the scruff of the neck.

Charlie says, "That's all they tell you?"

"I don't think McManus knows the whole truth even if he was willin' to talk."

Charlie says, "We ain't takin' nobody into our confidence either. Anybody wants to stick their nose where it don't belong, you tell 'em that the police were looking for Jack Diamond and got a little overzealous. Got that?"

Costello nods, pulls on his hat, and heads out. The Plaza Hotel's barber is waiting.

Charlie pours another cup of coffee and watches from his window as Costello blends into the Madison Avenue crowd. The cook sets out breakfast on the dining room table. Charlie ignores it. After weeks of dining alone, he is ready for a change, green face and all. He pulls on a suit jacket. His dark brown fedora sits low on his forehead. Charlie flips up the collar of his jacket and makes his way downstairs and out into the swarm.

He has in mind a little diner near Times Square where working stiffs eat.

The diner throbs. Eager wage earners jam into every open space. They shovel hash and eggs using crisp toast and forks. They guzzle pots of hot coffee. Charlie spots a place at the counter and squeezes his way through the crowd.

"The special," he says, "and a cuppa Joe."

The hash slinger never looks up, never notices the green face. He scribbles the order across a white slip of paper that he then impales on the spindle in the pass-through. The short-order cook grabs the paper and goes to work, more hash, more eggs, crisp slices of bacon.

The chatter in the diner is familiar and soothing, idle chit-chat that fills the room with a humanness that Charlie finds comforting. People complain. Working conditions have not improved since the days Charlie hunted for a legitimate job. He studies those sitting numbly over breakfast awaiting the inevitable, another miserable day at a job they hate, and thanks his lucky stars that he has the backbone to rebel.

The hash slinger slops coffee into a clean cup, butters two slices of toast, flops it onto a hot plate next to a pair of staring yellow eggs on a little mountain of potatoes and beef, and delivers it all to Charlie, still with no eye contact, which is the whole idea of this place. Total anonymity.

Charlie jabs at the yellow orbs sitting atop the hash. The soft yolk spills down the side of the mountain. He shovels hash and eggs onto toast and regrets having sent Costello to do a man's job.

He imagines Costello in the Plaza, looking in the barber's mirror, satisfied with his haircut and manicure, making his way to the hotel restaurant where he'll sip coffee from a gold-rimmed cup and nibble delicate toast triangles spread thick with marmalade and a line of men will quietly wait to see him, each taking his turn to ask for a favor or present a sure-fire business opportunity. Costello will see them all, one by one.

Charlie drains the last of the coffee and makes his way to the nearest public phone. He drops a nickel in the slot and dials the number of the one man he trusts to keep a level head and a secret.

"Three twelve here," he says. "Meet me in ten minutes."

'312' is Charlie's code, the numbers that correspond to the letters of the alphabet that are his initials. C = 3. L = 12. 312. It comes in handy when the phone might be bugged or someone might be listening and he must get through to his contact because it is important.

Ten minutes later, Charlie and Meyer Lansky meet up a block from the Claridge Hotel.

Meyer says, "You're up early."

Charlie says, "Frank Costello."

Meyer raises his eyebrows.

"I gotta get things off my chest," Charlie says. "This is for the four of us. You and Benny, and I called Joe A. He's got a right to hear what I say. That's it for now."

They press through the morning crowd. The doorman at the Claridge greets them with a smile. Benny is at his desk when they walk through the door of their suite.

"Whose funeral?" Benny says, sweeping a pile of papers into a drawer.

"Mine," Charlie says. "Give Joe A. a call, will ya? Tell him to leave the broad he's with and get his ass over here. I think he's at the Plaza."

Charlie drops into one of the leather club chairs.

Benny says, "Big business, huh?"

Charlie says, "Who's in the back?"

"Nobody...yet. Just us weasels," Benny says. He pulls a Colt 1911A from his desk drawer. "Best goddamn example of self-loading stopping power the U.S. Army ever made. Whoever the cocksucker is, I'm happy to introduce him to John Moses Browning's rod. He'll be eating lunch with the devil."

Charlie says, "This ain't no call to action. Not yet, anyway."

Benny calls the Plaza. Shortly after that, Joe Adonis enters the suite. He looks at the solemn faces and drops into the chair next to Charlie's.

Charlie says, "I got one thought keeps runnin' through my brain. Why would a couple of micks work me over and leave me for dead just to find Legs Diamond? It don't make no sense. Narcotics squad my ass. I asked Frank Costello to sniff around and see if the Irish knew anything about that night."

Charlie paces the few steps between the chair and the window.

He says, "Who the hell wants me dead? I ain't got no beef with the Irish. I keep wonderin' if the Sicilians are the ones behind this somehow but it ain't like the Sicilians to use cops to do their dirty work. If they wanted me out of the way, I'd be dead. Who hires coppers? The only guy that comes to mind is Joe the Boss. These old Petes get nervous when you earn too much. They figure you're lookin' to take over. He made me and Joe A. and Frank Costello take a loyalty oath. It's that damned Mineo, I tell ya. He's got the ear of the Boss and he's whisperin' all kinds of bullshit into it. I could see that from the start. The guy's a no-good traitor to begin with. He snuck around to get Joe's permission to kill his boss then he knocked the guy off right in front of his whole family...two little kids in the car. What kind of shit is that?"

Meyer says, "It could be the narcotics squad. You get opium for Joe the Boss. It's no secret that Rothstein was bringing

heroin in to this country through his antique business and that
Jack Diamond was one of his distributors. You were cozy with
Arnold. And, at one time, with Jack Diamond. They picked
you up after Arnold's death, didn't they? Maybe they think
you really did bump off Arnold to take over his rackets."

"It's a good story," Charlie says. "But why kill me? They're
cops. Throw me in jail!"

Meyer says, "You're bumping up against the Rockefellers
when it comes to the drug trade. Maybe you don't realize this.
Why do you think there's such a big push to make opium illegal
in this country? Without opium to relieve their aches and
pains, the people have no choice but to go doctors and get
prescriptions. That's big business. Even Coca-Cola has been
forced to remove the cocaine in their drink. Think about it. Old
Bill Rockefeller was a flimflammer. In his early days, he bottled
raw petroleum and sold it as a cure for cancer. When that didn't
work, they called it a cure for constipation. I'm sure it was.
After that he got into the patent medicine racket. He listed
himself as a physician. Same old medicine, brand new label."

"Whadya mean?" Adonis says.

"It was in the papers," Meyer says. "The Bureau of Social
Hygiene went into business with the Division of Medical Sci-
ences for the sake of research. You know what they're devel-
oping? Narcotics. You know who's in bed with them? The
Rockefeller Foundation. You keep fooling around with narcotics you'll wind up dead, alright. Joe the Boss won't need the
Irish cops on the payroll to do it."

Charlie settles back into the big leather chair and lights a
Lucky Strike. This is all news to him. "I asked Jimmy Alo to
check with Johnny Dunn and Eddie McGrath to see what
they've heard, but so far they got nothing more than Costello
got."

"What about the cops that beat you?" Meyer says.

"They've been shuffled off to Siberia," Charlie says. "They're lucky I was laid up or I'd a taken care of them myself. Their captain knew the score. He sent them to cool their heels somewhere across the river." He looks at Benny. "You any good with that pea-shooter of yours?"

Benny laughs, "I put four bullets in a running target, didn't I? Is that good enough for you?"

Adonis says, "You really think it might be Joe the Boss?"

Charlie says, "These guys are always looking for ways to make you swallow your pride. You choke on it enough times, it changes you. You ain't the same guy you once were. I've had a belly full of his Sicilian bullshit even if it ain't him."

He gives Meyer the look. Benny shoves the Colt into his shoulder holster.

"I'm packed," Benny says.

Adonis gives a wry smile.

"I'm all for it but you do that and you won't live through the week," Adonis says.

"I ain't afraid of dyin'," Charlie says.

Meyer smokes and thinks.

"We just got this thing with Capone squared away," Meyer says. "Let's not give up the ship just yet. You've got that greaser in Brooklyn to think about, too. You kill your boss, you look like Mineo."

"That greaser in Brooklyn wants to get rid of Joe the Boss," Charlie says.

"Then we're halfway there," Meyer says.

"It's a possibility," Charlie says.

Meyer opens a window, allowing a fresh breeze to blow through the room. Benny waits for a sign that Meyer has sprung upon an idea. Adonis moves uneasily in his chair.

"I hate the cocksucker," Adonis says. "I'm ready to take him out."

"You want to wait," Meyer says.

"Here comes Clarence Darrow," Benny says.

"This ain't no monkey trial, Meyer," Charlie says.

"No?" Meyer says. "It's dogma against reason. You said it yourself, the Americanized guys don't like this bullshit any more than you do. They're the ones on the street risking their lives while these old greasers ask for more and more tribute. The Sicilians are dogmatic about family. They've got their rituals. They find meaning in their traditions. You can't set all that aside, the Italian fathers wouldn't trust you if you tried to get rid of their bullshit. But you can put it in its place. This is America. The question here isn't what makes us different but what do we have in common? We all want to earn. Get the Americanized guys talking about earning and you'll have them on your side. These old Sicilians are like a couple of bulls fighting for dominance. They forget this isn't Italy. Sicily may be the largest island in the Mediterranean, but that's barely more than the size of Massachusetts. Wars over territory are trouble for nothing. Cooperation is always better than war. Identify the guys that can agree on that and you'll know how strong you really are. The greasers never will because they don't stop to listen. Eliminate the head and the rest follows."

"How do we take out the head without starting a war?" Charlie says.

"Let *them* start the war," Meyer says. "You said yourself they're pushing for it."

"You said you want the violence off the street," Adonis says.

"When the Black Hand was making trouble, the police department created the Italian Squad. The law focused on the troublemakers. The greasers are the troublemakers. The law takes them off the street, we win. Now, who's stronger, Charlie? Maranzano or Joe the Boss?"

"I don't know," Charlie says. "The Cleveland meeting put a pretty good scare into Joe the Boss. But the old man is greedy. He's pushing the Sicilians for tribute and making plenty of enemies in the process. I'd say they're about even right now."

"O.K.," Meyer says.

"If Joe the Boss goes to war, I go right along with him," Charlie says.

"You have to be shrewd," Meyer says. "Whalen's got his secret police all over the street now. That's what Capone brought on us with Frankie Yale's murder. We've got to close the circle around us, keep things close to the vest."

Adonis says, "You know Maranzano drives around New York with a machine gun mounted in the back seat of an armor-plated Cadillac. He can make the Valentine's Day Massacre look like a schoolyard quarrel."

"Then we have work to do," Meyer says. "Who is with Joe the Boss?"

Charlie says, "Peter Morello and Al Mineo are his main advisors. They're strong but Maranzano is strong, too."

Meyer says, "If you're smart, you let the game get caught in its own trap."

The discussion goes for hours, then days. Meyer and Charlie debate the pros and cons of the drug trade. Meyer argues that drugs are bad for business. Who needs a war with the Rockefellers when there's plenty to be made in whiskey?

Time moves on. The green vanishes from Charlie's face and he begins circulating among the mobs again. He lunches with Peter Morello and Al Mineo. Then he dines with the Sicilians and makes inroads through conversations about honor, solidarity, and vengeance. A pattern of thought emerges among the men who embrace the ability to work the subtleties of diplomacy. As for the rigidity of Old World thinkers, Charlie makes mental notes.

Black Tuesday hits Wall Street like a bullet. The collapse of share prices puts the economy into freefall. The guys on the streets, always hungry, are now desperate to earn.

Brooklyn's waterfront rackets grow cutthroat. Vince Mangano, known simply as "the Executioner," digs his claws into the backs of the dock workers forcing them to pay a fee for work. He and the wannabe Caesar see eye-to-eye when it comes to kickbacks. With Mangano overseeing the docks, Maranzano can bring in more of his Sicilian paesans. The waterfront becomes his fief. He tracks the ships coming in and notes their cargo. His men redirect into their own trucks whatever strikes their fancy. It is a lucrative business that allows Mangano to grow in strength.

Mangano doesn't care to hide his hatred of Joe the Boss. Joe Profaci makes the rounds among the Sicilian fathers more as an opportunity to talk about his hometown of Palermo than to side with anyone who stands against the new Caesar's foe. Profaci is comfortable in his business. He has his men under control. His year in a Palermo prison, convicted on theft charges before he left his hometown, makes him happy to be in America.

"Why rock the boat," Profaci says.

And Maranzano replies, "Our honor is at stake."

Profaci soothes Maranzano's discontent with a dozen front-row Broadway tickets.

"Take your family," Profaci says. "Forget about Joe the Boss. The past is in the past. I'm a citizen of this country now. You should think about becoming the same."

Maranzano senses a prick to his Italian roots and decides he needs to step up his campaign for the old ways. He hears Tom Reina, from the Bronx, is unhappy with the moves Joe the Boss is making. He invites him to lunch.

Reina hails from Corleone. He arrived in America when he was ten and, eventually, took control of the ice box racket in the Bronx and East Harlem. He complains loudly about Joe the Boss. What had started as an alliance between him and Joe quickly descended into a troubled relationship. Reina has his own mob. Joe the Boss wants to dictate policy. Reina doesn't want the intrusion.

Reina says, "What have I to do with Joe the Boss?"

Maranzano looks over his demitasse espresso cup and raises his brow. The retort is obvious. We are Sicilians. We will not be conquered by anyone.

Ripples of the discontent roll across the East River and fall upon the ears of Joe the Boss. He bristles and schemes, thinking about ways to gain control. His solution is predictable. Sicilian pride must be broken.

Joe Bonanno, a young turk under Maranzano's tutelage, sizzles at the mention of Joe the Boss.

"New York is a volcano," he says. "One day it will erupt in his face."

Maranzano is pleased with Bonanno's insight. Surrounded by pistoleros, he and Bonanno circulate among the Brooklyn Sicilians. Maranzano talks about bringing the Sicilian fathers together much like the hierarchy of the Catholic Church, with him at the top, of course, as Pope, which not coincidentally means Father. In deference to Caesar, Maranzano cloaks the proposed order of his organization in military terms. Capo di tutti capi, which translates as head of all heads, is the top position. The boys on the street easily use the crasser boss of all bosses, a term Maranzano firmly rejects. A father is not a boss. His job carries the weight of counselor and protector. The capo famiglia is next in line. He makes all the important decisions for his family. Profaci would be a capo famiglia as would Vince Mangano and Tom Reina. The capo bastone is second in command in a family and is followed by the caporegime, or captain or lieutenant, who heads a group of soldiers. The soldiers are the lowest rank among the members.

All this is music to Tom Reina's ears.

Charlie brings the news of Maranzano's vision for the Italian unification to Meyer who scoffs.

"It will never work with one guy at the top," he tells Charlie. "He can try."

"And fail," Charlie says.

Meyer says, "He sets himself up for failure. One guy making all the decisions…and what happens when nobody likes his decrees?"

"He sends out soldiers," Charlie says.

"One more reason to hate the prince," Meyer says. "Never set yourself at the top. You instantly become the fall guy. The Jews have a better arrangement. We call it beth din. It means house of judgment. A counsel of men invested with legal powers in matters of religious litigation."

"A bunch of lawyers?" Charlie says. "The Italians ain't like the Jews."

Meyer nods.

Charlie says, "These guys fight to sit at the head of the table. This ain't King Arthur."

Meyer says, "Even if Maranzano wins, he loses. His ego has

carried him away. When he makes his move, and he will, the Jews will take care of business."

Just then Jimmy Alo walks into the Claridge suite.

Charlie says, "You got some kind of nerve showing your face around here." He turns to Meyer. "This bastard…last night me and Benny were at the Stork Club with a couple of broads, dancers, and we're workin' 'em pretty good. Jimmy, here, waltzes in with Joe A. Of course, we call them over to our table. A few hours later they walk off with our broads! Can you beat that? Those were our broads."

Benny says to Jimmy, "You guys stay in Brooklyn where you belong."

Alo laughs. "Forget those broads. I got a Broadway producer tryin' to get me to back his show, what with the market crash and all. I told him I'd give him the money if he can find half a dozen broads interested in a good time. He's gonna bring them around to the Stork Club tonight. You want to join us?"

"What time?" Benny says.

"Eight o'clock," Alo says.

"You came all the way over here just to soothe your conscience?" Charlie says.

"I don't need no enemies," Jimmy says with a casual laugh that disguises the true nature of his visit. "I got to talkin' with Joe A. last night. There's a couple of Irish guys I know real good, guys with connections with the Irish on the docks. These guys aren't lookin' for a fight but they won't run from one either. I'd like to bring Johnny and Eddie around sometime to see if we can work things out like gentlemen."

"Sure," Charlie says. "Bring them around."

He looks at his watch. It is a quarter to seven, just enough time to stop at Polly Adler's house to enjoy a little satisfaction.

✿

It is a short walk from the Claridge Hotel to the Grand Central Building where Salvatore Maranzano has set up a "real estate" office on the ninth floor. Meyer strolls through the terminal and into the building. The would-be Caesar has chosen to locate his headquarters where he can overlook Park Avenue and sit at the center of the web of tracks where trains arrive and depart, going well beyond the city of Cleveland and botched Mafioso gatherings. Grand Central is the gateway to the entire country.

From the ninth floor picture window outside the office, Meyer stops to take in the city. The people are as hard as the edifices they build: steel, limestone, brick, the building blocks of skyscrapers that dwarf humanity. It is no small irony that the Italian word for a very tall man is grattacielo which literally means "scraping the sky." Maranzano will not don a top hat to make him look more important. He has purposefully located himself at the hub of Manhattan to make that statement. If it were possible, he would try to take over the world. The hubris of the man drives Meyer's determination to make sure he doesn't.

November 4, 1929, exactly one year to the day since Arnold Rothstein was shot and killed by George McManus. Arnold's father kneels over his son's grave and prays for the magnification and sanctification of God's name. He has in mind the words of Ezekiel and the vision of God coming to save his children, Israel, in a fury of pestilences and rage.

"My son," he says to Arnold's decaying bones. "I pray you have put repentance in your heart, that you might be released from your Gehinnam into His mercy." He raises himself slowly to his feet and rests his hand on the tombstone. "The trial of your killer starts on the eighteenth. If you are in Olam Ha-Ba, this farce will mean nothing. But if you are thinking about coming back to this life and starting over, I say to you, go with Him."

Abe the Just mourns and hopes that God sees the sincerity in his heart.

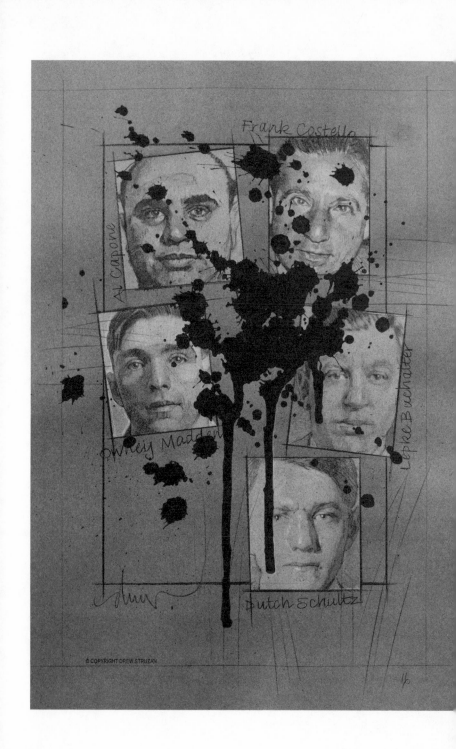

Frank Costella

Al Capone

Lepke Buchalter

Owney Madden

Dutch Schultz

1/6

Chapter Sixteen
In Vino Veritas

NOVEMBER 1929

The Puncheon Grotto, known simply as "No. 42" among the regulars, is smack in the middle of the piece of land where John D. Rockefeller Jr. intends to build a new opera house for the Metropolitan Opera.

Jack Kriendler and Charlie Berns, who own the Puncheon Grotto, grumble and hit the streets. They have been promised eleven thousand dollars if they will break their lease and move on.

"Do you think this thing with Wall Street is going to bust us, too?" Jack says.

Charlie Berns stuffs his hands in his coat pockets. Charlie has a bookish look, round face, thinning hair, dark-rimmed glasses. His look suits the financial end of the club. Jack, on the other hand, pours on the showmanship. The cousins have carefully built their clientele from New York's upper crust. They've come a long way since the days of the Red Head in Greenwich Village, which drew in the rowdy college crowd. A year later, they left the Village to open the Club Fronton at 88 Washington Place. Three years later they left Washington Place to open at 42 West 49th Street. And now they've got to move on.

"Do I look like I have a crystal ball?" Charlie Berns says. "I'll tell you one thing, people are going to need a drink now more than ever."

Broadway's neon signs make a hazy appearance in the mist that shrouds the city. They trudge to potential locations within walking distance. They want to see what these places look like at night, the way their customers will see them when the Puncheon closes its doors. They reject several before finding one that looks promising at 21 West 52nd Street. 21, 42—they can only hope the new club isn't just half the success the old one was.

They head back to the Puncheon to break the news to their customers. The regulars are unhappy. But Jack and Charlie accept their fate. You can't stand up to a Rockefeller and win. The Puncheon Grotto will be rubble, a mere anecdote of Prohibition, and Rockefeller's center will be born.

Charlie Lucky, not to be confused with Charlie Bern, steps from his Murray Hill apartment building right around midnight. The drizzling rain has cleared and given way to a black canopy studded with pinpricks of light.

"Taxi, Mr. Ross?" the doorman says.

Charlie looks around. It is a good three miles to Joe the Boss' penthouse. That's how far up in the world Joe has moved, twenty minutes by cab, an hour on foot.

"It's a good night for a walk," Charlie says.

Charlie heads north on Park Avenue. At Times Square, he hits a glut of mink and ermine. The Broadway crowd disperses into the local speakeasies like hungry vultures scenting a kill. Charlie stops to light a cigarette. This is his country, his realm. He knows what it takes to keep a good business going. He rubs the scar on his face and doesn't feel so lucky.

A month has passed and still he wonders who, besides the Irish cops that beat him, could be behind the trouble. His head swirls with rage. Maybe Meyer is right about the Rockefellers.

Maybe the drug trade isn't worth the risk. Or maybe the Rock-efellers are completely innocent. He laughs at that joke. Maybe Joe the Boss is to blame. Maybe Joe doesn't like his underling's strength or cash flow. Or maybe Al Mineo has been whispering sweet nothings about Charlie into the Boss' ear, triggering an ancient response. Keep 'em hungry and you keep 'em working for you. Loyal. Anything less and you take them out. Whatever the truth, Charlie doesn't need or want the trouble he has earned from the publicity.

He shakes off the illusion that he will ever know the truth and starts enumerating the men standing in the way of his success. Before he finishes, he is at the uptown apartment of Joe the Boss.

Charlie boards the elevator.

"Penthouse," Charlie says.

"Yes, sir."

The vestibule where the elevator boy deposits Charlie is filled with the nutty aroma of opium. Charlie knocks on the door. Joe's manservant, a burly guy with the manners of a Hun, ushers him in.

Charlie wades through smoke-filled rooms littered with Joe's guests who are stupefied beyond redemption. The man-servant sees Charlie to the balcony where Joe stands over-looking Central Park. He sips wine from the old country and pats himself on the back for his success. His rackets cover Manhattan like a dragnet. At fifty and still alive, he figures he is strong enough to demand the respect of the Castellam-marese. The Upper 80s, as these blocks of the Upper West Side are known, harbor the warm glow of insulated arrogance.

Joe gestures to his guests. Manhattan's finest have come to enjoy the party favors of the man in the penthouse. The rich and powerful sprawl across couches and lounge on chairs. They scoop Beluga caviar with small mother-of-pearl spoons onto perfectly toasted bread and sip Russian vodka, then wash it all down with an opium chaser.

Joe says, "You want to chase the dragon?"

"I gave it up for Lent," Charlie says.

"Lent is a long way off," Joe says. "Maybe a glass of wine? In vino veritas, Charlie. Your face is healing nicely. How is the neck?"

Charlie shrugs.

Joe waddles from the balcony to his private office. Opium paraphernalia is spread atop his heavy oak desk.

Joe barks, "We're expanding the opium business. Make sure we have plenty of men on the street. The Jews don't own the trade anymore."

"You mean Arnold Rothstein?" Charlie says.

"If that's the dead guy, that's who I mean," Joe the Boss says. "You see these people? They can afford whatever they want and what they want is opium."

"And whiskey," Charlie says.

"Yes," Joe says. "Whiskey and opium are good bedfellows, eh? With that kind of business, a man can control the world. I see by the look on your face you don't approve. I don't need nobody telling me which way the wind blows. That's high society out there, not a bunch of Lower East Side bums. We give them what they want."

Joe opens a silver container that holds the opium paste. The lid is decorated with the yin-yang motif and the cartouche on the side, as Joe points out, reads "Good Luck" in Chinese. Joe pokes at the paste with a long needle and withdraws a pea-sized ball which he holds over the flame of an opium lamp. The opium bubble swells and turns golden. Joe stretches the gooey mass into long strips and continues to cook it over the lamp.

When it reaches the right texture, he rolls it back into a ball and then jabs the little ball into the bowl of a bone pipe carved with the figures of two dragons chasing each others' tails. He takes a deep pull and then extends the pipe to Charlie. Smoke swirls through the room. The heady aroma beckons Charlie back to a long, lost dream.

Charlie shakes his head.

Joe says, "Opium is the gentleman's choice. We sell opium to gentlemen and heroin to the bums in the ghetto. Get 'em hooked. Who's gonna care about one less foot-dragger?"

Charlie says, "I ain't gonna smoke with you tonight, Joe."

Joe takes the tray, the paraphernalia, and lamp to a side table next to a lounge chair. He sprawls and heats the opium and puffs on the bone pipe.

"In vino veritas," Joe says. His small laugh sounds curdled. "What are you afraid of, Charlie? What you might say? Don't worry, there is no truth in wine or opium. Only escape. People smoke to run away from truth. They numb their senses and fill their minds with beautiful lies. But we know the truth, Charlie, you and me. We know the truth and we live with it."

Charlie says, "Whether we live or die has nothing to do with truth."

"Remember what I told you," Joe says, his face pinched suddenly into a mask of impatient command. "We are expanding our operations. Take care of it."

Joe waves Charlie off and takes another pull on the pipe. Charlie watches Joe fade into the dragon's dream and then slips from Joe's apartment. He walks the paths in Central Park. It takes nearly an hour to lose the stench of Joe's demands. After the long walk in the cold of the park, Charlie heads to the automat to appease the rumbling in his stomach. The great wall of little windows beckons with servings of mashed potatoes, creamed spinach, baked ham, chopped steak, coconut pie. The place buzzes like the zoo on a Saturday afternoon. Ever since the market fell, stockholders with empty palms have left off the high-end eateries in favor of the lowly automat. No shame here.

Charlie rummages for a handful of nickels and lays claim to a bowl of clam chowder.

Meyer strolls through the front door and straight to the dessert section. He slides his loose change into the slot and takes a custard pudding. On second thought, he buys one more. He looks around for a table and sees Charlie.

Charlie says, "What are you doing here?"

Meyer says, "She's got a craving."

Meyer drops into a chair. His eyes are bloodshot.

"Women," Charlie says with a chuckle.

"What would you know?" Meyer says. "Whores don't have babies."

"They're women, ain't they? Lots of broads get knocked up. You don't gotta marry them."

Meyer enjoys a cigarette. He grabs the spoon next to Charlie's coffee cup and dips into the custard.

"You have to do the right thing," Meyer says.

"Yeah," Charlie says. "Coffee?"

"Sure," Meyer says, throwing a handful of nickels on the table. It's going to be a long night.

The coffee is hot and fresh. Charlie sinks three spoonfuls of sugar into his cup.

He says, "I seen Joe the Boss tonight. He wants to expand the drug business. I got no choice but to do what he says."

"You always have choice," Meyer says. "You just don't like the consequences."

"Dead ain't a consequence," Charlie says. "It's a condition."

Meyer says, "Guys came back from the war hooked on the stuff. That's what made it popular. You've seen hoppies. Nobody wants that in their life. You've seen enough kids ruin their lives. What kinda guy wants to encourage that? Walk away. There are plenty of other guys willing to take the risk. I'm telling you, Charlie, the politicians are turning the public against the stuff."

"Didn't you hear what I said?" Charlie says. "You gotta understand one thing, even among the Italians, dealing drugs is frowned on. It's considered low class. The old greasers won't have nothing to do with the stuff. Joe ain't like that. You should hear the old greasers run him down."

"So, that's your answer," Meyer says.

"What was the question?" Charlie says.

"Sooner or later you're gonna have to get out from under this guy. From what you've been telling me, the deck is getting stacked against him. What's the lineup, Charlie? Who's with him and who's against him?"

"Tom Reina is against him, that's for sure," Charlie says. "He told me Salvatore Maranzano has set up a war chest and is looking for contributions."

"The wannabe Caesar wants a war?" Meyer says, almost delighted.

"If you were in his shoes, wouldn't you?" Charlie says.

"Do they have enough strength?"

Charlie shrugs. In his earlier estimation of his enemies, he hadn't looked at opposition in quite this way. Meyer pushes the empty custard bowl to the side of the table. He sits back and downs the last swallow of coffee. This could be the chance for which he's been waiting. The war will take more than strength; it will take wits.

Charlie runs through the Italian split.

"Maranzano is at the top of the heap in Brooklyn these days. Guys like Mangano and Profaci will side with him. Mangano is nothing. He has no choice but to go with Maranzano. He doesn't have the strength to stand on his own. Profaci is another story. He has his own business and don't want no partners muscling in on his business. He will throw some money at Maranzano's war chest but he won't stand up and start a fight with Joe the Boss. Joe the Boss has a couple of guys on his side. Carlo Gambino follows Al Mineo around like a puppy. And there are others. Maranzano is gonna have to have a pretty good plan before he makes any moves."

"And Chicago?" Meyer says.

"Capone considers himself Joe's ally," Charlie says. "But there's plenty of Sicilians in Chicago that don't like Joe *or* Al. And there's Cleveland and Detroit. Joe wants to exert his influence over these guys but they don't want nothin' to do with him."

Meyer listens. The Cleveland Mafia meeting had taken Meyer by surprise. The Americanized guys on the street never think twice about the old dons because the dons are strictly neighborhood thugs. The Cleveland meeting exposed their ambition to expand and their ability to organize.

Charlie says, "I'll tell you what's gonna happen. Masseria can't afford to let this little Caesar get too strong. Caesar wants the whole shebang. Joe will have to show he has superior strength."

"Then Joe will have to strengthen those around him," Meyer says. "That's good for us."

Charlie's web is made up of powerful guys with small but tough mobs. Adonis has forty, maybe fifty guys around him. Costello, with the help of Willie Moretti, has carved out a space in the Bronx. Vito Genovese and his boys go wherever Charlie goes. All these guys see Charlie as a fair dealer. They will muster around him if there is trouble, as long as they believe he has a good chance of coming out on top.

The war over New York's rackets is like a game of chess. The pieces line up. The pawns are organized to protect the big guys behind them.

"Trap the king," Meyer says.

"What?" Charlie says.

Meyer gives Charlie a quick chess lesson. Control the center. Develop your pieces. Protect your king. Castle quickly. In the process, give your opponent's king no way out. Checkmate.

"I haven't seen Jimmy Alo around," Meyer says.

"That's cuz he's on the lam," Charlie says. "One of his guys was in the can. He went to visit the guy. Next thing the cops know, the guy's got a gun."

"I see," Meyer says. "I know a lawyer."

"Jimmy ain't gonna want to go back to the can. I can't ask him to do that."

"I'll see what can be done. Then we'll ask Jimmy what he wants to do," Meyer says.

"You need him for something?" Charlie says.

"You need him," Meyer says. "You're gonna need the Irish, maybe not today or tomorrow, but soon."

Meyer scans the automat. The crowd has dissipated. The lonely corner where they have been sitting and discussing the politics of mob life is all the lonelier. Charlie stacks his empty plates. Meyer notices Anne's neglected bowl of custard.

"Stalemate," he says glancing at his watch. "I'll never hear the end of this. Call me in the afternoon. I'll know the score for Jimmy by then."

❋

Jimmy "Blue Eyes" Alo is biding his time in Westchester where he enjoys a good relationship with the local sheriff. Jimmy distributes beer and runs the numbers racket. No one in Westchester would know that the NYPD is looking for him for questioning.

Charlie and Meyer drive out to Westchester and meet Jimmy outside of town. They take Jimmy's Chris-Craft runabout for a trip to Long Island Sound and stop at David's Island. The usual steamboat excursions are closed for the season. The shore is abandoned. They wander the grounds and poke their noses into the buildings of Fort Slocum that once tended the wounded during the Civil War.

Meyer fills Jimmy in on the goings on in the city. He asks about Jimmy's business in Westchester. Jimmy laughs. Business is good. He and Eddie McGrath keep the flow of booze running smoothly. Everybody is happy.

Meyer says, "We'd like you to come back to the city."

Jimmy swallows hard and looks at Charlie.

Charlie says, "I told Meyer about your trouble."

Jimmy looks at Meyer who stands calmly, carefully weighing his words in the afternoon breeze.

"Charlie and I have been talking. We're going to be making some moves. We'd like your help."

Jimmy sighs in relief.

"Whatever you need," Jimmy says.

"It might not be that simple," Charlie says. "We got a greaser war brewing."

"That ain't nothin'," Jimmy says. "My guys are your guys."

Charlie says, "What about the Irish? There's a lot of ill will between Italians and Irish."

Jimmy says, "That's common knowledge."

"But they respect you," Meyer says.

"Yeah, I guess they do," Jimmy says.

"Can we count on the Irish to back us up when we move?" Meyer says.

Jimmy is quiet. It is a big question. The answer is uncertain.

Meyer says, "We want to bring you along. We think you can influence the Irish, identify those who will cooperate. Your case isn't as bad as it looks on the surface. I spoke with a lawyer and he thinks he can get you off. At the worst, you'll do a year."

Jimmy bristles, "I don't need a repeat performance in Dannemora. I'll be moving up the ladder with two strikes. One more and I'm gone for life."

Charlie says, "They can't prove you slipped the gun to the guy in the can. You got that on your side."

Jimmy says, "They can indict a ham sandwich."

Jimmy isn't so much a cynic as he is a realist. At twenty-three, he is no stranger to hard time and the assaults that brings into a kid's life.

Meyer grabs a cigarette and looks out at the Hudson River.

Meyer says, "Your parole officer is looking for you. The PD is looking for you."

Jimmy says, "I'd like to work with the Irish but I ain't lookin' for no bum's rush."

"You had a concealed weapon. That's a violation of the Sullivan Act. That's a one-year sentence. The lawyer is sure he can get you off especially since you can't be forced to testify against yourself. That's in the Constitution, the Fifth Amendment."

Jimmy says, "They had the priest come to me when I was in the can before. Wanted me to turn in my associates. I told him to go fuck himself. Fucking Siberia up there in the winter."

He gives a long, dark gaze. The memory of his prison life still haunts his daylight hours.

Jimmy says, "What if the other guy talks?"

Meyer says, "There's a law in New York. Nobody involved in a crime can testify against any other party that was involved in the same crime. If he does, and they try to use the evidence, you're free on a legal technicality because they violated your rights."

"Never stopped them before. Where'd you hear that?" Jimmy says.

"A good lawyer," Meyer says.

Charlie says, "You can trust Meyer. We ain't telling you what to do. You gotta do what you think is best. If you want to come along with us, then you gotta go back to New York and straighten things out with your parole officer. That means you're gonna get picked up for questioning. Our lawyer will go along with you, make sure your rights are not violated. Listen to him. He will make sure they don't trick you into saying anything that will incriminate you."

"You had a concealed weapon?" Meyer says. "Maybe the guy in the can is an excellent pickpocket. Maybe somebody else got the pistol and gave it to the guy. Whatever they think happened is all speculation on their part. They can't prove a thing."

Charlie says, "If they can give a guy like Al Capone just one year on a weapons charge, think of how easy it will be for you."

"I had a gun when I robbed the jewelry store," Jimmy says.

"Having a gun is not the same as conspiracy," Meyer says. "With the right judge, you may not do any time. Like Charlie said, we're not telling you what to do but we would like to use you when we make our moves. Can you do a year?"

Jimmy says, "Standing on my head," but he doesn't sound like he likes the idea. What ex-con would?

Charlie says, "Take a couple of days to think about it. If you want to go through with it after that, call me and let me know when you're coming into town. We'll set you up with the lawyer."

They board the Chris-Craft and motor back to Westchester looking much more like tourists than gangsters. Charlie and Meyer bid Jimmy goodbye.

Election Day in New York draws near. The theatrics continue to play themselves out. Fiorello waves his hat and promises food, housing, schools, parks, and sunlight. If he is elected, he will rid the city of dirty politics and focus on the corruption of Tammany Hall. And then he criticizes Jimmy Walker's wardrobe. Jimmy Walker disregards the Little Flower's allegations. He struts around Broadway entertaining the crowds with song. The crowds applaud. It's what New Yorkers do.

When the vote comes in, Jimmy Walker walks away with 865,549 votes. LaGuardia garners a mere 368,384. It is a clear victory for Beau James Walker, who is sworn in as mayor for another term, and for Frank Costello, who helped him get there.

With the election finished and Gentleman Jimmy back in the seat of power, the McManus trial gets underway. The case of Jimmy Alo is small potatoes by comparison.

Alo decides to take Meyer and Charlie's offer. He calls Charlie and reports to his parole officer. He hands the guy a cock-and-bull story that, for some reason, the guy accepts. Jimmy wonders if he was bought off or just resigned to the fact that more powerful men than him will make the choice about what to do with Jimmy Alo.

The lawyer sits by Jimmy's side while he is questioned by the police. In the end, they concede there is no case. The book is closed, the event over. Jimmy Alo stands a little taller. He calls the redheaded Eddie McGrath.

"We gotta talk," Jimmy says.

The East Village fills with drunken joy emanating from McSorley's Ale House. Eddie McGrath and Jimmy Alo head into the bar to join the rowdy celebration. It's Johnny Dunn's birthday. Eddie throws his arm around Jimmy's shoulder.

"Come on," he says. "This is a great day. You want the Irish with you, you gotta become Irish. Let's get inside before all the real beer is gone."

A sign posted on the wall reads: "Good Ale, Raw Onions, No Ladies."

Jimmy looks at Eddie dubiously.

"The fellas think more of speaking freely than making love when they got a belly full of beer," Eddie says.

A Rockefeller Christmas couldn't be any sweeter than the environment in the Ale House. Kettles of soup simmer on the potbellied stove. A sea of inebriated brawn sways between the pub's long, narrow walls. The atmosphere is as raw as the onions.

The boys steer to a back table where Johnny has already been celebrating. Eddie signals to the bartender for more beer. A waiter loads a tray and whisks it to the table. Charlie Lucky comes in a few minutes later and picks his way to them through the crowd.

Charlie buttonholes Eddie. "I heard a lot about you and Johnny on the street. Jimmy here says you guys are O.K. I believe him."

Eddie looks at Jimmy.

Jimmy nods.

Charlie says, "I heard you're with the Dutchman. What do

you say you stop by the Claridge tomorrow? We can talk there. Bring Jimmy with you. You know the place?"

Eddie finishes his pint, then knocks back another. Everybody hates the Dutchman, including him. But it wasn't always wise to admit as much to someone you just met, no matter who gives him the nod.

"I know the place," Eddie says. "You know the Dutchman?"

"I heard of him," Charlie says with a smile, "but that ain't the main thing. I'm always interested in reliable guys. Jimmy can vouch for that."

Jimmy says, "This is Charlie, I told you about him."

The name rings the bell in Eddie's head it was meant to. This is *the* Charlie, the guy with the cousin whose life Jimmy saved by standing up to the greasers on his behalf, shortly after he got out of the can. Eddie relaxes. He figures the meeting is a good thing. Maybe a very good thing. Mostly the Irish don't trust the Italians and with good reason. The two sides have fought for control over the docks around town for too long. But this Charlie isn't like most Italians. He has managed to develop a good reputation among many gangs. He runs an equal-opportunity mob.

"I'll give Jimmy the details," Charlie says. He stands and throws down a fin on the table, walks off.

Eddie asks Jimmy, "Is he always like that?"

"He don't beat around the bush much, if that's what you mean."

"Yeah," Eddie says. "It's different."

Jimmy says, "If you don't mind, I been outta town for a while. I wouldn't object to going someplace where they got broads."

It's a good call. The beer joint is just that. It lacks sophistication and doesn't care. Uptown are finer clubs with booze and music and all the other things Jimmy is looking for. The night runs late. The next morning, Eddie wakes with a pounding head. He shakes Bromo-Seltzer into a glass of water and then looks at his face in the mirror. He frowns. This is not the way he wanted to look for a business meeting with Charlie Lucky.

He calls Johnny Dunn.

"I'm coming with you," Johnny says.

"You weren't invited," Eddie says.

"Do I give a shite? You ain't goin' to see a guy like that without me!"

Johnny is small in stature by comparison to Eddie. Maybe that's what made him angry and tough, long years with bigger boys in Catholic reform schools.

Johnny says, "First a Jew and now an Italian?"

"And so what?"

"You can't trust any of them. The eyes give everything away. You didn't look in the Dutchman's eyes when you got involved. If you did, you wouldn't have gone with his mob. You'd a just delivered the beer like we talked about. Look this guy straight in the eye and ask 'im what you want to know. If he turns away and don't look back, don't trust him."

"Jimmy Alo knows this guy. They are very friendly," Eddie says. "You're not coming with me."

"I'm coming or you ain't goin'. If I gotta wait in the hall, I'm comin'."

Johnny has his eye on the piers in Greenwich Village and it's going to take strength to hold on to what he intends to take. Another Irish guy named O'Mara runs the docks to the north, the Chelsea District, down to around Twentieth Street. Chelsea isn't prime real estate but it is better than Greenwich. The best docks are above Forty-Second Street, where the big passenger liners come in. If Charlie Lucky is on the level, grabbing that big dream might come sooner rather than later.

Eddie stops at Johnny's warehouse on his way to the Claridge.

"Will ya come on?" Eddie says. "But get this straight. You ain't comin' in with me. Got that?"

Johnny pulls on the camelhair overcoat hanging on the hook in his office. The light brown coat makes him look like a pine box with legs. He grabs a blackjack from the shelf in the closet and slips it into an inner sleeve sewn into the coat for this purpose.

"Fer Christ's sake," Eddie says.

Jimmy is outside the Claridge when they arrive.

"Wild horses," Eddie says nodding toward Johnny.

Jimmy doesn't catch the drift.

"Wild horses couldn't stop him," Eddie says. "You never heard that expression?"

"Never," Jimmy says.

"There won't be no trouble," Eddie says.

"There'll be plenty of trouble if you need me," Johnny says.

Johnny stands guard in the hall. Charlie is enjoying coffee with Meyer, Joe A. and Benny in the Claridge office when the boys come through the door. Eddie's heart leaps into his throat. He recognizes every man there.

Jimmy says, "Johnny Dunn is waitin' in the hall if you're interested."

"Bring him in," Charlie says. Jimmy ducks out for a moment, returns with the other Irishman. "We got a shipment comin' in and we'd like to run it through you. Can you handle it?"

Meyer says, "We don't want to step on anybody's toes. If you have an exclusive agreement with the Dutchman…"

"We don't," Eddie says. "We can handle it." He looks to Johnny who nods his approval.

Benny looks at Johnny, "I heard you've been making moves on the docks."

"You heard right," Johnny says.

"Maybe we can help each other out," Charlie says. "Have you got enough guys to do the job?"

"There's plenty of guys willing to play deaf and dumb to avoid the soup lines," Johnny says.

"The Italians are making moves on the docks, too," Benny says.

Eddie doesn't flinch, "We still get things done, if that's what you mean."

Charlie says, "That's what we mean. I'll give you the details of where and when our shipment arrives. Keep a dozen cases for yourself. That'll be your cut. If it works out, there's plenty more where that came from."

That's how the conversation begins, a slow build in a frank discussion on what it takes to take over the docks. Benny weaves through a commonality with Johnny and Eddie, the strong belief that the only way to achieve one's goals is through force.

Meyer provides diplomacy.

"Sometimes you gotta sit down and talk it out," Meyer says. His eyes intense. "Like a little League of Nations."

Eddie says, "Sometimes you gotta get rid of the trouble-makers."

The boys stand on common ground. Charlie gives the Irish guys the specifics, a load of fine wine and Champagne coming in from Europe. Eddie wonders privately what he will do with cases of wine and Champagne since his customers are more partial to beer and Irish whiskey.

As the morning shapes up, Eddie hand-picks the guys who will offload Charlie's shipment and make sure it gets to the right trucks. The ship makes its way to the dock. The captain stands at the rail looking for his contact. Once moored and with the paperwork out of the way, Eddie sends Johnny to meet the captain.

"The sooner you get this off my ship, the happier I'll be," the Captain says. "There is nothing easy about sitting in a New York harbor with a thousand cases of illegal booze dribbling out to a stream of delivery trucks."

"You whine like a woman," Johnny says, passing off an envelope. "Point the way. I ain't got all day. I got the clerk to look the other way until we're done."

The Captain shouts orders to his crew. Eddie's longshoremen move into place. Using a system of pulleys and slides, cases of European wine are offloaded and transferred to waiting bakery trucks. Johnny keeps the Captain company on the bridge.

"No funny stuff and we'll get along just fine," Johnny says.

"You're the gunman?" the Captain says.

Johnny takes exception to the tone of the Captain's remark. He pulls a revolver, a Luger, the German choice of the world's deadliest weapon. The Captain frowns and pours two glasses of whiskey.

"I ain't in the mood," Johnny says.

The Captain slugs back the shot. "I am."

Whitey, a freelance bootlegger, gets wind of the shipment and stops by the docks. He finds Eddie and tells him he has an order for Jack Kriendler and Charlie Berns. Whitey is a small-time operator with a long overcoat lined with pockets sized for bottles. He deals only in what he can carry and delivers no further than he is able to walk.

"How the hell...?" Eddie says.

"I got my sources," Whitey says tipping his hat. "You ain't gonna make me tell you who it is, are ya, Eddie?"

"Hold on, Whitey," Eddie says. "As soon as I get this truck loaded, I'll load you up."

Whitey takes a roll of cash from his pocket and counts out the cost of a case of whiskey. Eddie helps load Whitey's jacket. Whitey balances his load and then waddles off in the direction of the Puncheon Grotto.

The shipment rolls through New York in the innocuous trucks. Charlie's guys are at the wheel. The wine settles into a New Jersey warehouse from which it will eventually be dispersed to fine clubs in New York's Tenderloin with a little extra set aside in case Samuel Bronfman is right and Prohibition ends.

With the success, Charlie and Meyer throw more work to the Irish. By the time Detective Sergeant Cordes is suspended for alleged laxity in the McManus case, Johnny and Eddie have offloaded Italian wines, Canadian whiskeys, and Caribbean rums.

They are part of the Claridge's well-oiled machine.

Jack Kriendler and Charlie Berns hold a party for the demolition of No. 42. It is New Year's Eve, a fitting time for celebrating the end of a great club, as well as the impending move three blocks north. Jack and Charlie insist their new "21 Club" will not only maintain the reputation of the 42, it will exceed it.

The bartender cranks out mint juleps and planter's punches and all manner of sours. Grown men strut through No. 42 wearing grass skirts and strumming ukuleles while singing "Aloha 'Oe."

While the elite hula the night away downtown, Al Mineo makes his way to the penthouse of Joe the Boss. Joe has his own party in motion. Mineo bides his time avoiding the opium and indulging in Champagne. When Joe finally takes Mineo aside for a serious chat, Mineo doesn't waste any time.

"I don't like what I've been hearing about Tom Reina," Mineo says, one schemer to another. "He is listening to the Castellammarese. He says, and please pardon me for what I am about to say but I think you should know how the Castellammarese are talking, he says you an incomplete man, a glutton feeding your belly, and a bully feeding your ego. We must quiet their tongues."

Joe looks out over Central Park. The trees are bare. Branches stab at the night sky. The party bellows behind him. Mineo's report stings his greedy ears. How dare they?

"Who is Tom Reina that he should take airs with me?" Joe says.

Mineo agrees. Reina is treading on dangerously thin ice. Mineo wonders out loud whether Charlie Lucky has also become a liability.

"What do you mean?" Joe says.

"The beating he took," Mineo says. "The police were looking for Jack Diamond, because he deals in drugs. They know Charlie is in that world. And you know the Sicilian fathers look down on drug dealers. They wonder if you know of Charlie's business in drugs and find further cause to mock you."

"What business is it of theirs what Charlie Luciano does?" Joe says.

Mineo backpedals.

"I'm only thinking of your reputation," Mineo says. "Charlie should be more careful. You cannot afford to let him lead the police to your doorstep."

Back at No. 42, as the hands of the clock creep toward midnight, Charlie Berns hands out crowbars, pickaxes, and hammers to writers, poets, and politicians who take to the walls of the Puncheon like a horde of drunken construction workers.

Charlie strolls by the Puncheon on his way to Polly Adler's, sticks his head into the club to see what the ruckus is all about, and decides Polly's is the better place to spend his holiday cheer. When he arrives, he finds Polly at the kitchen table, chin in hands, moaning.

Charlie takes a seat next to her. He reaches for the whiskey bottle next to her glass and pours a shot for himself and, upon making an estimation of Polly's misery, pours one for her.

Polly says, "I'm done. If it isn't the cops it's the petty thieves or the drunken johns or the damned stock market."

"You run the oldest business known to man," Charlie laughs. "You'll never be done."

Polly raises her glass to Charlie and blinks back the tears of life.

"Jesus, now there's a sad commentary on society," she says and faints dead away.

"Lion!" Charlie yells to Polly's maid. "Give me a hand, will ya?"

Charlie lifts the slight Polly from the kitchen chair.

"This way," Lion says, hefting Polly's arm around her shoulder. "She just needs some sleep and she'll be just fine. She had a big vacation planned but not no more on accounta the crash. I guess we all been hit real bad. You see the men sittin' around here drinkin'? That's all they do. Not much work for Polly's girls as long as everybody is short on cash. Maybe that's the plan, Mr. Charlie? They take all our money so we can't do what we want to do. You know what I mean?"

Charlie nods in agreement.

"Miss Polly don't usually drink but today she clean hid herself in that bottle."

"It ain't permanent," Charlie says, easing Polly into her peach sheets and down-filled comforter.

Lion sighs. She's seen Polly through raids and scandals, through hoodlum ransacking and ruffians. She knows how to handle Polly's excesses but this...this is something else.

"I'm a paying customer," Charlie says.

"Maybe you're the last one. And, yes, don't I know Miss Polly is grateful to you!"

A new girl steps into the room.

"Mr. Ross?" she says.

Charlie smiles and passes fifty dollars to Lion. The Ziegfeld dancer leads Charlie to the apple-green room.

"Polly is fond of fruit this season," she says. "All the rooms are some kinda fruity color. What do you like, Mr. Ross? I'm here to please."

She loosens the ribbon on her black lace teddy. The straps fall from her shoulders and the teddy slips to her ankles. She does a little Ziegfeld kick sending the garment flying across the room.

Charlie drops his pants to the floor. The dancer comes forward. Charlie grabs her hips and throws her on the bed. He is on top of her. She is warm and tight. She moans her pleasure in time with Charlie's thrusts.

The clock strikes midnight. A swell of cheers and bells and horns echoes through the cavern of Upper Manhattan's architecture. Blocks away, Anne Lansky sprawls on the floor of her Manhattan apartment. She rolls on her back and strokes her bulging belly.

"I look like I swallowed a watermelon," she says. "I wanted to do Times Square but here we are like some kind of old couple stuck in this stupid apartment. Pour the Champagne, Meyer. At least let us toast the New Year in!"

The crowd at No. 42 spills into the snow-filled street dragging pots and pans, bottles and chairs, glasses and table service. They heap the contents of No. 42 onto an open cart. A tuxedoed man has an epiphany.

"Let's take the iron gate," he shouts. "It belongs to us. It belongs to Jack and Charlie. We can't leave it behind for the Rockefellers. They won't respect it in the morning!"

The mayhem of reclaiming the iron gate that ensues could fill an entire vaudeville show.

Two weeks later, Anne Lansky gives birth to a son, Bernard Irving Lansky. Meyer stands at the window of the nursery and watches his son sleep. The baby is small but his sleep is sound, untroubled. Meyer admires the sleep of innocence. He wants nothing more for little Bernard than whatever the world has to offer him, even if that means becoming a tool and die worker, God forbid.

New parents fill the ward with nervous chatter. The nursery stirs. Babies are rolled out to meet their mothers. Bernard's bassinet is rolled to the door by the duty nurse. Another nurse checks the chart and wheels him down a long hall filled with mingling relatives of the newborns. Meyer follows silently behind.

Anne enjoys the quiet of a private room. She holds Bernard in his comfy cocoon and looks up at Meyer who is holding a vase filled with two dozen pink Stargazer lilies.

"It's January," he apologizes. "Nothing in blue."

The nurse smiles, takes the vase, and puts it in the window. She fluffs the chrysanthemums while Anne nervously cuddles Bernard.

"Don't worry, miss," she says, "he won't break."

She leaves Anne and Meyer to their conversation.

"I guess I better call the rabbi," Meyer says.

Jewish tradition demands a newborn son be circumcised on the eighth day of his life.

Anne says, "I'm sure my mother has already done that for you."

"We could pass on the whole thing and send him to a goy school," Meyer jokes.

Anne gives him the look.

"Not funny," she says.

"Maybe he should make his own choice. Let him figure out who he is," he says.

"He's Jewish," she says. "He'll always be Jewish. Soon enough he will be telling us what to do. What's that you're reading?"

Meyer hands her the book he's been carrying around, one of Dr. Watson's collections of advice for parents.

"It's got some good ideas," he says.

Meyer drags a crinkled copy of *The Mother's Magazine* from his jacket pocket.

Anne frowns, "Children aren't science experiments. I don't need a book."

"Don't you think it's a good idea to read up on parenting before you try to be one?" he says.

"What should we call him? Bernie?" she says. "That's American."

"I don't know." Meyer sighs. "Sounds a little soft to me."

"Oh, Meyer, stop worrying. You don't fool me with all this tough talk. He's going to be a strong boy. You'll see. He'll be our little buddy."

"Buddy," Meyer says. "That's who he is. Buddy."

Meyer sits on the side of the bed and lifts Buddy's tiny hand with his finger. It is the first warm interchange between Meyer and his wife since their honeymoon. Too soon, the nurse pokes her head into the room.

"Visiting hours are over," she says.

"Get some rest," Meyer says to Anne. "I'll see you tomorrow."

"Me and Buddy," she says. "You'll see me and Buddy tomorrow."

Meyer kisses Buddy's forehead. Buddy wiggles and his hands fly up and then settle back down into the warmth of his baby-blanket nest cradled in Mom's arms. The scene is, not oddly, that of the woman on the cover of the magazine. The illustrator got it right.

The next few days, Meyer spends at the Claridge talking with his boys about the possibilities confronting them. Charlie and the Italian situation is front and center. The greasers threaten to turn New York into another Chicago in sheer brutality.

Red argues that the Italians should be left to fight their own battles.

"Charlie is strong enough to stand up to these mobs," Red says.

Meyer says, "We stand behind Charlie, no matter what."

"We've got our own—"

"We stand with Charlie," Meyer repeats. "And we act like businessmen, not a bunch of ruffians."

Benny says, "Wait...what?"

"No massacres," Meyer says.

"Well, maybe one or two," Benny suggests.

"The Italians will eat us up if given half a chance, they are powerful enough. We're not going to win if it's a contest of pure firepower. We stick to our approach," Meyer says. "Take the violence off the street. No drive-by shootings. Settle differences peacefully whenever possible. And when the time comes, we will take care of the greaser that wins this war."

"And put Charlie in his place?" Benny says.

"We will do what needs to be done," Meyer says.

Chapter Seventeen
Yoo-Hoo, Is Anybody?

FEBRUARY 1930

There's a pop. The slug from a double-barreled shotgun rips through Tom Reina's chest, dislodging bits of flesh and imbedding the button of his shirt into his skin. He reels backwards, slams into a brick wall, and then stumbles forward. Adrenaline surges. Time slows. His mind snaps into sharp focus. Groping for the snub-nose .38 in his coat pocket, Reina searches through the low light of evening for his would-be assassin. He spots two ghostly shadows tucked behind a parked car.

The two men step from the shadows. One flips open his coat and pulls out a shotgun, twin to the one that just fired. He takes aim at Reina and pulls the first trigger. Shotgun pellets slam Reina's chest and stop him in his tracks. He staggers. The shooter pulls the second trigger. More buckshot. Bits of Reina's flesh go flying and Reina goes down, face first onto the frozen sidewalk, the snub-nose still clutched firmly in his hand. The second shooter rushes the body, firing nine more slugs point blank from a .38. Blood drenches Reina's shirt and handmade suit, floods the sidewalk, and runs down the curb.

The first shooter tosses the shotgun under a parked car and the two men flee.

For a moment, Reina's mind dawdles in this world. He thinks about the ten grand he was on his way to collect and the cash behind the basement furnace that his wife will never find. He knows his outspokenness against Joe the Boss has brought on the attack. He knows but doesn't care. His head swims in a mass of confusion as blood leaves his body and weakness sets in and then Reina's concerns disappear along with his heartbeat and his iron-clad hold on the ice distribution business in the Bronx.

Mrs. Ennis steps from a Sheridan Avenue apartment and screams. Her neighbors poke their heads outside their doors and shiver. Police arrive at the scene to take stock of the damage. Male, Italian descent, shot to death. He is identified as Gaetano Reina, forty years old, a wealthy wholesale ice dealer. The police interview witnesses and surmise a rival gang killing. It appears to them to be an open and shut case. A little cross-referencing back at the police station ties Reina to other crimes.

Reporters prod the police for details. They note the deceased's name as Gaetano, skipping the Americanized Tommy. They jot down the details of the murder that occurred outside Reina's office two weeks earlier when an ex-convict and a young woman companion were shot and killed. No one knows why. Detective Dominick Caso makes the supposition that Reina may have been shot by someone connected to the Barnett Baff murder case. The reporters make notes and then write their columns. It's all rather routine, nothing notable here.

Reina's death makes page three of the *New York Times*.

Charlie Lucky stops at the corner newsstand and picks up a paper. He tosses a nickel to the vendor. The guy in the small wooden booth, chomping on the butt of a cheap cigar, picks out three cents change from a tin of pennies.

"Keep it," Charlie says.

" 'Hit of the Week?' " the guy says.

Charlie masks his surprise.

"What?" Charlie says.

The guy hands him a newly minted unbreakable gramophone record. Charlie eyes the label. Don Voorhees Orchestra plays Dubin Burke's Fox-Trot "Tip-Toe through the Tulips with Me."

Charlie laughs. "A real toe-tapper."

"The people gotta have somethin'," the guy says. "Built to last, they say. Plays twice as long, they say. They're gonna put out a hit a week, they say."

"They say a lot of things," Charlie says bending the record back and forth in disbelief.

"Take it. The first one's free."

"Ain't nothin' free," Charlie says.

"Ain't that a fact," the guy says.

For a mere fifteen cents a week, Durium Products' brainstorm provides three minutes of popular music promising to keep workers skipping merrily along to their factory jobs. Charlie tucks the record under his arm along with the newspaper and then heads toward Times Square. He has an appointment with Meyer at the Claridge. The temperature is a balmy 60 degrees and cloudy, a nice day to hike the dozen or so blocks.

The doorman at the Claridge tips his hat as Charlie enters. In the hotel elevator, Charlie unfurls the paper and locates the article on Reina. He folds the paper in a neat square and gives the article a quick read.

The elevator doors slide open and Charlie steps out, satisfied that the police have not made the connection to the real reason for Reina's death. He swings out of the elevator and down the hall. A quick knock at Room 608 and he's inside talking to Meyer. The "Wealthy Ice Dealer" story is face up on the table next to Meyer's chair.

Charlie says, "Well, the fuse has been lit. The thorn in Joe the Boss' side has been eradicated. Expect fireworks."

The pastry cart near the front window beckons. Charlie grabs a bagel with a schmear before dropping into a deep leather club chair that faces Meyer.

"Did you read the story in the paper?" Meyer says.

Charlie nods. "I did."

Meyer says, "The detective on the Reina case thinks the murder has to do with Reina turning state's witness when they indicted him for the murder of Barnett Baff."

"That was years ago," Charlie says. "That was all those guys in the poultry business. That's a lotta horseshit. It just shows they don't know what's really going on in the Italian mobs."

"They shot the bastard in the middle of the market," Benny says. "Baff. Bunch of Italians were in on the job. They hated the guy right along with the Jews. The Italians wanted to send a message. I was there that day. I saw the whole thing."

A street car bell clangs on the street below, stopping conversation.

"It's a shame about Tommy," Charlie says. "He was a nice guy. He didn't deserve what he got but he didn't know when to keep his mouth shut. Lots of guys don't like Joe the Boss but they know better than to broadcast it. Reina was swayed by Maranzano's Sicilian bullshit. Tommy said stuff he shouldn't a said." Charlie shakes his head. "Maranzano is like this with Vito Cascioferro." Charlie twists two fingers around each other. "You remember, the guy who brought all that Black Hand shit into the neighborhoods and then ran back to Sicily after he stuffed a guy in a barrel?"

The "barrel murder" was notorious. The newspapers ran the story for weeks.

"I mention it because the two of them think alike. In the old country, Vito was like a revolutionary. He was sucked up by one of them Sicilian groups that were popular in the old days. They fought for democracy and socialism. That's why this guy thinks he's in the right all the time. If you listen to Maranzano, you hear the same story. He's on a righteous crusade to free the Sicilians and maybe he is. Joe the Boss ain't no saint but the truth is, they seen the money we're making and plotted on getting a piece of the action."

Benny grumbles, "What the hell does a guy in Italy think he's gonna do in the booze business in America?"

"We're making millions," Charlie says, letting the impact of the amount hang in the air. "And don't forget Mussolini came down on the Mafiosi so what are they gonna do in Italy? Their extortion rackets are gone. They come here to practice their trade. And here's the icin' on Maranzano's cake, Joe the Boss is backing a guy named Joe Pinzolo to take over Tom's mob because Pinzolo don't like Maranzano. Tom's boys call Pinzolo 'Fat Joe.' Just watch Fat Joe's world begin to crumble. I'll bet fifty bucks that Maranzano instigated the whole thing that got Tommy killed."

Meyer puts out his cigarette and lets the news sink in. Like a row of dominoes, the first tile has fallen.

Meyer says, "With Tommy dead, the other Sicilians are dragged into Maranzano's war games."

Charlie says, "He fancies himself a general."

Realizing that more soldiers for Maranzano could be bad for Charlie down the line, Meyer asks, "Do you trust anybody in Tom's mob?"

"Yeah. A guy named Tommy Lucchese," Charlie says. "He's a reasonable guy when he sees which way the wind blows. He's looking for a way into the garment industry."

Meyer says, "Maybe we can help him out."

Charlie pours himself a coffee.

"Joe's got you in a bad position," Meyer says.

"You don't gotta tell me," Charlie says. "These guys wanna know if I'm gonna go along with him or them. What can I say? Don't worry, if it comes to that I'm gonna take out my boss? Hell, even I don't know what I'm gonna do."

It's a chess move in the making. A pawn has been sacrificed. The next move must be Charlie's or it will be, by default, that of Joe the Boss.

"I understand the boys' dilemma," Charlie says. "What Joe the Boss done ain't right, but these guys don't see the big picture. They don't understand Maranzano is just the same."

"They'll understand when he puts his hand in their pockets," Meyer says.

"He already has," Charlie says. "Don't forget the war chest or the Cadillac with the machine gun. War ain't cheap."

Charlie sets his cup on the windowsill and looks at his watch. He turns back to Meyer and rubs his neck. Joe the Boss' yoke is beginning to chafe. The more money he makes, the more power he gains, the more nervous Joe gets and that's trouble.

Charlie grins. "I'd sure like to see these cocksuckers get what they deserve."

"They will. They still don't see that there are other players beyond Sicilians. That's an advantage. You've been on the street. You know what it takes to survive. Start peddling your own philosophy for peace and see how the guys respond," Meyer says.

Charlie finishes his coffee and chats with Benny about the day's orders. The warehouses are full and business is brisk. Attempts to end Prohibition have failed. Thousands of clubs fill the city. Their music fills the streets. The Stork serves its debutantes while the Cotton Club serves its bohemians. The boys walk through town as gentlemen. If it wasn't for the greasers, well, 'if it wasn't for the greasers' is a long, tall tale waiting to be spun.

Charlie hikes back to his flat. The housekeeper is busy cleaning when he arrives. The tall, slender bleached blonde that Polly Adler sent over to keep Charlie company for the afternoon is sitting on the couch, deep in the throes of *Life* magazine's search for the ideal American beauty. If *Life* is to be believed, this month's ideal is fair skinned, red lipped, and bob haired. She looks on the world with sultry eyes.

Life asks, "Do you know a girl who looks like this?"

The dancer sighs. Not her. Not any of Polly's girls. She throws the magazine on the floor.

"Happy Valentine's Day," she says to Charlie.

Charlie tosses his jacket onto the back of the wingback chair. The housekeeper puts a silver tray loaded with cheese and crackers and caviar on the coffee table.

"Will there be anything else, Mr. Charlie?" she says.

Charlie looks around.

"You can go, Hattie," Charlie says.

The housekeeper, a portly black woman in a neatly pressed black uniform and a starched white apron, picks up the magazine, reading the tagline and assessing the perfect girl's picture.

"Mmm mmm," she says shaking her head at the pale-faced girl. "The wind gonna blow that girl clean away."

She collects her coat and purse.

"See you tomorrow, Mr. Charlie."

The bleached blonde nibbles on cheese and then moves to the bedroom. Charlie follows.

"Rough day?" she says.

"It ain't the day, sweetheart, it's the people you gotta deal with," Charlie says.

She offers a shrug, "I guess a lot of people can say that."

She kicks off high heels and unbuttons her blouse. She tries out a sultry cover-girl look, loosens the starched collar of Charlie's shirt and works through the mother of pearl buttons. Charlie unfastens his cufflinks. His shirt drops to the floor. He wrestles with his belt and zipper and kicks his pants aside and then runs his hands up the blonde's long legs.

They drop onto the bed. She moves across him lithely.

He rewinds Reina's murder in his mind and wonders about Tommy Lucchese and the other mainstay of Reina's mob, another Tommy named Gagliano. The blonde gets between him and his troubles. She has skills.

The phone rings.

Charlie ignores it.

The ringing doesn't stop. He kicks at the phone. It falls to the floor. Someone on the other end keeps yelling "Hello?"

"What!" he says into the receiver.

It's Joe Adonis on the line. His voice is urgent.

"This ain't a good time," Charlie says.

Adonis says, "Twenty minutes?"

"Meet me at the Cotton Club."

The blonde throws out a pout.

"Half an hour," Charlie says and hangs up the receiver.

He's done in ten and sends the blonde packing with fifty bucks. Charlie showers, puts on a clean shirt and suit. Out on the street, he hails a cab.

Duke Ellington is in his third year at the Club. The jungle theme, successful from the start, is now ever-present in the stage show. Charlie wades through the crowd and finds Adonis at a front-row table ogling the all-black chorus line. Madden's rule of thumb: no dancer can be darker than a paper bag.

Charlie takes a seat and watches as the dancers gyrate. Adonis discreetly relays the message. Tommy Lucchese and Tommy Gagliano want to meet with Charlie. Willie Moretti, who circulates freely picking up gossip among the Sicilians, has told Adonis that the guys in Reina's mob think Vito Genovese, Charlie's underboss, was sent to take care of Reina.

"Is that it?" Charlie says.

He considers the situation. If he is going to play the game, he needs to know what these men are thinking. Gagliano is Old World, born in Corleone, Sicily. Lucchese was born in Palermo. With Willie Moretti in the mix, Maranzano is sure to be involved behind the scenes. He searches for a pack of cigarettes.

Duke Ellington and his orchestra take the stage and shake

the house with something they call the "Jubilee Stomp." The chorus line, clad in white satin shorts and matching halter tops dotted here and there with green glass gems to match their long feather tails, kicks its way through a new routine.

Charlie waits for the set to end.

He says, "Tell them I'll get back to them."

Adonis says, "One more thing. Maranzano is calling a meeting in Brooklyn."

Charlie nods. "Keep your ear to the ground."

Adonis eyes the two women sitting at the table next to them. They have no apparent escorts. He sends them a bottle of Champagne that is greeted with a smile. Just as he is about to make his move, Jimmy Alo walks up and takes a seat beside one of the girls.

"That son of a bitch," Adonis says. "He's moving in on my dime."

Charlie shakes his head. He has wrestled with the dragon of his jealousy and finds himself content with Polly's whores. He watches Joe A. make his move on the girls. Two girls. Two men. These women are no Dumb Doras. The real question remains, who has lured whom. Charlie doesn't care. He's got bigger concerns.

"Thanks for the Champagne," Jimmy says to Adonis.

Duke Ellington moves into another song. The chorus line pounds across the stage and then back again. Owney Madden comes down to the dining room and takes a seat next to Charlie.

Madden says, "I was just talkin' with Jimmy Alo. He wants to put Ellington on the radio. It's the new thing. He's got a guy at William Morris. You know him? He was best man at Jimmy's wedding. Jimmy's convinced this would double business overnight."

"Would it?" Charlie says.

"Look around," Madden says. "What would I do with more people? Besides, you can't see a chorus line on the radio."

Charlie shrugs. "You gonna do it?"

"What choice do I have?" he says.

Madden excuses himself. Business calls. Charlie leaves the broads to Joe Adonis and Jimmy Alo and steps outside to hail a cab. At Broadway and 34th, he gets out, walks through a cigar store, and drops a nickel in the pay phone in the back. Gaetano Gagliano, the guy who was Tom Reina's second in command, answers the call.

Charlie says, "I hear you wanna talk."

"Yeah," Gagliano says. Disgust fills the vacuum of his reply. "Meet me at Tommy's joint in the Bronx tomorrow at noon."

Charlie says, "I tell you where we're gonna meet, and when."

Charlie hangs up and calls in one of his boys. They meet at the automat.

"Tomorrow morning first thing I want you to run a little errand for me," Charlie says. "Be at the office at six."

Bright and early the guy shows up at Charlie's office, where Charlie and Tommy the Bull are waiting.

Charlie says, "I want you and Tommy the Bull to pick up a couple of guys for me. You know Tommy Gagliano and Tommy Lucchese? Go get them. Bring them to the South Street Seaport. I don't want no games. Don't give them time to think or make any phone calls. Get them to South Street. I'll be there. If you ain't there by nine-thirty, I'll figure something went wrong."

By eight-thirty, Gagliano and Lucchese are at the South Street docks watching small fishing vessels offload their fish for Manhattan's restaurants.

Gagliano says, "I ain't gonna beat around the bush. Were you responsible for what happened to Tommy?"

Charlie says, "You know I can't answer that."

Gagliano says, "Fat Joe is pushing himself to head up our family. He says Joe the Boss wants it that way. We ain't gonna listen to nothin' the Boss has to say. If he's behind this, he's gone too far."

Charlie says, "Why get caught up in a vendetta that's between Joe the Boss and Salvatore Maranzano?"

"Joe the Boss put us in the middle," Lucchese says. "He's forcing us to take sides and if we gotta choose, it won't be Joe. It's gonna be Maranzano. Maranzano don't want nothing from us. All he's asking for is respect for the Sicilian fathers."

"Don't kid yourself. All these old greasers are cut from the same cloth. Maranzano's got a war chest, don't he? He expects all you guys to pony up. He's already got his hand in your pocket and you don't even know it."

"Look, Charlie," Lucchese says. "We don't want no trouble with you. It's Joe the Boss that's the problem. We ain't gonna stand for Pinzolo telling us what to do. We thought you should know."

There it is, a declaration of independence against Joe the Boss.

"I'm going to pretend I didn't hear that," Charlie says. "Do what you gotta do but think of the consequences before you make your move. Nobody knows where all this is going to wind up."

Gagliano stares into Charlie's eyes hoping to find the truth about Charlie's guilt regarding Reina's death. It's an old Sicilian trick. Charlie stares back. His dark eyes reveal nothing one way or the other. The conference is over. Charlie heads back to the garage wondering if he should have tried a different approach, if he could have put forth a philosophy of peace. Gagliano and Lucchese return to the Bronx. One thing sticks with them,

Charlie's dismissal of their treason. "I'm going to pretend I didn't hear that," Charlie said. So it would seem to these men that Charlie doesn't wholly agree with his boss.

Meanwhile, at the Sabatini bakery, Fat Joe Pinzolo hems and haws with Joe the Boss over cannoli and espresso. He tries to convince Joe the Boss that he has control of Reina's mob but they both know it's a lie. Fat Joe is not in control. Joe the Boss sees his failure and worries. With every new ally, Salvatore Maranzano grows stronger and that is surely bad for business.

"They will do as they are told," Fat Joe insists.

Joe the Boss fumes silently.

Salvatore Maranzano rides through the streets of Brooklyn in the back seat of his armored Cadillac. A second car, filled with soldiers, follows behind. The cars cut dirty ruts through the freshly fallen snow. Maranzano straddles the machine gun, keeping an eagle eye out for trouble in the form of Joe the Boss or his henchmen.

Two bodyguards protectively flank Maranzano. On one side is Joe Bonanno, also from the old country, linked firmly to Maranzano by his admiration of Maranzano's great intellect. On the other side, a recruit fresh off the boat bringing news from the now-imprisoned Cascioferro.

"The Italy we knew no longer exists," the recruit says in Italian. "The Blackshirts have taken control of everything."

The car's driver maneuvers deftly along the icy roads. His destination is a restaurant located at the foot of the Manhattan Bridge on the Brooklyn side which Maranzano calls "a little taste of home." The soft yellow box of a building displays a pretense of elegance. It seems out of place among the piers and warehouses that line the river. The car skids to a stop close to the entrance. Joe Bonanno is the first to exit the car. His feet plunge into heavy slush. Icy water fills his shoes, drenching his socks and putting his feet into a deep freeze.

"There goes forty bucks," he says of his new shoes.

Maranzano steps from the car. The slush runs around the high rubber overshoes he wears. Snow continues to fall. The soldiers in the second car pour out of their vehicle and slog their way to the restaurant's kitchen entrance. The kitchen is used to the drill. Nothing is spared, from flour bins to the simmering soups and sauces. Everything is checked to ensure the safety of their family father.

Maranzano strolls toward the eatery like a conquering hero. He pauses to admire the string of lights dotting the Manhattan Bridge. On the other side of the East River, the city twinkles like a miniature scene in a glass globe.

"You see that?" Maranzano says with one arm outstretched. "The golden door. Brooklyn is just the beginning."

The soldiers trudge out from the kitchen. They stand at attention, hands folded to the front and feet slightly apart. They nod that the building is safe to enter.

Crisp white linens line the tables. Waiters scurry to accommodate the large group. Maranzano indicates a place in front of a large picture window. He looks out across the river and imagines Joe the Boss looking back, gloating over his control of the Italian rackets. Several tables are pushed together. Maranzano takes a seat at the head of the table.

The chef looks out from the kitchen. His cousin is Al Mineo and now that his cousin has aligned with Joe the Boss, the chef worries. Surely Salvatore Maranzano knows about Mineo's treachery. He closes his eyes and gathers his strength and then comes out to greet the great man who is taking over Brooklyn.

"You honor me with your presence," the chef says taking a deep breath. "Tonight, we have minestrone and fish soup. My cousin get frostbite, the fish is so fresh." He laughs nervously. "I make my grandmother's ravioli and my great aunt Dori's Torta de Mele. I think tonight you like the ricotta ravioli with meat sauce. My grandmother never serve ravioli without meat sauce. Maybe you like a little marinated eggplant to start?"

"Si." The Don nods his approval. "And some wine from Sicily. I want to taste the land of my birth."

"I bring it right out," the chef says.

Maranzano surveys the restaurant and the men guarding his life. His soldiers, for the most part, are young, strong, and barely fluent in English. They rank last in America's manual labor force but first in Maranzano's pick for war. By any standards, it is an impressive exhibition of force.

The other diners in the restaurant recognize the entourage. Excitement fueled by fear fills the air. All this satisfies Maranzano's longing for power. On this side of the river, in this restaurant, he has no equal.

He turns to Joe Bonanno and says, "The police have connected Frankie Yale's murder to the St. Valentine's Day Massacre, no?"

Bonanno listens with rapt interest as Maranzano recites facts from newspaper article after newspaper article. New York City Police Commissioner Whalen has announced the results of the ballistics test. The bullets brought from Chicago are a "definite and positive match" with the Yale bullet. For the first time, the New York police department cooperates with the Chicago police department. It is a coup d'état of sorts, an investigation driven by the new science and poised to overthrow the powerful Al Capone if the evidence can reach high enough up the ladder.

Maranzano says, "Neapolitans and Calabrese have no couth. We will hope the police take care of these barbarians so our friend, Joe Aiello, can advance his position in the Unione

Siciliana. Capone will finally get the message not to meddle in the affairs of New York."

Dinner is served in convenient waves. Eggplant and antipasto followed by minestrone. After the soup is the rather unusual pairing of the pasta and meat sauce. Maranzano sends his compliments to the chef. Marinated artichoke hearts come next. Finally, the table is filled with espressos and an apple torte.

Locals come and go. Maranzano sits back with brandy and a cigar. He turns his attention to the new soldier.

"Antonio," Maranzano says, "after tonight, you are Al Mineo's shadow. Where he goes, you go. I want to know everybody he sees, what he talks about, what business he has with Joe Masseria, the bigwig in Manhattan. I want to know how many times he screws his wife before he goes to sleep. I want to know everything. Capisce?"

Antonio nods. The next day, he rises early and parks near Mineo's home where he can clearly see the front door. Mineo leaves the house around nine o'clock, Antonio in tow, keeping a record of every stop, every face. For days Antonio follows Mineo and each night he returns to his small apartment, sits in the kitchen, boils water in his Napolentana for espresso, and transcribes his daily scribbles into a small notebook. Angela, his wife, sits on the musty couch and flips on the radio.

"Yoo-hoo, is anybody?" Angela calls.

Antonio rolls his eyes. Not again. Angela is hooked on *The Goldbergs*. She turns up the volume on the radio.

"Yoo-hoo, is anybody?" Molly Goldberg hollers from the radio.

"Yoo-hoo, I'm practice my English," Angela yells to Antonio.

The Goldbergs invades the small space. Antonio tries to ignore the intrusion. For fifteen minutes, while the episode airs, he records everything he remembers of Mineo's day: his morning stop at the bakery, a brief meeting with Joe the Boss that had something to do with Fat Joe Pinzolo, a stop in the Bronx to collect his share of the numbers racket, a visit to Pinzolo, a long lunch with Charlie Luciano at the Villa Nuevo, an afternoon at his office with regular visits from his underbosses, and finally dinner with the wife whom he enjoyed at least once before going to sleep.

Angela pulls the sleeves of her sweater over her hands and walks the five steps from the couch to the table where Antonio sits scribbling in his notebook. She snuggles against him. Antonio frowns.

She says, "What does that book have that I don't have?"

Antonio says, "Not now. I need to think."

She throws her arms around his shoulders and rubs up against him, "What can be so important?"

He bristles, "If I mess this up, I die."

Angela shrugs off his concern. She swings around and sits on the table in front of him.

"What kind of man would kill you for making love to your wife?" she pouts. "You say he is from Italy. In Italy making love is not forbidden like in America."

The espresso cup tips sideways sending a wash of coffee over the table. Angela's skirt is soaked along with the Mineo notebook. Tension fills the air. Angela looks at Antonio in horror and then breaks out laughing. The lovers embrace and waddle to the couch, a tangle of arms and legs and passion.

A knock at the door sends them scrambling. Antonio answers the door.

"Scusami," Antonio says pushing his hair back in place and tucking in his shirt.

Maranzano scans the small apartment. Angela disappears into the tiny bedroom. Antonio wipes the coffee-dampened pages of the notebook. Maranzano flips through the pages. He makes a note of Mineo's contacts then slides the notebook into his pocket.

Antonio drops his head.

Maranzano says, "Next time you start thinking with your *pene* instead of your head, make sure you're not taking care of my business."

"Si," Antonio says.

"Never hang you head," Maranzano says with a slap to Antonio's cheek. "Not even in shame. You don't know who is watching. If your enemy sees you shamed, he will know you are weak."

Antonio brings his eyes to meet Maranzano's, clenching his jaw in closed-lipped defiance. Maranzano nods his satisfaction.

"Remember that feeling," Maranzano says. "Use it the next time you are tempted to let a woman tell you what to do."

Maranzano leaves with the small black notebook. He orders the driver to take him to Cola Schiro's home. Maranzano has long since dismissed the quivering skeleton of a man from his position as head of the family if not officially then at least in his own dealings with the man.

Schiro takes Maranzano to the quiet of his library, where they discuss the family's business.

"Joe the Boss has demanded a tax," Schiro says.

"How much?" Maranzano says.

"Ten thousand," Schiro says.

"He'll bleed us dry," Maranzano says. "What are you going to do?"

"I will go and see Stefano. He will tell me what to do."

Stefano Magaddino is still, respectfully, the father of the Brooklyn family.

"Stefano is four hundred miles away. What does he know of our troubles? Can his arm reach to Brooklyn?"

Schiro says, "We cannot take matters into our own hands."

"Call a meeting of the fathers. We do not need Stefano to deal with this man who disgraces our tradition."

Schiro's eyes widen. He has made the estimation, and rightly so, that the Castellammarese are not strong enough to take on Joe the Boss, Peter Morello, and Charlie Luciano. Ten thousand dollars is a small price to pay when compared to the cost of a war and smaller still for the price of one's life. He does not need to call a meeting of the Sicilian fathers.

The phone rings.

Schiro's housekeeper appears at the door of the study.

"Signore," she says. "It is for you."

Schiro takes the phone. The news is bone-chilling. His knees wobble to the point of collapse.

"Gaspar Milazzo has been shot," he breathes at last. "He is dead."

Maranzano grabs the phone. These are men of his tradition. He must get to the bottom of things.

"Gaspar was in the fish market with Sasa Parrino when he was shot. We do not know who fired the shots," the voice on the other end of the line reports.

Maranzano's jaw tightens. His eyes narrow.

"This is a declaration of war," he says.

"I beg of you," Schiro says. "I will call Stefano. We will decide as a family."

Maranzano hangs up the phone. Milazzo's death is the spark he needs to light the fire under the complacent Sicilians.

"Please," Schiro utters. "Call Stefano."

But his pleas fall on deaf ears. The stoic Maranzano relishes the idea of being called away from daily life to live wildly in the heat of war, huddled in safe-houses, forsaking the luxury of Simmons comfort for raw ticking stuffed with anything cheap enough to leave behind when the enemy sniffs out the hideout.

"Can't you see what is going on?" Maranzano says. "Joe the Boss wants to exterminate us all. We must stand up and fight for what is ours." He looks at the quivering Schiro. "'Cowards die many times before their deaths. The valiant never taste of death but once.' Tell me, Cola, when you look in the mirror, do you find a corpse staring back?"

Cola hangs his head. Maranzano says nothing more.

Arthur Flegenheimer, otherwise known as the Dutchman, closes the ledgers on his desk and shoves them in the safe before heading to the john. The mirror over the sink reminds him of his long day. He splashes water on his face and wipes it off with a sour-smelling towel.

"Where the fuck's a clean towel?" he screams.

His armpits reek. He sloughs off his wrinkled jacket and drops his dirty shirt on the floor.

"Where are those towels?" he shrieks.

Bo Weinberg plays nursemaid to the Dutchman's demands. He passes the Dutchman a fresh stack of bleached white towels neatly wrapped in brown paper and tied with twine. The Dutchman rips the paper and throws it to the ground, stomping it underfoot. The Dutchman is a contradiction in terms, a slob with a fetish for cleanliness. He runs a towel under the faucet and rubs it with soap.

"Where's my shirt?" he yells.

"Hanging on the back of the door," Weinberg says.

The Dutchman swabs his armpits and throws the towel to the floor and then repeats the process until his pits pass the sniff-test.

"Get my car," he says. "I'm goin' to the bath house."

It is three o'clock in the morning and the New York Racquet

and Tennis Club on Park Avenue is still open for business. Bo Weinberg drives the Dutchman to the club, where the Dutchman indulges in a Turkish bath. The harder he's scrubbed, the better he feels. After half an hour of this treatment, he wraps a towel around his waist, pops chewing gum in his mouth, and ambles off to the steam room, his flat feet slapping hard on the tile floor.

Charlie Luciano sees him coming and chuckles.

"Watch it, Arthur. I seen a guy bust his skull wide open fallin' on this tile."

The Dutchman drops onto the hard seat like a polar bear landing on a cold fish. He wipes his forehead and stares at Charlie.

The Dutchman says, "You ever figure out why them cops beat you, Charlie? You get behind on their graft?"

"Them guys didn't need no excuse," Charlie says.

"I heard they was lookin' for Jack Diamond. Everybody knows that double-crossing cocksucker ran back to the Catskills right after he shot them guys at the Hotsy Totsy. Charlie Entratta coulda walked free if he hadn't a broke parole. They got him on associating with known gangsters. Who the hell is he gonna associate with? Choir boys?"

"Didn't Jack shoot them guys after he came back from the Catskills?"

The Dutchman is suddenly quiet, a great pensive mood sweeps over him. He hates being wrong and hates even more being corrected. Charlie leans his head back and soaks up the heat. His shoulders relax and calm sets in.

Suddenly, the Dutchman jumps back to life.

"Whatever way it was, Diamond's back in town and up to his old tricks," he says. "I got five bullets in the bastard and he's still causing me trouble. I woulda paid the bum what he wanted. Ain't no skin off my nose. Not now, not after Joey was killed. I ever see his face, I'll blow it clean off."

Jack has been the nagging sore on the belly of the Dutchman's oyster nearly since the beginning. The Dutchman wants him gone. The Dutchman generally gets his way. The Dutchman shifts in his towel and scratches his crotch.

"Whores," he says. "As if I ain't got enough problems I got this one, too."

"Jesus," says Charlie. "Show some respect. You ain't the only guy that comes here. Take care of yourself, for Christ's sake. And next time you want to get laid, go to a class joint where the broads are clean. Forget about the fifth-rate hotel tramps."

"Why pay for silk when cotton is just as good?" the Dutchman says. "One pussy's the same as the next."

"Apparently not, Arthur. If you want a good whore, you gotta spring for it. Call Polly Adler—after you get cleaned up. I don't need your troubles falling on me....Did you talk to the Guy lately?"

"About what?"

"The meetin' at Costello's office," Charlie says.

"Yeah."

"Do us all a favor," Charlie says. "Take care of yourself before you show up."

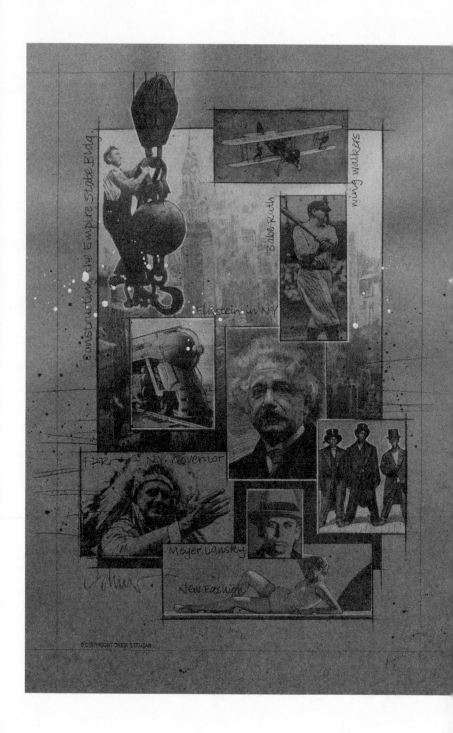

Constructing the Empire State Bldg.

wing walkers

Babe Ruth

Einstein in NY

FDR — N.Y. Governor

Meyer Lansky

New Fashion

Chapter Eighteen
Winner Takes All

SUMMER 1930

Cola Schiro coughs up the ten-thousand-dollar tribute and delivers it to Joe the Boss. Maranzano howls in disbelief. Peter "the Clutch Hand" Morello has allied himself with the detestable Mr. Joe, and that brings him more allies. Schiro still shivers at the grizzly Ignazio Lupo, known simply as the Wolf, who worked together with the Clutch Hand to remove their opposition. Enemies of the Morello gang were dismembered and shoved into barrels that were abandoned in back alleys or left on street corners or shipped to nonexistent addresses in another city with no one to perform the last rites.

Schiro frets and Maranzano fumes. Joe the Boss riffles through the envelope of cash, ten-thousand dollars' worth of sweet-smelling success. The acquiescence renews his staying power as he cruises the streets of Little Italy. He sees the Castellammarese as broken, disjointed, and quarreling. His thoughts turn to calculating. Salvatore Maranzano will not go quietly. He has greater ambitions than Cola Schiro ever imagined. Joe the Boss senses the need to school the arrogant Maranzano on criminal etiquette. He sends word to the budding Caesar demanding a "friendly" meeting.

Maranzano, in an egocentric haze, is convinced that Joe the Boss fears the strength of the Castellammarese and that's why Mr. Joe requested the meeting. Maranzano calls together the family fathers of his clan. Like a man crowned with a laurel wreath before the fact, he espouses his rage for the self-appointed rival capo di tutti capi and his cohort, Peter Morello. He declares he will meet the enemy face-to-face and gauge the fear behind his eyes. The fathers oppose the move. They are free to go about their business. What's ten thousand dollars to their millions. Maranzano tears their complacency to shreds.

In anticipation of the meeting, Joe the Boss brings in Italian delicacies: Cassata Siciliana; cannoli; a silver, gilt and ivory sugar bowl and milk jug atop a gold-framed mirror; and a row of gleaming forks and spoons. An oversized spray of fresh flowers sits atop the sideboard.

Maranzano arrives with Joe Bonanno in tow, a carefully chosen companion as Bonanno is Stefano Magaddino's cousin, and Maranzano thinks the famiglia tie will show Stefano Magaddino's solidarity with their cause, but Joe's bodyguards stop Bonanno at the door. Maranzano alone enters the room. Mr. Joe shows off his rich man's view of Central Park. Peter Morello lights a cigar and calls for espresso. Maranzano takes a seat. He is fresh, neatly groomed, organized. Morello is stern, unyielding, hardened from life and prison. Mr. Joe is confident but clumsy. His fat paunch strains the buttons of his vest.

Like giddy schoolgirls, Mr. Joe and Peter Morello circle the table and help themselves to cannoli. Morello takes a seat across from Maranzano. Joe the Boss speaks first. He gets right to the point. War would be foolish. As businessmen, they must accept recent events and work together.

Morello speaks of the changes in Italy now that Mussolini has waged war on the Italian fathers. In other words, now that Cascioferro is behind bars, the power of the Castellammarese is greatly diminished. Morello sees the rage in Maranzano's eye and grins.

The meeting, however, is not about Maranzano. It is a ploy

to get Stefano Magaddino to come to Manhattan in order to prove that Stefano, and not Maranzano, is still the head of the Brooklyn clan. The gauntlet is thrown down. Maranzano agrees to go to Magaddino. The Clutch Hand then confesses that the murder of Milazzo was done at his behest claiming Milazzo's intention was to kill Mr. Joe. The move was made in retaliation.

Maranzano shifts in his seat. With a surge of adrenaline, the general in him emerges.

After Joe the Boss calls for cordials, Maranzano collects Joe Bonanno and, in the car home, settles back into his rhythm.

"They are all dead men!" he says. "You will see."

Unwittingly, Mr. Joe and the Clutch Hand have thrust Maranzano into his element. He packs a small bag, stuffs it into the Cadillac's trunk, and kisses his wife goodbye. Maranzano, Joe Bonanno, and two bodyguards wind their way to Stefano Magaddino's Buffalo estate. The land is sprawling and green, wide open country where a man can see in all directions. The town rides the Canadian border separated by the raging Niagara Gorge. Stefano and Maranzano settle into a small café that overlooks Niagara Falls. Over a hearty lunch of meatball sandwiches and minestrone soup, Maranzano doles out the details of the friendly meeting.

Maranzano narrows his eyes. "Gaspar's murder will be the undoing of them both. Morello fears us, Stefano. I could smell the fear on him. When he made his threats, it was as if he were pleading for mercy."

"Why would Peter Morello fear us?" Stefano says.

"Because he knows he is on the losing side. Mr. Joe will destroy all who follow him. Mr. Joe claims the role of the capo di tutti. Even in that he slaps us in the face, calling himself boss of bosses. He sends word to you through me. Fear. He commands you come to New York for a clarification meeting or there will be bloodshed. Fear again."

Stefano Magaddino calls for another espresso and watches the raging water tumble over the falls.

Stefano says, "If he came crawling to me on his belly like the snake he is, I wouldn't give him the time of day."

"If you do not come to Manhattan, there will be war," Maranzano says, almost gleeful at the prospect. "Morello has given me that assurance."

There is darkness in Maranzano's eyes and readiness. The time is right for war.

"Then we must prepare," Stefano says.

Maranzano lays out his plan. The Sicilian orbit has been disturbed by the atmospheric drag not only of Joe the Boss but also Al Capone. Capone's release on March 17 signaled the return of Joe Aiello's problems. The *New York Times* may have buried the news of Capone's return to Chicago on page four among items of lesser interest and fashion ads but the news was not ignored by Salvatore Maranzano.

Maranzano says, "We have three enemies to neutralize, Mr. Joe, Peter Morello, and the Scarface who continues to interfere with the Unione Siciliana. We must clip his wings before it is too late and the Unione becomes the bastard child of a Neapolitan."

The afternoon fades into conversation of Old World politics and New World realities and other theories of relativity. They pass days in strategic discussions.

"You have my blessing to do what is necessary," Stefano says, to Maranzano's delight.

Charlie Lucky takes the news to Meyer and Benny at the Claridge.

Charlie says, "Joe don't trust nobody but Peter Morello now. The old greasers will stand up for Stefano."

Meyer says, "You have a pretty good sense of who is going along with our plan and who isn't. This is where the game gets interesting. When we make our move, all the other boys should make theirs. We take out the troublemakers all at once or our plan won't work. We give the signal. Let the dominoes fall where they may."

Charlie nods, "Joe expects Capone's support in this war but Al's got trouble of his own. A big Sicilian concern is trying to control the South Side of Chicago. It's the same guy who put a contract out on him. And the Chicago police are still waitin' to see if the peace pact between him and Bugs Moran is real."

Benny says, "He's gonna need eyes in the back of his head."

"He ain't got time to fight his battles and those of Joe the Boss, too. Has it struck you as kinda odd that you and Salvatore Maranzano are alike, Meyer?"

"I'm nothing like Maranzano," Meyer says.

"You're both great strategists," Charlie says. "I can see it. He comes from the Old World with all that history. You come from…where do you come from?"

"Grodno," Meyer says. "I grew up with the pogroms of Bialystok. The czar's soldiers took everything. I guess that influenced the way I think."

"Why you're always for the underdog," Charlie says. "Ain't it interesting that the guys call you the Little Guy and then you turn around and fight for the little guy."

Meyer shrugs. "I guess so. I never thought of it that way."

Charlie leaves the Claridge and drives out to Brooklyn, where he passes the afternoon at a Sicilian hangout fishing for contact with the Castellammarese. Joe Bonanno swings by around four o'clock in the afternoon for a few cups of espresso and a taste of antipasto. Charlie invites him to sit at his table. For the next two hours, they shoot the breeze and lament the discord among

Italians. Bonanno quotes Caesar and spouts Maranzano's philosophy as though it is his own. Charlie listens and nods, drawing his comments from things gone wrong in Italy that can be avoided with the application of honor in America.

Bonanno says, "New York is going to erupt, mark my words."

Charlie says, "And when the dust settles? Do we go back to fightin' or do we work out our differences like gentlemen?"

"If all men were men of honor, all men would act like gentlemen," Bonanno says.

Charlie says, "That's the way it should be but that ain't never the way it is."

"You don't think Maranzano can do it. You don't think he can change things for the good," Bonanno says.

"Let's just say I been around too long to underestimate the ability of things to go wrong," Charlie says. "Let me ask you this...let's say Maranzano is the right guy to lead your family. Let's say he comes to power, so to speak. What do you think he's gonna do?"

Bonanno sits in stunned silence. He ponders the question. Finally, the dutiful follower says, "Bring honor to our tradition."

"How does he do that?" Charlie says. "What we gotta do is find a way to protect our interests without interfering on other guys tryin' to do the same thing."

"Yes," Bonanno agrees. "And that is exactly what he will do."

Joe the Boss sends for Charlie and commands him to visit Tom Reina's mob to do what Fat Joe Pinzolo has been unable to do, quiet things down. Tommy Gagliano and Tommy Lucchese have split from the gang and started their own splinter group. Gagliano, the quiet diplomat, has no use for publicity and thus forsook the gathering of Sicilian fathers in Cleveland.

Charlie seeks out Gagliano first.

"These guys want to be big shots. What did they expect to happen in Cleveland? Bunch of Italians who barely speak English driving their fancy cars to a swanky hotel! For Christ's sake."

Charlie says, "They said they were there for the Unione Siciliana."

"That's bullshit and we know it. The life expectancy of the Unione president is a very short one anyway," he says. "Why bother?"

"Joe the Boss wants you and Lucchese to make nice, stop all this nonsense with Joe Pinzolo," Charlie says.

"Fuck him and that fat pig Pinzolo," Gagliano says. "Who is he to meddle in our business?"

"Is that what you want me to tell Joe?" Charlie says.

"Charlie," Gagliano says, "I ain't got no beef with you. You can tell Joe this ain't Sicily. He ain't no capo de tutti capi in my book. I run my own mob."

"These old Mustache Petes don't get that idea," Charlie says.

"Then fuck the whole lot of them," Gagliano says.

Charlie takes a breath, "Tommy," he says, "we're gonna make some moves. You got a level head. I'd like you to keep it on your shoulders. Can you settle the dispute for now while we work things out?"

"We?" Tommy says.

"Better if you don't know who I'm talkin' about," Charlie says. "Just trust me."

It's difficult for Gagliano to agree but the diplomat in him agrees to try.

The pushing and shoving between Joe the Boss and Salvatore Maranzano escalates. Meyer calls a meeting of his New York partners and associates. It's a small group of the heavy hitters that gather at Frank Costello's office in the Italian section of East Harlem.

Costello's headquarters resembles a model office, something put together to lure the reluctant shopper into thinking this is the look to have. Draperies hang on fancy rods. One perfect oak filing cabinet sits in the corner. A basalt and marble fireplace burns hard wood that crackles peacefully while keeping the room warm. Over the fireplace hangs an Allen Saalburg painting, mountains in Burma, donated in appreciation for a favor rendered. Someone has gone and completed the office furniture list: desk, chair, floor lamp, pen holder, fine pens, phone, desk set. It's all there, complete in its contents but somehow hollow, like it's all just for show, which it pretty much is.

A gangster's roundtable of allies fills the room at Charlie's behest. Frank Costello, Vito Genovese, Joe Adonis, Benny Siegel, Lepke Buchalter, and Lepke's strongarm, Gurrah Shapiro, the Dutchman and Bo Weinberg, Owney Madden and his partner, Big Frenchy DeMange. It is not by chance that the Italians, Jews, and Irish have representation. This concerns them all.

They gather around a small conference table set off to the side. It is a tight fit. Costello plays host with hot coffee and Cuban cigars.

Charlie says, "It ain't no secret that the Sicilians are gearing up for war. The war is mostly between Joe the Boss and Salvatore Maranzano, some of you might not know who Maranzano is. He came over from Italy a while back and took over the Brooklyn family that used to belong to Stefano Magaddino. Remember him? If not, it don't matter. What matters is this, if these guys go to war, we'll all be targets sooner or later. You can count on a lot of greaser violence. That means the coppers will all be up our asses tryin' to control the murders. These guys brought their war over from the old country but it's the same old problem. Maranzano has been smuggling his paesans into Brooklyn. We gotta decide right here and now to work together so this thing goes our way...not their way. I'm sure you heard about the shootings among the Italians."

Frank Costello says, "I don't even walk the streets anymore. Everybody associated with Joe the Boss has become the target of the Brooklyn boys."

"What didn't make the *Daily News* were the two Sicilians who were gunned down in a Detroit fish market. One of those guys used to be part of the Brooklyn mob a few years back. Joe the Boss was behind the assassinations. Salvatore Maranzano means to use this situation to get rid of Joe the Boss."

Vito says, "Sicilians are always scheming. They don't like Neapolitans and they don't like the Calabrese. That goes for Jews and Irish, too. We all got trouble."

Charlie says, "We don't need no greaseball war in New York but that's exactly what we're gonna have. The sea is parting. You're either for Maranzano or he sees you as against him. He's called a meeting of the family fathers to finish what they started in Cleveland. Since Joe the Boss admitted he was behind the Detroit murders, you know that's gonna be on the agenda, even though Joe called it self defense."

Meyer says, "Maranzano uses the idea that the honor of the Castellammarese has been sullied."

Charlie says, "This guy is already polishing his bullets."

Meyer says, "There's something else you should know about. The Chicago Crime Commission has created a public enemy list designed to enforce the law by stigma. Capone is Public Enemy Number One. A bunch of his guys are on the list, too."

"So what?" Madden says.

Meyer says, "Once the police connect Frankie Yale's shooting to the St. Valentine's Day Massacre, the stigma washes back on us if we become known as bootleggers."

Frank Costello very nearly gasps. He fancies himself a legitimate businessman. The local politicians rely on his favors. He can't afford to be associated with Chicago's Wild West massacres.

"Don't worry," the Dutchman says. "You won't have to get your hands dirty."

Madden says, "Capone's worst nightmare might be the tax collector. Wouldn't that be something?"

Charlie says, "He don't own much on paper. If they pinch him for what he does own, he'll pay a fine. That's what the rich do. He ain't goin' to jail for that."

Lepke says, "So what's the plan?"

Meyer says, "Charlie and I are keeping a close eye on what's going on between Joe the Boss and the Brooklyn Castellammarese. We're asking that, no matter what happens, you don't make a move without checking in with us."

The Dutchman grunts, "I ain't steppin' aside for no wop if he makes a move on me."

The room swirls with smoke and ash and overconfidence. Conversations swell and diminish over what should and shouldn't be done.

Charlie says, "Me and Meyer will take care of the greasers when the time is right."

Owney Madden worries, "These old bulls have been killin' each other as long as I've been alive. How are you going to change that?"

Charlie says, "Trust me, we want these guys outta the way as much as you do."

Madden says, "You got my vote, Charlie. Do what you gotta do."

The meeting winds down and begins to disperse.

Vito says to Charlie, "You need me to take care of anything?"

"I'll get in touch with you later, Vito. We got a lot to discuss."

Meyer stops Lepke at the door. "There's an Italian guy who's looking for action in the garment district. Can you throw him a bone?"

Lepke considers the request then says, "Give me a couple of days. I'll see what I can come up with."

Frank Costello wonders out loud, "What are the odds of pulling this thing off?"

"I give us a fifty-fifty chance. But keep it under your hat. We don't want nobody getting nervous," Charlie says. "And Frank, we're gonna need your help with some of the local politicians when all this goes down."

Costello says, "Nobody will miss these guys, Charlie."

"If we do it right," Charlie says, "nobody will even notice they're gone."

Meyer and Benny stop in at the Dutchman's hovel. Not much has changed since the last time they visited. The Dutchman's thugs sit around a corner table playing cards while Flegenheimer huddles in his office sorting the profits from his rackets. Bo Weinberg wanders through the saloon keeping an eye on business. Bo tips his hat to Meyer and nods toward the back room. Meyer and Benny follow the nod and step into the Dutchman's domain.

"What is it this time?" the Dutchman says. "Your Italian friend send you?"

Meyer ignores the insult.

"You don't think much of the Italians, do you, Arthur?" he says.

The Dutchman says, "Who gives a shit? I run my own business; they run theirs."

Bo Weinberg is drawn to the conversation. He leans against the door jamb and smokes a cigarette. Cold sweat seeps through the brick exterior of the saloon and casts a chill over the room. Meyer rummages for a pack of cigarettes and lights up. The Dutchman relinquishes his hold on numbers calculations. Bo offers him a cigarette. The Dutchman grabs the entire pack.

Meyer says, "I'm giving Benny the job of getting rid of the Brooklyn problem. We'd like to use Bo on this job."

The Dutchman bolts upright in his chair. He turns to look at Weinberg. The last thing the Dutchman wants is to cross swords with the calculating and volatile Siegel but Weinberg is his guy, not Meyer's…or Benny's. Weinberg smiles. He's in his element with Benny. The Dutchman sees the comradery and grouses.

"What do you need Bo for?" the Dutchman says.

"He's got a cool head and a dead aim. When the greasers make their moves, and they will, then we'll make ours…if they haven't taken each other out by then."

"We?" the Dutchman says.

"Me and Charlie," Meyer says. "In this case, Benny and a few guys of his choosing."

"You and the Italian. Ain't that chummy? Why Bo?" the Dutchman says.

"Meyer already told ya," Benny says. "Ain't it obvious?"

"It ain't obvious to me," the Dutchman counters.

"Charlie will take care of Joe the Boss. It's only right," Meyer says. "Jews should take care of the wannabe Caesar in Brooklyn. You have the toughest mob in Harlem. Lepke has the garment district. I'm asking for one of his guys, too. There will be four Jewish guys and one Irish guy. It sends a message. You fuck with Charlie you fuck with all of us."

Suspicion overcomes the Dutchman's better judgment. He gives Weinberg the once-over and then turns back to Meyer.

Benny says, "We ain't proposing marriage, for Christ's sake."

Weinberg shrugs, "Let's get these bastards."

"Let the Italians take care of their own dirty work," the Dutchman says.

Meyer says, "It's in all our interests not to let this guy get too much power. He wants to control the docks. Cooperation now will save you trouble later."

The Dutchman thinks hard. He moves on instinct and very little gray matter.

He says, "You gonna get one of Waxey's boys?"

Meyer says, "Waxey's got nothing to do with it."

The Dutchman grunts. He turns back to his ledger and the ancient Burroughs adding machine with the wobbling number keys battered and worn loose by the pounding of his merciless fingers.

"O.K.," the Dutchman sighs. "But I don't want no funny business."

Meyer says to Bo, "Drop by the garage tomorrow. Benny will fill you in."

Weinberg shows up at the Cannon Street garage the next day.

Benny revs the engine of a Model A that Sammy has modified into a fast getaway car. Red Levine waves Bo over to the vehicle.

"Come on," Benny says. "We'll pick up Lepke's guy and take a ride. I've got it all mapped out. Four Jews. We're gonna take Caesar down in broad daylight."

Benny is tough and ruthless. A man of action: independent, self-directed, and competitive. That's why Meyer put him in charge of taking down the wannabe Caesar. It's poetic justice to have the great general face an unpredictable adversary. Benny possesses a nimble intelligence. He lives in the moment. A tiger on the prowl willing to wait out his opportunity but when he moves, he brings with him great power and focus. Meyer admires this in Benny.

Weinberg hops into the Model A and Benny tears out of the garage. The plan is a good one. Although Maranzano busies himself with knowing all the men in his tradition, he has forgotten there are more than Italians interested in his plans. It's the blind spot of his ego not to notice what does not concern him and Meyer has noticed this trend to his advantage.

While Benny prepares the hit team, Meyer and Charlie turn their attention to Al Capone. They join the line of human cargo waiting to board the Broadway Limited heading to Chicago. The train leaves New York at 2:55 P.M. They settle in for the ensuing twenty hours of swaying and thumping as the heavy steel train powers across eight hundred miles of track. In the morning, they will present their strategy for getting rid of the greasers to Public Enemy Number One.

In the quiet of the drawing room that joins their sleeping compartments, they wrap their minds around the Chicago situation.

"The Ghost of Christmas Past ain't lettin' loose of the big man's brain," Charlie says.

Charlie is referring to the syphilitic corkscrew bacteria that are working their way through Capone's heart and brain and driving him slowly insane.

Meyer says, "He should be consulting a doctor instead of a medium."

"It's too late for a doctor," Charlie says. "We gotta focus on the power behind the throne."

Meyer says, "McGurn?"

"You saw the papers. He's on the public enemy list right

alongside Capone. If they take Capone, they'll take McGurn right along with him. Guzik won't skate free either. Who will take the throne when Capone falls? That's the question. I heard that Maranzano is turning heads talking about creating a Senate like they had in Rome. He's calling it a Commission."

Meyer says, "It's a good idea, Charlie. I told you the Jews have a court that helps people work out their problems. Here's the key. They work as a body, not one guy telling everybody else what to do."

Charlie says, "That's not how Italians work. Kiss the ring, do the ceremony. You'd think it was the Catholic Church!"

Meyer says, "So let them have their traditions. You can't take a child from his mother's tit until he's ready to go. Cut them off from that and they'll resent you. When we take these guys, we'll create a vacuum. They have to have somebody to look to and that somebody has to put an end to the senseless killing right away."

Charlie says, "There ain't no controlling these guys."

"The Commission, Charlie. You're Sicilian."

"The hell with that," Charlie says. "I don't need the publicity."

"You'll be Public Enemy Number One on Caesar's list in no time at all," Meyer says with a grin.

"That ain't funny," Charlie says.

"When this guy sees how strong you are, the first thing on his mind will be to cut you down to size. When that happens, you have two choices: die or take control. Didn't you tell me that self defense is a legitimate reason for killing someone?"

"These guys got all the words," Charlie says. "Honor. Tradition. It's all bullshit. If they had any honor, they wouldn't bleed the boys dry. How can you honor a guy that's robbin' ya? That's the problem right there."

Meyer says, "If Maranzano manages to bring the fathers together, your first move is to demand your position right along with the rest of them."

"How do I do that?"

"Switch sides. When war comes and Maranzano looks strong, you offer to take out your boss. Maranzano won't flinch. His ego is satisfied that you asked and he gets rid of Joe. It's what he wants more than anything else, your allegiance and Joe dead."

"Jesus," Charlie says. "But what if it's Joe the Boss and Morello that win the war?"

"Then we come up with another plan," Meyer says. "If it comes to that. Will it?"

"It's hard to say," Charlie says. "These guys are loose cannons. You don't give them what they want, you insult their honor. Maybe that comes from the old days of feuding. Who the hell knows? Honor covers a multitude of sins. That's what I know."

They head to the dining car where white tablecloths, crystal service, silver settings, and porcelain vases overcome the sensation of tight quarters. The waiter's white jacket, white shirt, black pants, and black bowtie further contribute to the illusion of a superb dining experience. The waiter heads to the table, impervious to the unrelenting swaying.

He says, "Tonight we are serving Lobster Newburg, Lemon Trout Almondine, Pepper Pot Louisianne, and sizzling New York steak. That comes with baked potato Parisienne and savory green beans. What can I get for you gentlemen?"

Charlie says. "What's Parisienne about the potato?"

"Fancy words for butter and parsley, sir."

Charlie says, "Steak and baked potato. And coffee."

Meyer nods.

"Yes, sir," the waiter says and glides back to the galley.

The train rumbles and whistles through Pennsylvania. This is farmland, inhabited by the people who, in a blind self-righteous zeal that appeared to be backed by the word of God, made Prohibition possible. By the time the train travels through the fields of Ohio, they are done with dinner and back in their car.

Meyer says, "Whatever else happens, you have to get out of the drug business."

"Ain't I heard this lecture before? 'I'll never have the respect of the Sicilians until I do. I won't be trusted. It's the way it has to be.' "

Meyer says, "You won't have the luxury of dreaming after we make our moves."

"Maybe I don't care if the Sicilians respect me," Charlie says.

"Charlie, you are going to be the man," Meyer says. "Wait and see."

The night train whistles and wails. Charlie and Meyer move to the observation car and smoke cigars. They sleep. Wake. Shave. They put on clean shirts and drink hot coffee. They indulge in poached eggs, toasted bread, and rashers of bacon. They plot and revise and strategize.

Charlie says, "If Maranzano gets Profaci and Reina's guys on his side, he gains a lot of strength."

"And their allies in Chicago?" Meyer says.

"The turmoil between Capone and the Chicago Sicilians is to our advantage. If they're busy dealing with Capone, they won't be able to throw as much strength to the Sicilian mob in New York."

The train rolls into Chicago's Union Station. Two of Capone's best, Rocco and Charlie Fischetti, meet Charlie and Meyer at the station. Rocco sinks boxing tickets into the breast pocket of Charlie's jacket. It is a quick alibi in case anybody notices a couple of New York gangsters in Chicago.

"The boss is waitin'," Rocco says, neither anxious nor burdened by the idea.

The Lexington Hotel, a ten-story building at the corner of Michigan Avenue and 22nd Street with four-hundred-fifty rooms and a claim of being one-hundred percent fireproof, is Capone's home away from home.

Tony Accardo, a Thompson by his side, keeps watch in the hotel lobby. Charlie nods to Tony as they walk past.

The Big Man's operation spreads through the Lexington like kudzu, climbing, coiling, and trailing through the third, fourth, and fifth floors. Capone has the necessities of gangster life: a shooting gallery, secret passages, and hidden vaults. Tunnels spread out like tentacles from the basement to neighboring taverns and whorehouses. No one is ever seen entering or leaving the hotel unless they want to be seen.

Suite 530 is Capone's personal refuge. A chandelier with smoked glass globes floats above a large oriental carpet. A stuffed deer head and two stuffed elk heads hang over a faux fireplace. Gold and reddish pink wallpaper form the backdrop for portraits of George Washington and Chicago's mayor, William Hale Thompson. The room reeks of insincere hominess.

"I made that guy what he is today," Capone says.

"You knew George Washington?" Charlie replies.

"Big Bill ain't no George Washington and that ain't half bad. He sure as hell knows how to take a bribe. We orchestrated the Pineapple Primary on his behalf," Capone laughs. "And worth every penny."

Grenades fueled the election that won the label. Sixty-two bombings prior to the primary. Two politicians killed in action. Capone wears the victory like a badge of honor. Rocco takes a seat by the fireplace and listens to Capone wax poetic about the affair. Charlie Fischetti hands Charlie Lucky the latest issue of

Time, featuring his boss on the front cover. The caption reads *Alphonse ("Scarface") Capone* beneath a photo of the man himself flashing a genial smile.

"You got me beat, Charlie," Capone says, rubbing his finger along his scar.

"Fifty-five," Charlie says. "If I remember, you only got thirty."

"Twenty-eight," Capone growls. "And these bastards gotta make a big deal of it on the cover of *Time*. How come Sigmund Freud didn't get no nickname when they ran his story?"

"How much you wanna bet your face sells more magazines than his?" Charlie says.

Capone doesn't want to think about Sigmund Freud or psychoanalysis. "You see the new kid in the lobby?"

"Tony Accardo?" Charlie says. "Sure, I seen him."

Capone says, "I call him Joe Batters. The kid's got real talent with a baseball bat. I'm thinkin' of bringing him up the ladder. You ever need a hitter, give me a call. I'll send him over, only don't show him to the Yankees. They might try to recruit him."

Capone lets out a belly laugh then summons three girls from the adjoining room. They glisten in the summer heat. The silk of their garments sticks to their flesh. Capone grabs the robust blonde wearing black silk suspender shorts and a puffy blouse. She falls onto the sofa and into Capone's arms.

"You got a nice ass," he growls with a slap to her derriere. "Don't let nobody tell you otherwise. You broads get lost for a couple of hours."

"Whatever you say," she says in a slow, Southern drawl.

She rises and the three girls leave arm in arm.

"I'm in the mood with that one," Capone says before turning unusually serious. "It's tougher than it used to be. Everybody's got their hand out. The cops, the press, the Sicilians...fucking

Sicilians. A pain in everybody's ass. I come home and I still got goddamn Aiello running around offering a bounty for my head. He figured I was washed up so he slipped back here to insinuate himself. That's the kinda coward he is. He thinks I lost my grip. That's why you're here, ain't it? Fucking Sicilians. Fucking scars. I'll tell you something, Charlie, a hundred years can pass and you'll still want revenge on the guy that cut you."

"Al," Charlie says, "we got a delicate situation in New York."

"You always got a delicate situation in New York," Capone says. "When are you gonna do what needs to be done?"

Charlie says, "We're lookin' to take care of the troublemakers once and for all."

The comment stops Capone in his tracks. For one brief moment, the syphilitic corkscrews lose their grip and Capone's mind snaps to attention.

"I'll be damned," he says.

Charlie says, "We'd like your cooperation while we work things out. That's why we're here. I'm asking you in all due respect, if you got something that needs taking care of in New York, consider lettin' us take care of it."

A grin fills Capone's face.

"Fucking cocksucker prancing around Brooklyn dreaming about another Sicilian Vesper? Won't he be surprised. I like this, Charlie. I was beginning to wonder if you had it in you anymore." Capone shoves the butt of his cigar into an ashtray and turns to Meyer. "You heard of Vespers? It's like evening prayers. Something Catholics do. The Sicilian Vespers, that's history. When the Pope crowned a French prince and made him king of Sicily and Naples, the Sicilians mounted an insurrection. It was back in 1282, or something like that. A bunch of farmers killed off most of the French on the island. They call it the Sicilian Vespers. It's a big deal with the Sicilians. Supposedly they struck while the French were saying their prayers, vespers, you know. The Neapolitans didn't fight off the French. That's where I come from, Naples. The Neapolitans used the French and Naples got to be a great city. The Sicilians wanted the Neapolitans to kill the French. They never forgave us for gettin' rich instead of gettin' dead."

Charlie peels off his jacket and hangs his head out the window to escape the heat.

"It's human nature," Meyer says.

"I'll tell you what's human nature," Capone says. "Two minutes after I get outta the can, Brooklyn's new Caesar sends word, you got that? Salvatore Maranzano sends me a warning that I better keep away from the conflict in New York. Now you come telling me to stay outta your way?"

Capone puffs hard on his stogie.

Charlie pulls his head back inside and says, "Al, I ain't askin' you to steer clear. I'm askin' you, with all due respect, if you would let him hold on to the misconception that he's in control while we pull the rug out from under him."

Capone studies Meyer and then Charlie. They have the gleam of war in their eyes and this pleases Capone. Again, he lets out a belly laugh.

He says, "I heard Joe Aiello is hiding out with his cousin in Buffalo. When the going gets tough, the chickens run to the farm, eh, Charlie? When he comes outta hiding, I'm going to blow his fucking head clean off and watch his body run around the barnyard."

Charlie shrugs, "Do what you gotta do; just don't do it in New York. That's all I ask."

Big Al rubs the back of his neck with his chubby fingers. He hasn't slept well since James Clark started reaching out from the grave. James Clark, whose face was obliterated by the blast of a shotgun on Valentine's Day, who was Moran's second-in-command, is keeping Capone up at night. The Big Man fights back with moans and threats but Clark continues to haunt his every dream. Nobody talks about it, especially Rocco, but they hear Capone's screams in the night.

Capone says, "If it was anybody else…"

Charlie nods, "I appreciate your cooperation, Al. I'll be thinking of you when we take Joe the Boss. By the way, we got an idea we'd like to run by you. When this thing goes down, we got the opportunity to set some new rules. Maranzano wants to build a Commission made up of the Sicilian fathers. It ain't a half bad idea."

"I don't need nobody tellin' me what to do in my own town," Capone says.

"Naturally," Charlie says. "He's talking about a Commission with him as the head. We got the idea of a Commission of equals. When somebody crosses the line and things get mixed up between mobs, we need a way to keep the peace. Everybody west of the Mississippi answers to Chicago. Everybody east of the Mississippi answers to New York. The mobs must sit down and work out their differences like gentlemen. No more killing without permission."

"You got big dreams," Capone says. "There ain't no way this will stop the violence."

Charlie says, "I ain't no fool, Al. You know me long enough to know that. But if we don't have an arrangement, we're gonna have anarchy the same as we got now. This ain't workin'. It brings heat on everybody. There's gotta be rules we can all agree on that even bosses are accountable to."

Capone throws his arm around Charlie's shoulder.

"Jesus Christ, Charlie, what got into you? I got a proposition. A friendly wager between you and me. Whoever loses takes the other guy to dinner. If I get Aiello first, you owe me. If you get Joe the Boss first, I owe you. Whadya say?"

"You got a deal," Charlie says. "One you'll probably win."

The Dutchman slams the newspaper down on his desk. Babe Ruth is pulling down an all-time high salary of $80,000 and he still can't dig the Yankees out of the hole they're in. Why this bothers the Dutchman baffles the imagination.

Bo Weinberg says, "Give him a break, Arthur. The Babe lost his wife last year in a fire. How's a guy supposed to deal with a situation like that?"

"Estranged wife," the Dutchman says. "He was remarried four months later. What's that got to do with baseball, anyway? What you don't know about the Babe's new wife is that she's got him on a tight leash. The Babe don't need no nursemaid. He needs to get laid by all them broads or he don't got the juice for the game."

Weinberg checks the news. The July 4th game against the Washington Senators ended in defeat. The season stands at 43 losses and 28 wins. Lou Gehrig, fourth in the batting lineup, can't seem to bring in any runs.

"They ain't gonna make it to the World Series this year," the Dutchman says. "They gotta free up Babe so he can get laid and then they gotta get a new pitcher. You got any idea how much money we would rake in takin' those bets! Maybe you oughta go out there and take the Babe to a good whorehouse."

The Dutchman ratchets the handle of the monstrous Burroughs adding machine. Numbers measure his success in tangible terms of dollars and cents. He doesn't like what he sees.

Weinberg says, "You don't waltz into professional baseball and take the star player to a whorehouse. They already got guys for that."

The Dutchman isn't listening. Profits are down. He's counting on the Italian lottery to boost them back up but he's running into trouble. There are thirty black policy banks in Harlem and the big ones aren't letting go of their grip on the game.

"Are them bankers lining up?" he says.

"I'm working on it," Weinberg says.

The Dutchman says, "I ain't lookin' for no battin' average. Take care of it."

"The small-timers are bowing out."

"Yeah? What about James Warner? And that black broad, Stephanie St. Clair, and her pimp friend?" the Dutchman says.

"One guy don't wanna play ball. He'll see the light soon enough."

"One guy? Black or white?" the Dutchman says punching in a new set of numbers.

Weinberg says, "The color of his heart or the color of his skin?"

"Don't try to be funny. It don't suit you," the Dutchman says. "Get Jimmy Hines to take care of the dumb mick."

"Jimmy has his hands full with Seabury," Weinberg says. "Besides, it's not a mick. It's a guy named Alejandro Pompez, a black banker. They call him Alex. He's no fool. He owns the Cuban Stars and the New York Cubans."

"What the hell do I care what he owns?"

Weinberg says, "He's got clout in Harlem."

The Dutchman stops punching numbers. His eyes narrow and his nose twitches in disgust.

"I ain't takin' nothing off no nigger." The Dutchman is up and moving around his cramped office.

"He's an attorney," Weinberg says.

"He ain't no saint," the Dutchman says. "I'm goin' to the Oswasco Democratic Club. Go get the nigger and bring him to me."

Weinberg gathers up his brother George and heads for the small club where Pompez operates his bookmaking rackets. The neighborhood is poor and dark by complexion. The two Jews stand out not only for the way they look but also the way they walk. They swagger with an air of trouble. Kids jumping rope stop and stare. A group of black men follow behind them as they make their way to the club. Pompez, a dapper man in his mid-thirties, is in a back room playing cards with three bodyguards.

Pompez looks up from his card game. "I already told you no. Now go on, get outta my establishment."

The bodyguards stand. The club comes to a standstill.

"This works better if you don't resist," Bo Weinberg says.

Pompez laughs.

"Your boss sent you out here to fetch me? Is that the game you're playing, boy? Fetch? I thought you Jews ran the world."

Bo Weinberg says, "The Dutchman didn't take business courses at Harvard. He's making it comfortable for you. A gentlemen's discussion at the Oswasco."

"Shit," Pompez says. "The Dutchman ain't never gonna be no gentleman."

Weinberg waits, assessing his options. If he pulls his .38, things will get ugly fast. He decides to avoid the morgue through reason.

"I'm just the messenger. Shooting me won't stop the Dutchman so why are we playing cat and mouse?"

"You're sweating," Pompez says.

"I'm wearing a suit in the middle of July," Bo Weinberg says.

Pompez stands. His boys rally.

"I'll drive myself, if you don't mind," Pompez says.

Bo Weinberg agrees to the compromise. The Weinbergs follow behind Pompez.

The Democratic Club, a Tammany stronghold, has the appeal

of a snake-charmer on market day. It is dark and musty and stinks of fraud but nobody seems able to turn away from the show.

The Dutchman is drinking beer with Solly Girsch, a Harlem policy banker with influence. The familiar face is intended to convince Pompez that protection money is money well spent. Pompez takes a seat across from the Dutchman. The two men lock gazes.

"Five hundred dollars a week for the privilege of staying in business. Think of it as a tax," the Dutchman says.

Pompez puts on his best courtroom demeanor.

He says, "I have no need of a partner and I won't be bullied into playing ball with you, Mr. Flegenheimer. My paltry business is not big enough for your concern."

Whatever hint of humanity the Dutchman might have had is completely gone. His glare is hollow, an all-consuming void that threatens to swallow Mr. Alejandro Pompez and his paltry business. The Dutchman doesn't flinch, doesn't wonder about his demands, doesn't care.

The Dutchman says, "Five hundred dollars a week in exchange for your life. You'll still be able to afford your fancy clothes and cheap broads."

Pompez stands and returns a blank face.

"I assume I will be hearing from you soon," Pompez says.

Once he's gone, the Dutchman says to Weinberg, "What was so hard about that?"

Weinberg says, "It must be your winning personality."

The Dutchman stands a round of shots for everyone. It is what businessmen do. His new attorney, Dixie Davis, has told him so and the Dutchman has taken his word as law. For the first time in his life, his suit is not from Sears, an extravagance for which Mr. Davis has lowered his usual twenty-five-dollar fee.

The Dutchman says, "Go get Ison. And when we're done with him, we'll deal with the Policy Queen. I've had enough of her shenanigans."

But Stephanie St. Clair refuses to yield to the Dutchman's advances. In a bid for autonomy, she has taken out an ad in the Harlem newspaper claiming the Dutchman is trying to steal her business. Tall, tough, and fast-talking, the French immigrant is sure that her gang, the Forty Thieves, can rout the bully.

"Roughing up broads ain't good for business," Weinberg says, showing his soft spot.

The Dutchman says, "I decide what's good for business."

Weinberg looks at his brother and then heads toward the door.

Charlie Luciano digs through his duffel bag after returning from Chicago and retrieves the envelope that Al Capone gave him to convey to Joe the Boss. Charlie thumbs through the stack of hundred dollar bills. The envelope feels light. He pads out the contents with more bills until the envelope feels fat and rich. He slips the packet into the inner pocket of his jacket and catches a taxi uptown to Joe's penthouse.

Joe the Boss listens quietly while Charlie relays the troubles Capone is having in Chicago. He laments the sad fact that Joseph Aiello is still running free and most likely hiding in Buffalo while holding out a contract on Capone's life.

Charlie hands over the fat envelope. The tribute is intoxicating.

"Cola Schiro has disappeared," Joe says. "He's smarter than I thought. Stefano Magaddino refuses my gesture for peace. Now I know why. Aiello is whispering in his ear. Stefano doesn't realize that Maranzano is a terrier at a rat hole waiting to seize the Brooklyn family."

"He wants more than Brooklyn," Charlie says.

The tune is music to Joe's ears.

"Joe Parrino will take over and calm the talk against me among Reina's boys," Joe says.

"He'll have a hard time of it," Charlie says. "I don't care what nobody says, no Sicilian ever forgives his brother's killer. These guys got memories like elephants. It don't matter that you didn't pull the trigger. It don't matter that you didn't pull the trigger on the gun that killed Sasa Gaspar that day at the Fish Market. Gaspar and Magaddino were allies. They worked the Brooklyn rackets together, and Magaddino won't forget."

To some degree, this is good news for Charlie. Stefano Magaddino and Salvatore Maranzano will always want Joe the Boss dead. If they get to the job before Charlie, that's one less situation to deal with.

Joe paces back and forth and wonders if Peter Morello was right in telling Maranzano that they are responsible for Gaspar's death. He steps out onto the balcony and takes in Central Park. The hum of the city drones in the background.

"I am going into hiding," Joe says, at last. "You will watch my interests. That is my decision."

"Whatever you say," Charlie replies.

"I knew you would understand. Now, my friend, let's take one last trip to Coney Island. Absence will be much easier on a bellyful of calamari."

Joe the Boss has pushed the Castellammarese too far. He fears Stefano Magaddino's reaction so he will go into hiding and leave Charlie to hang in the wind and draw off the heat.

They settle into a late afternoon meal at Gerado Scarpato's restaurant. Charlie watches the boss eat. Joe skirts the issues. He is entrenched in his afternoon ritual. Scarpato looks on, making sure the boss gets whatever he wants. Joe relaxes. He signals to Scarpato for espresso and cards.

Charlie loosens his necktie that tugs at the scar from the fifty-five stitches that remind him of the October night in 1929. He shuffles the cards and deals.

Chapter Nineteen
Now Is the Summer of Our Discontent

SUMMER 1930

Three days of triple-digit temperatures and high humidity and the residents of New York are ready for Bellevue. Those who can have taken refuge at the seashore. Those who can't swarm theaters and restaurants where man has triumphed over summer's reign of terror with something called refrigerated air. Architects celebrate by designing windowless buildings. The *New York Times* runs a pie-in-the-sky story promising "germ-free atmospheres and artificial sunlight for those who must spend much of their lives at work indoors." Of course, this news is not meant for those laboring in factories.

Joe Bonanno slings his suit jacket over his shoulder and sets out for his beloved Brooklyn restaurant on 84th Street. His shirt wilts across his chest as he walks. He wipes the sweat from his face with his handkerchief. Bonanno has spent the last few days visiting with one of his cousins, discussing the ins and outs of Maranzano's master plan. They are thrilled.

The small café fills daily with Italians who gather to discuss politics and economics and wolf down gobs of marinated artichokes and homemade pastas. A worn awning shades the front window. Cardboard signs on the windowsill tout the daily specials.

Bonanno pauses to catch his breath from the walk. The heat has left him woozy. Charlie Luciano, suit jacket off and shirtsleeves rolled to the elbow, is seated at a back table guzzling ice water. He sees Bonanno and waves him back. Bonanno dabs his forehead. It would be imprudent to dismiss the underboss of Joe Masseria this late in the game.

"How come you ain't at Lindy's?" Charlie says. "They got cool air over there."

He nods toward Manhattan and the luxurious lifestyle.

"I could ask the same of you," Bonanno says.

"Luigi's ravioli," Charlie says.

Enough said.

Luigi's wife, Gina, pounds out the rhythm of a hard-working woman with her stiff Oxford spectator pumps. She wears a neatly pressed readymade dress and bobbed hair. Not Fifth Avenue but definitely, now, American.

"Luigi, he make cold escarole and bean soup," she says, delivering two bowls, one for Charlie and one for Joe Bonanno. "I bring you antipasti, too, no? And then we see what else."

Charlie says, "What's the pasta?"

"What you think?" She winks. "Luigi make you ravioli, don't you worry."

She makes her way back to the kitchen. Charlie digs into the soup.

Bonanno says, "I heard that Joe has gone into hiding."

"Where did you hear that?" Charlie says.

"It's all over the street."

"Are you looking for him?" Charlie says.

Bonanno shakes his head.

"Aren't you concerned?" Bonanno says. "If Joe is afraid for his life. Why aren't you?"

"Me?" Charlie says. "I got nothing to be afraid of. Besides, Joe the Boss calls the shots. Hey, I hear the Castellammarese are pretty sore that Joe insisted on Pinzolo as the new head of Tom Reina's family."

Gina brings the antipasti. Charlie spreads roasted tomatoes and grilled eggplant on a piece of toasted bread.

Bonanno says, "The Clutch Hand should have known better but his good sense has failed him. The problem with Mr. Joe is that he lacks values. The way Tommy was gunned down, in front of his aunt's apartment, is that the act of a true father? Salvatore Maranzano has strong values. He would never do a thing like that. Even to a man who opposed him."

Charlie raises his eyebrows. "His aunt's house? He was gunned down in front of the apartment of his mistress. I guess Tommy didn't share Maranzano's values either. Maybe that's why he was gunned down. Who knows who pulled the trigger that night?"

Bonanno turns his gaze to the antipasti.

Charlie says, "Joe ain't gonna win no popularity contests. Everybody can see that. But these old guys aren't interested in what nobody else thinks but them. Joe has his reasons for backing Pinzolo. Maybe guys like you and me would handle things differently. Maybe if we were in their shoes we'd do just what they do."

Bonanno says, "You pay Joe."

"Plenty," Charlie says. "It's like a tax, the cost of doing business. It keeps things quiet, so to speak. Don't you kick in to your family?"

Bonanno snorts and lays out a list of grievances against Mr. Joe, Peter Morello, and Fat Joe Pinzolo, the latest greasy spot on the tablecloth of "Our Tradition."

Firemen pull up in front of the restaurant. All attention turns to the truck and the men climbing off it to the street. The fire they battle is not one that burns down buildings but one that overheats the local kids. They uncap a hydrant. Water blasts into the sky and then falls mercifully to earth, soaking the pavement and sidewalk. Neighborhood kids swarm to the oasis. The restaurant goes back to its conversation.

Bonanno says, "A little spark gives birth to a big flame. If

Mr. Joe had treated Joe Aiello with respect when they met in Chicago, we wouldn't be in this situation today."

"Joe Aiello ain't no saint," Charlie says. "As I understand it, and I'm just speaking about what I've heard on the street, there's a lot more to this than Joe Aiello's wounded ego. Let's start with the game Aiello is playing with Al Capone. Aiello demands Joe control Capone. Does he really think Joe the Boss has control over Chicago? Even if he wanted to, he can't tell Capone what to do. The Pope himself couldn't get Big Al to walk away from his rackets in Chicago. And what about the three musketeers? You know who I'm talking about."

"Guinta, Scalice, and Anselmi?"

Charlie says, "Who knocked those guys off? I heard the Sicilians who didn't want them mixing with Capone."

Bonanno says, "Capone killed those men."

"Sicilians bashed their heads in and then shot them for good measure."

Bonanno says, "Scalice and Anselmi were in on the massacre."

"Are you sayin' that the Sicilians paid them back because they rubbed out guys from an Irish mob? Then maybe it's true that Aiello has allied himself with the Irish to get rid of Capone."

Bonanno is silent.

Charlie says, "Look, maybe Maranzano don't see the difference between Sicily and America. There's a lot of mobs here and each one has its own territory. Trouble comes in when somebody wants to cross the line and take over somebody else. You get what I'm sayin'? The Castellammarese are expanding into bootleg. Those territories are already settled. If you cross that line, you have to pay for the privilege of working in somebody else's territory."

Bonanno says, "The way it looks to us, it's Mr. Joe that's crossing the line."

"And you want to be left alone," Charlie says. "I hear that but like I said, there's a lot of mobs around and they ain't all Sicilian. You gotta respect that or there's trouble. Maranzano has a lot of big words but he don't got a handle on what makes New York New York. Maranzano thinks he can take what belongs to the Jews if Italians are involved. He's got a head like Al Capone. He wants to control it all. It ain't gonna happen. What is yours? What is mine? What is the Dutchman's in Harlem? The Commission don't take the Dutchman into account, so what happens when the Castellammarese start movin' in on his territory on accounta the Italians there too? I already know what Maranzano thinks. What I wanna know is what you think."

A chill runs up Bonanno's spine. The half-truths he's been throwing around have fallen flat. He conjures an ambiguous reply, striving for neutral ground.

Bonanno says, "We came to America for freedom and found another Mussolini. You call him Joe the Boss. We call him Mr. Joe because he isn't our boss. We will defend what is ours."

Charlie says, "If Maranzano tries to install himself as head over all the families, there will be war. Are you going to support him in that?"

"The Commission is a great idea founded in Roman history. It is meant to solve problems, not create them," Bonanno says. "Someone has to break Mr. Joe's yoke."

"I'll tell you a little secret. There ain't gonna be no cooperation between Joe the Boss and Salvatore Maranzano. They're two bulls fighting for control of the golden heifer. One ain't no different from the other."

Bonanno says, "We don't want anything from anybody except to be left to our own business."

Charlie signals Gina to bring a bottle of wine. She pours two glasses.

"I think we can agree to a world without Fascism," Charlie says.

Bonanno nods, "Salute!"

"Pack a bag," Maranzano says after listening to Joe Bonanno's description of lunch with Charlie. "We're going to Long Island."

Within an hour, the Cadillac pulls up in front of Bonanno's building. Maranzano rolls down the back window.

"Get in, Peppino," he says, waving his broad hand in Bonanno's direction.

The driver takes Bonanno's duffel and places it in the trunk next to Maranzano's bag and a large metal box that holds ammunition for the machine gun. They head across the East River and out to where breezes blow and air is tolerable.

Maranzano settles in for the ride. He turns to Bonanno and asks for a repeat of the conversation.

"What was your impression?" Maranzano says. "He said many things but do you really believe he will turn against the over-stuffed capo di tutti? Perhaps he was testing your loyalty."

Bonanno says, "Charlie Luciano has no respect for the old man. If he respected the Chinese, he would defend him, but he does not. Don't you think that's telling?"

Mr. Joe has been dubbed "the Chinese" by Maranzano. It's an old trick. Erode respect for your enemy by lowering his social status in the eyes of others. Maranzano creates a carica-ture of Mr. Joe to insult him: "His face is so fat, his eyes squint like a Chinaman's."

"Indeed," Maranzano says. "Indeed. Tell me, Peppino, are you going to become a citizen of this country?"

"I am thinking of it," Bonanno says. "There is no place for me in Italy as long as Mussolini rules the country."

Maranzano laughs. "How true. But why this country? Why not Canada? There is no Prohibition in Canada."

"Yes, and we are making a very good living off Prohibition, aren't we?"

"We are indeed," Maranzano says. "And this is why Mr. Joe demands tribute. If we were like the other mobs, he would not even notice we exist. But we are not like other mobs and this is what irritates the glutton. We are a powerful family and we must remain united. We are going to visit the other men of honor. They must see who Mr. Joe really is and reject him. Tell me, Peppino, what did Charlie say to make you think he does not approve of Mr. Joe's actions? What were his exact words?"

"We talked about so many things," Bonanno says. "It is hard to remember just exactly what he said that gave me the impression. He did say that he is not interested in bulling anyone. That was his word. Are you familiar with the term?"

Maranzano shakes his head.

"No matter," Bonanno says. "He said it was too bad that we are headed for a war."

The first stop Maranzano makes is the summer estate of Vito Bonventre. The estate sits on the south side of the island in the town of Seaford where a small group of islands buffer the shore from the Atlantic Ocean. The location is perfect for offloading booze of all sorts, including wine from Italy. Any small launch can squeeze through Jones Inlet and hide from the Coast Guard, if necessary. The Coast Guard, however, is content with the graft so Bonventre's boats come and go freely.

Bonventre takes his ease on the patio, watching his grandchildren splash in the pool while he waits for his guests to settle in. The cook brings fresh bread rolls and lemonade spiked with mint. The afternoon sun flirts with the trees in a dappled dance that casts shadows across the land.

Maranzano is the first to join Bonventre. He delivers the news that Cola Schiro has gone into hiding. With no small amount of pride, Maranzano confides that he was voted to lead the family.

Bonventre watches the children play.

Maranzano starts again, "Joe demanded a ten-thousand-dollar tribute. Cola Schiro paid him. Then he demanded Stefano come to New York for a clarification parlay."

"He has no power over our family business," Bonventre says. "What kind of parlay? Clarification of what?"

"Has everyone in New York grown fat and complacent? Mr. Joe and the Clutch Hand took responsibility for the death of Gaspar in Detroit. He intends to devour our tradition."

"Relax," Bonventre says. "Please, you will upset the children. The families in Detroit will avenge Gaspar's death."

Vito Bonventre reaches for the lemonade. He is comfortable and, at this age, disinclined to involve himself in Maranzano's feud.

"Tell that to his four children," Maranzano says. "You can't trust these men. They have a war machine."

"He has a couple of thugs who intimidate the weak when the need arises."

Maranzano says, "I have looked in his eyes and I see what he wants. The Clutch Hand works him like a puppet. I knew of the Morello family in Sicily. The Clutch Hand was born in Corleone. He made his money counterfeiting. When he came to America, he spread out. Ignazio Lupo did his dirty work then and he does it now. The Clutch Hand has his fingers everywhere. Why not? He has been here for three decades. He will swallow us all."

Bonventre says, "You say Cola has paid the tribute? Then let it be. We would be wise not to stir the contempt of the Clutch Hand or Ignazio. They are nervous men. If he has not bothered us for three decades, why believe he will start bothering us now?"

"Forget Lupo," Maranzano says. "Joe will have us under his thumb or he will kill us all one by one."

"Why would Joe Masseria want to kill me?"

"You are the richest among us," Maranzano says. "Killing

you would eliminate the money that might otherwise be used against him in war."

"War? You worry too much. He would not dare to kill me. I do not threaten him or his aspirations. What would I gain by a war with Joe the Boss, or Peter Morello for that matter? Would you have me abandon my family, my business, and put my life in danger just to wage a war? You young men, you are too quick to the mattresses."

"Complacency is the old man's disease," Maranzano says. "This fat boss with slits for eyes will not be still forever. Even Charlie Luciano has turned from his boss."

"How do you know this?" Bonventre says.

"I have ears to hear what is being said on the streets of New York," Maranzano says.

"Be careful of rumors," Bonventre says. "Tom Reina jumped into your conflict and got himself killed. I will make my own assessment of business in our world."

"Am I to blame for Sasa Parrino and Gaspar Milazzo, too?" Maranzano says.

"Are you suggesting Chester LaMare is Joe Masseria's puppet, too?"

"The Clutch Hand took responsibility for the murder. Now Mr. Joe insists Sasa's brother head our clan when I was the one elected by our family," Maranzano says.

"We are a long way from Sicily. In America, there is plenty of room for everyone. As your success grows, you will see things differently."

"You are blind to the truth," Maranzano says.

Bonventre stares at the trees and then slowly and with determination he tells Maranzano, "We must call a meeting of the fathers at once. I put this in your hands. You know what you have to do." He stands. "Right now, I am going to take a swim."

The next morning, Maranzano bids Bonventre goodbye and

then, along with Joe Bonanno, heads for the luxurious estate of Joe Profaci. Profaci, ever the statesman, welcomes Maranzano while Joe Bonanno waits outside with Profaci's bodyguards.

The large living room with oversized beveled-glass windows that open to a garden dense with trees and shrubs is a welcoming place for Maranzano and Profaci to exchange pleasantries. But Maranzano is not content with chitchat. Still running hot from his encounter with Bonventre, Maranzano gets quickly to the point.

"I am worried about Bonventre," he says. "He is unprepared when he should be alert. He must take precautions to protect himself from this maniac but instead he swims with his grand-children."

Profaci says, "I lost everything when I left Italy. The state took it all. Look around. We have come to this country and made good. Why do you want to stir things up?"

"We are men of honor. We stand together."

Profaci says, "I have spoken with the fathers and they oppose this war of yours. It is you that must stand with us."

"I know you have no respect for the man who calls himself the Boss. Are you going to stand by and let this…thief roll over our family? Will you do nothing to help us?"

"Call a meeting and we will discuss the matter."

"Discuss, discuss. Is that all anyone has to say? We must take action or our inaction will condemn us all."

The Dutchman takes aim at Stephanie St. Clair in Harlem. As if her accusations in the local newspaper were not enough, she has taken aim at the corruption in the Harlem police precincts.

For that, she was slammed into the Women's Workhouse. Upon her release, she set off to Sing Sing to visit her ally, Bumpy Johnson. Bumpy runs numbers, pimps, burgles, and regularly spends time in jail. At last count, he has spent nearly half of his thirty years in prison. Bumpy doesn't quote from *The Divine Comedy* or *The Prince*. He doesn't make a pretense for his crimes. But he does try to convince Queenie that a deal with the likes of Dutch Schultz is inevitable.

"Bumpy," she says, "you better get your ass on up outta here. Harlem numbers are mine. Colored folks gotta stick together. You know as well as I do that we're the only ones can take back what belongs to us."

"Darlin'," Bumpy says, and he moves as close to Queenie as jail space allows, "you know I'm right. You just don't want to hear those words."

She leans forward until her face is barely an inch from his.

"Bumpy," she says, "you don't want this gruesome old white boy floating around Harlem for the rest of our lives, do you?"

"Our lives won't be worth spit if we try to stop him," Bumpy says. "I got a hot head and it lands me in all kinda trouble but I ain't got no death wish. The Dutchman's got the cops, bail bondsmen, lawyers, and all kinds a court officials in his pocket. He's got ties to the big New York mobs. We ain't goin' broke if we work with the Dutchman but we'll surely die if we work against him."

"I thought you liked it hot, Bumpy. You ain't one to lay down and take a beating from no white man. I know you been talkin' to that Schultz strongarm, Weinberg. Did he put you up to trying to sweet talk me into giving up?"

He says, "They're Jews and they stick together. They're as tough as they come."

"Since when?" she says.

"Queenie, a man don't spend half his life in Sing Sing and come out without having some say in how his life is gonna end. Part of somethin' is better 'n all of nothin'. You heard of the

Bugs and Meyer mob? Trust me, you don't want Benny Siegel comin' for revenge."

"I'm betting that Mr. Arthur Flegenheimer don't want nothing to do with Samuel Seabury."

Bumpy gives Queenie a hollow stare.

"That's right. I got the call. Mr. Seabury wants me to testify about what's been goin' on in Harlem," she says.

"Oh, Queenie, don't do it," Bumpy says. "You go in there, you're opening up a door you can't close again. This whole thing can come back at you. Lay low until I get outta here. Then we can talk. Then we'll do something about Mr. Arthur Flegenheimer."

"I'd make a bargain with the Devil if that's what it takes to spit on the Dutchman's grave."

"I hope you live long enough to get that chance," Bumpy says. "Go home, Queenie. Think things through. You play ball with the Dutchman for a few years, bankroll as much as you can. You'll have more than enough to duck out."

"Harlem is my home," Queenie says. "I got no place to duck out to."

The Queen goes back to Harlem. She mixes a drink and climbs out onto the fire escape. Over a red-hot sunset, she mulls Bumpy's proposal. The sun sets and the sky turns to gray. Her thoughts turn to Martinique, 1922, when she stuffed every penny she had into her purse and set out for America. The numbers racket has been good to her. She wears fine clothes and dines in the best restaurants. She has taste and respect.

She sets the empty glass on the windowsill and watches the traffic below. Blacks who migrated northward to escape the repression of the south fill the sidewalks with rowdy passion. They are poor and disillusioned. Drifts of people fall into the local clubs. Music and laughter rushes through the streets.

The more Queenie sees, the more she wants Schultz dead.

Alex Pompez is in the middle of a card game when she barges into his club. He waves her off. She sits, cross-legged, on a tabletop waiting for him to finish his hand. She is wearing a fitted silk dress, high heels, and large-brimmed brown hat.

"Somebody's gotta stand up to that white man," she says, tiring of the wait.

Pompez's men laugh and keep playing.

"Stephanie," Pompez says, folding his cards and leaving the game, "I have looked in the eye of the enemy. Give him his due."

"I'll settle for my foot in his big, fat Jewish ass," she says. "Are you going to sit there while this man runs us all out of business?"

Pompez's men look to their boss.

"What is it you expect me to do?" he says.

She stands and takes a place in front of Pompez. Her voice is low and focused.

"We pool our resources," she says coolly. "We do what he does. He strikes us. We strike him. He takes our runners. We take his. If we must, we close down his bankers. Blow up his beer drops. Hell, just do anything to let him know we ain't gonna lay down."

"It's a high-stakes game," Pompez says. "We'd be betting with our lives."

"Mon ami," she says, "we have always been betting with our lives. I heard you met the beast at the Democratic Club. If I was there, I would have spit in his face. What did you do?"

Pompez faces the Queen.

"Women are not allowed in the club. It's men only, so I don't see how you could spit in his face."

Her eyes flare and her skin flushes.

She says, "I am sitting down with Samuel Seabury. You know of him? He's heading the Hofstadter Committee investigating corruption in the courts and police departments. I'll give him an earful. I would hate to have to tell him about your operation, too."

Pompez sighs. "What is it you want from me?"

"Take one of the Dutchman's runners. Let him know us colored folks stick together."

Pompez sends out two of his thugs to target the Dutchman's runner. The kid, not more than thirteen years old, makes his way through a small neighborhood collecting bets. Queenie watches the kid and the shadows that follow him from a second-story window. He stops to take a bet from an old man who plays daily. The man digs through the worn pocket of his pants for the penny he is betting to get him out of poverty. Players choose a series of three numbers hoping to match the last three digits of the New York Stock Exchange numbers at the end of the day. The runner records the bet in his policy book and drops the penny in his leather pouch.

"O.K.," the runner says. "Tomorrow, Al."

"Tomorrow you'll be bringin' me my winnings," Al says. "I got it this time. I can feel it in my bones."

"Yeah," the runner says and moves on.

He's been collecting bets for six months and dreams of becoming a policy king. When he brings his bets to the Dutchman, he watches with wonder as Abbadabba Berman, the Dutchman's accountant, grabs numbers from the air like a magician. At night, he runs figures through his head to repeat Abbadabba's trick but always fails miserably.

He rounds the corner to the next street. Two black men block the sidewalk. He steps into the street to get around. The men grab the kid and push him into a back alley.

"What you doin' here in Harlem, boy?" the taller one says.

He grabs the policy book and looks through the bets. He grabs the leather pouch holding the loose change and upends it. Pennies, nickels, and dimes fall to the ground.

"We're gonna have to teach you a lesson," he says.

He delivers a sharp kick to the kid's knee. There is a loud crack. The kid's leg buckles and he falls onto the hard brick. Pain surges through his body. The men work him over. A gash to the face. A kick to the ribs. More kicks to his broken leg. The kid lies on the ground battered and bloody.

"Get the fuck outta here, white boy. We don't want your kind sucking up our policy game," the tall one says.

The men laugh and then walk away.

The Dutchman gets wind of the beating. He and Bo Weinberg drive over to the kid's house. The kid is laid up in bed with a cast on his leg.

"I can do my job," the kid says. "You don't have to worry about that, Mr. Schultz. I'll be on my feet in the morning."

"Who did this?" the Dutchman snarls.

The kid says, "I never saw them before."

Weinberg says, "If you saw them again, could you identify them?"

"Better believe I could," the kid says.

The Dutchman smiles.

He says to Weinberg, "Deal with it. Now."

Meyer reaches for his bankbook. Ada Hector is in the house and Anne is hanging on every word.

"These curtains will have to go," Ada says. "They simply will not do."

Ada walks through the house pointing out Anne's mis-matched sense of design. She makes notes in a leatherbound journal while Anne follows helplessly behind. Ada is Manhattan's latest whirlwind, an interior designer that is making her way through the pocketbooks of uptown New York.

Ada says, "I see why you called me, Mrs. Lansky. This apartment cries out for the touch of a professional. I don't know how you've managed to live with this décor for so long. I'll have my assistant gather up samples so we can set up an appointment. Will your maid be home this week, in case I need to make a measure?"

"Yes, of course," Anne says.

Ada slips the leather journal into an oversized tote.

Meyer waits near the front door, pen poised over a blank check.

"Oh, no, no, Mr. Lansky," Ada says. "No need for that. I will include my visit in your statement. I couldn't help but notice that you have quite a collection of books in your den. Are you a studious man?"

"I like to read," Meyer says.

"Fine, fine," she says. "These are important things to know."

"As long as the chair is comfortable and the lighting is good," Meyer says.

"Yes, of course," Ada says with a forced smile as she dips behind her big-brimmed hat. "Very nice chatting with you. Now remember, Anne, as much as you might be tempted, don't buy *anything* until you clear it with me."

Anne leans against the closed door. Meyer stands with crossed arms.

She says, "You're always trying to undermine my authority. You want our son to grow up with the best, don't you? He shouldn't have to feel different from the other children at school."

"Bad curtains don't leave scars, Anne."

"Ada is decorating Esther's place and Flo's, too. You don't see Benny or Jimmy standing around with a checkbook. I want this, Meyer. I need this. Buddy needs this."

Meyer says, "Why don't you take Buddy to the toy store and fill his life with the things he likes?"

Anne says, "You spoil him, Meyer. You spoil him and you torment me."

Vito Bonventre saunters through the kitchen of his Long Island estate. Salvatore Maranzano's visit is the furthest thing from his mind. Breakfast is on the table: a glass of freshly squeezed orange juice, frittata, basket of hard rolls, and a container of goat cheese. Bonventre pours coffee from the silver pot and, as his wife enters the room, he pours a cup for her.

Bonventre says, "Rockefeller is building again. He's got twelve acres for something called Radio City in midtown. Television. Can you believe he is putting two hundred fifty million in such an enterprise?"

She shrugs. "Where is the fruit? It's summer. Where is the fruit?"

Bonventre kicks off his shoes and rolls up his pant legs.

"Forget the fruit. Let's take a walk on the sand," he says.

They dawdle along the beach picking up shells and driftwood until the sun burns through the clouds and then they find a place on the patio where they enjoy sweet rolls and espresso.

"Don't go," she says. "We haven't enjoyed ourselves this much since we were children. Can't we forget about obligations just for a little while?"

Bonventre takes his wife's hand and pulls her up from her chair. He hums a familiar tune as he twirls her around the patio. The music in his head stops.

"What is it?" she says.

"I must go," he says. "I have business that requires my attention. But I won't be gone long. I promise, cara mia. Come with me. We will make Brooklyn our honeymoon suite."

She rolls her eyes. It is the middle of summer and Brooklyn is no honeymoon.

Bonventre brushes the sand from his feet, slips into socks and shoes. He lingers for a moment caressing his wife's long dark hair and then he is gone. As the distance between them grows, his mind turns to the business at hand. A liquor shipment never made it to port. He suspects foul play and, since Maranzano brought it up, wonders if Joe the Boss is at the root of his problems.

It's a balmy day in Brooklyn, seventy-five degrees, when he pulls into the driveway of his Brooklyn home. Before he can reach the front door, he is shot dead.

News of the funeral hits the second page of the *New York Times*. Nearly two hundred mourners are expected to gather at Mount Carmel Roman Catholic Church to grieve his passing. Detectives in the Eastern District and Greenpoint areas beef up forces in preparation for warfare.

Before the funeral, Joe Adonis meets Charlie at the Mulberry Street garage.

"Did you see the paper?" Adonis says. "Police are preparing for feud murders like the ones ten years ago."

"They better get ready for more than that," Charlie says.

"Morello?" Adonis says.

"He and Joe the Boss have been, shall we say, consulting with one another. It's best if you steer clear of the funeral."

"That's easy. I didn't get invited," Adonis says. "It's not like we were friends."

Charlie reads the news, all three paragraphs. Then he calls Meyer.

In the Lansky apartment furniture sits in the middle of the

room, covered with dropcloths, while workmen sling strips of wallpaper onto makeshift sawhorse tables and slather it with paste. The smell is sickly sweet.

Meyer says to Anne, "You think this is good for the baby?"

"He's fine," she says.

"Why don't you call Flo or Esther and get some fresh air." Meyer grabs his jacket.

"What shall I tell the cook?" Anne says half-panicked.

"Bring a gas mask."

Meyer meets Charlie at the usual bench in Central Park.

"Anybody know who's behind this?" Meyer says.

Charlie says, "It doesn't matter. Bonventre was a cornerstone to the Sicilian community. Joe A. came by earlier. Maranzano called a mandatory meeting of the Castellammarese. They went out to Profaci's place on Long Island. This is going to fan the flames of Maranzano's war. The fact that Fat Joe has taken over Reina's old mob will just add to the fervor."

"When Pinzolo is eradicated it will be Joe's turn to retaliate," Meyer says. "Like dominoes."

"This could take months," Charlie says. "It could take years."

"If I was Maranzano and I found out Joe the Boss went into hiding, I'd assume I have a pretty good shot at taking him down."

"You wouldn't be wrong," Charlie says.

Peter Morello's East Harlem office is modest, by all accounts. A few sticks of furniture, nothing special, a desk, chairs, a table. It is functional, not magnificent. At the end of the day, Morello is only interested in the cash receipts collected from various construction sites in the Bronx and Harlem.

It is a slow, hot August afternoon and the conversation in the office is as dull as the day. Half the population of New York is still at the seashore. The other half is in Saratoga drinking mint juleps and gambling. A friend of the Clutch Hand, Giuseppe

Periano, is hanging around the office biding his time while he waits for the boat that will take him back to Italy.

Morello's collector shows up with a small valise full of envelopes.

He says, "If you want bigger contracts, then you should talk with the architects. Kick back a few bucks to them. That's how you get to the big scores. The architect will have his clients eating out of your hand."

Morello makes a mental note. Tall buildings are gold mines. They require iron workers, plumbers, electrical workers, cement, and so on. They make great paydays.

Morello goes through the stack of receipts his collector has brought back. Profits are not as rich as he would like. A knock at the front door interrupts the count. Morello looks at his watch. Ten to four. He isn't expecting visitors. The street below his second-story window shows nothing more than an endless parade of foot traffic. He steps to one side and cracks open the door.

Two gunmen crash their way into the room. They open fire. The occupants are sitting ducks. In a flash of gunfire, four bullets rip through Morello's body. He goes down. The shooters empty fifteen rounds into the room that variously hit Morello, the collector, and Giuseppe. Giuseppe staggers across the room to get away. He dives through the second-story window and falls to the sidewalk below. The fall kills him instantly. One of the gunmen stands tall over Morello and takes aim. He fires one shot through Morello's forehead. He pauses to enjoy a moment of glory, Peter Morello dead once and for all.

The collector is left bleeding on the office floor. Nobody really cares if he lives or dies.

The *Times* article stretches across two pages. "Harlem Racket Gang Murders Two in Raid."

Word spreads through Brooklyn that Joe the Boss' war chief is dead and that Joe the Boss is still in hiding. The Boss has been crippled. This is good news for Tommy Gagliano, who still refuses to acknowledge Joe Pinzolo as the new boss of Tom Reina's old mob.

Joe waits out the war in a stripped-down apartment longing for his uptown penthouse. He sees his army as formidable. He's tired of onions and bread. Suddenly he has an epiphany. He makes a call to Charlie Lucky.

"Meet me in Coney Island," he says. "You know the place. I wanna talk to you."

By the time Charlie arrives, Joe has secured the restaurant inside and out. A dozen of his soldiers, trusted confidants who have fought with him on many occasions, are stationed outside each entrance. The only warm bodies inside the restaurant apart from Joe and Charlie are the chef and his wife.

Joe is twitchy. His life is on the line. Someone drops a plate in the kitchen and Joe jumps. His nerves are shattered.

"Everybody has gone crazy," Joe tells Charlie. "It's the doing of these Castellammarese. They boast of respect. There is no respect! If they had respect, they wouldn't have killed Joe Pinzolo. What did he do but try to help them with their business?"

Charlie says, "The newspaper said Tommy Lucchese leased the office where Pinzolo was killed."

Joe the Boss curses in Italian.

He says, "Lucchese leased the office months ago. They were planning this all along. They wanted to draw me into this fight. I will show them who's boss. I want you to go to Chicago. Tell Capone that he has my blessing to take out that no good Joe Aiello. Tell him he can't do it fast enough as far as I am concerned." Joe nods, "Eat. It is sacrilege to let pasta get cold."

"I'll say three Hail Marys on Sunday," Charlie says.

The blasphemy does little to deflect Joe's rage over Maranzano's recent victory. He figures, rightly so, that Stefano Magaddino and Joe Aiello are pumping money into the wannabe Caesar's war chest. Joe the Boss trembles with rage. No one kills Peter Morello and Joe Pinzolo with impunity. Case closed.

Charlie says, "With Aiello out of the picture, Maranzano won't have as much capital to work with."

"That's what I'm telling you," Joe says. "Take Aiello out. That'll put a crimp in this war. We got Bonventre, didn't we? He was stuffing the war chest. Now he's gone. We take out Aiello, that's another big bankroll gone. Let's see them fight when they can't afford soldiers."

Joe the Boss taps Peter Morello's soldiers for his next move. Their target lies in Brooklyn, two of Bonventre's associates, Patsy Tango Dauria and Frank Italiano, whose sphere of influence grew the minute Vito Bonventre died. They have heard that Joe the Boss is in hiding, a fact that emboldens the belief that Brooklyn is Maranzano's town.

"Cut the legs out from under him," Joe the Boss tells the soldiers. "The longer they walk around, the more money they gather, the easier it is for them to keep fighting."

Morello's boys roll through the neighborhood Dauria and Italiano have been known to frequent. They are spotted walking along Liberty Avenue. The driver stops a block away and two gunmen hit the streets.

Point blank, the gunmen fill the rivals with bullets, sixteen slugs for Dauria and nine for Italiano. The crowd on the street expands and then contracts. Police shove people aside to get to the bodies and assess the damage. Dauria is lying unconscious in the gutter. Italiano is nowhere to be seen. A trail of blood leads the policemen to a hallway off Linwood Street. Eventually they come upon the unconscious body of Frank Italiano. Meanwhile, Patsy Dauria is transported to the hospital. Twenty-four hours later, Dauria is dead.

Somehow Italiano manages to beat the odds and lives. More determined than ever, he joins with Maranzano to seek retaliation.

Al Capone creates a web of outposts around Chicago. The police call the outposts "machine gun nests." Capone boasts that Joe Aiello will be dead before Thanksgiving. Aiello makes the rounds among his paesans making his own plans to remove Capone from the face of the earth. He visits his friend, Pasquale "Presto" Prestogiacomo. He tells Presto that he is going to go to Mexico for a visit, just until things settle down between Joe the Boss and Salvatore Maranzano. The fact remains that while Al Capone holds the prized title Public Enemy Number One, Joe Aiello is not far behind, ranked at number seven on the Crime Commission's hit list.

They sit at the kitchen table and talk softly about the war that is raging in New York. Capone's brag has Aiello worried. Presto promises to watch over Aiello's rackets. Aiello thanks his friend and then calls for a cab. The cabbie pulls up to 205 Kolmar and walks up to the apartment. He stares at the buzzer plaque at the front door. All the card plates are missing so he returns to his cab and waits for the fare.

Aiello leaves the building through the alley door. From a second-story window across the street from Presto's building, a submachine gun explodes with a torrent of bullets that sprays the street below. Aiello is wounded but not cut down. He makes a mad dash for the front of the building, darting into a passageway. A second machine gun nest erupts. Giuseppe Aiello falls to the ground and bleeds out in a matter of minutes.

He is taken to Garfield Park Hospital as a matter of formality. After hours of tedious work, the coroner says with certainty that the 57 bullets dug from the victim's body were the sole cause of death.

"You coulda sunk him in Lake Michigan with that much lead," Capone says. "Congratulations, boys. I know it wasn't no picnic waiting for that bastard to show his face. Why don't you go to Florida and enjoy the sunshine for a couple of weeks?"

Salvatore Maranzano fumes. The North Side Alcohol King who contributed $5,000 a week to Maranzano's war chest will be sorely missed.

Charlie Lucky sends flowers. He picks up a celebratory meal from Nuova Villa Tammaro in Coney Island. The food is still warm when he arrives at Joe's safe house. Joe the Boss opens a bottle of Champagne and celebrates.

The following day, Charlie makes a beeline for the Cannon Street garage.

Charlie says, "Aiello's murder was a big deal. That's like Joe the Boss losing Capone's support. No telling what this will kick off in Chicago, or here. Tommy Lucchese says Maranzano makes a lot of promises but, so far, he's still taking everybody's money and stuffing it into his war chest. It sounds like he's spread pretty thin."

"I'd like to be a fly on the wall while Caesar works this one out," Meyer says.

"These old greasers are hemorrhaging money on this war. They've got soldiers stashed everywhere and runners on the streets. Everybody is involved. Cabbies make the best scouts. Good tips mean good rewards. How long can these guys afford to keep this up?"

"They're both eager to bring it to an end," Meyer says.

"Maranzano made a six-month promise to his men," Charlie says.

"Six months?" Meyer says.

"This guy is looking to create his own Sicilian Vesper," Charlie says.

"That makes it in the spring," Meyer says.

"That's right. That's when it happened in Sicily."

"If Maranzano is still around in the spring, then we know it's time to get rid of Joe the Boss."

"How do you figure?" Charlie says.

"This guy doesn't like to be wrong. He's interested in making a statement. He wants everything to be historical. If both greasers are still at war in the spring, you can be sure Caesar will give you the nod to take out your boss."

"Then we do a little Vesper of our own. We give the signal and all the mobs clean house just like we agreed. Once for all time. After that, no more killin' without permission."

Meyer nods.

Joe Valachi's stakeout finally yields paydirt. Joe the Boss Masseria and Stephen Ferrigno walk through the garden of the Alhambra Apartments where Valachi has been hiding in a ground-floor apartment. Valachi can't believe his good luck.

"Are you sure?" Bobby Doyle says as Valachi peeks through the blinds.

"I think so," Valachi mutters.

"Well go and find out."

"It's him," he tells Doyle returning to the apartment. "I'm sure of it."

The three men crouch in the apartment waiting for Joe the Boss to slip up and step in front of a barrage of bullets.

Finally, Stephen Ferrigno slips out of the apartment with Al Mineo.

"Shoot, shoot," Bobby Doyle shouts.

Buster pulls the trigger. Others are sucked into the fray. A volley of bullets crisscross the courtyard. Bodies fall. The boys in the first-floor apartment flee. Nobody wants to be left holding the shotgun when the police arrive.

Al Mineo and Stephen Ferrigno are shot dead. Whoever else was at the conference in Ferrigno's apartment have escaped.

Joe the Boss walks along Holland Avenue and thanks God for his good luck. The Man Who Dodges Bullets still has the touch. He smiles and stands a little taller.

"Racketeer War Hinted," the *Times* says. It's the first official acknowledgment of what's really going on. Meyer folds the paper and lays it on his desk as Benny strolls in from a run to New Jersey and a check on their warehouse supplies.

A fifty-mile gale sweeps torrents of rain through the city. Meyer stokes the potbellied stove, sits back, and relaxes.

"Joe the Boss escaped Maranzano's trap," Benny says. He sounds almost disappointed. "You think Maranzano is going to win this war?"

The flames of the fire lick the inside of the iron stove and send occasional sparks spewing through the grate.

"Maranzano is smart," Meyer says. "Smarter than Joe. Joe reacts. He is all emotion. Maranzano calculates. He makes a good general. It's Charlie that's getting buffeted around in this storm. He's caught in the middle of this thing."

"Charlie's got the respect of his men," Benny says. "These old greasers got nothing to gain from taking him out. Don't they know that?"

"Maranzano is a thinker," Meyer says. "He can see how powerful Charlie is. It would be a mistake to kill Charlie. Maranzano isn't as savvy as Charlie about what life is like here. It's an uphill battle for him. He needs Charlie if he is going to conquer this town. I'll bet on it."

"Then he won't take out Charlie," Benny says.

"Oh, he will," Meyer says. "Just not yet. Eventually. Only one guy wins at chess."

"When we take out Maranzano, let's do it at his office. Nobody will expect that, least of all the blowhard himself."

Meyer says, "I have to think about that."

Benny says, "We'll go in as cops. Who's gonna stop a cop?"

"Accountants," Meyer says. "Jews make better accountants than cops. Leave the cop business to the Irish." Meyer pauses and then says, "We get some friends of ours in the police department to spread a rumor about an audit. The Chicago boys are sweating it out while the government goes through their accounts looking for anything that will indict them. Let Maranzano sweat it out, too. He'll be anxious and won't notice the Colt under your jacket."

Benny likes where this is going.

"That's good," he says. "That's really good. You fuck around with Charlie, you fuck around with us all."

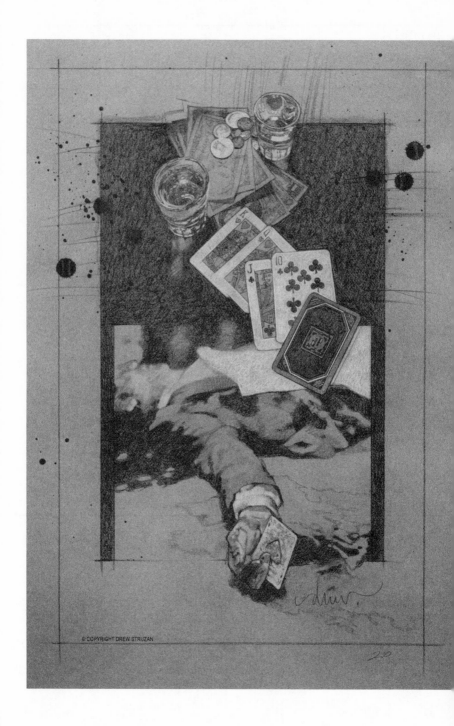

Chapter Twenty
Oh, Come All Ye Faithful

CHRISTMAS 1930

It's early November and the situation in the Italian world is still red hot. The Castellammarese continue the hunt for Mr. Joe but Joe remains elusive. The strength of his enemies has grown dramatically since Peter Morello was shot and killed in his East Harlem office. Joe had felt comfortable and nearly invincible up until then. He had relied not only on the Clutch Hand's strength but on his wisdom. The Clutch Hand knew the streets. He knew how to intimidate men. He had style.

To compensate for his loss, Joe the Boss surrounds himself with soldiers and worries about their trustworthiness. He mourns his bad luck and takes out his anger on the butt of a cheap cigar.

Charlie Lucky wades through the sea of security at Joe the Boss' safe house. The soldier to whom this home belongs has sent his family packing off to his mother-in-law's. Joe stands in front of the small fireplace and warms himself. The house has a pleasantly modest touch. Doilies protect the arms of the sofa and chairs. A Victrola in the corner next to the fireplace plays Caruso. It is 2 A.M. Joe the Boss reaches over to close the doors of the Victrola's speaker box. The mighty voice of the great tenor jars Joe's frazzled nerves as he sings a duet from *La forza del destino*.

Verdi's vision of the Power of Fate fails to lift Joe's spirits.

"I was at the Metropolitan opera when he sang this," Joe says. "What a voice the man has. 'Life is hell to those who are unhappy.' Truer words have not been spoken."

That Charlie never cared to personally hear Caruso sing is sacrilege. And now it is too late. Caruso has been dead for nearly a decade. What is left of the great tenor's voice sits on rigid shellac discs.

"Our destiny is to die," Joe says to Charlie. "Are we not men of war? And if we are, we are meant to die on the field of battle. I fear I may have dodged my last bullet."

Charlie says, "All them operas are nothing but love stories and the worst of it is the lovers never get around to loving. They all die one way or another. It don't seem to me our situation is anything like an opera."

After all, Joe the Boss is not on the street taking chances. He huddles with advisors and plots revenge and sends other men to do his bidding. He has soldiers on the rooftop, in the adjoining apartment, across the street, in parked cars. They have one purpose: protect the life of this one man.

Charlie pulls out a cigarette. Joe parts the closed curtains and peeks at the silent street below. One of his soldiers gives an 'all's clear.' The record ends. Joe the Boss lifts the needle to its cradle.

Joe says, "How many times I tell them not to make a signal? That's how people find out where I am hiding. What moves a man to run around Brooklyn pretending he's Napoleon Bonaparte?"

Charlie says, "I believe you mean Julius Caesar."

Joe ignores the correction. "Did you get Ben Gallo? That's what I want to know. Is he dead?"

"Shot in the back," Charlie says.

"Is he dead?" Joe falls into the chair across from Charlie. "Tell me."

Charlie doles out the story like crumbs to a beggar.

"The boys took in a show. *Smiles*, I think it was. You know that musical with Fred Astaire and Bob Hope. I saw them one night at the automat. Astaire was dancing all over the place. He musta been rehearsing."

Joe says, "What do I care about actors? This is life. Life and death."

"Right," Charlie says. His boss is restless, anxious. "Gallo was shot in the back. That's the story. He died on the spot. You can read about it in tomorrow's paper."

Joe paces the small living space. Silently, he calculates the Sicilian's losses. Will it be enough to end this ridiculous war? It was not for Maranzano to come to a new country and lay claim to Joe's territories. That's not how these things work.

He says, "What was it you told Tom Gagliano and Tommy Lucchese?"

"About Pinzolo? I told them exactly what you said…you give your blessing to Pinzolo."

Joe drops the philosophical meandering. The dragon he chases is the job of keeping the Sicilians from coalescing into a single, unmanageable mass. Maranzano chooses to defy him. This kind of treachery cannot stand.

Joe says, "Find the Sicilian responsible for this madness and kill him. You know who I am talking about. This war will only end when one of us is dead. I want to see his brains decorating a Brooklyn sidewalk. Then we'll see how bold the Castellammarese are."

Charlie says, "Maranzano has a lot of loyal soldiers that are eager and hungry."

Joe the Boss resents the rebuttal. He questions Charlie's allegiance.

"If I die, you die right along with me," Joe says. "Maybe you don't understand how this man thinks. Maranzano will never trust you or anybody in our family. When the boss dies, everyone around him dies right alongside him. You. Adonis. Moretti.

Costello. We all die. Maranzano's men found me, didn't they? Why can't we find this bastard and annihilate him?"

Act II has only just begun. The plot is not yet fully revealed. The battle between Joe and the wannabe Caesar takes center stage. Charlie is on the sideline. He chooses not to put Joe Adonis in harm's way, or Frank Costello, for that matter. And there's an uneasy truth here. Maranzano is better at fighting this war than Joe the Boss is.

Charlie says, "This guy's like a priest to his soldiers. It ain't likely they'll turn him in or screw up in public and reveal his whereabouts. Hell, the guys with him don't go out no more than he does and Maranzano don't go out at all. He communicates by phone. Only the guys with him know where he is. These are the same guys he had with him in Italy. They were soldiers there and they're soldiers here. People in the neighborhood work for him, too. Grocers, taxi drivers, you name it. They're all informers."

Joe bristles at this reality. His gut tells him the situation is terrible, intolerable, and unmanageable but not impossible. Never impossible. He can and has outsmarted the Sicilian Caesar. Joe has dodged bullets. Has his nemesis? Joe's mind runs back to Italy, back to his youth, to his own days as a soldier.

"Caesar is bunking with his men," he says. "Wherever you find his men, make sure someone is there to keep an eye on them. You will find his nest. Don't do nothin' else until that's done. Send Vito to do the job. He has the knowledge. The Camorra came out of Naples. His guys will know how to do the job. Get this son of a bitch before he gets me."

Charlie nods, "Don't worry. We will get the son of a bitch no matter how long it takes."

Charlie wants the war to end as much as anyone. He talks to his underboss, Vito Genovese, a man of action and brute force.

"I'll cover your interests," Charlie says. "I'll make sure your guys get their end of everything. You find Maranzano and let me know where he's hiding."

Vito nods, jumping at the chance to defeat the Sicilian's arrogance. But December rolls around and still Salvatore Maranzano is nowhere to be found.

Vito despairs, "This guy is squirreled away too tight, ain't nobody seen him and those that have ain't talkin'."

He is displeased. Irritated. He made a gamble and lost. Is it possible that the Sicilian Mafia has outwitted the Neapolitan Camorra? Vito sent out fingers across Brooklyn. Nothing concrete returned to him. He decides that Caesar must not be in Brooklyn.

The same day, Albert Einstein, his wife, and a small entourage board the *Belgenland* and head across the Atlantic Ocean. On the cold December morning the ship makes port in New York, the famous German scientist is ushered on deck and poses in front of the white exterior walls of the passenger compartments. The wind tousles his hair. Einstein focuses on the task at hand. He has arrived on the shores of America to reaffirm his faith in the ideal of a Jewish homeland. With his interpreter at the ready, Einstein faces the lineup of reporters and photographers.

Red Levine follows the Professor's brief visit with the passion of a devotee. Mayor Jimmy Walker officially welcomes Einstein in a ceremony at City Hall. Levine makes sure he is part of the crowd cheering Einstein on. After the ceremony, Red cuts a path to the Claridge Hotel to see Meyer, the one guy that completely shares his passion for a Jewish homeland.

"If I could be anyone in this world," Red says, "I would be Albert Einstein. Where does a brain like that come from? If I lived a thousand years, I'd never be half that smart."

"You want to be a scientist?" Meyer jokes.

Red bows his head. His heart is with Israel.

Meyer says, "It's a good thing for Zion that you became a bootlegger or we would still be sitting in the ghetto making someone else rich. How much have you contributed to the Zionist fund? Huh?"

Red nods.

Uptown, Anne Lansky dances around the tall Douglas fir delivered minutes ago to her apartment. Boxes of Bloomingdale ornaments spill across the floor: silver bells, snow-flocked red balls, a rosy-cheeked German Belsnickel Santa dressed in a red felt jacket and blue felt pants, bow-tied gold ribbons, green powdery glass pinecones from Japan, and a plethora of silver icicles.

Chanukah is days away. Not that it matters. Anne is doing her best Ada Hector Christmas while Buddy busies himself with a Fire Chief tin car Anne picked up from Schwarz Toy Bazaar on 23rd Street. Buddy is a quiet child who alternately watches his mother's antics and sleeps. When he needs feeding or changing, the nanny comes to his rescue.

Anne bounces from box to box laboring over each decision of what to put where. It is just after two o'clock and the sun is beginning to blaze through the room's picture window that overlooks Central Park. Bells and balls dance with reflected light.

Anne clicks on the radio and dials in Paul Whiteman, who fills the house with "Joy to the World." The maid sings along and dances with little Buddy in her arms. Tree branches bow under the weight of the ornaments. "O, Holy Night" follows Whiteman's song and then "Savoy Christmas Melody," a fox trot that lightens the mood. Anne kicks up the volume.

A knock at the door interrupts the joy of the season. Anne shuts the radio off. The maid answers the door while Anne slides the Menorah onto the long table in front of the window so that Israel's light can shine for all to see. She is just in time.

"Miz Lansky," the maid says, "yo mama is callin'."

Grandma Citron comes face-to-face with the Lansky living room. Her eyes widen. She is a small woman with dark brown hair that is pulled back away from her face. She wears a conservative gray dress.

"Oh my," Grandma Citron says. "Thank God your grandmother didn't live to see you with this…this…"

"Say it, mother," Anne says. "Christmas tree. It's a goddamn Christmas tree. You know, Christ mass tree. That's what it is and that's what I've got and I don't want to hear another word about it."

Buddy turns to Grandma Citron, eyes wide, confused by the sudden change of mood in the house.

"Don't flaunt your disrespect," Grandma Citron says.

A pile of little boxes containing silver icicles crown Anne's feet.

The wrapper is in German: "Christbaum—schmuck." Her mother picks up the box and marvels at the caption. In small letters, under the piercing German, is a literal translation into English: "Christian tree decoration." But every Jew knows the Yiddish meaning.

"Schmuck," Grandma says in a tone that would chill even the icicles. "That's what the gentiles think of you."

Anne turns an alarming shade of red and says, "Go home! You're not going to ruin this for me. We'll talk after Christmas, when you can be more civilized."

Outside, Meyer and Charlie walk through Central Park under a canopy of trees gone bare for the winter. Meyer keeps up constant contact with Charlie now that the two greasers have escalated their dispute to all-out war. Charlie has tried to locate

Maranzano, but to no avail. The leads Charlie's colleagues have followed up on haven't panned out.

In fact, Salvatore Maranzano is spending the holiday on the same farm in upstate New York where's he's been holed up from the start. He celebrates Christmas along with his victories over Mr. Joe. The holiday offers a small respite from his Spartan life as a warrior. The apartment where he has been dwelling since the war began consists of a main room with stiff chairs and several mattresses laid out for the soldiers' convenience. The kitchen holds a large, communal table where the men eat, share stories, and play cards. An innocuous stream of brown bags left on the doorstep with a knock keeps the refrigerator stocked. The sole bathroom serves a dozen men. Maranzano insists his home away from home be kept spotless by those inhabiting it.

Maranzano eats, sleeps, and prays in his own austere room containing a single bed with white sheets and a gray woolen blanket, a small table and chair, and a lampstand. To the side is Maranzano's not so meager arsenal.

Walking through the park, Meyer asks Charlie, "Have you found Maranzano?"

"There's a rumor he might be with Magaddino upstate. If he is, nobody saw him go. And nobody has seen him return," Charlie says. "He's riding high, right now. He ain't been on top of the world like this since before Mussolini came to power. He calls this a war of liberation."

"If you found him, you could offer him a Christmas present."

Charlie says, "I'd be the next in line to go."

"Maybe he'll offer Joe one."

"My luck, I'd still be the next to go," Charlie said.

"Maranzano must see your predicament. If you can't go

against your boss, how do you let him know you're all for liberation?"

"Gagliano and Lucchese know. If they know, Maranzano knows."

"You need to be ready with your terms," Meyer says. "He has to agree or continue to wage this war."

"The war chest ain't what it used to be," Charlie says. "Soldiers don't earn. Simple as that."

"What's the price he pays for you to end the war?"

"What do I want, you mean," Charlie says. "I want him to go his way and I'll go mine."

Six men crowd around the table at Maranzano's Brooklyn safehouse. Maranzano has just returned from visiting Stefano Magaddino and going over their war strategy. Stefano has agreed to allow Maranzano to lead the Brooklyn family that was once his. He returns to Brooklyn the victor.

A loaf of half-eaten bread sits on the kitchen counter. Next to it, a brick of hard cheese with a knife stuck into it. A musty odor hangs in the air. Maranzano kicks a brown bag sitting on the floor next to the refrigerator. Rotten trash.

"You expect your mother to come in here and wipe your butt, too?" Maranzano says.

He grabs the ear of the nearest soldier and points his head toward the bag. With the sweep of his hand, he sends the soldier to the floor.

"Clean up this mess," he says. "Wash the floor with soap and water and the counters, too. I don't expect to share my breakfast with the rats."

Soldiers scramble.

Maranzano fills an enamel coffee pot with water and puts it on the stove to boil. Stoically, he drops rounded spoons of ground coffee into the boiling water. Then, cup and pot in hand, he pads off to his room. He sets the pot on the corner of the small table.

Joe Bonanno stands at the door to Maranzano's room and watches as his leader rolls out the leather square kept in a valise next to the table. Maranzano pours a cup of coffee. The brew is weak, muddy, and bitter but only his belly misses the real thing. It is the spirit that counts and the spirit delights in the sacrifice of war.

In another apartment, someone plays a Caruso record. Maranzano pauses. His heart begins to fill with song. The wind whips the barren branches of a maple tree against his second-story window. He snaps to attention and focuses on the job at hand. The liturgy of Maranzano's Eucharist begins with preparing the altar. He sets out a loading press, 12-gauge for this evening's ammunition, a powder scale, hulls, powder, primers, wad, and shot. He offers thanksgiving for his men and his ability to lead them.

The kitchen erupts in horseplay.

Maranzano prays for patience. He sets a single brass casing in the loading press then loads the primer into the priming station. He pulls one complete stroke of the loading press handle to seat the primer before adding a measure of powder. The punched wad is pushed down and seated. The shell inspected, the shot added, one ounce, the optimal amount to propel the lead projectile through a man's flesh. If it is a good shot, it will take a life. Maranzano crimps the end of the hull before placing the cartridge on the left edge of the table, the first in line of this evening's work.

He picks up a new casing and places it in the press. Adds primer. Pulls a full stroke. Adds powder. Seats the wad, Inspects the shell. Adds the shot, one ounce. Makes the final crimp. A new casing. Primer. Stroke. Powder. Wad. Inspection. Shot. Crimp. Now there are three. Maranzano works into the night, Bonanno watching, until he has what he considers substantial firepower.

He forgoes the spaghetti and sauce simmering on the stove brought in by someone's mother. The men eat and play cards. The kitchen overflows with conversation.

Maranzano looks up and sees Bonanno.

"Aren't you going to eat, Pepito?" Maranzano says.

Bonanno shrugs.

Maranzano pours oil onto a cloth and begins to work on the raw metal of a 12-gauge shotgun. He doesn't have to ask if Joe Bonanno has never killed a man.

"When you shoot someone," Maranzano says, "you must be sure he is dead. An injured man is an angry man and an angry man will not rest without vengeance. Do you understand?"

Tough Bonanno has never seen war, but he has seen rage. He nods.

"The man who dodges bullets will not be able to dodge our bullets," Maranzano says. "We are smarter than he is."

Maranzano's next target is not Joe the Boss but a man named Joe Parrino who hates the war and threatens to join forces with Mr. Joe. His death will be an example to all would-be traitors.

It is the middle of January when Maranzano finds his opportunity. He slides a revolver into his coat pocket and takes an escort of four men with him to stand guard at the café where he is to meet with the cogs that will put into play his move against Parrino.

"Si, signore," the proprietor of the café says as Maranzano enters.

"Prima cosa," Maranzano says, "caffe!"

"Si." The proprietor smiles. He is proud of his latest acquisition, a brand new La Pavoni purchased in Italy for which he spent one thousand dollars. "Now nobody have to go to Greenwich Village for good coffee. They come to me."

A man coming through the door behind Maranzano calls out, "Due."

The man is Joe Parrino's underboss. His aspirations appeal to Maranzano's sense of efficiency. Following close behind him are two more men also eager to play a role in Maranzano's ascension.

"Quattro," the last man says.

"Is nobody want cappuccino?"

"Si," one of them says. "Si, cappuccino."

The four men sit at a small table. Maranzano breaks freshly baked bread and passes it around to the other men. The La Pavoni goes into action. Four perfect shots. The proprietor releases a valve which allows steam to whip the milk into a froth. The noise interrupts Maranzano's conversation. He protests with a look to no avail. The pride attached to the La Pavoni covers all sins.

The coffee arrives at the table. The men partake in silence.

Finally, Maranzano speaks. "Joe Parrino eats at Del Pezzo every Monday night, no?"

The men nod, none more so than the underboss. A wicked smile smacks across his face.

Maranzano says, "He is a man of routine, yes? Like clockwork, exactly at six he takes a seat near the door...in case he needs to escape. For a man who thinks he is invincible, it is rather comical, don't you think?"

Parrino, like most bosses, is not popular among his men. They call him "leccacazzi" behind his back which means bootlicker in polite society; for the more literally minded it means butt-licker. It is this energy that feeds Maranzano's scheme for the execution of the deserter. Del Pezzo is a second-story restaurant in midtown Manhattan frequented by the opera crowd.

"You know what to do?" Maranzano says.

Again, the men nod. They finish their bread and coffee and disperse.

Del Pezzo is already full of patrons desperate to make the first curtain call. Maranzano's men order a bowl of pasta fazul apiece and wait patiently for the crowd to thin.

They argue over the field that produces the best cannellini, the ones with the faint flavor of roasted chestnuts. They argue over the farm in Parma that produces the perfect cheese. And they argue whether it is marjoram or oregano in the sauce and then whether the herb is dried or fresh. It is then that Joe Parrino steps into the restaurant and takes his seat by the window.

The underboss takes the .38 from the coat pocket, and calmly aims it at Parrino. The first bullet flies wild. Parrino's body struggles to catch up with his mind as his underboss advances on him. The underboss shoots again, this time piercing Parrino's skull between the eyes. Parrino hits the floor, face first, with a thud. The underboss hovers over Parrino's body and puts two more slugs into the back of his head. He tosses the gun to the floor and walks out.

The death of Parrino pleases Maranzano. It fuels his ego. He begins to plot a demonstration of his power to the Americanized Italians. Frank Costello gets wind of the threat of harm and refuses to go to his Harlem office. He also refuses to keep his routine at the Plaza. He worries about his wife, his social life, and the meetings he holds with the rich and powerful of New York.

He flags down a cab.

"Broome Street," Costello tells the driver. "Let me off at Mulberry."

He hikes to Charlie's office and runs through a litany of complaints.

"I got trouble of my own," Charlie says. "This guy's declared open season on my rackets. Every time I turn around, some Sicilian is knocking over one of my joints."

"What are we waiting for?" Costello says. "We'll all be dead if something isn't done. What can Joe the Boss do in hiding? Does he even know what's going on?"

Joe Adonis bursts through the door to Charlie's office.

"You're gonna love this," he tells Charlie. "Maranzano just put word on the street. He's offering amnesty for the guy that knocks off Joe the Boss."

The news hangs in the air. There it is, just like Meyer and Charlie expected. Maranzano has lost patience with the war. He is eager to become the new Caesar.

"Amnesty," Charlie gloats. "Would you look at that!"

Vito, the Neapolitan, sits bolt upright in his chair. "New York would be a better place without either of these stronzi."

Charlie agrees, "Be patient. We don't want to appear too eager. We can't run around town blowing everybody away. Even Frank can't fix that kind of trouble."

It is a fact and Costello knows it, especially with Seabury poking around into every corrupt secret. Charlie turns to Vito.

"I think it's time you and me paid a visit to the new Caesar," he says.

Charlie says to Adonis, "Get word to Maranzano that I want to talk. Tell him we meet in a home in Brooklyn, none of this headquarters shit. Tell him I'll only come if we meet face-to-face and that Vito comes with me. Those are my terms."

Within days, Charlie is standing in front of Maranzano making a deal on Masseria's life. The talk is frank and to the point.

Charlie says, "I want to make one thing perfectly clear; I ain't lookin' to take Joe's place but naturally some of his guys are going to come along with me. I don't want nothin' from you or your family. And I don't want you to ask me for what's already mine. Where we come into conflict, we sit down like gentlemen and work things out. No more war over disagreements."

Maranzano nods.

"I'm acknowledging that Joe the Boss ain't helpin' this situation get resolved and if his death paves the way to peace, then that's the cost we pay."

Maranzano scrutinizes Charlie. If Charlie Luciano makes the move, the rest of Mr. Joe's camp will follow. If Maranzano ever questions Charlie's loyalty, he will have every right to kill the man who killed his own boss.

Charlie leaves Maranzano and calls Meyer. They meet at the Claridge under a cloudy sky and tepid temperatures. Charlie lays out his agreement with Maranzano.

"Are your boys ready?" Meyer says.

"As ready as we'll ever be," Charlie says.

Doing away with Joe the Boss must fall on Charlie's shoulders if Charlie is to continue in Joe's place. He has the most powerful mob of all the guys under Joe the Boss. Only Charlie can maintain control of the situation once Joe has been removed.

It is a Wednesday morning, early morning. An April morning. Smack in the middle of New York's concrete jungle, the warmth of spring has turned the park into an explosion of pink and fuchsia blooms. Meyer leaves a trail of stale bread for the birds to squabble over.

"If he thinks too many people got wind of his outing, he'll cancel again," Charlie says. "The good news is that he wants to hear my plan for getting rid of Maranzano. I sweetened the pot by suggesting it's a fine opportunity to enjoy Scarpato's cooking. It ain't easy getting the old greaser to budge from his sanctuary. He's entrenched in that place. Fortunately for us, he's had a taste of New York and he's missing the life he had here."

"Are you set, Charlie?"

"What's the worse could happen?" Charlie says. "I die. I been there before. I got Livorsi drivin'. Remember him? He drives for Terranova and ever since Terranova's nephew was killed by the other side, Joe trusts Terranova's loyalty. They gunned him down in front of his wife, so I don't go for that 'man of honor' bullshit Maranzano tries to pull. Terranova swore revenge on the killers. Ever since that, him and Joe have been together in the fight. We're in the shit now."

Charlie bids Meyer goodbye at the 110th Street park entrance and jumps into Vito Genovese's car. They head to the Fulton Fish Market, where Livorsi is waiting. The long drive gives Charlie plenty of time to think.

"I don't like you goin' in alone," Vito says.

"Just stick to the plan," Charlie says.

Vito says, "Drop you off, come back for your body? That ain't no plan. Let me do my job."

"This is somethin' I gotta do," Charlie says. "It's gotta be by my hand. That's the agreement I made with Maranzano. That's my absolution."

"What are you talking about?"

"Joe's blood must be on my hands. You just be sure you're there like we discussed. I don't need none of Joe's men jumping in to settle the score. I need you to keep an eye on Frank Livorsi. Make sure he don't do nothing stupid."

"O.K., Charlie," Vito says.

"Tell ya what, if I go down, you come in and take 'em all out."

Vito is satisfied with the option. They roll up to the fish

market and meet up with Ciro Terranova and Frank Livorsi. The four of them drive to the place Joe the Boss has called home for the past two months, on Second Avenue. The neighborhood is quiet for a Wednesday, not many cars on the street and the local kids have not yet filtered out from school.

Charlie and Terranova enter Joe's place as they always do. Joe doesn't say anything right away. Instead he pours tea and settles into a heavy rocking chair. Charlie and Terranova take a seat on the couch and watch Joe rock back and forth in silence.

"You want tea," Joe says, "there's cups in the kitchen."

Victorian wallpaper wraps the room in a blinding rush of rose, tan, burgundy, and silver on pink. The ceiling is heavy and dark, bronzed tin layered with the soot of too many New York winters. Fear hangs heavy in the air. Outside is spring. Outside is fear and freedom rolled into one.

Charlie says, "Let me send Vito over to Scarpato's. He can pick up whatever you want. We can eat here."

Joe jumps to his feet.

"We'll take my car," he says.

The steel-armored sedan drives up to the house. Inch thick plate glass provides Joe an added measure of peace of mind.

Charlie tells Livorsi to get Vito and meet him at the restaurant. Several cars fill with Joe's soldiers. Charlie and Terranova pile into the asylum of Joe's sedan. Almost immediately, Terranova begins to sweat.

The driver winds his way through the back streets of the city to Coney Island and pulls into a garage not far from Scarpato's restaurant. Joe, Charlie, and Terranova wait in the sedan while waves of soldiers scout the small café and surrounding neighborhood. When all is clear, they give the signal. Joe, Charlie, and Terranova step from the sedan. The breeze coming off the ocean is a relief from the cramped, hot quarters.

Soldiers surround Joe as he walks from the garage to the restaurant; Vito heads for the kitchen. Joe the Boss sends two of his soldiers to join Vito. Terranova nods to Livorsi to go with them. Scarpato and his mother are laboring over a hot stove.

Scarpato brings Chianti to the table. His mother brings the antipasti.

Charlie takes control of the wine. Scarpato scurries back to the kitchen.

Ciro sips wine and calms his nerves, "Maranzano's got us all jumpy. I'll be glad when he's out of the way. My nephew can rest in peace. Maybe I can get a good night's sleep, too."

It is a clever ruse and Joe falls for it.

Charlie says, "I got a few things that will interest you only I don't want nobody eavesdropping, not even the cook. Whadya say I tell Scarpato to take a hike? His mother is hard of hearing. She's the real cook anyway."

"Send one of the boys to keep him company," Joe says. "Make sure he doesn't make trouble. I don't need him makin' no phone calls."

Joe picks up the Chianti. He raises a salute and watches Terranova slug back the wine. Mama Scarpato brings out a lobster dish and then returns to the kitchen for the pasta dish.

The long, green awning that stretches from the front door across the sidewalk and ends at the curb serves as an effective barrier, blocking an outsider's view of the restaurant. Joe's guards stay on the far side of the leaded glass and make sure nobody enters. Charlie throws the heavy bolt on the front door while Mama Scarpato pulls the shades. She brings bowls of Zabaglione and cups of Italian coffee, then busies herself with scrubbing pots and pans. All the while the boys talk about the old days and their victories. Ceiling fans whirl lazily overhead.

"I have a couple of guys that will help us," Charlie says.

"Tommy Lucchese and a couple of his boys. They got no use for Maranzano either."

"Ha!" Joe says. "Lucchese is an opportunist. I wouldn't trust anyone from Tom Reina's family."

"Opportunity is the key to his loyalty," Charlie says. "And he's got a great cover story. You killed his boss. Maranzano will expect his loyalty to the cause. Lucchese will give up Maranzano's location. Then we make our move."

"That's your big idea?" Joe says. He looks at Terranova. "Do you go along with this? Tommy Lucchese turning over Salvatore Maranzano?"

Terranova nods. "Tommy and I go way back. He isn't interested in this war any more than the others."

"We have much to think about," Joe says. "How about a little Briscola while our meal settles?"

Charlie retrieves a deck of cards Mama Scarpato has brought from the old country for just such a purpose.

Charlie pulls a two from the deck, leaving the other 39 cards, to adjust for having three players. The deck consists of four suits: coins, cups, batons, and swords. Charlie deals three cards to each player and puts the remaining deck in the middle of the table with one card turned face up. The face card is the trump suit. For this round, it is batons.

Charlie smokes while he waits for Joe to make his move.

Joe stares at his cards and thinks of the men he's lost, a mental exercise that he performs daily to keep his rage fueled and his mind sharp.

Peter Morello, the Clutch Hand—shot dead sitting in his office with a couple of his paesans, including Terranova's stepbrother.

Joseph Pinzolo—murdered in the middle of the afternoon in the Brokaw.

Al Mineo and Stephen Ferrigno—ambushed at the Alhambra

apartments by Maranzano's men, who were hiding in an apartment on the first floor.

"It's your move," Charlie says.

Joe leads with the three of cups. The play moves to Terranova.

The Chianti flows freely as the card game proceeds. Charlie feeds cards to Joe and somewhere between the wine's buzz and a lucky feeling, Joe gets an idea.

"I should have listened to Morello in the beginning, God rest his soul. He warned me to kill this viper before he got too big. I thought I could cut him down to size. I was wrong. Charlie, I want you to get with Lucchese, but not with your plan. Tell Lucchese you want to meet with Maranzano. I hear he has offered amnesty to anyone who will kill me. Go to him. Tell him you are willing to give me up to them."

Charlie says, "I'll never get a gun past his men."

"Lucchese hands you the gun after you are searched," Joe the Boss says. "You shoot the bastard. It's all by the book, bing, bing, bing. I won't seek revenge."

Joe lays down the cards in his hand, victory in the Briscola match.

He is smug, almost bitter. The deal of the cards rotates to Terranova. Charlie slides a loaded revolver from a holster taped to the underside of the table.

"I never thanked you for all you done for me," Charlie says to Joe. "Not properly, anyway. You took me off the streets and showed me how to be a ruthless son of a bitch. I didn't always appreciate the lessons, especially when those micks beat the shit out of me."

He runs his finger along the scar on his face. His fingers bump over the irregular beard that sends his whiskers this way and that. Joe pours more Chianti and tips his glass toward Charlie.

"We toast the end of Maranzano's war," Joe says.

Charlie stands abruptly. His chair falls backwards to the floor. He raises the .38, takes aim, and fires. One bullet through the head, followed by four more through Joe's thick body as Vito and Ciro join in. Even in death, Joe's disgust with Charlie shows through. Tabula rasa. Clean slate.

The newspapers whip up fears of a gang war that never materializes. Two weeks pass and the only activity of any consequence is Al Smith celebrating the opening of the Empire State Building, an event that ignores the struggle for tenants as the economy slides deeper into Depression.

Meyer and Charlie take the elevator to the 86th floor of the new skyscraper and take in the view of New York. Across the Hudson is New Jersey, land of dispute between Waxey Gordon, Longy Zwillman, and Richie the Boot. Around the corner is Harlem and the rising conflict between the Dutchman and his Irish nemesis, Legs Diamond, who has sucked a new mick into the struggle, a guy named Vincent Coll.

No matter which direction you look, there is trouble.

Charlie says, "Something is gone in Terranova."

Meyer agrees. Some men are forged by battle; others are broken.

The sun disappears on the horizon and bathes the city in warm, rosy hues.

Charlie sets himself up in a new apartment, 115 Central Park West, The Majestic, and tries to guess how things will play out with Joe the Boss gone.

Charlie says, "What's next?"

Meyer says, "We give Maranzano his head. Let's see what he does with it."

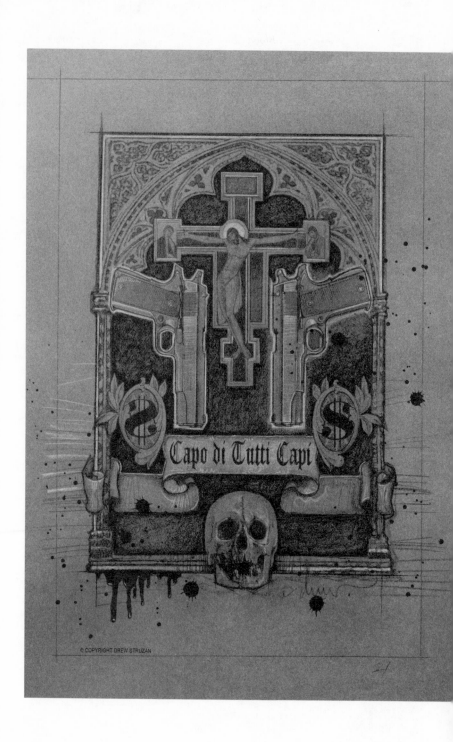

Capo di Tutti Capi

Chapter Twenty-One
A Clean Conscience Makes
a Comfortable Pillow

SPRING 1931

Like a phoenix, the Majestic, a twin-towered housing cooperative, rises from the ashes of the financial crisis. Would-be buyers are lured by the blaze of Art Deco splendor. Three stories of limestone underpin the twenty-six stories of light brown brick that gracefully reaches for the sky. Steelwork, perfected in the rise of the Empire State Building, sculpts luxurious wraparound corner windows and wide terraces on the upper floors.

The Majestic overlooks Central Park. Trees frame a view of the Lake. It is about as far from the Lower East Side as one can get without winding up in Harlem. Charlie buys a corner unit with a balcony overlooking Central Park West and settles into his new paradise.

"The neighborhood ain't half bad," he jokes to Meyer, who has come to see the place. "This started out as a hotel but that idea collapsed right along with Wall Street. After that they were going to build luxury apartments. Each unit was gonna have twenty-four rooms. What the hell would I do with twenty-four rooms? Open a whorehouse?"

Meyer has brought a bottle of 25-year-old Glenlivet and he opens it and pours two glasses.

Charlie shows off his collection of Persian rugs, Stickley furniture, Mica lamps, and William Morris wallpaper.

"When you're rich, even your furniture has names," Charlie says.

Meyer eases into the oak-and-leather chair snugged next to a reading table and lights a cigarette. The lamps cast a warm orange glow over the room. Meyer envies the distinctly masculine air.

Meyer says, "I'm betting Ada Hector didn't do the decorating."

"You see that light?" Charlie nods to the two-foot tall bronze lamp perched on a reading table.

The lamp is more of a sculpture than a light. The lamppost rises at a sixty-degree angle from the base. The pale-yellow globe atop the pole doesn't even try to come close to providing enough light for reading. This lamp is about the sleek nude pressing her hips to the lamppost, arching backwards while holding tight the top of the pole with both hands.

"Polly gave it to me," Charlie says. "She said the place needed some class."

Meyer says, "I thought you were paying tribute to the girls in Times Square."

Charlie laughs. The Claridge has become the place to play cards and hump whores. The quiet of the Majestic is much more to his liking.

Meyer says, "You never talked about Joe the Boss."

Charlie settles back on the couch. His droopy eye comes to life.

"I'll tell you, the old bastard sure as hell enjoyed his last meal. He was in hiding so long, he was losing weight. When I stood up to let him have it, he didn't say a word. He knew the score. I could see it in his eyes. If you ask me, I think he was relieved. All that Sicilian bullshit was taking its toll. The night Maranzano's guys got Mineo and Ferrigno really spooked him.

He almost got his head blown off. He was lucky that night. What were the odds of him surviving another attack like that one?"

Charlie tells the story of the Alhambra incident as if he is reliving the experience. Meyer wonders if Charlie might have been with Joe the Boss that night. Maybe his life was in as much danger as that of Joe the Boss. Maybe that prompted Charlie to meet with Salvatore Maranzano to bring the war to an end.

"It ain't easy to miss a target as big as Joe the Boss," Charlie says. "Not if you get a bead on him. Unless the shooter's too eager, or too far away. If you ain't got nothing bigger than a .38, you gotta get in close. If you can't get in close, take a sawed-off shotgun, a pump-gun, something you can tag the bastard with. Two bullets and the guy goes down. At the Alhambra, these guys were yelling and screaming. Bullets were flying everywhere. Joe was livid after. I don't think he thought he could be found. You saw he went deeper into hiding after that. Can you imagine if they would've cut him down that night? It would be an entirely different story today. We got lucky."

Meyer says. "Maranzano would have taken all the glory."

"He's still taking all the glory," Charlie says.

Charlie stares at the floor, the image of the lifeless body of Joe the Boss superimposed on his brain. Blood everywhere. The story of the death made front page news in the *Times*. Four bullets in his back and one in his head. That's what the paper wanted everyone to remember.

What Charlie remembered was something else altogether. He stood for the kill. Joe saw the gun and pushed back from the table to escape but Charlie was quicker. Joe's head flew backwards when the first bullet hit. Bits of bone and brain blew out the back of his skull and spattered across the floor. Vito bolted in from the kitchen, delivering two more shots that lodged in Joe's back. Terranova freed the revolver taped under the table in front of his seat and shot wildly. Two of his bullets went into Joe's back and the heaving mass of flesh fell to the floor. Blood soaked the tiles.

The shooters' car was found two miles away, abandoned, the paper said. Three discarded pistols were found in the back seat.

For the first time in as long as he can remember, Charlie answers to no one. He looks at Meyer in a confusion of relief and nervous anticipation. Here he is still alive, living in an uptown apartment. Without a doubt, he is one of the most powerful gangsters in New York.

Meyer says, "Have you talked with the new Caesar?"

"He got what he wanted. He's busy wallowing in his victory. There's a lot of guys eager to kiss his ring. Bunch of bullshit. He'd better enjoy it while it lasts." Charlie pours more whiskey. "Funny but I thought by the time we made it uptown a lot of this bullshit would be gone. The Boss ain't even cold in his grave and we got the Dutchman's brawl in the Bronx makin' the news already."

"It's Coll," Meyer says, meaning Vincent Coll, the latest defector from the Schultz mob. "Arthur didn't treat the kid right. Now he's got trouble. It was Madden who brought Coll along. It's Madden who will have to take him out."

Charlie says, "Fucking Irish. Too hot-headed for their own good. I don't want this to get in the way of taking out Maranzano. Did you notice that the newspapers are saying Joe the Boss was 'bigger than Al Capone'? Front page."

"One down," Meyer says. "One to go. When we're done, they can thank us."

Charlie says, "Yeah, they'll be shaking our hands through our prison bars."

✻

Vincent Coll and Fats McCarthy stake out a beer drop in the Bronx.

"Goddamn monkeys at the zoo eat better than we do," Coll says.

The twenty-two-year-old strawberry blond is frustrated. He wasn't getting his fair share of the beer take from the Dutchman's coffer. He paid his dues. After all, the Dutchman used Coll's gang to expand his influence in the Bronx, used them as enforcers, brought them in on the beer business, and then kicked them to the curb when the time came to pay up.

Coll and McCarthy wait in the bed of a canvas-back pickup truck half a block from John Soricelli's beer drop. Soricelli is still with the Dutchman. Coll reasons that whatever affects Soricelli affects the Dutchman. It's his theory of rob Peter to take down Paul.

"When will the Jews learn not to fuck with the Irish?" Coll says.

Coll has surrounded himself with the toughest of the Dutchman's Irishmen, and a few Italians to boot: Patsy Del Greco, Dominick Odierno, the Basile brothers, Frank Giordano, one and all disgruntled recruits.

"I think my arse is frozen tight to this fucking truck," McCarthy says.

McCarthy checks his watch. Owney Madden's beer truck is running late. It's nearly two o'clock in the morning. He pulls back the canvas top to take a better look around. In the distance, the construction work on the Triborough Bridge has stalled in the wake of the stock market crash. The area around the beer drop reflects the general neglect of property in the Bronx. McCarthy fears the drop has been abandoned.

Another hour rolls by. Coll throws off a knit cap and rubs his fingers hard atop his head, trying to shake the cold. McCarthy shifts his stiff legs and stretches his back. Coll smokes a cigarette and stares up at the moonlight. Outside there is nothing.

"Fuckin' traitor," Coll says. "What kind of man throws in with a German Jew over his own people just so he can have a nightclub? What the fuck? The Cotton Club is in the middle of Harlem. If he really is somebody, what the hell is he doing in Harlem?"

"He came from England," McCarthy says. "Never trust the English."

Coll lights another cigarette and breathes in a long drag.

"Count it up, Fats. At ten bucks a keg…son of a bitch, that's a couple of grand's worth of beer right there coming in on Madden's fucking truck and we've been freezing our asses off for a hundred-fifty a week. What kind of shit is that?" He snorts and falls back.

Suddenly the familiar rumble of a truck breaks the despair. Soricelli swings open the doors of the garage. The truck pulls into the yawning cavern. A faux brick wall separates two back-to-back garages. A handful of men swarm the trucks. The garage door closes.

McCarthy signals to the two other trucks filled with his boys.

Coll says, "You saw what Charlie Lucky did, din't ya? He knocked off his boss. He's no fool. You gotta take what belongs to you. The beer business in the Bronx belongs to us and we're taking it back."

McCarthy nods. Coll pulls a pipe bomb from a duffel. They shift to the front seat. Coll turns over the ignition and waves to the boys in the truck behind him. They pull out and position themselves. Madden's driver pulls out after them.

Coll rolls up alongside Madden's truck. McCarthy chucks the pipe bomb into the cab and Coll speeds away. Fire consumes the truck and sears the awnings off of a storefront. Coll whistles in delight and beats the roof of the truck with the flat of his palm.

"That'll show 'em," he yells.

Coll is on to his next target. Joey Rao, a 5'7", 190-pound thug who partners with Ciro Terranova to expand the Dutchman's interests in the Bronx, spends most of his waking hours at the Helmar Social Club on East 107th Street in Harlem. The Helmar is a hangout, plain and simple, a place where Rao can oversee his rackets: drug trafficking, policy banking, a bevy of slot machines in Harlem, and a booming beer business.

Coll decides on the moment of attack. Giordano fetches a stolen sedan. The gang piles in, each of them armed with a fully loaded Thompson. Coll takes the wheel. He eases into first gear, suppressing the surge of adrenaline pulsing through his veins. The heat of the July afternoon combines with the mass of bodies and turns the car into a furnace.

Nobody says a word.

They cruise through Harlem. Streets fill with kids escaping their own brick ovens to play in open fire hydrants.

Coll rounds the corner of Second Avenue and heads down 116th Street. Near Lexington, he spots Rao and Amato chatting. He hits the gas. A lineup of machine guns fills the car's open windows. Bullets fill the street with panic. Kids dive for shelter. Amato is hit in the neck and head and drops like a sack of potatoes. Rao is hit, too, but manages to take cover behind a car. Another of Rao's confidants staggers bleeding toward the Alpi Restaurant. The bullet in his back seems to have cut something necessary for coordination. He bursts through the door yelling for a doctor.

The Dutchman hears the news and bellows for DeRosa, his heavyset lieutenant who has a proclivity for inflicting pain.

"Take out those cocksucking turncoats. All of 'em. I'm done dancin' with these guys. Teach these fucking micks who's the boss."

DeRosa looks at Weinberg and nods. They hit the street in a near gallop, climb into a stolen apple-green Model A, and head for the Bronx.

DeRosa says, "We got two madmen at war with each other."

"One madman," Weinberg says, "and one goddamn turncoat."

"Vincent's brother drives through Harlem every day, down St. Nicholas Avenue. He's the guy we target. If we're lucky, Vincent will be in the car with him. Two birds with one stone."

Weinberg says, "Then let's hope it's our lucky day."

They circle the Bronx and then come back around to the Dutchman's headquarters to pick up another shooter. Weinberg drives. They park along Peter Coll's route. Right on schedule, Peter drives by, alone. Weinberg follows in quick pursuit. DeRosa hangs out the window and takes aim. Four bullets fly through the windshield and slam into Peter's chest. He is D.O.A. when the coroner arrives.

Vincent Coll is inconsolable. For an hour and a half, he wails and screams and smashes his fists into walls and cupboards and closet doors. Then he goes mute. Numb. His mind reels. When he was seven years old, he watched his mother die. Before he was twelve, he had watched five of his siblings die. After that, his father turned Vincent and Peter over to the state of New York and disappeared. Now he's got no one. Fucking no one.

Vincent Coll wipes his eyes.

"The Dago war is gonna look like child's play when I'm done," he says.

Somewhere around eleven o'clock in the evening, he and Fats McCarthy head for the first beer drop on Coll's list. Madden's driver doesn't notice Coll's dark shadow coming up behind him.

Coll slams a .38 into the driver's left temple. The driver goes pale but Fats McCarthy keeps him on his feet.

"Ah, no," Coll says. "I've got a job for you. Leave the beer and get to work ripping this truck apart."

Coll drops a bag of tools.

Coll says, "I said tear this fuckin' truck apart or I'll blow your fucking head off."

Coll uprights an abandoned chair and parks himself in it, the .38 trained on the driver. He pulls a pack of cigarettes from his pocket, balances on the back two legs of the chair, and lights up.

The driver attacks the truck with a vengeance. Every strut and filter, every tank and hose, every brake and tire, and every spring and gasket is strewn across the landscape. Coll breaks his newfound silence with a hysterical laugh.

"Get outta here," he says. "If I see you with the Dutchman again, it'll be you laying all over this field."

The driver runs while Coll takes potshots at him as he flees.

Within the next seventy-two hours, Coll and his gang demolish ten trucks and a hundred-fifty slot machines. The Dutchman sends DeRosa to find the bastards.

"If you wanna live to your next birthday, you'll find them bums," the Dutchman says. "I wanna know where they eat, sleep, and shit."

Coll's men know every inch of the forty-two square miles that make up the Bronx. They anticipate the Dutchman's every move. They count on the Dutchman sending guards to the beer drops.

Coll and his gang start making the rounds. It's sheer luck that they spot DeRosa before he spots them. The next morning, DeRosa is found in his car, flopped over dead, nine bullets heavier. The Dutchman rages out of control. He sends a new recruit on a beer run.

"And keep your goddamn eyes open!" he says.

Jacapraro creeps through the Bronx praying he won't be noticed.

He parks the beer truck and steps out. He turns up the collar of his jacket and then opens the back of the truck, gets ready to unload the beer. Suddenly he feels a .38 in his ribs.

"Play nice and you might make it through the night," an Irish voice says.

Jacapraro swings around with a wild punch that lands a left hook. The gun fires once. Jacapraro grabs his chest and staggers backwards.

Three more shots and Jacapraro is dead. They park his dead body in a sedan on Stratford Avenue. A few miles away they ditch the truck.

Coll picks up the boys, drops them at home. The next day they're at it again. Coll's only solace comes in the arms of his German-born lover, the only woman strong enough to understand he can't give up the fight.

They go at their rough play until the sun comes up. Then Coll moans and rails over the need for cash.

"Get a couple of cop uniforms," Lottie tells Vinnie.

He forgets his desperation and pushes her down on the bed.

"Let the rich make a little contribution to the Irish cause," she says, luring him closer.

He looks into her big blue eyes.

"What?"

"Take something they care about, enough that they'll pay to get it back," she says.

"You mean booze?"

"Jesus, no, not booze," she says, rising up and leaning on her elbows. "I'm talking about taking people, Vinnie. You want money, right? You dress the boys like coppers and put them to work grabbing celebrities. People who can pay."

Coll says, "Ah, Lottie, I love ya. You're a goddamn thinker."

"So who are we going to grab?" she says.

Coll sits on the side of the bed, pushes his hair back into place. "George Jessel or Eddie Cantor?"

"And that radio announcer, too, N.T.G. He was suing Western Union for a hundred grand because they didn't get a deposit to the bank in time."

"A hundred grand?" Coll whisks Lottie into his arms and kisses her hard on the lips.

Charlie and Meyer take Jimmy Alo for a boat ride on one of Frank Costello's luxury cruisers. They motor along the Sound and talk.

Charlie says, "We're all taking a lot of heat on account of Vincent Coll. What do the Irish say about what's going on?"

Jimmy says, "The Irish used to own this town."

Meyer says, "They still pretty much own this town. They have Tammany Hall and most of the police department."

"That ain't how they see it," Jimmy says. "They want the beer business and their share of the policy rackets. They understand Coll takin' back what was his before the Dutchman and Terranova took over."

"There's plenty of room for everybody," Meyer says.

"Tell that to the Dutchman," Jimmy says.

"Are the Irish lining up with Coll?" Charlie asks.

"Nah," Jimmy says, watching the coastline go by. "He's too, uh, unstable. That's what I heard. He ain't got many friends. He's a bully, you know what I mean? Got a chip on his shoulder. Who the hell knows why."

Charlie stops the engine and lets the boat float.

Charlie says, "You got a lotta Irish guys around you. What I'm gonna tell you is strictly between us now. Me and Meyer are working together to take out Salvatore Maranzano. We need to know if the Irish are going to be with us or against us. We ain't askin' for an answer right now. The beer war is spilling a lot of violence into the streets. When the time comes for us to make our move, we don't need the heat from the beer war interfering. We figure that Maranzano is going to start making his moves. He's got plans. If he starts tryin' to take over our rackets, he'll be joining Joe the Boss."

Jimmy says, "If? That guy ain't never gonna be anything but trouble."

"Do the Irish feel the same?" Meyer says.

"They don't know about these greasers like I do," Jimmy says. "But they been around the block with them. Wars on the waterfront and the like. There ain't no love lost between the Irish and the Italians."

"But they trust you," Charlie says.

"Oh, sure," Jimmy says.

Meyer says, "If Maranzano crosses the line, we're going to take him. Benny is in charge. We're pretty sure he's going to try to get rid of Charlie and all the Americanized guys. You're part of this, too. You want to send one of your guys along with our boys when we make our move, that's fine."

Jimmy nods, "All right. My guys will be all for what you're going to do. The Irish aren't gonna weep over one less greaser. They got respect for you and Charlie. They want to keep what's theirs. Who can blame 'em for that?"

Charlie turns on the engine and swings the cruiser toward Oyster Bay, where a driver is waiting at the dock.

❖

Salvatore Maranzano slips into a tub of hot water. Too many nights on bad mattresses have left him tired and sore. The war of liberation is over. After months of deprivation, he lies back to enjoy a fat torpedo sending waves of smoke racing along the surface of the water. A hot bath, a good smoke—it soothes his war-weary mind.

Holding the cigar in his dry hand, he sinks his head into the watery silence and looks up at the blurry Jesus hanging on the wall in front of the tub. He closes his eyes, letting warmth penetrate the folds of skin. He conjures the moment of Joe's death and wonders if Charlie Luciano made sure the old windbag acknowledged his defeat and saw that Charlie Luciano had been turned by the Castellammarese war hero.

In the silence, he remembers Mussolini's banner cry against the Mafia: Ferro e fucci. Steel and fire. Mussolini announced to the world that the Mafia was dead, slain by steel and fire, and that no force would be able to revive it. Mussolini was wrong. Victory runs in Maranzano's veins and controls his destiny. Of this he is certain.

He rises for a breath and takes another draw on his cigar. He's won the war but not the totality of Sicilian allegiance. He wants to see the troops, the clan of the Castellammarese that will form his Praetorian Guard. If history has taught him anything, it is that all powerful men endure small beginnings before becoming great leaders.

He decides on a hall on Washington Avenue as a good location for his coronation. It looks harmless, a place where locals go to listen to bands and to dance. A party will not be out of place. A crowd of Italians will never be noticed.

Maranzano rises from his bath, dries, and slips into a freshly starched shirt and a clean, new suit. He calls for his driver. He has the uneasy sensation that he's being watched. The sooner he has the Sicilian fathers on his side, the better.

He stops at the Washington Avenue hall and goes over his needs with the proprietor.

"Get rid of these tables and chairs," Maranzano says. "I will bring in my own."

Maranzano pads the rental fee and hands it off with a handshake. Fear keeps the proprietor from counting the profit in front of the Brooklyn boss. He squeezes the bundle of cash in his pocket and deems it sufficiently thick. No questions necessary. He hands over the key with a discreet bow. Maranzano dismisses him with the flick of a wrist and then turns to his driver.

"Nicky," he says, "go to the church and ask Father Bruno for ten or twenty paintings…pictures of Jesus and the Virgin Mary and all the saints. I want them hung all over the walls. Get Anthony to help you. He has an eye for these things."

"Yes, Sir," Nicky says.

"And Nicky," Maranzano says, "get a cross, too, a big one. Take Anthony's truck."

Nicky and Anthony round up the holy relics. Maranzano searches his attic for the piece de resistance that will adorn his stage, an X-shaped chair like the ones used by Roman commanders during long campaigns. The history lesson will be lost on the Americanized boys but no matter. The hand-carved lion heads on each arm are sure to lend the correct air to the ceremony.

Anthony is dutifully hanging the giant cross at the back of the stage when Maranzano arrives at the hall with the Savonarola chair.

"Anthony, what do you think of this chair?" Maranzano says.

Anthony takes a long look at the chair. He thinks it is old. The finish is cracking. The seat is small, cramped, and hard. The floral motif carved along the chair back looks more like something his grandmother would fawn over. No doubt about it, the chair is a piece of junk.

"It is very nice," Anthony says.

"But what do you think of when you look at this chair?" Maranzano says.

Anthony comes down from the ladder and takes a closer look.

"Only a man of great power could honestly rest his arms on the heads of lions."

"Bravo," Maranzano says, placing the Savonarola center stage.

"Why are we hanging pictures of Jesus?" Anthony asks.

"Remember what happened in Cleveland when the fathers tried to have a meeting at a hotel?" Maranzano says.

"Sure, I remember," Anthony says. "Joe Profaci had to grease a lot of politicians that day."

Maranzano says, "It is best not to rely too heavily on bribes. We are making history but not the kind that should fill the newspaper. Look out the window. What do you see?"

Pushcart vendors line the street. Traffic snarls. A local flat-foot is on patrol. A large crowd has gathered at the bank on Freeman Street.

Anthony turns back to Maranzano and shrugs, "You mean the people trying to get their money before the bank folds?"

Maranzano says, "You see everybody and nobody. We don't want people walking by wondering what a large congregation of Italian men might be doing. When they look in they will see the saints. They will think we are a religious order. You must use your head for these things."

The boys finish hanging the paintings and Maranzano places the Savonarola in front of the six-foot cross. The illusion is striking. Maranzano is satisfied. That night, when he crawls into his cozy bed and snuggles to his wife, he breathes a sigh of contentment. He takes his wife in his arms. Her body is smooth, albeit a little worn from childbearing and time. He makes love to her, secure in the sense of his personal honor and then the new Caesar sleeps like a baby.

On the other side of town, among those that fearlessly followed Joe the Boss into battle, a new fear surfaces. They have heard of the dinner Maranzano is holding for the four men that hold the most power in New York: Joe Profaci, Vincent Mangano, Gaetano Gagliano, and Charlie Luciano. The dinner is a celebration of the end of the war. Now that Joe the Boss has slipped into the earth at Woodlawn Cemetery in Queens, the men left of the Masseria family look at Charlie Luciano and wonder.

"What does Charlie Lucky want?" the fat man says into the phone.

The fat man drove Joe's widow to the church and then to the cemetery and now takes pity on her cries for revenge.

Joe's eldest son replies on the other end of the line, "This treacherous bastard…but the phone is not the place for this conversation."

The fat man agrees. Phone calls fly between the remnants of the gang. Like a gaggle of old women, they gossip over Charlie Luciano's intentions. In the dead of night, they slip out of the city and congregate at a summer house in Long Island. They gather around the massive oak dining table and air their grievances. The fat man heads the table, fancying himself the heir apparent.

"What does Charlie want?" the fat man says, this time to the entire complement of his cronies.

Joe the Boss' eldest son says with assurance, "Control."

They squabble over the lucrative rackets Joe the Boss has left behind. Women come and go with plates of ziti and antipasti and wine. As the men fill up, the discussion dies down. Espresso and brandy infuse a sense of compromise into the conversation. They wander out to the large patio.

"What does Charlie want?" the fat man repeats.

"Charlie doesn't want anything," the Quiet Don, Tommy Gagliano, says. "He says he'll leave us to our business if we leave him to his."

"How do you know this?" the fat man asks.

"I asked him. He told me," Gagliano says.

"And you believe him?" Joe's son says. "Just like that, you trust the man who murdered his own boss."

"I've got no reason to doubt him," Gagliano says.

"My father was a great man," the son says. "What we have, we have because of him. His biggest mistake was that he allowed the Americanized men to stand side by side with him. Charlie Luciano brought them in. Don't forget that. My father tolerated this new country but he never forgot the old ways. His heart was always Sicilian. Charlie Luciano has forsaken his true obligations. Why else would he side with the enemy?"

"Let's not bullshit ourselves," Gagliano says. "Your father was a ruthless killer. We do what we have to do. Let's not hang Charlie on the cross just yet. What would you have us do...continue the war until we are all dead? Have any of you been approached by Charlie? Is he trying to take anything from any of us?"

The family head from Brooklyn says, "Charlie Luciano might have pulled the trigger but it was Caesar himself who pulled the strings when he offered amnesty. Why didn't Charlie kill Maranzano when he had the chance?"

Joe's son nods, "Charlie sold us out. He deserves whatever he gets and I, for one, am happy to give it to him. You can bet that Salvatore Maranzano would be pleased for us to do the job ourselves, to take out the man who killed his boss."

The fat man laughs, "That's just the excuse this Caesar needs to put a contract on all of us. If you killed Charlie, Vito Genovese would take revenge. Let Caesar get rid of the traitor."

"What makes you think he will get rid of Charlie?" Joe's son says.

"How can he trust a man who was willing to kill his own boss?" the fat man says. "He will find a reason to do away with him. In the meantime, the best armor is to keep out of range."

Joe's son says, "Then we make Charlie the head of our family. Let him deal with Maranzano. When the wine of their romance matures, the wineskin will burst, and we will be the ones to enjoy the juice, eh?"

"Charlie controls the Tenderloin," the fat man says. "It is a temptation Caesar will not be able to resist."

The Quiet Don says, "Maybe the American men are right. Maybe Charlie did us all a favor. He stopped the war so we could all go about our business. Keep to your business and Charlie will keep to his. I'll tell you who you should fear, the man among us who wants to be the new boss."

"Don't be ridiculous," the fat man says.

The debate continues back and forth for a solid week. In desperation, they head to Charlie's Central Park West apartment and offer him the position of family head.

"Gentlemen," Charlie says, "I'm sure this offer is as hard for you to make as it is for me to accept so let me ease your minds by respectfully declining."

"We didn't make the choice," Joe's son says. "You made the choice when you killed my father. Salvatore Maranzano sees you as the one who has taken over. If we refuse you as head of the family, Maranzano will seek to destroy us all."

Charlie laughs at the suggestion.

"Salvatore Maranzano has exactly what he wants, control of the Brooklyn Castellammarese."

The room is suddenly silent. The odds have shifted. The band of leftovers is relegated to relying on Charlie's strength for their survival.

Charlie says, "I don't want nothing from you except that you leave me to get on with my business while you get on with yours."

There is something easy about Charlie that soothes the fear-driven members of the family who relied on the power of Joe the Boss and Peter Morello.

"This new Caesar," Gagliano says, "he has called a meeting of the prominent Sicilians in New York and ordered the family heads to assemble their soldiers. Will you attend this meeting and stand up for us?"

Charlie ponders the request. He knows these men and what they are capable of doing. They stood by Joe the Boss in the face of bitter odds. The Quiet Don makes a good point. Everyone in the room knows the significance of Maranzano's Bronx meeting. It would be a mistake not to solidify their bond if for no other reason than to let Caesar know he does not rule all of New York.

Charlie says, "We've had enough of war, and so has Caesar. He thinks he won the war but that don't mean he controls us."

"We would make it worth your while to take over as boss," Joe's son says.

"I appreciate the offer but I don't want to be no boss," Charlie says. "If Maranzano wants to think of me as a father, I ain't gonna tell him otherwise. But between you and me, we ain't got no boss. We are allies."

Charlie is talking but they are not listening. The tribe relents and accepts Charlie as an ally but in their mind's eye they see him as the new boss. Charlie manages their confusion by offering them a drink and toasting to a new era of plenty. The tribe shuffles off to their respective homes hoping for the best but planning on the worst.

Charlie throws on a coat and meets Meyer Lansky at the men's club blocks from his house. The club was once the hangout of Harvard grads but necessity has brought down the requirements for membership a notch or two.

"I don't got enough trouble without taking on that kind of bullshit," Charlie says to Meyer, slouching across the tile seat of the steam bath.

Trouble comes in many forms these days. The untidy problem of Vincent Coll has recently been complicated by the addition of Jack Diamond who, like Coll, needs cash. Jack has put pressure on the owners of the 21 Club. They have refused his advances and, in response, Jack Diamond has put out a contract on the club owners' lives.

"Maybe Jimmy can handle this," Meyer says. "He's a good negotiator."

"I'll set it up for tomorrow, the usual place," Charlie says. "After this I got a peace conference to attend."

Meyer stands and tightens the towel around his waist. He doesn't need the details of a Sicilian peace conference. He needs an antacid. After a shower and a shave, he slips into his suit and stops at the small dining room for a cup of hot water into which he stirs six Bell-Ans tablets. He downs the bitter concoction.

Charlie joins him and says, "Caesar took an office at Grand Central. How do you like that?"

The train station boasts a "city within a city." It houses commercial establishments, a police station, changing rooms, private offices, and apartments. But there is more to Maranzano's choice than convenience. The limestone-clad southern façade is modeled on a Roman triumphal arch. Mercury, the god of commerce, is supported by Minerva and Hercules. The symbolism is not lost on Italians who value their history. Minerva and Hercules represent mental and physical strength. The would-be Caesar has found the perfect palace to back his claim of Sicilian superiority.

Meyer says, "He can rent a place anywhere he likes, it doesn't make him a god."

Vito Genovese picks Charlie up from the club and takes him to a restaurant on Times Square, an upscale place with a private room where the New York Mafia heads of state, as defined by Salvatore Maranzano, gather. The hardwood floors, dark chocolate walls, and stiff leather chairs create an air of substance. Outside, the city shimmers.

Charlie sits between Joe Profaci and Vincent Mangano. Across from him is Tommy Gagliano. At the head of the table is Salvatore Maranzano. Five families. Maranzano is keeping it simple, manageable. The Mafia fathers break bread and raise Champagne glasses high.

"Gentlemen," Maranzano says in Italian, "we have been victorious. Let us celebrate with a meal of peace. Salute!"

The food comes in waves. Oysters on the half shell. King crab legs. Antipasti. Maranzano seizes the occasion to elevate the Sicilian ethic. After all, everyone present, save Charlie Luciano, is a transplant from the old country.

"I hope you can see the wisdom in what I am about to propose," Maranzano says.

Before he comes out with the proposal, Maranzano bobs and weaves, throwing a barrage of platitudes that stroke the egos of the Sicilian fathers.

"I propose we form a Commission," Maranzano finally says. "It will function like the Senate in Rome. It will be comprised of the five family heads. When we have a problem, we come together and resolve the problem."

Maranzano lauds the qualities he values in each man. Profaci's loyalty bailing out the men that were pinched in Cleveland is praised. Profaci's thriving olive oil business maintains valuable ties to Italy. Vincent Mangano holds the title of executioner which is highly useful when it comes to controlling the conflicts among the Irish on the waterfront. Tommy Gagliano is the epitome of quiet deception. He maintained the guise of loyalty with Joe the Boss Masseria while orchestrating his downfall. And Charlie Luciano is the power that controls the Americanized men.

Maranzano says, "It is not by chance that each of you has risen to head a family in America. We are destined for great things."

Champagne and wine and cigars and port follow, then the war stories. Maranzano weaves a web of loyalty and oaths and obligation, of wealth and exploitation, of a Promised Land and untapped opportunity. His Commission will be filled with soldiers in the fashion of the Roman legion. Capos, sottocapos, capodecinas, and decini. The street units will gather the spoils of war for presentation to the men of honor who will, in turn, be sure the soldiers have everything they need.

"In this way, we spread our influence all across this country. We bring men of honor to every city. This will give us the strength we need to succeed."

Charlie takes a long look at the man who intends to marshal the Sicilians by means of military conscription.

Maranzano says, "Destiny demands we come together and mend the past. Only this way can we command the future."

The greasers raise their glasses.

✿

A swarm of black touring cars invade the Bronx. Rough-looking men, dressed in expensive handmade suits, pour through the streets and head for the hall on Washington Avenue. In spite of Maranzano's predictions, locals do take note of the intrusion. Gossips dawdle at the entrance to the hall. Inside, Maranzano straightens the paintings and hushes the gathering mob.

A guy on the sidewalk, who would otherwise go unnoticed, catches Charlie's eye. It isn't his Sears and Roebuck suit or his worn shoes that make him stand out from the crowd. It is the large sandwich board he wears with a blaring message: RELIGION IS A SNARE AND A RACKET. The old man maneuvers the unwieldy missive through the gathering mob like some cumbersome weight on his conscience.

Walking by, Charlie says, "You ain't gonna make many friends with a message like that, old-timer."

The old man jabs a handbill in Charlie's direction and says, "The truth is never popular."

Charlie pockets the handbill and, with Vito Genovese and Joe Adonis flanking him, he ducks into the rented hall. Frank Costello is not far behind.

Joe Valachi, heavyset and looking more like a schoolyard bully than a man of war, stands wide-eyed at the spectacle of Maranzano's religious façade. He pokes his mob father, Joe Profaci, in the ribs and points to a painting of St. John gazing heavenward, clad in a radiant robe, hands clutched in prayer.

"You suppose St. John was brought in for the war, too?"

Profaci frowns at the physical contact.

"Don't ever touch me again," he says.

Valachi says, "See the fire floatin' between his hands? Don't it remind you of the oath? You know, how you say your vows and then burn the paper. The paper floats up just like that."

"Sure," Profaci says. "It's a holy communion to take your vows. Don't forget it."

Charlie makes his way to the stage and drops an envelope on the growing pile of tribute gathering on the table next to the Savonarola chair.

Ciro Terranova whispers into Charlie's ear, "Did you see this one coming? Says he has to replenish the war chest. I heard the Big Man himself sent six grand from Chicago. What war is Maranzano planning next?"

Nearly five hundred men are crammed into the hall when Maranzano nods to the door attendants. The doors are closed and locked. No coming in. No going out. Maranzano takes center stage.

He projects his voice like an actor quieting the crowd, and he's speaking in his native tongue. His message is clear. The war of liberation has changed everything. There is a new structure. Soldiers will now answer to their family heads. They will be held accountable for breaking the rules. Accountability includes death when the infraction involves certain of the new rules like talking with one's wife about Cosa Nostra, touching another man's wife, fighting with another member in anger.

Maranzano makes it clear that death is the penalty for not obeying. Death. The word reverberates in Charlie's ears. He sees the wisdom but also the treachery rolled into Maranzano's philosophy. The words are familial. Flattering. The bad guy is dead. Forget the past. This is a new day. "We are all brothers." Five hundred soldiers are distributed among the five family heads. But no matter how you cut up the pie, it is still Maranzano making the rules. And the rules are obey or die.

Ciro Terranova, who swore vengeance against Maranzano for the death of his nephew, turns to Charlie. The idea of forgive and forget is not part of his vocabulary. The man who shot Terranova's nephew is standing a few feet away. Joe Valachi, aka Joey Cargo, squirms and glances side to side.

Finally Maranzano completes the litany. "I am the father of the Castellammarese," he says.

Chapter Twenty-Two
Play Nice with Others...or Else

SUMMER 1931

Vincent Coll sits in the middle of Dutch Schultz territory guzzling beer in a Harlem saloon. He hasn't shaved for days. Jack "Legs" Diamond sits across from him wishing he wasn't downwind. Coll watches the suds slide down the side of his glass and laments the day he heard about the guinea meeting in the Bronx.

Coll says, "The hell with the guineas and the Jews. I say we go over to the Chop House right now and finish what you started with Joey Noe."

"Watch your mouth," Jack says, scanning the saloon.

"You afraid one of these barflies is gonna flutter over and whisper in the Dutchman's ear?"

The saloon is half-empty and harmless by Coll's standards. Jack is warier. He's been stung before by undercover cops and rival gang members posing as innocent diners, wolves in sheep's clothing.

Coll calls for another round.

He says, "What I woulda given to see the surprise on Noe's face when you let him have it. You set him up and then you knocked him down. Sheer poetry, my friend. And the Dutchman with nothing to do but weep. What a sight that musta been."

Jack leans back and smiles. The memory of the ambush at the Chateau Madrid pleases him, which is more than he can say for the beer in his glass. He longs for the old days when he was working for Rothstein and the drug business hummed along gainfully, the days before he was cast adrift to fend for himself.

Arnold Rothstein had hired him and his brother because they were ruthless. Rothstein thought he could harness their wildness. That was just another of a long line of miscalculations on the part of Rothstein, who thought everyone listened to reason and that he was at the center of reasonableness.

When Jack shot Joey Noe for invading the beer business in the Bronx, the Dutchman blamed Rothstein. It's the law of the street. Whatever a guy does reflects on his boss. The Dutchman expected Rothstein to take care of business but he didn't. And then Rothstein died.

After that, Jack tried to establish a relationship with Charlie Lucky. It never took. Jack can't resist the temptation to blow a relationship to hell and back. Jack is like that, desperate and stupid. Now he plies the other Jack and Charlie, the owners of the 21 Club, for protection money and tries to hold on to his territory in the Bronx. That's why he had to shoot Joey Noe and that's why he clings to his association with Vincent Coll.

Coll raises his soupy blue eyes and yells, "Two more, and then two more, and two more!" He trails off. "It was bad luck them coppers pinchin' eight of my boys. Bad luck, I tell ya. And if that weren't enough, they found our heaters. Took the whole lot of them."

"What did you expect," Jack says. "What the hell were you thinking, trying to grab a radio personality for ransom?"

"We need the money," Coll says. "It ain't that hard to understand."

"It isn't the kidnapping," Jack says. "It's the ridiculous notion that you can grab a celebrity and nobody is gonna notice. You gotta get your head on straight. We live in one world and they live in another. If you're going to grab somebody, make it somebody the cops don't give a rat's arse to protect. Get that through your thick mick head!"

A pack of black performers fall into the bar. The noise swells. Coll blinks hard trying to focus on Jack and the empty beer glasses. The bartender sidles up to the table and clears the mess. He taps his finger three times hard on the beer-soaked wood, holding back a new round until someone coughs up enough cash to cover the tab.

Coll stares at Jack. Jack pulls a wallet from his breast pocket and lays a bill on the tray.

"It'll take more than that," the bartender says. "He's been in every day for a week. I ain't got no more credit for a guy on the lam."

Jack drops a fin.

"You're right," Coll says. "You're goddamn right. I was a fool."

The bartender nods, leaving the pints to soothe whatever it is that ails Vincent Coll.

"Of course, I'm right," Jack says.

"We're washed up," Coll says. "Suckers on the downhill side of blown-out opportunities. Me with all the bad luck in the world and you a magnet for bullets."

Jack stiffens. "Don't put the whammy on me! Fifteen bullets and not a one could bury me." Jack knocks on the table. "What's wrong with you? You tryin' to jinx my future?"

"What future," Coll says. "We got no future. We got a guinea moving in on one side and a German Jew on the other. What they don't get, the coppers steal. What have we got when our own kind works against us?"

"Get off it. The greasers aren't interested in the beer business. You ain't seein' the big picture. The Dutchman ain't as invincible as he likes to think. Here's the kicker. You and me don't even have to make a move. That Caesar in Brooklyn is gonna do it for us."

"What are you talking about?" Coll says.

"Are you blind or just stupid," Jack says. "Harlem is full of guineas. This guy, Salvatore Maranzano, he wants the Italian policy racket. He's not going to sit around while a Jew bilks the guineas out of millions of dollars. I'll bet my dear mother's wedding ring on it."

Coll smiles. The waning ember of his ambition explodes with a new idea. He knows the Dutchman's business. Information like that can garner a bundle of cash from the new Caesar, enough to put him back in business in a heartbeat.

Coll says, "Spot me a couple hundred. I'm good for it."

"Jesus, I just got hit by a bunch of revenuers. Put the pinch on Madden, why don't ya?" Jack finishes the pint in front of him and stands. He gives Coll the once over and shakes his head. His kinsman is drowning in his sorrows. He peels a C-note from the roll of cash in his pocket and slides it to Coll.

"Don't say I never give you nothin'," Jack says. "Go home, Vinnie. Sleep it off. Take a shower and wash the cobwebs out of your head."

Jack is out the door before Coll can object.

Coll stumbles to the cramped bathroom, hangs his head over the sink and turns the water on full-blast. He aches for a good score. Jack's words swim through his miserable thoughts, piranhas in search of a carcass. Diamond had offered to sell Joey Noe the beer business but Joey had just laughed. It was hard to say which of the bullets killed him, the one that tore through his chest or the one that lodged in his spine. Either way, he lingered for a month before he passed on. Joey Noe got what he deserved.

"Now there's an interesting expression. Passed on to what?" Coll mutters to the reflection glaring back at him from the aging, freckled mirror.

The men coming and going pay no attention. Their minds are no clearer than Coll's. Coll runs the tips of his fingers across the stubble of his beard. He laments that Charlie Lucky has been caught up in the guinea web right after he freed himself from the likes of Joe the Boss. He resents the Irish who've gone along with the Italians and Jews. It's a crying shame. Coll crawls through the desperation of his wretched life and conceives a new plan.

Big Frenchy is the Siamese twin joined to Owney Madden's wallet. The right approach to Big Frenchy could put him on the road to recovery. Coll washes the self-pity from his face and calls his boys.

"Meet me for breakfast," he says, then heads home where he falls into a deep, restless sleep.

When he wakes, in the cold sweat of disorientation, he finds his boys playing cards at the table in the dump of a kitchen he calls home. It is still dark outside.

"I told ya to meet me for breakfast," Coll says, irritated by the intrusion.

"Ya just didn't tell us which day," Fats McCarthy says.

The darkness outside and the heavy coat on his tongue confirm the realization that he has slept through at least one day.

"What time is it?" Coll says.

"It's two in the morning," McCarthy says.

Coll rifles a small drawer in the kitchen cupboard then slams it shut. The boys go on with their game, waiting for him to cool down. Coll searches through the small flat, tearing through cabinets and books and small boxes. Half an hour later, he finds what he is looking for, a piece of torn paper with a phone number on it. It calms him.

"Listen up, you mugs," Coll says, taking a seat at the table. "The way I see it, you gotta look out for your own. Only fools don't know that much about life. We come to this country for opportunity. There's a cruel joke for ya. What are we? We're everybody's dogs. We labor on the docks and in the factories and what do we get? We get shit; that's what. Then when we finally get a break, fuckin' guineas and Jews want to cut us out. 'Play nice with others,' Madden says. 'Don't go makin' no trouble.' Easy for him to say, drivin' his fancy car and sittin' on top of the world in Harlem. What makes him any different from us? Why should he have all the breaks while we get none? That's the question I'm askin'. Well, let him put up a few dollars to help his own. Are you with me?"

The logic is indisputable. The mob ferries across town to a small hotel in Harlem where they huddle around a phone. Coll dials the number on the slip of paper, the number for the Club Argonaut on West 50th and Seventh Avenue in Manhattan. His boys, what's left of them, gather around.

Big Frenchy answers the phone. Coll hangs his head and cops a mournful tone, asks for a rendezvous. "Everything has gone to shite," he says to Frenchy. "The cops are after me. They missed me but they got my only means of defense against that Jew bastard. If the cops don't get me the Dutchman will. My life ain't worth a plugged nickel on the street. I ain't askin' for much. Just a fightin' chance, that's all. I ain't got nobody to turn to except you and Owney. You gotta know that. Whadya say?"

The sob story works. Frenchy grabs the pouch that holds the club's evening take. He counts out a grand and shoves it into an envelope. The pouch goes back into the safe next to the .38 Frenchy keeps for emergencies. He grabs that, too, wipes it clean with his handkerchief, then wraps the .38 and shoves it into his coat pocket.

A young dancer at the club watches the whole thing.

"Ain't you the big sucker?" she says.

"Yeah," Frenchy says. "I'm a real saint. Come on, we'll do our good deed for the night and then we'll go someplace special."

She nuzzles the big brute as they slide into the back seat of Frenchy's Cadillac. The bodyguard joins the driver in the front. But Coll's boys are on them before they can pull away from the club. Frenchy is dragged from the Cadillac and thrown into the back of Coll's getaway car. Coll's driver races up Riverside Drive and heads out of the city to a hideout in Westchester County.

"I got your cash," Frenchy says to Coll when the commotion ends. "What more do you want?"

"Our piece of the pie," Coll tells him. "Irish stick together."

"I ain't Irish," Frenchy says.

Frenchy has the face of a boxer, big and round, decorated with a continual snarl. He has the muscle to match, which comes in handy, often, but Frenchy prefers reason.

Coll smirks, "You ain't no Jew and you ain't no guinea. I bet you ain't no Frenchman, either. Where the fuck are you from?"

Frenchy scowls. "What difference does it make to you?"

"You and Owney are real cozy with that Jew bastard."

"It ain't like that," Frenchy says. "There's rules now. You gotta play by the rules. You wanted in with the Dutchman. Nobody twisted your arm. You want out, you gotta go through channels."

"Channels!" Coll says. "What the fuck are you talking about? Since when do we have channels?"

"Since now," Frenchy says. "We all agreed."

"I didn't agree. Maybe you didn't notice, this ain't no school-yard. We're playin' this my way," Coll says. "How much you got on ya?"

Frenchy pulls the envelope from his coat pocket and tosses it to Coll. Coll checks the contents and laughs.

"A thousand dollars? I want a hundred grand and I want it in small bills."

The Mad Dog isn't just mad anymore, he's rabid. He leaves Frenchy to contemplate the situation while he gets Madden on the phone.

"I got your boy here," Coll says. "If you want him back still breathin', you'll get me the cash."

Madden is rattled. He agrees to Coll's terms and the dropoff Coll has orchestrated. Satisfied with money in hand, Coll releases Big Frenchy and goes his way.

Madden is relieved to see his pal in one piece. But rumors about the kidnapping are circulating around Broadway. He makes a few calls. By Thursday, according to the *New York Times*, Assistant Chief Inspector John J. Sullivan denies the rumor that Big Frenchy was held for ransom.

"It's just common sense," Madden says to Frenchy as he folds the newspaper and lays it on his desk. "Who needs that kind of publicity in this town? Somebody would be grabbing you off the street every other week."

"The kid doesn't understand business," Big Frenchy says. "He's still livin' on the street. He'll never play ball. You know that, don't you? He crossed the line here. Charlie Lucky won't stand for it. That's the way it is now. That's the change we got on accounta the greaser war."

Halfway across town, Salvatore Maranzano reads of the incident and pushes Tommy Lucchese for clarification. Lucchese hems and haws. While he possesses a Sicilian pedigree, his parents immigrated to America when he was a boy, barely ten years old. The old ways are not sufficiently entrenched in his thinking as to outsmart an old fox like Maranzano.

"Most likely a kid named Vincent Coll," Lucchese says. "He's got a temper and he's low on cash. He tried to kidnap a radio announcer a little while back. Maybe you read about it. You know the Schultz–Coll beer wars? That's the kid. Vincent Coll. Irish guy. Hates the Dutchman."

Maranzano mulls over the implications of this new and promising situation. He trusts Tommy Lucchese, who has been with him since the beginning of the Castellammarese War. It was, after all, the death of Lucchese's boss that put the war in motion.

"What do you know about Coll?" Maranzano says. "What does he want?"

"Right now, he wants money," Lucchese says. "A couple of my guys heard him talking to Jack Diamond in a Bronx saloon. He wants to get rid of the Dutchman and maintain a hold on the Bronx beer market."

"The Irish lack discipline," Maranzano says.

"They're tough as nails," Lucchese says.

"Shifting sands," Maranzano says. "The Irish have never forged a great empire."

"They routed the British," Lucchese says.

"A country divided cannot stand," Maranzano says.

Charlie and Meyer drop in at the Dutchman's worn-out saloon surprised to find him sprawled behind his desk reading *Al Capone: The Biography of a Self-made Man*. The heavy spring of the swivel chair strains as the Dutchman leans back, feet propped on the desk's edge. Bo Weinberg sits on a dilapidated couch reading the newspaper.

"Picking up pointers?" Charlie says to the Dutchman.

Weinberg comes to attention.

The Dutchman says, "I gotta give the Big Guy credit. He's had his share of trouble with the Irish. Took the St. Valentine's Massacre to get things under control. I was just readin' about Yale, when he got knocked off by them four gunman on ac-counta double-crossin' Capone. For all the trouble with the Irish, it's the Sicilians you gotta watch out for. This part's all about Aiello. Says a crew slipped out of Brooklyn to take re-venge on Lombardo. Brooklyn! All on accounta the Unione Siciliana."

Meyer says, "You're big news, Arthur."

"It's Coll that's making the news," he says. "They write about me because nobody cares about a dumb mick."

"How about toning down the publicity at least until we deal with this other situation?"

"You don't run a beer business without breaking a few eggs," the Dutchman says. "I'll get Coll sooner or later."

"Leave it to Madden," Charlie says.

"The Killer ain't got the instinct for it no more," the Dutch-man says.

Charlie says, "Leave it to Madden. He knows how to reel Coll in."

The Dutchman moans, "When are you gonna take care of this other situation? Tell 'em, Bo."

Weinberg folds his paper and lays it beside him.

"There's a couple of new guineas running numbers out of a joint on 127th. They got quite an attitude about it, too. Say they're taking over the Italian numbers and if we have any sense at all, we'll butt out of their business. Either these knuckle-heads don't know who they're dealing with, which is highly unlikely, or they've been told to go forth and conquer. They set up shop in the back of a pharmacy on 127th."

The Dutchman says, "You shoulda taken out that cocksucker when you hit the other greaser."

Meyer says, "We want things to settle down."

"You're too soft, Meyer," the Dutchman says. "And let me tell you, things ain't settling down, or ain't you noticed? Hell, Charlie was there, at the big Bronx meeting, along with half the Italians in town."

Meyer says, "There are rules, now. Protocol. We'll take care of the greaser without starting a world war. We don't need the government trying to take care of it for us. They're going through New York like they went through Chicago. You of all people should know that. They're on your back for tax eva-sion."

The Dutchman looks at Weinberg.

Weinberg says, "Some of the boys say Caesar's compiling a hit list."

Charlie says, "Yeah and everybody in this room is on it."

The Dutchman says, "You play it too low key, nobody knows you're the guy in charge."

Meyer says, "Those that need to know, know."

The dullness of the Dutchman's foresight could fill a dozen books. But Meyer wouldn't need to read them. Life in the ghetto and a decade of Prohibition has been education enough.

Charlie says, "We'll move on Maranzano when the time is right. In the meantime, work with Madden on the Coll prob-lem."

The Dutchman curls back into his chair and opens his book.

"This greaser in Brooklyn ain't your only problem. Coll might be gunning for me but don't think he don't know that you're the one calling the shots, Charlie. Maybe him and that greaser have teamed up to take us all out. One hand washes the other. Vincent Coll gets the beer business in the Bronx and the Sicilian gets Manhattan. I'd watch my back if I was you."

"I'll take that under advisement," Charlie says. "Have we got your cooperation?"

The Dutchman shrugs in reluctant agreement.

Charlie and Meyer hit the sidewalk and make their way up the block to Charlie's car.

"I'm guessin' it's Gagliano's guys running the numbers. They filter over from the Bronx, push the limits, see what they can get away with. I'm sure they have Maranzano's blessing for this whole thing. I'll talk to him."

Charlie and Meyer have been working the undercurrent of discontent that runs through the foundation of Salvatore Maranzano's grand Sicilian dream. More than one guy in the neighborhood is restless over Maranzano's rise to power. Ciro Terranova still wants revenge for the death of his nephew. Tommy Lucchese and Tommy Gagliano bought into Maranzano's dream but Maranzano's death tirade at the Bronx meeting has them thinking. Joe Profaci never wanted war in the first place but he was nonetheless happy when Joe the Boss disappeared.

Maranzano argued Julius Caesar's position that "war gives the right to the conquerors to impose any condition they please upon the vanquished." The vanquished, who seemed to include all those gathered in the Bronx hall, were stunned into silence. Maranzano had praised them as the victors, then levied a host of dos and don'ts that choked the life right out of the victory celebration.

A lot of the old greasers died in the Castellammarese War and that's fine with the Americanized guys. In spite of Maranzano's chest beating, Charlie Luciano is looking more like the de facto victor. The Tenderloin belongs to him, a fact that has Caesar scheming.

"He wants to wipe out the opposition," Meyer says.

"Opposition to his taking over as capo di tutti capi," Charlie says. "War of liberation my ass. This incurs death, that incurs death. Who is he to set the rules for me?"

"He thinks he can stop the killing by decree," Meyer says. "There has to be equality among the families."

"That won't stop the killing either," Charlie says.

Meyer agrees. "But you can keep them from meddling in the business of other families. That's what the Commission should do. Those that won't go along with the plan have to be removed."

"But you said it yourself, you can't kill everybody."

"Guys that get a pass will think twice before causing trouble," Meyer says. "Maybe by then things will settle down in New York and we can get on with business."

"That'll be the day," Charlie says.

Maranzano sits in the back seat of his armored Cadillac and ruminates about all the little mobs around the city, a million little fingers that hold the Big Apple in a death grip. Joe Valachi is driving. They're approaching 107th Street when a shot rings out. Valachi ducks and looks around. He swings the car wildly, rushing away from the gawkers and nearly runs headlong into Central Park. He slides through the intersection onto 108th Street as a sedan races past him.

The next day, in a safehouse in Brooklyn, Maranzano reads the newspaper account of the near miss. "A bookmaker's feud," the newspaper calls it. The gunfire injured four children and killed another.

It takes the police two weeks to narrow their attention to

Vincent Coll as the likely culprit. By then, the Mad Mick is being referred to as the Baby Killer. A nationwide manhunt ensues. The Baby Killer is wanted dead or alive.

With a sigh of relief, Salvatore Maranzano returns to his Grand Central office to carry on the business. He calls Tommy Gagliano to a meeting. Tommy walks beneath Mercury, Minerva, and Hercules into Grand Central, the busiest terminal in the country. Gagliano looks up at the painted ceiling with glowing gold-leaf constellations of the night sky. He blends into the hustle and bustle of commuters. Shards of light filter through the tall, arched windows and create a godlike presence in the Main Concourse. The magic works. Gagliano is infused with determination as he makes his way to Maranzano's office.

Maranzano invites Gagliano in and closes the door to his private space. A large oak desk dominates the room. Behind him are bookcases filled with classical literature and historical books. One glance at the tomes tells whoever cares to know that Maranzano is a well-educated student of history.

"What do you think of Charlie Luciano?" Maranzano says.

The question comes out of left field.

"He's always been fair and square," Gagliano says.

"Yes, but what of his ties with Jews?"

Gagliano ponders the question. His reputation as the Quiet Don appeals to Maranzano's stoic sensibilities. With one eye on preserving his foothold in the Bronx and the other on what Maranzano might have in mind for the powerful Luciano, he considers his reply judiciously.

"It is always best to stick with your own kind," he says. "I have no immediate problem with Charlie. Are you concerned about his loyalty to Cosa Nostra?"

"Let us not be naive," Maranzano says. "This is a man who would kill his boss to advance to the forefront."

Maranzano's point is well taken.

"You offered him amnesty," Gagliano says. "I assume he wanted Joe the Boss dead as much as anyone else."

"You have interests in the Bronx. What is your position on the beer war?"

"It doesn't impact me one way or the other," Gagliano says.

"And Charlie Luciano?"

"He's more with the whiskey distribution," Gagliano says.

"But the Jews are tight, are they not? And there is a Jew in Harlem working the Italian lottery. We can use the situation in the Bronx to further our own business."

Gagliano is no fool. He has endured the murder of two bosses, Tom Reina and Joseph Pinzolo, and come out on top, which is exactly where he intends to stay. Does Maranzano intend to just fan the war or engage in it? If he engages, the Jews are unlikely to stand by and watch.

"Any publicity is bad publicity," Gagliano says. "On the other hand, the beer war draws attention away from us."

His answer pleases Maranzano who struts around his office like a peacock in spring. Gagliano recalls Caesar's decrees: The capo's word is indisputable. Death is the penalty for not obeying your caporegime. He need not wonder if the decree extends to Caesar's word. The look in Maranzano's eyes says it all.

Gagliano takes the problem back to his underboss, Tommy Lucchese.

"Maranzano wants the Harlem numbers racket. Isn't the Dutchman cozy with Charlie Lucky? If Maranzano routs the Dutchman, he's cutting off Charlie's influence in Harlem," he says. "Any way you look at this, it sounds like another war."

Lucchese leans back and sighs.

He says, "Every dime we make will go to support his war."

"Here's something else. Maranzano wants us to make loans on his behalf. He says who gets the money," Gagliano says.

"Fuck that," Lucchese says.

"He's Old World," Gagliano says. "He thinks he won the war and now he's the boss of everything."

"Are we back where we started?" Lucchese says.

"I don't know," Gagliano says.

Lucchese grumbles his discontent. When his boss leaves, he calls Charlie Luciano.

Charlie says, "What's your number there? I'll call you in fifteen minutes."

Charlie arranges a hasty meeting with Meyer. He calls Lucchese and tells him to meet them at the Claridge.

"Watch your back," Lucchese says and hangs up.

Meyer meets Charlie at the office.

Charlie says, "I don't remember it being this hot for this long. Remember when we used to cool off in the river?"

"That's before we knew what they were throwing in it," Meyer says.

"I got a call from Tommy Lucchese," Charlie says. "It looks like the war in the Bronx is going to get hotter. Maranzano is about to make his move on the Harlem numbers racket."

Lucchese knocks on the door. Charlie invites him in.

Lucchese looks Charlie in the eye and says, "There's a list and you're at the top."

"How do you like that?" Charlie says. "I was just telling the Dutchman the same thing. So there really is a list. Listen, tell Meyer what you told me."

"Maranzano moves around this town like Pancho Villa," Lucchese says. "He's got half a dozen bodyguards around him. He's got a machine gun mounted in a bulletproof car. The

Archduke of Austria toured with less firepower. He hasn't paid any of the soldiers like he promised he would. He keeps talking about war and conquering our enemies. He thinks he is in charge of everything. Bossing everybody around. He's trying to get in touch with Coll. It's like Aiello and the Bugs Moran mob. They made an alliance to get rid of Capone. Same thing. Since Coll is killing off the Dutchman's guys, I think Caesar is going to try to use him to take out everybody on his list. That means you, Charlie, and Costello and Joe A. and a lot of other guys."

Meyer looks at Charlie. Charlie nods.

"Are you ready?" Meyer says to Lucchese.

Lucchese knows there's a plan to take out Maranzano but lacks the details.

Meyer says, "Here's how it's going to go. Capone is facing charges on tax evasion. That's big news. It's also been in the news in New York. The government has their own list of fifteen hundred racketeers. The list includes Jack Diamond, Dutch Schultz, Vannie Higgins and Larry Fay. Make sure Maranzano is aware that the same federal men that got Capone have come here to get us. Let him get nervous. Our friends in high places will leak the information that Maranzano is on the list. Our guys will come in dressed as IRS agents. We need you to tell us when. We want to hit the office at a time when it is least populated."

Lucchese nods. He's ready to play his part.

"Maranzano had a good idea with the Commission," Meyer says. "His trouble is that he wants to be at the top."

Charlie says, "We been talking about a board where everybody is equal. Each family takes care of itself. Keep your nose in your own business. Use the Commission the way it's supposed to be used, when there's a problem between families.

Then the fathers get together and work it out. But no one is on the top, tellin' anyone what to do."

"You're talking to Sicilians, Charlie," Lucchese says.

"Two of the biggest Sicilians around will be dead. What's the body count already? They purged themselves. There isn't that much more that needs to be done. We can't stop the killing but we can make business a little more civilized," Meyer says.

Walking through Grand Central Terminal in broad daylight is Salvatore Maranzano's greatest pleasure. At eight o'clock every morning, he comes through the 42nd Street entrance under the gaze of Mercury, Minerva, and Hercules. The main concourse is alive with the dance of a thousand commuters occupied with the business of life. Maranzano stops to help a little boy who has dropped a toy train. Joe Valachi stops for newspapers and coffee.

There is no rush on Valachi's part. He nods to his boss and heads to the café where he orders a large breakfast and reads the news. He bides his time chatting up the waitress until it's time to check in with his boss. Maranzano gives him the afternoon off. A little after noon, he heads down to the Oyster Bar for lunch. Lucchese, who has been on hand for Maranzano's morning meetings, tags along.

They settle in at the Oyster Bar's long counter and order soft-shell crabs, coleslaw, and beer. The guy behind the counter grabs near beer from the cooler under the counter and flips off the caps for his customers. Valachi takes a swig.

"That's some piss poor imitation," he says.

Three cops a few seats away give him a look. Valachi goes back to his crab. The cops finish their clam chowder and laugh over the fate of some poor unfortunate they put away.

Maranzano's name pops from their boisterous conversation.

Valachi strains to eavesdrop on the conversation but can't make out the details. The cops get up to leave.

"You'll find me in the privy," one of them says.

"Good idea," another says.

The blue suits head for the john.

Lucchese gives a nod to Valachi, "Follow 'em. See what you can find out."

Standing at the porcelain troughs, the blue suits talk about the upcoming audits and how they're going to laugh their asses off watching the racket guys squirm. The performance is worthy of a Broadway play. The talk centers on Frank Wilson, the accountant who has been calculating Capone's net worth and expenditures. Word on the street is, after three years of undercover work, the Chicago Outfit is about to be taken down. Ballistics has tied a machine gun used in the St. Valentine's Day Massacre to the slaying of Frankie Yale. It is only a matter of time before the Italian kingpins in New York face a similar fate. Maranzano's is one of the names thrown around as they piss and flush and wash their filthy cop hands.

Like a teenage girl who has just experienced a run-in with Rudolph Valentino, Valachi races back to Lucchese with his news.

"I gotta get back," he says.

When Maranzano hears, he ducks into the silence of his office and begins to sort papers. Valachi and Lucchese sit on the couch in the reception area trading glances. Eventually Maranzano calls them in.

Maranzano says, "Are you sure they're coming after me?"

Valachi shrugs, "They mentioned you along with Capone. They said there's a crackdown all over the city on accounta all the violence. You know how Seabury's been tryin' to clean up the corruption. It's all part of the deal. All the big guys. The Dutchman. Larry Fay. Owney Madden."

"How did they get my name?" Maranzano says.

"I don't know," Valachi says. "They were talkin' about the Seabury investigations and all them interviews."

"Who do we know that can back up the story?" Maranzano says.

Lucchese says, "I know a couple of guys."

Maranzano says, "This is a real estate office. The police come in here, it should look like one. Understand? Nobody brings guns to the office."

But the auditors don't show. Time drags on. Maranzano begins to relax. The oppressive heat breaks, just about the time Maranzano manages to get word to Vincent Coll on a matter of mutual interest, their combined desire to eliminate the competition. Maranzano makes Coll a generous offer from the coffers of his war chest. For the extra income, Coll is happy to accept contracts for all of Maranzano's problems. Vincent Coll slips in and out of the ninth floor of the New York Central Building with a large deposit on a new life.

Salvatore Maranzano calls Charlie Luciano and requests a clarification meeting to be held in his Grand Central office on September 10th. Charlie agrees to the meeting, which is intended to clear up the territories in dispute in Harlem.

"You've got the go-ahead," Charlie tells Meyer.

The four Jews and one Irishman destined to change the course of organized crime are called in. Meyer watches with eager anticipation as the assassins don the garb of IRS agents.

Meyer says, "You have the stiletto?"

Red Levine says, "If you want to give the guy a buckwheat, why not take him out to Coney Island and do it right?"

"This isn't a buckwheat," Meyer says. "This is a message to anybody who thinks he's going to set himself up as Caesar. We're taking him down in his office so everybody knows nobody is out of reach. It's a history lesson. Caesar always dies in the end."

Benny says, "You want us to wear togas, too?"

He shimmies the sheath in place along the small of his back then arranges the stiletto's handle to make sure it is positioned correctly. Satisfied with the easy release, he focuses on the 1911 Colt, making sure the chamber is cocked and ready for work. Jack Adams, the guy from Jimmy Alo's mob, drives the getaway car.

"Plug 'em," Charlie says. "Lucchese says there's maybe half a dozen guys around him and one girl at the front desk." He looks at Gurrah Shapiro, "Put 'em up against the wall and hold them there. They don't get killed. Gagliano has drawn off Joe Valachi for the day."

The boys add silencers to their weapons and Bo and Red are given knives.

"Keep it tight, Benny," Meyer says. "We don't need the newspaper blowing this thing out of proportion."

Benny laughs. "Let me get this straight. I'm stabbing and shooting the strongest Mustache Pete in New York and you don't want it blown out of proportion? That's funny. This will go down as the greatest mob hit in all of fucking history." Benny shakes his head as he slides the Colt into a modified shoulder holster. "What the hell was that line again, Meyer? Liberty, freedom, and what?"

"Liberty, freedom, tyranny is dead," Red says. "It's fucking Shakespeare."

Jack Adams rips the cover from the stolen car parked in the garage. He checks the tires and starts the engine like he's done every day since the car was appropriated for the Maranzano hit. Sammy has fiddled with the engine so the car can outrun just about anything.

Jack releases the hand brake and rolls the car forward. Four Lower East Side gunsels, from each of New York's powerful Jewish mobs, pile in. Briefcases line the floorboard.

At 3:45 in the afternoon, four accountants hit Maranzano's office on the ninth floor. They put seven men and one female against the wall.

Gurrah says, "Keep it zipped and nobody gets hurt."

Benny, Bo Weinberg, and Red Levine push their way into Maranzano's office. Benny pulls the stiletto and plunges it into Maranzano's belly. It stops at the hilt. Bo and Red follow suit, plunging their knifes into the staggering Sicilian.

"Liberty, freedom, tyranny is almost dead, you fat cocksucker," Benny says. "Did you really think you were going to get away with screwing the Jew mob out of business?"

Maranzano grabs Benny by the throat. His grip is strong. Benny struggles to pull him off. He rips the stiletto from Maranzano's body and plants it again and again into his abdomen. Maranzano falls forward, clearing his desk with wild swipes of his arms. Benny and Red slam Maranzano backwards. He falls into his chair. Benny starts blasting.

Weinberg holds a .38 to Maranzano's chest and fires.

"Let's get out of here," Benny says.

They retreat through the outer office, releasing their hostages. The secretary runs to Maranzano's aid while the seven men flee.

Over the next few days, the ranks of the New York families are purged of Old World thinking. Not many have to die. The *New York Times* connects Maranzano's killing with an alien smuggling ring and then to Chicago because a couple of hats which bore Chicago hat store labels flew off the assassins as they ran out the door.

Charlie tells Meyer, "The Night of the Vespers is finally over. The peasants revolted and got their land back. We don't want no more bullshit."

When the dust settles, Charlie sets up a celebratory dinner at the 21 Club.

Jack Kriendler works the 18-inch wire that releases the lock that allows the two-ton brick wall to slide open. Behind the wall is the wine cellar. A large table sits in the middle, decked in high style with the club's best linens and tableware.

Charlie, Joe Adonis, Vito Genovese, Meyer Lansky, Benny Siegel, and Jimmy Alo make their way into what is fondly called "Jimmy Walker's hideaway." Frank Costello gloats over the fact that it was his idea to disguise the cellar that is actually located in the basement of the neighboring building. He lets everyone know he arranged for the electronically controlled disappearing bar upstairs that drops all liquor bottles down a chute and away from the club. You can't get arrested for fumes.

Jack lets him brag. It is good business.

The cellar not only holds the wealth of the club, it displays the vested interest of some of New York's finest clientele. Cubbyholes from floor to ceiling line the walls, each filled with bottles of wine. Most sport bronze tags but there are also some with small pieces of tape with handwritten names or, in Charlie's case, numbers. Charlie takes a seat at the long dining table. Behind him the cubby labeled "312," Charlie's personal stash for special occasions, several bottles from which are already on the table, ready for pouring.

Charlie says, "We might have Frank to thank for this cozy

hideaway but we got a few other guys to thank tonight for a different kind of freedom."

Jack Kriendler personally pours the wine for Charlie's party, a fine French Bordeaux. Then he disappears, closing the two-ton wall behind him.

Charlie raises his glass. "I was beginning to wonder if I'd ever get to enjoy this stuff. I got one guy to thank. That's Meyer Lansky. Without him, we'd all still be swimming in Sicilian swill. Gentlemen," he says, "we did it."

It is a cheer heard around the city but most deeply felt by Meyer. The days of squalor are so much water under the bridge, and a wild-hair of an idea that brought Meyer and Charlie together, fostered by a "noble experiment" gone wrong, has brought them both to this pinnacle of success. Though it's an unusual pinnacle, what with it being celebrated in hiding, underground.

Charlie points to the neatly wrapped boxes at each table setting.

"A little something for you boys," he says. "A token of my gratitude."

Inside each box is a gold watch.

The meal begins with blue points and a lobster cocktail followed by pâté de foie gras and supreme of melon maraschino. Then soup, a potage of new peas. Roast prime ribs of beef Jardiniere. A family-style collection of vegetables and potatoes au gratin. Desserts range from peach melba to caramel custard. A demitasse settles the load before the girls come in.

Vito says, "You deserve to be the boss. Look what you done."

Charlie says, "Get that idea out of your head. I don't need that kinda trouble."

Vito says, "This ain't the end of the trouble. There's a Mad Mick running around town."

Charlie pours another glass of wine. He looks down the blouse of the girl on his lap.

"That's for another day. Right now, I'm gonna enjoy the night."

Charlie Luciano

Meyer Lansky

© COPYRIGHT DREW STRUZAN

Chapter Twenty-Three
A Snowball's Chance

FALL 1931

The Night of the Vespers is not so much an excuse for personal vengeance as a cleansing of Old World domination and thinking. Meyer's philosophy is simple and to the point. Don't kill more than is necessary. Don't draw attention. Do what is best for everyone. Thanks to the war, most of the Old World power-houses are already gone.

Stefano Magaddino enjoys an unannounced absence from his Buffalo estate in order to meet Charlie Lucky in Manhattan and discuss private matters. Charlie's place looks lived in. Books are scattered around the room. Jazzy music plays on the radio. There is the lingering scent of perfume from a scarf left behind by one of Polly's girls. Magaddino smiles at the telltale sign of Charlie's lifestyle even though he disagrees with Charlie's insistence on an unattached life.

"Congratulations, Lucky," Magaddino says.

Charlie says, "It wasn't luck that kept me alive. It was Meyer's insight. If it was up to me, I'd a blown everybody away from the beginning, but then we'd never really know what kinda guy Salvatore Maranzano turned out to be, would we? Meyer kept tellin' me to wait. You know how hard that is for a guy like me? The final straw was gettin' word that Maranzano was ready to bump us off. We struck first, that's all. Self-defense. The Jews did a helluva job. A helluva job. We took a big chance but it paid off."

"Power went to Salvatore's head," Magaddino insists, not at all sorry that Brooklyn is voting on a new father.

The fact is, Stefano didn't like the direction Maranzano was taking the family. He was a source of contention and conflict from the beginning. Magaddino notices the wear and tear in Charlie's face. The war was hard on all of them. Anyone who says otherwise is a liar.

"You got stugots," Magaddino says not expecting a reply. "We're all better off for it."

Magaddino is tough. Ruthless. But somehow reasonable by Mafia standards. That's what keeps him alive. That's what kept him from making a move on Maranzano before the time was right.

Charlie says, "If you ask me, Maranzano never got over what happened in Sicily when Mussolini came in. He came here but he couldn't manage to live and let live. The guy was always afraid somebody was gonna take somethin' away from him. He couldn't trust nobody. That's why he had to be in control, of everything. He ain't in control no more. What's Caruso gonna do now that Maranzano's gone?"

Caruso, not the singer, was Maranzano's second in command and normal circumstances would dictate that he would ascend to lead the family. But these aren't normal circumstances.

Magaddino says, "He'll step aside. What choice does he have?"

Charlie pours whiskeys. They sit in comfortably worn leather chairs. Charlie and Magaddino go way back. They understand the street. They know who is around whom and what resources they have. Magaddino continues to influence the Brooklyn Castellammarese from as far away as Buffalo. His power is undeniable, as is Charlie's.

"Let's hope whoever steps up agrees to keep the peace," Charlie says. "I've had enough of this bullshit."

"Life is short," Magaddino says.

"It's the business we're in," Charlie says.

Magaddino raises his glass. "Alla tua salute!"

Charlie says, "Salute," and downs his whiskey. "I wonder how long it will take for Maranzano to be canonized. You can bet the Castellammarese will be singin' hymns to his glory."

Magaddino shakes his head, "Not all of them. It ain't ever easy, Charlie. It still ain't easy. You still got trouble in New York. Lots of it."

He means the Irish guy and the German Jew. He means who is going to take over the Bronx? The beautiful Bronx. He means the end to the violence has not yet come to pass.

Charlie stays mum. Coll's death is only a matter of time, now. Nobody can tame the Mad Dog. The German Jew will keep the Bronx. Coll's mob, should they survive, will be pushed aside. The worst of it is that nobody likes the Dutchman, not even his own men. Once that's settled, then what? Who will rise to contend for control somewhere else? Some things never end. Some things never say, "Enough." Trouble and violence are two of them.

"How about a steak?" Charlie says.

Magaddino agrees. "We'll pretend we're normal guys with normal jobs like all the other businessmen."

The Castellammarese fathers gather to vote their choice for a new head. Caruso's resignation opens the way for Joe Bonanno to stand up. Bonanno is twenty-six. He has roots in old-world sensibilities but is too young to be fully entrenched in old-world politics. Perhaps that's why Charlie had given him a pass in the purge.

The Sicilians grumble. Bonanno treads the razor's edge between allegiance to his family and respect for Charlie Luciano's strength. With few real choices, the Castellammarese agree to support Bonanno to lead the family.

Time drifts quietly by without incident, allowing the Italians to go about their business without fear of retribution. The Brooklyn-based family that was once headed by Al Mineo sobers to a new reality. Slapped like ping-pong balls from one side of the war to the other, they now settle down with Vince Mangano as their head. Charlie agreed to give Scalice the pass if he agreed to quietly allow Mangano to take over. The Mad Hatter, Albert Anastasia, favored Charlie's decision. Scalice gave a quick Hail Mary and passed the reins to Mangano, his underboss. It was only common sense. Better a living member than a dead boss.

Tommy Gagliano thanked Charlie for the peace and went about his business.

Joe Profaci held onto his position and acted as though nothing out of the ordinary had taken place.

Thus, the five main New York families are cemented more or less by Charlie's decree. From there, ripples fan out through the rest of the country, except for Chicago. It is agreed that the little mobs that fall under Chicago's jurisdiction will wait to see if the Big Man is going to get jail time for tax evasion or if, as anticipated, he will pay a fine and skate free. It is understood that whoever leads Chicago leads the small mobs west of the Mississippi.

Meyer and Charlie shuffle through the thick carpet of leaves that cover Central Park. The setting sun plays peekaboo with the narrow shafts that run between buildings, lighting up autumn's foliage with brilliant shades of orange and red. Rain trickles from the heavens, saturating the air. Rain doesn't matter. Charlie walks through the park with an air of ease. His overcoat keeps out the cold and wet. His fedora shields his eyes. Even his cigarette seems invincible to the weather.

He says, "Why waste the taxpayers' money running Capone through a trial when syphilis is doing the job for free?"

"Publicity," Meyer says, popping open his umbrella. "The government needs a conviction to win public trust. Let's say Capone gets jail time, will Nitti take over?"

"He's a figurehead," Charlie says. "With Capone and Jack McGurn out of the picture, the strength is with the Fischetti brothers. Further down the line is Paul the Waiter and Tony Accardo."

"They call Nitti 'the Enforcer,'" Meyer says.

"Ha! That's like the government. It's good for his reputation. Nitti gets things done but he don't pull the trigger," Charlie says. "He's weak. Everybody knows it. They call him the Enforcer to get respect."

Squirrels scamper through the leaves and up trees and disappear. Central Park shifts into low gear and quiets for the night. Even birds refuse their songs. Street lights kick on. Office buildings shine like otherworldly beacons at the end of Poets' Walk.

"Maranzano had some good ideas," Meyer says. "If he would have kept his head, he could have had a nice slice of this town."

"The whole damn country is looking to see what New York is going to do now."

"Keep the Commission," Meyer says.

Charlie says, "Burn the paper. Kiss the ring. Sicilians feel all cozy with that Catholic shit. I ain't Catholic. I ain't even religious."

Meyer says, "Don't throw out the baby with the bathwater. Let them have their traditions in their own families. That doesn't affect you. They're tired of war. Most of them are broke. They're relieved you didn't stick your hand in their pocket. The fewer changes you make, the better."

"You're probably right," Charlie says. "Whatever happened to playing it low key? Avoiding the spotlight? We're in it now, Meyer. Everybody in this goddamned city knows who we are."

They sit on a park bench and smoke.

"The Commission is still a good idea," Meyer says.

Charlie squirms. "It's old-world."

Meyer says, "It has a laundry list of problems."

"That's puttin' it lightly."

"Think of it as the League of Nations. It's there to maintain peace. Each country has an equal say."

"Now you're just playin' with me," Charlie says. "Aren't you the guy that says let them settle their own disagreements? Never take sides. How is the Commission going to stop the killing?"

"It can't any more than the League of Nations can stop war," Meyer says. "But that's not the point. It creates a place where guys can solve problems that crop up."

"They'll be scheming by the next morning."

"They'll feel important. Respected. Honored. The strength lies with the five New York families and Chicago. Everybody else falls into place under them. Detroit. Cleveland. Philadelphia. All the major cities."

"What I don't get is why you think I should be a part of it."

Meyer says, "Like it or not, you're already part of it. Are you going to step away now and let them make the rules? We'd be back to square one."

"You think this can hold together?" Charlie says.

Meyer says, "The Americanized guys are with us. They're all thanking you."

Charlie takes the compliment with a grain of salt.

They walk back to the Majestic and wait for Aaron Sapiro to knock. He's their lawyer now. Meyer figures if a guy like Henry Ford can't beat a guy like Sapiro then Sapiro sounds like a pretty good choice to set up their corporations. And if he is good at corporations, then he must equally be good at working out the agreements between CEOs, which is what Meyer is calling each of the five New York family heads plus Chicago and Buffalo, using the title in the same manner as U.S. Steel Corporation. "Chief" has a nice ring to it.

It's eight o'clock in the evening when Aaron Sapiro lays out an array of pens and paper on Charlie's dining room table and starts asking questions.

"Where are you with this thing?" Sapiro says.

Meyer has been talking with Sapiro, hammering out the technical details of the arrangement he and Charlie hope to forge with the Italians now that Maranzano is out of the picture.

Charlie says, "Think of it as the League of Nations."

"But not delegates," Meyer says. "We need tougher standards. These aren't politicians. And no one guy is stronger than the others."

Sapiro says, "Then you can create a Board of Directors with an appointed Chairman." He looks at Charlie. "The position can rotate through the various members. The Chairman is purely administrative. He doesn't hold power over the other members of the board. I assume everyone has an interest in a common goal."

"Yeah," Charlie says. "Everybody wants to keep livin'."

Sapiro says, "What are the problem areas? How will the board function? You need to decide what circumstances require the board's involvement. You should have an accountability structure.

In other words, everybody ultimately answers to the board and then the board decides how to handle the problems that arise. How often you meet is up to you. I guess there's no real reason to talk about the term of the directors?"

Charlie laughs. "Anything in that black bag of yours that keeps guys from scheming?"

"Accountability," Sapiro says. "Best I can do. And penalties for breaking the rules. Honestly, as you probably already know, even that is meager policing."

The conversation rambles through loopholes and hard reality. Charlie doesn't expect the Sicilians to agree with him. He expects them to adhere to his proposal, though. Whether out of fear or respect, it really doesn't matter.

Al Capone plays host to the budding Commission. Nearly a hundred men show up in Chicago to hear Charlie out and to discuss the nature of the Commission. Charlie is the brazen radical among the conservative Sicilian families. He populates his mob with Neapolitans and Calabrese and makes alliances with Jews and Irishmen. He isn't married. Has no son to inherit his empire. He has no stage, no throne, no throng of deferential soldiers. What he brings to the meeting is common sense.

The men gather in a hotel banquet room. Capone entertains as a country entertains visiting royalty. Gold silverware and gold-rimmed china plates, crystal glasses filled with Dom Perignon, appetizers and hors d'oeuvre, a serving staff of hundreds that roll through the main event like the smoothest-operating machine. Afterward, the men sit back with dessert and cigars.

Charlie stands before the crowd. The clinking of forks and the prattle of chitchat falls into silence. All eyes are on Charlie Lucky, the man that both killed his boss and takes responsibility for the assassination of Salvatore Maranzano.

Charlie says, "I didn't come here to be proclaimed the boss so let's take that off the table right at the start. You're here for the same reason I'm here. We've had enough of war. It's time for peace and the profits that go along with it. You could say we are no different from any other major corporation. We have business interests that need protecting. We all see the need to stop the killing and start running our businesses like gentlemen. That don't mean that we ain't gonna have disagreements. It's how we resolve these disagreements that will either destroy us or move business forward. We have a vested interest in keeping the peace, as they say. To keep the peace, we have to agree on certain rules.

"We can all agree that Salvatore Maranzano had a good idea. He knew history. He knew how Caesar organized his army. That's what he based Our Thing on, that structure with the capos and all. We all tried to make sure that all the families got a fair shake in organizing the men under them. Nothing is gonna change in that regard. We agreed to that before there was more trouble. It's a good thing so let's keep it that way.

"What went wrong is that Maranzano wanted everybody to toe his line. That's the trouble with a boss among bosses, or capo di tutti capi if you prefer the Italian way of saying things. Nobody here wants to be Caesar. It's bad for business. What we're going to try for is agreement among equals. We don't live individually in little provinces where our word is law. We live together in big American cities. If we war with one another for control there won't be no time for our men to earn. Killing ain't the way to settle our differences. Maranzano agreed on that point. The killing has to stop.

"America is a big country with lots of opportunities. As we spread out, we need to watch out we don't step on each other's toes. When there is a dispute within a family, it stays in that family. When there is a dispute between families, it comes up the ladder to the Commission. The guys in the dispute will sit before the family heads and try to work out their differences. If they fail, it is up to the Commission to make a decision and their decision stands. I'm not here to tell you what incurs death and what don't. That's up to each family except when a matter comes before the Commission. Then the Commission will have to decide on consequences. I want to make that perfectly clear. We're gonna knock heads and then we're gonna sit down and work things out.

"We ain't choir boys. It ain't gonna be easy to tame things down but that's what we gotta do. Say an opportunity comes your way and two guys from different families make a deal with each other. Everything has to be put on the table right then and there. If you don't put it on the table, it doesn't exist. Nobody can come along later and say 'but I thought this or that.' The pie's already been cut up. There ain't no more pieces left. We can make millions if we can work out this one simple thing."

The fathers listen and like what they hear.

The next day, Charlie meets with the heads of the five New York families, Chicago, and Buffalo. Everybody else will fall in line with one of these mobs. Places like St. Louis, Philadelphia, New England, Detroit, Pittsburgh, and Cleveland have a chain of command that leads to representation on the Commission.

Charlie distributes the outline of ideas that Aaron Sapiro has written up in official jargon that reads like every agreement between major corporations. Some of Maranzano's rules remain. Screwing another man's wife, violating his daughter, disgracing his family, these things remain strictly off limits with the standard consequence. Disrespect of any kind against another member will not be tolerated. These matters are self-evident.

The fathers adjourn and talk over the details. Maranzano's vision, the parts that the Sicilians bought into, is still intact but it has been fortified with the ability to protect individual gangs from a power grab.

Meyer, a non-participant in the Italian world, stays in the background. Still, the link is obvious. When there is trouble between Jews and Italians, Meyer will stand up for the Jews.

"And the Irish?" Gagliano says.

Charlie says, "What about the Polacks? And the Chinese? Who else is around? The guys that want to join us, can. Then they're under the same rules as you and me. The Irish ain't joiners. They don't want to be no part of us. They want to be on their own. Let them do what they want to do. When there's trouble, we reason with them the same way we reason with everybody else."

Gagliano says, "The way Capone reasoned with Bugs Moran?"

"We're here to prevent another massacre," Charlie says. "We gotta be patient and smart. Seabury is diggin' into the corruption in Tammany Hall. A lot of Irish power will fade with that investigation. The Irish are mostly interested in the beer business anyway, that and the docks. It's been their business all along."

Gagliano nods. The fathers reconvene and accept Charlie's terms.

Charlie says, "If anybody has a beef, speak up now. After today, we all agree to toe the line."

Nobody says a word.

The beer war in the Bronx continues. Tales of the battle fill newspapers. Manhattanites worry that New York has become as violent as Chicago. The public outcry against the Baby

Killer reaches its crescendo, a shout so loud it reaches Governor Roosevelt in Albany. Roosevelt commands the boys in blue to deal with the "damnable outrage." If they do not, he will appeal to Washington for Federal aid and bring in troops that will stop the violence. Vincent Coll disappears from public view.

Meyer Lansky meets up with Charlie Luciano at a candy store on the corner of Second Avenue and St. Marks Place. They shoot the breeze and enjoy an egg cream.

"Madden might need help with Vincent Coll," Meyer says. "Why don't we bring in a couple of Jimmy Alo's guys? Eddie McGrath and Johnny Dunn? Maybe they can reason with the guy."

Charlie nods. It's a good idea. Jimmy is tight with the Irish on the street. And besides, Jimmy has a flourishing beer business with interests in the Bronx.

"He's become quite the diplomat," Meyer says.

Jimmy is in the thick of a game of gin opposite Ben Siegel when Charlie and Meyer walk in. They discuss the Irish situation with Jimmy.

Meyer says, "What's the feeling about Vincent Coll among the Irish?"

"From what I understand, everybody thinks highly of Coll," Jimmy says. "I don't know him personally but people say he's a smart guy. They blame the trouble on the Dutchman for killin' Coll's brother. The kid was all right before that. The Dutchman treated them guys like slaves. I guess they got tired and rebelled."

Charlie says, "Coll crossed the line when he kidnapped Frenchy."

Jimmy says, "He was broke. What else could he do?"

Charlie says, "He shoulda come to us."

Jimmy says, "The Dutchman would kill him for that."

The conversation isn't what Charlie expected. He grouses. He hasn't seen a pillow since yesterday afternoon following an unusually long night on the town. The dancer was exceptionally limber, he recalls.

Meyer is torn. His sympathy lies with Coll, the underdog, but the situation favors the Dutchman. Coll has gone over the edge. In the public eye, he is the Baby Killer. The war has brought the governor's threats down on them. The real question is whether Coll's death will cause commotion among the Irish.

"Coll ain't never gonna walk a chalk line," Jimmy says. "Not after what they done to his brother."

Charlie says, "The cops are hot on his trail. The Governor is threatening to bring in troops. It's Madden's game but we're gonna have to work together to get Coll off the street."

"I'll see what I can find out," Jimmy says.

"Jimmy," Charlie says. "Me and Meyer would like you to bring Eddie McGrath and Johnny Dunn in on this situation. We want to make sure there's not going to be trouble with the Irish."

Jimmy nods.

It turns out that Vincent is hiding in plain sight not far from McSorley's Old Ale House. Eddie becomes a regular fixture at the place, waiting and watching for Vincent or his boys. His patience pays off and he contacts Jimmy with the news. They meet at the Claridge.

Eddie takes in a deep breath and exhales the betrayal: "Mike Basile is ready to play ball. Since his brothers were shot, he doesn't have the stomach for it anymore. I could see it in his face. Here's the number."

Eddie hands off a piece of paper to Charlie. Mike's phone number is scribbled across the sheet. Charlie notes the number and puts the paper in his jacket pocket and thanks Eddie. They've got their inside man.

Charlie thinks long and hard about the logistics of Owney Madden getting the jump on Vincent Coll. He sets up a meeting with the principal players who now congregate at the Cotton Club. It's midweek and hours before the club opens. Madden is in the middle of a renovation. Duke Ellington has flown the coop now that his radio broadcasts have given him a national audience. Madden works a series of new acts into what he is calling the Cotton Club Parade. Carpenters whittle a new look for the stage while Cab Calloway breaks in a new singer.

The club's chef works on lunch for Madden and his guests. The members of the quorum file in randomly: Meyer Lansky, Ben Siegel, Charlie, Joe A., Arthur Flegenheimer, Bo Weinberg, and Big Frenchy.

Madden pours whiskey. They sit around a large round table in the back quarter of the club, far enough away from prying ears but close enough for Madden to keep an eye on the new show.

"I welcome your suggestions," Madden says, only somewhat facetiously.

Benny says, "The guy is desperate for money. Ain't that right?"

Frenchy's voice is cold: "You could say that."

Benny says, "Put word out on the street that you think he's gotten a bum deal and that you'd like to help out."

The Dutchman snarls at the accusation.

Madden says, "Let's say he didn't smell a rat and shows up

on my doorstep. What do you want me to do, shoot him in the middle of the third act?" Madden gestures to the club.

Benny says, "He ain't gonna just show up. It's too dangerous. Everybody is lookin' for him. He's gonna call you first, to make sure the offer is legit. You keep him talkin'. Our guys will get to him before he hangs up the phone."

A round of clam chowder graces the table.

Madden says, "It's a damn shame. I like the kid."

The Dutchman snarls, "I'll be glad to get this scab off my back."

The Dutchman has a way with words. He's been hiding ever since he found out that Coll was walking around town with a machine gun strapped to his arm. He knows the kid will go anywhere to kill him. He doesn't regret Coll's big mistake, that of grabbing Big Frenchy for ransom. He knows Madden would have given him the money anyway but the blunder was better. It made Coll the fly in everybody's ointment.

The club's singer takes the stage. She is nervous. She holds the microphone too tight, scoots in too close, and clears her throat. Calloway holds the orchestra until she is settled then he waves his wand. The first few words wobble but then her voice clears, the song smooth and brilliant.

"The kid had potential," Madden says with no small measure of regret. "He's fearless. Coulda made somethin' of himself."

Two young men take the stage after the singer. They confer with Calloway and then the boys take a seat at a table close to the stage.

"You gotta see this," Madden says. "Couple o' colored guys from Philly. I caught their act in Lafayette. Just watchin' 'em wears me out."

Calloway waves the conductor's wand and the band blasts a

rousing introduction that rolls into a number called "Bugle Call Rag." Calloway sings and with infectious energy introduces the Nicholas Brothers, Fayard and Harold. The boys stand. Fayard jumps up onto the table and begins a tap dance; Harold does the same on the chair. Calloway scats while Fayard jumps across to another table and Harold leaps from the chair to the table. Fayard jumps down to the stage where they tap and flip and spin using chairs and stools as props. Then they work their way through the orchestra pit jumping across a series of platforms in front of the orchestra. All the while, Calloway is scatting and the orchestra is rolling through their number.

Harold is barely ten years old. His acrobatic finesse and his ability to sync with his brother's moves boggles the mind. Madden watches with a showman's interest. Calloway dismisses the orchestra and the room clears of talent.

Madden turns to Big Frenchy, "Remind me later that the stage needs to be higher."

The Dutchman groans, "A couple of kids stompin' their feet. What's the big deal?"

Big Frenchy's eyes roll hard in their sockets.

Charlie says, "We got a guy willin' to give us Coll's location."

Madden is almost disappointed.

"You think you can keep Coll on the phone long enough for us to get to him?" Meyer says.

"I run a nightclub, don't I?" Madden says. "I got the gift of gab."

Meyer says, "Make sure there's enough cash in the safe in case he gets here. We'll be following his every move."

"I'll be sure," Madden says.

Charlie says, "Eddie McGrath and Johnny Dunn can be here while everything goes down, in case."

Madden considers the offer and declines. He doesn't need Coll spooked should he come to the club. It's bad for business when the shooting starts.

Madden thinly hides his disgust that the Bronx will again belong to the Dutchman when this is over. If you're rich and you don't live on Madison Avenue or Park Avenue, you live in the Bronx. It's where the wealthy have always lived, a little slice of country smack in the middle of civilization. But these days, the Bronx resembles the Wild West more than it does the cradle of civilization, and the Dutchman's a big part of why.

"Are we settled?" Charlie says.

Madden resigns himself to the end of Coll's possibilities.

"We're settled," Madden says.

From the time Coll's name appeared in the newspapers in August, the boys in blue have been in hot pursuit of the Irishman. Almost by chance, they find a witness, a drug dealer turned useful informer, who can identify the shooters behind the drive-by that killed little Michael Vengalli. The informer names two of Coll's men, Dominick Odierno and Frank Giordano. The cops gloat. The informer tries to press charges against them that he had been kicked and beaten into the confession. Nobody seems to care. The fact that Vincent Coll and Joey Rao were absolved of the boy's murder has everyone hot and bothered.

Police Commissioner Mulrooney smiles at the press conference and declares war on the gangs. Mulrooney introduces a new squad of sharpshooters armed with pump guns who will cruise each of twenty neighborhoods known to be hot spots for gang violence. The sharpshooters form a line with their heavily armored Harley-Davidsons, each with its sidecar where the sharpshooter will sit.

"The problem must be attacked at its roots," Mulrooney says as photographers snap away. "It's all in a day's work, boys."

The first tip the sharpshooters get takes them to Greene County where someone claims to have seen Vincent Coll trying to take over Jack Diamond's beer and applejack racket. Jack has been convicted on a charge of second-degree assault and sentenced to four years in prison. But the lead falls flat.

Still clutching their pump guns, they return to the Bronx and hang around Coll's house on Randall Street. Their due diligence nets little more than saddle sores. While the sharpshooters chase phantoms, the undercover squad busts open the case on Coll's gang. In an unlikely tangle of conflicting eyewitness accounts, a license plate number appears that belongs to two separate crimes, once in the shooting death of Joseph Mullens and once in connection with a pipe bomb lobbed into the Majestic Garage, known as a Schultz beer drop. A general alarm goes out for a green Buick bearing those plates. A patrolman visiting the Penn Post Garage on Ninth Avenue spots the Buick and the plates. Undercover detectives swarm the garage. When Vincent de Lucia calls to pick up the car, he is arrested. De Lucia quickly spills his guts.

From then on, Coll's gang falls like pins at a bowling alley.

Police find Mike Basile and Patsy Del Greco at the Ledonia Hotel.

Then they grab Frank Giordano along with five pistols at the Mason Apartments.

Odierno and the Baby Killer himself are picked up at the Cornish Arms Hotel.

Giordano and Odierno are put on trial for the Mullens murder. By the end of November, they face the chair at Sing Sing. Coll and Giordano go on trial for the murder of Michael Vengalli while the Dutchman, the Broadway mob, and Owney Madden watch from a safe distance. Samuel Leibowitz, the lawyer that got Capone and his men off in the murder of Peg Leg Lonergan, tries for an acquittal for Vincent Coll.

The Dutchman grins. "I'd like to be in the audience when these guys ride Sing Sing's hot squat."

Two thousand volts. Fifteen seconds. That's all it takes.

But Leibowitz is good and Coll is back on the street by Christmas. The Dutchman can't believe his bad luck. He handpicks half a dozen guys and sends them forth like apostles with nothing to do but find Vincent Coll. Coll proves as difficult to find as a black mamba on a moonless night. Not even the fifty-thousand-dollar bounty the Dutchman has put on Coll's head yields results.

By mid-December, Jack Diamond faces his third jury in four months. This time, he is under the gun for kidnapping James Duncan. The news of Jack's trials has been read, examined, debated, scoffed at, envied, abhorred, and otherwise received by a vast web of his enemies. The Dutchman gets word of where Jack's living and ruminates over the double-crossing he received at Diamond's hands. He promises revenge for the death of his partner, Joey Noe.

Diamond, riding high on his two previous acquittals, dresses in a blue pinstriped suit, gray spats, and checkered cap when he faces his jury.

The Dutchman yells for Bo Weinberg.

"Get me Spitale and Bitz," he barks.

Salvy Spitale and Irving Bitz had, at one time, partnered with Diamond only to find their investment spirited away by the son of a bitch. The fact of Diamond's poverty is inescapable now that he has moved from the luxurious Kenmore Hotel into an ordinary and quite seedy boarding house where he has two rooms, one for himself and his wife, Alice, and another for his younger brother and sister-in-law. Kiki, his mistress, is stashed in a rooming house not far away. This is good news for the Dutchman who figures Spitale and Bitz will jump at the chance to get back their missing cash.

"He owes you eleven grand," the Dutchman says. "He's holed up in a boarding house in Albany, 76 Dove Street. The bastard has fifty-seven thousand tied up in bail. He ain't got nobody left around him and he can't afford to hire nobody. I got fifty grand on his head. You can't lose."

Spitale and Bitz are speechless. It has been over a year since they last shot Diamond, after which he had taunted them to everyone within earshot.

They don't bother to pack, just head straight to Albany. They make it to the Kenmore Hotel in a record three hours and fifteen minutes. They cruise by 76 Dove Street.

"You sure this is the right address," Spitale says in disbelief.

Bitz looks at the Dutchman's scrawl.

"This is Dove Street, ain't it?" he says.

Spitale nods.

"Then this is it," Bitz says.

"The Dutchman said he was livin' in a hole. Holy shit, he wasn't kiddin'."

Spitale pulls the car around to a side street and parks. It is nearly nine before Diamond drags home from his day in court with Alice, Kitty, and Eddie Jr. in tow.

Bitz nods at the parade. With Diamond safely inside his new dump, Spitale and Bitz return to the hotel for a good night's rest. They wake in the morning and enjoy bacon and eggs with hash browns for breakfast. Spitale peruses the newspaper for the details of Diamond's trial. They drink coffee and chat. The radio informs them that the jurors have gone into deliberation. An hour passes. Two hours. They find a place for lunch. The jury remains in deliberation.

"He ain't goin' to jail. That's good news for us," Spitale says.

"How do you figure?" Bitz says.

"No jury would take this long to find a guy like that guilty. They're gonna let him off. We'll be able to collect on his debt. I wonder if he will get his bail money back before he leaves court."

"Sure he will," Bitz say. "The law can't hold your money once you're acquitted."

Spitale smiles. This is just getting better and better.

It takes the jury five hours in all to find Jack "Legs" Diamond not guilty. Diamond leaves the courtroom with his bail money in hand and a lilt in his step. He chats with reporters. Says he's going to move to the Carolinas for his health. He poses for a few photos before he imagines he's seen the Dutchman in the crowd. He ducks behind a policeman just as the pop of a flashbulb explodes.

Diamond heads for a local speakeasy. Long about midnight, plenty of drinks gone, Jack blinks back sleepy eyes. He has more holes in him than a moth-eaten sweater, but he's alive and he's free.

Jack flees around the corner to Kiki's bed where he entertains his dancer mistress with the story of his courtroom victory. She keeps the Champagne coming. By 4:30, spent and satisfied, Jack dresses and leaves Kiki to sleep off her stupor.

"Take me home," he tells his driver. Even in his poverty, Diamond has held on to this one last luxury, his car and driver.

"Livin' in a dog house suits him," Spitale says as Diamond and his driver pass by where they're lying in wait.

Bitz unhinges the cylinder of his .38 and rotates it clockwise, double-checking that each chamber is fully loaded. Satisfied, he snaps the barrel in place and sights the front door of 76 Dove Street.

"Nervous?" Spitale says.

"I'm gonna unload everything I got into that cocksucker. I picked up dumdums," Bitz says, meaning the bullets that expand on impact. "Good for dumb-dumbs like Jack."

Diamond stumbles from the back seat, then wobbles to the front door, pulls it shut behind him. Spitale checks his watch. Much longer and the people of Albany will be waking.

"Let's go," Spitale says and Bitz agrees.

They leave the car and cross the street, their breath visible in the cold morning air. The boarding house is unlocked. Bitz steps into the entry hall and takes out the bare bulb that hangs from the ceiling, casting the stairs into darkness. The men climb the darkened stairs to Jack's room. Apparently, Jack was too drunk to close this door behind him, or maybe Jack just doesn't care anymore. He's sprawled sideways across the bed.

The wife isn't with him, a small mercy. Though they would carry out the job just the same if she was.

Bitz drags a pillow over Jack's head to contain the mess and fires. The dumdum rips through Jack's right ear. Bitz fires again, from the other side. This bullet pierces Jack's left temple. He fires again. The dumdum rips through Jack's right jaw and lodges in his spinal cord. Blood runs everywhere. So much for containing the mess.

The noise shakes the boarding house residents awake. Spitale starts for the door.

Bitz yells, "I got three more bullets."

Spitale says, "That's fucking enough."

They race down the dark staircase and past the boarding-house proprietor who stands in stunned silence at the bottom of the steps. An hour passes before the police arrive. They catalogue the crime scene and send Jack's dead body to the morgue. The list of suspects is long and ignominious, yet not one of them can be tied to the murder.

Two weeks later, the Dutchman sits in his ramshackle bar quietly enjoying a cigar. He's already counted the take from an operation that once belonged to Jack Diamond. Abbadabba Berman is busy counting cash and entering numbers into a ledger.

"Not bad for a pretzel, eh?" the Dutchman says.

"A pretzel?" Abbadabba says offhandedly, more interested in the figures in the book than a conversation with the Dutchman or an illumination on what being a pretzel might mean.

"A German," the Dutchman says. "Ain't you ever heard that expression before?"

"Never," Abbadabba says scratching his ear and rechecking his figures.

"Well you heard it now," the Dutchman says. "What's our take?"

"Enough," Abbadabba says.

"Don't ever tell me it's enough," the Dutchman says. "There ain't no such thing as enough. There's only how much we got and how much we can get. That's what I want to know. Ain't you some kinda genius with numbers? Ain't that what I pay you for?"

Meanwhile, over on 52nd Street, Jack and Charlie, the two guys that own the 21 Club, pour themselves a drink.

"Here's to freedom from fear," Charlie says.

"There's always fear," Jack says. "Here's to no more Jack Diamond."

Meyer Lansky drives out to Prospect Park in Brooklyn to deal with a matter of no small importance. He knocks on the front door of a modest apartment. His mother answers.

"I made blintzes," she says.

The apartment is simple and immaculate. Yetta Lansky doesn't like fluff. She doesn't like clutter. A place for everything and everything in its place.

Meyer says, "Sit down, Mama. We need to talk."

"I sit when my work is done," she says.

"I can't stay that long," Meyer says.

"You can stay long enough to eat. You spoil your wife, Meyer. You give her too much money. She doesn't know the value of hard work."

"Mama," Meyer says, "I came to find out why you fire every cook I hire for you. I want to make your life easier. You deserve that."

"I work my whole life. What, I can't do a little more? I don't need the best of everything. This apartment is already too much. Besides, I'm not blind. Don't think I don't know where you get your money." Yetta raises an eyebrow. "The government knows, too. Every day they see you living the good life and they remember how much money they used to make on all those taxes when alcohol was legal. Don't kid yourself. And now they've got sixteen percent unemployment. Someday they are going to want their money back, then what? What will Anne do if she can't go out to eat every day and every night? All this fuss over a dry worker. There is no such thing. The government will do the Mendelssohn March with the brewers, you wait and see, and when they do, all the Germans who were put out of work when they lost their breweries will be so happy, they'll forget what happened to them during the war. Don't look so surprised, Meyer Suchowljanski. I didn't get off the boat yesterday. I listen to Walter Winchell, too. And I can vote in an election, for all the good it will do. I would vote for Hoover just so you can keep your job but Tammany Hall wants to run Al Smith. He's what you call a wet candidate. What if he's the next president? No more Prohibition, I can tell you that."

Meyer says, "We'll be O.K., Mama."

Yetta says, "I come from the old country. What politicians say and what they do are two different things. I didn't raise a stupid son. You've been the Shabbat goy, Meyer. Shabbat is almost over."

Yetta's analogy is keen. The Jews, who are forbidden to do certain types of work on the Sabbath, hire non-Jews to do the work for them. The work gets done. The Jewish household remains blameless before God. The only catch in this whole diversion is that the goy, the non-believer, can never really be clean in the eyes of God.

Meyer says, "Tell the cook she can have her job back."

Yetta says, "Does this cook know that a little lemon zest is the secret to a good blintz? Even Ratner, with his fancy restaurant, doesn't know that. I know that."

"Then teach her, Mama, but don't fire her. Shabbat isn't over yet."

Yetta softens.

"Come back later," she says. "We can play cribbage with Papa."

"Sure, Mama," Meyer says, but he won't return. "I have to go."

On the elevator, Meyer rustles through his pockets looking for the small tin of antacids he carries for emotional encounters.

He checks his watch, the gold watch given to him by Charlie on the occasion of their victory over Salvatore Maranzano. It is barely eleven o'clock in the morning. Low-hanging gray clouds wrap the city in gloom and threaten snow.

Meyer climbs into the 1931 closed-coupe Chrysler and heads to 301 Park Avenue, Suite 39C, Charlie Luciano's suite at the Waldorf. He tucks the cashmere scarf into his camel-hair coat and steps from the car. A valet whisks the car to the garage.

Meyer takes the elevator to Charlie's residential suite. The place is littered with moving boxes. Contents spill onto the floor.

Charlie says, "I hate moving, but you gotta love the place."

He shuffles through the kitchen looking for a coffee pot.

Meyer says, "Vincent Coll was acquitted."

"I thought they threw him in the can for violation of the Sullivan Act."

"They did," Meyer says, "but he's out on a sixty-thousand-dollar bond."

"Madden?" Charlie says.

"Probably."

Charlie says, "Are the guys ready?"

Meyer nods.

Charlie pokes through the refrigerator. "Hungry?" he says. "We got a lot of choices in this joint. I got room service."

The new hotel is stunning, over two thousand rooms including three hundred residential suites and numerous ballrooms, dining rooms, restaurants, kitchens, foyers, lounges, corridors, stairways, club rooms, and private entertaining suites. The Waldorf Astoria takes up an entire city block, from 49th to 50th Streets and Park to Lexington Avenues, twenty million cubic feet of modernity in the heart of Manhattan.

Charlie slips on his shoes.

"Let's go out," he says. "I'm gettin' stir crazy."

Outside is the luxury of living, the constant din of a city always at work, at play, generating fortunes, generating sorrow. Neighborhoods bursting with Charlie's history, uptown and ghetto all mixed into one, a heartbeat that constantly throbs "I'm alive."

Chapter Twenty-Four
What's Yet to Come Is Always a Gamble

1932—1933 (REPEAL)

The year starts with Vincent Coll riding high on the victory of his acquittal. Leibowitz, Owney Madden's lawyer, has made sure no one can continue to pin Coll with the Baby Killer moniker. The NYPD maintains a different view. The police inspector tells Coll that he will be arrested whenever he is spotted in New York City.

Coll picks up his beloved Lottie and marries her in a civil ceremony. The newlyweds check into the Cornish Arms Hotel as Mr. and Mrs. Moran. The hotel, on West 23rd Street, is one stop from Penn Station. Great for a quick escape should the need arise. Although the specter of little Michael Vengalli no longer hangs over them, thanks to the sole witness admitting to lying on the stand, the Mad Dog remains a hunted man. It's not so much that the Dutchman wants him dead. That's a given. Nobody leaves the Dutchman and lives to tell about it. The Baby Killer and Big Frenchy abductor, however, must answer to a higher power, the New York boys, because now there are rules.

The double room in the Cornish Arms becomes their haven and their hell, thirteen stories of moderate rates (a buck fifty to be exact), comfort, courtesy, and service, or so the advertising says.

Mr. and Mrs. Moran kick back and try to relax. They shoot the breeze over current events like every other married couple.

Coll says, "After all we been through, I gotta say the Killer ain't half as bad as I thought he was." He means Owney Madden. "What kinda guy gives up his own lawyer to fight another guy's battle? But that's what he done. Madden gave me one slick son-of-a-bitch lawyer. Did you listen to him in court? Jesus. I wish I could talk like that. Make people believe me. I never had the gift of gab. Some of the guys say Madden put a price on my head. I don't believe it. I'd believe it if somebody said the Dutchman put a price on my head. That bastard. He don't stop at nothing. If we want peace, Lottie, I'm gonna have to get rid of the bastard. It's gonna take planning. Don't worry, Lottie, my lass, ain't nobody gonna take me away from you. You give me somethin' to live for. I ain't never had that before. I didn't care if I got killed. Now I care."

Lottie gives Vincent a playful shove that topples him back-wards onto their austere bed, covered in lemon-yellow chenille trimmed with a ribbon-and-bow design. It is well suited for the honeymoon suite.

"You're a sucker, you know," she says. "I don't know why I married you. Only a fool would think Madden's your best friend just because he bought you a lawyer. For one thing, the guy's probably on the payroll. For another, Madden had no choice. Don't you see, Vinnie? These guys gotta look good to keep the heat off. If you look bad, they look bad. If you look good, they look good. If a guy gives me a pretty dress, it doesn't make me the Queen of England, and it sure as hell doesn't make the guy a prince. You're on cloud nine because you got acquitted, that's all. Just remember: I'm your friend, not these other guys, and you best not forget it. Wake up and smell the coffee."

Coll hangs his head like a kicked dog. Lottie flings her shoes from her feet and then stands on the bed and starts a striptease. Living on the edge excites her and Coll knows it. She drops her

skirt, her sweater, the shoulder strap of her silk teddy. She falls
to her knees, crawls across the lemon-yellow bedspread with
the raised chenille bows, and then pounces on top of Coll. Coll
rolls over and plays hard to get. Lottie creeps over the top of
Coll's shoulders and slides down in front of him, a vamp move
she's learned from Anita Page on the silver screen.

"Let's make love and order up room service," she says.

Coll rolls over, stares at her, impassioned. Love is a go, and
then it isn't. Coll's mind drifts to his pals, Frank and Dominic,
who are still in jail on a murder rap. The electric chair has entered the discussion. Lottie sees their troubles cloud his eyes.
She rises to her knees and gives Coll a stern warning.

"Don't," she says. "Can't we have one day where we pretend
we're the only people in the world? You beat the rap. You're
free. Jesus Christ, just once let us act like normal people."

Coll frowns. Lottie runs her fingers through his thick, dark
hair and grabs a hank, holding his head back as she rolls over
his body and kisses him hard on the lips. Coll pushes her away
and then pulls her back, ripping off the silk teddy. She tears at
his shirt, stripping the buttons away as they get naked and make
love, roughly, wildly, and then fall apart in utter exhaustion.

Coll says, "Yeah, we're just a couple of normal Joes."

By February, the Dutchman is crazed that the hunt for Vincent
Coll has netted nothing but rumors. He gets word that Coll and
his men are hiding out in a two-story house in the Bronx. He
sends out a horde of his best shooters. Five assassins bust in on
a small dinner party. They hit the jackpot. Two members of
Coll's gang, Patsy Del Greco and Fiore Basile, celebrating with
a group of friends. The assassins open fire. Women scream and
children cry. One woman jumps in front of Patsy to save him
from the bullet. The bullet shoots through her skull. Another

bullet goes through Patsy and then Basile is shot. Three people lie on the floor bleeding but Coll is nowhere to be found.

The story of the slaughter hits the front page as yet another headline of the beer war raging between the Irishman and the Jew. The story speculates that there is a fifty-grand bounty on Vincent Coll's head. No one knows who has offered the bounty.

Meyer Lansky reads the article and grumbles to Charlie, "The city will be overrun with bounty hunters. We have to find Vincent Coll and put an end to this. We have rules that need to be maintained. If we ignore the violence among our own mobs, how can we enforce violations in other mobs? It will undo everything we've done."

Charlie says, "At least Del Greco and Basile won't be any more trouble."

Charlie talks with Jimmy Alo and Jimmy talks with Eddie McGrath. Eddie finds Vincent hanging out in a broken-down saloon in the Bronx. Eddie sips Madden's Number One Brew and listens to the drunks trying to harmonize a song they picked up from a revue that ran for five days at the Shubert Theater.

Eddie says to Coll, "How's Lottie taking all this?"

"Ah, she's fine," Coll says, staring at his beer. "The Germans are tough, you know. She's as tough as any man I know. Tougher."

Eddie says, "Women aren't cut out for this sort of life."

"Don't you worry about Lottie. She's been with me night and day, down by the Grand Opera, hidin' in plain sight—how many women got that kind of steel? She calls me the Great Conqueror. Says that's what Vincent means in Latin. She makes me laugh, ya know. The woman's brilliant. She's every bit the schemer Maranzano was. He had a laundry list of guys he wanted moved out of his way. All the top guys. I coulda made a fortune. He could see I could do the job."

Eddie shakes his head, "There ain't no pot of gold at the end of the rainbow. He'd a used you and then taken you out of the way. He wanted to be Caesar, for Christ's sake. He believed his own publicity."

Coll says, "Next thing I know you'll be tellin' me to play nice."

Eddie says, "You see what's goin' on. Do you have any idea what kind of power the guys have that walked into Grand Central and took down the toughest guinea in New York?"

"Ach, not you, too? The trash still needs taking out. We ain't nothing but second-class citizens. Eejits. Riffraff."

"What about Patsy and Basile," Eddie says.

"Cryin' shame but it 'tis what it 'tis and I can't change that. The Bronx belongs to the Irish. Madden will cough up the dough for the tools if I ask him."

Eddie crushes another cigarette on the saloon floor and throws back a pint. "Maybe he will and maybe he won't. Let me give you a little free advice, some of them guineas aren't half bad."

"Yeah? They ain't half good either."

"You've got it wrong," Eddie says. "Who do you think Jimmy Alo was covering for those three and half years he spent in the can? Irish guys. And he's done all right by me and Johnny. He can do all right by you, too."

"Sure," Coll says, "as long as you toe the line. Run back to your masters and tell 'em I'll be in touch. I'll catch you later, Eddie. I gotta take a piss."

Coll stands. He hesitates. He scribbles a phone number on a piece of paper and slides it to Eddie.

"Give this to Madden and tell him to call me." Then he staggers away. Eddie watches him go. Eddie takes the news to Madden. Madden calls a guy named Tough Tommy Protheroe who stakes out the Grand Opera House on Eighth Avenue and 23rd Street. Across from the Opera House is the London Pharmacy and

Candy Shop. Protheroe watches as Coll pads back and forth between the Cornish Arms Hotel and the pharmacy to use the phone. Tough Tommy lies low and takes notes.

Meyer looks at his watch. Anne will have had dinner on the table for…well, no doubt it's gone by now. Buddy is playing on the floor when Meyer walks through the front door. He picks up his son and takes him to the picture window that overlooks the park. Buddy is two and still doesn't walk. The doctors call it cerebral palsy, a disconnect between Buddy's brain and his arms, legs, and other moving parts. Meyer calls it a "condition" and spends his days in the public library reading up on it.

"I thought you were coming home for dinner," Anne says.

"I had business," he says.

Anne glares. "You should spend time with your son."

"He's happy enough," Meyer says.

Anne says, "I've heard of a doctor that helps kids like Buddy. He's at Boston Children's Hospital. He says he can make the lame walk."

Meyer says, "You sure it's a doctor and not Jesus Christ?"

Anne says, "Dr. Carruthers. I want to take Buddy to see him."

"Do you want to go see Dr. Carruthers, Buddy?" Meyer says, jiggling Buddy into a smile.

Buddy's eyes go wide. "Ride?"

"Ride, Buddy. We can eat hot dogs and watch the Red Sox play at Fenway Park."

"Don't listen to Daddy," Anne says. "It's a stupid game and their hot dogs aren't kosher."

Meyer puts Buddy back on the floor to play with his Woodsy-Wee Zoo collection. Buddy fumbles with the lion, pushing him along the carpet until the metal hook intended to link the animals together in a neat little train catches on his pajama bottoms and gets stuck.

Anne untangles the mess. Buddy's disability is wearing hard on her nerves. She sits on the floor and connects the train for Buddy, then helps him push it along.

She complains, "God is punishing us."

Meyer says, "What kind of god harms a child for the sins of the parents?"

"The sins of the father," Anne quotes from the Hebrew scriptures. "Maybe if you went to temple once in a while. Gave up your gangster friends."

Meyer says, "What would it accomplish if I went to temple? How do you know God isn't punishing us for Christmas? How the hell is anybody supposed to know what God thinks, if there is a God at all."

"Shhh," Anne says. Her guilt shudders through the room.

Meyer says, "Stop worrying."

Anne says, "What if Hoover isn't re-elected? It could happen. His promise to end poverty was bupkes. The democrats will bring in repeal. Then what will we do. We'll be broke. No doctor will touch Buddy if we're broke!"

Meyer says, "I'm telling you, don't worry."

"You think you're so smart," she says, half admiring and half despising Meyer's boldness. "You may live on Central Park West but you're still ghetto. You need to get into a legitimate business now."

"I've never flown under any false colors. Look around." He gestures to their creature comforts. "How do you think we got here? It wasn't by being legit."

She says, "Legitimate people live here, too."

"Legitimate doesn't necessarily mean ethical."

"My father runs a legitimate business," Anne shouts.

"I'm going out."

Meyer grabs his coat and hat.

"You just came in," she says. "We're having a discussion. Where are you going?"

"Out," Meyer says. "This isn't a discussion."

And he's gone, through the door, down the elevator, and out onto the street. The Shabbat goy wanders along Central Park West. After yesterday's freeze and today's howling wind, few people have braved the outdoors. Meyer turns his back on the buildings and takes to Central Park. A thin film of ice coats the fountains and ponds. The trees huddle around him, shoving aside the world of the Upper West Side. Meyer shuffles through the hoarfrost on the pathway. He hunches his shoulders against the wind and buries his mind in thoughts of life on the Lower East Side, and before that Grodno.

The rabbis got it right. Poverty is a kind of death. It steals opportunity and quietly eats away at the soul. No one should be impoverished, they would say, and then encourage industry and cleverness. Meyer's father came to this country with hope. How is it that the only gold street was the one paved with illegal money?

"You'll die young from the tailor's disease," his father had said, discouraging Meyer from the needle trade. "Get a job where you can use your mind. You'll be better off."

It was the only good thing his father had said during Meyer's entire childhood. Sweatshop conditions were the cause of the tuberculosis Jews were thought to breed. Just like Italians were said to breed polio and Irish caused cholera.

Meyer shakes off the memory. He stops to listen to the silence of the park. He lights a cigarette. The possibility of Repeal is a bitter pill to swallow especially now that the greasers are gone. If it wasn't for the beer war, the life of crime would be downright peaceful.

If Repeal does pass, legitimacy will return and the bootleg business will fold. Anne has a point. Her father is a grocer. Distillers will need supplies once Repeal passes: grains, hops, and sugar. Sugar from the Caribbean is profitable. The bootleg business has created inroads in the Caribbean.

Meyer passes the pond where Waxey Gordon and Maxie Greenberg made their deal with Arnold Rothstein in a bid to control Manhattan's bootleggers. They didn't count on Emory Buckner's trial, which disrupted Waxey's connections and sent him fleeing to New Jersey in search of a new headquarters.

At 59th Street, the Plaza shines like a beacon in the night sky. Meyer leaves the park, heads down Fifth Avenue to 58th, and crosses over to Bergdorf Goodman's where the fur trade shows off the latest collection: a white fox drape, a collar of mink, two fox jackets, one in white and one in black, and a brown fox fur shrug.

"It's enough to make a girl faint," says Flo Alo, coming up from behind him.

Meyer turns. Jimmy Alo and his wife are on their way home from a play.

"*The Devil Passes*," Flo says to Meyer. "Don't bother."

"All right," Meyer says. "I'll be sure to miss it."

The Lanskys, Siegels, and Alos are fast friends. Flo, Esther, and Anne are constant companions with very few secrets between them.

Flo says, "I hear you're going to Boston to see that doctor for Buddy."

Meyer says, "I guess that's the plan."

Flo says, "I thought I'd stop in and visit the boy. Are they home now?"

"Last time I checked," Meyer says. "By the way, Anne is pregnant again."

Flo smiles. "I know." She turns to Jimmy. "Do you mind?"

He doesn't mind. He never minds. Flo bids the boys farewell and heads to the Lansky house while Jimmy hails a cab to go home.

Meyer says, "When I go up to Boston to see this doctor, I would like you to ride along. There are some guys there you should meet."

As long as there's going to be a trip to Boston, it might as well include some business. Meeting Hymie Abrams and Charles "King" Solomon, the major Jews that hold sway in New England, will bump up Jimmy's reputation. Solomon, a Russian Jew, is well established in gambling and narcotics and bootlegging. Abrams is one of Solomon's lieutenants.

Jimmy says, "I'll pack a bag."

Coll makes late-night excursions regularly from his hotel to the pharmacy across the street, where he connects with his mates via the pay telephones lined up in a series of booths at the back of the store. This is convenient for Owney Madden, whose job it is to deal with the Mad Mick.

"You got the opera crowd to think about at some times of night," Tough Tommy says to Madden. "But Coll ain't no fool. He don't go out in a crowd. He hot-foots it over to the pharmacy when there ain't too many people around to identify him."

"You know what needs to be done," Madden says.

Madden hangs up with Tough Tommy and calls Charlie. Charlie sends Eddie McGrath to the Cotton Club to cover for Madden should things go wrong. Eddie reads the *New York Times* and the *Daily News* and gawks at the chorus line.

Madden pours a couple of whiskeys and hands one to Eddie. Madden sits on the edge of his desk, one leg supporting him, the other dangling down the side.

He says, "You gotta hand it to Coll. He gave the Dutchman a

helluva run for his money. Son of a bitch won't listen to a word
I say. I was just like him when I was a kid. Then I wound up full
of holes and landed in Sing Sing. It changes a guy. Puts a little
more sense in your head."

Eddie says, "So they tell me."

"I didn't want it to come to this," Madden says. "I didn't."

Eddie shrinks back to the newspaper. After years with the
Dutchman, all the bullshit, all the craziness, he hates what is
about to happen mostly because he hates that he is powerless
to have any control over the consequences Coll has brought
upon himself.

Music rises through the club as Cab Calloway and his orchestra tune up.

"Hi de hidee hidee ho," Calloway sings out.

Madden dials the Cornish Arms Hotel and asks for the honeymoon suite. Coll answers the phone.

Madden says, "Are we gonna talk or what?"

Coll hesitates. The rhythm of the orchestra wafts through
the phone's receiver. The Hi-De-Ho man belts out another
chorus.

"I'll call you back in ten minutes," Coll says.

Big Frenchy slips away from his duties and joins Madden
and Eddie in the office.

Outside the honeymoon suite of the Cornish Arms, Mike
Basile waits for Coll to appear. Lottie stands in front of the
suite's door. Coll comes to the door and kisses Lottie hard on
the lips then takes her shoulders and moves her to the side. He
opens the suite's door and nods to Basile. It is Monday night.
The opera house is silent. Ice lines the street and sidewalk. A
cab pulls up and drops four guests at the hotel. From the looks
of it, they're part of the theater crowd.

Coll hikes up the collar of his jacket, pinching it closed

around his chin. He nestles his nose into the thick wool, tugs the brim of his hat down over his eyes, and strolls over to the pharmacy.

Coll says to Basile, "You might as well get a cup of coffee. I don't expect he'll ante up right away."

"Maybe he'll throw in the Duesy," Basile says.

Basile takes a seat at the long soda fountain counter where two men eat pie and mourn the state of the economy and the ongoing Depression. Basile keeps one eye on Coll and the other on the front door. Coll rifles his pockets for loose change. He throws two dimes, a quarter and five nickels on the metal shelf just below the phone. He's in no hurry to call Madden. Something doesn't feel right. He thinks Madden is too eager and then dismisses the idea. Madden is always eager. He's a night-club man.

Coll lights a cigarette and sits in the small booth blowing smoke rings. He twirls the quarter through his fingers. A customer pays for bicarbonate of soda and mooches a glass of water from the soda jerk behind the counter. Basile nods an "all's well" to Coll. Coll drops a nickel into the phone's coin slot. The coin chimes its way through the phone's innards. Coll dials the Cotton Club from memory.

Madden lets it ring a few times before picking up.

Coll says, "Whadya say we drop the bullshit and talk about what really matters. I know you hate this double-crossing Jew bastard in Harlem as much as I do, so why don't you give me the hundred grand I need to do the job and I'll give Harlem back to the Irish."

Madden says, "The Dutchman has a big web. What makes you think you can waltz in and make him go away?"

The Cotton Club clamors with Calloway's music, the dancers on the stage, and the rowdy crowd.

"I blew a goddamn hole the size of Lough Neagh in the Dutchman's beer operation with a lot less," Coll says.

"You took down plenty of my guys, too. What's to prevent you from a repeat performance?"

"Give me the cash," Coll says. "I earned it."

"What assurances do I get?" Madden says.

There is an uneasy silence between Madden and Coll. Coll shifts in the small booth, dangles his feet outside. He wants to go into a tirade, hang up on Madden, but he's made a promise to Lottie. He is going to take down the Dutchman.

Outside the pharmacy, Tough Tommy and two of his boys spill out of their car into the early morning chill.

"What's the matter, kid?" Madden says. "Cat got your tongue?"

Coll says, "I'll tell you something about these guinea friends of yours. When the chips are down, they'll sacrifice you quicker than ale turns to piss. They ain't your friends. Don't you get it? They're in business for themselves. They don't give a shit about no mick."

Coll watches a tenement kid working a ten-finger discount for a can of pomade.

He says, "The Irish have a saying. I'll put it into words you can understand. Marry a guinea and you marry the whole bunch of them."

Madden doesn't respond. Coll says, "You don't think the dagos and kikes give a shit about your sorry arse, do you?"

Madden says, "I could buy the whole of the Irish Republican Army for a hundred grand."

Coll says, "And then what? Where's 'the Killer' now? Fat and happy and sucking on the tit of success."

"That ain't so bad, kid. Listen to me when I tell ya, it ain't the years that wear you down, it's the lead you collect getting through them."

"You sound like an old washerwoman."

Coll scans the pharmacy. The lunch counter is empty. Mike Basile is gone. The dawdlers who have been milling about the store stand frozen in fear, a scattering of cemetery statues gazing at the only moving figure in the whole store. Tough Tommy, Thompson machine gun held high, is moving fast toward Coll's phone booth.

Coll screams into the receiver, "You dirty bastard."

Tommy pulls hard on the Thompson's trigger. A steady stream of bullets slams into the phone booth. The first few bullets scatter through Coll's legs, then a short burst fills his abdomen with bullets and then his heart. The Baby Killer bounces like a tin target in a shooting game. Fifteen steel-jacketed bullets riddle his body. Before Coll's lifeless corpse hits the floor, Tough Tommy is gone, out the door and swallowed by the darkness.

The pharmacy's customers shake and jitter. The tenement kid fills his pockets with candy and makes a quick escape.

Sirens wail as police race to the scene of the crime. They interrogate the witnesses but nobody is either willing or able to identify the shooter although some are fairly sure it is the Baby Killer slumped over and bleeding all over the phone booth.

Lottie runs into the pharmacy just as the local police flood the scene. She is frantic. Screaming for her husband. She is held back. Flashbulbs pop. The mass of mangled flesh is hoisted onto a stretcher and hauled away. Police prod Lottie with questions. She stares blankly into the distance.

Morning dawns and finds Lottie still walking the streets of Hell's Kitchen in a state of shock. Coll is examined and catalogued. Each bullet entry and exit wound is graphed on the outline body that fills the coroner's worksheet. All pertinent information is attached to a clipboard and hung on the end of the coroner's exam table. Coll is gone and there is no bringing him back.

Meyer Lansky, away in Boston to meet with Dr. Carruthers, picks up the morning edition of the *New York Times*. Vincent Coll is front and center.

It is done.

The sun bathes Boston with a warm glow. Meyer meets Dr. Carruthers at the children's hospital. Carruthers turns out to be quite charismatic. He describes a series of medical procedures developed to help children overcome illness just like Buddy's. As a Christian Scientist, for him this means changing Buddy's mind.

"He's two years old," Meyer says.

"Age doesn't matter. It's the mind that matters. I bet this little boy of yours is smart...smarter than you think."

"He's smart, all right. How exactly do you convince a two-year-old that his illness is all in his head?" Meyer says.

The doctor lets out an all-knowing smile.

"You must trust me," he says. "All things in due time. Now, when can I see this young man of yours?"

Meyer makes an appointment for Buddy to meet the doctor and calls Anne with the news.

"When are you coming home?" Anne says.

"Soon," he says.

"When, Meyer?" Anne repeats. "When are you coming home?"

"Soon," he says.

The line goes dead, as usual these days when Anne doesn't like the direction of Meyer's conversation.

Meyer picks Jimmy Alo up at the hotel and they join the hordes of workers who swarm the streets in search of beaneries, hash-joints, eateries, nosh bars, and greasy spoons, anything that will alleviate the gnawing in the pit of their stomachs. They stop at a small diner downtown where they indulge in roast beef sandwiches.

"Did you see the paper this morning?" Meyer says.

Jimmy shakes his head.

Meyer says, "Hoover's got the Justice Department and the Internal Revenue Service searching for gangsters. That's how Capone and a lot of his boys were taken down. The greasers brought all that attention to New York with the war."

They pay for lunch. A cab ride away is the Charles River Esplanade where they meet up with Charles Solomon.

Solomon is neatly dressed in suit and tie. His eyes are bright. He blends easily with Boston's elite, who find the esplanade an escape from the rigors of business.

"Who've you got here?" Solomon says.

Meyer says, "Jimmy Alo."

Jimmy stands tall, his shoulders back.

"What do you do?" Solomon says eyeing the Italian.

"A little of this. A little of that," Jimmy says.

"Booze?" Solomon says.

"Beer," Jimmy says.

Solomon says, "I hope you have more than that. We're all going to feel the crunch when Roosevelt steps into office."

"I've got my eye on a few things," Jimmy says.

"He's got a friend in the William Morris Agency," Meyer says.

"Ah," Solomon says. "I see how that could be useful."

They stroll along the river and then across the stone bridge to a narrow strip of land that runs parallel to the shore. They stand alone under barren trees. Boston fans out from the giant hub, reaching its tentacles into neighboring towns.

"Are you ready for Repeal?" Solomon says.

"Does it matter?" Meyer says.

"Gambling, Meyer," Solomon says. "That's where the money is. What do you think, Jimmy?"

"We've got the numbers in White Plains and those little towns up there."

"Small time," Solomon says. "Abe Zwillman has the right idea. You need a roadhouse, a place where people can come and spend money all night long."

Jimmy says, "We were makin' so much with the numbers that we had to cut down the percentage. You can't lose even if you try."

Solomon jingles the change in his pocket, "If you can do that with small change, think of what can be done with millions."

They while away the afternoon in speculation. Meyer and Charles Solomon go back nearly to the beginning of Prohibition. They have protected each other and scratched each other's backs.

At the end of the day, Jimmy and Meyer sit by the pool and talk about whatever comes to mind.

Jimmy says, "I did a favor for a guy. His name is Julian but everybody calls him Potatoes. Nice guy. Son of a millionaire. No mob guy but he got in trouble with the Outfit. He was running a ritzy joint in Irish territory, kicking back to Bugs Moran to stay in business. Capone wanted to take out his beef with Bugs Moran on Julian. They woulda killed him. I talked to Charlie. I figure the only way this guy can keep breathing is if he starts up a new joint and cuts the Outfit in on the profits. Spread a little good will, you know. Charlie talks to Charlie Fischetti who could see the value in the move. They cut Potatoes a break. Now he's in Florida. He's got a sheriff in his pocket. Wants me to come down and take a look at the operation. You wanna come? We can get out of the cold for a few days."

"Florida?" Meyer says. "Mosquitos."

"Not so bad this time of year. The whole state is depressed. Julian bought an old tomato packing plant. He wants to fix it up and call it the Plantation. He's got the idea of bringing acts down from New York. The snow birds go for that kind of thing.

George, that's my friend at William Morris, can get all kinds of acts. Whatever we want. You, me, Charlie, the Fischettis. We cut this up like a Christmas pie. Julian won't have no more worries about the Outfit coming after him."

It sounds interesting but Meyer prefers to let Jimmy go it alone. Besides, he hasn't packed for the humid tropical weather.

Jimmy takes the morning train from Boston to Ft. Lauderdale, a day and a half of travel. Julian is waiting at the station when he arrives.

The Plantation is a big barnlike structure that once served as a packing shed for cabbages and tomatoes. Julian has given the place a facelift. The gambling consists of a roulette wheel, a few crap tables, a blackjack table, and poker tables. Off to one side is a bingo parlor.

"People down here love bingo," Julian says.

"Where's the stage?" Jimmy says.

"I got a guy coming in over this afternoon to lay it out," Julian says.

"A good act can pack the place," Jimmy says. "Where's the kitchen?"

"What kitchen?" Julian says.

"You gotta feed 'em, Potatoes. There ain't no place else around to take care of this much business."

Julian scratches his head and looks around. The joint was never meant to be fancy. He worries about the competition up the road, Capone's joint.

Jimmy laughs. "Don't you read the papers? Capone's in the can."

It's true. The Big Man is cooling his heels in the Cook County jail, where he enjoys an oversized cell in the fifth-floor hospital ward. Charlie Fischetti is the man in charge until things shake out for the Outfit. Capone expects to beat the rap.

"He's got a long reach," Julian says. "Nobody knows that better 'n me."

"Don't worry. I told you that Charlie Fischetti worked it out. You no longer have a problem with the Outfit. Let's get this joint up and running. Put in a dance floor and a kitchen and a stage. We'll get Sophie Tucker down here as an opening act."

"We'll need a band," Julian says. "Do these guys really come this far south?"

"They'll come as far as they're told to come," Jimmy assures him.

Back in New York, Meyer runs down the business plan. Gambling has to be run square. None of this Capone stuff. Word spreads fast about crooked joints. Whatever is done is done right. It's only common sense. He likes the idea of gambling in Florida. Saratoga has been good to him but it is strictly upscale clientele. Florida will be different. Florida will cater to the common man. Meyer puts his money on the line.

May arrives with clouds and the probability of evening showers. Frank Costello sits at a dining table at the Waldorf and hovers over the front page of the *New York Times*.

Three items in the paper pique Frank's interest.

The first item is labeled "Great Transit Monopoly." Frank has followed Samuel Seabury's investigations from the moment Roosevelt brought Seabury back to continue the fight against New York's corruption. As the lead investigator of the Hofstadter Committee, Seabury has laid bare, among other things, the attempts of the Equitable Coach Company's bid to control New York's transportation system. If successful, the Equitable estimates they will make a ten-year profit of nearly twenty million dollars. Senator John Hastings has received a third interest in the project. The Senator, for his part in clearing the way, stands to make $200,000 a year. There's another $6,380,000 that will come from his 70,000 shares over the next ten years.

Mayor Jimmy Walker shows up in the list of complicit politicians, too. Costello shakes his head. Samuel Seabury is systematically dismantling Tammany Hall's grip on the City and, along with it, much of Costello's political power.

Costello lingers over a second cup of coffee and the next item of interest, the presidential primaries. Franklin Delano Roosevelt has not yet been confirmed by the Democratic Party. The vote is split between Roosevelt, Al Smith, and Speaker Garner. Roosevelt has made known he opposes Tammany's grip on New York City.

While the democrats argue, President Hoover shifts the blame for the worsening economy to an ineffective Congress. The public rallies behind him. The hope for a "dry" president lingers in the air with the fragrance of spring blossoms.

Costello rubs his head and squares his shoulders and takes the next piece of news on the chin.

Al Capone is no longer a guest of the Cook County jail. His hope for a commuted sentence has been dashed to pieces by the Supreme Court's denial of his petition for appeal. Capone is heading to the Atlanta Penitentiary. He tells reporters that he is "glad to get started" on his sentence—eleven years, plus an additional six months for a contempt charge.

Frank Nitti steps up to lead the Chicago mob.

Costello calls for a third cup of coffee and turns to the Sports section of the *Daily News*. Lou Gehrig connects his first four times at bat and nearly a fifth time in the ninth inning. Finally, something Costello can cheer about. And there's a bonus. The Kentucky Derby will be heard on the radio thanks to the National Broadcasting Company and the Columbia Broadcasting System. This will increase betting. Costello signals to one of his runners.

"See what you can find out about the Derby. I want to know if any of the horses have a chance at the Triple Crown. I wanna know who looks best for the Derby and the Preakness. Get that information to Walter Winchell pronto. And make sure the information is passed on to J. Edgar Hoover."

Mr. Schedule checks his watch. Three minutes to ten o'clock. He folds the newspapers into a tidy pile, takes the napkin from his lap and places it on the table, and then heads to the Waldorf's barber shop for a shave, haircut, manicure and shoeshine. Once groomed, he opens himself to meetings with assemblymen, judges, racketeers, moguls, mayors, democrats, republicans, anyone…everyone. Costello's philosophy is simple. A favor granted is a favor earned.

Louisiana's Senator Huey Long is the first in line. The King-fish, as he is called, wants to organize gambling in New Orleans so it will bring in revenue to fund social programs. Huey Long calls his operation "spreading the wealth."

"Little children need education," he says. "We need roads, bridges, hospitals, schools. You, Mr. Costello, can help me make these promises a reality."

Long is energetic, captivating, and determined.

"New Orleans has a long history of gambling," he says. "I believe we can make things happen for the good people of this country if we work together. Mr. Costello, I'd like to consider you a friend of Louisiana and this good country of ours. Do I have your attention?"

Costello nods, "I might be able to put you in touch with someone."

"I believe you can. I certainly do. We have many poor people in this country. I intend to see them get their fair share of the American dream. Sir, I thank you for your time." Long reaches into his vest pocket and procures a business card that he hands to Costello. "When you find that man who can help the great state of Louisiana, give him my number. Have him call me anytime, sir. Anytime."

Huey Long continues on his way. Costello calls the man destined to help Louisiana and Huey Long spread the wealth. His name is Philip Kastel, the same man who has placed 25,000 slot machines throughout New York City.

Kastel is suave, no-nonsense, and practical. He wears the title "Dandy" Phil like he wears a white linen suit on Memorial Day. Dandy Phil scouts around Louisiana and New Orleans and finds a potentially profitable situation.

"Huey Long is no saint," he tells Costello. "We can make plenty of moves but we'll need Charlie Lucky. The Italians are strong in New Orleans and have been for a long time."

"I'll send Willie Moretti to talk to the Italians," Costello says.

Kastel frowns, "This is bigger than Willie, Frank. We're gonna need Charlie and the Little Guy, too. They got respect and they got strength. And they ain't greedy."

Frank's ego sizzles. Kastel leaves it alone. Costello checks his watch. He's most likely to find Meyer and Charlie lunching at Dinty Moore's. He hails a cab and soon enough he is walking through the green double doors of James Moore's restaurant.

Moore says, "If you're lookin' for the boys…" He nods toward the upstairs room.

Costello sits with Meyer and Charlie. He lays out the conversation with Huey Long and the estimation of the gambling opportunities in New Orleans according to Dandy Phil Kastel.

Costello says, "There's a Sicilian in New Orleans by the name of Corrado Giacona. I can send Phil down with Frank Erickson to get things going but without Giacona's nod we're just asking for trouble."

Charlie says, "It's his town. Before we come in, he's got it all to himself. I'll talk to him and let him know we're interested.

Give the guy a percentage of whatever the take is and make sure he knows who's bringing the envelope to him. And Frank, never fail to give him what you promise. If you do, it will reflect badly on all of us."

Costello thanks Charlie and heads back to the Waldorf.

Meyer says, "We'll never see a dime from this."

"Swamps and mosquitoes," Charlie says. "Let him have it."

Meyer says, "Nevada repealed their ban on gambling last year. I'm sending Nig Rosen to take a look around. I'd like Jimmy to go along."

"Nevada?" Charlie says.

"We fly the Hollywood crowd over. They step into an air-conditioned casino. Spend the night. Fly home. And it's all legal."

Charlie says, "Sandstorms and rattlesnakes."

By September, Gentleman Jimmy has danced his last waltz with Samuel Seabury and Governor Roosevelt. He calls his trial a travesty and, with a single sentence, resigns as Mayor of the City of New York, effective immediately. FDR sighs in relief. The bitter debate between Walker and Roosevelt gradually dissipates and then disappears.

Paul Lansky is born healthy and happy. God's judgment has been lifted from the Lansky household.

November brings the presidential election. Franklin D. Roosevelt sweeps the electoral votes, 472 to Hoover's 59. The new president is eager to dispense with Prohibition so he can sit down and have a proper drink, legally. Repeal looms on the horizon. Depending on which side of the tracks one finds oneself on, the news is either good or hauntingly awful.

Ever the optimist, Flo Alo, detecting the shift in her friends, decides it's time for a getaway.

"A cruise," she says at a Lindy's lunch. "If it's good enough for Jimmy Walker, it's good enough for me."

"I have a tiny baby," Anne says.

Flo says, "It's a weekend trip. It's cold in New York and heavenly in Havana. Booze cruise. It's all the rage."

"Paul is two months old," Anne says.

Flo says, "Grandma can watch the boys for a weekend! You aren't nursing, are you? If you are, bring Grandma and Paul and let's go."

Esther says, "A Christmas booze cruise. Your mother will die! Let's do it."

Anne laughs.

Flo says, "I once saw Clark Gable on deck on one of our cruises."

Anne hems and haws for a good five minutes before finally relenting to the pressures of the life of luxury. Over the next two weeks, the girls shop. And shop. Nothing is out of bounds. Anne buys a Madeleine Vionnet silk dress, because she can and because she has lost her baby belly and because all the girls are doing it. The silk is creamy smooth and makes her feel like a million bucks. Then Anne finds a matching Lilly Dache hat. Bingo. Jake, Meyer's brother in the fur trade, contributes a white mink shawl. The girls spend hours in the salon: pedicures, manicures, and waved hair.

With suitcases loaded to bulging, they board the Morrow Castle cruise ship headed for Havana and settle into their respective staterooms. Just past the twelve-mile-limit, the waiter brings Champagne to all those taking in the breeze on deck.

The frigid air sweeps across rosy cheeks and bundled passengers. Soon enough they are cruising by the Bahamas and relaxing over lobster dinners.

Anne raises her glass in a toast.

"Here's to Prohibition. May bygones be bygones," she says.

Esther, the more practical one, says, "Not too far gone. I've grown accustomed to this life. Next up is Paris. I'm taking French lessons. You should, too."

Meyer says, "Don't you think you should learn English first?"

Esther glares, "What's the point of having money if you can't better yourself? Do you imagine we should cease becoming fully formed people?"

Meyer says, "What does speaking French have to do with it?"

Esther says, "For me, it is something. For you, apparently nothing. For our kids…they have a shot at a different life. Don't be a hypocrite. You want that for Buddy and little whoever we have here. We eat the best food. Wear the best clothes. Why not speak French and become Continental?"

Benny says, "That's the bubbles talking."

Esther says, "I asked Meyer a question. Why not?"

Meyer says, "You can't hide who you are…or where you're from. Sooner or later people find out and then what? You live and die on what these people think of you and I'm telling you, you don't want to know what they really think. They don't want you in their clubs or on their streets or in their hair. Money doesn't buy you a way in. Do you know why they give kids an I.Q. in school? Speaking of speaking French. The French had the test created to help them identify mental retardation. You know what the leisure class expected from the test, why they gave it to all of us school kids? They thought they would find out they were intelligent and entitled to their riches and that the rest of us would prove to be idiots destined for nothing more than to slave in their mills. When we surprised them with high I.Q.'s, they dismissed the test. I bet you didn't learn that in French class."

Flo, a little nervous over Meyer's reply, asks Jimmy to dance.

"Hold on," Jimmy says.

Esther considers Meyer's point and then says, "We're not so different, you and me. You think we are but we aren't. We came from the ghetto and we're not going back. You are mistaken if you think I care about their clubs. You hate the establishment, not me. I may hate what they do at times but there are still decent people in this world. You don't want to get in; you want to get even." Esther raises her glass, "Well, here's to getting what we want…whatever that may be."

Meyer says, "I said I don't find a need to be accepted by those that set the gold standard."

"To each his own," Esther says. "I figure you and Benny and Jimmy take care of one side of the tracks and we girls take care of the other. What will you do when Repeal takes all this away?"

Meyer says, "Rudyard Kipling said it better than I ever could. 'If you can keep your head when all about you are losing theirs and blaming it on you…' I'll keep my head. Will you?"

It's a standoff that loses steam once the ship docks in Havana. The city is sophisticated. The couples stroll along narrow streets barely wide enough for one car let alone the hordes of people wandering from shop to open-front shop where the climate puts beauty parlors, flower shops, grocery stores, and cigar stores within arm's reach.

Meyer buys a box of cigars. The girls indulge in perfumes and soaps.

Flo and Jimmy take everybody to Sloppy Joe's Bar, renowned among tourists. The place is packed. A long mahogany cabinet, maybe the longest in the world if legend holds, spotlights the bar's collection of booze.

"Take your time," Flo says. "It's Cuba, not New York."

Sloppy Joe, Jr., the four-year-old son of the owner, prances across the bar carrying Champagne cocktails to tourists.

"Cute kid," Benny says but he doesn't mean it.

"Drink up," Flo says. "We're off to El Floridita. And then La Bodeguita del Medio. After that, you can go home content unless you want to stay here and eat ropa vieja which means old clothes and tastes about the same."

Benny says, "My mother has been cooking that for years."

Esther says, "Relax, this is Cuba, not New York."

Abe Zwillman, the guy that used to take protection money from pushcart vendors to chase off pilfering thugs, mostly Italian, sits in his Claridge Hotel office a few doors down from the Bugs and Meyer headquarters. It's been a long time since he beat up a kid taking advantage of an old man. During that time, the man known on the streets as Longy has made a success of himself. His nails are manicured. His hair swept back in neat wavy rows. He controls a vast portion of New Jersey's gambling and bootleg operations.

What's got Abe hot and bothered is the news he is receiving from one of his booze runners in Jersey. Some mob guys associated with Max Greenberg and Waxey Gordon are making moves on their beer customers.

Zwillman sighs. He doesn't relish a war. For God's sake, the wars have finally stopped. But Gordon's mob is tough, ruthless, and filled with ex-cons. The Maxey–Waxey combo is more than capable of bumping off the competition, making themselves the only show in town.

"Maxey always was a cretin," Zwillman says.

The runner says, "Customers are throwing their business to the cretin. They don't want no trouble, either."

Zwillman says, "How much are we losing?"

The runner scowls. "Too much."

Zwillman says, "Let it go for now. Come back tomorrow and I'll have an answer for you."

Zwillman gathers his wits and walks down the hall to see Ben and Meyer. He tells them what's going on.

Benny says, "Fucking ingrate. We coulda made his life miserable after Buckner but we didn't. We gave him Jersey. I'll talk to him."

Zwillman says, "You can't talk to a guy like Waxey."

Meyer says, "When Benny says he'll talk to him, he isn't doing that much talking."

"Oh," Zwillman says.

Charlie Lucky walks in. "Am I interruptin' somethin'?"

A waft of Pinaud Lilac cologne floats through the room.

"Might as well take a seat," Benny says.

Charlie notices Zwillman's tie.

"Are those bull's-eyes?" he says.

Zwillman looks down at the black, blue and white concentric circles cut in half by the tie's fold and laughs.

"I guess they are," he says. "Never thought of it that way."

"What can be worse than that tie?" Charlie says.

Charlie hears Zwillman's predicament. Benny stands and paces the room. Boxcars of liquor, their liquor, come through Jersey. They have warehouses in Jersey full of the booze they've been storing away for the days when Repeal sets in. The unholy trifecta in Jersey, the combined might of Waxey Gordon, Max Greenberg, and Max Hassel, threatens their distribution arm and their livelihood.

Meyer says, "Hoover's got the Department of Justice working to pin a tax evasion charge on Waxey."

The papers are full of the news. Investigators have tracked down two million dollars deposited into five separate bank accounts that could only be related to something illicit. The government claims the money belongs to Gordon and pressures the Hoboken banker for information. The banker refuses to answer the government's demands. He is charged with contempt of court and sentenced to 90 days. The U.S. Circuit Court of Appeals backs the judgment. Frederick S. Lang of the Jefferson Trust Company must either turn over the information he has on the deposits of the fictitious Harry Forbes or go to jail.

"What are you saying?" Benny says.

"Waxey would be crazy to make a war out of this when he's under that kind of scrutiny," Meyer says.

Benny laughs, "Since when did Waxey have any common sense?"

It doesn't matter that Waxey and Maxey rake in millions annually. It doesn't matter that they lost count on their fingers and toes of the total sum of breweries and distilleries they own.

The wind howls along Times Square and rattles the hotel windows. The neon of the automat flickers in the distance. A cloudburst drenches the city with a pounding rain.

Meyer glares. "Talk to him, Benny."

Benny smiles. It isn't often that Meyer gives his O.K. this quickly. Benny looks at Charlie and then at Zwillman. Everybody agrees.

"Maxey's set up in the Carteret Hotel. You know the place? In Elizabeth?" Abe says.

Benny goes to Elizabeth and confronts Maxey in his Carteret suite.

"You still kickin', kid?" Maxey says, deliberately mocking the twenty-four-year old.

"Big Maxey Greenberg," Benny says. "Some of your guys are putting some of our guys outta business."

"Must be some mistake," Maxey says.

"No mistake," Benny says. "Fix it or I'll fix it."

"What got into you?" Maxey says. "I never saw you as the

negotiator type. You shoulda joined up with us when you had the chance, kid. You could be livin' the high life by now."

The calm of the Carteret does little to soften the antagonism between the men. Gordon, Greenberg, and Hassel own the local politicians and run their business through an endless chain of tunnels that snake their way under the county and beyond. Maxey sees little need to bend to Benny's demand.

Benny smiles, "I never liked your mob."

"Ya got me right here," Maxey mocks, pounding his chest.

Benny turns on his heel and leaves Maxey to contemplate his future.

Waxey gets off the elevator just as Benny gets on. They pass each other in silence. Waxey, the big, round-faced thug with the cheap haircut and snarling face, pounds his way down the hall and into Maxey's suite.

"What did he want?" Waxey says.

"Cocksucker," Maxey says. "Come up here pushin' his weight around."

Gordon tugs at his collar, loosening the stranglehold of his tie.

Waxey says, "Ever since they bumped off them old dons, they been prancin' around Manhattan like the cock of the walk."

"So we cut 'em down to size. We ain't got no use for them no more," Maxey says.

"Easier now than after Prohibition ends," Waxey says.

Meyer's growing family moves to a spacious Boston home with a view of the Charles River.

The days are long in Boston, longer than they are in New York. Perhaps Einstein is right, time is relative. Meyer is restless. He calls Benny at the Claridge.

"Need any help?" he says.

Benny laughs. "WASPs got you down?"

"My wife believes in Jesus," Meyer says.

"Costello has a beef with that Kennedy he's been dealing with. Some deal gone wrong," Benny says.

"That's it? I was thinking of taking the train down," Meyer says.

"Something's going on in Brooklyn. Red and I are heading over to check it out. I'll touch base with you when I know what it is."

That's the extent of the conversation. Nothing serious. Benny and Red Levine head to Brooklyn and drop in at the home of one of their Brooklyn distributors. The apartment is small, a tenement joined to other tenements. The sum total of rooms is two, with one window to the outside world. That's it. A sash window divides the rooms so that light can filter through the apartment and so that the room can be closed off to create the illusion of privacy when necessary.

The distributor, a guy named Bernie, is a tall Jew with swept-back hair and blue eyes. His wife is nervous. She wipes her hands on a flour-spotted apron and smiles. The house smells of freshly baked bread, cinnamon, and chocolate.

"I made babka," she says. "And coffee."

She gestures at the small table in front of the fireplace where another man, named Izzy, stands sentinel over the sliced bread. Izzy nods.

"Esther is my wife," Bernie says.

"Esther?" Benny says. "I'm married to an Esther."

Benny's smile softens Esther's uneasiness.

Esther removes her apron, folds it neatly, and lays it across the inner windowsill. She retrieves the coffeepot from the small stove and fills the four cups sitting next to the four plates on the table in front of the fireplace and then places the pot on a thick crocheted square.

"I hope you like the babka," she says. "It's my mother's recipe."

She departs quickly out the door and down the hallway, leaving the men alone to do whatever it is men do. Benny and Red sit at the small table next to the cleanly swept hearth. They talk over the rumors circulating about Waxey and Maxey and Max Hassel.

"You ask me, it's Max Hassel that's the problem," Bernie says.

"What's Hassel got to do with it?" Benny says.

"He's got everything to do with it," Bernie says. "You don't think the other two goons know what's going on, do you? Waxey's squirreled away in his castle behind a moat. Maxey stays in the hotel surrounded by bodyguards. What's he afraid of, I'd like to know. Mob full of ex-cons. What the hell is he afraid of?"

"What's that got to do with Max Hassel?" Red says. "He's a numbers guy. He's bought up a bunch of little breweries in Philadelphia. Wants to be some kind of beer baron."

Bernie says, "Waxey is still a big goon. When he wants something, he sends his guys in blasting. Greenberg can't get out of his own way. Hassel figures the numbers, right? He's the one calculating the odds. Goddamn gunsels want to take over the beer business. That's what this is about. I'll bet my last dollar on it."

"They're making millions," Benny says.

"Hassel screwed the government out of the taxes he owed. You know how he walked away from his tax lien?" Izzy says.

"What lien?" Benny says.

"The lien the government put on him for over a million bucks in unpaid income taxes. Hassel ignored it. Bought himself the Berkshire Hotel instead. That's why the government came after him. The lawyers went back and forth for years. In the end,

Hassel got off for under five grand. Five fucking grand. He's brilliant, I tell you."

"He's lucky," Benny says.

Bernie says, "He's using that lawyer guy Meyer uses. Sapiro."

"Sapiro is a corporate lawyer," Benny says. "What does he know about tax evasion?"

"He's a lawyer, ain't he?" Izzy says. "Lawyers got a lot of tricks. They're born negotiators. This guy…"

There's a rattle in the chimney and then a clang on the hearth. Benny sees the bomb and jumps from the table as the bomb explodes. Bricks fly through the room like missiles. The window explodes, piercing the living with glass shards. The concussion of the blast rattles brains and causes ears to ring. The wall between Bernie's apartment and the neighboring tenement blows out completely. The floor gives way. The boys fall into the apartment below, pinned under a mountain of bricks and furniture. They scratch their way through debris. They are bleeding and half-deaf.

The entire neighborhood has been rocked. Benny, barely able to walk, manages to disappear into the gathering crowd as firemen and police arrive at the scene. Neighborhood men are frantically digging for survivors. Nine people are pulled from the debris and then shuttled to Gouverneur Hospital for care. Red Levine is among the battered survivors. The names of the wounded, minus Benny, are collected and appear in the newspaper article the following day.

It takes nearly two weeks for Benny to track down the bombers. They had followed Benny and Red to Bernie's tenement and then carefully and stealthily climbed the fire escape, found the chimney that rose from Bernie's apartment, and dropped the bomb, making their escape across the tenement roofs.

Benny takes the two men to an open field in New Jersey and shoots them dead.

The War of the Jews shifts into high gear.

Two of Abe Zwillman's runners are shot and killed. He calls Benny and hisses into the phone.

"I've got two more widows on the payroll. And then I find out that the holy trifecta is in bed with a guy from the State Beer Control Commission. You know what that means? As soon as Roosevelt is elected and makes beer legal, they're going to roll over everybody. They're arranging a fucking monopoly."

Benny massages Zwillman's wounds with words of revenge. Before Benny can formulate a plan for New Jersey, Nig Rosen is at the Claridge with complaints of his own. Waxey and Maxey are making moves on Rosen's beer business in Philadelphia.

Charlie Luciano and Joe Adonis enter the Claridge suite just as Nig Rosen spews, "They think they're too powerful to be taken out."

"Who?" says Charlie.

"Waxey, Maxey, and Max Hassel," Benny says.

"I know a couple greasers thought the same thing," Adonis says.

Adonis says, "Knock 'em outta the box. They won't be so rich after that."

Benny rubs the back of his neck and cocks his head back and forth. "Those bastards. My ears are still ringin'."

"You talk to Meyer?" Charlie says.

Benny says, "He's got his own troubles."

Rosen says, "They've got the fucking Piccadilly, don't they? Seven hundred fucking rooms in the middle of Times Square. All the guys hang out there. That ain't enough for them?"

Adonis says, "If we bury them they won't give us no more trouble."

Just then, Meyer comes through the door.

"What trouble?" he says, taking a seat.

Benny fills him in on recent events.

Joe Adonis says, "He's givin' us the finger, plantin' the Piccadilly on 45th Street. Look out the window. What do you see?"

Meyer says, "Waxey is giving Emory Buckner the finger with the Piccadilly. It's revenge for shutting down his operation. Everybody goes to the Piccadilly, celebrities, politicians, you, me. This isn't about the Piccadilly."

Benny says, "Then what?"

"Waxey wants it all. Always has. I didn't see it before. He was up there in Jersey building his empire. Prohibition is about to end so he's making his move. He's a clever son of a bitch. He means to take us all out."

"That's what I said," Adonis says. "They gotta go. All of 'em."

Rosen says, "I heard Hassel has been trying to get citizenship so he can travel to Germany and hire brew masters. His guys are all over the layout in Pennsylvania."

Abe Zwillman steps in and joins the powwow.

Meyer smokes and runs through the facts. The government is intent on taking Waxey down for tax evasion. He is the latest Al Capone. The beer war has the president's attention. Police now see the beer war as a territorial fight between the Dutchman and Waxey Gordon.

Jimmy Alo pops in. Catching sight of the group, he turns to leave.

"Stay," Benny says, realizing Jimmy has a thriving beer business. "Are you having any trouble with Waxey Gordon's guys?"

"Yeah," Jimmy says with a shrug. "They've been making moves in White Plains and the little towns around it. I got a lot of business in those towns. They're trying to take over."

Meyer says, "Do these guys know that you're with us?"

Jimmy says, "I didn't bother to ask."

"How much trouble you got?" Charlie asks.

"Me and Moey Dimples had a few run-ins. The trouble-makers won't be bothering anybody anymore. I'll put it that way."

Charlie and Meyer exchange a glance.

Benny says, "Take the head, right, Meyer?"

Meyer says, "Right, but we have to do this the right way since the government is all over Waxey's business."

"I got a guy who's friendly with Max Hassel," Zwillman says.

"How friendly?" Meyer says.

"They pal around together," Zwillman says.

Meyer says, "See what you can find out."

"The time for findin' things out is over," Benny says. "I got this covered."

And so, the conflict escalates.

Waxey saunters around Broadway and the Piccadilly with a broad smile, a new wardrobe, a new haircut, and a brand-new image but money has only changed him superficially. When Franklin Delano Roosevelt swept the election in November, he threw an epic party at the Piccadilly, a meet-and-greet with potential political allies.

Back in the Carteret Hotel, Waxey Gordon keeps in earshot of his Brown Bakelite Egyptian Air King Sky Scraper tube radio. He is waiting for the news that FDR has begun the process of legalizing beer. He intends to be first in line for permits. He's sure the Dutchman, Jimmy Alo, and all the Irish dubs have not taken advantage of the law to legalize their business. If he can squeeze in ahead of them, he can corner the market.

Maxey Greenberg sits on the couch in Waxey's suite listening to Roosevelt's first fireside chat. Waxey, still in his silk pajamas and wearing his leather slippers, pads through the room in search of coffee.

"Who cares about banking?" Waxey says. "When's he gonna get down to legalizing beer? I thought that was gonna be his priority. Where's the goddamn coffee?"

Greenberg says, "It's on the cart in the corner."

"You're going to D.C. with that shyster lawyer Sapiro to make sure he says the right things to the right people. You got that? He's got a silver tongue but we still ain't got our permits. Go to Washington and make sure we get beer permits for our operations in Pennsylvania and Jersey. And don't come back 'til you got them in your hand."

Greenberg says, "How hard can it be to get a bunch of beer permits?"

"We can't move forward in Newark or Paterson until we get them permits for brewing and distribution. Got that? I want this set up before Repeal. I want the whole goddamned thing on my desk yesterday."

"Sapiro's gotta file papers. There's protocol," Greenberg says.

Waxey fumbles a cigar from the wooden box on the side table. The stubble on his face says he hasn't been out in public for a day, maybe two.

"I don't give a damn. Just get it done before them yahoos figure things out," Waxey says.

By the end of March, the Cullen–Harrison Act makes 3.2 percent beer and wine legal. Yuengling Beer Company sends a truckload of "Winner Beer" to the White House. Nobody bothers to mention that it takes three weeks for Yuengling's beer to brew and age but that the truck arrives instantly after legalization. Nobody cares. Happy times are here again.

Max Hassel, fondly known as the Beer Baron of Berks County, pumps out beer from his breweries, at least twenty-three in

Pennsylvania and New Jersey alone. He pushes ever harder for citizenship. The well-mannered Max is determined to make a success of legitimacy. Five days after beer is legalized, Max visits the Harrison Brewery in Harrison, New Jersey, pleased in the knowledge that he no longer has to look over his shoulder and pay out hush money while he turns a profit. He heads back to the Carteret Hotel in Elizabeth and settles into his room secure behind a door with an electronic lock.

These are difficult times.

Maxey Greenberg drops by to discuss business. Hassel buzzes him in. Greenberg makes himself comfortable, pouring two glasses of whiskey before taking a seat at Hassel's desk.

"We got it made, huh, Max?" Greenberg says. "We got our permits. We got our breweries. If only we could get rid of the Dutchman, we could take over the Bronx. Before you know it, we'd have the whole Eastern Seaboard."

Hassel downs his whiskey and pours another.

"Why not leave well enough alone?" Hassel says.

"You're missin' the point, Max," Greenberg says. "How long you been fightin' with the government for a passport? You still ain't gettin' one. What does that tell you? Once a criminal, always a criminal. Forget dreamin' about becomin' a brewer. How long we been in this business? Legal don't mean nothin'. Why do you think all them banks failed anyway? You heard the president. Whole damn country's a mess on accounta Wall Street. You know how many banks closed, Max? Four thousand. Four fucking thousand banks closed on accounta Wall Street. You think them shysters care? There was two and a half billion dollars of lost deposits when them banks closed. Billion, Max. What's our crime compared to that? Son of a bitch. I just don't get what's wrong with people."

"That's what you tell yourself so you don't feel like a failure," Hassel says.

"Tread lightly, Max," Greenberg says. "Have you forgotten the favor we done for you when Duffy tried to muscle in on your brewery? Don't forget your money come from the same place mine come from. A leopard can't change his spots. Goin' legit ain't gonna change yours."

There's a knock at the door, the secret knock known only to a select few.

"You expectin' somebody?" Greenberg says.

Hassel shakes his head.

"Who is it?" Hassel demands.

"Joe," the voice behind the door says, muffled by the double thickness.

"Stassi," Hassel says. "I forgot he was coming by."

Joe Stassi, the guy in Zwillman's mob who is close to Max Hassel, lives downstairs. At Stassi's suggestion, the two men are going to the Piccadilly for lunch with a guy that Stassi is certain will be able to secure citizenship for the Beer Baron of Berks County.

"Push the button and let him in," Hassel says to Greenberg.

"Stassi?" Greenberg says. "What the fuck are you thinkin' lettin' in a guy from Longy's mob? This guy ain't changing sides, is he?"

"It isn't like that," Hassel says. "Push the damned button."

Greenberg pushes the button that releases the electronic lock that allows Joe Stassi to enter the room, only it isn't Joe Stassi but Benny Siegel who storms through the door waving a .38 caliber handgun fitted with a Maxim silencer marketed as the "gentleman's way of target shooting."

Benny aims and fires, putting one bullet through Maxey Greenberg's head. The .38 kicks hard. The silencer suppresses the pressure wave of the escaping gasses but does nothing about the sonic crack created as the bullet tears through the air. Greenberg falls face-first onto the rolltop desk. Hassel turns to run. Benny puts a bullet through Hassel's head. Hassel cascades to the floor, sprawled out like a ragdoll.

"Tough luck, Max," Benny says to Hassel with honest regret. "You mighta been good with numbers but you were lousy at choosing business partners."

Benny steps over Max and unloads what remains in the six-shooter into the slumped-over Greenberg, four extra shots to extirpate the rage over the bomb intended to kill him and Red Levine. Benny hunts through the suite but Waxey is nowhere to be found. He drops the gun to the floor and quickly exits the building through a service door before the police can be summoned.

Waxey, spooked by the commotion and hiding a few rooms away from Hassel's suite, climbs out a window to escape the gunplay.

Benny meets up with Meyer, Charlie, and Abe Zwillman back in the Claridge.

"Waxey got away," Benny says. "He was fucking some broad in another room. You ever try one of these goddamned silencers? Silence my ass. Piece of shit!"

Benny plots another attack while Waxey's beer continues to flood the market in the Bronx and Yorkville in unswerving competition with the Dutchman. The Bugs and Meyer mob spreads its tentacles in all directions. The Internal Revenue Service does likewise. After two years of prepping for the case against Waxey Gordon, they aren't about to lose their man over what they are calling a territorial dispute. Word goes out to law enforcement agencies to be on the lookout.

Waxey lies low in the Catskills. He listens to the birds sing and the wind blow through the trees, and the beating of his own black heart. Three weeks pass in quiet solitude. As far as the town knows, he's just another tourist escaping the city to enjoy a little rest and relaxation in the Mansion House in White Lake. That's the theory, anyway.

The trouble with Waxey's theory is that it doesn't take into account the uncomplicated nature of a resort town. Tourists who spend $1,500 renting a property are a curiosity. Tourists living in complete isolation are fodder for speculation. Tourists with bodyguards and fast cars and speedboats tied up at the dock in front of the lodge are definitely running from the law.

People talk. Talk gets around. The police find out. Soon enough, the IRS gets involved. The hotel is staked out. It doesn't take long to confirm the presence of Waxey Gordon, even with a two-day growth. Troopers surround the lodge. In the early morning, before Waxey or his men stir, the police make their move. With weapons drawn, they push open the front door and find a sullen, dark-faced man who gives up readily, hands in the air. Upstairs, they find another man just getting out of bed. Under his pillow they find a .38 caliber revolver.

Moving to the next room, they come upon Waxey Gordon still fast asleep.

Waxey blinks awake, "What is it? What's this all about?"

It's all about, of course, turning Waxey Gordon and his men over to the Internal Revenue agents so he can be charged with tax evasion on $1,427,531.48 from the year 1931.

The broad-shouldered, thick-jawed Gordon chews on a cigar. The inconvenience of fingerprinting and mug shots annoy him, even more so the fact that he's been caught by a bunch of yokels.

On April 27, three pedestrians are wounded in a shootout at 81st Street and Broadway in New York City. The attackers ditch their machine guns, rifle shells, and two bloody hats, one bearing a Newark store label. It's the only lead the police have. Since the incident occurs close to the Dutchman's known hangout, police assume the violence is related to the beer war. Therefore it must involve either the Dutchman's men or those of Waxey Gordon.

On June 4, a cool Tuesday, William Oppenheim is found dead in front of his house. He is a big man, 350 pounds big, which explains the nickname "Big Bill." His last rendezvous, at 4 A.M., was with friends in a confectionery shop three blocks from his house. Police say his assailants jumped from a car and fired five shots into his face as Big Bill arrived home. Bill fell onto the stone steps leading up to his apartment and fractured his skull. The shooters fired five more shots into Bill's chest before leaving the scene. Bill died on the spot.

It turns out that Big Bill was an ex-con and was running beer as part of Waxey Gordon's mob. His murder is quickly linked to a feud resulting over his invasion into the Bronx and Westchester beer territories. This ties him to the murders of Charles Brady and Abe Durst. The Jersey-Bronx connection confirms the police suspicion that the murders are tied to the beer war.

On June 9, with three loaded pistols to keep him company, Gus Berger uses a pair of field glasses to keep watch. Three gunmen break into his apartment. Gus fires. Someone stumbles and returns fire. Gus takes a bullet in the shoulder. His assailants flee.

Murray Marks is not so lucky. He gets his on June 30, as he steps from a city bus that has stopped in front of Pelham Bank. Five shots ring out. Three of the bullets land in the unfortunate Marks. Gordon gets the news while he waits for his tax evasion trial to begin. The annoyance of fingerprinting and mug shots pales in comparison.

Thomas E. Dewey, the new Chief Assistant U.S. Attorney, has been assigned as the prosecutor in Waxey Gordon's case. The murders leave him guessing as to who it is that is systematically taking out his key witnesses. When Waxey's lawyer asks for a "list of particulars," Dewey replies with a clever rebuttal. Since Gordon claims he was an underling, and, indeed his name appears on nothing, a list of particulars is impossible to produce. This ploy keeps his list of witnesses secret.

The police theorize that the killings are being carried out by thugs once on Gordon's payroll who used to make $50 to $100 a week. Once beer became legal and the men lost work, they started killing Gordon's friends. It's a long shot but they stick with the idea anyway.

Then Murray Marks is tied to the opium trade and the police shift to a new theory. This time they make a connection to a mob called "Bugs Meyers" and a guy named "Bugs Spiegel" and another thug known as "Dimples." They believe all these men were on Gordon's payroll.

Right gang. Wrong reason.

Waxey's trial begins in earnest. The evidence the IRS brings against him is overwhelming. They meticulously trace everything down to the gasoline and tires purchased for Gordon's trucks. The agents call their detective work "a footrace with Gordon's men." It is anyone's guess who will get to the evidence first. Sometimes they win. Sometimes they lose. And on it goes, the corruption, the interference, the undeniable evidence against the bootlegger and tax evader. It takes the jury a mere 51 minutes to decide Irving Wexler, aka Waxey Gordon, is guilty of tax evasion.

Meyer follows the trial in the *Daily News* and the *New York Times*. It seems Meyer's age-old nemesis will no longer darken his path, not this side of Repeal anyway, not for ten more years. And so it is that the government, and not Meyer Lansky, delivers the final blow to what the underworld calls the Jew War.

✱

In 1924, Clarence Darrow had debated Prohibition with John Haynes Holmes. Darrow dared to question the philosophy of government itself. Darrow had argued that Prohibitionists didn't know when to stop telling others what to do. There was legislation against smoking. In New England, a law was passed that forced people go to church. They even picked out the church and threw people in jail if they didn't go...to that one church approved for all.

Darrow's argument struck a chord with Meyer. Something so small as a single law that denies a man his freedom to drink fuels Meyer's rage over ancient wrongs levied against an entire people, his people. Prohibition provided the crucible that allowed Meyer to embrace an illicit personal freedom by defying the law. Now it's over. The Eighteenth Amendment has been repealed. What direction lies ahead? Will Meyer embrace something as mundane as legitimacy? Or will he continue to battle the unseen enemy? Those are the questions in front of him now that this Shabbat goy is out of a job.

Jimmy Alo stops at the Cannon Street garage where Meyer and Moe Sedway are closing down shop. A fan belt and an assortment of odd tires litter the floor. The factory desk in Meyer's cramped office sits idle alongside the relic of a potbellied stove. The smell of crankshaft oil and metal lingers in the walls and floor, a reminder of what it took to move booze through the streets of New York.

Moe Sedway looks around and says, "Kinda feels funny after all these years."

Moe slides the rolling door across the garage entrance. The boys head for Ratner's Deli.

"How's the kid," Jimmy asks.

Meyer says, "He's tough as nails, that little guy, which is more than I can say for his mother. She's falling apart."

Jimmy says, "Women can't take that kind of pressure, watching their baby in pain."

Meyer says, "The doctor made her believe in miracles. They're all religious in that hospital. Mind over matter. It's the kid that has his head on straight. He will never walk. Let him find another way to get around. Why continue to torture the little guy? His mother wants me to repent. To her, that means going legit."

"Will you?"

"Nah," Meyer says. "Not entirely anyway. I'm going down to Cuba to secure sugar rights. The guy running the place is easy enough to bribe. It's a poor country."

Jimmy nods.

Meyer gets the sugar rights. He forms a legal corporation and calls it Molaska. The Cleveland mob and the Jersey mob are brought in on the deal. Sapiro guides them in what they can and cannot do. Meyer is in business with his father-in-law, Moses Citron, to provide molasses to distillers. Molaska Corporation is official. Anne is beside herself with joy.

But the new frontier, as Meyer sees it, is not beer or even legitimacy, it's gambling. New York settles into a new rhythm. Freedom of thought. Freedom of speech. Freedom to buy a goddamn drink whenever one wants.

A young boy walks into a candy store and stops dead in his tracks. Beyond the lollipops, the peppermint sticks, the chocolates, the Boston Baked Beans and Licorice Snaps and Red Hots, the Valomilk Candy Cups and Choward's Violet Mints, sits something new, a bright yellow slot machine embossed with a brilliant red eagle holding a bellyful of loose change. The boy wonders at the machine.

"It's called the War Eagle," the man behind the counter says. "It's tempting, isn't it?"

The man wears a white apron over a well-worn suit. He has a broad smile and a desire to keep his business.

"What is it?" the kid says.

"It's called a trade simulator," the man says.

A trade simulator avoids entanglements with gambling laws by diversion.

The boy marvels and then says, "How do I get those quarters?"

"The War Eagle doesn't give up his bounty easily," the man says. "You see that slot at the top? You drop your quarter in and pull the handle down. If you're lucky, and the fruit in the windows is all the same, you get a prize."

The boy licks his lips. "What kind of prize?"

"You trade it in for gum or candy," the man says.

"Not quarters?" the boy says.

"You get the value of the quarters when you trade for candy," the man says.

The boy rubs his fingers across the quarter in his pocket. The eagle's wings spread out across the face of the machine in brilliant red and shiny silver that takes on the shape of an Indian headdress. In the center of the headdress is another red circle around a black core, each division lined by silver metal that looks like razor wire.

The three windows above the eagle show a non-paying play: cherries, a blue plum, and a yellow bell. The boy rubs the quarter again and then looks hard at the candy case.

The man behind the counter says, "You can spend the quarter in your pocket or you can take a chance. Maybe you'll get more quarters and you can trade for more candy. What'll it be, son?"

Judging from the coins in the Eagle's belly, with a stroke of luck, the boy could buy the whole candy store, he's sure of it.

"Well, son?" the man says again.

The kid drags a stool over to the one-armed bandit, holds his quarter over the slot and hesitates. He wipes sweat from his forehead and then drops the quarter into the shiny silvery machine and grabs the lever. Down he pulls it. The fruit whirls around and then clicks into place: orange, orange, bell.

"Too bad, sonny," the man says. "Maybe next time."

The boy hangs his head in defeat and walks out empty-handed just as Mayor Fiorello LaGuardia walks in. He's seen it all before. With a pack of reporters, a moving truck, and a slogan, LaGuardia makes his moves.

Ceremoniously, LaGuardia confiscates the War Eagle from the candy shop and hauls it to a waiting truck. The Eagle joins a growing mountain of slot machines. LaGuardia scales the mountainous pile and waves a sledge hammer for the waiting photographers. As they trigger their shutters, he attacks the Eagle, bludgeoning the belly of change, spilling Frank Costello's interests onto the street below.

The kid who lost his quarter smiles, grabs a handful of change, and scurries away.

LaGuardia sifts through the nickels and dimes and quarters raising handfuls high above his head. Loose change slips through his fingers. Flashbulbs pop, freezing the moment in time. The Little Flower gloats. He's finally getting his revenge on Frank Costello for the election he lost to Jimmy Walker in 1929 when Costello split the vote.

His next cause will be the fight against all the K.G.'s.

"K.G.?" a reporter says to the cop standing beside him.

"Known gambler," the cop says. "It's part of his reform platform."

The cop winks. The photographer smiles. The plundered slot machines are loaded onto a municipal barge and dumped into the sea.

LaGuardia is hailed as a modern St. George, conquering the dragons of immorality and vice.

Meyer and Charlie read the news of LaGuardia's victory in

the papers. Charlie opens a box of Cuban cigars and offers one to Meyer.

"Were they?" Charlie says.

"Rolled on hot thighs?" Meyer says. "What do you think?"

"It's the stuff that fires the imagination," Charlie says.